FANTASY ONLINE
3&4

HARMON COOPER

Copyright © 2023 Harmon Cooper
Copyright © 2023 Boycott Books
edited by Andi Marlowe
Cover Art by Richard Sashigane
Font by Shawn King
Interior art by Sor Cooper
Print design by Joshua Diles
Audiobook produced by Soundbooth Theater and narrated by Jeff Hays and Annie Ellicot

www.harmoncooper.com

All rights reserved. This is a work of fiction. Names, characters, places, and incidents either are products of the author's imagination or are used fictitiously.

MAP OF HYPERBOREA

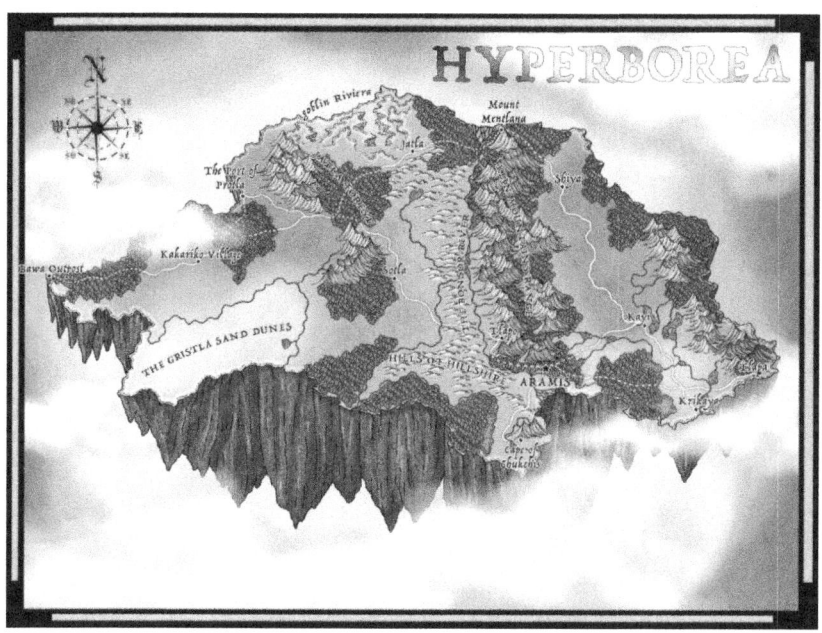

MAP OF POLYNYA

MAP OF ULTIMA THULE

"Continents, three,
Float over the Endless Sea,
Hyperborea, Polynya, and Ultima Thule."
--A famous Tritanian poem

"Takha bae bitakh novlaa rakh Aya Bortaetae,
Huborakha, Polonkhya, Hutamae Dulekh."
--Written in Romanized Thulean

BOOK THREE
THE RUNESTONES
OF TRITINAKH

CHAPTER 1: TO WARINGTLA BY WAY OF TOKYO

THE LAST THING RYUK WANTS TO SEE is Hiccup's naked ass sprawled out on the floor.

Luckily, he's on his belly, Ryuk thinks as his avatar takes shape.

Everything that has happened over the last few hours comes to him in a sudden flash. He recalls taking Hajime to the repair facility using the instructions the humandroid sent him over iNet.

He was so calm, so collected, Ryuk thinks. He then feels stupid for thinking this: *Of course Hajime was calm and collected; he isn't real, or at least, he doesn't feel the same emotions we do.*

After Ryuk released him to the repair facility, Hajime walked him through the next steps he needed to take.

First, Ryuk installed the most powerful encryption apps available on the dark web. He then booked a Proxima capsule hotel not far from Hajime's location under a false name using fake life chip info and a chip masker.

He even had a fabricated life story just in case someone asked him (he was a college student visiting a sick relative, his alias was Madara Uchiha). Ryuk was instructed to stay logged in until Hajime recovered, twelve hours total, which would still give him time to meet FeeTwix and Sophia in person under Hajime's watchful eye.

And that was that. Hajime would pick him up tomorrow and they'd continue their new, fugitive-esque lives in Tokyo.

Whatever that entails.

Ryuk hasn't really figured out what happens yet or where they'll go. His brother will be looking for him; Hajime was certain that Tesla would be repaired, and she'd be looking for them as well.

Then there was his mother. Her assistant had already contacted him demanding answers. If Kodai couldn't find him, his mother could. She was resourceful; she had connections across the city.

As Hajime had told him over iNet: *it is imperative to keep a low profile.*

"Yoy, yoy, yoy," Hiccup mumbles in his sleep.

The cranky goblin is in the Knights of Non Compos Mentis' secret guildhall alone, likely having cleared everyone out with a blast from the past. In this case, the 'past' meaning something he ingested earlier.

Damn goblin.

Hiccup rubs his belly, says 'yoy' a few more times, and lets out a painful squeaker.

"Wake up," Ryuk tells him, his nose twitching as Hiccup's stank reaches his nostrils.

"You can't have my chalupa, Barry!" The goblin kicks awake, wild-eyed and ready to fight. He's on his feet now, two tomahawks at the ready.

Ryuk glances away immediately, barely catching a glimpse of the goblin's chalupa.

"Fick, Marbles! What happened to my clothes?" Hiccup tosses his tomahawks over his shoulder. One cuts into a table; the other skitters across the floor.

"I was going to ask you that," Ryuk says hurriedly, his eyes shut tight.

"Well, if I fickin' knew where they were, I wouldn't ask you. Gee, Marbles, you sure can be a fickwit. Actually, come to think of it, I think I lost my clothes to Snake Eyes, you know, that ninja guy."

"His name is Aiden."

"Yeah, Brandon, whatever."

"Aiden."

"Stop interrupting me, Marbles. Fick, where was I?" Hiccup's eyebrows narrowed. "That's right, my clothes. Pretty sure I just lost my pants. Dunno who took my underoos and my top."

Ryuk sighs. "Where are the others?"

"Back in Kayi with Elfy, Wolfy, Snowballs, and Conan."

"And who is Barry? You were saying something about that when I woke you up."

"Who's Barry? Ha! There's a question you won't like the answer to, Marbles. Barry is an evil ass bumfick ink shadow who tried to steal my chalupa about a day or so before all this shit happened—and by 'all this shit' I mean all the shit you and Tammy caused. Long story long: two days before we set off on our little ficked up adventure, I technically lost my chalupa to an ink shadow. I then had to put together a ton of shit, including a parade, a massage, a Michelin star dinner and a stay at Jatla's best hotel, to appease octopus squirt so I could keep said chalupa."

"Jatla has a best hotel?" Ryuk cringes, his eyes still closed.

"Fick yeah it does. All dirty, greasy, filthy places have an expensive spot for the richkins to rub their elbows and dip their chalupas in the locals' special sauce. I'm sure Japan has tons of places like that."

"Okay. Will you put some fucking clothes on?"

"Jeez, Marbles, you act like you've never seen a chalupa before. Well, I guess it's hard if yours is always tucked between your legs. Ha! Anyfickin' hoo, that's who I was screaming about, an ink shadow named Barry. And you can open your eyes now. I put on some clothes I had stashed in my list. I didn't like this monkey suit before, but now I'm kind of digging it."

Ryuk very carefully cracks an eye open to find Hiccup in the white potato sack he got from the Empress' designers. A thought comes to him.

"Why are you looking at me like I got your sister pregnant?" Hiccup asks.

"What you were saying earlier about Barry the ink shadow...it was pretty grueling, right?"

"Fick yeah, it was grueling."

Ryuk points a finger at him. "Could this be why you were sleeping when Tamana was abducted? A little too much excitement the night before?"

Hiccup burps. "Ha! You could say that. But fick, Marbles, if you want my fickin' backstory, I'll let you borrow my diary. And if you're trying to blame me for the Shinigami kidnapping Tamana's flat but fine Japanese ass, then point that finger somewhere else. That shit wasn't my fault."

Ryuk feels the urge to argue more but bites his tongue. *It is useless to argue with a goblin,* he reminds himself.

"Damn thing." Hiccup holds up his mechanical arm. "It vibrates a bit while I sleep, which was why I was sleeping on my belly. But if I sleep on my side, it wakes me up. Can't win with this damn contraption."

"Then sleep on your other side."

"You sleep on your other side! Sheesh, Marbles, your tone is uncalled for, and definitely safe space inducing. But I'll discuss that with my fickin' therapist later." The goblin hawks a loogie on the floor. "Look, the maids here can clean that up. We need to get a move on, to Kayi. Get this horse and pony show on the road."

Ryuk looks around at the grand room, from the elaborate furniture to the floor to ceiling windows overlooking the courtyard outside. "I was wondering why you were resting here."

"Why wouldn't I rest here? It's warm, there are no elves, there's absolutely no chance someone will stab me, and I mean, let's be honest, Marbles, our guild is slowly filling up with immiNPC fickbags, commoners that haven't been properly vetted, huckster-ass-fickboys, two lizards, and your poofty fruit ass. So I needed a little peace and quiet. Fickin' sue me."

"Let's go, Hiccup." Ryuk lifts his finger and a spawning point appears, the location of the rest of his guild appearing in gold letters.

"Wait, before we go to Kayi, let me at least fickin' steal something!"

"Seriously?"

"Yes, *seriously*. Who knows when we'll be back. Fick, when in doubt, loot. Am I right? Look the other way if you're scared the Knights will give a shit."

The goblin waddles over to a cashmere throw blanket on the couch. He rubs the blanket against his cheek, considers its softness, and tosses it into his list.

"Come on, Hiccup, *let's go*."

"Fick, Marbles, never rush an artist mid-loot!"

(0)___(0)

"Hold up, everybody!" Black-eyed FeeTwix says to the mirror in his hand. "Ryuk has left the building. I mean, Ryuk has entered the building!"

Zaena, who sits on Enway's couch, chuckles. She's next to the high elf, and she still wears her sexy white dress from the DJ Ride the Lightning and Holo-Beatles concert. Oric is nowhere to be found, nor are Wolf and Yangu.

"What the twix are you going on about, Ficky? Fick! You know what I mean. I fickin' hate your name. Sounds like a breakfast cereal. Actually, I like breakfast cereals, so I retract my previous statement: I like your name. 'Sup, Twixy."

The two bump fists.

"Wazzup! Sorry for leaving you back there, Hiccup. The place was ..." The Swede clears his throat.

"Was what?"

"A bit odorous, goblin," says Zaena.

"Well excuse me, Princess, but some of us eat well and have evidence of how well we eat."

"How is stuffing your face full of dragon wings eating well?"

"I know this sounds a bit carnivorous, Liz, or should I say cannibalistic? But you get my fickin' point: dragon wings are good eating, and you don't need to be a fickered snowflake foodie to know that. Now, before I can be judged or shamed anymore, I'm out."

Hiccup leaves, heading straight into what Ryuk assumes is Enway's bedroom.

The entire guild's stats appear and Ryuk quickly scans them, remembering where they all stand:

Ryuk Matsuzaki Level 19 Ballistics Mage

HP: 602/602

ATK: 118

MATK: 149

DEF: 89

MDF: 73

LUCK: 24

FeeTwix Fajer Level 21 Berserker Mystic

HP: 815/815

ATK: 170

MATK: 30

DEF: 88

MDF: 51

LUCK: 23

Hiccup Level 18 Shield Thief

HP: 888/888

ATK: 110

MATK: 17

DEF: 241

MDF: 113

LUCK: 38

Zaena Morozon Level 20 Brawler Assassin

HP: 786/786

ATK: 214

MATK: 9

DEF: 119

MDF: 44

LUCK: 24

Enway Zoltan Rosa Level 15 White Mage

HP: 411/435

MANA: 251/268

ATK: 63

MATK: 78

DEF: 55

MDF: 106

LUCK: 19

Oric Rune Level 58 Warrior Berserker

HP: 304/3104

ATK: 554

MATK: 11

DEF: 467

MDF: 389

LUCK: 31

Wolf Level 38

HP: 2296/2296

ATK: 679

MATK: 0

DEF: 521

MDF: 236

LUCK: 19

Enway laughs. "Hiccup is not going to like what he finds in there."

"No, he won't," says FeeTwix. "Now, like I was telling you all, Krunkin' Kronuts has a special this month. It's winter time, and *burrrrr* is it cold! Warm your happy ass up—ha!—with a gingerbread mocha pumpkin spice latte with a maple drizzle, and Krunkin' Kronuts winter exclusive St. Valentine's Day Massacre Kronut with cherry blossom icing, white peppermint sprinkles and a red velvet molten chocolate core. Get you some! Mention #FeeTwixRox at checkout to get a thirty percent discount on the set. This promo is worldwide, people, so whether you're in Seoul, South Korea or Stamford, Connecticut, you get the same discount. Okay, everyone, new contest coming soon. Review my feed for anything you've missed, and I'll be back in a jiffy!"

"We need to talk," Ryuk says as soon as FeeTwix's eyes have gone blue.

"Why the fick is Oric in my bed?" Hiccup asks, stomping back into the room.

"He still isn't well," Enway tells him. "Plus, that's not your bed. You can have my seat if you'd like."

"And sit next to a princess? Don't mind if I do!"

Enway stands and Hiccup plops down into her seat. "You've got yourself quite the warm ass there, Elfy. Wait a minute: that's not sexual harassment, is it?"

Zaena shrugs.

"Fick me, you never can be too careful today. Now, where were we? Someone was saying something."

"I was," Ryuk tells the goblin. "And if you'd be quiet for a moment, I'd be able to finish what I'm saying."

Hiccup chortles. "Damn, Marbles, say your piece. Don't let Uncle Goblin stop you."

"So, there's been a further complication in Tokyo."

Ryuk explains to the guild how Kodai's humandroid assaulted his humandroid, how he intervened, and how he is now hiding out using a fake identity until Hajime is well again.

"So, the robots fought? Fick yeah, I'd pay to see me a good robot fight."

"And you aren't worried about your brother watching FeeTwix's feed and seeing that you're here?" Enway asks.

"I am worried about that, which is why we should move now. It's almost morning, and if we're going to go after the Runestones of Tritinakh, we should start up now. Maybe go up to the Sabors."

"Where were the other two?" FeeTwix asks Ryuk.

"One location is unknown."

"I can have my fans help me with that."

Ryuk nods. "The other is at the easternmost part of the catacombs, under Waringtla, most likely."

"Fick the catacombs and fick ink shadows. Also, did you just say your brother beat your ass again using a robot? Am I following this right? Marbles, you've got to get that dirty fickin' brother of yours in check! If I were you, I'd leave a fickin' IED on his doorstep. Problem solved."

"I don't want to kill him, Hiccup."

"Why the fick not? If this were a goblin issue, it'd already be solved by now. Someone would be 'sleeping with the fishes in the Endless Sea,' if you get my drift."

"Did you say Waringtla?" Oric, now on a crutch, stands in the hallway that leads to Enway's bedroom.

"Glad you could fickin' join us, Tarzan. How's my bed?"

"It's *my* bed," Enway reminds him. "You've never slept in it."

"That's because you didn't let me. Part of the paperwork you signed when you went through your extreme vetting process was about goblin bedding, FYI."

"You're kidding."

Hiccup grins. "It was in Thulean."

"Enough, Hiccup," says FeeTwix. "Yes, Oric, we were talking about Waringtla. Know anything about the place?"

Oric coughs into his arm. "I have an old friend in Waringtla named Lothar who runs a bakery called the Occult Bakery and Athenaeum. He'll definitely know more about the Runestones and their location. Plus, he has a book I'd like to give one of you."

"I love reading," Hiccup says, "as long as it involves a harem, is self-published, barely edited, and combines genres one wouldn't normally think of combining, I'm fickin' sold."

"The book isn't for you." Oric turns to Enway. "It's for you; I believe it would give you quite the leg up, and my friend, Lothar, should be able to explain some of it to you."

"For me?" She smiles at Oric and Ryuk feels a pang of jealousy. "Thanks, Oric!"

"So back to what we were kind of discussing earlier," FeeTwix says, his eyes still blue. "My feed was on when Ryuk arrived. If your brother—"

"—Kodai."

Hiccup snorts. "What kind of poofty ass Japanese name is that? Isn't sushi a Japanese word? I'd love me some fresh lamb sushi."

Lamb sushi? Ryuk cringed at the thought. "Anyway, if Kodai is monitoring my feed, he'll know we were here."

"Which means we need to get on the closest airship out of here," Enway says.

"I'll stay," says Oric, "even with my illness, those fuckers don't stand a chance."

"Well look who is all of a sudden the most confident member of the Mitherfickers," Hiccup stage whispers to Ryuk. "He is a member, right? I'm losing track. If anything, we should let that ninja guy in."

"Yes, Oric is a member, and no, Aiden can't join us."

"Remember when I called him Afternoon Delight?"

"No."

"You're really no fun, Marbles." The goblin slowly stands, his hand on his lower back. "Listen up, Mitherfickers, someone has to take charge here, and that someone is me. Let's go!"

With that the goblin marches to the door, swings it wide open, squeezes out a parting poot, and steps into the streets.

(0)___(x)

"Maybe we should just let him march down the street and right off a cliff. There is a cliff here, correct?" Zaena asks Enway.

"And another thing," Hiccup says as he lets himself back into Enway's antique shop. "Where the fick are Snowballs and Wolfballs?"

Oric points to the back door.

"Good, just checking. The wolf is coming with us, right?" he asks, making his way to the back door. "Not that I like him or anything, but...he's useful. Cute too. Useful and cute. Kind of like me."

"He should probably stay here and protect Oric," FeeTwix says.

"You heard Conan over here, the big man can handle himself. I need a fickin' ride. If we are going a long distance, I don't plan to use these two bow-legged ficksticks to carry me the entire way. No sir. Too much walking."

Hiccup opens the back door and shrieks as a donkey-sized wolf presses through, knocking the goblin on his back.

"Yoy!"

Wolf stands over Hiccup now, licking his face.

"That's adorable!" Enway says to Zaena's laughter.

"You have finally found a friend, goblin," says the Thulean.

And before Hiccup can start up the curse train, a young dragon nearly Wolf's size crashes through the back door, taking both Wolf and Hiccup out.

"Yooooy!"

"Yangu?" Ryuk gasps.

"I forget to tell you that part," says FeeTwix as he places his arm around Ryuk's shoulder. "Yangu is growing."

"Get the fick off me!" Hiccup swats at Wolf until he lets him up. Once on his knees, Hiccup comes face to face with the icy blue snow dragon. "Holy shit, Snowballs, someone needs to put your fat ass on a fickin' diet."

Yangu pulls his neck back, the scales on the back of his forehead lifting. His cheeks puff out, and he blows a small cloud over Hiccup's head, which rains snowflakes onto the goblin's pink topknot.

Back on his feet, Hiccup scoots behind Ryuk, putting the Ballistics Mage between the snow dragon and him.

"You scared, Hiccup?" Ryuk asks.

"No, he's not a fickin' ghost! Just don't want to get my hair all icy. I heard that's a great way to kickstart male-goblin-pattern-baldness. I'll keep my pink topknot, thank you very much. Fick, let's get out of here."

Again, the goblin exits. Yangu approaches Ryuk and drops on the floor before him, showing him his white-blue belly. The snow dragon's tongue falls out of its mouth, and it coos as it looks up at Ryuk, to the collective 'aw's of Enway and Zaena.

"You know," Oric says, once he's sure that Hiccup won't barge back in, "you could leave the goblin here, and I could get him wasted and ship him off to New Gotha."

"Or back to Jatla," Ryuk suggests.

"What are you talking about, guys?" the Swede asks. "Everyone loves Hiccup! His followers have even started a Wikipedia page for him. I think one of them is compiling Hiccup hijinks and quotes into a videobook."

"I agree with Oric," says Zaena. "He is useless, and his disappearance or death would be better for our guild all around."

Wolf barks.

Oric glances down at his towering canine and frowns. "Really?"

"You two can communicate?" Enway asks.

"We've been together for six years now so yes, in a way."

"Well, what did he say?" asks FeeTwix. "And next time you two talk, let me know so I can record it. People love dogs. Add a cute pup to anything and people will love it. Not as click-worthy as kittens, but shit, kittens are gold."

"He indicated that he doesn't dislike the goblin."

Zaena stands. "Let's settle this now, either Wolf goes or stays, but we definitely must go. Who has an airship schedule?"

"I do," says Enway as she takes a slip of paper from her inventory list. "Ah, we can take the shuttle at the Hour of the Mana, not long from now. The ship doesn't go straight to Waringtla; it stops outside the Jatla Forest before it turns south to Talini. That should work, though."

"Good," Ryuk says, turning to the door. "Let's do this then."

Wolf tears past Ryuk and hops over Yangu, who still lies on the ground with his belly up.

Oric laughs. "I guess he is going with you guys then. I'll keep an eye on the snow dragon." He coughs into his hand. "Yangu, correct?"

"Or Snowballs," says FeeTwix as his eyes turn black. "I'm back, everyone! Did you miss me? I missed you, and you, and you, especially you, Kay. That's a great gif, Bobby. Hiya, Todd! Hello, Don, Chi-raq, am I right? Jay, you my bae!"

"What the bloody fick is he going on about?" Hiccup asks as he reenters the space. "And for the love of fick, let's go already."

(x)___(x)

Just as Ryuk expected, their first battle happens just about the moment they touch down in a clearing outside the Attla Forest.

It was a quick trip, their speed bolstered by the fact that the airship didn't have any further stops it needed to make along the way. Hiccup napped on Wolf most of the trip, so their shared cabin was relatively quiet, albeit aromatic at times. FeeTwix mostly spoke to his fans as Zaena lay in his lap. This left Enway and Ryuk to converse, which was mostly her asking him questions about Tokyo and him answering, and then wishing he'd answered in a better way.

"Fick you, spiders!" FeeTwix screams, his tactical vest on and an L85 under each arm. The bullpup assault rifles shred the approaching spiders, acid green ooze spritzing out of the their bodies with each hit they take.

-35 HP! -53 HP! -21 HP! - 38 HP! -72 HP!

The gun-crazed Swede finishes his mags and tosses his weapons aside.

A healing potion appears in his hand and he throws it back, finishing half of it before tossing the potion in the air to Hiccup, who catches it with one hand and back-swings his ax into the multi-eyed face of a spider that's just dropped from a tree.

Instakill!

"Fick yeah!" Wolf zips in front of Hiccup and the goblin latches on, somehow managing to pull his weight up to a full-on ride.

A spider leaps for Hiccup and Wolf just as Ryuk fires a gravity marble at it.

-49 HP!

The gravity marble creates a clear bubble in the air that explodes, sending the spider backwards into a low-hanging branch.

-315 HP! Critical hit!

Using her ghost limbs to propel her forward, Zaena cuts through a cluster of spiders that have surrounded Enway. The Thulean flips and comes down, superhero landing on a spider's body with her swords pointing downward.

Instakill!

"Fickin' Thuleans always showing off. Watch this shit, Lizzy!" Hiccup drops close to Wolf's ear. "Now, do it like I told you, boy."

Wolf speeds up and skids to a halt, catapulting the goblin at a big motherfucking spider with fangs dripping with venom and a shit-ton of angry red eyes. Hiccup's shield appears just in time for him to clobber the spider.

-63 HP!

He follows this up with a series of quick tomahawk attacks, severing most of the spider's legs. The goblin jumps, and squashes the spider's skull with his feet.

Instakill!

"Get you some, Marbles! Fick you, Liz!" he cries as Ryuk unloads a mag of sword marbles at six spiders dropping from the branches.

Insta-Insta-Instakill!

An arc of white light forms in the air over Enway and she floats a few feet above the ground, white mana coursing through her body. The magic spreads outward, covering the Mitherfickers.

Ryuk suddenly feels his stamina increasing, his will to fight strengthening, the muscles in his arms and legs increasing.

His Magic Slingshot out, he fires a direct shot at a spider crawling out of a mangled tree trunk.

Instakill!

Skill level up!

Skill: Gory Headshot

Level Two: Odds of Instakill increase with level.

Odds of Instakill: 59% if enemy is less than level 30; 32% if enemy is greater than level 30.

Caveat: Must be within five meters of opponent's head.

Zaena tosses one of her throwing knives and it zips by, *inches* away from Ryuk's face.

Instakill!

He doesn't have to turn to see that she's killed a spider on the trunk behind him.

"What happens if their venom gets on you again?" Enway asks, now at Ryuk's side.

FeeTwix charges past with his double-bladed sword. He swings it left and right, cutting the limbs off spiders, and leaps back just in time to avoid an attack.

With a flourish, his blades separate from the hilt of his sword and take off. The drone-like blades twist in the air and descend upon the spiders, cutting through their bodies as FeeTwix goes for a sawed-off shotgun.

"If the venom gets on you, you are forced to log out for like a week or something. Careful."

"Got it!"

A molten black marble mag in his gun, Ryuk explodes and melts one of the larger sources of the spiders, which just so happens to be a hole in the ground surrounded by discarded armor and webbing.

Clickety-boom!

"Now is the time, friends, to save at Wendy's Huts worldwide!" the Swede cries as he takes out another spider. "Thought about trying a pizza burger with cheese-y crust and maple bacon on top? How about Dave's single pie with Dave's signature sauce—"

"Ha! I'll give you some signature sauce, Twixy!" Hiccup cries as he rides by on wolfback. "Now quit selling, start fickin' killing."

Clickety-boom!

"As I was saying, Dave's single pie with Dave's signature sauce and a side of Frosty-filled fries? What about ALL OF THE ABOVE for the price of ONE OF THE ABOVE!?"

"Fick yeah, I love bogo!"

Enway looks at Ryuk and laughs. "Are you guys always this fun to fight with?"

A smile spreads across Ryuk's face as he brains another spider. "Not always, but usually."

"That's right, for a limited time, mention #FeeTwixRox at checkout or in-store to get the biggest bogo you've ever got! Son of a ficklord! That spider almost got me. Fick you, spider!"

Clickety-boom!

"'Fick' is my word!" Hiccup says as he comes down hard on a spider, cutting off three of its legs.

Critical hit!

"Dirty filthy creatures." Zaena spins with her blades, cutting through webbing like she's Doctor Octopus.

"I love you too, Liz!" Hiccup and Wolf skid to a halt just in time to avoid a blast from Ryuk's marble gun.

Insta-Instakill!

"Whew! Good work, Marbles, you just may grow a pair yet."

CHAPTER 2: FALLEN ANGEL

TESLA IS LIGHT IN KODAI'S ARMS, much lighter than he thought she'd be. Her eyes are closed, her mouth frozen open, her pupils dilated.

He stares down at her expressionless face and swallows hard. Yugio is with him, standing guard at the door. More hired goons are on the way; his mother arranged this without asking him. Mother knew as soon as Tesla went down.

"The motherfucker." Kodai wipes the hair out of Tesla's face as he holds her like she's a fallen angel.

Yugio turns away from his boss, his hands behind his back.

"She can be fixed." Kodai clears his throat and stands. "Yugio, clean this up. I can't fucking look at it anymore. Check all surveillance footage regarding Ryuk and his exit. It was hasty. I can tell because he left his fucking rig here."

"Yes, Kodai."

"His stupid fucking rig…" As Kodai turns away from Tesla, he quickly fires off a message to Lorem Ipsum, the head of MercSecure Asia.

Kodai: I need a repair.

Lorem Ipsum: It's late. If you are having trouble with Tesla, please contact our services department.

Kodai: It isn't just trouble; she was hit by a Humgun.

Lorem Ispum: I see, and I can safely assume this was during some type of physical combat? I have to ask because of Japanese law. If it wasn't because of physical combat, then you can send the humandroid through normal channels for repair.

Kodai: It was through physical combat.

Lorem Ipsum: In that case, I'll have the service department handle this. Is it possible to have her body delivered to our repair facility near Shimokitazawa?

Kodai: It is.

Lorem Ipsum: Done. <u>Here are the rest of the details you need to know.</u> Good luck.

"It's handled," Kodai tells Yugio. "Please have Tesla brought down. Quickly too. I don't expect a visit from the authorities, but I'd like to make certain that is not a possibility. Let's move fast."

(0)__(0)

Kodai and a small army of goons arrive at the MercSecure repair facility outside Shimokitazawa. A light snow blows flurries into the air and a crisp, familiar coldness meets his face as he stepped out of the vehicle.

He is greeted by an older American man in a parka, who does nothing to hide the assault rifle in his hands.

"Let's move," the man says instead of hello.

Kodai recognizes him from his rooftop breakfast with Lorem Ipsum.

"We've met before," he says as they enter the facility and turn left into a featureless, gray hallway. A woman in MercSecure fatigues takes the man's weapon from him, and he offers her a short nod.

"Walt," the man says. "And it is nice to see you again, Kodai."

Kodai looks over his shoulder. "Should my men...?"

"Your men have already been given their instructions."

"And where are we going?"

"To a viewing room." Walt, a grizzled mercenary if there ever was one, turns to Kodai and smiles briskly. "Wouldn't you like to see how all this happened in the first place?"

"I would."

"Then follow me."

They take a left, a right, another left, and eventually arrive at a room with the number six on the door.

"After you," Walt says as he opens the door.

The room overlooks a gurney and various medical tools, cables, monitors, and even a 3-D rendering machine.

An operating theater.

Kodai sits and a series of lights flick on in the operating theater. Two MercSecure engineers roll in Tesla's body and transfer it to the main gurney. Using a large pair of scissors, they remove her clothing and begin hooking her up to a grouping of tubes.

A woman doctor enters, decked in seafoam green scrubs.

"Is this really that serious?" Kodai asks, no hint of sarcasm in his voice. He has no idea what goes into rebooting a humandroid.

"Precautions. MercSecure treats the recovery aspect of humandroids as they would any of their representatives. Protocol, really, but it is important to maintain the status quo, and it is equally important to bill the client accordingly."

"Heh. I figured that much."

"Ah, this should be interesting," Walt says as the female doctor scans the side of Tesla's neck with a small device that looks like a divining rod. The red light on Tesla's nearly translucent skin turns green, indicating that the upload is complete.

"The encrypted recording from her iNet feed," Walt explains.

"Good," says Kodai, "let's see what happened."

The window in front of them blackens as Tesla's video recording plays. The video shows her first-person struggle with Hajime, a struggle she is about to win when Ryuk gets involved.

"My younger brother?" Kodai shakes his head.

"With the humgun? Interesting."

Kodai and Walt watch as Ryuk points the weapon at Tesla. Her feed suddenly fizzles out.

"So, it *was* him. I thought Hajime did it, assumed he had done it."

Walt nods. "I would have thought that as well. Little known fact, I've actually fought Hajime, once, when we were on opposite sides of a conflict in eastern Ukraine."

"You fought a humandroid?"

The blue eyed mercenary bites his lip. "I did, and I'm lucky I only lost one leg." He knocks on his right thigh. "If it hadn't been for my team, Hajime would have ended it."

"And now you two work together?"

Walt grimaces. "We work for the same company, not together. But back to the video. I must admit, especially after seeing Hajime in action, it was almost like he wasn't trying to fight back. As I've said, I've seen what that humandroid can do. Even with her power, the Hajime I know would have ended it."

"Why would he let her overpower him like that?"

Walt shrugs. "Maybe he was toying with her."

"Toying with her? She *completely* disabled him."

"She did do that." Walt considers this for a moment as the video plays back. "In that case, then, she got lucky."

"How long until she is fully operational again?"

"Not today. It takes up to twenty-four hours for a complete reboot."

"But she'll be her old self again tomorrow?" Kodai asks, desperation in his voice.

"Yes, I believe so."

CHAPTER 3:
BUGBEARS ARE ASSHOLES

EVEN THOUGH IT IS EARLY MORNING, the foliage of the Attla Forest keeps the ground bathed in shadows. Walking ahead are FeeTwix and Zaena, followed by Hiccup on Wolf's back and then Enway and Ryuk, who have been instructed to hang towards the back because of their classes.

It is good advice, actually, and even though he's technically the leader, or at least everyone treats him like he is, Ryuk lets Zaena take the lead on this one.

If she has changed any since revealing she's a princess, he really can't tell.

The fact that she's threatened to throttle Hiccup multiple times for mentioning the word 'princess' only reminds Ryuk of how powerful the word is to her, and how little she'd like others to acknowledge her background.

I get that, Ryuk thinks. He too would like to forget his background, his mother and his brother, the sick business that has made his family wealthy to the point that he's never even considered the cost of things.

He acts as if he's your average college dropout barely making ends meet, his motto remaining something along the lines of: I didn't ask for this, all this came to me.

Sometimes, there is no other way to cope.

"Ever see that episode of *Flight Feet* in which they fight their way to Spider Skull Island? I love that one!" Enway smiles at Ryuk, the ends of her white skirt bouncing as she steps lightly from one rock to the next. "The queen spider is so freaky..."

"They always play that episode," Ryuk says, recalling when he went to the Tokyo International Anime Fair with Tamana, and the fun they had there. A pang of sadness spreads through him: *things were so much simpler at that time.*

"Yeah, well if anyone is asking, I hate spiders too," Hiccup says, having a one-sided conversation with Wolf. "You're right, pal, I should fickin' clarify my hatred before Princess Liz over there says I'm some sort of bigot. Racist, yes, Liz, maybe, but I'm no bigot. Spiders are ficked."

Zaena stops, her fists clenched at her sides. "You are the very definition of bigot, Hiccup. I wouldn't be surprised if your name really was Hiccupanaratabigot." She laughs at her own joke. FeeTwix grins like Liz just dropped a dad joke, which only makes her laugh harder.

"Laugh it up, Liztard. We'll see who is the bigot once I get to meet your family."

"Meet my family?" she shakes her head. "I hope there is never such a day."

"Don't listen to her, Wolfy," Hiccup says as he trots forward on wolfback. "Haters gonna hate, but you already knew that. All dogs know that. I mean, you fickers have cats to deal with. And fick cats, unless we're speaking about kittens, because they're cute as fick. Delicious too."

"Gross," Enway whispers.

The cantankerous goblin pauses for a moment as he tries to remember the point he was trying to make. "Where was I, Twixy?"

"Beats me, Hiccup. I tuned you out long ago, old pal."

"Is that any way to speak to an elder? Don't they have respect for distinguished members of society in Swedish culture? Okay then, um, Marbles, catch me up to speed," Hiccup calls over his shoulder. "What the fick was I talking about?"

"I'm not your notepad, Hiccup."

"Like fick you aren't. You're practically my legal assistant over there, and if you really want to know how to get a whiff of Enway's lady choop, it starts with charity towards your elders."

Enway shakes her head. "I'm offended and at the same time *finally* happy you learned to use the word chalupa correctly. Yes, Hiccup, I have a chalupa, or lady choop, as you call it. And you have a churro."

Ryuk steps around a curious stump in their path. Thulean script is carved into the stump, and upon reading it, Hiccup announces that this was the very same path the Knights of Non Compos Mentis traversed over fifteen years ago.

"See kids, it is helpful to be able to read," he says, matter-of-factly.

"We can all read, Hiccup. I'm assuming at least a few of us can read in multiple languages," says FeeTwix. "I know I can."

"Same here," says Enway.

"I can read English," Ryuk adds, "but maybe my speaking isn't so good."

"I'm sure it's fine, pal," FeeTwix says. "And we're going to find out soon enough. I'll be in Tokyo in a couple of hours. I'm already at the airport, awaiting my flight. I'll be logged in the entire time aside from takeoff and landing. I'll go on auto-level for those times. Can't miss a beat!"

Propping up FeeTwix's perfectly arranged blond hair is his Reaper skull, which is now latched to his forehead thanks to Enway's handiwork back in Kayi.

"I too understand several languages," Zaena adds. "Thulean, English, and ancient Thulean."

"Fick me, I try to make a point and you three drill it into the ground. Come on, Wolfy, let's ride ahead. If you feel the need to relieve yourself, now would be an appropriate time."

Wolf comes to a halt, nearly bucking Hiccup off. He barks as his ears flick back.

"Keep your cool, Wolfy, there are no bitches in this forest. Ha! Finally, *finally,* I can use that word in its proper context."

"Riptak jatla blanktakh boomboom morrha."

"Fick me thrice and call me Dumbledick. How many times do I have to tell you, Liz? Calling me a 'filthy goblin' is a compliment in my neck of the woods. And my mother wasn't a whore. Or at least I don't think she was."

Wolf barks again and starts backing up.

"Whoa! Keep your red rocket in its socket, Wolf, there's nothing to get fickin' worked up about!"

To prove his point, Hiccup hops down from the immiNPC canine and waddles out into the main path.

"See? Yoooooooy!"

Hiccup's shout disappears as the ground gives way beneath him. The rest of the Mitherfickers hear a sickening splat followed by Hiccup's cursing as he hits the bottom of the hole.

"Yoy ...yoy...fick me!"

"It's a trap!" FeeTwix shouts, his eyes black as ever. "I know, guys, I know," he tells his fans. "I'll try again. 'It's a trap!' Copyright DisNike. Better? Don't want any lawsuits." A Gatling gun with a hand crank forms in FeeTwix's hand and he starts cranking it up. "Hang on, Hiccup! We're going to clear the area!"

"Don't fickin' clear the area!" Hiccup shouts up from the bottom of the hole. "What's the cranking sound? Fick! There could be ghosts in this hole. Ever heard of hole ghosts? Ha! I know a hole ghost joke about a brothel that burned down in the Red Lamp District, but that's a joke for another day. Fick! What just touched me?"

"Thank me later," Zaena says, clearly not happy to use her ghost limbs to lift the goblin out of the hole.

Enway turns left, a sphere of magic forming at her wrist. Ryuk keeps his eyes on their three o'clock, his Marble Gun aimed at the dark forest.

"Give me something to shoot at," FeeTwix says, biting his lip as he keeps the muzzle of his steampunk gun aimed to the left. "Come on..."

Zaena drops Hiccup onto the ground and the goblin cushions his landing with a spicy concussive blast from his nethercheeks.

"Goblin!"

"Fick you, Liz. What did you expect when you lift my ass out of a hole and drop me on the ground? The air has to go somewhere."

Enway's nose scrunches up. "Ewww..."

"Sorry," Ryuk says, suppressing the urge to bow on Hiccup's behalf.

"Stop farting, Hiccup, and get your ass ready!" FeeTwix shouts, the partial Reaper skull over his face. "Bugbears. Nine o'clock!"

(0)___(0)

Three bugbears step out of the shadows, ugly fuckers with odd patches of hair on their loinclothed bodies and big, bloodshot eyes under bushy eyebrows. If *Deliverance* were set in a Proxima fantasy world, these three would be offered starring roles.

Shit, Ryuk thinks as the two level twenty bugbears brandish clubs made of Sabor Mammoth bone. The third, a level thirty bugbear, goes for a blade made of polished ivory nearly the size of a buster sword. Armor crafted from rib cages, skulls, and various dragon parts form on their bodies as the one with the sword steps forward.

"Fick! Bugbears," Hiccup says, pushing to the front of the group. "Just follow my lead, Mitherfickers. While I don't care to admit it too often, bugbears are actually distant cousins of goblins."

"This better be good," Zaena tells him.

"Fellas! I'm going to go ahead and guess it was you fickers who set the trap back there." Hiccup nods at the three, impressed. "But a little sage advice from a goblin with a penchant for being right and a 154-year track record to back it up: if you are going to set a hole-in-the-ground trap, then put some fickin' spikes down there. Shit. Look at your bone weapons. I'm guessing there are plenty more where those came from. All I'm saying here is to put a few of those fickers in the hole next time. I would have been skewered as fick, if you get my drift."

Ryuk looks at Enway, anger furrowing his brow.

"Why is he giving them advice?" asks Enway.

"I don't know, *but this ends now*." Ryuk lifts his Marble Gun and fires four explosive marbles over Hiccup's head.

-215 HP! -173 HP! -115 HP!

New skill learned!

Skill: Preemptive Strike

Level One: Distract your enemies, or have your guildmates distract them and receive a fifteen percent bonus on your attack.

Requirements: Level 18 Mage, LUCK > 20.

"Premature ejaculation, Marbles!" Hiccup shouts, jumping sideways to avoid any bits of bone from the bugbear's armor.

Click, CLANK, click, CLANK, click, CLANK!

FeeTwix's hand-crank Gatling gun makes its presence known.

His feed being broadcast to all his fans, FeeTwix laughs as he cranks the weapon and more bullets tear into the bugbears, two of whom dive left as the biggest and most badass bugbear takes the brunt of FeeTwix's bullets.

Zaena goes to engage the first bugbear. He swipes his femur club at her, and she just barely manages to stop it with her blades.

Baring her teeth, Zaena's ghost limbs fly over her, blades twisting in the air. The bugbear goes to block them, only to pause briefly as the swords go *over him*.

She comes up and over, crying out as she lands behind the creature and swipes her swords at his back.

-149 HP! Critical hit!

"Roarrrrrr!"

The bugbear stumbles forward; Zaena pulls her ghost limb blades from the ground and gets in a battle-ready position, one leg before the other.

Whooosh!

Her opponent is tossed forward by a white blast from Enway.

Zaena's reaction is immediate. The Thulean warrior princess twists; the bugbear's head goes flying, purple blood spraying out the other end.

Instakill!

The other bugbear with a clubbing bone tries to hit Hiccup, who scoots by on Wolf and barely dodges the blow.

"Fick you!" the goblin cries as he goes back around for another swipe.

With limited combat room, Wolf is hitting all sorts of stops and pivots to keep the bugbear at bay. Meanwhile, FeeTwix has a Terry Funk barbed wire wrapped baseball bat, which he uses to engage the largest bugbear.

It doesn't make the greatest weapon, but FeeTwix, as always, is going for style over practicality.

The big bugbear swings his bone buster sword at the Swede.

FeeTwix steps out of the way just in time, and is about to bring his barbed baseball bat onto the back of the big fucker's head, when the bugbear taps him in the chin with an elbow.

"Shit!" Ryuk aims his Marble Gun at the bugbear just as FeeTwix flies backwards, hits the ground, and tumbles.

-49 HP!

Without the boost from his preemptive strike, Ryuk's black marble does considerably less damage than before. It does stop the bugbear's advance, giving FeeTwix the time he needs to roll out of the way.

"Fick! Fick!" Hiccup shouts, running towards Ryuk.

Enway points, and Ryuk sees what has got the goblin so worked up.

The other bugbear has equipped a bag of bees and is in the process of letting them go on the battlefield.

(0)__(x)

"I've got this!" An industrial sized can of Raid flying insect killer materializes in FeeTwix's hand. He takes aim at the oncoming swarm and lets them have it.

"Fick yeah, Twixy, give those fickers the money shot!"

He keeps laying down a thick stream of foam as he shouts, "That's not what that's called!"

Enway looks to Ryuk, who is tracking the biggest bugbear with his Marble Gun. The bugbear leader has taken a step back, still recovering from Ryuk's last attack.

After the bees are handled, a poll appears before the trigger-happy Swede.

"Really guys? You went with the pinecone? And over an R. Moore signature pedo-pistol? It's so small, antiquated, and pathetic! Roll tide, bitches! And what's wrong with Hacksaw Jim Duggan's 2x4? Fine, pinecone it is."

The pinecone appears in FeeTwix's hand, and Ryuk immediately sees that there is more to this pinecone than meets the eye.

"*Konoshlo duka duchaka!*" Zaena cartwheels over to the second bug bear and moves into a four-blade attack that comes coupled with a Thulean battle cry.

"Fick, Liz, save the orgasm for Twixy, ha!" Hiccup pats Wolf's head. "Get ready, boy, we're about do us some fickin' killing."

A message flashes on Ryuk's vision pane.

FeeTwix: Okay, distract the big fucker and I'll deliver the package.

Ryuk: The pinecone?

FeeTwix: Not just any pinecone, this is a pinecone IED from Unigaea! Enway gave it to me. Thanks, Enway.

Enway: No problem!

Ryuk: An IED?

FeeTwix: Improvised Explosive Device!

Hiccup: I don't remember Elfy giving you shit. Why the fick didn't I get a gift? It's close to Valentine's Day, right? Or has that already passed?

Enway: I'm having a churro made especially for you. It's shaped like a heart.

Hiccup: Fick, Elfy, what part of *no fake news on the chat screen* do you fail to understand? Speaking of alternative facts: anyone ever thought about how it's fickin' odd that I, an NPC goblin, can communicate this way? I mean, sure, you guys are logged in, fick-faced commoners and whatnot, but no one ever says anything about how weird it is for NPCs to send messages on vision panes. Princess Velociraptor included.

Zaena: Stop talking, goblin, you're distracting me!

Hiccup: Just saying, Lizzy. It's like one of the Proxima developers didn't really think this one through. Too much chalupa, probably. I'll bet video game developers in your world get all the lady choop. Probably high-quality guys too, who are clearly not overweight and who practice good hygiene. Definitely not losers.

Ryuk: Shut up, Hiccup!

-184 HP!

"No!" Zaena cries as she's struck in the gut by the second bugbear.

"Fick!" Hiccup launches into overdrive, concern splashed across his face. "I've got Liz, you three fickers kill that other ficker!" Twisting around a branch jutting out of the ground, Hiccup goes to Zaena's rescue.

Wolf's fast, fast enough that the hefty goblin reaches Zaena before the bugbear can hit her again. "If anyone is killing her, it's me!" the goblin says as he launches off Wolf onto the bugbear.

"Yooooy!"

The monster easily tosses the gassy goblin off his shoulders and Hiccup flies into a tree, the sound of his snapping back barely muffled by the dense forest.

The bugbear leader looks at FeeTwix and then at Ryuk and Enway.

"Distraction, Ryuk!"

FeeTwix floats like a butterfly to sting like a bee as he goes from foot to foot, pinecone in hand as he sizes the biggest bugbear up. The fantasy monstrosity roars, spit flying from its mouth.

"Now!" A lighter in his left hand, the crazy ass Swede lights the end of the pinecone and backpedals for a moment as Ryuk lines up his shot.

Four shots later and the ground before the bugbear explodes into dust.

"Catch, mitherficker!" FeeTwix baseball-slides to the right of the bugbear, the pinecone making a perfect arc in the air.

The pinecone explodes in the bugbear's hands, sending his arms flying and spritzing the air with blood.

"Fick yeah, Twixy," Hiccup wheezes as the now armless bugbear stumbles away.

"Get behind me," Ryuk says as the only bugbear with arms left stomps over to Enway.

Ryuk can see Zaena behind the creature, on the ground and holding her side.

FeeTwix is focused on the bugbear trying to get away, and Ryuk has no idea where Wolf ran off to.

"Get behind me, Enway!" he shouts.

A hand pushes Ryuk to the side and he turns just in time to see the high elf floating towards the bugbear, white magic radiating off her hands.

A glowing cloud of ivory white needles forms around Enway's body. With a flick of both of her wrists, she fires the luminescent points at the bugbear.

They connect, and the bugbear pauses dead in his tracks.

"Fick you, you fickered fickbag!" Hiccup, seemingly out of nowhere, latches onto the bugbear's legs.

He bites and claws the temporarily frozen bugbear, growling as he does so.

-8 HP! - 6 HP! -7 HP! -5 HP! -30 HP! -9 HP!

Enway's freezing spell only lasts about twenty seconds, and as the bugbear regains movement, Wolf leaps up and grabs the monster's jugular, his body mass causing the creature to stumble backwards over Hiccup.

Instakill!

Wolf snarls as he continues to rip into the bugbear's throat.

"Say hello to my little friend!" the Swede bellows in an Italian accent.

VOOMSH!

Instakill!

FeeTwix cuts the armless bugbear down with a ball of green plasma.

He lowers his off-world weapon, drops to a knee and immediately goes for a healing potion. Once he's taken a swig, the Swede hobbles over to Zaena, helps her up, and lets her finish the potion.

"Where's my fickin' cut?" Hiccup asks, finally out from under the now throatless bugbear.

"Here you go, Hiccup, a bacon-flavored Cherry Apollos with your name on it!" FeeTwix tosses the goblin a fresh healing potion.

"Bacon-flavored? Fick yeah!" Hiccup downs the bottle, burps, and tosses it over his shoulder, where it plinks off the dead bugbear's skull. "Yom, everybody, I got a fickin' level up!"

"Me too," says FeeTwix. "Anyone else?"

"Same," Enway says, slightly out of breath.

CHAPTER 4: OCCULT BAKERY AND ATHENAEUM

As the five Mitherfickers walk towards the giant city of Waringtla, Ryuk gets to hear more than he'd like to hear about bugbear history, anatomical differences, stool consistencies and how to spot droppings in the wild.

It is a long history, and for the most part he tunes the often-irreverent goblin out, focusing more on the journey that lies ahead and the occasional sidelong glance from Enway, who he can say with certainty has taken a liking to him.

"On the airplane right now," FeeTwix says as they approach the Waringtla city gates. "I hope your ass is ready to meet me in person, because I'm definitely ready to meet you."

"My ass is ready to meet anyone and everyone." Hiccup laughs. "I'm a funny guy, Liz, believe me."

Ryuk turns to FeeTwix to confirm his eyes are indeed blue.

"What? You thought I was going to give you away? Come on, what kind of brother from a different mother would I be if I gave my homeboy away?"

"Homeboy? What kind of fruity poofcake word is that, Twixy? In Jatla, a 'homeboy' is a younger goblin one percenters keep under the stairs. Whenever they go upstairs to their bedrooms or come down for the day, the homeboy cleans their feet using brushes made of, you guessed it, dragon scales. They also fick him. Well, some do. Not everyone, but some."

"That sounds terrible, goblin."

"Fick me, Liz, here I was just about to compliment your species on their nice skin and its practical uses—including, but not limited to: perineum polishing, underarm exfoliation, goblin BSD&M, souvenirs, and general flogging purposes—and you have to go and put the racist hat on. Next thing we know, you'll be calling drows 'darkies' and elves 'crackers.' Anyone ever notice how elves are always white? Seems fishy, if you ask me, Liz."

"Hush, goblin, your voice gives me a headache."

"Hiccup," FeeTwix says, stepping around the goblin. "Your fans want to say hi!" His eyes a soulless black, the Swede bends over so Hiccup can deliver a message to his fans.

"Out of my way, Twixy!"

"Oh, come on, don't you want to say something to your fans?"

"Fick yeah, I do." He bites his lip for a moment as he thinks. "Okay, here it is: look kiddos, for some reason, all thirty—was it thirty thousand?"

"Now it is sixty thousand!"

"All sixty thousand of you have somehow, in your sad little lives, found time to embrace a goblin who isn't even real in your world. Fick. Can you believe that? But you know what, Uncle Goblin is here for you anyway, that is, if you happen to be sexy or sexy-ish, and can meet me in Waringtla tonight."

"Hiccup!" Ryuk says.

"What? Marbles? Let me spell it out to you in words you can understand: Chalupa plus dry equals bad. I need to dampen it, if you get my drift."

FeeTwix's eyes flash blue. "Please, Hiccup, do not ask my fans to come sleep with you. It is a great power you wield over them and many would likely take you up on your offer."

"Why the fick not? Why get all this power if I'm not going to get downright evil with it? They have diseases or something? Fick, at my age, any disease I get now will just be added to the stack."

Enway pushes past Hiccup. "I'd rather not hear about your love life at the moment."

"I'm a romantic at heart."

She skips ahead and Ryuk jogs to catch up with her.

"He can be hard to deal with," Ryuk says as soon as he reaches her. They now stand directly beneath a guard tower easily the height of an eight-story building.

"It's fine," she says, "just needed a breath of fresh air."

"You were downwind?"

"I was." She pinches her nose, a strand of her blonde hair falling into her face. "I'll say this while we have some privacy: you and I should spend more time together someday." Her face goes red. "Not like that! I mean, I just want to know more about you, and it's hard in the guild setting, with so many different types of, um, members."

"You down there!" The two look up to see a giant eye looking down on them. On second glance, Ryuk realizes it's a giant looking at them through a mounted spyglass.

"Hi!" Enway says, waving at the giant.

"What brings you to these parts?" asks the giant.

"Who the fick is saying that?" Hiccup asks as he approaches. The goblin is short of breath, a bead of sweat trailing down the side of his head.

Ryuk considers this for a moment as his Extreme Focus skill kicks into gear. *How did he work up a sweat riding Wolf?*

"Hello, Mr. Giant!" FeeTwix calls up to the man.

"Enough formalities, what brings you to these parts?" the booming voice calls down.

"Do your thing, Liz." Hiccup elbows in her direction, too lazy to actually move over to her.

"Ahem, I am Princess Renata of the Thulean Royal Family, and I request expedited entry into the city along with my traveling companions."

"Fick yeah, Liz," the goblin whispers. He wipes a fake tear away. "Fickin' making your uncle proud over here."

"You may enter!"

Hiccup trots through the city gates, still on wolfback. Ryuk glances up to the top of the tower and back to the entrance, wondering how they would have been prevented from entering in the first place.

(0)__(0)

The streets of Waringtla are divided into three lanes: the far-left lane for giants, the middle lane for commercial goods transport, and the far-right lane for normal-sized people. Shops line the streets, most with two entrances, one for giants and the other for everyone else.

"You fickers ever seen so much segregation? Giant door here, small person door there, 'no small people allowed.' Fick if this isn't a repressive ass city, nothing like Jatla, which treats everyone equally."

"Like shit?" Ryuk asks.

"Fick, Marbles, you get a little future booty confidence from Elfy over there and you get emboldened enough to talk back to your elders. Sad! Don't make me open up a can of whoopass, kiddo. Believe you me, I may be relatively handsome, short in stature, a stable genius, with a full head of pink hair and a mechanical arm, but I'm no blowhard."

"I think the word you mean is pushover," says FeeTwix. "Blowhard is something else entirely."

Zaena laughs. "Actually, blowhard defines you quite well."

Offended, Hiccup lifts his nose in the air and tells Wolf to trot ahead. Ryuk watches them pass, admiring the wolf and his healthy coat of black hair and his blue-green eyes. Wolf hasn't really warmed up to Ryuk, but then again, he hasn't really tried to make friends.

This thought triggers an image of Yangu the dragon, and the fact that Ryuk has spent little time with his familiar. *Maybe Hiccup was right, maybe I am an absent father.*

The goblin places two booger-encrusted fingers in his mouth and whistles at a passing female goblin, who is a head taller than Hiccup.

"What the fick do you want?" the goblinita asks.

"Fick, lady, there's a lot of things I want, starting with a nuru massage followed by a hot waxing, but that's not the point. What the fick is a goblin doing in Waringtla?"

The lady goblin, who wears a push up bra which adds quite a bit of skin to her otherwise normal peasant's dress, brushes a strand of hair from her face. "For your information, I'm in Waringtla to see Og Lemon. What the fick is a washed up old goblin with pink hair riding a fickin' wolf doing here? That's the real question."

FeeTwix pauses, his mirror appearing in his hand. "Okay, everyone, we're in a giant city, is it better if I say 'city of giants?' Speaking of giants, I want to tell you fickers—sorry, too much time around Hiccup—about a giant offer from CVSgreens! CVSgreens are longtime supporters of the feed, and hell, just about the best one-stop pharmaceutical company slash late night condom purchasing spot. You'll love what they're offering worldwide audiences! And really, what goes better with a bag of LoCal Non-GMO chili cheese Dorito-dusted Cheetos with molten cheddar cheese cores, than a high octane zero carb vitamin enhanced energy drink?"

"Ignore him," Hiccup tells the female goblin, "and I'll ignore your question about my pink hair and my traveling preference. Og Lemon is an old friend of mine."

The way Hiccup says this makes Ryuk think that Og is not in fact an old friend.

"A friend, huh?" she asks, her mood lightening.

"Yeah, Og and I go way back, and that ficker owes me after what happened last time."

"Well," she says with a flirty thrust of her shoulder, "if you need someone to join you for dinner, you can find me at the $Hotel on Stater Street."

"Yeah, I'll have my people talk to your people," Hiccup says, no longer paying attention to the gobliness. "Let's go, Mitherfickers."

Hiccup rides forward and the others eventually catch up.

"You had yourself a date there, goblin, I hope you don't blow it."

"Not now, Liz," says Hiccup.

"Come on, she seemed genuinely interested."

"Maybe, but she's no better than one of Twixy's bandwagon fickboys. Look, if I'm going to go on a date, I want the lady to like me. Otherwise, I'll just pay for it. I don't like being used. Speaking of which, Marbles, I have a little side quest for you and me."

Ryuk places his hands on his hips. "Us? What's the reward?"

"The reward? Pfft! The *reward* is getting to spend time with an elder, something I thought you Japanese appreciated. Look, the guy the goblinita was talking about, Og Lemon, the ficktard severely ficked me over. I almost lost my chalupa because of that fickered ficktwat. Remember the ink shadow I told you about? The one that I almost lost my chalupa to? Well, Og Lemon's fickered ass is to blame there."

"We are sort of busy right now," Ryuk says, annoyed at the goblin.

"Too busy to get revenge?"

Enway says, "Let's just meet the giant Oric wanted us to meet, then we can figure out our night from there."

"Of course she wants to meet the giant, he's got a gift for her. Come on, Wolf, you and I are out of here."

Wolf stops, even though Hiccup drives his heels into his sides.

"The beast is more loyal than you are, goblin!" Zaena laughs.

"What the fick ever," Hiccup says, giving up.

"Okay, according to my map, again provided by Jack S., Cartographer extraordinaire, the Occult Bakery and Athenaeum should be just a few blocks from here." FeeTwix stops to admire a passing giant, who carries an uprooted tree at his side. "You know, I've never fought a giant. Quantum Hughes did, though."

"I've told you my thoughts on that man," Zaena says bitterly. "He cheated in a fight against my sister. Also, there's something I haven't told you about him."

"Gee fick, you act like he porked you and things went poorly, Liz. Get over it."

"Pork? What is this pork you speak of, goblin, and what does it have to do with Quantum Hughes?"

"Never mind, babe!" FeeTwix says, leading her away from the goblin. He looks at Hiccup when Zaena can't see and gives him the 'I'll cut your throat' hand gesture.

Ryuk laughs.

"Laugh it up, Marbles. Twixy knows better than to bring it to me. We may be besties and possibly the most useful members of this guild, but I'd kill that vain ficker in a heartbeat."

"Let's just get to the bakery," says Ryuk. He glances at Enway as a light smile spreads across her face.

(0)__(x)

"It's *yuge*," Hiccup says once he spots the bakery.

His tongue hanging out of the side of his mouth, Wolf looks exhausted from carting the goblin's fat ass around. He pants, tries to sit, but Hiccup tells him to keep on all fours.

"Give Wolf a break," Enway says. "You can walk up those stairs."

The stairs aren't really stairs per se, they are three giant steps with a ramp that travels to the top for commoners. Hiccup grumbles about extreme vetting as he dismounts from Wolf. He stretches his arms over his head, yawns, burps, and begins walking up the ramp.

A passing giant looks down at the Mitherfickers and frowns at the pink-haired, mechanically armed goblin.

"Is he maddoggin' me?" Hiccup asks Ryuk, who is a comfortable distance behind him so as not to be blasted if the goblin decides to exhume the dinner corpse.

"Did you say maddogging?"

"Keep with the lingo, Marbles, I'm a copesetic ficker who uses big words bigly. We clear?" The goblin eyes him for a moment, then with a big huff, he takes another step forward.

"He's grumpy today," Enway tells Ryuk once the goblin is out of hearing range.

"No, he's Hiccup."

The Occult Bakery and Athenaeum is located in a two-story building, and two stories by giant standards means that it is about the same height as a five to six story building for commoners.

There are dual entrances, one for commoners, the other for giants, and the exterior of the building has recently been upgraded, the walls now featuring a stucco lace texture.

As the Mitherfickers enter, they're greeted by a bespeckled giant behind the counter. The giant has red hair and a chin covered with beard stubble. He wears a bright red apron over dark blue robes.

"Wolf?" he asks almost immediately.

Wolf barks himself into a frenzy upon seeing the giant.

He runs in a circle, his tail wagging, and as soon as the giant has stepped around the counter, Wolf comes tearing across the lobby to him.

"You must be Lothar," FeeTwix says as he scans the giant with jet black eyes. "Oric sent us."

"Ah, Oric! Which would explain Wolf," the giant says, as he bends down to pet Wolf with his finger.

"Yes, it would," Hiccup stage whispers to Ryuk. "Methinks the giant's brain doesn't match his size."

"Ha! And a cranky goblin in the midst, huh? I assure you, goblin, my brain is adequate for my body size."

"The name is Hiccup."

"Short for Hiccupanaratapana, yes?"

"I thought someone said he was from fickin' Unigaea. Didn't Conan say that? I'm fickin' hearing things." Hiccup sticks his pinky in his ear, twists, and comes back with a bring orange glob of earwax, which he proceeds to flick at FeeTwix.

"Quiet, goblin," the Thulean warrior princess says. "Lothar, it is a pleasure to meet you. My name is Zaena."

"Another shortened name. You are of Thulean royalty, yes?" The giant finishes petting Wolf with his finger and gets back to his feet, his hands now at his sides.

Zaena runs her hands over the front of her armor. "I am. It is short for Zaechana."

"Empress? Your name means *empress*?" Hiccup snorts.

"It means *queen*. 'Empress' is a southern interpretation of the word."

"You are a princess who is named Queen," Lothar says, stroking his beard. "Is this a Thulean joke?"

Zaena nods, the look on her face indecipherable. "I am the youngest of my family. The likelihood of me becoming the queen, like my older sister Renata, is close to zero. So, my parents named me 'Zaechana' or 'Zaena' for short."

"Fick me," Hiccup uses his clawed finger to scratch at a food stain on his mechanical hand. "That's what's called an absentee parent right there, kind of like how Marbles is to Snowballs, and kind of like how I was to Spew Gorge."

"I thought Spew Gorge was your cousin?" FeeTwix asks.

"Yeah, and my son. Then again, he may not be. Beats the fick out of me. There isn't a fickin' way to do a paternity test in Jatla unless you have healthcare, and I don't have healthcare." He glares at Ryuk. "Which is another complaint I plan to register once my current complaints and grievances are all addressed."

"No one said anything to me about healthcare," Ryuk says, on the defensive.

"It's called employee perks, Marbles, and like other employers in Jatla, you could at least provide a starfish scrub, a three-day weekend, or hell, a fickin' ten-minute break after a long shift. But nope, you and Tammy are a 'right to work' kind of employer, so I don't even get that. All I'm saying is healthcare is a basic goblin right, as is getting your chalupa regularly jerked, and the occasional three-day weekend. Fick." Hiccup's nostrils flare. "By the way, Big Guy, it smells yummy in here. Howzabout hooking some of Tarzan's best pals up with some grub?"

"Tarzan?"

"The barbarian guy; the wolf's owner."

"You mean Oric."

"Sure, call him that, but it sounds too much like orc and I'm not a fan of those fickers. Where the fick were we?"

"I'll take over from here," FeeTwix says, stepping around Hiccup. "Hello again, Lothar! Oric said you may have some details regarding the Runestones of Tritinakh. He also said you'd have book for us."

"A book?" Lothar asks.

"That's what he said."

The giant looks at each of them and then turns back to the counter. Once he's on the other side, he swings open the kitchen door and calls out, "Gadsaa, I'm taking guests to the library. Is that okay, dear?"

After he has received a response, he turns to a spiral staircase in the corner of the bakery and tells the Mitherfickers to follow him.

"Not another staircase," Hiccup grumbles.

(x)__(x)

"So, a little background," Lothar says as he sits on a large leather sofa chair set behind an enormous polar bear rug. With no place to sit, the Mitherfickers take a seat on the fur. Zaena remains standing, her arms crossed over her chest.

"No backstories, please," Hiccup laments. His boots are already off, his funkified feet fouling up the air. Surprisingly, only Wolf tolerates the smell, which goes to show just how dumbly loyal dogs can be.

The others sit on the other side of the rug, as far from the funk as possible without triggering the goblin.

"It all began on a relatively warm winter day on a trip from the city of giants known as Tael to the city of scholars known as Solidus. The Red Plague was moving towards the southern lands of Unigaea, and I did not know at the time that Florin Talonas, governor of Stater, was working to take all of Unigaea."

"Fick me, is this guy serious?" Hiccup asks Wolf. "Like anyone gives a bloody fick about Unigaea. I mean, Tritania is clearly better. We got orclins with quad-tits, if you get my drift, Wolfy, and judging by your size, I'm pretty sure you had your fair share of teat when you were a pup."

"I met Oric and Wolf on that fateful day, and my world was forever changed!" Lothar laughs for a moment at his own joke. "It was Oric who sent me, and later Gadsaa, my future wife, to Tritania. And not a moment too soon. Unigaea was completely destroyed soon after that, and once I adjusted to Tritania, and undertook a few adventures, I opened this bakery with an upstairs library."

Hiccup shifts his body so he can use Wolf as a headrest. His crusty feet now face the other Mitherfickers.

"I was a scholar in Unigaea. In Tritania, I'm a baker *by choice*, mind you, as I've been offered an emeritus position at the Polynian Technical Academy in Porthos. That said, my studies have opened up some very interesting discoveries in Tritania and its three floating continents. So, let's begin with the Runestones of Tritinakh. Are you aware what Tritinakh means?"

"Tritania," Hiccup says, his eyes closed. "If these fickers can't decipher that from context clues, they need to go back to Hyperborea. Let's get to the fruit of this chalupa, Big Guy."

"Very well." Lothar removes his glasses and polishes the lenses. "Then I will cut to the chase: the first runestone is beneath Waringtla, in the catacombs that double as a sewer under the city."

"Sewers? Looks like I need to get out the hazmat." As if he has been planning it all along, FeeTwix snaps his fingers and a hazmat suit appears on his body.

"Too orange, Twixy," Hiccup says, shielding his eyes. "Reminds me of my first girlfriend's makeup."

"Spew Gorge's mom?" Ryuk calls over to him.

"Hey! Keep your jokes to yourself, Marbles, I'm in my fickin' safe space here and you know what they say about throwing rocks in glass houses: it's a perfectly good waste of rock! Fick me, now that's a joke." The goblin's eyes flash and confusion forms on his face.

"We're in Lothar's library," FeeTwix tells him quickly. "Lothar is Oric's friend, Oric is Wolf's owner."

"I know who Wolfy's owner is," Hiccup grumbles. "And thanks for the updates. Who's the elf? Oh, that's right, the one who wasn't vetted properly."

Lothar takes a deep breath. "The first runestone should be easy for you to get. It's guarded by an underground giant named Fafner. He's a Unigaea outcast, a former friend of mine who was able to make his way to Tritania."

"A friend of yours is guarding the first runestone?" Ryuk asks.

Lothar sighs. "That he is. Fafner used to run the museum of sorts in Tael. He was obsessed with Busty Gazongas, and was so offended by, well, Oric's comments on her painting, that he kind of went off the deep end."

"What did Oric say that offended him?" asks Ryuk.

"Something about her breasts."

"Fick, did you say Busty Gazongas? As in, *the Busty Gazongas*?" Hiccup makes a hand gesture in front of his chest.

"Yes, Hiccup, the same one that giants in Tritania look up to."

"I'd look up to those things too!"

"And this ex-friend of yours is guarding the runestone?" FeeTwix asks, his voice muffled by his hazmat suit.

"He believes it gives him power, and will do anything to defend it."

"And does it actually give him power?" asks Enway.

"No, but like many things in many worlds, yours and the ones I've visited, the belief of power given has led to power had."

Hiccup yawns, and turns to his other side.

"Once you've made it through the catacombs, you'll come out near Bluwid, the predominantly goblin city on the easternmost coast of Polynya. This is good for you. The second runestone is there."

Hiccup flips back over. "We're going to Bluwid? I have family all over that shithole!"

The giant nods. "Last I heard, a goblin shaman has been using the runestone to cure various goblin ailments, such as Goblinheimer's."

"Cure Goblinheimer's? Pfft, like that will work." Hiccup squints up at Lothar. "Will it do anything for warts?"

"*Baka!*"

"Fick you, Marbles! I've got warts, okay? There, I've said it. Not big ones, and these are clearly sexually transmitted, so they can't be dangerous, I mean, at least for chalupas, they aren't. Female choops could be different. But what can you do, really?"

FeeTwix clears his throat and speaks, his voice still muffled. "And now would be as good a time as any to remind everyone watching my feed that G. Todd has created an app that filters *in live time*, people, anything filthy the goblin says!"

"The goblin has a fickin' name!" Hiccup pounds his fist against the ground. Wolf looks up, huffs, and goes back to resting.

"That's right, if you don't want to hear about goblin chalupa warts, install G. Todd's app now!"

Lothar chuckles. "I don't know if this goblin shaman can cure warts, but before you take the runestone from her, you can definitely ask."

"I just might," Hiccup growls. "Now we got places to go, people to see, and I've got a little revenge to get."

"Later, goblin."

"Lizzy, I swear to the Empress' fantastic fun bags, if you don't stop it with the racism, I'll … I'll talk to HR."

"HR?" The Thulean rolls her eyes.

"We don't have HR in our guild, Hiccup. Please quit interrupting," Ryuk says. "Who has a healing potion? If we give you a healing potion, will you shut up?"

"You can't fickin' bribe me, and yes, if you give me a healing potion, I'll shut up. So gimme, gimme, gimme."

FeeTwix equips a potion and tosses it over to the goblin, who examines it, mumbles about it being the store brand, twists the top off and throws it back. His stomach grumbles, he beats his chest with his mechanical fist, and he sighs bitterly as he tosses the bottle over his head.

"So, the first runestone is beneath Waringtla, the second in Bluwid, and the final runestone is in the Sabors. This one will be considerably more difficult to get. Come and see me before you go for that one, after you have acquired the first two."

"Cool, so let's go." Hiccup stands and wipes his hands. "Wait. We're good here, right? Isn't there some other shit that was supposed to go down?"

"There's one more thing," Lothar says, his eyes dropping onto Enway. "The Book of Time."

CHAPTER 5:
THE POO FIGHTERS

LOTHAR ASKS RYUK to climb a ladder to a top shelf of his bookcase and bring down a small wooden box wrapped in black chains.

"You sure you don't need any help up there?" FeeTwix asks. The Swede has removed the face mask of his hazmat suit but still wears the rest of his bright orange getup.

"I've got it." Once he's up there, Ryuk places the box under one arm, and with a quick look down, he begins his descent. The box isn't heavy, but it is bulky, and about halfway down the ladder, he misses one of the rungs and falls to the floor.

-93 HP!

"Ryuk!" Enway cries.

"My word! Are you okay, Ryuk?" Lothar asks.

The wooden box still in his hands, Ryuk sits up, his face flaming with embarrassment. He gives the giant a very pathetic thumbs up.

"You okay?" Enway asks, now at his side. Zaena has also joined her.

"Fick me, Marbles, you fall like a goblin." Hiccup cracks up. "Tell me you recorded that, Twixy. The Fickers will love it."

FeeTwix points at his eyes. "I've gone blue. I know that Ryuk's brother watches my feed. Sure, he'll eventually figure out whatever it is this book does, but like any good author knows: show don't tell! Also, I'm pretty sure I mentioned we were in Waringtla. Or at least a giant city. I really need someone to filter my feed."

"Here's the box," Ryuk says as he approaches the giant.

"Good, just hold onto it for a moment." Lothar looks the Mitherfickers over. "I'm guessing by your character classes that only one of you is truly able to use this book." His eyes land on Enway. "This book has done a lot of good, and it has also done a lot of bad. It's best that it remain locked, but if Oric sent you to retrieve it, then I'll readily relinquish it. Now." He claps his hands together, startling Hiccup and Wolf.

"Fick!" The goblin leaps up, draws his toe knife, and twists around. "I thought, fick, I don't know what I thought. Ghosts don't clap. They're depressed. No one who is depressed claps. I hate fickers that are depressed. Just take a look outside, am I right? Great big world, lots of lady choops or chalupas, if you're into that. Some people are more desperate than others, uglier too."

"Quiet, goblin."

"Liz?" He looks to her and the Thulean returns his glare. As usual, Zaena is the first to look away.

"Um, yes, let's move on," says Lothar. "You can argue amongst yourselves later. The key is over there."

Enway moves to get the key, but Zaena's ghost limb beats her to it. The Thulean drops the key in her hands and ruffles the goblin's pink top knot.

"Hands to your fickin' self!"

"The key should be the only golden one on the ring," Lothar says as soon as Zaena has handed the key ring to Enway.

"Found it."

"You want me to, um, hold it while you open it?" asks Ryuk.

"Fick me to tears, Twixy, you hear that?"

FeeTwix winks at the goblin and nods.

"Holding it is fine," Enway says softly as she sticks the key in its proper place and pops the top open.

"Let me see!" Hiccup nearly shoves Enway aside as he approaches the box. "Bring it down lower, Ryuk, not all of us are tall as a giraffe's ass."

Enway shakes her head. "Is that how you'd describe me?"

"It's one way I'd describe you," the goblin says as Ryuk lowers the box to reveal a leather-bound book with a closed eye on its cover.

"Fick, that's spooky."

"The Book of Time, yes?" asks Zaena, who stands on the other side of Enway now.

"It is a relic from Unigaea," explains Lothar. "It is less powerful here, thankfully, and that's a story for another day, but in Unigaea, it possibly the strongest weapon available—if used correctly, of course. Some of its more frightening abilities have been stripped from the book here in Tritania. The greatest wielder of the Book of Time in my lifetime was Sam Raid. There were others, but in her brief time with the book, she did more with it than anyone would have imagined."

Enway reaches into the wooden box and takes the book out. "How do I use it?"

Lothar, who is hunched over the Mitherfickers intently watching the proceedings, takes another deep breath. "From what I recall, I believe it is the book that uses you."

As her hand hovers over the closed eye on the book's cover, the eye flickers open, squints, and rolls back, turning white.

A wisp of pink and yellow magic curls up Enway's arms and forms two sharp needles that lift off her shoulders and point at her head like a cobra ready to strike.

"Fick!" Hiccup ducks for cover as the magic zips into Enway's skull.

She stumbles backwards, only to be caught by Zaena's ghost limbs. Once righted, Enway immediately sits to ground herself.

A red tear drop forms in the center of her forehead; her hair darkens, her skin turns a caramel color, and an hourglass necklace takes shape over her bosom.

Enway's sclerae fill with red ink. Her eyes stay this way, no pupils present. The last thing to take shape is a wand. The receiving end is black, rotten, yet the handle is light brown, a fresh piece of wood.

She turns it over in her hands for a moment, admiring it.

"A fickin' demon wench? Welp, I'm done. Wolfy, get over here. We're going to the orchouse. Fick this." Hiccup turns to Wolf, walks past the beast, and whistles for him once he reaches the non-people stairs.

After Wolf doesn't come, and curiosity gets the best of the goblin, he waddles back over to the Mitherfickers and takes his place behind Ryuk. They're all in front of Lothar now, who peers over their shoulders at the seated Enway.

"Look, fickers, once people's eyes start going all *Exorcist*, I'm fickin' out. Hear me? Out. I already told you guys, I don't get paid for this," Hiccup complains. "No fickin' overtime, no healthcare, no complimentary chalupa relief, no 401K, no reduced summer hours, no nothing. And that's not to mention the fact that none of the new members have been properly vetted. Very bad people, folks, real losers, and now we have a red-eyed demon."

"My eyes are red? I wasn't even focused on that, I was focused on the fact that I gained four levels from the transformation." An ivory mirror materializes in Enway's hand and she looks herself over. "My god. And this necklace..."

"Your god is right," Hiccup says, nervous as ever. "Shit is fickin' ficked up."

"Four levels?" asks Ryuk, trying to change the subject away from her appearance. "Not bad at all from an artifact. Usually, only sponsored items have properties like that."

"Will her eyes stay red?" FeeTwix asks. "Cause I have some pretty badass Ray-Bans you can wear if you don't like the color." The Swede equips a pair of Wayfarers and tosses them over to Enway, who tries them on and nods at her reflection in the mirror.

"Better."

"You are concerned about style right now when you possess one of the most powerful books in the Proxima Galaxy?" Lothar asks, no hint of disappointment in his voice.

"I like your eyes better without glasses," Zaena adds.

Enway shrugs and hands the sunglasses back to the Swede. "What about this necklace?"

"Ah, good question. When you cast a spell, the sand in the necklace will begin to fall to the other side. Once it has completely depleted itself, you can cast another spell."

She begins flipping through the pages. "And this is the Unigaean language?"

"It is," says Lothar.

"Why can I understand it?"

"Because you are now Tritania's one and only Time Mage, or as it was known in Unigaea, an Hourglass Mage. To be an Hourglass Mage, one must have a basic understanding of the Unigaean language."

Enway stops at the end of the book. "Why are the last few pages missing?"

"Because those spells aren't necessary for a Time Mage to possess. I've had them removed, locked away."

"There's some very interesting stuff in here," she says as she skims through another page.

"There is, and I hope it is useful to your guild and your cause. Now, Gadsaa is going to be angry if I don't go downstairs and man the front. We will meet shortly, after you've recovered the first two runestones, and we can discuss more then." The giant stands. "Until that time, I wish you all luck."

"That's it?" Hiccup asks as everyone starts to turn to the exit stairs. "No fickin' pastries or anything? I need carbs, dammit!"

Lothar laughs. "Later, Hiccup, once you all return with the first two runestones."

(0)__(0)

"So just hop in anywhere, huh?" FeeTwix asks, still in his hazmat suit. The Mitherfickers have gathered around a manhole not far from Lothar's bakery. The sun is at its apex in the sky, and while it's still a warm day, a cold breeze has blown in from the east. Wolf seems rejuvenated, and looks especially happy that the goblin decided not to ride him on their short walk over.

"There's no way in fick I'm going in that shithole, and seriously, it is a shithole. All sewers are shitholes."

"Jatla is a shithole," Ryuk says.

"Watch your fickin' mouth, Marbles!"

"Relax, Hiccup, there aren't ghosts in the sewers," says the Swede as he lowers the mask on his suit and seals it up. "We're just going to work our way through to the easternmost point."

"I know there aren't any ghosts in the sewers, Twixy. I'm just opposed to bad smells. Also, anyone ever think it was funny how they call these things manholes? That's not what I call a manhole! Ha!"

Zaena sighs. "I find it incredibly hard to believe that you don't like bad smells, goblin, considering your company."

"I agree, you four kiddos are some very stinky mitherfickers. Wolf's breath smells bad, a little like aged fupa sweat kept in a bottle for a decade, but that's something I don't really have much of a problem with."

"Aged fupa?" Ryuk asks. FeeTwix gives him the head shake that means 'you don't want to know.'

"I was referring to you, goblin, you keep your own company."

"Makes no sense, Liz, sorry. I don't speak dumbass."

"Okay, everyone, enough bickering." Enway smiles at the group. "Let's get through the sewers as quickly as possible."

"Now that's something I can fickin' agree with."

Ryuk looks at Enway, still curious about her new avatar. She acts the same, but looks completely different with her dark hair, bronze skin, red eyes and red tear on her forehead.

"Say, you don't have another hazmat suit, do you?" Hiccup calls down to FeeTwix once he has descended into the hole.

"Sorry, Hiccup!"

Ryuk goes in the manhole next, after a sidelong glance at Enway, who still has her Book of Time stuffed under her arm. She smiles, and he's just about to smile back when Zaena sidles up next to him.

"Are you going to go into the sewers or are you going to smile at the Hourglass Mage?"

Ryuk nearly jumps out of his dream armor. "I'm going!"

Down the hole he goes, two rungs at a time until he lands in a long, dreadfully odorous tunnel. FeeTwix aims the headlamp on his hazmat suit at a giant piece of shit floating by.

"That's a lot of shit," he says, "and if you need to shit a lot, there's no better time than right now to pick up a package of Super Strength Pumpkin Spice Ex-Lax, available exclusively at WalMacy's and WalMacy's online! You can't get this flavor anywhere else, and if you're tired of P. Spice, choose from a dozen other flavors including Tropickle, Birthday Cake, Red Banana, and Pepto Bismol. Do what Hiccup does every day—clear that bowel and let it all out!"

"I heard that!" the goblin shouts from the top.

"And remember, fan-migos, mention #FeeTwixRox at checkout and get, I *shit* you not, 35% off your first two packages! Stock up now, and be ready for anything! Terms and conditions apply. Please see WalMacy for details. Offer valid online and in all fifty states and territories excluding Afghanistan, Puerto Rico, American Korea, the Midway Islands, and the Green Zone. Not valid with any other offer or discount. The claims made by the WalMacy Bowel Clearance Department have not been evaluated by the United States Food and Drug Administration and are not approved to diagnose, treat, cure or prevent any disease. WalMacy's is not liable for any information ad-libbed by the host of this ad, nor should you use this ad to diagnose any symptoms you may be experiencing. If symptoms persist, please consult a healthcare professional. Whew!"

"That was quite the disclaimer," Enway says after she's stepped off the last rung. Zaena is above her, and as usual, the Thulean uses her ghost limbs to quickly climb down the ladder.

"Yeah, some advertisers are more difficult than others…"

"How the fick are we going to get Wolf down?" Hiccup calls down the hole.

"Hmmm …" FeeTwix turns to Ryuk. "Any ideas?"

"Do you have a crane in your list?"

Enway laughs at Ryuk's joke and he smiles.

"Ha! That'd be something. Any ideas, babe? I believe your limbs aren't long enough."

The Thulean shakes her head. "What about one of Ryuk's gravity marbles."

Ryuk unhooks his slingshot. "That may work, but what about Wolf? On second thought, that won't work."

"Git your ass down there!"

The Mitherfickers look up to see Hiccup trying to push Wolf into the hole.

"That won't work, Hiccup," the Swede calls up to him. "Okay, okay, I'll handle this. Do you guys think I can lift him?"

"Who? Hiccup?" Ryuk shakes his head.

"The goblin is a fatass. I believe Wolf weighs more, but that is just because he is mostly muscle."

"Good point, babe. Now I don't want to go with my Steamsuit. A little overkill. I could go with my flying boots from Steam, but again, I'd have to carry both of them separately."

"Git in that fickin' hole, or I'm sending your ass back to Kayi!"

Wolf looks in the hole, barks, and with a nervous glance at the goblin, he places his front paws on the first rung.

"Not gonna work, Hiccup!" FeeTwix calls up.

"Like fick it won't work. Wolfy, I'm fickin' warning you, if you ever want to put your red rocket in another silo, you'd better git in that hole!"

Wolf barks.

"This is animal cruelty," says Enway.

"Git! Git!"

Wolf takes another step down just as digital gravity kicks in.

"Shit!" Hiccup cries out as Wolf falls all the way to the bottom of the sewer, a good seven meters. "Is he okay?"

Enway races over to Wolf just as he stands. The big black canine shakes his head and falls back down again.

"I'm coming, Wolfy! Someone get that dog a potion!" Hiccup says as his fat ass clings to the rungs.

The goblin reaches the ground in record time. He rushes over to Wolf, drops to his side and snaps his mechanical fingers at FeeTwix. "Potion, now, the good stuff. A Hopkins', dammit!"

FeeTwix tosses over the grenade-shaped bottle and Hiccup shoves it in Wolf's mouth. Soon the dog is better, his tail thumping against the ground.

"Fick me, Wolfy, that wasn't my idea. No one told me you couldn't climb a ladder. Blame Marbles over there." He turns Wolf's head toward Ryuk. "That's the ficker that told me to force you down."

"Hiccup, stop fucking around!"

"Marbles," the goblin says as he gets to his feet, "I know you're trying to show off in front of your new lady friend who has recently become exotic with her dark hair and burnt butter skin, but really, kid, you don't want it with me. I'll fickin' murder your poofty ass. Fick! What the fick was that?" Hiccup jumps back, his leap accompanied by a cloud of doom. He swiftly unsheathes his toe knife.

A giant mound of poo lifts from the stream of waste traveling through the sewer. The eyeless creature roars, filth and debris spraying out of its mouth.

"Fick! It's a shit monster!"

(0)__(x)

Fecal Creature Level 7
HP: 192/192
ATK: 48
MATK: 0
DEF: 29
MDF: 38
LUCK: 2

Leaping into action, Ryuk goes for his slingshot and looses two sword marbles that pass straight through the center of the poo monster. The fecal terror cries out, brings a droopy arm back, and responds to Ryuk's attack with a blistering stink attack of its own.

Ryuk's dream armor barely blocks the hunks of partially digested bone that hit it.

The armor morphs as the Ballistics Mage dives left, only to be struck by the partially digested skull of a land dragon.

-59 HP!

Ryuk slams into a group of pipes. One of the pipes bursts open, covering him in urine and feces.

"Fick me, Marbles, that's called a golden-brown shower where I'm from!"

Rather than fight, the goblin has dipped into one of the emergency drainage systems. He has a healing potion in his hand, sipping it as he watches the ensuing mayhem.

"*Baka!* Don't just sit there!"

"Fick you and your 'baka,' Marbles. No one here even knows what that fickin' means!" He puckers his lips and takes another small sip of the potion. "And don't get your underoos in a wad; I'll join the fight when I see an opening, just like Lizzy."

Ryuk looks the other way to see Zaena standing on the sidelines. She pivots from foot to foot, waiting for her chance to strike as FeeTwix does his thing.

"Burn in hell, mitherficker!"

The Swede now holds a Model CR-24 Flame Rifle. With a pull of the trigger, a great ball of fire bursts from the weapon's receiving end, only to backfire because of all the flammable gas in the air causing a minor explosion.

"Fick!" Hiccup shouts as FeeTwix is thrown into a side wall, his hazmat suit now on fire.

Like a stuntman in a movie about firefighters, FeeTwix stumbles around as flames rage off his suit, his hands waving in the air above him.

Ryuk quickly fires off a message to FeeTwix.

Ryuk: You okay?

FeeTwix: I'll be okay. I'm wearing a flame retardant undersuit.

Hiccup: You looked like a retard batting your hands at the air while your body was on fire. Don't cringe from across the way, Marbles, *retard* is only offensive to retards, and ficktards for that matter. Everyone else secretly uses the word, kind of like racial slurs."

"Shut up, goblin!" Zaena's battle cry is atypical for her, yet apropos.

Her swords spinning, and her nose held high likely due to the stink, the Thulean warrior princess uses her ghost limbs to fling herself at the towering feces foe, only to be swiped by the creature's beefy, sewage enhanced hand.

-78 HP!

"Aye!"

The Thulean is tossed into the running stream of filth cutting through the sewer. Gasping for air after she comes up, Zaena quickly uses her ghost limbs to pull herself out of the stream of feces.

The monster roars and Wolf barks loudly in response.

The big black wolf stands as far away from the stream of waste cutting through the sewer as he possibly can.

"You will die for this," Zaena says as she flicks a bit of bathroom matter off her brow.

Her wand at the ready, and sparking pink magic twisting around her arm, Enway fires off a blast of chromatic goodness, which fizzles away before it can reach the angry poo beast.

"You're going to need to work on your magic there, Elfy," Hiccup comments from the sidelines.

"Just watch," the Hourglass Mage calls over her shoulder.

-103 HP!

Suddenly, her chromatic energy takes a shoulder off the shit monster.

"Fick!"

"Delayed Strike," she says just about as coolly as Ryuk has ever heard someone say the name of their last attack.

Feeling emboldened, the Ballistics Mage steps up, Marble Gun at the ready. Ryuk fires three opaque marbles at their increasingly shitty foe.

The marbles connect, and the scheisse monster lifts into the air, slamming into the ceiling of the sewers and causing the entire tunnel to shake.

-151 HP! Critical hit!

Rather than fall back down, the crap creature stays stuck to the ceiling, hurling globs of after dinner goo down on the Mitherfickers.

Everyone who can dive, dives for cover.

Hiccup, still in his tunnel, finishes his potion and tosses it aside.

"I've got this," he growls as he straightens up. While everyone is either ducking for cover and trying to avoid flying feces, or in Wolf's case, barking maniacally, the most gaseous goblin this side of Athos equips one of his throwing tomahawks.

Even as shit flies all around him, he beats his chest for a moment, grumbling about potion-induced heartburn.

"Now where are you, you little ficker?" The goblin's eyes trained on the energetic egesta, he pulls back his arm and overhand tosses his tomahawk into the center of the dung demon's chest.

The ceiling-bound monster screeches as it falls to the ground, shit whirling in a tornado around its body.

Instakill!

One legendary explosion of odorous ordure later, and the Mitherfickers see a small fairy float into the air.

She spins, golden dust and any leftover residue flying off her body.

"Just as I thought," Hiccup grumbles, "a fickin' stinkerbell. It's safe to come out, everyone. I've won the fight here."

"Stinkerbell?" FeeTwix asks, his eyes quivering as he reads messages from his fans. "Ah! I see, they collect treasure in sewers and sometimes become possessed by shit. That can't be right."

"It's right," Hiccup says as he takes a few steps closer to the fairy. "These little fickers love going through butt truffles in search of rare stones and whatnot."

"Are you the one that freed me?" the fairy asks, dropping down before the goblin so she's now at eye level.

"That's right," he says, a mischievous grin on his face.

"Thanks!"

Hiccup plucks her out of the air, and before she can zip away, he tosses her in his mouth and swallows her whole.

"What the hell are you doing!?"

"Relax, Marbles, swallowing these things is great for digestion. It's illegal in Jatla, but that's because of the fairy lobby and the fairy union there. Fickers."

"Did he just swallow that shit fairy?" Enway asks.

Zaena nods, disgust evident on her face.

"When you two are fickin' done judging me, you can *thank me* for winning the fight for the Mitherfickers. How many times do I have to save everyone's asses again? Gee, let me think. It's been at least three times, and I'm a barely functional part of the team, aside from comic relief. It's like a played-out trope, here comes Hiccup to save the day."

"No one thinks you are funny," Zaena reminds him while cleaning her dirty arm with one of FeeTwix's rags and a canteen of water from her own list.

"Yeah? Says you." Hiccup burps, slams his mechanical fist into his belly, and turns east. "If we run into any more of those fecal fickers, aim for the heart, that's usually where the pixies are trapped."

"Good to know, Hiccup!"

"You're fickin' welcome, Twixy." The goblin burps. "Shit, she's really putting up a fight in there." He punches his stomach again. "Better. Now, are we going or what? Don't you fickers worry about me eating faeries. If you need safe spaces, you can book one once we get in Bluwid. Fick."

CHAPTER 6: TAMANA'S TEST

Kodai waits nervously for Tesla's diagnosis. Walt, the older MercSecure mercenary who met him at their repair facility, assured Kodai that she'd be fine, but he still lets out a sigh of relief when he is told he can come see her.

It's early morning now, and while Kodai was planning an assault on his rival Ginko's estate, he doesn't know if he still has it in him. And besides, if Tesla isn't there...

But Walt assured me she'd be fine relatively quickly due to the advanced tech they have in this facility, he thinks as he's led down another hallway into Tesla's room.

She's sitting up when he enters, a MercSecure scientist busying himself with the holoscreen tablet affixed to her gurney.

"Kodai," Tesla says, a smile taking shape on her face. Her eyes flash black as she scans his vitals.

"Easy," the scientist reminds her, "you've just booted up."

"How are you?" Kodai asks, his hatred for Hajime and Ryuk growing as he reaches her side.

"I'm fine. Are we still on for later today?" she asks, cutting to the point.

"We discussed all that before," he swallows hard, "before this happened. Now, I don't know. Maybe we should wait a few days."

The scientist, a thin man with glasses and a beard, looks at Kodai and frowns. "She needs to take it easy."

"Thanks, Dr. Taylor," Walt says. "We've got it from here."

"You most certainly *do not* have it from here."

Walt clears his throat and Dr. Taylor is out of there before the grizzled mercenary can say whatever he was planning to say.

"I can go in her place," Walt offers Kodai. "Whatever it is you were planning to do, I've been instructed to act as Tesla until she can be adequately repaired."

"That won't be necessary," Tesla says. "I am ready now to proceed with my mission."

Kodai smiles at her. *She has drive, I'll give her that.* Still, he knows that she probably needs at least a few more hours of rest.

He turns to Walt. "How about this? I have some things I need to do in a Proxima world, which I'm sure you at least know something about."

He nods.

"Good, you can escort me home." He turns back to the female humandroid. "Once you are ready and have been cleared, you can meet me at home. I can also pick you up here on my way to our next visit."

"That would work better. At eleven?"

Kodai's calendar pops up on his iNet screen. Messages from his men appear, as do a series of available times. "That will work. I'll be back then."

(0)__(0)

FeeTwix's feed plays on his iNet screen as Kodai makes his way home in an aerosSUV. Walt sits up front, and a vehicle follows behind them, added security courtesy of MercSecure.

Kodai doesn't always agree with America and their aggressive military habits, but over the last century, the country had created some of the best security companies the world has ever seen.

The American private security companies are light years ahead of Japanese and Korean ones, and just about the only country that gives them a run for their money is Great Britain, mostly because they have an agreement in which they hire from the same pool and are able to skip visa, regulatory, and other protocols.

Walt is a notable example of this.

Kodai assumes he is American, and he detects an American accent when he speaks Japanese, but regardless, the guy is a seasoned professional. He feels just as safe with Walt as he does with Tesla, which is saying something.

The fact that Walt is a cyborg only adds to Kodai's confidence in his abilities.

From what Kodai can tell Walt has had his arm, both legs, and his eyes replaced, and those are just the most visible portions. The seasoned vet may be reaching a new problem for the modern day, war-ravaged soldier: just how much of his body is human and how much is otherwise, and if it is predominantly otherwise, does that still make him human?

The aeros lands and Kodai is shuffled inside.

Once he is in his penthouse apartment, he immediately goes over to his favorite chair and places his haptic gloves and NV Visor on. The

Proxima login screen appears, and after a few moments trapped in the Empyrean, he stands in his avatar at the mouth of the Sabors.

Kodai Matsuzaki Level 15 Ballistics Mage

HP: 830/830

ATK: 213

MATK: 176

DEF: 98

MDF: 105

LUCK: 7

Tamana Nakamura Level 15 White Warrior

HP: 410/410

MANA: 389/389

ATK: 117

DEF: 134

MATK: 149

MDF: 108

LUCK: 6

Tomas Romero Level 51 Shield Warrior

HP: 2167/2167

ATK: 593

MATK: 10

DEF: 740

MDF: 555

LUCK: 21

Dark Mage Level 35

HP: 590/590

MANA: 315/325

ATK: 19

MATK: 137

DEF: 166

MDF: 283

LUCK: 22

Berserker Mage Level 38

HP: 843/843

MANA: 81/81

ATK: 146

MATK: 12

DEF: 251

MDF: 237

LUCK: 4

A wild wind whips around him, the air filled with snow flurries.

Kodai knows his brother's infantile guild will be here at some point; he's watched the Swede's feed long enough to pick up on that, and even if he hadn't, the Swede's fans have already run polls and compiled video showing FeeTwix and company discussing this.

He almost starts to laugh at the Mitherfickers' stupidity, but keeps a serious face as he checks out his guild members. There are the two mages provided by the serpent women. These two are NPCs and neither have ever spoken to Kodai.

Tomas wears his rare, Tagvornin armor which didn't seem to help him in the fight against the Mitherfickers last time, and Tamana is in reflective armor made from the scales of their former dragon, Mirror.

Even though the NPC dragon flew off, the NPC mages were smart enough to take some of the scales from her belly while she was in captivity. According to the blacksmith who crafted this armor, it should cut damage taken down by thirty percent, something Kodai now wanted to test.

"Attack Tamana," he instructs his guildmates. "Tamana, defend yourself."

Wielding her ironing board of a sword, Tamana goes for one of the mages, who blasts her backwards with a huge fireball.

-95 HP!

"Fight back, Tamana!" Kodai growls at her. "Fight!"

Back on her feet, Tamana swings her sword at Tomas, who quickly parries her attack. A white flash and his legs are swept out from under him.

With the magic coming from her free hand, Tamana lifts Tomas by the feet as if she has him with a lasso. She tosses him into the armed mage, who, rather than try to help his guildmate, swipes him out of the air.

-211 HP! Critical hit!

"Tomas, you weak fuck!" screams Kodai.

As a huge hammer forms in the Berserker Mage's hands, Kodai walks over to Tomas and unlatches his slingshot.

A knife marble in his hand, Kodai shoots a blade into the ground. His foot connects with Tomas' chest and he reminds him to do better next time.

The Berserker Mage swings his hammer and connects with Tamana's chest.

-102 HP!

"Ahhh!" she cries as she flies backwards.

She hits the ground hard and rolls back up onto her feet, kicking snow away in the process.

Her armor reflecting bits of light, Tamana spins towards the spellsword and meets his weapon head on. While he's a much higher level than her, she holds her ground, and is just about to overpower him when another fiery blast from the other mage cuts her down.

-81 HP!

The armor is working, Kodai thinks as he makes his way over to Tamana.

As she gets to her feet, he kicks at the back of her knees, slamming her face first into the snow.

Kodai grabs the back of her hair and pulls her neck back, smiling as fear takes shape behind her eyes. He curls his other fist and punches her in the throat.

-250 HP! Critical hit!

Badly off now and coughing blood, Tamana tries to crawl away from Kodai.

"Fight me!" he screams at her, yet she refuses.

-34 HP!

A kick to her stomach sends her back to the ground. Kodai stomps on her back, drops to his knee and pulls her hair back again. "When I tell you to fight me," he whispers in her ear, "*I expect you to obey orders.*"

He slams her face into the ground, tainting the white, powdery snow with her blood. A healing potion appears in his hand and he drops it on her head.

"Drink up, now." Kodai turns to the others. "Once she's healed, attack her again."

CHAPTER 7: BRO DOWN

"THIS IS THE BEST IDEA we've had in weeks," says Hiccup as all his clothes drop to the ground. The Mitherfickers are in Zaena's Sotlian Pocket Spa, which they haven't used since their battle against the cherry blossom ninjas in the Jatla Forest.

Rather than look at Hiccup's blemished, naked ass, Ryuk pulls up their stats.

After two hours of battling various sewer creatures, including a couple more shit monsters and even a possessed beardadillo skeleton, the guild's deets are looking up.

Ryuk Matsuzaki Level 22 Ballistics Mage
HP: 746/746
ATK: 135
MATK: 178
DEF: 104
MDF: 81
LUCK: 24

FeeTwix Fajer Level 24 Berserker Mystic

HP: 1052/1052

ATK: 187

MATK: 33

DEF: 102

MDF: 58

LUCK: 27

Hiccup Level 20 Shield Thief

HP: 1118/1118

ATK: 116

MATK: 17

DEF: 253

MDF: 122

LUCK: 38

Zaena Morozon Level 23 Brawler Assassin

HP: 915/915

ATK: 228

MATK: 10

DEF: 125

MDF: 47

LUCK: 24

Enway Zoltan Rosa Level 21 Hourglass Mage

HP: 732/732

MANA: 411/506

ATK: 71

MATK: 149

DEF: 64

MDF: 174

LUCK: 22

Wolf Level 39

HP: 2354/2354

ATK: 685

MATK: 0

DEF: 526

MDF: 240

LUCK: 19

Not bad, Ryuk thinks, he even managed to get some levels in a few of his skills, including his Cherry Poppin' Daddy, Splash Back, Gory Headshot (courtesy of a Rat Thing), and One in a Million when he took out a sewer snake from a good fifty meters with his slingshot.

He still hasn't used the skill given to him by Empress Thun, the Knights in White Satin skill, but he plans to test that out once they finally reach the giant guarding the runestone.

Another thing that has been interesting for Ryuk is watching Enway use some of her new spells.

Her Delayed Strike is especially helpful, as is her Youth spell. She actually turned a giant cockroach back into a baby, allowing Hiccup to easily squash it and, thankfully, *not* eat it. While she doesn't have the healing capabilities of her former avatar, her Speed Heal spell definitely helps.

Even with her ability to still heal the guild, the Mitherfickers have taken quite a beating. If it weren't for the three cases of top grade healing potions a fan named S. Reid sent over to FeeTwix, they would have had to take a break long ago.

"Am I the only one getting naked?" Hiccup asks, as he waddles into the spa.

"Shower first," Zaena reminds him.

"What's the fickin' point of that when I can just sweat it out?"

"I'm serious, Hiccup, rinse off over there."

The goblin turns to her, his ears twitching. "Slap me on the ass and call me fickered fickboy, did you just call me by my actual name?"

"Yes," the Thulean says, a smile stretching across her face. Her orange slit eyes have even softened some, which is something Ryuk doesn't see too often.

"Well, in that case, Liz, my liddle Thulean princess, I will do as you requested." He turns to a shower and uses his mechanical hand to turn the hot water on. "Fick yeah, that's the good stuff!"

"Wait, what? I don't know why you guys want to watch Hiccup shower, but it is your feed, and your wish is my command. Those with filters on, you won't be catching this exclusive content, but maybe you're better off that way." The Swede, his eyes blacker than a politician's soul, turns to Hiccup.

"Hey!" Hiccup says, covering his man-tits. "You know, a smart goblin would charge for this kind of access. Hell, I could probably make a fickton of rupees if I washed myself in front of strangers. I'm robust, I get that, but it's a goblin body type that is considered attractive."

A hand on Ryuk's shoulder startles him.

He spins around to find Enway in a one-piece bathing suit, her breasts much ampler than he was expecting them to be. This gets him wondering if they grew when she changed her avatar, or if they've always looked like this.

You're worse than Hiccup, he thinks as his mouth stretches into a grin.

"So, you don't mind my red eyes?" she asks.

Even though he wasn't looking at her eyes, which he now feels incredibly ashamed for and would bow for if it didn't give him away, Ryuk nods. "Yes, they're fine."

"Sunglasses in the spa, Elfy," Hiccup calls over. "I can't do the demon thing while I'm relaxing. Gives me the willies."

"You'll be fine, Hiccup," says FeeTwix, who now wears a speedo with a big Swedish flag on his ass. "I got you a matching pair too, babe."

He presents Zaena with a small box, which she opens to find a two-piece, Swedish themed bathing suit.

"Try it on," he encourages her.

"Okay." Her head held high, Zaena walks into an attached changing room and returns moments later, looking hot as a dragon woman can look in her two-piece, Swedish bathing suit.

"Someone's been doing crunches," Hiccup says as he moves from the shower into the spa. "And I'm talking about me, not you, Liz, and your washboard princess abs. Can anyone tell I've lost weight?"

Wolf barks.

"He can't come into the spa," Zaena says.

"And why the fick not? He's part of the Mitherfickers now, a much bigger part than Marbles, I might add."

"Because the heat isn't good for him."

"Don't worry, Wolf." FeeTwix steps over to one of the free showers and whistles for him to come over. Wolf barks and takes a few steps back. "I'm just going to bathe you, boy, nothing more."

"You know," Hiccup says, still naked as ever with his little chalupa dangling between his stubby legs. "I noticed that ficker was afraid of the sewer stream as well. Is that what it's called? Fick, you know what I mean."

"Maybe he's afraid of water," says the Swede.

"Duh, Twixy, that's what I was trying to say."

Enway drops next to Wolf and pats him on the head. "Let's just get cleaned up," she tells him, "you won't have to swim or anything."

He licks his lips and starts panting.

"What a fickin' poofcake! Cats are supposed to be afraid of water, not mutts. Whatever," Hiccup says, entering the sauna. "It's time for a little me-time."

With Ryuk's help, Enway eventually coaxes Wolf over to the shower. The four Mitherfickers gather around, Zaena using her ghost limbs to hold him in place.

"I don't know when you were last washed," says FeeTwix, "but my fans are fickin' loving this. LOVING this. Hello to all three million viewers! While you watch us bathe Wolf—and don't worry, we'll be gentle—I want to tell you about an exclusive offer from Time Warner Comcast T&T. These guys control everything, it's no secret, and because they're a good, trustworthy corporation that essentially runs a monopoly, they're able to offer you the best prices of your lifetime!"

Zaena gives FeeTwix a funny look.

"Subscribe now to any one of their wonderful services and get twenty dollars, euros, pounds, yuan, yen, won, rubles, crypto—whatever you use—off your first twelve bills! Now remember, this is a three-year contract, so the second twelve bills will be double priced, and the final twelve, triple priced! But don't focus on that, focus instead on the money you'll be saving that first year. It's like you're getting it at a third of the price, and that's *before* the twenty bones discount! It's the deal of the century, if you ask me! So, hit up Time Warner Comcast T&T now and tell them #FeeTwixRox!"

"Sounds like a fickin' rip off!" Hiccup shouts from inside the sauna. "Fick, Twixy, I know you're getting more famous and shit and there's more to shill, but don't do your fans like I did Spew Gorge's mom. What you just regurgitated right there is called a goblin bargain. Fick, where's that other healing potion I had. Ah, there it is. Love that Cherry Apollos."

Once Wolf is cleaned, the rest of the Mitherfickers head into the sauna to find that Hiccup's *parfum de merde* is not a strong as it normally is. Sure, it's there, but the humidity of the sauna and an expensive blue melon lotion Zaena has since rubbed on her body has somehow met the stank, not overpowered it in any sense of the word, but if Ryuk tilts his head away from Hiccup, he can almost not smell the now hot and sweaty goblin.

"I'm in Tokyo now," FeeTwix says, his eyes blue again. "I thought I'd let you know. When are we meeting up?"

Ryuk runs his hand through his black hair. "Um, you were auto-leveling back there?"

"Only for about five minutes. I landed and already went through immigration, which was fast as fick."

"Twixy, where I'm from, your constant over-usage of my favorite word is called *cultural appropriation*. Now, if only I could fickin' trademark the word 'fick,' to make sure that I had control over the word and all of its subsequent usages. But it's pretty difficult to trademark a commonly used word, even in a shithole like Jatla, especially if the word is one that everyone uses to describe something that everyone enjoys. Fick me, am I right?" A pair of reading glasses appear on the bridge of Hiccup's nose, a copy of *Wet Goblin Holes: Orclins Gone Wild* in his hands.

"What? There are quality editorials in the Wild edition," he reminds both Enway and Zaena, who now look at him skeptically.

"Anyway," says the Swede, "immigration was quick, and I jumped back in once I got in my taxi. I do a lot of Proxima stuff through iNet, to be frank. Carting an NV Visor around is cumbersome."

"Anyone here like cummerbunds?" the goblin asks as he turns his copy of *Wet Goblin Holes* vertical. "Those things never seem to fit me."

"Most things that go around your waist don't fit you, goblin."

"And it's Liz with the fickin' fat shaming again. You know, not all of us can afford the high fiber, low fat diets of Thulean royalty."

"Self-starvation would be a helpful diet for you, goblin."

"Enough." Ryuk clears his throat. "I should be able to meet soon, FeeTwix. I believe Hajime is close to being released from his repair facility. We have to be very careful about this." He gulps. "My brother can't technically hurt us in here, but he can up there, and he may not hurt me, but he wouldn't be opposed to hurting someone I care about."

"Welp, Elfy, looks like your boy is all about puckered starfishes and chalupa tucking. Back to the drawing board, am I right? Maybe Tarzan is more your type."

Enway frowns at the goblin.

"What?"

"Keep up the bullshit, Hiccup, and I'll cast Temporal Decay on your steampunk arm."

Everyone turns to Enway, who is normally happy-go-lucky.

Zaena is the first to laugh. "Ha! That is great. Yes, now you know how to interact with our lovely little goblin."

"Don't pinch my fickin' cheek, Liz!"

Ryuk stands. "Join me outside real quick, FeeTwix. We keep getting *interrupted* in here."

"Safe space!" Hiccup coughs into his hand as FeeTwix and Ryuk exit.

Wolf immediately joins them once they are in the changing portion of the spa. "You were saying?" FeeTwix drops his hand to the beast's head and starts scratching behind his ears.

"So, we have to be really careful, which means, shit, I don't know how we can do it, but we have to make sure he-who-shall-not-be-named doesn't blurt out the fact that we're together, which would be live on your feed, which my brother would then see."

"Ah, I see. He-who-is-always-smelt must be tricked in some way. Easy."

"Easy how?" Ryuk asks, watching as a mischievous smile forms on FeeTwix's face.

"You're overthinking this. The goblin doesn't really even know what Tokyo is."

"Well, he knows you were at the airport."

"But does he? This is one of the times that we should fall back on his Goblinheimer's."

"So then, we just don't talk about it anymore?"

The Swede nods. "Exactly, Ryuk. Easy peasy. If you need to tell me something about it, message me on a private channel."

"Got it."

"Now where should we meet up? I'd love to go to a cat cafe or a maid cafe. That would be crazy!"

Ryuk cringes as he thinks of the awkward maid cafes in Akihabara.

"You won't like a maid cafe."

"What's not to like? Cute girls dressed in maid outfits, food, music—am I missing something here?"

"Cat cafes are quieter, but it might be helpful for us to be in a place where we can blend in better. Fine, a maid cafe. Have you received word from Sophia?"

The leader of the Knights of Non Compos Mentis should be interesting in person, Ryuk thought.

"Yes! Her flight was delayed, and she'll be in later. So, you and I can meet in the real world, in Akihabara, and then we can easily get to Ueno, which is where she'll stop on her way from Narita to the city. At least that's where I'm staying."

"You're in Ueno now?"

"I am, near the station. Where are you?"

"Shinjuku. Okay, after we're done here, Hajime and I will pick you up and we can go to Akihabara. Does that suit you?"

"It suits me just fine." The Swede claps his arm around Ryuk's shoulders. "Now let's get back in there and enjoy the sauna. Nothing like some rest before a boss battle!"

(0)__(0)

The Mitherfickers respawn in a narrow tunnel, a far east shoot off of the main catacombs that, according to FeeTwix's intel, is a shortcut to the end.

The Swede's black eyes flash as he reads incoming messages from his fans. "I'm sorry, guys! Ryuk and I had some important stuff to talk about. You checked out the bonus content, right? That's a clip from a particularly gruesome night in Dead City. Scary, right? Yeah, I didn't see that last zombie coming either! Almost shit myself, in the real world and in the Proxima Galaxy."

"A double shit," Hiccup says. "Can't say I've done that, but I have shit myself before. I think there is no better way to combat existential arguments than to shit one's self."

"Doesn't even make sense," Zaena mumbles, taking the lead.

The Mitherfickers are out of the sewers, the brick walls replaced by rock carved ages ago. Both Hiccup and Zaena have had trouble reading some of the Thulean down here. It's an older dialect, and the script that is still legible has been hard to understand.

According to Hiccup, the vertical script carved into the rockface to their immediate left says that the easternmost exit lies in the chamber ahead, which is why they decided to hit up Zaena's pocket sauna, all keenly aware that a good ol' fashioned boss battle lies in their future.

"So, we go in guns a-blazing, right?" asks FeeTwix, who is in his normal overcoat and fingerless gloves but has also gone with Punisher-inspired body armor. To match it, he wears his half Reaper skull, affixed to the other side of his face by the leather strap Enway devised.

"Let's do it," Ryuk says, dropping to one knee.

He takes out backup magazines, pops a few of the marbles out, and loads up three of them with combo explosive and sword marbles. Knowing that he'll likely need to use his Spitfire spell, he latches a leather wristband he owns with a pouch on it to his right wrist.

He hasn't used it before, but he was thinking about it back in the sauna and figured it'd be perfect for accessing marbles quickly.

He holsters his Marble gun, fills his wristband pouch with warm, molten marbles, and takes a deep breath, hoping to activate his Extreme Focus skill at the drop of a hat.

Zaena practices drawing and sheathing her swords, flourishing each of them as she re-familiarizes herself with their weight.

Enway, her Book of Time in hand, uses a light provided by a drone FeeTwix has hovering over them to go over her available spells. The drone provides a cone of light for the Mitherfickers as it silently performs its role as an eye in the sky.

For his part, Hiccup equips two healing potions, finishes one, complains that it is the store brand, and tosses it over his shoulder as he takes a sip from the next one.

"We just healed up," Ryuk reminds him.

"Marbles, first of all, fick you and the high horse you rode in on. Second, it's called topping off the tank. Third, fick me and the wolf I'm about to ride in on. Wolfy," Hiccup places his hand on Wolf's neck, "be a goblin's best friend and let me get on top."

Wolf obliges, dropping to his belly so the goblin can climb on.

"You're a good dog, I'll give you that. A poofty snowfruit because of your fear of water, but we all got things that scare us, so I fickin' get that." An ax appears in his left hand, a dinner platter-sized shield in his mechanical hand. "Now git!"

The goblin on wolfback takes off towards the next corridor, the Mitherfickers doing their best to keep up.

They move into a smaller room, barely high enough for Zaena to stand upright.

From there, the catacomb opens up into a large space similar to the worship room the Mitherfickers discovered last time they were in the catacombs, back when they were making their way to Porthos via Katiyana.

Only this time, all the statues have been decapitated and tossed aside, the walls now covered in repeat paintings of a giant nude woman stomping a village, milk spraying from her exposed breasts. The painting has been replicated in several different sizes and styles, from floor to ceiling to small, Dali-esque designs.

A giant man squats in the center of the large prayer room, his kibbles and bits out as he glares at the Mitherfickers. Tangles of hair cover his face and his skin is covered in brown smudges and scars.

Fafner Level 25
HP: 1459/1459
ATK: 192
MATK: 0
DEF: 155
MDF: 141
LUCK: 8

"Who's doing the talking here?" Hiccup whispers.

"I've got this," Ryuk says, stepping forward.

"Like fick you do. Fine, I'll do it. Okay you big dirty ficker," the goblin says, looking up at the squatting giant, "we've got places to go and people to see. If you'll kindly point us to the runestone, we'll get our fickin' asses out of your hair."

The giant growls.

"Hiccup!"

"Quiet, Marbles, let the adults talk. You're Fafner, right? Is that what Lothar said your name would be? How the fick did I remember that? Twixy, I'm getting better!"

The goblin turns to FeeTwix and gives him the thumbs up with his shielded hand. FeeTwix nods, impressed.

"Lothar sent you?" Fafner asks in an angry, scratchy voice.

"Fick yeah, he sent us. Now seriously, I'm impressed, your chalupa is bigger than mine, but if you'd kindly get the fick out of our way, we'll *be* on our merry way. Nice art? Did I say that? I'm a big Busty Gazongas fan, believe you me."

"Quiet, goblin," Zaena hisses.

"What do you know about Busty?" the giant says, getting to his feet. He's a good five meters tall, his head only about a meter away from the rounded top of the worship room.

Ryuk steps up. "Let us pass, or we will be forced to fight you."

Hiccup chortles. "Fick, Marbles, you've got to work on your tough guy act if you ever hope to stick a hand up Elfy's lustrous robe."

Fafner hunches over, his form clearly affected by the years he's spent underground.

"You sure about this, big guy?" FeeTwix says, his bowie knife mutant hack materializing in his hand. The weapon begins to bubble upwards, pulsing and writhing as it forms an enormous blaster.

"You DARE threaten me?" Fafner screams.

-359 HP! *Critical hit!*

The blistering blast from FeeTwix's mutant hack tears Fafner's leg clean off.

What's left of the giant's leg flies into the wall, splattering the Busty Gazongas paintings with blood, and shaking the room.

Fafner crashes to the ground, hits hard, and screeches in anger as he throws a fist in FeeTwix's direction. Still coming down from the spread of his mutant hack, the Swede meets the giant's hit full on and slams into a wall, killing him instantly.

Instakill!

"Oh my god, they killed Twixy! You bastard!"

"No!" Ryuk fires swords and explosives at the giant.

-56 HP! -62 HP! -41 HP! - 49 HP!

The explosions don't do anything, and the swords, even though they are insignificant compared to his size, now jut out of his sinewy shoulders.

One Thulean war cry later and Zaena is charging at the grounded giant, blades spinning all around her. She boosts herself up with one of her *konoshlo* and meets the giant with a wall of blades.

"You won't beat me!" the giant bellows. Grounded but still able to use one of his hands, Fafner backhands Zaena into the same wall that killed FeeTwix.

-526 HP! Critical hit!

Winded, the Thulean warrior princess falls onto FeeTwix's dead body and rolls right, just in time to miss Fafner's crashing fist.

The ground rumbles; debris falls from the top of the worship room adding a layer of dust to the air.

A pink blast of magic cuts through the dust; Fafner screams and starts beating his fist against the side of his head.

"Make it stop! Make it stop!" the giant screams.

"What the fick was that?" Hiccup calls over to Enway.

"Arcane Tide!"

"Whatever the fick it was, fick yeah! We're up, Wolfy, let's tag team that big mitherficker, and no, Marbles, I don't mean we're running train on the giant. You're sick in the fickin' head!" he cries as the wolfbound goblin moves in for his attack.

"Don't mind him." Ryuk looks at Enway and she shrugs.

"I never do," she says, her wand at the ready. Ryuk catches a glimpse of her hourglass necklace, the sand now cascading to the other side so she can cast another chromatic spell.

Wolf leaps towards the giant and grabs hold of one of his nostrils. He and Hiccup swing right as Fafner roars, giving the goblin the opening he needs to stab his ax into the giant's right eye.

-115 HP!

Wolf lets go of Fafner's nostril; he and Hiccup fall a good two and a half meters. Wolf lands like a cat, even with the top-heavy goblin on his back.

"You see that shit, Marbles? I got that ficker in the eye! We call that one an instant eye cream in Jatla!"

"Damn you!" Fafner swipes his free hand towards Hiccup's voice.

-420 HP! Critical hit!

"Yooooy!" Hiccup and Wolf flip sideways. They hit the ground, roll, and eventually Wolf lands on top of the goblin. "Yoy," the goblin mutters, a healing potion appearing in his hand. Wolf tries to get to his feet but falls sideways. "Fickered ficktard giant fick-faced kiddy fickin' salad tosser!"

He throws back the healing potion, burps, and tosses the potion over his shoulder.

"Cover me, Marbles!"

Ryuk looks skeptically from the goblin to Zaena, who is still trying to get her second wind. Fafner isn't looking too good himself, his eye a bloody mess and his leg blasted off at the knee.

The giant is trying to stabilize himself with one hand and fight with the other, and while Ryuk could probably end it by firing all he has directly at the giant's face—that or laying down cover for Hiccup—he decides instead to go with the spell granted to him by the Empress.

Only she never told him how to cast it.

Ryuk raises a finger in the air, takes a breath in, and shouts, "Knights in White Satin!"

"The fick you just say?" Hiccup glares at the Ballistics Mage. "Have you lost your fickin' marbles, you emo-twated ficktard? What part of 'lay down cover' do you fail to understand, soldier!?"

"Um," Ryuk looks to Enway, who has no idea what he is going on about. "I, um, I call on the Knights!"

"What in the actual fick is wrong with you, son?" Hiccup throws his hands up in the air. "Fick, he's truly lost it, Twixy. That's fine, I'm okay with that. Just saying: I'm not going to take care of him or visit the poor liddle ficker when he's in the crazy home, but at least I can know, from afar, that he's in the right place." The goblin shakes his head. "Elfy, your man has lost it, which means you're up. Lay down some fickin' cover!"

"Dammit, Hiccup, shut up!" Ryuk bites his lip, steels himself, and points at the giant. "Knights attack!"

Clouds of white smoke add to the dust already in the air.

A squad of the Empress' White Knights pixelate into existence, each with a pike aimed at the giant. They're in ivory plate armor with the requisite white satin capes, the edges of the capes embroidered with golden threads.

Their leader lifts his broadsword and the squad attacks, each coming in from a different angle.

Once they have Fafner the giant skewered, it doesn't take them long to finish the job.

Instakill!

Fafner falls, and as soon as he does, the leader knight takes a knee before Ryuk.

"Thank you!" Ryuk says, bowing. "Thank you very much."

The knight nods and disappears, the others following suit.

(0)__(x)

"Not too bad, kid," the goblin says as soon as the knights are gone. "I take back what I said about committing you to a crazy home."

"Really?"

"Ha! If you could only see your face right now, Marbles. Of course I don't take back what I said! Don't start yelling crazy shit again, or I'll have you committed. We clear? You could have messaged us and told us what you were fickin' doing."

"It was a good attack," Zaena says as she hobbles over to FeeTwix. She drops to his side just as he wakes up.

"That was fickin' glorious, Ryuk," FeeTwix says, his voice scratchy as he goes for a potion.

"'Fick' is not your word to appropriate, Twixy," the goblin reminds the Swede. He is next to Wolf now, trying to coax a healing potion into his mouth. "What kind of stupid fickin' mutt doesn't like healing potions? Can you fickers believe this shit? Also, I'd check the giant for loot, but he's naked, and I'm not sticking my hand up in a giant's bunghole, especially this one. Ryuk, on the other hand…"

"I'm not looting his corpse, Hiccup, especially in that way."

"What the fick ever. Judge me. Go on. Fick, Wolfy, drink the potion!"

Wolf sneezes and pushes Hiccup away with his maw.

"That was a great spell," Enway says as she approaches Ryuk. "The Empress gave it to you, right? Those were her knights."

"She did, but it can only be used once a day. I just wanted to test it, actually."

"It was killer," says FeeTwix as his wounds heal up. "My fans are going crazy for your performance."

"You were still filming?"

"Of course I was. I fell in a way that would allow my fans to catch the rest of the action." He points at his black eyes. "Clever, huh?"

"Twixy, you're dumber than this weretiger I once knew named Simba. Look, Wolf, if you aren't going to drink the potion, I will." To prove his point, Hiccup takes a long sip from the generic potion. "See? That isn't so bad, is it?" He examines the bottle. "Shop 'n Save, huh? That sounds like a store brand. Not too shabby, though. Kind of a grape flavor. I like grape."

Hiccup finishes Wolf's potion and tosses it over his shoulder. He's the first to enter the next corridor, and once he's there, Ryuk hears him cry out in anger.

"That's it?"

"Let me see!" FeeTwix races forward, Zaena not too far behind him.

In the center of the adjoining room is a small pedestal with a rectangular stone sitting on top of it. About fifteen centimeters tall, the thin, black stone is polished to the point that it is reflective.

"That looks like, you know what, there are kids around, I'm not going to say what it fickin' looks like. Hint—chalupa. An oddly shaped, drow chalupa. Heard those fickers were hung as fick. Real talk, Twixy."

"Can we touch it?" Enway asks. She stands at the back of the group, her red eyes shining in the brightly lit cavern.

The Polynian surface is near, evident in the undergrowth jutting from rocks on the ground, the light, and a fresh breeze whistling into the space, carrying with it a grassy smell.

"Rather than answer Elfie's question with a dirty joke, I'd like to point out that it would have been much fickin' easier to just spawn outside the catacomb entrance—I'm sure you have the deets on the location, Twixy—and send just one of us down here to get the stone and completely avoid the giant. Again, real talk."

"We went through the catacombs to level up too," Ryuk reminds him. "We need to be at level thirty-five to get to Ultima Thule."

"Am I the only one that has no idea why we need to go to that cold fickhole? It's warm down south, lots more racism down south too, which you guys know, I'm combating against."

"Sure you are, Hiccup, sure you are." A yellow latex glove appears on the Swede's hand, followed by the rest of his hazmat suit. "Just in case it is toxic," he says, once the mask has formed over his face.

The Swede grabs the runestone, looks it over, and just as he's about to put it in his list, Enway steps up with an off-world device that looks like a steampunk-themed divination wand.

"Let me run this over it," she says.

"By all means."

"And before anyone asks: I collect rare artifacts. This is something I picked up in the Bawa Outpost."

"The Bawa Outpost?" Hiccup shakes his head. "Only losers and sandfickers hang out there."

"Rare artifacts hang out there as well." She scans the wand over the black stone and shrugs.

"Well?" Ryuk asks.

"Nothing. I don't think it is enchanted, at least not currently. We should be able to touch it."

The runestone lifts into the air seemingly of its own volition.

"Damn, Liz, you're going to get us all killed, you know that?"

Zaena drops the stone on his head and he shrieks. "My hair!" Oblivious to the fact that the stone is still falling, Hiccup pats his head down, making damn sure that his pink topknot is still in place.

Of course, Zaena catches the stone just in time.

"Fick!" Hiccup continues to pat at his head. "Marbles, look me square in the eye and tell me that there's no marks on my head. We're going to Bluwid. There are lady goblins there. I just gotsta look good, feel me?"

"You'll be fine," Ryuk says, as Zaena drops the runestone in his hand.

There is nothing special about it at first touch. It isn't warm, it doesn't glow, and there is no indication it is anything but a rock.

"How come he gets to hold on to it?"

"Because he's our leader, goblin."

Ryuk starts to smile at Zaena, but returns his focus to the runestone instead. *It is definitely interesting,* he thinks as he looks it over. He inventories the runestone and looks to FeeTwix.

"You ready?" he asks as the Swede's eyes flash blue.

"Sure am. Let's meet up in Tokyo. Our avatars will still be here walking to Bluwid with you all, but Ryuk and I are about to bro down in the Land of the Rising Sun!"

"Come on, Wolfy," Hiccup says as he mounts up. "Keep clear of poofters and anyone who uses the phrase 'bro down.' Fick me."

THE RUNESTONES OF TRITINAKH

CHAPTER 8: THE MAID CAFE IN AKIHABARA

RYUK LOGS OUT AND TAKES a deep breath in through his nostrils. His iNet screen comes alive and he pretty much ignores it, tired of the constant barrage of updates and notifications. He removes his borrowed NV Visor—his is still in his duffle bag—and makes sure not to catch his arm or leg on any cords in his small, Proxima capsule bunk.

A message from Hajime blinks on his iNet screen, and he reads it as he gets down from the bed.

Hajime: I am in the lobby.

Ryuk: You should have sent me a message earlier. I would have logged out.

Hajime: I've just arrived. Perfect timing, I suppose. It gave me time to think of a good Oblique Quote.

Ryuk stretches his arms over his head and looks at the row of Proxima capsules across from him. The room is by no means large, but it does have enough space to fit fifteen capsules, three to a wall and six on the lengthiest wall of the room.

Other players are in the bunks, logged into their chosen worlds. A holoscreen next to the bunk indicates playtime and somnium skipbox usage. This is for legalities, but most gamers know that the skipbox monitors are rigged and never actually meet their supposed time cut offs.

Ryuk: Do you mind if I take a quick shower? We will be meeting my friend FeeTwix at a maid cafe in Akihabara in about thirty minutes.

Hajime: A maid cafe? That is a very public space.

Ryuk: Hidden in plain sight, that's what we were going for.

Hajime: I see. Let me do some research regarding cafes with the best exit points. I will make the decision on the cafe based on how it easy it would be to escape.

Ryuk: Sounds good.

A foreigner walks by, a thirty-something with pale skin and long, brown hair. He belches, excuses himself, and climbs into the nearest bunk without making eye contact with Ryuk.

Once he's in the hallway, Ryuk turns left into the male shower rooms.

Each shower is private, but the changing area is shared, and as he enters, he catches a glimpse of a stocky Japanese guy who almost reminds him of Hiccup.

This thought bothers him in two ways: One, he doesn't like the fact that he's just checked out some guy's chalupa by accident; two, the damn goblin has somehow worked his way into Ryuk's psyche enough that people are starting to remind him of Hiccup.

"Damn goblin," he says, a grin spreading on his face as he removes his clothing. While he secretly has started to find Hiccup amusing—well, at least some of the time—he doesn't like it when he teases him about Enway.

I wonder what she looks like in real life, he thinks after he's removed his clothes. *Maybe she looks a bit like her avatar after she became an Hourglass Mage.*

Ryuk slips into a pair of 3-D printed sandals dispensed by a machine in the corner. From there, he hops into the shower, turns the water on, and immediately sits on the stool in the middle of the shower, letting the water sluice over him.

A quick glance around for soap and he finds the dispenser.

The smell is a bit weird, some type of fruity melon with a hint of mint, but at least he's clean and it feels good for his muscles to have hot water on them, especially after being logged in for so long.

While he lets the water run over his head, he checks a few of the feeds he follows on GoogleFace, including the Tritania leaderboard. He's never been one to take part in the leaderboard competitions, preferring to stick with the classic guild-building and leveling strategy.

"The Mitherfickers," he whispers.

It is a stupid name, but such a motley crew could hardly be named anything else. Where it goes from here, especially after they've gotten the runestones and figured out a way to free Tamana...

Ryuk swallows this thought down.

He hasn't been very verbal about it, but it has been at the back of his mind and he knows that Tamana, the Tamana he knew, would never have betrayed them.

It was Kodai, he thinks, his fists tightening. Kodai or the serpent woman, *that's why Tamana is the way she is now.*

"And if we stop them," he whispers to himself, "then she will be freed."

And then what? a voice at the back of his mind asks.

Ryuk doesn't know the answer to this question, and to further complicate matters, he has no idea how Tamana will be received by his guildmates once she's back on their team. Hiccup and Zaena will never trust her again. FeeTwix would, as would Oric and Enway.

Enway.

His thoughts skip to Enway and her transformation. Red-eyed with a big crimson tear on her forehead, Enway looks nothing like she looked when they first met, back when she was trying to loot someone in Aramis.

And this new power of hers? Why did Lothar take some of her spells away? How powerful could an Hourglass Mage truly be?

Ryuk recalls the couple of times he has used his wild card marble to freeze time. He hasn't been able to replicate this spell in a while, but then again, he's been using his gun more and more.

Funny that. Just like anyone anywhere at any time in the history of humankind, given the choice of a gun over slingshot, Ryuk has chosen the gun.

Maybe I should load a mag with clear marbles, he thinks.

His teammates might not like it, but his luck has increased some since he started out, and with his level, he's gotten better control over his avatar.

The steaming water goes cold, indicating to Ryuk that his shower is over. He towels off, puts his clothes back on, and once he's given himself a hard look in the mirror, he pops his black hood up to conceal his face a little.

"A maid cafe it is," he tells himself in the mirror.

(0)__(0)

Ryuk gets the urge to hug Hajime but he suppresses it. He bows instead, a long graceful bow that shows just how much respect he has for the humandroid. Hajime returns the bow, both of them now in the lobby of the Proxima capsule hotel.

The clerk, a humandroid female with a perfectly formed face and dimples, smiles at the two and looks away. She is a far cry from the older gamer manning the front desk last night, and as Hajime and Ryuk step out into the streets, she calls goodbye to them in a high-pitched voice.

The Uberyota waits for them curbside. It is a black affair, with suicide doors and polished chrome accents.

"Riding in style, huh?" Ryuk asks.

"Only the best when we are secretly siphoning money from your family's accounts."

"We are?"

The door opens and Ryuk gets in, followed by Hajime.

"Yes, but the way I have it set up, it won't be noticeable for some time. We've spoken before of what I'm capable of, and what humandroids in general are able to do. I want our current transactions to blend in with other transactions normally accrued by higher-ups in your family's organization. Here is one way we accrue it."

After they are reminded to place their safety belts on, the Uberyota lifts into the air, settling into its appropriate airlane. Advertisements flash on the inside of the front windshield, hawking everything from in-country vacation destinations, such as a trip to Kobe, to Sumi Haigou Settuken charcoal bar soap.

Ryuk settles into his seat, and as he does, Hajime hands him a pair of sunglasses and a black surgical mask.

While it would be odd for Ryuk to walk around in any other country in the world in a surgical mask, aside from polluted-ass China, it is something that is perfectly common in Tokyo. Take a slice of any busy subway station in Tokyo and the odds that half the people surveyed are wearing the mask is high.

"You think the glasses are too much?" Ryuk asks, the surgical mask now on his face.

"They're just for when we go from the aeros to the maid cafe. You can take them off once we arrive." Hajime takes a deep breath. "Now, we need to discuss your Oblique Quote. I do not have a card to write it on today, so I chose something simple, something you'd easily remember."

"Sure."

"Listen to the quiet voice."

"The quiet voice?"

"Yes, that voice at the back of your head hidden behind all of your thoughts. Listen to this voice."

"That's easy."

Hajime chuckles. "It may not be as easy as you think."

The two are quiet for a moment as their Uberyota races across the expansive city. Aeros moving both horizontally and vertically add a sense of wonder to the cityscape. Neo-Tokyo a city of the future built on the ashes of the past.

Buildings cluttering the airspace add a touch of grandeur to the city, mystery too, as every building has the shadow it casts, and every shadow has its secret.

Snow flurries whip around the aeros as it passes over the subway station and nears the outer rim of Akihabara, the anime and tech hub of the famous city.

Five story tall holoscreens are attached to the sides of many of the buildings, flashing video game and anime advertisements. Kawaii teen girls pose on a few of the advertisements, winking at passing aeros. Ryuk knows better than to focus on them, lest he be bombarded with iNet popup adds.

It's a lot to take in, and every time he comes to Akihabara, he gets the urge to hit up some of the arcades or peruse some of the electronic parts shops for the latest Proxima rig mods. Everything from custom visors to more illicit items, such as ones that create artificially heightened sensations for those engaging in Proxima dreamworld sex, are on offer in this famous ward.

Anything can be modified, improved, tricked out; Akihabara is proof of that.

This part of the city is famous for the maid cafes, an odd Japanese invention that pairs restaurant and entertainment with fetishism. The dozens of maid cafes in Akihabara cater to a variety of crowds. Those who want anime-themed and anime-anatomically enhanced waitresses rub elbows with those who simply are looking to spend time with young girls.

The girls employed by maid cafes are most certainly under the age of eighteen. The traditional cafe—if it can be referred to as such—features six teenage bombshells dressed in maid outfits. Fishnet stockings, push up bras, a ruffled dress, different colored wigs (pigtails a must), white gloves, contact lenses to make their pupils look larger: there are many variations of maid outfit, but they all fit the same theme.

The oddity of it all, at least for a westerner, is the fact that there is no sexual exchange nor is there a hint of this exchange in maid cafes. The girls that work there are hired to be cute, *not* to offer sexual services.

Which, in a way, aligns them more with geishas, famous for their ability to converse and entertain, rather than with sex workers, such as the women Kodai employs.

As my family employs, Ryuk reminds himself as the aeros sets down before a maid cafe. Hajime steps out first to scan the perimeter. Once it is clear, he sticks his hand in and motions Ryuk forward.

"Remember," he says, "sunglasses."

Feeling like some sort of celebrity, Ryuk steps into the streets of Akihabara. The sidewalk is wet from the light snowfall, the breaths of the people passing visible in the air. The smell of cooking meat immediately reaches his nose. He naturally turns to the left to see a man with a small alleyway yakitori stand.

"We'll order inside," says Hajime, his hand now on Ryuk's arm.

"Got it."

They approach the first maid cafe and are greeted by a teenage girl in a light blue maid outfit and six-inch heels, her hair in a ponytail. She's added just about as much blush as humanly possible to her cheeks, but other than that, her skin is milky white, clearly the results of an intense cosmetic session.

"Welcome!" she says in just about the highest pitched voice she can. *"Irrashaimase!"*

She bows deeply, hops back to her heels and smiles at Ryuk in a flirty way.

"Yes, um, we're meeting someone," he says. "A foreigner."

"Hai! Follow me!"

She swivels and marches into the maid cafe. As she passes the front door hostess, she's handed a set of menus.

A swift glance around and Ryuk sees there are five other maids working, one of whom is preparing to sing a song onstage. Sitting near the stage is who can only be FeeTwix, who stands out even more as he's the only foreigner in the room.

"Ryuk?" he asks, his voice pretty much the same as it is in Tritania.

FeeTwix has brown hair in real life, shaved on the sides but longer on top and combed over. He wears black rimmed glasses and his face actually resembles that of his avatar. If it weren't for the hair, his height, and the fact that real life FeeTwix is about five to ten kilos heavier than Proxima FeeTwix, they'd look almost like identical twins.

"Um, hi," Ryuk says, suddenly ashamed of his English. He knows it is accented, and he can't speak as well as his brother, but for words he doesn't understand, he has an app running on his iNet screen translating in real time.

The app runs now, the words FeeTwix says appearing in scrolling Japanese characters, almost as if he were taking part in a movie. Possible responses also appear, written in katakana so he can pronounce them correctly.

"I am sorry, my English is no, ahem, not so good."

"It's fine, Ryuk! And where's my hug? What's this bowing stuff, buddy? You act like we're in Japan or something!" The Swede laughs, and the maid, who stands next to him with the menu pressed against her bosom, laughs as well. "See? She gets me!"

Ryuk turns to Hajime, who has a thin grin on his face.

"And you must be Ryuk's killer droid friend. He's told us all about you. Hajime, is it?"

Hajime nods.

"You, sir, are an utter badass."

"You have no idea."

FeeTwix laughs awkwardly. "You're right, I really don't! Now let's get down to business. Sophia has arrived, and wants to meet in an hour in Ueno in a lab at Tokyo University. She didn't tell me what she'd be testing, but she did say to come prepared to log in for a while, which as you know, I kind of make a living being logged in for a while so no problems there, feel me? Also, I'm starved, and I'm ready to hear whatever song Kiko has promised to sing!"

He switches to Japanese and begins talking to the girl standing on stage behind a microphone stand decorated in flowers.

"Nihongo o hanasemasu ka?" Ryuk asks.

"GoogleFace translate, buddy, just like you're using," FeeTwix says in English. "What language do you prefer? English or Japanese? Actually, Sophia will likely speak English, so we should probably stick to that. One minute, Kiko! Just let me catch up with my friend. *Sumimasen! Gomenasai!* I want to hear something super cool. Shit, Ryuk, what song should I listen to?"

"I do not really listen to pop music," he says as he removes his sunglasses.

"And what's with the mask? You sick or something? Kidding, kidding, I get it, you're incognito." FeeTwix sits and Ryuk does the same, Hajime remaining standing.

"You can sit with us, Hajime," Ryuk says.

"I'll stand near the door," the humandroid says. "I've checked everyone in the maid cafe. We should be safe for now."

"Cool!" The Swede eyes Ryuk for a moment. "Ryuk, if someone hasn't already told you today, let me be the first to say that you are one cool mitherficker. You too, Hajime!"

"Um, thanks," Hajime says over his shoulder.

"Here's the menu!" The maid in the blue outfit drops two menus on the table and backs away, waving with both hands.

"She's a cutie, so is she, and so is she. But I have to say, Ryuk, this is weird as fuck. They aren't actually, um, what would Hiccup say? Orc chippies?"

Ryuk clears his throat, his face going pale. "Of course not, this is just a job some of the cuter girls in high school get. Nothing, um, sexual."

"Yeah, aside from all of it. Kiko! You sing whatever you want. I'm all ears!" FeeTwix gives the girl on the stage a double thumbs up.

"What do you want to eat?" Ryuk asks. "Omelet or instant ramen? They also have okonomiyaki."

"Let's keep it simple. How about an omelet and a couple of beers?"

"I am too young to drink. I am nineteen."

"Well, it looks like I'm boozing alone this time."

The maid waitress comes and Ryuk orders. Just as his order is placed, Kiko starts up her song, which Ryuk recognizes as *Sukiyaki*, a famous song from the 20th century, albeit a poppier version sung with a schoolgirl voice.

"What's the song mean?" FeeTwix asks Ryuk.

"It's about your girl going away and leaving you lonely."

"Ah." FeeTwix's face grows serious for once. "It isn't bothering you or anything, is it?"

"Why would it?" Ryuk gulps, instantly thinking of Tamana. "No, it is not bothering me. I am over that."

"Are you? Because you don't have to be. Look, I know that we get pretty wrapped up in our typical guild shit-talking. Actually, that is all the goblin's fault, but you get my point."

"He is a ficker."

FeeTwix laughs. "Yes, yes, he really is. But like I was saying, we get wrapped up in the shit-talk and don't really discuss serious things, like Tamana, like Tomas. Those two...I know they are being brainwashed and forced to work for Kodai against their will. Tomas would never attack me, and Tamana..."

"Yes?" Ryuk asks, a fluttering sensation in his chest.

"I know she wouldn't attack you like that. The others, Hiccup and Zaena, really, may think so, but I know there's more to this story. We just have to get strong enough to go after them."

"I agree," he says, conviction in his voice.

"We brought the fight to the Shinigami once, back when we were a much weaker guild. We also beat Tomas and Tamana back in Kayi. Now, I'm not stupid enough to think they don't have some tricks up their sleeves, but after we get the runestones, I think we should bring the fight again to the Shinigami, and end it."

"Get Tamana and Tomas back," Ryuk whispers.

"Yes, both of them. The Shinigami will pay."

"—My brother will pay."

"Him too. This shit is going to be going down real soon, and when it does, I'm fucking game."

The maid waitress brings back a beer for FeeTwix and a vitamin enhanced blueberry soda for Ryuk.

"You game?"

"Definitely," Ryuk says. "We just have to get to the point where we can take them on."

CHAPTER 9: BLUWID IS AN ACTUAL SHITHOLE
(NOT LIKE JATLA)

"CAN I WEAR A SURGICAL MASK TOO?" FeeTwix asks as they exit the shop. "I didn't think to conceal the fact that I'm in Tokyo."

Hajime pauses. "Do your fans know what you look like in real life?"

"Well, I look pretty much the same. That's bad, right?"

Hajime nods as he sticks his hand into his front jacket pocket. Trying to blend in as best he can, the humandroid is dressed minimally: a black parka, a pair of ever-so-lightly distressed jeans and a pair of black winter boots with fur-lined uppers.

"You can wear this mask."

FeeTwix takes the mask from Hajime and puts it on as he gets into the waiting Uberyota. The vehicle is a different model from the one Ryuk and Hajime came in, an SUV version with back seats that face one another and no steering wheel.

"And now you can take it off," the humandroid says as the aeros lifts into the air.

"I'll keep mine on; it's warm! You know, we really should wear these in Sweden. It gets pretty cold there, not that I go out much." His blue eyes light up.

"What is it?" Ryuk asks. He sits across from FeeTwix, his back towards the front windshield.

"Just looking at the pictures of the omelet we ate back at the maid cafe. Who knew Kiko could be so talented with ketchup. It's kawaii, Ryuk!"

"You are the same in the Proxima Galaxy as you are here in the real world," he tells the Swede.

"What? You're not? You seem the same too: quiet, loyal, brooding—I mean that in a good way. A lot of people try to reinvent themselves online to find that they're only an extension of who they were in the first place. Sure, there are some fickboys—copyright Hiccup the goblin—but most people only change a few things about their appearance, at least now. I think it was different back in the 2040s, when people were just getting their feet wet in the galaxy."

"The 2040s," Hajime murmurs. Their vehicle drops to a lower airlane, the change in gravity felt in their chests.

"Back when Quantum Hughes was kicking ass and taking names! The OG Dream Team. You guys ever see the Netflix Hulu series about the Dream Team? No? Well, they changed the names, even a damn catchy name like Quantum Hughes, but anyway, that's what those shows were based on. Shit, I would have fought in the Battle for Tritania if I had been old enough. I mean, I was logging in in 2058, but those were mostly to kiddy worlds. Fun places, kid worlds. Whew, I feel like Hiccup at the moment!"

"Why's that?" Ryuk asks.

"I'm the only one talking."

"Sorry."

Their aeros lands a few minutes later in a parking lot next to a slick lab with walls made of blackened motoglass. Standing in front of the lab is a middle aged Asian woman with, of all things, a puffy afro. She wears a white lab coat, high-waisted slacks, and a pair of Converse high-tops.

The doors pop open and FeeTwix jumps out, the surgical mask still on his face.

"Hey Sophia, what's going on?"

"Let's get inside," she says instead of hello.

Ryuk and Hajime approach, and as they do, she begins talking to her personal iNet-based AI in Mandarin.

The three follow her through a sliding metal door. They turn down a wide corridor, and from there, down a stairwell and onto a polished concrete floor.

A hovering drone approaches Sophia and scans her retina.

She continues to speak in Mandarin to herself as they enter a lab with lofty ceilings and several dive vats.

"You're going to log in, both of you, actually."

"Sweet," says FeeTwix. "I was hoping you'd say that."

"You and your guild can go about their business as I monitor Ryuk and go through the last two weeks of data. Once I've done that, I'll give you my diagnosis."

"That's it?" asks Ryuk.

She cocks an eyebrow at him. "Were you expecting something else?"

"I really don't know what I was expecting."

"I've come here to work, and luckily for you two, that work means that you need to be logged in." She turns to two dive vats. "Shall we?" Once she realizes that they aren't following her, Sophia turns back around. "What is it?"

Ryuk and FeeTwix exchange glances.

"We get to *dive* dive? As in, use a dive vat? That's awesome!" The Swede pumps his hand in the air. "I've used one before, but not for a while."

"I've never used one," says Ryuk.

"Yes, you both get to use one. Um, Evan, can you help me get them strapped up?" Sophia calls out.

A slim humandroid Ryuk hadn't seen before steps into the room. He's fit, his shirt is tucked into his pants, and his light hair is combed to the side. He holds a pair of NV Visors, and as he walks over to the dive vats, he smiles at Sophia. "No problem, honey."

Sophia's face softens as she takes in the humandroid. Ryuk and FeeTwix exchange glances; a message immediately appears on his iNet screen.

FeeTwix: Pretty sure she has something going on with the humandroid.

Ryuk: Good observation.

"I'll go first," the Swede announces. He walks over to the dive vat and starts stripping.

"We have to undress?" Ryuk asks.

"Yes, just down to your underwear" says Evan, the humandroid. "If you care for some privacy, you can use the office."

"Um," Ryuk looks from Hajime to FeeTwix to Sophia, whose smile has thinned. "Sure, I'll use the office."

(0)__(0)

"That was different …" Ryuk says as soon as his avatar takes shape.

The dive vat was almost like being submerged in a small pool, aside from the fact that the liquid was thick and gooey. Even though he now stands on solid, digital ground, the weightlessness associated with being suspended in the vat is still throwing his center of gravity off.

He takes a step back as the Mitherfickers' stats appear before him. With no changes since he last checked, he swipes them away.

"Fick, Marbles, did your big bro hand you your candy ass again?" Hiccup turns to Ryuk and laughs. "You look like you've seen a ghost."

The mention of the word 'ghost,' even though he was the one to mention it, brings terror to the portly, pink-haired goblin's face.

Ryuk sighs deeply. "Nice to see you too, Hiccup."

"Fick, must be nice to not actually have to do all the walking yourself. I wish I could just log out and have my avatar do the dirty work. There are a lot of tasks I need to accomplish that I'd prefer not to do myself including trimming my toenails."

"Quiet, goblin," Zaena says, now out of habit.

Enway laughs as she moves over to Ryuk. "How are you? Any changes up there?"

"Not, um, not that I'm aware of. I met FeeTwix in person."

As if he were Beetlejuice, the mere mention of the Swede's name causes him to appear, his avatar slowly pixilating into existence. His eyes instantly go black. "Fick yeah, everybody! We're back, and while I was gone, I hope you guys kept track of what Hiccup was doing and saying. Never can be too sure of that goblin."

"Hey! Fick you, Twixy!"

"Okay people, so we're outside Bluwid and night is coming, which will likely lead to some battles and some asshattery, or fickery, if I do say so myself."

Hiccup throws his hands up in the air and mumbles about FeeTwix owing him royalties for using his favorite word.

"And we all know what I like to do at night. That's right, folks, sleep! And if you are having trouble sleeping, McStarbucks has you covered. Melatonin lattes and McFlurries are on sale worldwide! And you don't even need to mention #FeeTwixRox to get the discount!"

"Then what's the fickin' point of this ad?" Hiccup asks. "And what the fick is Melatonin?"

"I'm glad you asked," FeeTwix says as he places his arm around Hiccup's shoulder and turns to him. The goblin glares into the Swede's black, soulless eyes.

"Why are you fickin' staring at me like that?"

"If you *do* mention #FeeTwixRox at checkout, you'll get—and I really can't tell you guys how excited I am to share this—you'll get a bogo offer! Bogo bogo! What better way to spend than bogo!?"

Hiccup tears himself from FeeTwix's grip. "Ficker." He whistles for Wolf to come over to him but the Unigaean beast stays away.

"What happened there?" Ryuk asks as FeeTwix continues to tell his fans of what drinks qualify for the buy one, get one free offer.

"Hiccup pissed the wolf off," Zaena says.

"I didn't piss 'the wolf' off, I accidently pissed *on* 'the wolf,'" Hiccup argues. "And it was a fickin' accident. I don't need adult diapers or shit like that. I thought I saw a fick-faced ghoul back in the brush we passed through. Everyone has personal fears. Mine trigger bowel movements."

"It was a deer."

"Yes, Liz, we later discovered that after you fickin' tossed a sword at it and killed it. But at the time, I thought it was a ghost and I fickin' hate ghosts. Thanks for the deer meat though, it is best uncooked."

"So, you peed on Wolf?" Ryuk asks.

"Fick, why is everyone judging me? It was just a little and I pissed myself too, which is why I'm walking the way I'm walking."

"I thought you walked that way because you were bow-legged," Zaena says, a mischievous smile forming on her face.

Hiccup's face turns red. "I had fickin' rickets when I was a young goblin and now you're making fun of me for this? Fick! There are no safe spaces in this guild, not that I need one, but just fickin' saying." He sniffs loudly. "Fick everyone that isn't me."

With that, the goblin crosses his arms over his chests and waits for the others to walk past him. Once they are a good five meters away, he slowly starts to pick up his pace.

"How long do you think he'll stay quiet?" Zaena asks.

"No idea."

A message appears on Ryuk's vision pane.

Sophia: I have started downloading your feed. The download process won't take long, but viewing and interpreting the data will take a fair amount of time. Please refrain from logging out while it is being interpreted. Like I explained before you logged in, we are storing your feed's data in real time. If you log out, we won't have enough available space to completely process your feed. Trust me, I'm an expert.

Ryuk: I do trust you.

Sophia: Be sure not to log out.

Ryuk: I wasn't planning on it. Are you viewing my feed?

Sophia: Not your current feed.

"You've got that look on your face, Ryuk," says FeeTwix.

"Which look?"

"Like you're annoyed."

"It's ..." Ryuk points up at the sky.

"Ah, cool, cool, cool. Fick 'em, as our goblin friend says. And yes," the Swede calls over his shoulder, "you're still my friend."

Seeing that Hiccup won't join the group, Wolf turns back to the goblin. Once he reaches him, he lowers his body so Hiccup can climb up.

"Good Wolfy," Hiccup says as he pets his head. "At least you get me. I'll let you know if I feel a piss coming on."

(0)__(x)

The goblin has more or less cheered up by the time they reach the Bluwid city limits. Ryuk's nose twitches at the stench that hovers over this city like a big cloud of pollution. There are hints of Jatla in the smell, but the Bluwid stank is more pronounced, thicker, and Ryuk instantly wishes he wore the surgical mask he had back in Tokyo.

"Whew!" Zaena says. "It is quite pungent here."

The goblin's nostrils flare. "Yeah, yeah. Jatla may be a shithole, but Bluwid is an actual shithole. People shit in holes in the alleys."

"Why don't they install bathrooms?" Enway watches a goblin on a purple cockatrice ride by. He wears chainmail and spiked arm bracers. A scowl on his face, the rider grumbles, "Get the fick out of the way," as he passes them.

"No one is in your way, you fickered dotard!" Hiccup calls after him.

"Shit, Hiccup, please don't pick fights."

Hiccup raises an eyebrow at Ryuk. "Pick fights? That's a fickin' greeting where I'm from." His voice grows louder. "And if the cup-fickin' dirty finger banger has anything else to say, he'll say it to our faces!"

The goblin on the cockatrice tells Hiccup to "fick off," and just when it seems like a fight is about to break out, FeeTwix whips out a 9mm Luger he had tucked into the back of his pants and caps the goblin.

Bang!

Instakill!

"Fick, Twixy, we were just fickin' around!"

"No one threatens my friends," FeeTwix says as he returns the gun to its hiding place. "And no one talks shit about the Mitherfickers."

Hiccup considers this as he rides past on Wolf. "I'm with you there, Twixy, I'm all about jingoism, however minute it may be. Extreme force too. Shoot first, don't ask questions—good motto."

"Tossers tonight! Tossers tonight!" a young girl goblin yells out. She has her hair in pigtails and she wears a tattered, hand-me-down leather tunic.

"Tossers is tonight?" Hiccup runs his mechanical hand over his pin topknot. "Fick yeah! Who wants to go to Tossers?"

"Oh, that's what it is," FeeTwix says, his eyes flashing as his fans explain. "I'll pass."

"Dare I ask?" Enway grins at Ryuk, her red eyes softening.

"Better you than me," he jokes.

"What is Tossers?" she asks as they come to a checkpoint manned by a pair of sleeping goblins. A couple of emptied steins on the table tell a story of late afternoon debauchery. One of the checkpoint guards has his thumb in his mouth.

"Doesn't know what Tossers is." Hiccup rubs his hands together. "Tossers is the name for public executions in Bluwid. Fun shit."

"It's not a game?" Zaena asks. "Everything you mention sounds like a game."

"No, it's not, Liz, and I wish you, of all people, would turn the prejudice down a hair. Any-fickin'-hoo, *Tossers* is where you put someone convicted of a crime in a giant slingshot and shoot them off the continental shelf."

"That's it?" asks Ryuk as they pass a goblin perched on a carpet selling severed bugbear heads.

"Yes, Marbles, that's it. Any other questions?"

"And this is a game?"

"No, it's a public execution. What the fick is wrong with you?"

"Nothing is wrong with me; it just sounded like a game."

"Well, people bet on it. Bets like, how loud will the goblin scream, how far will they fly—those sort of things. Fick, I need to get new pants. Stop arguing with me, Marbles. Where's the pants store? Or does this guild say *trousers*? I wish we could all agree on a name for the shit we put on our legs to cover our chalupas."

FeeTwix flips open a map and it floats in the air before him. He scrolls through the map, which is backlit, roads and buildings highlighted in green. "Ah, Bluwid, it feels like I know you intimately now."

Hiccup takes a look at the map. "Not bad, but it doesn't show all the shortcuts." He squints as the map zooms in on their current location. "Liz, I need some reptilian eyes over here. Hey! Limbs off the hair. Fick. Okay, does that say Wild Cherry Oriental Massage?"

Hiccup points at a building a few blocks away.

"It does. You can clearly read it, goblin."

He licks his lips. "Then that's where we are going first. I know the guy that runs Wild Cherry and he, of all goblins, is a real fickboy. Old friend too, goes by the name Dougbug." Hiccup whistles. "Sorry, Wolf, we'll need to wait on pants. To Wild Cherry! And Liz, fick you and the dragon you rode in on. Let's go, Mitherfickers!"

"Fick you!" a cranky goblin begging by the side of the road shouts.

"Fick the poor!" is Hiccup's response.

"Yeah, fick them!"

"The locals are very hostile," Enway says as they follow the wolfbound goblin.

Ryuk laughs. "It reminds me of home."

"Tokyo is this bad?"

"No! Not that home, um, I meant our guildhall in Jatla. I can't believe I've just referred to that place as home. We need a new guildhall, in fact..." Ryuk catches up with FeeTwix, who walks beside Zaena holding her hand.

"What's up, Ryuk?" FeeTwix says after he sees the eager look in his eyes.

"We need a new guildhall, something not in Jatla. Let's never go back to Jatla again."

Zaena nods. "I agree. We should get a place in Valhalla, in Porthos."

"Pretty expensive there," Ryuk says.

"Price is not an issue." FeeTwix smiles at both of them. "We need a suitable location that has access to amenities and other guilds. We also need a place that isn't filthy as fick, like Jatla."

Hiccup slows, his big ears twitching ever so slightly. "Did I hear someone say something about Jatla? It ain't that bad, folks, but believe whatever fake media outlet you want. I'm sick of waging war against the lamestream media. I mean, really, you've seen the shit they said about Dirty Dave, right, Liz?"

"No."

"And we all met Dirty Dave, and he's a high-quality guy. Clearly not a drug dealer, good people, the best of people."

Ryuk sighs. "He is a drug dealer. We protected his shipment of wizardous as part of a quest, remember? In the Port of Corpses, as you called it."

"Maybe *you* protected his shipment, but I didn't see shit, Marbles."

"Hiccup, you yourself pointed out the fact that orcs were loading drugs into an airship."

"See what I'm talking about, Twixy? Ryuk's clearly been poisoned by fake news. Shit, I bet he believes the world is round."

"Whose world?" Ryuk asks, his eyes narrowing on the back of the goblin's head.

"Anyone's world. I'm walking on a flat surface. The world is flat. It's not fickin' rocket science, whatever a fickin' rocket is. Sheesh. Okay, stop picking fights with me. You fickers see that place up there with the big red cherry on the window?"

"Yes," FeeTwix says. "And no offense, Hiccup, but I may be re-equipping my hazmat suit. It is toxic over here!"

"None taken. I'd equip one too if you had one for short and round guys. Here's the plan: let me do all the talking with Dougbug."

"Dougbug?" Enway asks.

"Keep up, Red Eyes. Ooo, I like that name. Anyfick, Dougbug is my friend, and he may be pissed at me, so let me do the talking."

"Why are we going to see this 'Dougbug' anyway, goblin?"

"Fick, Liz, read between the lines for once. We're trying to find intel on the goblin shaman who has this fickin' runestone you three and the giant in Waringtla were drooling over. If anyone knows where this shaman is, Dougbug will know. But it may take some bartering."

"I'm sorry. I lose track of what we are doing the longer you ramble."

"Did you say bartering?" FeeTwix asks. "Because that's my specialty."

"Maybe, maybe not, Twixy. Let me put my feelers out first."

(0)__(x)

"I will not give him a massage," Zaena says, her hand on the hilt of her sword. "How *dare* you even propose such a thing, Hiccup!"

Hiccup turns to Dougbug and shrugs. "I told you she wouldn't be down."

Dougbug is a short goblin with a full head of hair and nice clothes too. He wasn't initially too enthused to see Hiccup, but once he laid eyes on Zaena, his tune changed.

From what Ryuk could gather from the brief exchange between the two goblins, Dougbug's animosity stemmed from the fact that Hiccup was responsible for destroying Dougbug's last relationship with an orc masseuse. Something about an ink shadow named Barry, and something about a massage gone horribly wrong after Barry tried to stick his chalupa in the masseuse's ear.

Such a stupid story, was Ryuk's thought at the time, and he's just about to tell Hiccup to stop being a dumbass when a message flashes on his vision pane.

Hiccup: Fick, Liz, play along. What part of "play along" did you not understand from before? We need info, and unless you want to spend the rest of the night trying to shake loose some intel in the mean streets of

Bluwid—which is a lot more difficult than just beating up a drunk in Aramis—then you'll do Uncle Goblin a solid and at least pretend you'll give him a massage.

Zaena crosses her arms over her chest and glares at both the goblins.

"No massage, no information," Dougbug says, a crooked, toothy grin stretching across his cheeks.

Grease stains across his tunic are all that's left of the fried dragon skins he was munching when they entered his establishment. Even though he was angry when they first entered, he offered some of the gluten-free dragon skins to Hiccup, who readily obliged.

"Dougy, goblin to goblin, we've been through a lot of bullshit," Hiccup says, getting on his knees. "And I'm here to..." He throws himself at Dougbug's feet. "Please, please, please, fick, please give us the info!"

"You purebred poofty fruitflake ... get your ass up! There is no begging in Wild Cherry's. Fick. Can't have employees or clients seeing that you can just beg your way to success here."

"Please, Dougy, please!"

"Nope, you'll have to get your information the old-fashioned way: killing, cheating, robbing, tricking. Not necessarily in that order, but you get what I'm saying."

"But Dougy, that could take all night! Come on, do a solid for your old pal."

"I don't owe you any favors, not after Jatla."

"Get up, Hiccup," Ryuk says under his breath. "You're embarrassing us."

Hiccup stops fake crying long enough to exchange glances with Dougbug. Not seconds later, he's beating the floor with his fist and laughing alongside his old friend. Dougbug soon joins him, both goblins laughing and rolling around on the floor.

"What in the hell are they doing?" Enway asks.

"Being goblins, I believe," is FeeTwix's reply.

"Fick, Marbles! You're such a sorry excuse for a strongman. Fick. I told you this one was a real starfish sniffer, Dougy. Didn't I tell you?"

"Ha! Yes, you did. Fick. I thought you were exaggerating," Dougbug says as he helps Hiccup to his feet, both their faces red from laughter. "This one couldn't get laid by his own right hand. Fick me. Where's the other? You said there was a female, I believe."

"Tammy, a traitor-ass bitch. She's no longer with us."

"Fick, I hate a traitor, but it happens to the best of us." Dougbug shrugs. "Anyfick, like I said, massage for info. Sorry, Hiccup, no more favors."

"Fick me, Dougy, we could pay you."

"I have plenty of money." His eyes narrow on Zaena. "What I want is a four-handed Thulean massage."

FeeTwix glances from Zaena to Dougbug. "Not going to happen, Dougbug, that's my girlfriend there. If anyone's getting a massage, it's me! Ain't that right, bae?"

Dougbug's face softens. "He says 'bae' too? I love that word!"

"Fick you both, and yes, Twixy says it too. Says a lot of stupid shit. Sells a lot of stupid stuff too. Look, Dougy, fick, what do you want from us? You name it, you got it. Hell, have Marbles. Straight up. I'm giving him away. He can be a fluffer around here or something. You have fluffers, right?"

"I told you what I'd like, Hiccup." Dougbug's eyes light up. "What's that?" He relaxes some and stretches his shoulders back. "Feels good … mmmm … damn good."

His mouth agape, Hiccup looks from Dougbug to Zaena, who still has her arms crossed over her chest.

"Yeah, feels really good." Dougbug starts tapping his foot. "Oh yeah, harder, harder. Shit! SHIT! TOO FICKIN' HARD! FICK! Okay…okay …better …ah, that's the spot, Thulean. Lots of stress there. Feel that knot? Big league, am I right? Sometimes I have to take over for the orcs when their arms are tired…ahhh …lots of yanking…hurts your back muscles. Hey! Why'd you stop?"

Hiccup points his mechanical finger at the shorter goblin. "Fick that. Did you just say you *take over* for the girls? You chalupa-tugging in here, Dougy? 'Cause if the madams, or in your case, misters—pretty sure that's what you call yourself—are taking part in the tugging, I'm fickin' taking my business elsewhere."

"You can't afford a massage here, Hiccup. Need I remind you? And don't fickin' judge me!" Dougbug growls.

Zaena clears her throat. "There will be plenty more massages where that came from, if, and only if, you tell us where the shaman lives."

"Fick." Dougbug runs his hand through his hair. "Fine, fine. You got me there. I know lots of shamans. Which one are you looking for?"

The Mitherfickers exchange glances. Wolf, who is near the door, yawns and drops onto the ground to rest.

"The goblin in question can cure Goblinheimer's, possibly chalupa warts. Although that last part is hearsay, because I made that part up. Fick. Oh, they use a runestone, or there is a runestone around them. Something like that. What you got, Dougy?" Hiccup asks.

"Easy, her name is Sugar Spur," he says, a note of intense severity to his voice.

Ryuk suppresses a sigh and fails.

"What the hell is wrong with the emo poof-flake?" Dougbug asks.

"Someone dropped him on his head when he was a wee little ficker," Hiccup laments. "He's been half-ficktarded ever since. Continue, Dougy."

"She goes by the name Sugar Spur, and word on the street is she can cure chalupa warts and has helped several overcome Goblinheimer's."

"Fick. Yeah. Point us in the right direction."

Dougbug snorts. "You're going to see her? Appointment only, Hiccup. The waitlist is at least a fortnight."

"No, we're going to..." Hiccup's pink topknot lifts. "Hey! Hands off the hair, Lizzy."

"Ah, your hair. And your arm. Things I meant to comment on." Dougbug sighs. "But what the fick ever, look, if you guys want to see Sugar Spur and cure your chalupa warts, you'll need to make an appointment. Luckily, Sugar lives in a dungeon on the hill to the northwest. Can't miss it. You can make your appointment directly at the gate. Now..." He rubs his hands together. "Where's that massage?"

Instakill!

Dougbug's head flies off his shoulders, a splatter of blood staining the wall. Zaena flicks the blood off her sword and quickly sheathes it.

"Fick, Liz! You weren't supposed to kill him!" Hiccup shakes his head as he makes his way over to his old friend's body. "But if I don't check him for loot, someone else will."

CHAPTER 10: UPGRADE

"...And that, everyone, is why you should try Krunkin' Kronuts' new post-V-Day latte and Krunked Up Kronut of the month! Heartbreak, or maybe an October/November baby on the way, you can never go wrong with these yummy yummy donuts. Cream? Check. Non-GMO flour ingredients? Definite. Kosher halal vitamin-enhanced icing with added nutrients created in a donut shop with a focus on Feng Shui? You bet your fickin' ass! #FeeTwixRox at counter gets you half-off an additional donut, to share with that special someone or to share with yourself in hopes of finding a special someone next year!"

Hiccup pulls the Swede aside. "Look, Twix, I'm not the type that would tell their kid to not follow their dreams, even if their dream consisted of becoming a vape artist or getting a liberal arts degree, whatever the fick that is, but seriously, Twixy, we're in the mean and dirty streets of Bluwid, and you'll draw attention to us with all that selling nonsense. Read between the lines of what I've just said: shut the fick up. Also, what's a kronut?"

The Mitherfickers, led by Hiccup, are navigating the alleys that connect the shantytown of the city to the main thoroughfares. Wolf trails at the rear, not ridden by the goblin for once.

Hiccup promised it'd be a shorter distance, but Ryuk is starting to doubt whether the goblin even has a vague sense of basic cardinal directions.

They've been walking a good thirty minutes now, and while no one has challenged them to a fight, they have encountered a roving group of pickpockets; a handful of busty and busted orc prostitutes; a couple of bloated dead bodies; a good amount of bodily excrement; ubiquitous shitting holes; a few suspicious puddles; and several Wizardous fiends sitting on the ground with their arms clutched around their knees.

"A kronut is something that you would really like, Hiccup."

"That sentence doesn't tell me anything. We talking sour, tangy, sweet? Can you snort it?"

"Sweet and delicious, and I suppose you could snort it. Also, while I have you, anything you'd like to say to the Fickers?" FeeTwix asks as he bends over towards Hiccup's face. Instead of streetlamps, the slums that surround the city center of Bluwid are lit by paper lamps, a fire hazard, but then again, everything in Bluwid is hazardous in some way.

The paper lamp above them twists as a breeze blows by, startling Wolf. He barks, the Mitherfickers turn back to him, and FeeTwix and Hiccup continue their conversation.

"Say to the Fickers...hmmm...How many are there now?"

"Nearly forty-five thousand, not too shabby, especially for someone like you, who doesn't seem too keen on providing a steady stream of content."

"*Providing content?* What kind of doublespeak fickery is that? We've been at this how long? A couple weeks?"

"Less than a week," Ryuk reminds him.

"Fick, Marbles, if I needed a virtual assistant, I'd hire one."

Ryuk turns to Enway and she grins softly at him. Something about her red eyes strikes him every time he looks at her.

Zaena slips by, catlike and graceful. "I don't care about what the goblin needs to say to his misled followers. If there ever were a basket of deplorables…"

"Ignore the dragon woman, kiddos," Hiccup says, looking FeeTwix square in his black eyes. "And I can't say I disagree with Liz, you are a basket of deplorables, and if any of you ever want to dampen your chalupas, you'll stop watching this ficker's feed and get out there and get you some." He points his mechanical finger at the Swede's face. "So, stay in school, and if school's too hard, bribe your teacher. Fick, Twixy, what do you want me to say? If these fickers started hooking me up in terms of women, drugs, and healing potions, I'd be a much better role model."

A goblin passing by on a crutch lifts into the air. He screams and starts crying almost immediately. Wolf starts barking, circling the suspended goblin.

"Fick! Ghosts!" Hiccup hits the ground, his golden helm appearing on his head. Once he realizes he's the only one that has hit the deck, he glances around from beneath his loose-fitting helm and narrows his eyes at Zaena.

"Put your fickin' konoshlo away, Liz!"

"I will set you down," the Thulean tells the suspended goblin, "when you tell us where Sugar Spur's dungeon is located."

The handicapped goblin, an older man with a long white beard, realizes pretty quickly what's going on after he sees the Thulean. "Fick you, lizard bitch. Yoy, yoy, yoy! Put me down, you rotten taint stain!"

"Ha!" Hiccup slowly gets to his feet. "That last one just rolls off the tongue."

"Where is Sugar Spur?"

"Fick if I know!" the older goblin cries out. "I was just visiting Dirty Dave." His voice drops an octave as his eyes roll back into his head. *"You should visit Dirty Dave too. His shop is two blocks away on the left. Now, please set me down so that I may get on my way."*

Zaena does as instructed almost immediately.

As soon as the possessed older goblin's feet touch the pavement, his eyes return to their normal state as does his voice. "Fick you!" he shouts at the Mitherfickers as he scuttles away.

FeeTwix cheers. "Hell yes, Dirty Dave has summoned us!"

"Liz, we are going to need to discuss your enhanced interrogation techniques. In the last hour, you've decapitated an old buddy of mine *and* you've harassed a distinguished member of the goblin community, triggering a cryptic message from Dirty Dave. Now, I approve of enhanced interrogation for immiNPCs, but not goblins. No fickin' way. We're people too, you know?"

Hiccup continues and Ryuk tunes him out. As they move in the direction that Dirty Dave has sent them, he recalls giving the infamous weapons dealer a few of his marbles back in the Port of Protla.

Who knows what Dirty Dave will present us with next, he thinks as he steps around a puddle of blood.

Why there is a random puddle of blood in the back streets of Bluwid could be attributed to a dead or sleeping goblin near the puddle, a discarded knife a few meters away, or a butcher's shop in a yard that faces the street.

Ryuk's Magic Eye skill working in tandem with his Extreme Focus ability sheds light on a lot of things, and in places like Bluwid, it'd be nice to turn off.

The problem is that he can't turn it off.

Whereas before he'd have to focus to get it to work, as Ryuk has leveled, the skills have become more pronounced, more readily available. Sure, he can "think" it into working, but it is pretty much ever-present at the moment, which makes things like normal conversations a bit annoying because he's constantly seeing magical outlines around various items and people.

"There it is," Enway says, breaking his train of thought. The Chromatic Mage carries the same smile on her face that he's grown accustomed to seeing. Her hair pulled back with a braid, similar to the way Tamana's avatar wore her hair, tugs at Ryuk's heartstrings.

He's well aware that their guild has its own priorities, and there is the overarching quest of stopping the Shinigami and preventing them from spreading to the real world, but Ryuk can't help but tack *Save Tamana* on the end of that list.

It began with her, and it very well may end with her.

"This Dirty Dave's is a lot less impressive than the one in Aramis," Hiccup comments. "I mean, where are the fickin' fauns on the top of the building? Where's the big vault door? That said, I admire the fact that this one is next to a DD BBQ. Don't mind if I fickin' do, am I right? Who's in for a fifty pack of Lemon Pepper dragon wings?"

"They're not lining up," Ryuk says, his Japanese sense of order perturbed by the mob outside DD's BBQ. The goblins have swelled around the entrance, a few fists and angry elbows readily exchanged.

Just as Hiccup turns to join the mob, his trajectory is corrected by Zaena's ghost limbs.

"Liz! What the fick? I'm starved over here."

"Dirty Dave told us to see him, *not* for us to visit his meat establishment."

Hiccup goes from angry to half-grin. "Meat establishment. Sorry, Liz, that phrase brings out a younger, more obnoxious goblin than the gentleman who stands before you. And fick, I'm getting fed before we go to the dungeon, believe you me. Maybe I'll just put an order in with Davey Boy himself."

"Let's just see what Dirty Dave has to offer." FeeTwix is the first to enter the weapon's shop. He's followed by Hiccup, who has elbowed his way to the front, then Zaena, Enway, Ryuk and Wolf.

Completely the opposite of his shop in Aramis, Dirty Dave's Bluwid Weapon Emporium would make the Steve Jobs Museum appear cluttered. Aside from a white counter near the back corner of the room, the place is completely bare.

"Where the fick is he?"

"Maybe he had legal matters to see to," Zaena says.

"You know, Liz, those kinds of offhand remarks are what sway public opinion and generate fake news. If you ever decide to get out of the princess business, there's definitely a place for you in the lamestream media. Am I right, Twixy?"

Instead of responding, FeeTwix moves to the front counter. "Hello? We got your message, Dirty Dave."

"Hmmm, so this is the same guy who owns the barbeque place in Kayi?" Enway asks.

"And most of the weapons shops across all three continents, and the inventor of wizardous," Ryuk explains.

"The narcotic?" she asks.

"Fick, Marbles, what ever happened to the due process of law in Tritania? Innocent until proven guilty? Sure, we don't practice that in Jatla, instead going for guilty until proven innocent, but that's a case for another day." Hiccup's eyes glaze over and he bites his bottom lip. "Where are we again? Why isn't there anything in this room? Twixy..."

"Don't worry, Hiccup, we're... " FeeTwix smiles as he pats the goblin on the shoulder. "We're in the quiet zone. Also, you've already eaten. You ate so much. You must be very full."

"Don't feel full," Hiccup says, rubbing his hairy belly. He jiggles it for a moment. "Are you sure I ate?"

"You ate big league, Hiccup."

The goblin's eyes narrow at FeeTwix. "Are you trying to trick me?"

"Why would I ever do that, Hiccup?"

"The quiet zone, huh? I see what's going on here, Twixy, and if I had recently eaten, there'd be a stain on the front of my tunic." Hiccup looks down at his designer white tunic, which is difficult because of the rolls of fat around his neck. "No stain, no food. And I smell food." His nostrils flare.

"Maybe Dave wants you to turn off your feed," Ryuk suggests.

Ding! Ding! Ding! Please turn of all live feeds. Ding! Ding! Ding!

The voice is like that of a female humandroid.

"Where the fick did that sound come from?"

"Ah, sorry, Dave, and sorry, fans, I'll be right back. In the meantime, be sure to check out my newest contest called *Count the Ficks*. I've had G. Todd, who has been running all my contests, see just how many times our favorite goblin used the word 'fick' yesterday. For the first ten people to get the number right, you'll get a six-month TwitchTubeRed membership for free. Since most of you are already members, as is required by your cable/internet provider, your next six billing cycles will be comped! So, get cracking, count those ficks, and I'll be right back!"

His eyes flash blue, and before Hiccup can berate him for cultural appropriation, a door that wasn't there just moments ago slides open behind the counter.

Dirty Dave, his face as predatory as ever and his hair slicked back, steps into the room. He wears a bathrobe open at the chest, revealing a copious number of tattoos, so many in fact that his skin is almost reptilian. The main piece, a skull with gaping mouth and fangs across his chest, grins as Dirty Dave places his hands on the counter.

"How can I help you?" he asks, his voice that same sinister tone Ryuk's heard twice before.

(0)__(0)

"Fickin-a, Mr. Dirty, or is it Mr. Dave? Davey Boy? Dirty D? Double D? Ha! I like that one. The Dirtiest Dave this side of Porthos?"

The level 99 weapons dealer grins at the goblin and the smile of the tattoo across his chest thins. "Dave, just call me Dave. Now, I know the six of you have a dungeon to get to, so I will make this quick."

"Just let me get my checkbook out." A quill pen appears in one hand and a binder of partially filled out company checks in FeeTwix's other arm. The phrase Mitherfickers LLC is written in golden letters on the front cover.

"No need," Dave says, "your items have already been paid for by the Knights of Non Compos Mentis."

"So that rude biotch Sophia has finally come through with her promise," Hiccup says. "I was fickin' wondering when the Knights would hook us the fick up."

"Quiet, goblin, have some respect for their guild," Liz hisses.

"The ninja killer dude seems cool enough, as did the faun. Sophia was a hell no."

Dirty Dave laughs. "I've had my run-ins with Sophia as well. She is a necessary evil..." The famed weapons dealer runs his hand along his chin. "As are many evils, if you think about it."

Hiccup claps his hands together. "I couldn't agree more, Dave. Now, I'm not going to say something like *gimme, gimme, gimme*, but, fick, I'm ready for my present, Santa!"

Damn, goblin. Ryuk glares at Hiccup, who continues to rub his hands together. It doesn't take long for his glare to twist up into a half-smile. The goblin, while generally obnoxious, does grow on you. *But so do warts.*

As Ryuk tries to remember where he heard that, possibly from Hiccup himself, an ax drops down from the ceiling and slices into the countertop.

"Fick!"

Dirty Dave smiles. "Fick is right, Hiccup. To go along with your golden helm, which you still wear, correct?"

"Always!" The golden helm appears on Hiccup's misshapen head. "And disregard whatever Marbles wrote in his LiveJournal about it, whatever the fick that emo poofty thing is. Fick. Where was I?"

FeeTwix taps on his head and Hiccup picks up the cue. "Yep! My helm. Always have it on, rain or shine, crazed Thulean or semi-sexy Mexican elf with red hot ojos."

"Where did you learn the word *ojos*?"

"Fick if I know. I just somehow speak Spanish. Could be the fact that my parents are from El Salvador. Kidding."

Enway crosses her arms over her chest as she raises an eyebrow at the goblin, an eyebrow he can't see, as he's front and center now, still rubbing his grubby paws together as he looks the ax over.

"This is a genuine Gilius Thunderhead Ax," says Dirty Dave. "It will greatly improve your chance for a critical hit. While it has electric powers, because you aren't a magic caster, that aspect of the weapon doesn't work. However, simply equipping it will lower the damage you take from a magic attack."

The silver, double-bitted ax is huge, nearly half Hiccup's size.

As he takes it off the counter, the goblin gets into a battle pose and practices a few swipes holding the ax with both hands. "Fick yeah! A little heavy, and I won't be able to use a shield with it, but fick yeah, Davey Boy. You done hooked a brother up again!"

"I'm glad you enjoy it." As he says this, the tattooed skull on Dave's chest bares its sharp teeth.

Hiccup eyes him funny. "Welp, that's creepy as fick. As much as I'd like to stick around and look at your heroine-chic chest, Dave, someone has to eat your barbeque, and that someone is me. FeeTwix, rupees."

"No need," says Dirty Dave, "I will bill the Knights."

"Fick to the yeah. In that case, I'll double my order. See you kiddos in a bitto." Hiccup tosses the ax over his shoulder, heads to the door, and kicks it open.

"The air is noticeably cleaner," Zaena says as soon as he's gone.

Enway nods in agreement. "It totally is."

"You guys are too harsh," says FeeTwix. "Then again, I've just learned to breathe out of my mouth when he-who-shall-not-be-named is present."

"Moving right along," Dirty Dave says, his eyes and the eyes of his chest tattoo narrowing at Zaena, "I believe the Thulean princess has a gift in store."

"You knew all along," Ryuk asks. "Sorry, dumb question."

"Yes, I knew all along." He clears his throat. "And there are more things I know that will be revealed to you at the proper place and time. Anyway, some new armor is in store for the tank of the group."

"Hiccup's not the tank?" FeeTwix asks.

Dirty Dave considers this. "I suppose he can take the most damage, given his shields. In that case, I'd say your group has two tanks, one for defense and the other for offense, which would be you, Princess Zaena."

"Please, just Zaena."

"As you wish," Dave whispers. With the snap of his finger, a female mannequin decked out in armor appears. The armor is form-fitting, the tasset almost skirt-like and inlaid with incredibly tiny jewels.

"It is a work of art," says Zaena. "It wasn't designed by anyone from this world, was it?"

"You are correct. It was designed by Olivas, a Unigaean immigrant who still creates pieces from time to time. I believe one of the reasons it is such a fine piece is because he originally designed it for an illusionist named Sam Raid, who was one of the great leaders of Unigaea. She died before he could have the piece delivered, and when Oric, your guildmate, brought the Unigaeans here, Olivas carried the piece with him."

"Oric brought them here?" Enway asks, looking to Wolf. "He never mentioned that."

"There is quite a bit Oric hasn't told you, but yes, it would have been six years ago in your world that he brought the Unigaeans. But that is a tale for another day. Care to try the piece on?"

A room divider pixelates into existence in front of the armor.

"We'll close our eyes." Dirty Dave's eyes and the eyes of the skull on his chest tattoo cement shut as Zaena steps behind the curtain.

She emerges a few moments later with the new armor. As she takes it in, Ryuk pulls up her main stats to see that her defense has increased by a hundred points.

Zaena Morozon Level 23 Brawler Assassin

HP: 915/915

ATK: 228

MATK: 10

DEF: 225

MDF: 47

LUCK: 24

"I love it," Zaena says softly. "It is an absolute specimen."

"Damn, babe, you look hella great!"

FeeTwix opens his arms wide and Zaena approaches him. She stops before him, her hands on her hips, and with a deep breath in, she collapses into his arms. He catches her, leans her back and kisses her.

FeeTwix pulls back a little after she bites at his kiss.

"Ha! Careful!"

"There are people around," she reminds him.

"You're the one who fell into my arms, not the other way around."

"Now," Dave says, "I don't have anything for you, Enway, but the book Lothar has given you and your new avatar should keep you entertained for a while. That leaves two more members, and a big Tagvornin wolf. For Wolf, all I can offer is some of the best steak I've ever had the pleasure of tasting."

A platter materializes into shape on the floor. The top lifts; Wolf runs over to it and digs in.

"That leaves you two," Dave says to FeeTwix and Ryuk. "We'll begin with FeeTwix, as I'd like to save the best for last."

(0)__(x)

"What do you get the man that has everything?" Dave asks, his hands now behind his back.

"That's the same question I ask myself every year on my birthday," says FeeTwix.

"Guns, blades, explosives—you can get any of that through your extensive network of fans."

"Correct."

"But there is a weapon not available to most weapon owners, namely because I invented it and I've kept its distribution network very narrow."

"Go on..." the Swede says, his eyes lighting up.

"It was a weapon your hero Quantum Hughes once used."

Zaena scoffs.

"Not to defeat your sister," Dirty Dave says, "but to destroy Steam Enforcers. It is called the Almost Universal Solvent hose gun, or AUS hose gun."

Dave taps his long nail on the table and a brass reservoir with a backpack strap appears on the table. A cable connects the reservoir to a nozzle, similar to the way a firehose operates.

"Another little hack I added is within the reservoir itself. It never, and I mean never, runs out."

"And you just pull the trigger?"

"Correct."

"Let me show you how it works."

A heavily armored warrior appears in a flash of smoke. Carrying two broadswords, he gets into a battle pose and charges Dirty Dave. Without strapping the reservoir to his back, Dave simply turns the hose's nozzle towards the towering warrior.

A pixilated liquid steams out of the gun.

As soon as it reaches the warrior's body his armor melts away, followed by his flesh and bones. He screams in agony until he has completely dissolved into a puddle of steaming blood and fleshy discharges.

"Yes, yes, yes, and yes! Yes! Yes. Double fuck yes. I will take it!" FeeTwix practically hops into the shoulder strap.

He adjusts the weight of the reservoir over his shoulder, and before he can comment on its awkward placement, Dirty Dave shows him how to hold it so that he can pretty much, like an over-the-shoulder pump sprayer, hose down anything in a two to three meter vicinity.

Enway laughs. "You're like a rich boy at his birthday party."

"Hell yes, I am." FeeTwix pretend-sprays the counter. He pivots, and turns to spray the wall. "I am going to fick some shit up with this thing, Dirty Dave."

"I'm glad I can aid in the, um, ficking up of shit. Now, last but not least, Ryuk."

"Me?" Ryuk gulps. He knows Dave probably has a pretty good weapon in store for him, but he has no earthly idea of what it could be.

"Everyone follow me into my shooting range."

"Your ... Oh, I see it now," FeeTwix says as the back wall elongates, adding about ten meters of space to the room.

As if he were holding it all this time, Dirty Dave now has a shotgun featuring a revolving cylinder. The recoil pad has been modified to provide extra cushion, and the front grip is encased in leather.

"That thing shoots marbles?" Zaena asks. "It looks like..."

"It looks like something I'd use to take on an army of zombies," says FeeTwix.

"Its design is based on the Armsel Striker, a 12-gauge shotgun with a revolving cylinder designed for riot control. It's easy to load. Rotate it, drop a marble in. Two full revolutions and you have yourself twenty-four available shots. I recommend loading it with similar marbles, i.e. all explosive or all sword, but a mix would could also come in handy. The molten and explosive mix you've been doing would be especially brutal."

"I've received a new marble since we last met," Ryuk says as he steps over to Dirty Dave. "A gravity marble."

"I wouldn't put that, nor would I put your clear marbles in here." Dave considers what he just said. "Although, that last one could be interesting."

The infamous weapons dealer demonstrates how to hold the weapon. After he's pointed it away from the Mitherfickers, he squeezes the trigger, which produces two clicks.

"The first click is the cylinder rotating and the second click is the ammo dropping. Anyway, load it up."

He hands the weapon to Ryuk and the Ballistics Mage quickly figures out how to use the weapon.

It is relatively straightforward.

After hitting a small lever, he starts dropping marbles into the loading port, this time going with all black explosive marbles. Less than a minute later, he's fully loaded.

"And then I just squeeze the trigger?"

"Yep. I keep things simple. I know your marble gun is triggerless and uses algomagic, but I'm a trigger guy. Squeeze and boom."

A bag of popcorn appears in FeeTwix's hand. "I can't wait to see this," he says as he starts funneling popcorn into his mouth. A few pieces float into the air as Zaena uses her ghost limbs to sample the off-world food.

"This is great!" she says as she stuffs more into her mouth.

Woosh! Woosh! Woosh!

Three targets pop up in the firing range.

Click-click. BOOM! Click-click. BOOM! Click-click. BOOM!

The explosions obliterate the three targets.

"That's amazing!" FeeTwix says, popcorn dropping out of his mouth.

"You're a natural, kid," says Dirty Dave, a satisfied grin on his face and the face of his chest tattoo. His eyes narrow. "Now, finish the round."

A dozen *live* imps drop from the ceiling and Ryuk lays them all out.

Insta-Insta-Insta-Insta-Instakill!

"Whoo-hoo!" FeeTwix shouts.

A live orc, a few heads taller than Zaena, rises from the ground. He flexes his muscles and roars.

Instakill!

Ryuk puts the fucker down before he can take another step.

"There is one last thing," Dirty Dave says as he extends his arm and turns his palm around. "Your guild needs to level, and unfortunately, the ray gun I had in Aramis is malfunctioning. Therefore, I've turned to narcotics."

Five bullet-sized pills now sit in his open palm. They are blue with a white stripe through their centers.

"What do they do?" Enway asks.

"They are leveling pills. Very rare, and very addictive. They decrease the experience points needed to level up by sixty percent. They will only last for the next two hours, so eat them when you get to the dungeon."

THE RUNESTONES OF TRITINAKH

CHAPTER 11: DUNGEONS AND GOBLINS

"I really wish I had kept that collar on him," says FeeTwix as the Mitherfickers leave Dirty Dave's Weapons Emporium. The Swede was referring to the collar he'd placed on Hiccup at the DJ Ride the Lightning concert, a collar which instantly dragged the goblin back to FeeTwix, no matter how far away he was.

His Marble Shotgun attached to a shoulder strap and now at his hip, Ryuk looks just about as badass as a Ballistics Mage can possibly look. The canister fully loaded, mostly with explosive marbles but a few sword marbles just for shiggles, Ryuk is as ready for business as he'll ever be.

Unfortunately, without the goblin, the Mitherfickers are incomplete. And while they may normally go to the dungeon without him, a goblin dungeon is a whole 'nother story, and Hiccup's expertise should come in handy. "I could clear the air." He points the muzzle of his Marble Shotgun at the sky.

"That could work," says FeeTwix.

"It could also bring the authorities," Enway chimes in. "I don't know what type of authorities there are in Bluwid, but I have a feeling doing a little Arabic wedding celebration is one surefire way, pun intended, to bring them. Then again..."

"It is a goblin shithole, I agree," says Zaena. "I know what we'll do. FeeTwix, dear, please release your drone."

"Release the drones!"

She smiles at him. "And once you spot his pink topknot in the crowd, hover over him and I'll send my limbs in."

"Excellent idea."

"Wait," says Ryuk as he notices more goblins getting in line. "You guys actually think he's in line."

"It hasn't been *that* long," the Thulean princess says.

"Yeah, but he's Hiccup."

Zaena nods. "And Hiccup would never wait in line when there is free food to be had somewhere else. Good point, Ryuk. Let's check the back of the restaurant."

"Are we talking dumpster diving here?" Enway asks as the Mitherfickers and Wolf step into the alley separating DD's BBQ from a barred up pawn shop next door.

"I will release the drone anyway!" FeeTwix's sticks his finger in the air just as a drone appears. It lifts off, and quickly clears the top of the building. "Just a little further."

His half-formed Reaper skull takes shape on his head, handshakes with the drone, and soon, FeeTwix announces his discovery.

"Luckily for us, murder is legal in Bluwid!"

"*Jatla blantakh trek tata ganakh blotae suutakh,*" Zaena laments as she turns the corner to find Hiccup sitting on an overturned crate, a pair of teenage goblins before him, knife wounds in their backs.

"Fick!" He spits a dragon wing out as soon as he sees the Thulean. Naturally, she dodges the projectile, and it just so happens to smack Ryuk in the face.

"Dammit, Hiccup!"

"Ha! Fick, kid, my bad. And Liz, did you just call me a dirty goblin with tits filled with sour milk?" Hiccup snorts. "That's fickin' one of the cruelest ones you've come up with yet! I'll have to totally, *totally,* use that on Spew Gorge next time I see him. I told you all he's technically my son, didn't I?" Hiccup asks with his mouth full.

Enway gasps. "You murdered these young goblins and…stole their food?"

"Who fickin' died and made you the morality police? Oh wait, they did. Fick yes I robbed these little ankle-biters fair and square. Any goblin with a half-ounce of brain matter knows better than to eat barbeque in a Bluwid back alley. There's loads of gentrification here, Elfy, and one can never be too safe. Me? I'm all about gentrification, as long as I'm not the one forced out by high rent prices."

FeeTwix's drone lands and he returns it to his list. "Wish I could have used you longer, buddy," he tells the device.

"So, we ready?" Hiccup hops down from the crate and burps. Nursing his lower back as he picks up his new Gilius Thunderhead Axe, which he has set sideways across a trashcan. "Besides, I had to test this shit out." He burps again. "Fick, never eat dragon wings two at a time, kiddos."

"I hate you."

"Yeah, Liz? Well, I hate you, you hate me, we're a happy family. And fick, did Dave give you some new duds? You look fine as a lizard can look!"

Zaena's angry glare softens. "He did. Do you like them?"

"Do I like them? Fick yes, I do. I'd hate to see the kind of stuff Twixy's fans do when they watch his feed."

"This way," FeeTwix says, instead of engaging the goblin.

"Well, at least let me clean my fickin' paws." Hiccup slowly bends over and wipes his filthy, dragon wingy hands onto one of the dead goblin's tunics. The process of standing squeezes a small juicy squeak from the goblin's nethercheeks, which he quickly blames on Wolf.

"Just this way, I believe," FeeTwix says as they exit the alley at its northeastern entrance. His eyes turn black. "I'm back everyone, just in time to tell you about an exclusive offer from McStarbucks! Ever heard of overpriced coffee? Of course you have, but you've never heard anyone complaining about McStarbucks selling overpriced coffee. Sure, they're basically charging you eight to ten dollars for a few centimeters of milk and a couple inches of condensed coffee, but you've never been the type to question your retail overlords, and that's why I, for one, welcome McStarbucks' newest item, the Happy Latte McMuffin!"

"That sounds interesting," Zaena says as she hooks her hand around FeeTwix's arm.

Hiccup elbows up next to Ryuk. "What do you want, Hiccup?"

"Easy, kid, just checking to see what Dirty D hooked you up with. Tell me he gave you a pair of truck nuts to hang from your lady choop."

"He gave me a shotgun," Ryuk says, unaware of the term 'truck nuts.'

"Whatever happened to gun laws in Tritania? That shit doesn't have a bump stock, does it? I've been writing my congressgoblin ever since I met that vain Swede: we need stricter gun laws here, believe you me."

He places two mechanical fingers in his mouth and whistles. "Wolfy, I need you." Wolf approaches and Hiccup climbs on. "There, that's better. Need to save my stamina for the fight."

FeeTwix finishes his ad read just about the time the Mitherfickers reach a narrow lane. Health code violations disguised as restaurants line the right hand side of the street; tchotchke shops and secondhand stores the other.

Goblins seem to like a wide variety of collectables and used items, which may partially explain Hiccup's constant looting.

Enway stops in front of one of the thrift stores. "There's always something interesting in Bluwid," she tells Ryuk.

"I believe that."

"And that, everyone, is what I call a dungeon." FeeTwix nods to a two-story building on a hill. Lit by torches, the building is made of yellow and gray bricks. While it isn't very tall, it is exceedingly large, easily the length and width of an entire city block.

"What's the plan?" Zaena asks, her chest inflating as she takes the lead. "The more goblins killed, the better."

"Hey!" Hiccup shrugs. "Actually, you're right. Less goblins equal more poontang, loot, healing potions, and glory for me. I'm with Liz, let's kill us some fickboys!" The goblin points his finger at the dungeon and Wolf charges.

"Hiccup!" Ryuk clenches his fist as the goblin and the wolf continue up the hill.

"Looks like we have a classic Mitherfickers plan here," says FeeTwix.

"What's that again?" Enway asks, unable to hide the skepticism in her voice.

"Kick ass, and then take names! Babe, can you hand out the leveling pills Dave gave us?"

FeeTwix takes his pill and the others lift into the air, each finding their recipient.

"It's too big to swallow," Ryuk says as he judges the size of the blue pill.

"That's what healing potions are for." FeeTwix pops his pill in and takes a sip from a fresh potion. He passes the potion to Zaena, who does the same before passing it to Enway, who passes it to Ryuk.

Once the pills are ingested, FeeTwix takes the lead. "Let's go, and please, give the goblin his pill once we catch up to him!"

(0)__(0)

Hiccup has already started the first fight by the time the Mitherfickers reach him. The sky above them is dark, the battle lit by torches and interrupted by the shadows of passing foes.

Now dismounted from Wolf, the goblin swings his big axe, both hands gripped tightly around the handle.

Instakill!

The head of a robed goblin sprays right just as Wolf leaps into the air to catch it. He lands, and starts whipping the head left and right.

"Fick, Wolfy, I already killed that one!"

"Goblin, eat your pill!"

"Pill?" Hiccup calls over his shoulder.

"From your hero, Dave."

"He is my hero, and I'll take just about any pill he gives me." Hiccup rolls his neck back and opens his big mouth. "Toss it in, Liz." He gulps as soon as Zaena uses her ghost limb to transfer the pill over to his hungry mouth. She drops it; he swallows the pill without the help of a potion. "Fick yeah."

"Don't expect me to ever do that again."

"Come on, Liz, you fickin' liked it and you know it!"

FeeTwix springs right into action with his new AUS hose gun. The metal canister on his back, he hoses down a horde of goblins approaching from the western gate.

Insta-Insta-Instakill!

The ones that aren't hit start freaking out.

"Fick! Fick!"

"Yoy!"

"Fick, yoy, fick!"

Hiccup joins in the chorus of ficks. "Fick yeah, Twixy, fick those liddle fickered fickturds up! Red team, go! Blue team, go!"

Red team? Blue team? Ryuk looks around to try and figure out what the goblin is shouting about.

-232 HP! Critical hit!

Hiccup takes the arm off an especially muscular goblin just as a message appears on Ryuk's pane of vision.

Hiccup: Marbles, fick me. You're blue team because you're emo. Elfy is red team because she has demon eyes. Red team, blue team, go. Get it?

"Fuck you, Hiccup!" Ryuk lays down a cluster of goblins now spilling out of the front of the shaman's dungeon.

Click-click. BOOM! Click-click. BOOM!

"That's the spirit kid...Yoooooy!" A robed goblin punches Hiccup in the stomach and sends the Mitherfickers' loudest member flying backwards with an uppercut.

-69 HP!

Hiccup gets his bearings as he stands, his legs wide. "Ha! Sixty-nine, fickers! I've been waiting for someone to get that number…shit! Shit, shit, shit! Front and center, Marbles, we got a fickin' trojan horse coming out of the main gate. Elf, where the fick are you? Magic out the wazoo, pronto! Twixy, ballistics. Wolf, chomp, chomp!"

Ryuk hears the squeak of the wheels before he sees the large wooden horse tear out of the gate, a good ten goblins riding the wooden horse's back and who knows how many of the fuckers inside.

Click-click. BOOM! Click-click. BOOM! Click-click. BOOM! Click-click. BOOM!

Splinters of wood mixed with bits of flesh tear away from the wooden horse as Ryuk unloads his entire cylinder of black and sword marbles at the odd goblin transport.

Insta-Instakill!

Zaena launches into action.

With a one armed front flip to boost herself forward, she springboards and hits the air, coming down blades a-spinning like a damn helicopter crash.

Imagine the sharpest ceiling fan in the world coming loose and falling onto a tightly packed barnyard full of angry, snorting pigs. The red "instakills" that appear on Ryuk's vision pane are too many to count, unsettling to say the least.

Zaena lands on the horse, balances on it like a surfboard, and then backflips to the ground, just in time to greet the goblins funneling out of its ass.

Snarling, Wolf drags a goblin across the battlefield and quickly rips his throat out.

Instakill!

"Fick that bitch up, Wolfy!"

For his part, FeeTwix has equipped a croquet mallet, which he uses to knock the living goblin out of any Bluwid local who dares approach.

-46 HP! -29 HP! -58 HP!

"That's right everybody, three point five million viewers! Tell your friends, family members, enemies, frenemies, queens, kings, and failed government leaders! Tell your doctors, lawyers, baristas, soldiers, and law enforcement officers. If we reach four mil by the end of this, I'm doing one big ass giveaway!"

Taking cover now so he can reload his Marble Shotgun, Ryuk catches Enway shift *in and out of time.*

One moment she's here, the next moment she's somewhere else, zigzagging her way to the back of the battle. Once she's there, she slips into a shadow cast from an open door.

Ryuk sees the glint of her hourglass necklace, and as it glows, a mist of pink magic falls over a troupe of goblins tearing out of the open gate.

The "ficks" and "yoys" that follow are almost too much to bear.

His Magic Eye skill activated, Ryuk can tell that Enway has cast some type of algomagic, which usually affects the psyche. It's once the goblins start killing each other that he comes to the quick realization that this isn't your ordinary spell.

Ryuk: What did you just cast?

Enway: Arcane Tide. It forces the enemy to relive a traumatic experience and can cause madness.

"Fick, that's some seriously psycho shit right there, Elfy." Hiccup says as he pulls a healing potion out of thin air. He takes a swig from it, waits a moment, and once a female goblin separates from the fray, he domes her with the empty potion bottle.

Instakill!

"Fick yeah, level up, baby. Anybody else feeling that golden shower of levels raining from above?"

"I got a level up," Enway says, a big smile on her face as her hourglass necklace recharges, the sand falling in the opposite direction now.

"Golden shower? What in the fick are you talking about?" a fat goblin, who has just arrived on the scene, screams.

"Fick you, fatty!" is Hiccup's reply.

"You're fatter than I am you two-ton, pink-haired, humpty dumpty fickcake!"

"Humpty dumpty fickcake?" Hiccup snarls. "Marbles, put a cap in his candy fickered ass!"

Click-click. BOOM! Click-click. BOOM!

Instakill!

Ryuk sends the fat goblin flying backwards, a hole the size of a basketball where his center mass used to be.

"Fick yeah plus one! Marbles, I take back all the nasty things I said, especially the part about attaching a pair of truck nuts to your female choop." The goblin looks around. "Now, where were we? That's right. The gates are open, Mitherfickers, let's get in there, fillet some Jonestown fickboys, get us some mad loot, and grab the runestone while we're at it!"

FeeTwix knocks the crap out of a goblin with his croquet mallet. "Hell yes!"

"Aye! Aye! Aye!" Zaena shouts, all four blades in the air.

"That's the idea, Liz," Hiccup says as Wolf pulls up to his side, his maw wet with blood. "Now, Twixy—potion me, pronto; Marbles—reload your shooty thing and no funny business when we're inside; Enway—stop looking at me with your Exorcist eyes; Liz—slice and dice, you know the drill; Wolf—you'd better bring me back some goblin throats. Let's do this!"

(0)___(x)

The Mitherfickers quickly clear out the dungeon entrance, putting a dozen more goblins in early graves and leaving their trojan horse in flames. Everyone has gained a level now, and Ryuk suspects they'll gain several more as they make their way through the dungeon.

It has been relatively straightforward so far, without a lot of routes to take. This changes when they hit a trapdoor and the six fall several stories down.

"Yoy!" Hiccup rolls sideways and decompresses by airing his grievances, which instantly muck up the already foul air of the deep hole.

"*Boombakh toll.*"

Hiccup chortles. "An elephant anus, huh? You sure are creative for a princess. Most I've met had a silver spoon up their *toll*."

"I'm curious, how many princesses have you met, goblin?" Zaena has not only saved herself from the fall, she also used her ghost limbs to save FeeTwix, who now stands by her side in his sleeveless overcoat.

"Let me see," Hiccup says as he gets to his feet. "You, Ryuk, and the Empress."

"*Baka,*" Ryuk whispers as he sits up.

"I don't speak Chinese, kid, but I do love me some spicy Asian dragon wings. Shit is yum in my tum."

Ryuk gets the urge to pistol whip the goblin but he's instantly calmed by Enway's cool touch. The chromatic mage helps him up and dusts his shoulder off. "You okay?"

"Yeah, I'll be fine." His dream armor took the brunt of the fall, easing his landing.

"So cute, you two, really. But what is a well-endowed, stable genius like myself to do? Let's get back to the top of the dungeon before the shaman's followers start tossing shit onto us. And by shit, I mean 'feces.' Most of what Liz says about goblins is true: they are dirty fickers."

A headlamp now on his head and casting a bluish cone of light, FeeTwix quickly finds an exit point from the hole they've fallen down. To reach it, Ryuk goes for his gravity marble, the Swede his steam boots, and Zaena her limbs, which of course leaves Enway, Hiccup and Wolf still at the bottom of the hole.

"Not to worry, guildmates!" FeeTwix rolls out a ladder, which Enway climbs with relative ease.

"How the fick is that supposed to help your four-legged friends down here?" Hiccup calls up to them.

"The goblin doesn't have four legs," Zaena comments matter-of-factly, "but for once, I do see his point: he would either destroy your ladder or overexert himself by climbing up."

"Good point, babe," FeeTwix says as he looks over the edge into the hole.

"I can hear people talking up there, but no one is tossing me down a ghost limb, cough, cough, hint, hint, Liz."

Zaena looks to FeeTwix and cringes.

"I have some hand sanitizer," Enway offers.

"Fine. I will touch him. But if he says anything remotely sensual I will drop him, and we will finally be rid of the goblin."

Wolf barks and Ryuk hears his paws scuffling at the bottom of the hole. The Ballistics Mage looks down and his Extreme Focus skill kicks into high gear, illuminating the trapped space.

When his Magic Eye skill kicks in, he notices that there are a few rocks illuminated in green algomagic.

Strange, he thinks, as Zaena lugs the goblin up.

"Careful, Liz, I'm fickin' ticklish and I can be held responsible for what I do if I'm tickled."

When she gets Hiccup over the platform, the Thulean is sure to drop him in a way that adds insult to injury.

"Yoy!" He grabs his knee. "I think it's broken, Twixy, better hit me with a potion."

"You've had too many potions, Hiccup."

"Oh, so you're my doctor now?" The goblin moans as he gets to his feet. "That's right, I guess you are my doctor, seeing as how Marbles here doesn't provided healthcare to his employees."

"Quiet, goblin, before I toss you back into the hole. How should I lift Wolf?" Zaena asks FeeTwix.

"Well, I have a doggy harness, but that's for the pooch I had back in Dead City. Um ... how about a blanket? I have a fire blanket that you could wrap around him."

"This isn't some sort of culturally inappropriate remake of Pocahontas, Twixy. Just grab him by the belly, Liz. He's a dog, treat him like one."

Pocahontas? What in the hell is the goblin talking about? Ryuk glances at Enway and they both shrug at the same time. He's the first to laugh, and soon, she's laughing alongside him.

This brings a big smile to the goblin's face.

"You finally get my joke, don't you, Marbles?" He sniffles. "Fick me to tears, I've never felt so honored."

"Um, yeah, sure. I get your joke, Hiccup. Sure."

Enway laughs again. "You're clearly the funniest member here."

By the time Hiccup gets done fake crying and thanking the Academy for nominating him, FeeTwix and Zaena have gone with FeeTwix's idea and used the blanket to get Wolf to the platform.

Ryuk looks down into the hole one more time and sees the wall accented by green algomagic.

Something is in there, he thinks, but instead of telling the others, he lets FeeTwix take the lead.

"Let's get back to the top," says the Swede, the beam of blue light still on his head. The Mitherfickers make their way up a winding passage and come out a side door just behind the dungeon's main gate.

Ryuk surveys the bodies of the dead goblins and shudders, there are a lot of them and he has a feeling that come morning, the sight of this many goblins will attract attention.

A creaking sound nearly causes Hiccup to leap into Ryuk's arms. "Marbles, did you hear that?" the short goblin asks as he pulls at his sleeve. "The place may be fickin' haunted." The goblin whispers something in Thulean.

"Your prayers won't work against ghosts," Zaena says as she walks past him, her hips swaying. It is still strikes Ryuk as odd to see the Thulean next to Hiccup, her grace versus his sloppy disarray. Even now, one pant leg is half tucked into his boot, there are dark stains on the back of his tunic, his chainmail is too tight, and while he does wear his golden helm, it's tilted sideways, almost to the point of falling off his head.

Hiccup is just about to rant when Ryuk steps on a creaky stone. The goblin jumps around and nearly punches Ryuk in the face.

"Marbles! Fick, kid, I almost KO'd your ass. Careful, bro."

"Bro?" Ryuk asks, instantly reminded of Kodai. Before he can say anything else to the goblin, a wall opens up behind them and a dozen orcs and orclins storm out.

The heavily armored fuckers are armed to the teeth and raring to go. Their leader, an orc with a side ponytail, is the only one that speaks.

"Your appointment with Sugar Spur is cancelled," he says with a snarl. The orcs around him cheer and clink their weapons together.

Hiccup snorts and looks around at his guildmates. "Yeah, yeah, what the fick ever. Say, Marbles, got anything to say to Chester the sheep molester over here?"

Ryuk lifts his Marble Shotgun and points it at the leader. "How's this?" he asks as squeezes the trigger.

Click-click. BOOM!

(0)__(x)

Wolf takes down an orclin and goes straight for the guy's face, ripping it to shreds as the orclin tries to beat him off.

Click-click. BOOM! Click-click. BOOM!

-122 HP! -38 HP! -87 HP! -44 HP!

Ryuk lays down some cover fire as Zaena spins into action to protect Wolf from the orclins that have descended upon him.

"Say hello to my little friend!" FeeTwix shouts, a tommy gun in his hand.

Brrrat! Brrrat! Brrrat!

-8 HP! 6 HP! 7 HP! 5 HP! 30 HP! 9 HP!

"Did I already use that catchphrase? Oh well!" A wild look in his eyes, the Swede continues spraying a cloud of metal unhappiness at the orcs, who are all trying to scatter yet who have also found themselves in a fatal funnel.

FeeTwix drops to a knee, takes a swig from a healing potion and throws to Hiccup, who catches it, takes a huge chug from it, tosses it over his shoulder, and cracks the living shit out of an orc with his tomahawk.

Instakill!

Brrrat! Brrrat! Brrrat!

The Swede fires quick bursts at his opponents. Once his mag is out, he tosses his weapon behind his shoulder and comes back with a Slice Bang, his eyes livestreaming the mayhem. "Holy fick everybody! Have you entered my bigass giveaway yet? Just how many ficks can a goblin say? Be sure to enter, and don't forget…" He ducks a club and counterattacks with an incredible stab that cuts through an orc's armor and brings him to the ground.

-219 HP! Critical hit!

"Whew! That was close. Don't forget to tell everyone you know about the Mitherfickers' live stream! Help make us the most popular guild in all of Tritania. Love you guys. Whoa!" FeeTwix bends backwards just in time to miss a swing from the orc leader. Unfortunately, he doesn't miss a big, gnarled follow up fist from the orc.

The punch sends him straight to the ground.

The orc steps over the Swede, a wicked grin spreading across his scarred face. He brings his weapon overhead with both hands.

Zap!

A bolt of pink magic hits the orc and his weapon crumbles into dust, the sudden change in gravity throwing him off balance.

He falls next to FeeTwix and the Swede pulls the trigger of his Slice Bang.

Instakill!

"Thanks, Enway!"

Ryuk fires at a couple of orcs who have turned the other way.

-95 HP! -110 HP!

Level up!

He manages to get one in the back of his head, sending the orc face first onto the cold stone floor.

Propelled by the urge to loot, a bit of adrenaline, and as always, an ass blast of barbeque aftermath, Hiccup races over to the downed orc. He drops onto the orc, and using his toe knife, he stabs the orc repeatedly in the back until he's covered in blood.

Instakill!

"Fick, that was fun." Hiccup says, a wide grin forming on his face.

"Let's finish them off," Ryuk shouts to the others, confidence growing inside him. "Only a few more orcs left!"

THE RUNESTONES OF TRITINAKH

CHAPTER 12: NO ONE WANT TO LIVE NEXT TO A GANGSTER

"You don't have to join us for this trip, Walt," Kodai tells the seasoned MercSecure rep. They have returned to the repair facility near Shinagawa to pick up Tesla, who now sits in the backseat of the aerosSUV in front of Kodai.

Kodai tries to hide his excitement in seeing her. She's as beautiful as the day they first met, her features a blend of East and West, her body tight and her posture perfect.

"I believe I may be of use to you in whatever it is you plan to do next," the mercenary says. "And you have my services until three. Normally, since you have adequate protection, I'd call it a day. But I must admit, I'm intrigued."

"You don't even know what it is I'm planning to do," Kodai tells Walt.

"From context clues, I've concluded that it has to do with a rival. Tesla is solid, and you don't really need the men who are in the vehicle behind us. But if you do need any additional manpower, like I said, my services have already been paid for."

Kodai considers this for a moment as he looks Tesla over. She continues to intrigue him, and soon, he'll act on this intrigue. But for now, there are things that need to be accomplished, including hitting Gintoki where it hurts.

It was only yesterday that Gintoki attacked Kodai's bar, killing a good many of his employees, including Sarah the Australian.

"Fine," Kodai tells Walt, "you can come. Sync with Tesla to get the details of the assignment. I'd like to have a moment to reflect on how I'd like to handle things once we get into the compound."

"You've got it."

The aerosSUV lifts into the air, snow twirling past its windshield.

Walt, grizzled as ever in his MercSecure gear, closes his eyes as he gets the briefing from Tesla. Meanwhile, Kodai stares out the window, occasionally facing frontward to see Tesla, her beautiful face and her dilated black eyes.

She smiles at him on one of his glances and he smiles back. Because of the company in the vehicle, he quickly fires off a message over iNet.

Kodai: I am glad to see you are okay.

Tesla: I am just as glad to see you.

Kodai: You are?

Tesla: I am.

Kodai: Let's discuss this later.

Tesla: Let's.

He can't help but grin at her as he turns back to the window, gazing out at the world class city.

Kodai knows damn well what he is going to do once he arrives at Gintoki's place. The young crime lord is out for the day, checking on some of his businesses in Okinawa. This is the opportunity he has been waiting for.

Hit them where it hurts. Kodai's father told him this once, while speaking to Kodai about best business practices, especially when it comes to dealing with hostile competition.

A smile spreads on Kodai's face as he realizes just how well he's following his late father's business model.

Not five minutes later, the SUV lands on a quiet residential street in Setagaya, one of Tokyo's biggest wards. Sangen-Jaya Station is a particularly well known location in the district, with its many shops, restaurants, and the fact that it leads directly to Shimokitazawa, a neighborhood that has become the vintage and indie fashion hub of Tokyo.

Even now, Kodai can hear the announcements from the train station near them, the small local train aimed at the Sangen-Jaya Station. While he notices the sound, he's much more focused on the SUV that has landed before him.

Clad in black suits, four of his men get out and Walt quickly joins them.

There is no pointing, and there is no real indication what they may be up to, if one doesn't consider their numbers.

The group moves towards a strikingly large home protected from the street by a stone wall and a gaudy torii gate inspired entrance.

It's then that Kodai sees his other team, the group that has been staking out the place since last night. They're already inside the complex, and once they've given the okay, Tesla speaks.

"They're ready for us now," she says.

"Good. Let's handle this rapidly."

Out of the vehicle now, Tesla opens Kodai's door once two of his men have returned. The two form a perimeter around him, and alongside Tesla, they quickly slip into the residence.

It is a bigger show than Kodai would like to put on, but the neighbors have already been warned, and from his intel, Kodai has learned that the neighbors don't like the fact Gintoki has a residence here anyway.

After all, no one wants to live next to a gangster.

(0)__(x)

Kodai passes Gintoki's men. The ones that are still alive have been tied and gagged. They sit under a tree beside the driveway, their faces awash with fear.

"Handle them, Walt," he tells the mercenary.

"Done." Walt walks over to the first man and lifts his assault rifle. A suppressor has been placed on the receiving end, but it's still a bit percussive as he tears the first one down. The second man tries to scream, falls sideways, and attempts to caterpillar crawl away.

Walt finishes him off and moves to the third man, who refuses to react yet who has a puddle of piss spreading across his pant legs.

Walt puts him down, and does the same to the last man, who's already bleeding so badly that he barely registers he's about to be shot.

"Are they ready for me?" he asks the thug named Yugio, who stands near the door, his hands crossed in front of his groin and a pistol in his left hand.

"They are."

Kodai and Tesla pass into a grand foyer with a floor to ceiling painting of a Greek statue. From there, they head through the kitchen to a dining room area, where the table has been overturned.

Tied and gagged, sitting with her back to the table, is Gintoki's wife, Fumi. She's beautiful, with a fake rack, perfect skin, and long, white legs. In front of her are her two children, a boy and a girl, both tied.

"These are Gintoki's children?" Kodai asks Yugio, who has now stepped into the dining room.

"Yes."

"Good." Kodai opens his palm toward Yugio, and once Tesla has placed a glove on his hand, he takes Yugio's pistol.

He walks over to the boy, who has been tied so that he lies on his belly on the ground.

Bang!

Fumi screams out, her voice muffled by the gag as she watches the pool of blood form around her young son's head.

"Fumi," Kodai says, dropping before her.

To his right, Fumi's daughter gives a muffled scream and kicks her feet against the ground.

"Fumi, Fumi, Fumi. You realize I had to do this, right? Gintoki came after me yesterday, in my place of business and I hate to admit this, but he nearly had me. I didn't do anything to provoke this," he lies. "And now, as you have painfully become aware of, I feel the urge to retaliate. Do you want to say something?"

She cries, her face puffy red, her mouth moving as she tries to spit the gag out.

"Sorry, I can't hear you."

She screams, her voice muffled.

"Since you won't speak to me, I guess I'm going to have to kill your daughter too."

Kodai stands and points the pistol at her daughter.

Bang!

Fumi shrieks until she's hoarse. Kodai drops before her again and she tries to kick at him.

"You shouldn't have done that." He backhands her with his free hand and calls Yugio over. "Here," he says, handing him the pistol. Kodai smiles once more at Fumi. "It was nice seeing you."

With that, he stands and turns to the kitchen. Fumi shrieks again, kicking her feet against the stone floor.

"And what do you want me to do with Fumi, boss?" Yugio gulps. "Finish the job?"

Kodai places his hands behind his back and nods Yugio forward. "No, that'd be too easy. Have her placed in a coffin and delivered to Gintoki's headquarters in Shinjuku. Make sure she's alive. *I'm serious about that part.* That said, do whatever else you'd like with her."

CHAPTER 13: QUEEN OF THE RINGS

"Fick! Not another hole in the ground."

"I think it's the same hole," FeeTwix says as he dusts his pants off.

"I'm getting that same feeling too." His head still spinning, Ryuk sits up and massages his temples for a moment. The guild's stats appear, and Ryuk notices that even Wolf has gained a level.

Ryuk Matsuzaki Level 25 Ballistics Mage
HP: 848/967
ATK: 146
MATK: 189
DEF: 110
MDF: 83
LUCK: 24

FeeTwix Fajer Level 26 Berserker Mystic
HP: 1200/1284
ATK: 204

MATK: 36

DEF: 108

MDF: 63

LUCK: 28

Hiccup Level 22 Shield Thief

HP: 1345/1345

ATK: 125

MATK: 17

DEF: 268

MDF: 134

LUCK: 39

Zaena Morozon Level 25 Brawler Assassin

HP: 1017/1231

ATK: 251

MATK: 10

DEF: 229

MDF: 51

LUCK: 26

Enway Zoltan Rosa Level 24 Hourglass Mage

HP: 916/950

MANA: 494/555

ATK: 74

MATK: 167

DEF: 68

MDF: 178

LUCK: 23

Wolf Level 40
HP: 2221/2402
ATK: 699
MATK: 0
DEF: 534
MDF: 241
LUCK: 19

Again, he sees the subtle green outline of the rock wall before him. Zaena has already lifted herself out of the hole to the upper platform when Ryuk tells everyone to hold it for a moment.

"The wall is enchanted."

"Marbles, I've had just about enough of your crazy talk. If the wall was enchanted, it'd have done something by now, you dumbass. This is the fifth. No sixth."

"Seventh!" FeeTwix says.

"*Eighth* time we've fallen in this hole. Now I may be dumber than a pair of Jatlan bearadillo anus traps, but you Marbles, oh you. Poor kid," Hiccup tells Zaena. "He'll never be like the others."

Ryuk shoulders past Hiccup, sending him to the ground.

"Ha! Kick his ass, Ryuk."

"Hey! I thought you were on my side, Twixy!"

"Like a good parent, Hiccup, I don't take sides."

"Good parent my ass. Okay, that's how we're going to do this, huh? Fine. I'll get the 'secret enchanted door' open, or whatever the fick

Marbles is going on about. Ahem." Hiccup kicks the wall. "Yoy!" He falls, and Wolf comes over to sniff him.

Enway laughs. "This guild...I don't think I've ever been part of a guild that so eloquently puts the 'fun' in dysfunction."

"It is mostly one member," Zaena says as she touches the wall with her hands, and what Ryuk assumes are her ghost limbs. "Imagine if there weren't a goblin in the guild. How successful would we be? It is a nice thought to entertain. How much more would we have accomplished? We'd probably have the third runestone by now."

"The third runestone?" Hiccup laughs. "Liz, even for a princess, you are *way* too convinced of your own badassery. Let me be clear: I'm the glue that holds this guild together, the stilts that keep this shit-house up in a hurricane, the ficker in charge of scraping the snow off the driveway after a blizzard. And Marbles, next time you think it's a promising idea to shove an elder, just remember that I know where you live, I know how to use a shiv, and I know how to get rid of a corpse."

Ryuk sighs. "Good to know."

Hiccup pounds his mechanical fist against the wall. "Open up! I fickin' hate dungeons."

"Everyone stand back." His legs wide, FeeTwix hoists his favorite bazooka over his shoulder.

"Twixy, I swear to the Empress' expertly crafted and perfectly maintained fun bags, if you shoot that damn thing off..."

"Relax, Hiccup, a little kablooey never hurt nobody."

"I think it uses some type of magic spell to activate it," Ryuk says as he goes for his slingshot. "We could try a clear marble."

"Nope," says the Swede. "Too much time wasted in this dungeon and I'm sick of killing orcs and goblins. Viewership is dropping. The fans want a boss battle! Hiccup, equip your biggest shield. Everyone else, get to the ledge up there and take cover."

"What about Wolfy?"

"He can fit behind your shield."

"I guess you're right, Twixy." Hiccup's scutum appears in the air and drops onto the ground. "But I prefer the space to myself. Also, you have other types of explosives. Why the fick are you aiming a rocket launcher at a wall less than two meters away?"

"Because sometimes, Hiccup, a man has to take matters into his own hands. Actually. This is a horrible idea. Who has an idea for how we can open this door?"

"I already said I did, *reveal door*!"

Ryuk looses a clear marble. As soon as the clear marble touches the wall, a pink moss spreads from all directions. With the moss comes yellow and purple flowers, which bloom, release a floral scent, and die.

"Welp, that's just about the poofiest thing I've seen all day, and I won't mention the fact that it came from Marbles."

"At least it cleared the air of your stench, Hiccup," Ryuk bites back.

Zaena laughs hard at this. "It is actually refreshing for once!"

"Laugh it up, Liz," Hiccup says, trying to hide how offended he is by turning away from the others and cursing under his breath.

"Just let me try again." Ryuk loads another clear marble into the slingshot. "Reveal door!"

A Simple Request!

Skill level up!

Skill: A Simple Request

Level Five: 1 in 5.95 chance of a request being granted.

Caveat: Only works with a clear marble.

Requirements: LUCK > 15

The moss boils away releasing a fragrant scent that quickly turns sour. By the time the Mitherfickers are done coughing and Hiccup's finished lamenting the rotten stench, a giant hole has formed in the wall, a faint light visible at its other end.

(0)__(0)

An assault rifle with a night vision scope in his hands, the Swede slips into the hole, ready for things to get rowdy at the drop of a hat. Zaena is next, followed by Enway and Ryuk. Hiccup scuttles in last, behind Wolf, whose tongue hangs out of his mouth as he walks.

"It's nice having a dog in the group," Hiccup says. "He's quiet, and believe you me, I'm a fan of quiet fickers."

With nobody commenting on his statement, Hiccup quickly runs out of things to say. He pops open a healing potion, takes a swig, burps, and mumbles about heartburn and cheap potions.

"Where do you think it leads?" Enway asks, after the Mitherfickers have walked for a few minutes.

FeeTwix's maps don't work down here, and from what Ryuk can tell, they seem to be spiraling downward. At least it feels like they are going deeper into the ground, mainly due to the change in temperature.

Wolf barks and zips around FeeTwix. His eye pressed to his night vision scope, FeeTwix tracks the big dog as he disappears around a corner. "I can send a drone," he says. "You picking up anything, Ryuk?"

"No magical readings. Zaena? Do you sense anything?"

"Only that there have been more goblins in this hole than I'd care to admit."

Hiccup nearly falls over laughing at that last line. "Liz, you make this shit *way* too easy!"

"What do you mean?" she hisses.

"Never mind, babe. Let's just focus on getting out of this hole; it's fickin' terrible for live-streaming. What's that? Ah, that's right everyone! You can order items off the Old Banana Navy Gap Republic webstore from the deepest hole on planet Earth and *still* get a 15% off discount and twenty-five Old Banana Bucks to use for your next purchase by mentioning #FeeTwixRox at checkout! If you order now, you'll get an exclusive Mitherfickers T-shirt featuring Hiccup's two skulls deepthroating a sword design *free* with any purchase over a hundred bones. Wow, what a fantastic shirt! Did I mention I'll be digitally signing the first fifty to go out? It's the holy hole sale with prices practically at wholesale! #FeeTwixRox, people, you know what to fickin' do."

Hiccup burps and tosses his healing potion over his shoulder. "Twixy, first, fick you and the way you just polluted this hole with your bullshit. Second."

"—I believe you're the one with the polluted hole, goblin."

"That was actually pretty good, Liz. Ha! Who knew Thuleans had a sense of humor. Crap. Where was I? Can't remember. Wait. I got it. Something about not signing a merchandising agreement and having my attorney contact Old Banana Fick in the Box and FeeTwixRox LLC about royalties and other damages that come with having one's IP exploited. FICK! Anyone feel that!?"

Ryuk *definitely* felt it. Although it had no aura, something magical just moved through the dark passage.

The hair on the back of his neck prickles; he naturally pulls his Marble Shotgun closer to his chest. Focusing as hard as he can, he now senses a faint green magic all around them.

Her red eyes flaring up, Enway raises her wand, and suddenly, time speeds up and the Mitherfickers are standing at the exit point to the cavern.

Wolf whimpers and scratches his paws against the ground. Hiccup lets loose a string of curses peppered with the putrid stench of nervous toots. Zaena pulls out all four of her blades.

FeeTwix gulps as he realizes how close he just came to firing a short burst of gunfire in Ryuk's general direction. The Ballistics Mage gulps, an algomagic-laced aura filtering off his body.

"How...what just happened?" Zaena asked.

"Sorry," Enway says hurriedly. "We needed to get out of there."

"And what in? Where in the actual? FICK! I'm at a loss for words. Fick." Hiccup sits down onto the ground, and rubs his temples.

"I cast Time Skip," Enway says before he can curse any more. "I transported us forward in time to the natural exit point of wherever the hell we just were."

"We can teleport?" FeeTwix asks. "Because if we can, I can finally get rid of my DeLorean. I never could get the damn flux capacitor to work."

"The spell said that I needed to touch everyone to do it."

"So that's what that weird sensation was," Ryuk says.

She nods. "It was an addition to the original spell. Whereas before, to cast Time Skip on a party, I think the Chromatic Mage had to touch whomever she wanted to transport. Now, I can just cast the spell and visualize who will go with me." She shows them her hourglass necklace.

"It's regenerating much more slowly than normal, though, probably because of mana expenditure."

"Okay, fine, I'm fine with that, but just fickin' warn us next time. And another thing, why can't you just Time Skip us to the end of the battle that's coming? Because boy fick, I know there's a battle coming."

Enway bites her lip for a moment as she thinks. "The spell doesn't take anything into account aside from the physical act of moving. It was probably a handicap put into place to prevent someone from just beating every monster on the continent."

"Makes sense," Zaena says, as they enter the main corridor.

The Thulean glances up at a red door with Thulean script cut into its surface.

"You thinking what I'm thinking?" FeeTwix asks, his free arm now around Ryuk's shoulder. "Cause that looks like a door that leads straight to a boss battle, and you know how much I like boss battles. You want to take the lead here, or should I? You feel like giving a pep talk? My fans *love* our pep talks."

"Please, go ahead," Ryuk says, his Japanese politeness again making its presence known.

"Mitherfickin' Mitherfickers and fans of the FeeTwixRox brand of entertainment products, listen up! Ryuk and I believe, based on absolutely no evidence aside from the fact that both of us are seasoned gamers, that whatever boss this goblin dungeon contains lies on the other side of that door. So, top off your health bars, equip your weapons, tell your friends to get back on the feed, and let's get ready to do what the Mitherfickers were put in Tritania to do!"

"Don't have to ask me twice," Hiccup says, guzzling another potion and belching. "Fick yeah!"

Where does he keep getting these potions? Ryuk wonders as the goblin sticks his tongue into the bottle to get the very last drop.

"And to quote St. George of Carlin, or better yet, to paraphrase St. George of Carlin, *boss battles are a zero sum game.*"

Brrrrat!

The Swede fires a quick burst of gunfire into the ceiling, much to Hiccup's dismay. "Let's do this!"

"Aye! Aye! Aye!"

(0)__(x)

"We just came to talk," Hiccup tells the female goblin in the center of the next room. Getting through the red door had been relatively pain free—it simply popped open when they approached it.

Sugar Spur Level 31
HP: 2400/2400
MANA: 856/856
ATK: 143
MATK: 331
DEF: 154
MDF: 192
LUCK: 17

The female shaman known as Sugar Spur sits midair with her legs crossed. The room is much larger than Ryuk anticipated it would be, easily forty meters across, and the walls are covered in tapestries depicting the famous goblin shaman in a variety of yogic poses.

She's nude from the waist up, her black nipples pierced with golden rings. These rings match the rings hanging from her droopy earlobes, and they're the exact same as the single ring jutting from her belly button, an outie, only accented more by the fact that she, like Hiccup, is a good thirty to forty kilos overweight.

"Lookin' good too," Hiccup says, turning the charm up. "I've seen a lot of goblins in my day, but none as fit and sensually robust as you, Sugar."

She bares her teeth as her eyes start to roll into the back of her head.

"Hey, keep cool, Sugar, I'm just here to have a few troublesome chalupa warts removed. Also, and fick me if this isn't the case, my Goblinheimer's has been flaring up as of late. Heard you could handle that too. Hell, some days, I even forget to take a shit! Just a joke there, but seriously, it's bad. Ask these fickers." He tosses his mechanical thumb over his shoulder.

"I know what you've come for, goblin," Sugar hisses. "You've come for my runestone!"

"Rune-what? Take a load off, Sugar, and cool floating technique, by the way. Never heard of a fickin' runestone. For fick's sake, I can barely remember my own name. Pretty sure it's Spew Gorge, just in case you want to get revenge after ... Twixy, go! Marbles, go! Liz, Elfy, go!"

FeeTwix and Ryuk, as they planned, lay down the heavy ordnance. FeeTwix has gone with a grenade launcher, Ryuk with his Marble Shotgun filled with explosive marbles.

Sure, they desperately need a new opening attack strategy, especially since the 'Hiccup distracts them while we shoot them' technique seems to be on the first page of the Mitherfickers' playbook, but it works, and the explosions definitely add confusion to the fight.

Unfortunately, from what Ryuk can see, Sugar Spur hasn't taken a lick of damage. In fact, when the smoke clears, she's the same as she was at the start of the fight—floating midair, her legs crossed, a calm yet wicked smile across her pockmarked face.

"My turn," she says, her voice suddenly piping out of every corner of the room.

Slats in the wall open and robed goblins pour in carrying a smorgasbord of weapons, from daggers to hammers to broomsticks.

The goblin shaman casts a spell that throws Enway and Zaena five meters back into a wall.

"Wolf, git over here!"

The big black wolf with blue-green eyes takes two running steps forward, and slides up next to Hiccup just in time for the goblin to hop on.

Once he's secure, they take off towards the incoming goblins, and like a perfectly thrown bowling ball, Hiccup kicks off Wolf, his golden helm on his head as he dives forward, tucks, and rolls into the fray.

Wolf follows suit, tearing into the goblins and taking out a good many with his sheer size. As FeeTwix lays down more heavy ordnance, sending fireballs, dust, and detritus into the air, Ryuk drops, clicks open the revolving canister on his shotgun and quickly pops more black marbles in.

He comes up a few moments later, his Marble Gun in one hand, his Marble Shotgun in the other, the recoil pad pressed into the nook under his arm. If there were bonus attack points available for style alone, the Ballistics Mage would get it for his current pose, both weapons trained on Sugar Spur.

"I've got this, FeeTwix!"

Click, click. BOOM! Click, click. BOOM!

The rapid-fire marbles do as much if not more damage than FeeTwix's camouflage-colored Milkor MGL.

Despite all the heavy firepower, and even as Hiccup and Wolf pretty much handle the goblins filing out of the walls, Sugar Spur is completely unaffected by Ryuk and FeeTwix's attack.

Enway's wand comes up and she fires a pink blast at Sugar Spur, a blast which fizzles out before it hits her.

"Bitch!" Zaena fires an arrow that strikes Sugar Spur directly between the eyes.

Critical hit!

Everyone stops and turns to the goblin shaman as a single trickle of blood drips down the bridge of her nose, over her lips, and stops at her chin.

The arrow pushes itself out, the wound heals up, and her eyes roll completely back in her head.

A portal opens up behind Sugar Spur and a pink blast of magic strikes her in the back of the head, nearly tossing her off her invisible perch. Ryuk looks to Enway and she gives him the thumbs up.

Delayed Strike, he thinks, having used a similar attack as a Ninja Warrior.

"She's invincible to all our attacks," Zaena shouts.

"We'll see about that!" is FeeTwix's reply as he equips the mutant hack Bowie knife given to him by Dirty Dave back in Aramis.

A panel on the opposite wall spins and more goblins tumble out. This group wears loose-fitting battle armor and holds Molotov cocktails, flames sparking at their tips.

"Fick!" Hiccup cries. "Suicide fickboys…Watch your choop, Marbles!"

Instakill! Instakill! Insta-Instakill!

Four of the suicide fickboys explode before they can reach the Mitherfickers, spraying the air with limbs, bits of armor, and gobs of flesh.

Watch my choop? Ryuk gets the notion to fire a sword marble at Hiccup, but is too distracted by the fat goblins holding explosives who are advancing towards him.

Wham!

-265 HP!

Ryuk is knocked sideways by a hammer.

Seeing stars, he tries to right himself only to be tossed backwards by an exploding suicide fickboy.

-112 HP! Critical hit!

A tingling sensation pulls him back from the brink. His eyes blink open to find Enway crouched before him, pink magic sprinkling from her wand and a warm smile on her face. She's close enough now that he can see that the red tear drop on her head is pulsating.

+250 HP!

"That's right," he says as the tingling sensation continues to move through him. "You can still heal."

"Speed Heal," she says. "It's pretty good, no?"

Fwhipp! Fwhipp! Fwhipp!

Insta-Insta-Instakill!

Zaena is due for the guild's 'Most Headshots in a Single Battle Award' if they can ever get a hit in on Sugar Spur. The well-trained Thulean takes out suicide fickboys like she's auditioning for a role as the *White Death*.

They keep falling, their bodies exploding and sending shrapnel, bone, and flesh into the air.

A searing green blast cuts through the mayhem and meets Sugar Spur head on. Her body boils as FeeTwix's mutant hack attack does its damage.

"We did it!" Hiccup says, pumping his fist in the air. "Fick yeah!"

His exuberance quickly disappears when it becomes increasingly clear that the goblin shaman has survived the blast.

"Impossible," FeeTwix says as his hack melts away.

It's then that Ryuk notices the faintest outline of algomagic surrounding the golden ring hanging from Sugar Spur's earlobe.

His eyes dart right and then down to her sagging breasts and her extended belly to see that *all her rings have a green tint to them.*

"Get them, my children! Pull their entrails out and bathe in their blood! Skull fick them to death!"

-95 HP!

Hiccup swings wide, both hands on his golden axe, cutting down a muscular goblin. "Skull fick that, you fickered fickhead!"

Instakill!

He brains the next goblin, pulls his blade out, and goes for another. Wolf jumps over him and takes out another goblin, snarling as he rips his leg to shreds.

His Marble Gun holstered at his side and his Marble Shotgun slung over his shoulder, Ryuk goes for the stock weapon that came with his avatar. A molten marble in the pocket, the Ballistics Mage takes aim at Sugar Spur's right earlobe with his slingshot.

A targeting reticle appears and even as chaos swells all around him, and more goblins file out of the panels in the walls, Ryuk cuts a molten marble across the battlefield, connecting with Sugar Spur's ear.

-400 HP!

Skill level up!

Skill level up!

"YEEEEOOOOOOY!" the female goblin shaman screeches as the golden hoop melts away.

Her earlobe quickly reforms, but the damage she's taken remains the same.

Hiccup's eyes light up as he looks from the floating Sugar Spur to Ryuk. "Fick me twice and call me grumpy after a long nap, Queen of the Rings!"

"Queen of the what?" FeeTwix calls over to him.

"Fick, Twixy, no time to explain. Take out all her golden rings!"

(x)__(x)

"I'm on goblin duty!" FeeTwix, now with his tommy gun one hand and a healing potion in the other, delivers a little swift justice to a group of suicide fickboys that have just swarmed into the room.

Insta-Insta-Instakill!

"I just want to remind all four million of you live-streaming this battle that I'll be picking a winner of the Count the Ficks contest after! And don't forget, WalMacy's is having a spring sale, and boy, is it a sale you don't want to miss! Sure," FeeTwix tears through another swarm of goblins, "everyone is already familiar with WalMacy's falling prices, but did you know you can save an additional three percent by signing up for their store card! Just think of what you can do with three percent!"

"No one can do fick all with three percent, Twixy!" Hiccup shouts once FeeTwix pauses to reload his tommy gun.

"Ignore the goblin, everybody! If you sign up for a WalMacy's store card in the next twenty-four hours, WalMacy's will add an additional one percent to this offer for the first year and waive the yearly fee! Talk about saving a hundred dollars *and* four percent! How much better is four percent than three percent?"

FeeTwix kicks in the face of a goblin that has somehow crawled over to him during his ad read. "One percent better, that's how much! You know the code. people: #FeeTwixRox!"

As the Swede lays down more cover fire, Zaena focuses on getting closer to Sugar Spur. This is proving difficult, especially since the goblins have started to pile up around her, forming a protective shield of bodies.

The Thulean warrior princess slices and dices her way closer to the goblin shaman, her ass saved once by a blast from Enway's wand. Ryuk too has taken a supporting role, knowing all too well that there's too much mayhem now to get in a good hit.

Instakill!

Level up!

New marble acquired!

The level up and the two skill level ups he just received start to fade away.

Skill: One in a Million

Level Two: Use your slingshot and any marble of your choosing to take an impossible shot. Odds of connecting increase with each point you gain in LUCK.

Requirements: Level 10 Mage, LUCK > 17.

Skill: Extreme Focus

Level Four: Can detect approach of camouflaged / concealed / stealthed enemies and objects.

Mage bonus: Higher levels allow sleuthing and increased accuracy. Also increases magic detection range when used in tandem with Magic Eye.

He very briefly reads the details of his new marble.

New marble acquired! Aqua marbles are water based marbles capable of a number of feats, including drowning an enemy and extinguishing fires.

A message from Sophia pops up on Ryuk's viewing pane.

Sophia: Please log out now. I am done running the tests I need to run for the day.

Ryuk: We're kind of in the middle of something.

Sophia: Is it a boss battle? If it's a boss battle, finish it then log out.

Ryuk: Will do!

I'll have to check out my new marble later, Ryuk thinks as he pops a mag full of sword marbles into his Marble Gun, and tries to take out some of the goblins on the outer edge of the wall of flesh surrounding Sugar Spur.

These goblins fall, only to land on those trying to climb up below.

Sugar Spur still floats on top, a furious look on her face as a serpent made of magic begins to swirl around her body.

Using a goblin's head as a springboard, Zaena hits the air, flips, and comes down with a slice that takes *both* the shaman goblin's nipple rings off.

-800 HP! Critical hit!

"Yeeeeeeeoooooooooy!" Sugar Spur shrieks and shrieks. Her nipples reform, but the golden rings are long gone.

"Holy fick, Zaena, I mean, Liz! Fick! Keep that up and I'll start calling you Princess Zaena!"

The Thulean lands, cuts a goblin wielding a morning star down, and uses her ghost limbs to lift back into the air. This time, she tosses one of her blades, which zips through Sugar Spur's other earlobe.

-400 HP!

A look of utter anguish spreading across her face, Sugar Spur manages to fire off her serpent of magic, which zips around the room, eventually taking a hundred or more HP from each Mitherficker.

Ryuk is thrown sideways, only to be dogpiled by stinky, robe-clad goblins.

"Fuck!" he shouts as he's being smothered. Firing blindly into the stack of bodies, he finishes the rest of his mag of sword marbles.

Insta-Insta-Instakill!

Unable to adequately reload his weapon, Ryuk, amidst being bitten, scratched, poked and prodded, is able to stick two molten marbles in his mouth.

His spitfire spell does the rest.

Fire scorching from his lips, Ryuk torches the goblins off him, rolls right, and manages to come up away from the pile of burning, screaming goblins.

One more golden ring, he thinks, as he goes for his slingshot. The ring is affixed to Sugar Spur's belly button, so an explosive marble should do the trick.

But first...

To get some leverage, and get away from the goblins descending upon him, Ryuk places a couple of gravity marbles in his mouth. He lifts into the air, his slingshot aimed at Sugar Spur's belly.

The goblin shaman sees him and points as a blistering spiral of energy twists around her arm.

"Not today," Ryuk whispers.

His black marble hits her belly and explodes, flesh flying everywhere.

-400 HP!

Sugar Spur screeches and falls from the air. She lands in the pile of goblins beneath her and they quickly work to cover her body.

"She's still not dead?" Ryuk asks as he steps back down to the ground.

He glances to Hiccup, who is doing the math on his mechanical fingers. Wolf is beside him, cutting down any goblin who dares approach.

"Fick," Hiccup finally says. He gulps loud enough for Ryuk to hear him a good four meters away. "That means there's another ring."

"Another ring?" asks Zaena, who has just touched down between the two. FeeTwix, to Ryuk's right, grabs his Glock and puts three shots directly into the forehead of an approaching goblin.

Instakill!

"Marbles, Twixy, cover me!" Hiccup says as he waddles over to the wall of goblins. The most cantankerous goblin this side of the Port of Corpses shakes his head in disgust. "It can only be one fickin' place."

FeeTwix gets it before Ryuk does. He finishes his round and calls over to Hiccup, "Are you sure?"

The goblin swallows hard. "I was born for this moment, Twixy," he says, his eyes reflecting the growing chaos of the goblin dogpile forming around Sugar Spur. "If I don't make it out of there, Twixy, tell Spewy that I'm his father and that I don't approve of his life choices."

With that, Hiccup bites down on his toe knife, gets into a diving position, and leaps into the goblins that have swarmed around the powerful shaman.

"What in the fuck is he doing?" Ryuk asks, still capping goblins as he sees fit.

"The final ring," FeeTwix says, pointing to his groin. "It's there…"

"Seriously?" Enway asks. "Her chalupa?"

Ryuk can't decide whether to be disgusted or to laugh out loud.

"Filthy creatures!" is Zaena's response as she decapitates two approaching goblins, their blood spritzing the wall.

But that's not the instakill that gets Ryuk's attention. About a minute later, a mini nuclear explosion spits goblin limbs, goblin weapons, and entrails through the air.

Instakill!

Hiccup flies out of the mess, smacks into the ceiling, cries out in pain, and lands on the ground, a meter away from Wolf. Any robed goblin left standing quickly exits the room.

"Yoy…" Hiccup says as he throws his mechanical hand out to reveal the runestone.

FeeTwix rushes over to him and helps him up.

"Are you okay?"

The goblin puckers his lips.

"Fine, healing potion." The Swede takes a healing potion out of thin air and jams it into Hiccup's mouth. He livestreams the close-up of the goblin, much to his fans' approval—well, at least the Fickers. "Drink up, baby goblin!"

"Yoy!" Hiccup spits some of the healing potion into FeeTwix's face. "That was…fick me, that was crazy. And Twixy, I've said it once and I'll say it again: I'm nobody's little fickboy. Any-fickin'-hoo…" He shows FeeTwix the runestone. "You fickheads wouldn't believe where this was buried, and I ain't talking about her female choop either. That was the golden ring. I had to get that one off with my toe knife. The runestone…"

"It was there?" Zaena asks, disgusted.

"Like a hemorrhoid, Liz. Fick, talk about a damp, hairy, filthy place I never want to visit again." The goblin shudders and wipes blood from his brow. "Who wants the stone?"

"I do?" Ryuk asks, not too keen on taking the shit-covered stone from Hiccup.

"Welp, here you go, Marbles. Fetch!"

The runestone flies through the air, and luckily for Ryuk, Zaena catches it with her ghost limb. She holds it there for a moment as she gets a cleaning towel from FeeTwix. "I figured you didn't want it in *that* condition, and FeeTwix, please burn this towel after I'm finished."

"Will do, babe."

"Thanks," Ryuk says as Zaena hands him the clean runestone. This one is bigger than the first, and once he has equipped the first one, he notices that it fits perfectly into the grooves across the face of the second runestone.

"So, they fit together," Enway says as she approaches him. "Not bad."

"Yeah," Ryuk says as he turns the attached runestones over in his hands. "I wonder what they do when we get the third."

Enway shrugs. "No telling. Hey, did anyone else get levels? I got two!"

"One for me," says the Swede.

"Two for me," Zaena says.

"Three for Uncle Goblin. I think I got some type of bonus for hopping into that pile of fickboys. BOGO, am I right? Wait, that's not buy one, get one. That's like buy one, get two. Fick. Algebra is a bitch."

Ryuk takes a deep breath. "FeeTwix and I need to log out to see Sophia. We'll be back in a little while. In the meantime, the guild should make their way back to Waringtla to see Lothar, but not through the sewers."

"For once, I agree with Marbles. Let's get on the first train out of here, Mitherfickers, and since there are no trains, we're going to have to take an airship."

"Good," Ryuk says as he lifts his finger to log out. "See you guys in Waringtla."

The Japanese youth takes one more look at the room and the piles upon piles of goblin bodies, closes his eyes, realizes he will never forget that memory, and logs out.

THE RUNESTONES OF TRITINAKH

CHAPTER 14: RAMEN REVELATIONS

THE LOGGING OUT PROCESS while in a dive vat is something Ryuk didn't quite expect. He sees the same exit screen, and goes through the same spiraling vortex, but rather than waking up in his bed, he wakes up in a pool of sticky liquid with a breathing apparatus jammed into his mouth.

His first instinct is to try to rip his body free, but he quickly reminds himself where he is, and it isn't long before Sophia's humandroid friend, Evan, is by his side, removing cords stuck into the back of his NV Visor and returning Ryuk's breathing apparatus to its hook on the side of the vat.

His lips exceedingly dry, he feels an intense thirst coming on. His thirst is quickly met with a glass of lukewarm water from Evan.

"Drink up," the humandroid says, "and I'll see to your friend. Once you are ready, you may climb out of the vat on your own. There are showers over there. I suggest washing the conducting substance off your body. It can get very sticky if it is kept on for too long."

Ryuk does as instructed, and once he's showered, he meets Hajime, Evan and Sophia at the front of the room, all of whom are waiting for FeeTwix to finish up.

"How was your dive?" Hajime asks. "Did you listen to the quiet voice?"

The Oblique Quote. Ryuk scratched the back of his head. "Um, not exactly, but we did get two of the runestones."

"Impressive," Sophia says, even though her facial expression doesn't make it seem like she's very impressed.

"And I'm assuming you have one more to go?"

"Yep," Ryuk tells Hajime. "The three runestones of Tritinakh. No idea what they'll do once we get them all together, but the first two actually fit into one another."

"I'm familiar with them," says Sophia, "but I've never known someone to actually go after them. There are tons of quests and rare items like that in Tritania. I've been diving to Tritania for, jeez, almost two decades. That makes me sound so old, but that's how long I've been going there. I don't know if I already told you, but I own an apartment in Valhalla."

"Nice," Ryuk says, familiar with the most famous district in Porthos, the capital of Polynya. Out of all the capitals of the continent, Aramis in Hyperborea and Athos in Ultima Thule, Porthos is by far the most expensive.

"I agree, it is nice. Evan, have you chosen a restaurant for us?"

"Yes, Hajime and I conferred and decided on a ramen restaurant in Nippori. Is that to your liking?" he asks Ryuk.

"Of course. I love ramen."

"I've been craving ramen since we arrived," Sophia admits. "I'm not Japanese. Don't know if I told you that, but my family is from Taiwan and I was born in America."

"Okay."

"But I love ramen. I think all Asians love ramen, at least all Asians I know. I guess it sounds like I'm stereotyping them because I am." She grins. "And I love ramen."

"Me too," Ryuk says, just as FeeTwix walks out of the shower room.

"That is one hot shower! Whew! What's on the agenda for dinner tonight, fam? My fans have told me about some really delicious monjayaki in the Tsukishima District."

"I thought you weren't telling your fans you were coming here," Ryuk says.

"Relax, Ryuk, just a really close group of fans. These guys and gals know everything I'm up to. It's a private group. No squealers there, I promise."

"Monjayaki is good," Ryuk says, "but maybe okonomiyaki is better."

"Interesting. I'd try them both 'cause I am starved! Not starved like a pink-haired goblin who shall remain nameless, but I'd definitely eat my weight in just about anything Japanese, aside from fermented beans."

"*Natto.*"

"Yeah, I'll pass on that. Ha! And we can totally discuss this later, but really, Ryuk, can you believe how we ended up defeating that last boss?"

"What happened?" Sophia asks as they step out of the dive facility.

FeeTwix quickly explains the Queen of the Rings battle, much to Sophia's chagrin towards the end of his explanation.

"So, if it wasn't clear, Hiccup had to squirm through a pile of goblins to remove the golden ring from her, um, lady part and then he had to take the runestone from her—"

"Goblins continue to be the bane of my existence, even though I no longer associate with them. I never told many people this, but once, as a test from the Sage—"

"The Sage?" FeeTwix asks Sophia.

"The NVA Seed of Tritania," Ryuk says.

"Ah, okay, continue—"

"I was once forced to babysit dozens of baby goblins as a test of my patience. It was..." Sophia shudders. "Horrifying."

"Did you pass the test?" Evan asks as they step outside of the lab.

"No, I failed. But Quantum passed his test, so we were able to solve the riddle."

FeeTwix's eyes go wide. "That sounds so awesome. I wish I could meet Quantum Hughes."

"You could, if you go to America."

"He doesn't dive anymore?"

Sophia turns to FeeTwix and shrugs. "No comment."

Once they reach the parking lot, a cold burst of air moves past the five; swirling snow presses into the front of Ryuk's sweater. The Uberyota SUV awaits them at the curb and they can't get in soon enough.

"It's getting colder out there," FeeTwix says as he puts on the mask Hajime gave him.

In response to his statement, a weather forecast appears on the inside of the windshield as the aeros lifts into the air. The weather is read in English, followed by Japanese.

"Tokyo is so pretty at night," Sophia says, looking out the window. "I really wish I had more time to do a little shopping but..." she sighs.

"What is it, dear?" Evan asks.

"You know exactly what it is. My work calls. My work always calls."

"Did you discover something?" Ryuk asks. "I mean, what you were looking for. Did you discover this?"

"I did," she says with a grimace, "and it's not what I expected. Look, we'll get into all the details at the restaurant."

"But I am okay, yes?"

She smiles at the young man. "Yes, you are okay."

"No, I mean my..." Ryuk fires off the word in Japanese to Hajime.

"His digital hallucination," the humandroid says.

"Yes, sorry, I forgot the word hallucination."

"You will be fine regarding your hallucinations," Sophia says. "It is what lies behind these hallucinations that has me worried."

(0)__(0)

The steamy air from the ramen shop brushes past Ryuk's face as the door slides open. Two men sit at the counter slurping from their bowls while a trio of ramen chefs busy themselves by chopping ingredients.

"Welcome!" a female chef calls out. She wears a black apron and has her hair pulled back by a matching black bandana.

The space in the ramen restaurant is tight, and there are only two tables and some seating at the counter, but the place is cozy, quaint, and it smells fucking phenomenal. It has been a while since Ryuk went to a ramen shop, his last visit being one with Tamana.

As he normally does with Tamana memories, he quickly swallows it down.

As they discussed in the ride over, Hajime stands near the door and Evan takes the furthest seat at the counter. *Two humandroid bodyguards,* Ryuk thinks as he sits with his back to the door. FeeTwix is next to him, and Sophia Wang across from them.

"You'll do the honors, right?" Sophia asks.

"Honors?"

"Order," she tells Ryuk. "You'll order for us."

"Sure. What do you want?"

"Miso ramen and gyoza, lots of gyoza. How much comes on a platter again? Six?"

"Yes, six."

"Order me two platters then."

"Okay. FeeTwix?"

The Swede turns a laminated menu on the table over. "I have no earthly idea what I'm looking at...kidding! I activated my real time Japanese language reading app which, seriously you two, I recommend the hell out of this app. I swear it can read everything, from Swahili to Cantonese. Sorry, they once sponsored a slot on my live feed. It does work well though. Okay, sorry again. What will you have, Ryuk?"

"Ramen."

"I figured that. Which kind of ramen?"

"Secret broth," he says, licking his lips. "It is a pork broth, I believe."

"Yep, I'm all in. Secret broth it is and fried dumplings."

"Gyoza."

"Sure, let's order a ton of those."

The female chef comes around with a pad. After suggesting the shoyu broth, she takes their order, and calls it out to the other chefs as she returns to the counter.

Finished with his bowl, one of the salarymen at the counter stands, thanks the chefs for their food, bows, and exits the restaurant, a newspaper tucked under his arm.

"Let's get down to business then," Sophia says, settling her gaze on Ryuk. "I went through your feed since you took your new avatar, and I noted a couple of things."

"Okay," he says nervously.

"You recall the woman behind the door in the Shinigami's guild."

"Yes, the snake woman. I think she looked like a snake, at least from here down," Ryuk says, touching his stomach.

"I'm just going to flat out tell you everything I know about this person. Her last known handle was 'Veenure,' her real name is Victoria Mays."

"Veenure?" Ryuk asks.

"Wait," she says as FeeTwix's mouth opens to ask a question. "Let me finish, because it is about to get a lot more complicated. Veenure was, or quite possibly still is, a Reaper. Now, I know you know about the Reapers, FeeTwix, especially being a Quantum Hughes fanboy. But for Ryuk, an explanation is important."

"I know a little. I was a Knight, remember?"

Sophia continues her explanation anyway. "The Reapers were the name for what was essentially a murder/slavery guild formed in the 2050s by Strata Godsick. Remember that name, because it is about to come up again. Strata formed the Reapers during the search for his son, Luther. The Reapers worked for a company known as the Revenue Corporation, of which Strata was the CEO, which exploited people who were trapped in Proxima Worlds."

"I've heard about being trapped," FeeTwix says.

"Being 'trapped' used to be a thing. The Reapers usually enslaved those who were trapped, and tried to use clever, algorithm changing weapons to trap more players, so they could extract insurance money from them. There were shell companies upon shell companies, and a public scandal happened once all this was revealed in late 2058, plus a system-wide change from the Proxima Company. Any questions so far?"

FeeTwix and Ryuk shake their heads.

"Now back to the serpent woman and how she relates to all this. Veenure was Strata's daughter, Luther's half-sister. She was actually part of the Knights of Non Compos Mentis. Now for a little background on that, the Knights were formed when Quantum and the rest of the federally funded DREAM Team, that's Dream Recovery Extraction and Management Team, went to Tritania in search of Strata's son, Luther."

"Why did they want his son?" FeeTwix asks.

"Leverage and because we—yes, I was a DREAM Team member—were tasked with freeing people trapped in Proxima worlds. So, helping Luther would have been twofold: freeing him and also giving us leverage on Strata and the Reapers. Anyway, not long after Quantum and company spawned, they met Veenure, who tricked us all and joined our guild, getting intel from the inside." Sophia gulps. "She later ended up killing my dive partner, Zedic Woods."

"She killed your partner?" Ryuk asks, seeing the troubled look on her face.

Sophia nods slowly. "There is more to it than that, but yes, Veenure killed him in the OMIB, and he didn't have an RPC set to respond."

"Orthogonal Matrix Inverse Base."

"Yes, FeeTwix, OMIB. Remember that word, because I'm about to get back to it."

The gyoza comes, and after taking her wooden chopsticks from their package, Sophia dunks the first one in soy sauce and eats it right away. "Okay, so as I was saying, Veenure, who I believe is this woman you encountered, Ryuk, is Strata's daughter."

"So how did she end up in the OMIB?" FeeTwix asks, his mouth full of piping hot gyoza. "It's sooooo good!"

"We put her in the OMIB. Remember Doc? You met him yesterday."

"Yep," says FeeTwix. "The faun."

Ryuk recalls the faun they met back at the Knights' guildhall, the one in the tactical vest similar to the vest FeeTwix wears to reduce damage taken from the firearms penalty.

"Doc is a..." Sophia bites down on her lip as she considers how to describe him. "He is the original Proxima hacker, that's how I'd describe him. He was born in the 80s, as in 1980s, and he was one of the first to really toy with what the Proxima Company created."

"And he was a DREAM Team member?" asks the Swede.

"Not exactly," Sophia says, her mouth full. Once she swallows, she continues the information dump. "He was never an official member because that would have made him a target. Instead, he was a contractor for the DREAM Team, and in his free time, aside from spending time with his goats." She cringes. "He had one named Sally that I wasn't the biggest fan of. Again, a story for another day. Like I was saying, aside from spending time with his goats, Doc liked to tinker with algo weapons."

FeeTwix stuffs another gyoza in his mouth. "Mutant hacks."

"That's right, FeeTwix, and while the one you have in your inventory list..."

"I have two."

"Okay, so you know what they're capable of. Doc created a type of mutant hack he called the 'Golden Goosinator,' which we also called a 'Reaper Hack.' The Reaper Hack was relatively straightforward at first. Blast a Reaper, and it tracks their real world location and gives them a life bar penalty when they log into any Proxima world. But it got cooler as Doc tinkered with the weapon's effects."

"Did he fry their NV Visors?" FeeTwix asks.

"Fry?" asks Ryuk.

"Electrocute to death. You know, um, zzz, zzz, zzz!" FeeTwix flashes his hand around his head to illustrate what he means.

"I see."

"No, he didn't design hacks to kill them, although he could have, and I believe he contemplated doing so for a while." Sophia sets her chopsticks down. "But he didn't do it; instead, he designed a mutant hack that not only logged their location, it also force-spawned the Reaper in the OMIB, meaning they could *never* return to the Proxima Galaxy proper. Let me rephrase: after being struck with this weapon, they could return to any Proxima world, but they couldn't actually function with normal players. Instead, they would automatically spawn in the OMIB, and if you've ever been in the OMIB..."

Sorrow flashes across Sophia's eyes.

"What?" FeeTwix asks.

"If you've ever been stuck in the OMIB for a considerable time, it can be quite harrowing."

"So how does this relate to Veenure?" the Swede asks.

"Once we discovered she was a Reaper, there was a pretty big battle in which we blasted her with one of these hacks, I believe it was Quantum who got her."

"Hell yes, it was Quantum!" FeeTwix says, his mouth full of gyoza.

"Veenure was never able to log into a Proxima world proper; rather, she could only log into the OMIB."

"So that's where she is now?"

"Correct, Ryuk, but there's one more layer to this. Doc and Quantum, using the DREAM Team's jurisdiction, went after Veenure in California. They planned to bring federal charges against her for killing my divemate, Zedic. But just as they were about to capture her, Veenure killed herself."

The color drains from FeeTwix's face. "And she had a Reborn Player Character who force-spawned in the OMIB, essentially trapping her there for eternity."

"Exactly. Now, she could still use her dashboard to terminate her account, but I believe she's been using her time in the OMIB to grow stronger and to figure out a way to come back to our world."

"Whoa," FeeTwix says. "You think she's trying to come back here?"

Sophia takes a deep breath and looks at Ryuk. "And this is exactly what happened to your friend Tamana just before her death. You and Tamana were resetters, and just like the data Hajime showed me, these digital hallucinations are *only* happening to resetters, those who decide to start over with new avatars. And I believe it is Veenure causing this."

"Why resetters?" Ryuk asks. "Why is she trying to come through resetters?"

Sophia's brow furrows as she tries to think of the best way to water down her explanation. She gives up, and goes with the more technical explanation.

"The answer to this question involves an avatar's digital neuronal autoconstruct system, or D-NAS. New avatars are created in real time, their D-NAS not passing through the OMIB as portions are recycled. Once someone becomes a resetter, their D-NAS is partially processed in the OMIB. No avatar is ever completely destroyed, which is why you, Ryuk, have likely noticed a few similar characteristics between your current avatar and your last Tritanian avatar."

Ryuk nods, recalling his Extreme Focus skill.

"Most people only have a sliver of this past-avatar residue, but it's there, and it passes through the OMIB, which is how Veenure has caught onto it. It's how she found you and Tamana. She has tried with you as well, Ryuk, but continues to fail. She appears to be trying to use an NPC to come through a person's iNet feed and take over their body. Thing is, this isn't possible." Sophia grins smugly. "Trust me, I know."

"I'll bet," FeeTwix says as he finishes the last gyoza.

She takes a sip from her glass of water to clear her throat. "Let's backtrack, just a bit, to my successful experiment from the 2050s. If you recall, I was able to have an NPC spawn inside a humandroid's body."

Ryuk remembers going over this with Hajime and later sharing it with the guild.

"As I told you, FeeTwix, Quantum Hughes did this for a time as well. He got stuck in a Proxima world and returned to our world using a humandroid's body. So theoretically, an RPC *would* be able to take a humandroid's body, but *not* a human's. That's the problem here: Veenure is trying to come through human bodies, which doesn't work. If she tried a humandroid's body, it could work. I proved that it was possible.

"Veenure is an RPC. Remember, she's dead. She killed herself in California in 2058. I've already proven that an NPC can r-dive, or reverse dive. Aiden did it in the 2050s, and Quantum was a regular player character, and he did it too. So, I've proven both NPCs and PCs can come to our world using a humandroid's body.

"Point is, an RPC could *definitely* do it, which is what Veenure should try to do if she really wants to spawn in this world. But she doesn't know this. All she knows is that she's been able to use NPCs to distort a person's live iNet feed." She offers a rare smile. "Which, in itself, is quite the discovery. Oh, the ramen has come!"

The waitress sets the three bowls of ramen on the table and asks them to enjoy their dinner.

"*Arigato gozaimasu,*" Ryuk says as she leaves.

"What's next?" asks FeeTwix. "I mean, what are we supposed to do about this now, as in, after dinner."

"That's really up to you two," says Sophia. "If you have things to do in Tritania, you could go back. Or you could sleep. We've discussed both options, *we* being Evan, Hajime and me. Until you've left Japan, FeeTwix, Hajime will also be looking after you."

The Swede finishes slurping up his noodles and looks to the door. "I get a bodyguard?" he asks, grinning at Hajime.

Ryuk laughs. "He is much more than a bodyguard."

"What do you mean?"

"Never mind." Ryuk thinks for a moment as he takes another sip from his bowl of ramen. "We can go back to Tritania after. Do you need to run more tests?"

"No," Sophia says, "but it wouldn't hurt to monitor you some more. Plus, I want to spend some time tinkering with your iNet interface, to see just how these NPCs from Tritania are coming here. I'm also interested in how they've augmented reality to make it appear as if they are interacting with the real world. That is one part I find incredibly interesting about all this, and it's also a great angle for a future research project."

CHAPTER 15: KODAI GETS LUCKY

"So, they're in Tokyo."

Kodai can't believe his luck. Hours spent watching FeeTwix's live feed hadn't garnered much. He hated the goblin, that was for sure, and he despised the Swede's ad reads, but finally, after a long afternoon of watching and simultaneously monitoring the Shinigami's progress in leveling up in the Sabors, he finally got the information he needed.

Sitting in his chair and taking in his beautiful view of Tokyo, Kodai plays the feed again just to confirm, for the sixth time, he's heard what he thinks he's heard:

"FeeTwix and I need to log out to see Sophia. We'll be back in a little while. In the meantime, the guild should make their way back to Waringtla to see Lothar, but not through the sewers."

How could you be so stupid, Ryuk? He thinks as he plays the clip again. He already knew they were in Waringtla, and he knew they were going after the runestones—another reason he had his team positioned in the Sabors—but he had no idea FeeTwix was in Tokyo, and Sophia...

It didn't take him long to deduce she was the leader of the Knights of Non Compos Mentis, and he only needed to ask one of his contacts at MercSecure, a security analyst named Ian, to do a little digging. Ian had run info for him before, and Kodai paid him handsomely to do so.

"Sophia Wang," he says as he feels a hand drop onto his shoulder. He looks up to see Tesla, nude, her body completely cleanshaven. The humandroid wears a small collar with a chain that trails down her back.

"Are you ready?" she asks.

"Something big has come up."

"Oh?"

"I'll catch you up rapidly." Kodai activates an app on his iNet screen which transfers all the data he's poured through over the last hour, plus the clip of his brother saying that FeeTwix and Sophia are in Tokyo.

"And do you know where they are yet?" Tesla asks, her eyes dilating.

"Ian was able to get me some information regarding her arrival, but there hasn't been much since. I think someone, or possibly some AI, is covering her tracks. It appears as if she left from the airport in fifteen aeros taxis. All the trips were paid for by someone named War Faun, and they all have a transaction number that ends with DOC."

"Odd. And what does your intelligence analyst think of this?"

"He's checked all the taxi's destinations and each of them have a drop off point that is either in a body of water or in a public park."

"And he is going through all live cam data from the parks?"

"As of now, yes, but that's going to be hard to filter through. We will focus instead on finding FeeTwix going forward."

Kodai places his hand on the small of Tesla's back and latches onto the chain hanging from her neck. He pulls back slightly, and she lets out a small cry for help. He laughs.

"You could kill me in a heartbeat," he reminds her.

"You don't want me to play along?"

"No, but I want to touch your skin again."

She sits in his lap, the second time she's done so today. After this morning's gruesome murder, Kodai needed his Nikko whiskey like he's never needed it before. He's a bit drunk now, but not drunk enough that he can't make decisions.

"Then touch it," she says, turning her breasts towards him.

He doesn't say what's on his mind: *they feel so real.*

That would be an amateur move, but he does think it, and he does bend forward to kiss her breasts, only to find that they are warm, that if he presses his head to her chest he can hear something akin to a heartbeat, that goosebumps form around her nipples after he's sucked on them for a moment, that the place between her legs is wet.

It is something else.

And even as he puts his fingers in, as he continues fondling her, as he stops and looks deep into her soulless eyes, a business idea is ballooning at the back of his mind. *This is the way of the future.* And his competitor, Gintoki, how smart he was for employing these droids at his pink salon!

He gets the notion in that instant to fire a message off to Lorem Ipsum, but he resists the urge, knowing that he's already bothered the man a great deal and that, while he pays Lorem's company a lot of money, it'd be better for him *not* to be a nuisance.

The proper channels, he thinks as Tesla turns, her back to him.

She moves her body back and forth on his lap, across his erection.

He hasn't gone all the way with her yet; that's what this evening is about. He's saved it, took care of his business for the day, which just so happened to be murder, and spent the rest of the afternoon spying on his brother's guilds.

"Are you ready?" she asks, her hands dropping to his belt.

"You can read my mind too?"

She smiles. "No, but I can scan your vitals."

"You don't need to scan much to see that I'm ready."

"Then let's try it."

"You ever done this before?"

She laughs. "Actually, no. No, I haven't. I am not a humandroid built for sex work, but I have met a few. We're actually quite similar."

"How's that?" he asks as she pulls his pants down.

"They don't have violence governors."

"They don't? Why?"

She smiles as she places her warm hands on the seam of his boxers.

"So that they can do whatever a person asks of them," Kodai says, answering his own question. "It's brilliant."

"It is."

"You're beautiful."

"Thank you."

"I want you so bad." He bites his lip, ashamed of how primal he's being.

"I'm already yours." Tesla pulls his pants off and gets on top of him. Soon, he's inside, and less to his surprise than he would have expected, *it feels the exact same.*

Or at least, it feels the same as he remembers it. Kodai hasn't had sex in quite a while, preferring to watch women of his choosing do vile things to himself.

He cancels that thought now alongside the images of the things he's asked people to do for him. What is happening now is completely alien, something that he can barely comprehend but something that seems so right, so *now*.

And no, it isn't odd for a human to have sex with a mechanical device, nor is it really odd for a human to have sex with a humandroid, especially approaching the 22nd century.

What strikes Kodai as odd is how attached he feels to Tesla, that he *actually cares for her*, that he may even love her, and more frighteningly, the fact that he doesn't know why he feels this way.

"Just enjoy." She drops her hands to his shoulders, so she can work even harder. "Don't think so much about it," she says, breathing hard. "And regarding your brother, and the others, we'll get to them after this." She grins as she thrusts her body harder into his.

"This is fucking wonderful."

"It is, Kodai, it is."

THE RUNESTONES OF TRITINAKH

CHAPTER 16: PASTRIES AND A SIDE QUEST

FEETWIX AND RYUK spawn on an airship just as it is dropping into Waringtla. The sudden change in gravity, even though they've theoretically just traveled from the real world to algorithmic dream world, is something that definitely causes Ryuk's stomach to turn.

Ryuk Matsuzaki Level 26 Ballistics Mage
HP: 1030/1030
ATK: 150
MATK: 198
DEF: 113
MDF: 85
LUCK: 24

FeeTwix Fajer Level 27 Berserker Mystic
HP: 1311/1311
ATK: 209

MATK: 37

DEF: 113

MDF: 68

LUCK: 28

Hiccup Level 25 Shield Thief

HP: 1690/1690

ATK: 133

MATK: 17

DEF: 299

MDF: 152

LUCK: 39

Zaena Morozon Level 27 Brawler Assassin

HP: 1334/1334

ATK: 264

MATK: 10

DEF: 233

MDF: 53

LUCK: 27

Enway Zoltan Rosa Level 26 Hourglass Mage

HP: 1005/1005

MANA: 571/571

ATK: 82

MATK: 177

DEF: 69

MDF: 183

LUCK: 24

Wolf Level 40
HP: 2402/2402
ATK: 699
MATK: 0
DEF: 534
MDF: 241
LUCK: 19

Still feeling a bit of nausea, Ryuk places his hand on his belly and turns away from Hiccup, who sits at the small table across from Zaena. Red-eyed Enway in her sexy-ish monk robes sits on the ground, her Book of Time open across her lap. Wolf lies next to her, sleeping lightly.

Enway looks up at Ryuk and smiles. "How was it up there?"

"Good."

She laughs.

"Marbles isn't one for words, Elfie. There's a word in Jatla for a quiet ficker like him, but I'm not going to say it here," says the cranky goblin.

"Hi to you too, Hiccup." Ryuk flashes him a not so subtle middle finger, which Hiccup ignores, so focused is he on shifting through a set of scrolls on the table before him.

"What? You want a hug or something? Goblins don't hug, Marbles, and even if I did want a hug, which I don't. Twixy! No! Bad Swede! Do not...!"

FeeTwix tackles Hiccup with a hug, taking him out of the chair. Using her ghost limbs, Zaena stops them from completely toppling the table over.

"Hands off, you vile kiddy ficker!"

"What's this you got here..." FeeTwix starts rifling through the scrolls on the table in front of Hiccup.

"That's personal!"

Zaena laughs. "The goblin is trying to design a guild logo for a future tattoo. All he can come up with is two flying skulls surrounding a sword."

"Ah," FeeTwix says, holding the picture in question. "The old skulls deepthroating a sword logo, eh?"

"Fick! An artist shouldn't be judged until, *until*, he's finished his masterpieces. I'm still working on the fickin' design, Twixy," Hiccup says, scooping the scrolls into his arms.

"Relax, Hiccup, my fans have already copied your design and made it better."

"The fick you just say? They have?"

An image flashes in front of FeeTwix and Hiccup looks it over for a moment.

"Fick me, that's actually not too bad, Twixster, but I'd make the sword veinier."

"Swords don't have veins, Hiccup. If you add veins, it will look like a *chalupa,* as you put it."

The ground shakes and the image FeeTwix is showing Hiccup disappears.

"Good, we've landed. About fickin' time too. So sick of being judged for my art. But you guys liked it, right?" Hiccup asks, his eyes softening. "Been working on it for a while now. An artist needs the proper tools to create, but all the fickin' Mexican elf could conjure up were some crayons. Forgot to mention that. What do you guys think?"

"We fickin' love it, Hiccup!" FeeTwix says, his eyes solid black.

"It is goblin art," says Zaena.

"Um, thanks? Marbles?"

"It's fine."

"Marbles." The goblin curls his mechanical hand. "Fick, I hate you, even though I think of you kind of like a son. This guy couldn't tell Monet from Manet. Am I right, people? Elfie?"

"I agree with Zaena."

Hiccup throws his hands into the air. "Is this about the extreme vetting? Because if it is, listen, kid, we can't keep letting people into our guild, especially people from certain countries that practice certain religions. I mean other people, people that believe what I believe, like Wolf over there and Oric, we can relax restrictions on them. But you."

"I'm from Mexico."

"When I hear Mexico I think bad hombres, and I don't even know what that means. Any-fickin'-hoo, never agree with Liz. Remember, she's royalty, the one percent of the one percent. She wipes her starfish with caviar, if you get my drift. She'll never think like us."

Liz approaches Hiccup, her hand on the hilt of her sword. "You know, goblin."

"Fick, Liz, if you're going to do it, fickin' do it! I was born ready to die, and I'd consider it an honor to be killed by Thulean royalty, especially a pretty Thulean such as yourself. FeeTwix told you how beautiful you are today, right? Tall, slender, strong, sexy fine facial features, powerful orange eyes, slick orange hair, soft lips, extra delicate hands. If you were my main squeeze, I'd tell you how hot you were every day of the fickin' week."

Ryuk glances over to FeeTwix, whose look is indecipherable. From there he looks to Enway, who seems to be trying to contain laughter.

The goblin and the Thulean hold each other's gaze for a moment, and as usual, Zaena ends up looking away. "The logo is fine," she says as she turns to the door. "Make the sword sharper, and no veins. Thanks for the compliment. Your pink hair is better than having no hair."

"Fick yes, it is. And they say flattery won't get you anywhere. Listen up, Mitherfickers." Wolf howls, startling the four of them. Hiccup quickly recovers. "That's right, Wolfy, we've got a logo!"

(0)__(0)

. Lothar's Occult Bakery and Athenaeum is relatively easy to find, especially as the airship drop off point is only a few blocks away. It is very early morning, and the streets of Waringtla are empty. About the only person the Mitherfickers pass is a drunk giant, snoring with the right side of his face pressed into the pavement.

"I'd loot him if he weren't so big," Hiccup says. "Never looted a giant before."

"You think it's too early?" Enway asks as they stop in front of the commoner-sized door, which is cut into the giant door.

"I can smell pastries," says Ryuk.

"Oh, that's right, bakers get up early to start their day's work."

"Yep, and even if he wasn't awake, we got fickin' places to go and people to see. So we'd wake him."

"Rude," says Zaena, "but I agree with the goblin."

"The goblin who has a name, but you know what? You complimented my topknot back in the airship, so I'm going to let this one slide. Now. Let's get in there."

FeeTwix is the first to go through the door. He finds Lothar's wife, Gadsaa, arranging scones behind the counter.

"We aren't open yet—oh, it's you all. Lothar, honey, you have visitors!"

Lothar comes out of the swinging backroom door, his apron covered in flour. His red hair is a mess and there's even some flour on his oval glasses. "You've already gotten the runestones?" he asks as he wipes his hands on his apron.

"Yep, and that shit wasn't fickin' easy," the goblin says. "First, we had to kill your friend, Fafner, or whatever his name was."

Gadsaa looks to Lothar. "They did what?"

"Never mind, dear."

"And then we had to fight this crazyass goblin bitch with a bunch of golden rings that we had to cut off one at a time." Hiccup shudders. "The last one was the worse; I had to get *up in it*, if you get my drift, and seriously, Big Guy, I will never be the same after that. The therapist bills alone."

"That's great!" Lothar claps his hands together and the air fills with flour. "Let's get upstairs and I will tell you about the final runestone."

"Honey, we open in two hours."

"I can help," Zaena offers. "My *konoshlo* should be of some use."

Gadsaa and Lothar exchange glances.

"Thulean royalty shouldn't have to help in the kitchen," Lothar's wife finally says.

"Fick yeah she should, and another thing, don't forget that we, as in at least one of you Mitherfickers and me, have a little side quest we need to take after this. Og Lemon is in town. I want my revenge."

"Revenge?" Lothar asks. "Did you say Og Lemon, the famous orclin chef?"

"Long story, and yes, that's the ficker I've got beef with. Let's just hear about the runestone and we'll be on our way. Liz, you staying or going?"

"I'll stay and help."

"You really don't have to, princess," Gadsaa says.

"It's fine."

"I promised everyone pastries," Lothar smiles, "and I just so happened to take the commoner sized batch out of the oven already today. I'll meet you four—five, you too, Wolf—in my library."

Wolf barks, a look of excitement plastered across his face. He has clearly eaten giant pastries before, evident in the way he beats his tail. FeeTwix leads the group up the stairs, and as they did before, they take a seat on the carpet in front of Lothar's big chair.

Ryuk again notices the golden scepter on the wall, cast behind a pane of glass. Something tells him that he wouldn't be able to get to the item just by breaking the glass.

"I meant to ask you last time," he tells Enway, who sits next to him, "but have you ever seen anything like that?"

"I was wondering about that myself," she says.

"My fans don't seem to recognize it either," says FeeTwix.

"It's a beating stick. Plain and fickin' simple. Just hold it by the bottom and beat someone across the head with the ruby side. That, or take the ruby off and pawn that shit. You guys know rubies are worth good money here in Tritania, right? Especially Polynya. Take that shit to New Gotha and..."

They hear a giant footstep behind them and feel the vibration on the floor.

"Ah," Lothar says, a tray in his hand. "You were discussing the First Artifact. A fine piece, isn't it?"

"What does it do?" Enway asks.

"*Did* it do, would be more appropriate. It lies dormant at the moment. As to what it did," he smiles fondly, "that's a story for another day."

As soon as Lothar has set the platter on the ground, Hiccup goes for a croissant and stuffs it in his mouth. "Fick, that's fickin' good. Got any lemon pepper sauce I can fickin' add to it? Fick. Okay, that's right. Look, Giant, if you can keep your explanation," Hiccup swallows, "to under thirty seconds, I'd love to hear about your beating stick."

"That is a *scepter*, not a beating stick, and it is called the First Artifact. Long story incredibly short, it was the item used to bring Unigaeans to Tritania."

"The Max Exodus?" Zaena asks, a cream-covered pastry floating in front of her. She takes a small nibble of it and sighs. "It is wonderful."

"The Max Exodus," Lothar says, "that's what people here call it. That item was the first item created by the NVA Seed of Unigaea. Her name was the Obelisk. Oric, your guildmate, used it to bring people here, but only *after* it had been activated by a spell from the woman who also held the Book of Time. Sam Raid. I'm sure you've seen her name in the book."

Enway nods.

"So that's the simplest explanation. A more scientific explanation is that it is an advanced algo weapon, but you want the short one, and I give you the short one."

"I am the short one!" Hiccup laughs, crumbs flying from his mouth.

"Now, about the final runestone. The final runestone is located in the Sabors, which I've told you before. It is heavily guarded by Skadi's minions."

"Skadi?" FeeTwix takes a bite of a scone glazed in orange icing. "Why does that sound familiar?"

"You are from a former Norse region of your world, are you not?"

"Sweden."

"Skadi is a Norse mountain goddess. She has protected the runestone since it came to this world. The other two that you possess have changed hands. Not the third and final stone."

"How did the runestones come here?" Enway is the only one who hasn't eaten anything.

"Please, eat, the pastries will give you a boost in willpower." Lothar laughs. "At least that's what I always tell people. To answer your question, the runestones came here from Unigaea. They were some of the items smuggled by a pair of gnomes."

"Fickin' Unigaean gnomes."

"One of the many things that made Unigaea different from Tritania was the quests and some of the items available. The items that were found, and I believe there were a good many items and quests that died with that world, were brought here. These items now make up some of the most powerful items in Tritania. I suppose you could call these a benefit of the Max Exodus."

"Fake news," Hiccup coughs into his hand, which causes him to choke on the pastry in his mouth. The goblin beats his chest, coughs until his face is red, and finally spits out a garbled hunk of pastry into his lap. "Fick!" He clears his throat and flicks the garbled bit of pastry away. Wolf greedily eats it. "Ha! My leftovers."

Ryuk shakes his head. The urge to apologize for Hiccup's behavior rises in his chest, but Lothar doesn't seem to give two flying fucks about how nasty the goblin can be.

Once the commotion has settled, the giant continues his explanation: "You won't be able to defeat Skadi using traditional methods. You'll have to think creatively. Please proceed with caution."

"What happens when we get the third runestone?" Enway asks.

"That I do not know. No one, aside from the gnomes—husband and wife, I believe—ever had the runestones together at the same time."

"Any idea why they got rid of the runestones?" asks FeeTwix as he chews another bite of scone.

"I believe they sold them, separately, because they needed money. Their Unigaean money, known as lira, was no good here. All they had were the items they carried on their person." Lothar stands. "I have to get back to my own wife because we'll be opening soon. There is an airship leaving for the Sabors in three hours. You can relax here in the meantime, if you'd like."

"Three hours? That should be enough time," Hiccup says as he gets to his feet. "Okay, so who is going with me?"

FeeTwix finishes his scone and licks his fingers. "So good! Hiccup, as much as I'd like to help you get revenge, I'm going to visit Dirty Dave's place again and see if I can't use his shooting range."

"That's not a bad idea, actually."

"Nope, Marbles, you're coming with me."

"Really, Hiccup?"

"It's a side quest. Hell, you may get levels here, and believe you me, you need to level up. Elfie, you in?"

"I will port back to Kayi to check on Oric and Yangu."

"Snowballs."

That's right, Ryuk thinks, *we can instantly travel to any location if a guildmate is already there.*

Since the Mitherfickers had formed, they'd usually been together. But they could have ported rather than take an airship the last time they went to Kayi. Ryuk frowns. He's the only one that would have known this, so that wasted time was definitely his fault.

"Wolfy?"

Wolf, who now stands on the platter eating what's left of the pastries, falls to his side, his stomach distended.

"Fick, Wolfy, you ate your fickin' weight in pastries. Fine, fine. Whatever. It looks like it is you and me, Marbles. Probably Liz too."

"You three should join me back in Kayi if there is still time after you've, um, gotten your revenge," Enway says. "I'm sure you'd like to check on Yangu."

"How long do you think this revenge will take, Hiccup?" asks Ryuk.

The goblin considers this for a moment. "Well, one can't really put a timeframe on revenge, but I'd say, especially if we hurry, it won't take more than an hour."

Ryuk nods. "Then it's settled. FeeTwix, enjoy your shooting. Enway, we'll meet you in Kayi. Hiccup, let's grab Zaena and, I can't believe I'm saying this, let's get revenge."

Hiccup lifts his mechanical hand to his ear. "Everyone hear that? Marbles' marbles just dropped!"

THE RUNESTONES OF TRITINAKH

CHAPTER 17: LUBED UP SABOTAGE

"Okay, here's the deal." Hiccup scratches his ass a few seconds longer than necessary. "You know, I may hate Twixy for giving me this mechanical hand," he says as he places his ass-scratching hand into his nose to dig around for a second, "but fick, can it scratch. Good at scratching your brain too. Where was I? Fick? Marbles, help me here."

Ryuk is in a back alley behind a fancy restaurant. Zaena is next to him, a disapproving look on her face, and Hiccup stands before them, his finger still in his nose.

"There it is." He flicks a booger at Ryuk and continues. "Sorry, better to go in ready to kick some ass."

"And jamming your finger in your nose helps you kick ass how?"

"That's a weird sentence, Liz, but I get what you're asking. Cleaning out the nostrils," he places his finger on his left nostril and blows air out the right, "helps me open the airways. Look, kiddos, we need to be realistic. Without FeeTwix, someone has to be the best member in the team."

"I believe that would be me."

"You would say that, Liz; excessive confidence runs in your blood. But that's beside the point. I'm taking the lead here, and I'll pick my nose whenever I goddamn like. We good?"

Damn goblin. Ryuk crosses his arms over his chest.

"That's the spirit, you poofty emo kronut. Ha! I still don't know what a kronut is. Regardless, here's how this revenge side quest is going to work: we need to sabotage whatever it is Og Lemon is planning."

"Who is this Og again?"

"Og is the guy who nearly caused me to lose my chalupa back in Jatla. He was supposed to provide a nice, Michelin star dinner for me and my guest, who just so happened to be an ink shadow. Well, he ended up ficking me over."

"Did you deserve it?" Ryuk asks.

"What!? What kind of ficked up question is that? Of course I *deserved* it. I fickin' stole his spicy sauce." A bottle of red sauce appears in his hand. "This spicy sauce, to be exact."

"What's so special about this sauce? I will overlook the fact that whatever Og did, you likely deserved it."

"Thanks for the vote of confidence, Liz. Now, this isn't any hot sauce, this stuff is called HotAzz Ballz sauce, and boy fick does it live up to its name. One fickin' sip of this stuff, and you'll be burping fire. Kind of like when Marbles swallows his fire marble, or whatever the fick it's called, and starts spitting fire."

"Bullshit," Ryuk says. He hears voices somewhere and presses further into the shadows provided by the alley.

"Inside voices, Marbles, this is about to be a heist. Fick, *Ocean's Three*, if you get my drift. Wait. That doesn't make sense. We're not stealing anything, we're sabotaging. Anyfick, I don't have a filter, sorry. What did you just ask me?"

"I didn't ask you anything, Hiccup, I said that I don't believe your hot sauce actually works."

"The fick you say?" Hiccup uncorks the hot sauce and holds in front of him. "Okay, Marbles, two can play at this game. You really want to see what this shit is capable of?"

"I do," Zaena says.

Hiccup takes a small swig and turns to the wall behind him. One burp later and a giant fireball exits his lips, nearly setting his eyebrows on fire. "Fick!" he burps again and another fireball flies from his mouth, this one hitting an overturned trash can.

Zaena's eyes go wide. "Wow! It is like magic."

"Shit is good too," Hiccup says, about to burp. He beats his chest instead. "Okay, I'm better. Anyway, the plan is simple. We break into the restaurant and we add this shit to whatever he's going to serve his guests. Needs to be something premade, and not something he'd taste before giving it out. Now let's figure out how we're going to get inside."

Like a fat man adjusting his belt, Hiccup fiddles with his pants for a moment. He shoots Zaena a look that says, "don't judge me," and turns to the back door of the restaurant.

"Can you pick it?" Ryuk asks. "It's a lion lock, right?"

Hiccup stares at the lock for a moment and its golden lion face. The metal lion opens its mouth and licks its metallic lips. "Nope, not going anywhere fickin' near that thing. Looks like we have to go in from the front."

Ryuk hears the voices again and his Extreme Focus skill kicks in. It feels even more powerful than before, and as everything is bathed in shadow, Ryuk can sense that the voices are coming from the front of the restaurant.

"We're going to have to fight our way in." Ryuk equips his Marble Shotgun and begins loading the canister.

"Fick. Marbles, you sure have become trigger happy since getting that damn thing. Whatever happened to the old Marbles, the one happy with his slingshot?"

"I was never happy with my slingshot," Ryuk says as he checks his weapon to make sure everything is in place.

"Let's try the rooftop," Zaena suggests. "We may not have to fight if we go that route, and if we do have to fight, we'll have advantage."

"We should fight, if we can. After all, we need more levels."

"That's the problem with leveling up," Hiccup says as Zaena lifts herself to the roof. "Just getting a couple is never enough. Fick, it's like capitalism in that regard. Always wanting more. Fick me, I'm happy with my fair share, as long as my fair share is bigger than other people's fair shares, am I right? Hey! Fick, Lizzy, careful with the goods."

As Liz begrudgingly lifts Hiccup to the rooftop, Ryuk pops a gravity marble in and floats up.

(0)__(0)

"There are no other entrances up here," Zaena reminds Hiccup as they duck behind the parapet that overlooks the entrance to the restaurant. A giant guard stands at the front, a huge club in his hands.

"Yeah, I get that," he says as he takes another peek at the courtyard. "But how in the fick are we supposed to take out a giant? More importantly, if we do take out a giant, how are we going to make it look like it was a mistake?"

"Why would we do that?" Ryuk asks.

"Gee, I don't know. If we go down there and hand him his ass, then Og Lemon, or the owners of the restaurant, will be suspicious. They'll know that something is up. Now, if we had more time, I think we could kill him, cut his body up, and then make those parts disappear, but then again, morning is near and we're running out of time."

"We're not dismembering a giant."

"Marbles, you sure get sensitive when I drop truth bombs and good ideas. How else are we supposed to get in there?"

"Let me look around."

Ryuk stands and moves back into the shadows. He can see the giant in the courtyard below, a muscular man in armor with a logo on the back. *DD Security, huh?* He shakes his head. Dirty Dave has his fingers in a lot of pies, and this is one that Ryuk would rather not bring his guild into.

"There has to be a way," he says to himself as he walks along the rooftop.

His Extreme Focus kicks in and he begins looking for any sign, any chance of getting in. It takes him a good five minutes, but he is rewarded when he finds a vent covered by a wooden crate. He moves the wooden crate over and presses his head into the bars of the vent, hoping to sense what is on the other side.

It's a kitchen, he realizes, as soon as the outlines of various kitchen appliances take shape in his mind's eye.

Ryuk returns to Hiccup and Zaena. "There's another way in, through a vent that was covered by a crate. From what I can detect, the crate was just moved there recently. I think the vent leads directly to the kitchen, although it may be a storage room in the kitchen. Either way, it's our only option."

The three quickly move over to the vent and Hiccup laments the fact he's not going to be able to squeeze in there.

"The vent isn't fickin' big enough."

"Translation: you're too fat to fit."

"Liz, for the sake of all ficks given in and around Tritania, if you keep up the fat-shaming, you're going to be responsible for the death of a goblin with at least forty thousand real world fans, who will come after you. You want that?"

She pats him on the head with her own hand, for once. "I'll tell you what, Hiccup, because Ryuk and I like you so much, we'll go down there and handle this for you."

"You'd do something like that for me?"

Ryuk and Zaena exchange glances. "For sure," he says, "as long as you can keep quiet up here. In fact, how about you just leave this to us and, um, leave all together."

"But this is my side quest!"

"And that's fine, it's still your side quest, but you can't fit in there."

"Like fick I can't. Liz, remove the manhole cover."

"It isn't a manhole cover."

"Liz, remove the vent cover. I'm going in there whether you two like it or not."

The goblin's clothes fall off his body.

"Why are you taking your clothes off?" Zaena asks, turning away from him.

"Just remove the cover and get down there. Once you're there, see if you can't find something lubricated, like some butter or some fickin' lard. Send it up and I'll handle the rest. We can spawn out of here, rather than try to get back out." He eyes Ryuk and Zaena. "We good?"

"I guess?" says Ryuk.

"I might be lazy, but this is my revenge to get, and I'd be no better than one of those fickboys in the Shinigami or your bitch-titted older brother if I let someone else do my dirty work. Now get down there and find me some lube!"

(0)__(x)

"Don't get any sicko ideas after I'm all lubed up, Marbles," Hiccup calls down the ventilation shaft.

"Fucking idiot," Ryuk says as he and Zaena search for something lube-worthy.

Just as Ryuk had predicted, the shaft actually led to a storage room attached to the kitchen. It's a pretty small place, but it's well-stocked, and it doesn't take Zaena long to find an unopened bucket of lard.

Using one of her throwing knives, she cracks the lid open and lifts the bucket up the ventilation shaft.

"Fick yeah, Liz, how'd you know I was a fan of Aramis lard? Way better than the rich people shit they make in Porthos. Fick yeah, tastes like my childhood."

"This should be interesting," Zaena says as she steps over to the door, just about as far away as she can get from the exit point of the ventilation shaft overhead. It was a pretty straight shot for them to go from the rooftop to here, so as long as Hiccup can get adequately lubed, and as long as he can somehow fit his very round girth into a very square entry point, he should be good to go.

Ryuk starts to laugh.

"What?" Zaena asks, a warm smile forming on her face as her cheeks lift.

Something soft flickers behind her orange eyes. Ryuk is quite fond of her, and she of him, but they're usually overwhelmed by louder guild members to the point where they don't communicate much.

"This is the stupidest thing we've ever done."

"Is it?" Zaena thinks. "There may have been stupider things, but I haven't kept track. One day at a time."

"Okay, fickers, I'm lubed up and ready to get my ass down there. Marbles, hold your arms wide and be ready to catch me."

"Um, sure," Ryuk says, also moving just about as far away from the exit point as he can. "Go ahead."

They hear some struggling and the creak of the ventilation shaft. For a moment, nothing happens. Ryuk glances at Zaena just as a whooshing sound fills the room.

-236 HP! Critical hit!

Hiccup's almost naked ass hits the tile floor hard, and for a moment, the glistening hunk of grade A goblin meat flaps around like a fish.

"Yoooooooooooy! Fick, Marbles! Fick!"

Hiccup gets his bearings and throws his arms out, belly facing up as if he were auditioning for the role of Patrick Star in a SpongeBob Squarenuts live action feature.

He groans some more as a healing potion appears in his mechanical hand. He pops the generic potion in his mouth and slowly begins to regain his strength. Hiccup sits up and finishes the bottle.

"You done yet?" Zaena asks.

"Hard to drink lying down." He's just about to toss the healing potion over his shoulder when he decides to return it to his list instead. "And for the love of fick, what part of 'catch me with open arms' do you fail to comprehend? My fick that was painful. Marbles. Your stupid move almost put me in retirement. Don't be surprised if I schedule a meeting with HR over this shit. The people who work for the guilds of Jatla are protected, albeit loosely, by OSHA laws."

"Quit bitching. This was your idea."

"You're right there, Liz," Hiccup says as he stands.

A greasy imprint of his body still on the floor, the goblin finds a mop and wipes the lard away. He does so without putting clothes on.

"Please, goblin, clothes."

"The name..."

"Hiccup, please put clothes on," Zaena says, still averting her gaze.

"Later, Liz, I'm busy here!" He tosses the mop over his shoulder. "Let's find some food to sabotage."

They enter larger kitchen and Hiccup's nostrils flare.

"The food smells great," Zaena says.

"Og Lemon is a damn good chef," Hiccup says as he scratches his well-oiled belly. "He's half orc, half goblin, an orclin, and believe you me, those fickers can cook. Okay, like I said, we can't make this fickin' obvious."

Ryuk stops in front of a large tuna resting on a block of ice. "Too obvious."

"You're thinking right, kid, desserts. That's how we'll do it. I want this shit to go down at the end." Hiccup thinks for a moment. "I can imagine it now: Og has all his lunch guests, he serves their courses, and he serves the dessert all at the same time. Boom. Fire breath. Gonna be a scorcher, folks. Fick, I wish I could be here to smell it."

"Gross."

"Marbles, you've made it this far, and you'll likely be my accomplice in a number of deaths tomorrow, so don't start sticking your nose up at it now. Remember that, after about lunch time tomorrow, you're technically a murderer."

I'm glad there isn't such a thing as "infamy" in Tritania, Ryuk thinks as he heads into a room designed for a pastry chef. A huge wooden board on the table before them already has a bowl of dough on it, left to rise overnight.

Ryuk enters a smaller room, and it's here that he finds tarts with a red sauce already on them. There are other desserts, such as macaroons, but the tart looks to be the best way to hide the fiery hot sauce.

HotAzz Ballz? Ryuk tries to remember the name. *Why does everything stemming from Jatla have to be so ridiculous?*

A macaroon lifts into the air and Ryuk turns to see the Thulean enjoying it. "You sure love those things."

"They are wonderful," Zaena says.

"Yeah, those things are what caused you to turn in your V Club membership to FeeTwix."

Zaena spins around. "Watch it, goblin."

"Fick! Sorry, Liz, I didn't know that was actually true."

"I didn't say it was true!"

"But you didn't say it wasn't, which where I'm from is basically the same thing as the truth. Marbles, hurry the fick up in there. You finding anything that will work?"

"This should do," Ryuk says, lifting the tray of tarts.

"Fick yes, it will. Okay, let's douse these fickers with the HotAzz Ballz sauce and get the fick to Kayi. Don't do the ones from the front; the pastry chef may taste those ones. Do the ones in the middle, yeah, those ones, and let's hope for something ficked up to happen tomorrow."

CHAPTER 18: KAYI REGROUP

"Are you three hungry?" Enway stands in her living room wearing an apron. Ryuk can smell a soup boiling in the kitchen. They're in Kayi now, and he still feels a little guilty for what he just did in Og Lemon's kitchen. "The soup I've made has a special ingredient in it called Karuna Basil. It will increase our LUCK for the next few hours."

"I'll have some," Ryuk says, a grin spreading across his face as he takes Enway in. They haven't been apart very long, but for some reason, he's missed her. Just having her around gives him a sense of comfort.

"Fick yeah, I'll increase my luck any day." The almost nude, very oiled goblin steps into Enway's kitchen, leaving greasy footprints in his wake.

"Do I need to ask?"

Zaena sits on Enway's couch. "We had to lube him up to get him down a ventilation shaft."

"I lubed myself up, Liz, thank-you-very-much," Hiccup calls from the kitchen. "I'm nobody's liddle fickboy, got that?"

"You may want to put a tarp down."

"Good idea." Enway takes a large canvas tarp from a cabinet and places it on the couch just as Hiccup is about to plop down. Zaena instinctively stands.

"You could put clothes on, *Hiccup*."

"Good, Liz, you're learning how to talk to me like an adult and use my real name. Sure, I'll take your request, but I was getting comfortable in my birthday suit." He snaps his mechanical fingers and his normal get-up appears on his body. His neck and any visible portion of his skin is still greasy.

"What's with the goblin?" Oric asks as he enters the living room. He looks better than he did yesterday and the color in his face has returned. "Why is he so greasy?"

"Greasy? Look, Conan, you try to fit your chiseled chest down a ventilation shaft." Hiccup throws back a big spoonful of Enway's soup. "Wow! Not too fickin' shabby. Needs salt, but then again, everything needs salt."

Oric turns to Ryuk. "So that's what happened here?"

"It is, and also, I wanted to thank you for introducing us to Lothar. He was very helpful, and his information made it very easy for us to find the first two runestones."

"And the third? There are three, correct?"

"That's right, Conan," Hiccup says as soup dribbles down his chest.

"And where is Wolf?" Oric asks, a hint of worry in his voice.

"He is resting at Lothar's," Zaena says. "We are all going back there soon to take the airship to the Sabors. We will meet Wolf and FeeTwix there."

"FeeTwix is with him?"

"Wrong again, Tarzan! FeeTwix is at the shooting range with Dirty Dave, fickin' shit up."

"Okay."

"What? Don't believe me?"

"I didn't say that." Oric places both hands on his hips. "I'd like to join you in the Sabors, if that's possible."

"Definitely," says Ryuk as Oric's stats appear.

Oric Rune Level 58 Warrior Berserker
HP: 3104/3104
ATK: 554
MATK: 11
DEF: 467
MDF: 389
LUCK: 31

He's level fifty, so that means enemies will be harder, but we'll also have Oric and Wolf to help out for the toughest battles. Ryuk remembers what Lothar said about the battle ahead being especially tough. "We could actually use you there."

Spoon in his mouth, Hiccup counts the Mitherfickers up. "Twixy, Liz, Wolfy, Elfie, He-Man, Marbles, Uncle Goblin. Fick me, seven is my lucky number!"

Enway, who has just brought a bowl of soup to Zaena, laughs. "Seven is everyone's lucky number."

"Alternative fact. Goblins hate the number seven. Notice there were no seven-story buildings in Jatla?"

Ryuk shakes his head. "I noticed there were no four-story buildings in Jatla."

"Four is also an unlucky number. Point is, kiddos, most goblins don't like the number seven, those superstitious fickers. Me? No problem with the number seven. I don't like the number six, though."

So, goblins that don't like the number seven are superstitious, but a goblin who doesn't like the number six isn't? Ryuk sighs. *Goblin logic.*

Oric nods to Ryuk. "Come, I want to show you something."

"Don't you want some soup, Ryuk?" Enway asks.

"I'll have his if he ain't eating." Hiccup finishes his bowl and is just about to toss it over his shoulder when Zaena gives him a dirty look. "Fine, I'll behave."

"I'll have it in just a moment," Ryuk says. "After, let's get to Waringtla and regroup with FeeTwix and Wolf."

Zaena smiles at the mention of FeeTwix's name. "Sounds good."

(0)__(0)

"He's huge now," Ryuk says as he takes in Yangu. Now bigger than Wolf, the snow dragon is easily big enough for a single person to ride. How he has grown so fast is beyond the Ballistics Mage. He knew they were supposed to mature quickly, and even though he was aware that it would only take a few in-game days, he's still shocked to see Yangu so large.

"Yeah, he's pretty awesome." Oric drops to his knees and the snow dragon comes running over to him.

Yangu stops when he sees Ryuk, and goes to the Ballistics Mage instead.

"Ah, I figured you bonded with him."

"I did." Ryuk places his hand on Yangu's snout. The snow dragon's scales are icy cold, his eyes as red as Enway's. As Ryuk touches his face, Yangu makes a purring sound in his chest.

"They grow so quickly here in Tritania, unnaturally so," says Oric. "He should be able to speak to you in a day or so."

"Was it different in Unigaea?"

"It was, but that's neither here nor there." A grimace spreads across the Unigaean's face.

"I see."

"There are a couple things I wanted to discuss with you. First, I see that Enway has taken on the powers of an Hourglass Mage."

"Lothar said you had some experience with this. Is it dangerous?"

Oric smiles and Ryuk swears he sees something flash across his eyes. "It is, but the power has been stripped of some of its potential here, and rightfully so."

"I think Lothar said that some of the pages had been taken out of her Book of Time."

Yangu falls onto his side and rolls over, letting Ryuk touch his soft belly.

"Yes, some pages have been removed." Oric smiles grimly. "There's a lot you don't know about me and my relationship with that book. Let's just say that, at least for now, it's better to not have access to all the spells. Now onto my second question: what is your guild's, or should I say *our* guild's, fighting style?"

"Fighting style?" Ryuk bites his lip as he thinks of a way to describe it.

"How does everyone fight?"

"Well, Zaena uses her swords. She has four swords. I'd say she's our tank, even if Hiccup is better armored."

"Right, she's Thulean. And Enway is an Hourglass Mage, so I know what she's capable of. What about the Swedish one?"

"FeeTwix has an endless inventory list. He uses firearms a lot and drinks potions to cover the damage penalty. Sometimes, he does ad reads during combat. Um, what else? His list can be pretty helpful because he has a lot of different items, not just guns."

"Interesting. And Hiccup?"

Ryuk thinks for a moment as to how he could describe Hiccup's fighting style. "He uses shields and axes. He is kind of our wildcard. If someone needs to be sent in as bait, or we need someone to come in for a rogue-like knife in the back, that's Hiccup. He's also our laziest member yet, for some reason, he seems to save the day quite a bit."

"And you?"

"I shoot marbles." Ryuk clears his throat. "Let me rephrase: I am a Ballistics Mage. My first weapon was a slingshot. One of FeeTwix's fans made me a Marble Gun, and Dirty Dave recently gave me a Marble Shotgun." Ryuk equips the shotgun and proudly shows Oric how it works.

"And your marble types? I am assuming there are types."

"I have explosive marbles, molten lava marbles, aqua marbles, gravity marbles, sword marbles, and clear marbles, which are wildcards."

"Like Hiccup?"

"Yes, unpredictable."

"Show me the sword marble."

Ryuk's Marble Shotgun pixelates out of existence and he takes his slingshot off his belt. He places the gray sword marble in the slingshot.

As he pulls back on the pocket, a sword stretches into existence.

Thwhip!

The sword digs into Enway's fence, startling Yangu. The snow dragon's natural response is to coat the sword with a sheet of ice.

"Damn," Oric says. "That was impressive."

"The dragon or the marble?"

"Both. I don't think Yangu is going to stay this size for long. He could come in handy in the Sabors…"

"Are you suggesting what I think you are suggesting?" Ryuk asks, his eyebrow raising.

Oric nods, a grin spreading across his face. "Let's bring him too."

CHAPTER 19: SWORDS AT PLAY

THE MITHERFICKERS, along with Oric and Yangu, spawn in Waringtla. If the passing giants are fazed by seeing such a motley crew, none of them say anything about it. Most are either on their way to work, to travel, or returning home to Waringtla. The richer giants have people carrying their bags, the poorer ones carry their bags themselves.

"Just goes to show you that classism is a giant issue. Ha! Like what I did there? Also, Snowballs is mine to ride, Ryuk. When he's bigger, you can saddle up next to me, but no fickery."

"Hiccup, no one said you could ride anything."

"That's why I'm calling dibs. And really, think about it. Zaena is too tall to ride, plus she's half lizard so that's some sort of species abuse."

"Thuleans ride dragons, goblin."

"And she's racist, and a young and moldable mind like the one Snowballs has doesn't need to deal with that bullshit. Besides, you shouldn't ride him because you need the exercise."

Ryuk shakes his head. "I need the exercise?"

"Marbles, you're never going to bulk up like Conan over here if you don't put the time in." Hiccup waddles over to Yangu. He blows some snot into his hands, flicks it out, and places the same hand on the dragon's neck. "Don't worry, boy, it's just you and me. Ignore these fickers."

"And why can't I ride it?" Enway asks.

"Because you're a high elf. High elves are too hoity toity to ride dragons. Have some self-respect. Okay, Snowballs, drop a little so your elder can hop on."

"Hiccup, we only have to walk like fifty meters to get to our airship."

"Marbles, let me have my fun."

The dragon responds to Hiccup's command, and soon, the only thing keeping the goblin's lemon pepper diffuser away from Yangu's upper back is a thin layer of fabric.

FeeTwix and Wolf spawn. "Fick! We got a dragon everybody! Looking good on there, Hiccup. The Fickers are going to love this."

"Want me to pose?"

"Do it!" the Swede says, his eyes black as a starless night.

While Hiccup poses, Wolf quickly makes his way over to Oric.

The two greet each other, and Ryuk notices a deep, genuine smile spread across Oric's face. The warrior drops to one knee next to his canine companion and begins stroking the fur on the side of his neck.

"Get a room, you two!" Hiccup calls over to them. "Now, Snowballs, to the airship!"

The ice dragon turns to the airships just as Zaena approaches him from the right. The Thulean makes a cooing sound and Yangu responds.

"Liz, quit distracting him with your cookie monster talk."

"We're not going to be able to take him on," Enway says, pulling Ryuk aside.

"Trust me, we'll get it on," Oric assures her. "Service animal, works every time."

"For a dragon?" FeeTwix asks skeptically. "I mean, maybe a pug or possibly a Yorkshire terrier, but a dragon?"

"Just say the goblin has a mental disorder and the dragon makes him feel better." Oric thinks for a moment. "Or better, that it stops him from lashing out."

Ryuk laughs. "I don't think anyone will believe that."

"Just trust me," Oric says, turning towards the ships. "Someone booked a ship for us, right?"

The Mitherfickers exchange glances. Enway finally says, "Really, guys? No one?"

"I was busy shooting my guns," FeeTwix says. "Also, one of my fans just won big league! She actually guessed how many times Hiccup said 'fick' yesterday. Congrats Ciayraa J.P.!"

"Oh, what the fick ever, Twixy. I hardly use that word. And what kind of name is J.P. anyway?"

"Those are called initials, Hiccup!"

"I thought you or Ryuk would be booking the tickets," the Thulean princess tells FeeTwix, interrupting the goblin just as he was about to start up a rant.

Ryuk shrugs. "That was the last thing on my mind."

"What was the first thing?" Hiccup asks.

"Helping you get revenge on Og."

The goblin chortles. "That's right! Fick would I like to be a fly on the wall when all those one percenters dig into their dessert tomorrow and light each other on fire."

"What?" Oric asks, an eyebrow raising.

"Long story, that I'll gladly tell you on the airship over to the Sabors. Now, who the fick has the tickets? Because I sure as fick don't, and Snowballs here can't speak yet, so he doesn't."

Wolf barks.

Wolf has the tickets? Ryuk looks at the big black beast just as a small envelope materializes in his maw.

"You've got to be fickin' kidding me."

Oric takes the envelope from Wolf's mouth. It is surprisingly not very wet. "It's from Lothar."

"And it has the tickets?" Zaena asks.

"It does, six to be exact."

"How the hell does a dog have an inventory list?" FeeTwix asks.

"If anyone knows," says Oric, "it's Lothar."

"Six tickets, eh? That's a bad number right there." Hiccup shudders. "And what about Snowballs and Wolfballs?"

"Service animals, like I said." Oric tucks the envelope down the front of his armor. He's worn the same leather armor since Ryuk first met him. It's high quality, but it doesn't look like it would protect him much. "Trust me on the service animals part. Just play along. Wait, you know what? Just be yourself. I'll handle it from there."

(0)__(0)

Oric indeed handles the situation once they reach the ticket gate. With a terrible cough, he explains that he has a bond with the wolf and it's the only thing keeping him alive, that they're going to visit a shaman in the Sabors who can cure him. He then explains that the snow dragon is Hiccup's comfort pet, that he gets really grouchy if Yangu isn't around.

"That seems feasible," the giant at the ticket counter says. He is heavyset with a soul patch that he's shaped into a pretty wicked spike. "You may all pass."

"Fick yeah," Hiccup whispers.

Because of the size of Wolf and Yangu, the Mitherfickers are told that they need to stay on the main deck. Ryuk would be fine with this if it weren't for the fact that they are heading to the northeastern quadrant of Polynya, where it is much colder than the southern half.

As the airship lifts into the air, he can feel the bitter cold of the northern slopes descending upon them.

Not that he hasn't felt this kind of cold before—there are parts of Ultima Thule that are even colder than this—but it's the humidity that makes it feel ten degrees colder.

Even now, as the rudders of the airship flap and the captain calls out for the masts to change direction, Ryuk can feel his chattering teeth as the sharp cold cuts into his bones.

"Marbles is turning blue. Who has a jacket?" asks Hiccup, who now sits on an overturned bucket next to Yangu.

FeeTwix, already in a parka, albeit sleeveless, raises his hand. One pixel-ly flash later and he holds a thick, white, fur-lined jacket. "How's this?" He tosses the jacket to Ryuk and the Ballistics Mage readily puts it on.

"Better," he says, still shivering.

Zaena now wears a robe, the neck of which is lined with a shiny, sable-like fur. Enway also has a parka, off white and form fitting.

"Yep, it's going to be cold," Oric says, going for a lavender cloak.

"Ha!" Hiccup points at the warrior's long cloak. "Never thought of you as a purple guy."

"Laugh all you want, goblin. I'll be warm while you'll be freezing your ass off."

"My ass is just fine, thank-you-very-much. And I don't need a jacket like you poofters. I have natural warmth." He touches his considerable girth. "Although my head is getting a little cold." He tries a gold helm but realizes quickly that this won't help. "Got any cool warm hats, FeeTwix?"

"I have a balaclava."

"A what? Keep the fickery to a minimum please, I'm looking for something warm."

FeeTwix shows Hiccup the balaclava, black with holes where the eyes, nose, and mouth should be.

"Oh, that's a balaclava!"

"You should know what it is, goblin. It is your nickname for Aiden."

"Who?" he asks Zaena. "Oh, you mean the Knight's ninja man? Fick, I don't remember calling him that. At any rate, hand that shit over."

Hiccup, still on an overturned bucket, puts the balaclava on and stretches it out in the process. "Nice, keeps my nose warm too."

"So, what's the plan when we get in the Sabors?" Ryuk asks, taking the lead.

Oric is the first to answer. "I'm assuming we will have to fight our way to the person who holds the runestone."

"Skadi," Enway says, "at least that is what Lothar told us."

"If Lothar told you this, it is true. He is rarely wrong," Oric says solemnly. "I've already discussed fighting strategy with Ryuk."

"Have you?" Zaena asks.

"Yes, and I'm aware of your fighting styles."

"And what's your style?" she asks, her eyes narrowing as she looks him over.

"Similar to yours. I'll go in front for maximum advantage. My weapon is short." He brandishes his buster sword, the tip of which is broken into three distinct peaks.

"That's right, it's broken."

"It is," he says as he admires the blade, "and I've purposefully kept it this way."

Zaena looks at him suspiciously. "That seems like a terrible idea."

"Do you want to see it in action?" he asks, not a hint of animosity in his voice.

A snarl now on her face, Zaena brandishes two blades, the *schwing* of which nearly causes Hiccup to hop off his stool. "Shit! You two are going at it? Damn, this is going to be fickin' tighter than a Jatlan chalupa trap. Twix, I got fickin' fifty thousand rupees on Liz. Marbles, popcorn, now."

"Relax, Hiccup, they're not actually going to fight each other...are they?" The Swede eyes Zaena suspiciously.

The Thulean drops into a battle stance, and using a move Ryuk has seen her do countless times, she propels her body forward with her ghost limbs. She comes down hard with both blades.

Much to her surprise, Oric manages to catch them *both* in the grooves of his buster sword.

"Ha!" Zaena kicks off his chest, but the warrior from Unigaea holds his ground. His legs spread wide, he gets into a defensive position, awaiting Zaena's next move.

"Kick his chiseled ass, Liz!"

Chiseled ass? Ryuk shakes his head.

"I'm glad to see the guild has warmed up to me. Are we finished here yet?" Oric asks, breathing heavily now.

Two more blades appear in the air above Zaena, held by her invisible ghost limbs.

"I guess not," Oric says, blowing a strand of hair out of his face.

"Easy, Babe!" FeeTwix says as the Thulean warrior princess spins into action.

Zaena performs an aerial blade attack which Oric swipes down as if she were a fly.

She flies backwards and is caught by FeeTwix, who takes a good bit of damage from one of her blades.

"Shit just got real!" Hiccup cracks up. "Marbles, popcorn, pronto."

"Shut up, Hiccup!"

Hiccup looks to Wolf, and Ryuk swears a grin spreads on Wolf's face.

Not you too, he thinks as Zaena springs back into action, this time going for a series of quick thrusts to distract from the fact that she's trying to use her ghost limbs to stab Oric from behind.

With little effort, Oric swings wide to knock her first blades aside; he follows his blade around to take out the ones now descending upon him from behind.

His strike connects and Zaena actually loses one of her blades, the first time Ryuk can recall seeing this happen.

She curses in Thulean as she backflips away.

"Everyone should bring it down a notch," Enway says.

"Like fick they should. We want blood! We want blood!"

The fact that this is happening on the deck of an airship doesn't seem to bother the Thulean. While some patrons have gathered to watch the fight from the upper deck, most ignore the clink and clank of the swords.

"Can we finish up now?" Oric asks.

Zaena bares her teeth.

"Fick, Liz, there's probably a dentist in Jatla that could fix that grill up for you. Cheap too. Don't even need healthcare, *Marbles*, to visit the dentist I know."

"Quiet!" Zaena rolls her neck back and goes for an attack that mirrors the way a cobra strikes.

She attempts multiple times to stab her blades at Oric, each attack blocked or parried.

Oric fights in a self-taught way, a style of combat that can only be developed from years and years of hand-to-hand combat.

He's broken a sweat, at least Zaena can say that, but he doesn't appear to be struggling other than that.

Zaena tries again for an aerial attack and Oric manages to strike both of her blades away.

Taken over by animosity, she lets loose a trio of throwing knives, which Oric easily blocks. With this as her distraction, the Thulean tries, scorpion-like, to drive her final blade into the top of Oric's head.

Flourishing his blade, he pulls right just as she increases her force, and uses her downward momentum to knock the blade from her ghost limb.

"Aye!" Zaena comes in with fists this time, which Oric dodges.

"Shit," FeeTwix says, concern growing on his face. "Hey, let's chill out, everybody! Who's up for, um, a game of Three Cards?"

"Fick yeah, Twixy, but you better have some jewels and only after somebody in this fight dies. I've got two dogs in this fight."

"What?" Ryuk asks as Oric blocks Zaena's chop with his forearm. "You mean Wolf?"

"Fick, Marbles, it's an expression. Shit, Liz, uppercut! Knock that ficker's mullet off! Thatta girl!" Hiccup uses his good hand to whistle for Zaena. "Chalupa, get that ficker's chalupa!"

Wolf barks, his comical expression from earlier all but gone. Ryuk looks at Wolf and his aggressive stance.

He's clearly looking for an opening, Ryuk gulps. *If I don't stop this soon...*

Before Ryuk can say anything, Oric knocks Zaena's arms out of the way and brings his splintered sword to a spot just beneath her chin.

She lifts her nose just a bit, still defiant as she stares him down with her orange eyes.

"You are strong," she says, not flinching.

Ryuk, on the other hand, feels the tension strike him like a wave. One glance at Enway and he sees her gasp.

"And you are fast and formidable," Oric says. "Shall we end this now?"

Zaena's face hardens. "If we must."

"We can pick it back up another day."

"Promise?"

"Promise." Oric sheathes his blade and turns away, not at all afraid of the fact that he's exposed his back to her.

He walks over to Wolf and places a hand on his head. "Easy, boy," he says as Wolf sits onto his back legs.

Zaena turns to FeeTwix; he comes in to hug her, but she holds him back with her ghost limbs. "He's strong," she says, bitterly.

"You're strong too, babe. Don't worry. Don't let it get to you."

Hiccup chortles. "Fick me, Liz, don't get your thong up in a bunch. You wear a thong, right? I used to, but that shit caused some massive chafing down south, so I had to leave it in Spewy's mailbox. Point is:

everyone loses, and everyone is a loser. Including He-Man over there. I'm sure he's had his ass handed to him."

"I have," Oric says as he runs his hand through his hair, "multiple times."

"See?"

"Quiet, goblin," she says half-heartedly.

"Come on, Lizzy, don't let that beefed up pug ficker get the best of you. Let me get the best of you instead! Howzabout a game of Three Cards? Who's in? We'll play for favors this time. Everyone has one favor they can give away or collect. Fick yes, this will be awesome. Marbles, get some paper and write everyone's name."

"I don't have any paper."

Hiccup shakes his head incredulously at Marbles. "What part of 'I'm trying to cheer Liz up' do you not comprehend? Find some paper. Shit, I'm sure someone has some. Fick, I bet I have some. Ask me for some paper."

Ryuk sighs. "Can I have some paper?"

"Fick no, Marbles, get your own paper!"

(0)__(x)

The airship stops at the entrance to the Sabors, which from what Ryuk can gather is the far end of a glacier. The icy ground hasn't prevented Unigaeans from thriving here, at least in the safer part of the territory. Like humans back in the real world, they'll live anywhere as long as they can get access to basics such as food and water.

"We'd better stock up," FeeTwix says as he turns towards the small village of nomadic herders. Similar to the herders they saw riding griffins at Lake Klattenhoff, back when Ryuk first tested his gravity marbles, the

Polynian herders are a hardy bunch, stout with faces that have been heavily lashed by the cold winds.

"Good idea," Hiccup says as he kicks over a snowdrift. He wears the balaclava FeeTwix gave him, and as usual, the bottom of his belly is visible. "Chalupa is going to shrivel if I don't get something warm in me."

"There isn't time to eat, goblin," says the Thulean, who walks at his side. Still reeling from her loss to Oric, Zaena hasn't said much over the last hour.

"Liz, if there's time to fick, time to shop, time to drink, or time to fight, there's time to eat. I'll get it to-go. If we're fickin' lucky, Dirty Dave will have a pop-up barbeque shop around here. I loves me a fickin' food truck."

Hiccup looks around at the scattering of yurts and the four or five buildings made of wood. The small settlement seems as if it can be deconstructed overnight and quickly moved to another location.

"Fick, I'm guessing there's no DD's BBQ, and the locals don't look so tasty either. Whatever. We'd better get some food in me, if we want to keep my mood stable."

Oric laughs. "You are the worst member of this group, aren't you?"

"No comment," says the Swede, who quickly turns back to the mirror in his hand so he can finish his ad read, something about a credit card offer from Chase Bank of America Fargo with a low interest rate of 35%, after an introductory interest rate of 25%, and other perks from using the card including a complicated point system that only kicks in if you maintain a credit balance that is at least 75% of the credit limit.

"Fick you, Twixy, and anyone stupid enough to consider what you just said a good offer. To answer your questions, Conan, the worst members of the Mitherfickers in order are Marbles, Elfie, Liz, Twixy, Snowballs, Wolf, you, and me. Who'd I miss?" He counts on his mechanical fingers for a moment. "Fick, two's company, three's a crowd, but eight is a fickin' orgy. Japanese orgy probably. Those fickers are probably into all sorts of weird sex shit. I would be if I lived on an island."

Ryuk rolls his eyes. "First, how did you know Japan is an island, and second, you do live on an island, a floating island?"

"It's a fickin' continent, Marbles, and while Tritania may not be contiguous—go ahead, I'll wait for you to look that word up—it doesn't mean it's a fickin' island." Hiccup's nostrils flare. "I smell food. Meat. Find the meat, Wolfy!"

Wolf barks and circles around the goblin.

"He usually doesn't like new people, at least goblins."

"What's that supposed to mean?" Hiccup asks Oric.

"He has liked women in the past."

"Have you seen the size of Wolf's red rocket? Fick yes he likes women, and I'd bet they like him too."

"Red rocket?" Enway looks to Ryuk, but before he can say anything, Yangu races forward. "Hey!" he calls after the ice dragon.

"Snowballs, get your ass over here."

Surprisingly, the dragon obeys Hiccup. He stops, and the goblin places his hand on his snout. "I know he has been a bad father, an absent dad, and I know we can't really say his name right now because he could retaliate, but I need you to be on good behavior, okay?"

Yangu coos.

"Good, we're on the same fickin' page."

"There's an item shop!" FeeTwix points at a small building with a carved sign over the door that reads WARES.

"That's right!" A gnome steps out from the back of the group, startling everyone but Oric.

"Fick." Hiccup bristles. "Don't do shit like that, Shorty!"

"Actually, the name is Walley, and that's my shop. Walley's Wares. Will you be joining me?"

Ryuk looks at the small wooden building, no larger than a shed. "There are eight of us."

"No problem, kiddo, there's plenty of room in Walley's Wares, no matter your guild count. We've crammed fifteen in there before. Let's go!"

Walley snaps his fingers, and suddenly the Mitherfickers are standing inside a huge shop, easily the size of Seiyu. Just to confirm they haven't actually left the village, Ryuk looks to the windows, which are now floor to ceiling, and beyond them to confirm the spot they were just standing. The air smells of apples and cinnamon, a crisp and inviting scent that leaves Ryuk smiling.

"I love Tritania," Enway says, and Ryuk can't help but agree with her.

"We'll cut to the chase, Walley, because we have places to go and quests to slay. We need potions," FeeTwix tells the gnome. "And lots of them."

"Fick yeah, and not the shitty ones," says the goblin. "Hopkins' or Cherry Apollos, bacon-flavor if you have them."

Walley runs his hand through his beard. He's in similar clothing to the herders they saw outside, but there's something very custom about it, as if he's gone to a good tailor but told him to make sure he blends in with the locals. "I have two cases of Apollos, one Hopkins'. Will you take the lot?"

"Bacon-flavored?" Hiccup asks.

"I was going to suggest we don't get bacon-flavored, but Wolf may like it," Oric adds. The Unigaean warrior stands on the outer rim of the group.

He seems a bit distant, and Ryuk has a feeling that he will always be this way.

As Walley informs Hiccup that one of the cases is bacon-flavored, Wolf and Yangu begin to play.

Wolf makes sure the growing snow dragon doesn't knock anything over, but fails miserably to prevent the dragon from freezing a mannequin in a fur-lined parka.

"That's all right," Walley says, his smile shattering. "But if you could get your animals under control... "

"Yangu." As soon as Ryuk says the words, the dragon rushes over to him and stops at his side. He sits, his blue scaled tale curling around to the front. As he looks up at Ryuk, Enway approaches and places a hand on his head.

Yangu bares his teeth in what looks to be a smile.

"So, three cases of healing potions. And what else, adventurers? Weapons? Tents?"

"Mana potions," Enway says, "just in case."

"A case you said?"

"No, just *in case*."

"A case will be fine," FeeTwix says. "And we're good with the other items."

"I see." Walley busies himself for a moment as he whips up a bill of sale. "There is one thing I like to offer all my guests, and that is a cup of Walley's Special Apple Cider."

"Does it have meat?" the goblin asks.

"No, but it will instantly increase your stamina and reduce hunger for the next several hours."

"Great, but I need meat. This body doesn't fuel itself, and especially not on fickin' apple juice."

"Um, very well, the rest of you may enjoy the cider and you, goblin, shall enjoy a bowl of Saborian dumpling soup made with ice fox jerky."

"I'll have what he's having," Oric says.

"Same," says Zaena.

"I see." Walley clears his throat. "Then that settles it, cider and dumpling soup!"

CHAPTER 20: FLAMING ZOMBIE DWARVES AND A SAD GAME OF TOUCH CHEST

"Fick me thrice and slather me in holy water, that soup was good!"

The Mitherfickers now stand on the outskirts of the small village, near a sign warning to be careful when entering the Sabors. From where they stand, the entrance is about thirty meters away, through a small gully that has been frozen over for ages. The air is bitingly cold, even with the fact that the sun is high in the sky.

While the cider did warm Ryuk some, it has done little to stop his face from feeling cold and his eyelashes from occasionally getting icy.

The guild continues forward, FeeTwix in the lead and now wearing a pair of knee-high snow boots, an impulse buy at Walley's Wares.

They hardly make it thirty meters before Hiccup complains about the pain in his back and calls Yangu over. The goblin mounts up and goes for one of the Cherry Apollos, which he eventually throws over his shoulder, almost hitting Ryuk in the head.

"Do you see that?" Oric asks about twenty minutes later, interrupting Hiccup's diatribe about child labor laws in Tritania and how more children should work so older people don't have to.

Ryuk pauses, his Extreme Focus skill kicking into gear. The world around him thins to a dark whisper as his eyes gloss over every small detail in the terrain. *Listen to the quiet voice* —Hajime's Oblique Quote comes to him.

It is then that he notices some of the snow on the ground has frozen over, and that the frozen snow looks to be in the shape of melted footprints.

"What could do that?" he asks.

"Everyone, get ready!" Armor forms on Oric's body. Thick pauldrons, a muscled breastplate, gauntlets, and tassets with gold inlay, Oric's armor makes him look incredibly formidable.

"What the fick is everyone going on about?" Hiccup asks, his eyes wide with fear under his black balaclava.

"The afflicted are near," Oric whispers.

"The afflicted?" Zaena's orange eyes settle on a bend in the road.

"Afflicted, huh?" FeeTwix's brow furrows as he reads messages from his fans. "Damn, that sounds bad, everybody."

A group of pyro-afflicted dwarves, six in total, step onto the path. Ryuk tries to get a read on the six flaming dwarves, but fails.

Their stats aren't listed, and there are no icons above their heads. *They could be any level,* he thinks, as he empties one of his mags and fills it with aqua marbles. *If anything will work, it'll be my new marbles.*

"Are they zombies?" the Swede asks, his shotgun appearing in his other hand. Like he was auditioning for a role in a zompac flick that hit all the tropes, FeeTwix does the one-handed shotgun pump with considerable flare.

"They're not exactly zombies." Oric flourishes his splintered buster sword. "Pyro affliction is a virus that causes the person's body to burn eternally. They are still alive, even though they are on fire."

"Did you say it's a virus? I've never heard of this shit," Hiccup says, fear evident on his face even though he wears a black mask.

"It's a virus from Unigaea, a sickness that came with one of the people I brought here."

"Are you fickin' kidding me?" Hiccup throws his hands in the air. "Does everyone now understand what I mean when I say immiNPCs bring disease, and that extreme vetting is pretty much the only way to make Tritania great again?"

"Just get ready, goblin!"

"Fick, Liz, when you put it like that." A small tomahawk appears in his mechanical hand, a shield the size of a stop sign on his left arm. He's still on Yangu's back; the dragon doesn't really know how to respond other than to observe the approaching dwarves cautiously.

"How do we kill the fire dwarves?" Zaena asks, all four of her swords now equipped. The flames lick off their bodies, obscuring their faces. "And why haven't they attacked us?"

"They haven't attacked us because their leader hasn't instructed them too," Oric says, his sword at the ready.

Their leader?

His Extreme Focus takes over his viewing pane, and Ryuk sees that one of the dwarves has a different glow than the others. He's a bigger dwarf too, the flames flickering off his body only adding to his size.

Zaena slashes her swords together. "Neutralize them?"

Oric nods at the Thulean, his fist tightening around his sword as an electrically charged shield appears on his free arm. "Arms and legs have to go, head too. One more thing: don't let them touch you. If they touch you, you become one of them."

"For how long?" Ryuk asks quickly.

He swallows hard, fear writ large on his face. "Don't know. In Unigaea, you could never use that same avatar again. I don't know what happens here, though. Wolf, stay back. Zaena, come with me."

Oric charges forward and meets the first afflicted dwarf, Zaena on his heels.

(0)__(0)

The Thulean warrior princess uses her limbs to springboard over Oric. She finishes her forward flip and takes off the arms of the afflicted engaging Oric.

The man falls and scoots on the ground towards Oric, hellbent on reaching the Unigaean warrior.

Six shots later and Ryuk quickly realizes that his aqua marbles have little effect on the afflicted. As soon as the marbles hit, they instantly dissolve, the air filling with steam.

Wolf barks from the sidelines just as Enway hits one of the smaller afflicted with a pink blast of magic.

The dwarf shrieks as the fires on his body rage even harder.

"What was that?" Ryuk calls over to her.

"Metastasize wound. It doesn't seem to be working though."

Oric hops right just as Zaena takes the legs from the afflicted that already lost his arms.

"Defensive magic only," he calls to Enway. "Time magic won't work on these fuckers. Wolf!"

The towering black wolf races by and Oric latches on to his body.

He rides Wolf like Hiccup? Ryuk thinks as the two sprint by, smoke, steam, and fire filling the air around them.

"Fuck you, fuck you, you're cool, I'm out!" FeeTwix laughs maniacally.

Clickety-boom!

The Swede creates a basketball-sized hole in the chest of one of the afflicted. He one-arm pumps his shotgun and blows another dwarf away. "Headshots work, people! And that goes for all three million of you watching my feed. When faced with zombies, or creatures based on zombies, your good ol' fashioned headshot will do the trick! Speaking of headshots..."

One of the afflicted comes up behind FeeTwix and he spins, popping the afflicted dwarf in the chest with his fire extinguisher. "Where was I? Ah! Speaking of headshots, it's time to tweak that resume! Employers care how you look, and what better way to show them how stunning you are than a high quality, professional headshot from Walgreens CVS. Now I know what you're thinking, you're thinking..."

"Fickin' huckster ass fickboy, Twixy, fick, stop doing ad reads and start killing the flaming zombie dwarves!" Hiccup's eyes go wide. "We've got company, Mitherfickers, more dwarves approaching."

"I've got it, Hiccup!" A grenade appears in FeeTwix's hand. He pulls the ring with his teeth, aims, and throws.

Shit, shit, shit, Ryuk thinks as he quickly races through his options. *My gravity marbles could help, as could my sword and clear marbles.*

The problem is, he's so used to going with ballistics that he doesn't really have these loaded up. His shotgun is loaded with explosive marbles, and all but one of his Marble Gun mags are either molten marbles, molten black mix, or black and sword marbles.

BOOM!

FeeTwix's explosion sends flaming dwarves and debris into the air.

"Headshots work! Grenades too!" FeeTwix shouts to either his fans or the Mitherfickers. Ryuk really can't tell.

Wolf skids to a halt and Oric uses the forward momentum to toss himself forward. His splintered sword in hand, he swipes his beast of a weapon at the leader of the afflicted. The dwarf, his fists in flames, tries to catch Oric's blade.

The dwarf's hands fly away, hit the ground and pulse.

Oric, nearly as fast as Zaena, jukes the leader out, making him think his next attack is going to come in from the right. When it comes in from the left, the leader dwarf is caught off guard, resulting in a downward swipe from Oric, which takes the dwarf's head and arm off.

"Hiccup, I need Yangu!"

"Fick you, Marbles, this is my ride!"

Ryuk grits his teeth. "Dammit, Hiccup! Yangu, here, now!"

The snow dragon stops dead in his tracks and bucks up, throwing the goblin off.

"Yoy!" Hiccup crash-lands into a boulder-sized hunk of ice. The goblin's mechanical hand immediately comes to his lower back; he groans and moans as a healing potion takes shape in his hand.

Once he's finished his first potion, he equips a second.

"What are you thinking?" Enway calls over to Ryuk as Yangu races over to him. Not knowing how she can help, Enway has her wand at the ready, tracking the combat.

Meanwhile, Zaena has taken on three pyro-afflicted dwarves. She hops around like a doped up Russian gymnast, simultaneously engaging and dodging a myriad of sloppy attacks.

"Aye!" The Thulean throws her whole body into an attack and cuts the arms and head off a dwarf still in a horned helm.

"I've got a plan!" Ryuk points at the afflicted about fifty meters away, their numbers strengthening as they swell towards the Mitherfickers. "Yangu," Ryuk asks, looking into the eyes of the snow dragon. "Are you ready to do this?"

"What are you going to do?" Enway asks, concern in her eyes.

The dragon barks, his eyes now tracking the approaching afflicted. Ryuk loads three aqua marbles into his slingshot and pulls back on the pouch.

"You know what to do?" he asks Yangu.

A vicious smile stretches across the dragon's face.

"Then let's do this!"

(0)__(x)

Ryuk pulls back until the slingshot is at its breaking point. Images from the last few days flash across his mind's eye: Tamana standing over him, Tesla about to decommission Hajime, his brother punching him.

His muscles tense as he pulls back even further.

Warmth spreads from the slingshot to his hand and he ignores it.

I've got this.

He looses the three aqua marbles and they soar through the air.

Yangu rears his head back and spits a thick stream of blue flames at the aqua marbles. As soon as his blue fire connects with the marbles, a four meter long ice scythe takes shape.

Ryuk hardly has time to lower his slingshot before the ice scythe sails through the air, decapitating nearly every pyro-afflicted dwarf advancing on the Mitherfickers.

Skill level up!

New skill learned!

Level up!

Ryuk quickly notices his Bonding Trust has moved to level two.

He's also gotten a new skill.

Skill: Ice Scythe

Level One: Work in tandem with your bonded animal to create a scythe made of ice.

Requirements: Level 20 Mage, Bonding Trust level two or higher.

"Wow!" Enway cheers. "That was awesome!"

"Three more to kill!" A bewildered look in her eyes, Zaena flings herself towards the remaining flaming dwarves using her ghost limbs.

She spins into action, her swords flailing all around her and she goes from limb to limb. The Thulean finishes the last afflicted and drops to her haunches, her back to the group.

"Damn, Liz, if only you'd done that back there to Conan. Ha! And fick me, Marbles, if it weren't for the fact you just saved our asses, I'd be pissed about the way you stole Yangu out from under me, but seeing how I didn't get my ass burnt and I got to enjoy a few potions, I'm good. Liz..."

Hiccup's mocking smile fades as the Thulean turns to them. "Shit! Zaena, I mean, Liz, shit! Are you okay?"

Ryuk gasps as the Thulean approaches, an infection visible on her right hand. Her skin has cracked, and beneath it, moving lava pulses, some portions bright red and the others charcoal.

"Babe!" FeeTwix cries out.

"Don't touch it," Oric says.

"Get out of my way!" FeeTwix cries. He tries to move around Oric, but the Unigaean warrior steps in front of him again.

"Relax," Oric says, his hand rising to the sword on his back.

The Swede pumps his shotgun one-handed and presses it to Oric's chest. His eyes flash blue. "Out of my way," he says, his voice drained of all its normal color.

"Put your gun down," Oric grits. "And don't do anything stupid. We don't know how the infection works in Tritania. It could spread if you touch her hand, or it could spread if you touch any part of her."

"I'm warning you."

"Cool it, FeeTwix. Think this through, and please lower your gun."

Wolf circles around to FeeTwix's side, his head down, his lips raised in a snarl.

"Relax, FeeTwix," Ryuk starts to say.

"Please, FeeTwix," says Enway, "think about what you're doing."

The Swede glances at Wolf and back to Oric.

"That's right, FeeTwix. That dog and I have been doing this for quite a while. If I don't get you," Oric wraps his hand around the handle of his sword, "he will."

Hiccup claps his hands together, startling everyone. "First of all, fick you, Tarzan, and the wolf you rode in on. Second, I'll fickin' test it."

The goblin's chainmail disappears.

"Liz, don't listen to He-Man, touch me with your non-infected hand and let's see if it spreads. If it doesn't, keep touching me. And while we're at it, Marbles, bring me a healing potion."

Ryuk starts to tell the goblin he can equip his own potion but decides otherwise, especially after seeing the goblin take another step closer to Zaena.

"Here," he says, healing potion in hand. A look left and he sees that FeeTwix has lowered his weapon, his face white with shock.

"In my mouth, Marbles, put the potion directly in my mouth."

"You can still use your hands."

"I'm aware, but if I'm about to turn into a flaming goblin with a healthy head of pink hair, I want to go out on a fickin' bang, and that bang is having someone feed me a potion!" He puckers his lips. "Now pour."

"Hiccup, this is a serious moment," Ryuk says, his voice lowering. Zaena stands in front of them now, shock still evident in the way she holds her shoulders.

"Dammit, Marbles," Hiccup says, a hint of something genuine behind his normal goblin snarl, "I know this is serious, kid. I just...I just wanted to make her laugh. Fick. We may have to kill her right here, and if that's the case, I get to do the honors because, you know, goblins versus lizards and whatnot."

"I will kill you two years before you kill me," Zaena says, her voice quivering.

"Yeah, whatever, Liz, I'm just trying to make Marbles laugh over here, everyone lighten up a bit."

"Are you serious right now?" Ryuk whispers.

"Marbles, if you haven't figured it out already, I handle tragedy with comedy. Now, stop acting like a genderfluid bush beater and feed me the potion."

Oric clears his throat.

"Quiet, Tarzan, and I don't see you stepping in to stop her from touching me like you did FeeTwix."

"That's because I don't like you."

"Well, fick, someone bring out the Festivus pole, so we can all air our grievances. Marbles, potion, pronto."

The potion lifts out of Ryuk's hand.

"I'll give it to you..." Liz says with a hint of sadness in her voice. "Hiccup."

"That'll work too," he says, his voice lower than before.

"You ready?" Zaena asks.

"I was born ready to die, Mitherfickers." The goblin opens his mouth wide, and from where he's standing, Ryuk can see that Hiccup has a few rotten molars, which may explain the smell that usually wafts around him.

No, those are farts, Ryuk reminds himself as Zaena pours the potion into Hiccup's mouth.

"Damn." Hiccup burps and Wolf barks. "See that, Conan? You may not like me, but your pooch and I, fick, let me be the first to tell you, we go way back. Way back. Rode that bitch all the way through the catacombs connecting Kayi to Polynya."

"Whatever."

Hiccup pulls his shoulders back and shows Zaena his bare chest. "Now fickin' do it, Liz, do it!"

"Are you sure?" She lifts her *non* pyro-afflicted hand.

"Fick yes, I'm sure," the goblin says, tears in his eyes. He sniffs, sucks back some snot, and sniffs again.

"Someone tell Spewy that...fick...don't tell him I love him, but *do* tell him that I think of the liddle ficker fondly every now and then. And not in a poofty fruit bat way. I'm charging you with that, Twixy. Spewy lives in Jatla, in the Venom Spur District. Remember that. And Marbles, Spewy gets the five percent you promised me after all is said and done."

"Two percent."

"Four."

"Three."

"Fine." Hiccup slams his fist against his chest. "Fick, Liz, do it already, *do it*. I'm losing my nerve over here! Touch my chest!"

CHAPTER 21: NEW RECRUITS FOR THE SHINIGAMI

Kodai stands before the serpent woman, a vicious sneer on his face. "I have news, news I believe you would like to hear."

An image of naked Tesla on top of him, her hands pressed against his shoulders flashes across his mind's eye. He blinks it away.

Now isn't the time.

"Sophia is in Tokyo, yes?"

The woman slithers towards Kodai, her breasts swaying as she moves through the OMIB. It is still something Kodai has to get used to, the OMIB, the endless galaxy around them even as they stand on relatively solid ground.

He looks down to see stars beneath him, as if he were standing on a glass floor overlooking the Milky Way.

Only in a digital world...

"That's right." Kodai touches his temples, afraid that she's read his mind to the point that she knows about his relationship with Tesla. If she has, she doesn't offer any indication that it bothers her.

"Yes, since we've bonded, I can read your thoughts. But back to the information you have brought me: FeeTwix and Sophia have both come to Tokyo to meet your brother." She grins, green algomagic flashing across her eyes. Her face is normally obscured by shadow but today he can see her features, her solemn expression, her vampiric fangs. "You realize what this means, right?"

"Not quite," Kodai admits. "I know that the Mitherfickers have met with the Knights, and that Ryuk used to be in the Knights, but I don't see why it is they have joined together in the real world."

"Sophia used to work for the DREAM Team. Are you familiar with this?"

"No."

"Dream Recovery Extraction and Management Team, a program funded by America's Federal Corporate Government, or the FCG, to help free players who were trapped in digital worlds. Since the Proxima Company held the biggest number of digital worlds, the Dream Team mostly focused on freeing people who were trapped in those."

"I don't understand what this has to do with the Knights."

"Sophia knows what she is doing, I'll give her that. The Knights are the guild that was started by the Dream Team when the team first came to Tritania."

"Why did they come to Tritania?"

"In search of my brother, Luther. My father, Strata Godsick, founder of the Reapers and the Revenue Corporation…"

Kodai nods. He is all too familiar with the Reapers, having listened to the serpent woman's explanation of the murder guild after their first encounter.

The name of their guild, the Shinigami, was in homage to the Reapers, the Japanese word Shinigami meaning "god of death," a common translation of the word "reaper." He also knew that some of the tech they had, weapons they had yet to use, were originally created by Strata Godsick in conjunction with his Meridian Circle.

The woman's expression sours. "My father was hellbent on finding my brother. Luther was the favorite of the family. Anyway, that's how the Knights of Non Compos Mentis were formed, and I was once part of their guild."

"You were a Knight?"

"For a time." She laughs. "A short time, really. I got close to them using a Dark Mage avatar that I'd worked on for a while named Veenure."

"So your name is Veenure?"

"No, my name is Victoria, but you may call me Veenure. I created the name to pay homage to my father's company, the Revenue Corporation."

"How does that name pay homage?"

"It's an anagram, but we can discuss my time in the Knights later. The point is that Doc, one of the members of the Knights and the old fucker in charge of tech for the Dream Team, developed a weapon..." She clenches her fists together. "He developed a weapon that trapped people in the OMIB, in this space."

"That's why you're here?"

"Yes, after my true identity was revealed, I was shot by the weapon Doc invented, cursed to spawn in the OMIB eternally."

Kodai grinds his teeth together. With FeeTwix and Sophia in Tokyo, now is the time to take them out, to act on this information. "We can go after them as soon as tonight. I have people at MercSecure who will be able to trace Sophia."

"You won't be able to trace Sophia," Veenure says. "Doc would never allow that."

"Is Doc still alive?"

"No, Doc is dead. But his RPC, a faun, is alive and well. I don't think he spends much time in Tritania though. I only see the flash of his D-NAS every now and then. My point is," she hisses, "it will be impossible to find Sophia because of Doc. I hate that fucking faun, but he is an expert, and he doesn't make mistakes."

"FeeTwix," Kodai says suddenly.

"Yes, FeeTwix, that's who you should be going after. Doc may have put some identity hiding protocols in place, but then again, maybe not. Find FeeTwix while he is in Tokyo and that will lead you to Sophia, who may very well hold the missing piece to the puzzle."

"I've thought of another way we can get this missing piece," Kodai says.

"As have I." She offers the young crime lord a rare smile. "I like your idea, though, you first."

Kodai places his hands behind his back and stares at Veenure's face, aware that she has already read his thoughts, but still excited to share his idea with her. Behind her, a black hole opens up, a purple rim of energy around it as it fades back into the starry galaxy.

"There is one member in the Mitherfickers who I am one hundred percent positive we could break," he says. "I don't know what he knows, but I assume he knows something."

"Even if he doesn't or can't remember, I may be able to get inside his head and go through what has been discussed around him. The goblin should be our target then."

"I fucking hate that goblin, but he's got a big mouth, and I don't think we'd even need to use your powers to figure out what the Mitherfickers are hiding, or why Sophia is in Tokyo."

"Then we'll get the goblin, now, while they are in the Sabors."

"You said you had an idea, right?" Kodai asks, now mesmerized by the green glow of her eyes.

"I do," she hisses. "With the Knights in the picture, and the fact that they don't seem to be going anywhere, we need to increase our strength. Many of the Knights are level ninety or higher. This was also something I received when I was a member of the guild. We were all granted an incredible, once in a lifetime level increase. Further, if the Knights are ever truly in trouble, they can call upon a large group of NPCs, from British Assassins to the infamous Dirty Dave to help them. We need leverage, and that leverage could come through stronger members."

"But where will we get stronger members?"

Veenure's hand comes up and a sliver of silver magic forms into a small balloon. The balloon floats over to Kodai, and as soon as he touches it, it turns to ink and spreads up his arm.

Everything is suddenly clear to him.

"The Drachma Killers?" he asks. "Who are they?"

"A murder guild from Unigaea, the same world that Oric Rune and his Tagvornin wolf have come from. They've operated in Tritania from time to time, and using old tech provided by Proxima Smugglers, they've leveled quite nicely."

"And they will cost real world money, correct?" Kodai asks, the silver magic pooling in his sclerae.

"Yes, but I thought this may be something you can arrange."

"It is most definitely something I can arrange."

"Good," she says, "then it is settled. We'll work on recruiting the Killers, and in the meantime, you'll get the goblin."

CHAPTER 22: SAMSQUANCH

ZAENA LOWERS HER HAND. Hiccup's eyes still squeezed shut, the goblin asks Ryuk to come take a look at his chest to see if the pyro affliction has spread to him.

"I told you it didn't, goblin."

"Fick, Liz, I'm getting a second opinion here. Everyone should get a second opinion, especially if they have healthcare provided by their employer, ahem. Marbles."

"Whatever." Ryuk steps forward and examines Hiccup's chest. Other than a few curled hairs, he seems fine. "The infection didn't spread."

"Whoo!" Hiccup does his best Ric Flair impression. "Uncle Goblin lives to see another fickin' day. Good thing too, I enjoy barbeque, but would prefer not to become it."

"There has to be something we can do," FeeTwix says as he scans messages from his fans. He nods, bites his lip, and hunches over, his shotgun nearly touching the ground. "Fuck."

"Nothing?" Oric asks.

"Nearly four million people and none of them have heard of a cure for this." FeeTwix's mirror appears in his hand and he looks down at it. "Everyone, I'm signing off for a moment while I deal with this. Please understand."

"Take her to Lothar, he'll know what to do," Oric says.

FeeTwix approaches Zaena and takes her infection-free hand.

"You don't have to come with me," she says, "I can go back to the airships alone."

"No way," he tells her. "The rest of you can continue on." The Swede turns to Ryuk. "I'll join the party as soon as I can." The look on his face is something Ryuk has never seen before, and he truly feels for him.

"I understand." Ryuk steps in front of Zaena and bows to her. "Good luck."

"She'll get through this," Hiccup mumbles, "we'll get through this too. Twixy, Liz, good fickin' luck, and put a fickin' glove on that hand or something. Fick, I think I may have an oven mitt in my list here."

Hiccup's mechanical hand comes up as an oven mitt takes shape.

"Where did you get that?" she asks.

"Og's kitchen. What? You think I'd get all lubed up to go down a ventilation shaft and *not* steal something?"

The oven mitt lifts into the air and Zaena quickly places it on her afflicted hand.

"It may catch fire," she says.

"Well, that's just something you'll have to deal with later. Fick, this is a tragedy. Don't worry, Hiccup, you'll get through this." The goblin looks at Ryuk. "What? My therapist told me speaking to myself in third person is the best way to deal with situations like this."

"I can try my Speed Heal spell," Enway says.

"It won't work," says Oric, who stands a few feet away from them next to Wolf. There are still bodies burning all around the Mitherfickers, and it is an odd place to be having a conversation.

"Let's freeze your hand for now," Ryuk suggests. "And then put it in the oven mitt."

"Freeze it?"

"Not fully, just to cool it down. Yangu can do it." He places his hand on the snow dragon's neck.

"That sounds like a great fickin' way to lose a limb."

"I may already lose a limb," Zaena reminds him.

"Hey, it ain't so bad." The goblin knocks on his mechanical arm. "Fick me! Twix, you got another arm in that list of yours?"

"No, I don't," he says his eyes filling with hope. "But that could work."

"A mechanical arm?" Zaena takes a deep breath.

"Trust me, Liz, it ain't so bad. Shit gets cold at night though if you don't sleep on it. Also, if you've forgotten you have it, and you go to wipe your starfish, that can be a liddle ficked."

"Starfish? What the hell is this starfish you always talk about?" Ryuk asks.

"Fick me, Marbles, you don't know what a starfish is? It's goblin slang for asshole."

Ryuk drops his head into his hands. "So every time you've mentioned starfish, you're talking about an asshole?

"Yes, as in 'your brother is a dirty starfish banger.' But let's not open the urban goblin dictionary at the moment. Point is, Lizzy, having a mechanical arm ain't too shabby."

"I can go to Steam now," FeeTwix says, his finger lifting to log out.

"But," Zaena gulps, "I don't want a mechanical arm."

"Selfish much, Liz? Do you think I wanted this goddamn contraption? You don't hear me bitching."

"You always bitch," Oric says.

"He-Man again? Fick, I knew we should have left you back in Kayi."

"We need to keep moving forward," Oric says, "and I'd suggest you see Lothar before you get a mechanical arm. Also, we don't know if pyro affliction is a blood based disease or not. You may take her arm only to realize it has already spread to other parts of her body. I'm sorry to sound harsh here, but the more we stand around and argue about this, the less time we have."

"He's right," Ryuk says. "You two get to Waringtla and see Lothar. We'll join you as soon as we're done here."

"And I'll rejoin you guys if I'm able," FeeTwix says.

"I want to fight too." Her voice quivering, Zaena turns away from her guildmates. "I'm sorry for this."

"It's not your fault," Enway says. "If anyone will know what to do, it's Lothar. You saw all his books. Just don't lose hope."

After another round of goodbyes, FeeTwix and Zaena turn back to the entrance of the Sabors, still holding hands.

(0)___(0)

Our dynamics are definitely different, Ryuk thinks about an hour later, after they've had a few more fights. He's leveled again—the enemies here are really hooking it up with EXP—as have Enway, Hiccup and Yangu.

Wolf and Oric have fallen into their own groove, providing some pretty incredible offense. Years of digital combat under their belts, the two cut through most of the enemies they've come into contact with, leaving the scraps for the rest of the Mitherfickers.

But the others have their specialties as well. Enway provides backup support, her delayed strike ability continuing to take enemies off guard. Unlike the army of flaming dwarves at the beginning of the Sabors, the enemies deeper in have been rather weak, mostly ice-based or some type of abominable animal.

They even fought a polar bear, which was an easy kill for Oric and Wolf.

Ryuk has mostly provided backup support, but hasn't used his bond with Yangu as much as he would have liked. This is due to Hiccup, who again has taken to riding the growing young dragon so he doesn't have to walk.

"Up ahead," Oric says, his face red from the cold.

Ryuk follows his finger to a castle cut into the ice.

A flurry of snow blows past the group, whipping at Ryuk's hood and blurring his view. Enway steps forward and equips a mana potion.

"Gimme, gimme, gimme," Hiccup says from his perch on the snow dragon's back. "I need a boost now that I've seen a castle made of ice. Getting jelly over here."

"You don't even use magic," Ryuk reminds him.

"Mana potions are an acquired taste, Marbles."

"And you've somehow acquired it?"

"Fick yes, I have."

"Sorry, all gone," Enway says, finishing the bottle.

"I see how it is," Hiccup says, equipping his own bottle.

"How many of those have you drunk in the last hour?" asks Oric.

"I have a problem, okay? And no, I'm not ashamed to admit it. I have a fickin' problem and that's that. With Liz gone, Conan over here has taken it upon himself to press my buttons. Look, pal, we got bigger problems, such as the fact that the tower you're going on about sits on top of a freaking wall of ice blocking our path."

A wall of ice? Ryuk was so busy using his Extreme Focus to cover their three and nine that he has failed miserably to look at their twelve.

Sure enough, the ice is solid, with no real option that he can sense to enter the tower. *Even Zaena with her ghost limbs would have a problem scaling that wall.*

The thought of the Thulean and her infection hits Ryuk hard.

"She won't die," he reminds himself as he looks up at the wall of ice. "She'll make it through this."

The message he just received from FeeTwix flashes again, awaiting his response.

FeeTwix: We're close to Waringtla. It was the last airship of the day, faster than the morning one. I'll be in touch as soon as I know what happens next.

Ryuk quickly fires off a message.

Ryuk: Tell Zaena good luck. Don't let her beat herself up over this.

"Talking to yourself again, Marbles, or are you trying to figure out a way for us to get to the top of that wall of ice? Fick, you know I'm not one for climbing."

"See any other way?" Oric asks Enway. Their breaths visible, the Hourglass Mage and the Unigaean warrior take another look around.

"Not currently," the Hourglass Mage says as she knocks on the wall of ice.

"Fick me, what good is that going to do?"

"Testing its thickness, Hiccup."

"Nope," the goblin snorts. "Not going to make a thickness joke. I'm above that type of toilet humor. Marbles, you're in charge here, right?"

"Um, sure?" Ryuk looks to Oric and Oric shrugs.

While the Unigaean warrior took charge earlier when FeeTwix tried to run to Zaena, he's since relaxed a bit. The more Ryuk watches him fight, the more he realizes that this odd combination of control and free-for-all is not only ingrained in his psyche, it's also ingrained in his fighting style.

"Well, fick, tell us what to do then!"

"We need to get to the top of that wall of ice."

"Gee, you think, Marbles?"

"And I need Yangu to do it."

Hiccup considers this. "He is my ride, you know."

"Hiccup."

"Marbles."

The two lock eyes and for the first time in their guild's history, *Hiccup* is the first to look away.

Skill level up!

Skill: Inspire Others

Level Four: By inspiring others, you induce them to follow your orders. Higher levels allow for manipulation of enemies and random strangers.

Requirements: LUCK > 20

"Great, you win, Marbles," Hiccup says as he gets down from Yangu. "But this better be fickin' good."

Ryuk places his hand on Yangu's neck and bends so they are now face to face. He stares deeply into the ice dragon's red eyes as he thinks the phrase: *make some stairs.*

The dragon's left eyebrow rises.

"Make some stairs," Ryuk whispers.

Wolf barks and he ignores him.

"I can help." Ryuk shows Yangu his Marble Shotgun.

He pops the canister open and quickly gets to replacing the explosive marbles with aqua marbles. Once he's loaded all twenty-four available slots, he aims his weapon at a natural starting point and fires his aqua marble at the wall.

Yangu freezes it upon impact and as Ryuk predicted, it makes a single stair, thinner on one side than the other, but a stair nonetheless.

"Brilliant," Oric says. "That will totally work."

Ryuk nods to Yangu and they begin.

After another canister, the two have made a set of stairs all the way to the top. They then focus on improving the stairs, making them wide so Wolf and Yangu can use them.

"And to think that soon, you'll be able to fly, eliminating the need for these stairs all together," Ryuk says as they start a fourth round of solidifying the platforms.

Once they're done, Enway is the first to test them out. She starts up the ice wall, going from step to step with little effort, stopping in the middle. "You guys coming?" she calls down to them.

"It's inventive, I'll give you that," Hiccup sighs. "But now I have to walk up a flight of stairs, which is a great way to give a 154-year-old goblin a heart attack."

"It will be good for you," Ryuk says.

"You sure you can't give me a piggyback ride?"

"No."

"Fick, fine." The goblin adjusts his considerable girth, burps, and snorts. "Stairs it is."

(0)__(0)

After some clever footwork, and a lot of grumbling from the goblin, the Mitherfickers reach the top of the ice wall. They now stand about ten meters away from a gate made of ice. The gate is closed, frozen over, and it is times like this that FeeTwix's near limitless inventory list would come in handy.

But he's not the only one with quick access to fire.

Ryuk grabs his Magic Slingshot and puts a pair of molten marbles in. "Everyone stand back."

"Fick, I'm just trying to stand," Hiccup says, out of breath. "That was quite the fickin' climb. Boy fick, I don't think a goblin half my age could get their tosh up that wall. It was clearly not designed for the distinguished members of our guild." A healing potion appears in his hand. "Fick, don't say anything, Tarzan. Just let me warm my belly."

He drinks the potion and tosses it over his shoulder, where it plinks off one of the ice steps and falls into the valley below.

A valley. Ryuk can see now, from their vantage point, that the ice wall and its castle have been built into the wedge of a narrow valley.

Looking at the ice below, and the way it has been smoothed over again and again, it's hard to tell that there was ever anything but a wall in the space.

"Everyone ready?" Ryuk asks, returning to the task at hand.

His hand warmed by the molten marbles, he waits to get the confirmation from Enway and Oric. Once they give him the nod, he fires off the molten marbles at the gate of ice.

A terrible scream rocks the valley as the ground shakes. Snow from the surrounding cliffs begins to fall.

"Fick, Marbles, you caused a damn avalanche!"

"No, it's not that," Oric says, his splintered sword in one hand and his electric shield in the other. "He's awoken something."

"Fick!" Hiccup quickly gets as close to Oric as he can.

"What are you gathering around me for?" the Unigaean warrior asks, his shoulders bristling.

"Fick, I'm not. Just, fick, did you hear that scream? It couldn't be. It couldn't fickin' be."

"Couldn't be what?" Enway asks. Wolf barks himself into a frenzy as the gate begins to melt away.

"Not gonna say it because fick those things."

"Dammit, Hiccup, give us some insight here!"

"Sheesh, Marbles, you sure know how to talk to an elder. Fick. You want insight? I'll tell you what my superstitious ass thinks it is." He gulps, fear in his eyes. "I think it's a..."

The gates crumble forward and a towering creature, just a few heads shorter than Lothar, breaks through the wall. The creature has the face of an older bodybuilder, his head puny atop his muscled body.

"Jesus Murphy, it's a samsquanch!" Hiccup hauls ass over to the edge of the ice wall. He hops down to the first stair he can reach and hides.

Samsquanch Level 39

HP: 2399/2399

ATK: 287

MATK: 0

DEF: 341

MDF: 382

LUCK: 6

The beast drops to his two front arms like a gorilla. His head rears back and he roars, spit hurtling from his open mouth.

"Got it!" Ryuk zips an aqua marble into the samsquanch's mouth and the beast starts choking.

New skill learned!

Skill: Waterboard

Level One: Fire an aqua marble into an enemy's mouth and simulate drowning, causing a momentary stunning effect

Requirements: LUCK > 21

While no damage is taken, the samsquanch can't seem to get a grip on his choking. So distracted is he by the water caught in his throat, the beast hardly sees Oric run towards him, broken buster sword in hand.

The Unigaean warrior drives his three-pronged sword into the back of the creature's leg, ripping through its calf muscle.

-181 HP! Critical hit!

The samsquanch roars in pain and swipes at Oric. He misses, but is able to get the warrior on his second swing.

Oric flies right, but recovers with a roll. Meanwhile, Wolf advances towards the beast, raring to go. He jumps, latches onto the samsquanch's wrist, and is also tossed aside.

-89 HP!

A pink blast of delayed magic hits the samsquanch in the back of the head, courtesy of Enway.

Ryuk follows up her attack by firing a mag of sword and black marbles, which the creature tries to block with its bony forearm.

The monster cries out as the marbles explode and the blades pierce its flesh. One of Ryuk's blades, propelled by a marble explosion, is flung into the creature's eye, popping it like a zit.

-199 HP!

He quickly glances to see where Hiccup has run off to. *Damn goblin,* he thinks when he can't locate him.

Yangu, still on the outskirts of the battle, waits for Ryuk's instruction to attack. An aqua marble now in the pocket of his slingshot, he whistles for Yangu to get ready.

Ryuk pulls back and looses the marble; Yangu blasts it and it forms a giant ice pick, which pierces the samsquanch's chest.

-178 HP!

"We've got this!" Oric calls out as he gets back to his feet.

He doesn't see the woman now sitting in one of the windows, her legs hanging out as she watches the battle with a disgusted look on her face.

As Oric approaches the snow monster, his blade at the ready and his electric shield in his free hand, a great blast of blackened lightning tears through his body.

Instakill!

Held by a small black cloud, the woman lowers to the ground in front of the critically injured samsquanch.

The mysterious woman wears white fur and her bosom is exposed. Her clothing is tight, her legs wrapped in furry boots. Around her neck, attached to a golden band, is the final runestone.

Instakill!

She finishes off the samsquanch and turns to Ryuk with a grin on her face. "You've brought me the other two runestones, yes?"

Skadi Level 48

HP: 3315/3315

ATK: 217

MATK: 369

DEF: 281

MDF: 413

LUCK: 28

It's her! Ryuk's mind cries.

Fury in his eyes, Wolf rushes towards the woman and is tossed backwards by a great bolt of black lightning.

Instakill!

Enway points her wand at the woman, her hand trembling. "Give us the final runestone."

Skadi laughs. "If only it were that simple." Her lips lift into a snarl. "But I will make this quick."

Black lightning swirls up her arms and groups around her neck. Sleek, electrified dark armor moves down her body until it appears as if she's in a sparkling black bodysuit.

Her eyes flash yellow and a sinister smile forms on her face. "Ready?"

CHAPTER 23: CLASS ACT

YANGU CRIES OUT and lowers his head, his throat puffing as he prepares to freeze Skadi solid. Ryuk's never seen him so focused, so charged. The blue scales on the back of his neck have lifted, his red eyes are fixed and furious.

"No!"

Ryuk watches in horror as a bolt of black lightning strikes the young snow dragon. His scales sizzle, and he screeches in agony as he falls to the ground.

Yangu's body quivers as he tries to get back up off the ground.

Instakill!

"Fuck you!" Ryuk unloads a magazine of explosive molten marbles at the woman, his marbles completely absorbed as they connect with her electric black armor.

Once his round is finished, bubbles of magic begin moving across the front of her armor. She stands, her legs wide and her chest now exposed.

The bubbles lift off her chest plate and fly back towards Ryuk.

-253 HP! Critical hit!

Getting a taste of his own medicine is something Ryuk didn't expect from the powerful mage. He sails backwards, his Dream Armor barely stopping the spread of the molten marble.

"Ryuk!" Enway points her wand at the terrible mage. *"Chrono Statis!"*

The woman grins as she absorbs the pink magic. "Interesting spell," she says, her brow furrowing. Skadi points her finger at Enway and whispers, "Chrono Stasis."

Ryuk, still trying to get his bearings, looks to see Enway completely frozen in time. Even though she can't move, he can see fear in her eyes.

Skadi takes a few steps closer to Enway, and as she does, Ryuk fires off a message to Hiccup.

Ryuk: Everyone is dead. Enway is almost gone. Where the fuck are you?

Ryuk goes for his Magic Slingshot and loads a clear marble in it. *Come on*, he thinks as he pulls back on the pocket.

"Remove buff!"

Fwhiip!

The marble strikes the woman and bounces off the front of her armor. She stops and turns to Ryuk, just as he comes up with his Marble Gun, this time with a mag of half black and half sword marbles.

The sword marble is the first to leave the weapon.

It stretches into its full capacity as it zips through the air towards Skadi.

Ryuk gasps as the powerful mage *sidesteps* his attack.

Able to move again, Enway tries to pivot away from Skadi just as a black bolt of lightning strikes her in the back.

Instakill!

"Shit!"

Ryuk: FeeTwix, we're dying here!

FeeTwix: I'm almost at Lothar's. I'll be there as soon as I can! Just hold them off; run if you have to.

Ryuk look over his shoulder at the wall of rock and ice.

He glances right to the edge of the ice wall. His Extreme Focus causes something on the ice castle wall to light up and an idea comes to him.

"It is useless," Skadi says, lifting her hand.

A determined look on his face, Ryuk points to his eleven o'clock and finishes his mag. His sword and explosive marbles strike the exposed ledge, which causes a small avalanche of snow and ice to descend upon Skadi.

Figuring this is the distraction he needs, Ryuk turns right, his fingers jamming into the pouch of gravity marbles on his waist. *Just need to make it to the ledge,* he thinks as he gets ready to jam the marble in his mouth.

He's two meters away when a bolt of black lightning strikes him in the back, sending him to the ground and instantly taking his life.

Ryuk spirit lifts out of his body, and like he did back at the Port of Corpses, he now hovers above the battle.

Hiccup.

The goblin now stands five meters behind Skadi, his Gilius Thunderhead Axe in his hands.

"What the fick is with the bodysuit, lady?" the goblin asks, out of breath again.

Skadi turns to the goblin and narrows her eyes. "You are the last of them?"

"Bitch, I'm the first of them!"

"What did you say to me?" the terrible mage asks Hiccup.

"Fick me, lady. Never was a latex guy, more of a chainmail head. Add a good amount of chainmail to any orc chippie and I'll be fickin' til my chalupa no longer works."

Black lightning cackles over Skadi's body.

We're so fucked, Ryuk thinks as his spirit floats above the battle. If Hiccup dies, they'll have to start again at the entrance to the Sabors.

Hiccup snorts. "You know, fick, since everyone else is dead, I guess I'll be the one to tell you: there's a reason you're up here by yourself with not much more than a samsquanch to fick. If you ever want to get that lady choop of yours filled, you're going to need to drop the whole 'I'm an evil bitch who lives in an ice castle' schtick. I mean, seriously, who the fick wants to live in the Sabors? This place is a cold ass fickhole, and believe me, I'm from Jatla, so I've seen my fair share of fickholes, warm and cold."

A bolt of black lightning strikes the ground before Hiccup.

He gulps and continues. "Fine, if that's how it's going to be, then so be it. But before I kill your twisted ass, I just want to put it out there that I'd love to take you out on a nice date. I mean, if you ever get over this 'ice queen living in the middle of fickin' nowhere and making dildos out of stalactites' gimmick you've got going."

"Enough!" Skadi blasts Hiccup with a bolt of black lightning and his ax *completely* absorbs the strike.

"Thank you, Dirty Dave," Hiccup says as he points the ax at her. "See you in hell, biotch."

Hiccup deflects the bolt of dark lightning back towards Skadi, and for a moment, nothing happens. The strike hits her and she just stares at him, her mouth agape as they both wait to see what happens next.

Instakill!

Skadi's skull explodes into kibbles and bits and her body falls backwards.

"Fick yeah!"

Enway, Oric, Ryuk, Wolf, and Yangu respawn.

"What the hell did you just do?" Oric asks, his eyes wide with surprise. He smooths his hand through his disheveled hair. "That was amazing!"

"Fick yes, it was," Hiccup says as he waddles over to the woman's body. "And that's probably one thing these fickers didn't tell you about me: it's practically a battle strategy now that the goblin saves the day."

"Hiccup! You did it!" Enway runs over to him and gives him a hug.

"Whoa, whoa, Elfy, if you think hugging me is going to stop my anti-immigration rhetoric, you're right!" Hiccup kisses her on the cheek and she immediately moves away. "What? In Jatla, a hug is always followed by a kiss."

"Hiccup, how...how did you know your ax would absorb her magic?" Ryuk asks.

Yangu at his side now, Ryuk equips a healing potion, finishes it, and equips another to feed to Yangu.

"Don't you listen, Marbles? When Dirty Dave, blessed be his fickin' name, gave me this big ass ax—try saying that three times fast—he claimed that it had electric properties, but that I couldn't use it because I don't have any mana. Well, fick, I figured it would absorb her black lightning, and as you fickers can see, I was right."

"And if it didn't?" Oric asks.

"Well, then she would have fried my ass and we would have all been ficked."

"You risked everything on an untested assumption?"

"Of course I did. To quote a song I heard a fickin' ogre singing back in Jatla: *It's my life, and it's now or never. I don't want to live forever.* Fick, I don't know the rest of the song, Tarzan, but you get the point. Actually, I don't like that song. Ogre songs are terrible, but you get my point, YOLO, mitherficker."

Ryuk shakes his head. *I can't believe that worked.*

"And I already got a hug from Enway, so I expect some shit from you two as well," Hiccup tells Ryuk and Oric as he slowly bends down to look at Skadi's decapitated body. "I swear to fick if I had a rupee for every time I saved this guild's ass, I'd be living in the Richman District and drinking drorikh out of a high elf's skull."

The goblin checks what's left of Skadi's body. "Fick, looks like I'm going in deep." He equips his toe knife, removes the woman's chest plate and stomach armor. "Don't get any sick ideas, Marbles, no one likes a necrophiliac."

He drives his knife into her gut, and once he's made a pretty good sized opening, he sticks his hand in. "There it is." He returns with the final runestone.

"How did you know it'd be in her stomach?" Oric asks. Wolf is near Hiccup now, sniffing a bit of flesh leftover from Skadi's exploded head. "I thought it was around her neck ... "

"Marbles, tell He-Man 'I drink and I know things,' so that I don't have to say it. Okay, I'll say it. The one around her neck was a fake." Hiccup wipes the runestone on a bottom piece of his tunic. "Wolfy, don't eat that. Whatever it is, save it for me."

He finishes cleaning the final runestone. "Who's keeping these things anyway? That you, kiddo?"

"Yes."

Hiccup tosses the runestone at Ryuk, who just barely manages to catch it. Still wet with blood and viscera, Ryuk tries to wipe the runestone against a patch of snow. Hiccup snorts at this, but doesn't say anything.

Enway joins him seconds later. "This is going to be interesting," she says, watching as the other runestones appear in Ryuk's free hand.

Once he has the three runestones together, he notices a strange tension spread up his arms.

A magnetic force pulls the runestones towards each other, even before he can figure out how the third and final piece fits into the equation.

As soon as the third piece is put into place, Ryuk feels as though someone is ripping his spine from his body. His shoulders rise, and he leans back as a column of white magic strikes him.

The magic twists through his body and a prompt appears before him:

How would you like to respawn?

1) A Berserker Warrior

2) A Ballistics Mage

3) A Dark Mage

4) A White Mage

Ryuk's hand trembles as he looks to Enway and Oric, who has now joined them.

"What should I do?" Ryuk asks.

"Try it," Oric says, "try to spawn as a warrior."

Enway gasps. "I know exactly what it is! The runestones allow you to change classes freely."

"And you think I can change back?" he asks.

"I know you can. I've seen this same prompt before. Another smuggler who has a shop in Shiya once had an object that did just this.

He showed it to me. You can change classes freely, but your mana, for example, carries over, as does your health."

"Okay," Ryuk nods as he lifts his hand, "let's try warrior."

(0)__(0)

Ryuk touches the prompt and his body starts to morph.

His muscles bulge and his Dream Armor opens up in the middle of his chest, allowing for the three attached runestones to settle in place across his breast.

A sword takes shape in his right hand, the hilt golden, and a dagger takes shape in his left. His hair grows, and as muscles are added to his body, his hood shrinks and the clothing under his armor reaches its tearing point.

Ryuk Matsuzaki Level 28 Berserker Warrior
HP: 1156/1156
ATK: 157+75
MATK: 211
DEF: 118
MDF: 89
LUCK: 24

"Holy fick, Marbles, you're stacked!"

My attack power has increased, Ryuk thinks as he examines his chiseled arm and the sword gripped tightly in his right hand.

"Not bad." Oric claps his hands together. "I have legitimately never seen something like that before."

"Marbles, I take back anything I ever said about your marbles not dropping. Your marbles have officially dropped, kid. Congrats. Prepare to open up your world to a legendary amount of poontang. Fick."

Hiccup licks his fingers and runs them through his eyebrows. "You know I'm down as fick to play wingman. Just say the word and we'll hit all the good clubs in Jatla, I'm talking about the ones with a door charge and adequate security. Ladies like those places."

Ryuk sheathes his dagger and touches the runestone on his chest. The prompt appears again, and he selects Dark Mage.

His muscles shrink, and his hood swells up and over his armor. Robes form on his body, and soon, he's shrunk in size, even shorter than he normally is. He now notices a strange, heavy sensation moving through his body. A sense of cold moves down his shoulders and settles at his wrists.

Ryuk Matsuzaki Level 28 Dark Mage
HP: 1156/1156
ATK: 157
MANA: 375/375
MATK: 211+75
DEF: 118
MDF: 89
LUCK: 24

Ryuk lifts his hand and curls his fingers.

Dark magic courses through his veins and he notices a light reticle take shape on the dead samsquanch's body. As if he were auditioning for a role as a young Padawan learner in whatever DisNike Star Wars flick is set to be released in the summer of 2075, Ryuk slightly tightens his hand and a giant bolt of lightning cuts into the samsquanch.

"Fick me, Marbles! Watch it with the evil shit. I was going to get some meat from that ficker and now you've gone and toasted it. You know how much a goblin would pay for samsquanch organs? No? Well, neither do I, and now we both will never know. Fick."

Hiccup throws his hands in the air and turns away from the samsquanch's carcass.

"Nice," Ryuk says.

"And a cleric, right?" Enway asks.

Ryuk touches his chest and selects the White Mage option. He experiences a similar transformation; his robes lighten as a sense of hopefulness sears through his avatar. The feeling is light, carefree, fresh, *healing*.

His stats appear before him:

Ryuk Matsuzaki Level 28 White Mage

HP: 1156/1156

ATK: 157

MANA: 363/375

MATK: 211

DEF: 118

MDF: 89+75

LUCK: 24

He lifts his hand above him and a cloud springs out of his fingers. The cloud rains light down onto the Mitherfickers.

"I can group heal," he whispers.

"That was the poofiest thing I've seen all day," Hiccup says, trying to dodge the sparkling magic but failing. "Fick! It touched me. Does that mean I'll become a snowflake?" He laughs. "Kidding, Marbles."

Ryuk touches his chest again and he returns to his normal form as a Ballistics Mage.

"It's an amazing ability," Enway says.

"It really is."

"So, are we going to Waringtla then? FeeTwix and Zaena should be there by now." Oric's hand coming up to spawn at the location of their other guildmates.

"Sure," Ryuk starts to say as a portal opens up across from them. His brother steps out, followed by Tamana, Tomas, and the two mages.

"I thought you'd still be here," Kodai says, his marble slingshot appearing in his hand.

Ryuk raises his hand to touch his chest, but decides to go for his Marble Gun instead.

CHAPTER 24: COSMIC DUST

"Tamana, take Ryuk. Tomas, Oric. I'll take the goblin. You two handle the rest." Kodai says the last to the two mages they fought back in the Shinigami's rented guild.

Hiccup chortles. "I'll take the emo-twated fick dick with the slingshot and the microscopic chalupa. Oric, I don't even know who that other guy is, but kill him good. Elfie, Yangu, Wolfy—those two mages might look tough, but we killed them fickers dead as fick back in Aramis when we were hardly level fifteen. Like their bitch-titted mama's boy of a leader, they are fickboys of the highest degree. Marbles, whip Tammy's perfectly-shaped ass." The goblin tightens his grip on his big axe.

Take Tamana? Ryuk gulps as he aims his Marble Gun at his former best friend. He wishes he had time to load his shotgun, and he may do so if he gets a chance. *No, this will have to do.*

"Well, fick, people? Who's going to strike first?" Hiccup narrows his eyes at Kodai and laughs again. "I can't wait to cut your head off and shit down your neck, you fickered fick-faced queef-farming poof-flake!"

A sinister smile takes shape on Kodai's face. "You will eat your words, goblin."

"And you will eat my shit, or at least your neck will. Fick, that's gruesome, but you get the picture. BRING IT, FICKER!"

Tamana charges and Ryuk unloads a clip of molten black marbles at her. She's thrown backwards just as Ryuk's hand comes to his chest.

He chooses the Berserker Warrior and feels his muscles swell under his Dream Armor.

His blade isn't the same size as Tamana's ironing board of a sword, but it is big enough to block her first attack.

Fuck, she's strong! Ryuk thinks as their blades meet and Tamana grunts and tries to kick Ryuk.

He instinctively stretches backwards to avoid the kick, and it's at this point that he realizes that not only has he become a warrior, he has also, through the runestones, picked up the instincts and characteristics of the class.

Trust your class.

Oblivious to the fight that is happening around him, Ryuk pivots onto his left foot, well aware that they are four meters away from the edge of the ice wall, and brings his blade in an upward swoop.

Tamana blocks him just in time but is caught off guard.

As she stumbles backwards, he approaches, both hands on his blade and ready to end it there. Digital adrenaline surges through him; he brings his weapon back and is just about to deliver a finishing strike when he stops.

It can't be.

Ryuk swears that he saw something flash behind Tamana's eyes.

Instead of finishing the job, he brings his weapon down, still at the ready, so he can get another glimpse of her.

"Tamana?" he whispers.

"Fick, Marbles, stop undressing Tammy with your eyes and kill that turncoat-ass bia bia!" Hiccup has replaced his bigass ax with his bigass shield. He hides behind his scutum now as Kodai continues to fire black marbles at it.

Meanwhile, Oric and Tomas are all out brawling, their blades clinking and clanking as the evenly matched warriors try to get the upper hand.

Enway is doing relatively well against the Dark Mage. She's cast her quick movement spell—Ryuk believes she called it Light Shadow—and moves in and out of reality as she avoids attacks from the mage.

Her hourglass necklace glowing, she blasts the mage from behind, -**127 HP!**, and again dips out of reality.

Wolf and Yangu have teamed up on the Berserker Mage, Yangu hitting him with streams of molten ice. The snow dragon's attacks aren't very strong, but he is able to provide enough of a distraction for Wolf to move on the mage.

"Ryuk?" Tamana asks as her eyes quiver, a look of confusion spreading across her face.

"Tamana!"

She bares her teeth at Ryuk and brings her buster sword over her shoulder, as if it were a baseball bat.

-266 HP!

The strike from Tamana's sword sends Ryuk over the side of the ice wall. He hits the ice stair he created and tries to dig his free hand into the ice.

No such luck.

Ryuk's body slides across the stair and he falls backwards, down to the very bottom of the ice wall, landing on his back.

-551 HP! Critical hit!

(0)__(0)

Tweety birds and a galaxy of stars swirl around Ryuk's head as he sits up.

He's down eight hundred hit points, and his first instinct is to go for a healing potion. Oblivious to his surroundings, he equips the healing potion and is just about to throw it back when he gets a boot to the face.

-48 HP!

The healing potion flies from his hand and he drops to the right.

Far away from the others now, Tamana stands over him, a familiar image if there ever was one, and before Ryuk can react, she grabs him by the back of his hair and sits him up.

His former friend brings her fist back, and as she does, Ryuk places his hand on the runestone on his chest and selects select Dark Mage.

Tamana is just about to strike him when his form starts to morph.

Startled, she brings her fist back again, giving Ryuk the time he needs to strike her with a bolt of black lightning.

-297 HP!

She's thrown sideways and Ryuk goes for his potion. One hand still trained on her, ready to blast her at a moment's notice, he gulps the potion down.

+500 HP!

He hasn't had a chance to go through the spells the Dark Mage has, and truth be told, he hasn't quite figured out how the avatar switching affects skillsets.

Regardless, he knows that the lightning works, and as Tamana struggles to get to her feet, he strikes her again.

-167 HP!

"Ryuk?" she asks as she pushes herself up.

Her armor is now blackened and blood flows freely from her lips. She wipes her mouth, and somehow, accidentally transfers some of the blood to her white hair.

"Not going to work this time," Ryuk says, standing.

He can hear his guildmates fighting above him. He doesn't know how well they're doing, but if what he saw before he was tossed over the wall is any indication of their performance, the Mitherfickers will beat the Shinigami today.

He shoots his hand out before him and curls his fingers. Another bolt of lightning strikes Tamana.

-222 HP!

"Please," she whispers. "Ryuk."

She looks at him, blood smeared across her face, and at that moment, his heart breaks. He can barely look at her in that state. He lowers his head, ashamed of what he's done. Tamana falls forward onto her chest; the snow around her face quickly turns crimson.

As snow whirls all around, Ryuk makes an impulsive decision.

He presses his hand into the runestone on his chest and changes to his Cleric form.

Standing in his gray robes, light mana surging through his veins, Ryuk slowly lifts his hand over Tamana.

+250 HP!

She pushes herself up, now in a prone position with her knees and hands still on the ground.

Ryuk heals her again.

+274 HP!

Tamana gets to her feet, her fists at her side. Her buster sword is still on the ground; if she moved quickly, she'd be able to get it before Ryuk could change avatars.

+150 HP!

Ryuk heals her again, tears streaming down his face.

He sees the Tamana he used to know, the Tamana who would meet him at the arcade, who'd go eat ramen in Shinjuku with him, who'd meet him for breakfast, who fought beside him as a Knight, who went to first year classes with him, who had always been there for him since they first met.

And as he looks at her, hardly able to see through vision blurred by tears, Tamana does something that will affect him for the rest of his life.

She lifts a trembling hand and a yellow light appears.

"Don't," Ryuk asks, knowing exactly what she's doing. "Please, Tamana, no!"

"Goodbye, Ryuk." Tamana's hand extends to the yellow blip of light and Ryuk rushes to her.

He tackles her to the ground and pulls her into his arms, sobbing as he tries to hold her back.

"Please, don't!" he screams, the yellow reflecting in her eyes. "Please, Tamana, no!" He presses his forehead to hers. "Please, don't do it, you can't, I need you here."

"Ryuk..."

The light is still shining behind his head, and Ryuk can sense that she's still trying to reach for it.

He tries again to move her away from the light, to use all his strength to push her away, but he is so wrapped up in trying to save her that he doesn't compute that the light is a part of her dashboard, that no matter what he does, *he can't actually stop her from completely deleting herself.*

All Reborn Player Characters are able to permanently delete their base avatar and actually die, never to respawn again in a Proxima world.

"I'm sorry, Ryuk."

"You don't have to do this," he pleads with her, "we can fix your avatar. Please, Tamana."

He feels a burning sensation in his chest as she begins to fade away.

"Why?" he asks, barely able to make out the words.

Tamana presses her finger into the center of his forehead. "I'll always be here," she whispers. She removes her finger and leans forward to kiss Ryuk. As she kisses him, her body turns semitransparent. Her avatar starts to crumble and pixelate as her body turns to cosmic dust.

Ryuk falls to the right, sobbing as the cosmic dust settles all around him.

He places his hand on his wounds, white healing magic quickly patching it up.

In front of him, still lying in the snow, is Tamana's buster sword.

CHAPTER 25: WITH A LITTLE HELP FROM MY FRIENDS

Rather than climb to the top of the stairs, Ryuk switches to Ballistics Mage, places a gravity marble in his mouth, and floats up. Once the marble starts to lose steam, he places another marble in his mouth.

He stops before reaching the top and moves onto an ice step.

Tears still stinging his face, and quickly starting to freeze, Ryuk crouches and loads his Marble Shotgun. He hears the clink and clank of swords above him, and he's received no indication that any of the Mitherfickers have died.

Still, Tamana's actual death, the fact that she deleted her RPC, is going to make it hard to fight. He will still be able to fight, but what he really needs is time to unpack what he's just witnessed.

No time, he reminds himself as he finishes loading the canister full of gravity and black marbles. It is a combination he hasn't tried yet, but he feels almost certain that it will put forth the damage he is looking to cause.

Another gravity marble in his mouth and he floats to the top, focusing on one thing and one thing only.

Kodai.

His brother continues to fire marbles at Hiccup even though the goblin is blocking them with his shield.

Hell, Hiccup has gotten so accustomed to just blocking that he now has the scutum held up with one shoulder, so he can chug a healing potion.

He sees Ryuk and gives him the "well it's about fickin' time you show up" face. Ryuk hardly acknowledges the goblin. He pulls the trigger on his Marble Shotgun and unloads the entire mag at his brother.

The combo of explosions and shifts in gravity works in just the way he predicted. His brother is thrown into the air and quickly sucked back down to the ground, thrown into the air again, and again brought back down.

He's bad off by the time everything is said and done, but Ryuk's too busy watching the mayhem take place notice any of the damage prompts. He knows it isn't enough, but killing his brother now will at least give the Mitherfickers a much needed victory.

The problem is the mages.

As soon as Kodai looks like he's about to go down, the Dark Mage casts a shield of purple mana that blocks Kodai from any incoming hits. The Berserker Mage kicks Wolf into the rock wall, knocking the breath out of the beast.

He slams his two axes together and a searing flash of light flings Yangu over the edge of the snow wall. For his part, Oric has managed to get one of Tomas' swords free, but struggles to get the other, as Tomas whips into a frenzied, multi-blade attack.

Enway.

Ryuk sees that she is down, blood dribbling down her chin as she sucks in air. He instinctively touches the runestone on his chest, changes into a cleric, and as white magic fills his soul, he sprinkles a cloud of healing magic onto Enway.

The wound on the side of her head heals up and she gets back to her feet.

Ryuk touches the runestone on his chest and turns into the warrior, Tamana's buster sword in his hand.

Kodai's eyes go wide as he takes in Ryuk's new ability. His shock quickly settles into a wicked grin as a portal in the sky opens.

The OMIB? Ryuk thinks as he looks up at the portal and the star-filled galaxy inside of it. He sees the outline of the serpent woman, Veenure.

Her eyes flash green and spears of electric green magic rain down upon the battlefield.

-310 HP!

Ryuk takes a direct hit to the chest.

He hits the ground, but the warrior's stamina and ability to take damage is much different than his base avatar. He's back on his feet in seconds, a white magic glowing around the hilt of his buster sword.

I will guide you, Ryuk.

"Tamana?" he gulps and looks down at the glowing weapon.

There's a flash a few feet away from him and FeeTwix steps out, two bandoliers of bullets across his chest, a RE4 Hand Cannon in his right hand and a Lancer chainsaw/assault rifle combo in his other hand.

The Lancer's chainsaw kicks into gear. "To quote Hiccup," the Swede says, a huge grin spreading across his face, "Fick everyone who isn't me!"

FeeTwix lays down some major firepower as he alternatively takes huge .50 caliber shots from his Hand Cannon. He focuses his bullets on the portal in the sky, which momentarily takes Veenure off guard.

Once the Swede's rounds are spent, he throws his Hand Cannon over his head and chugs a healing potion.

"Fick, Twixy, share some of that!" Hiccup says from his place behind the scutum.

"You're on your own for now, goblin, I've got some mages to kill!"

"Ha! *Viewers are surging,* am I right? Fine, fine, New Marbles, you're fickin' dead!" Seeing that Kodai is still blocked by the mages, the cantankerous goblin drops to his hands and knees and scurries around them.

Normally, the mages would catch him and squash him like a cockroach, but FeeTwix has started to engage both of them with his Slice Bang. He cuts into the first, blasts at the second, and even as he moves, his free hand scrolls through his inventory list until it stops at his Steamsuit.

The Steamsuit materializes around him and he's instantly in the cockpit. His face fills with fury as the docking station secures itself. The Berserker Mage comes in for a swipe and FeeTwix *grabs him* with his free hand (the other hand actually being a giant sword).

Propelled by steam from his mahoosive metal feet, FeeTwix takes off into the air, the Berserker Mage tucked under one hand.

Once he's about a hundred meters up, the mage struggling all the way, FeeTwix does a one eighty and blasts off towards the ground.

Instakill!

He drives the mage headfirst into the parts of the tower that haven't already been destroyed, doing damage to himself in the process.

"Fickin' show off," Hiccup says as he points his mechanical finger at Kodai, who is still protected by the Dark Mage's barrier. "Get out from behind that magic shield, you dirty snowflake ficktard!"

Tomas' second blade flies out of his hand and Oric moves in for the kill, only to be thwarted by Tomas' speed.

With a loud grunt, and a louder nethergrunt from his starfish, Hiccup takes off towards Kodai, his huge axe held tightly between his grimy paws.

A snarl across his face, he's just about to swing his weapon when a pink blast from Enway blazes over the battlefield, directly into the open OMIB portal.

The screeching sound that follows grounds everyone still fighting.

Ryuk hits the deck, his hands over his ears as the sound boils through him. A million angry voices screaming inside his head, Ryuk tries to lift his weapon in Kodai's direction.

The buster sword is surprisingly light, but the trauma from the ear-piercing scream from Veenure makes it nearly impossible for him to focus.

What the hell did Enway hit her with? he thinks as he tries to get back to his feet.

"Fick you, let go of me, you ficker! Fick! FICK!"

Ryuk glances right just in time to see Kodai with his hand around Hiccup's mouth. The two disappear in a flash, and as soon as they're gone, the Dark Mage and Tomas also bow out.

The portal closes and the Mitherfickers are left tattered and goblin-less.

(0)__(0)

FeeTwix lands his Steamsuit and the front clamshell opens with a hiss.

"They took Hiccup?" he asks, rage in his eyes.

Ryuk, still reeling from the auditory wave, finally gets back to his feet. "They took him. My brother fucking took him."

"That's your brother?" Oric asks, his face drenched with blood. "Somehow I missed that part of the narrative."

"My older brother."

"He seemed like a dick."

FeeTwix nods at the Unigaean warrior. "He's a real asshole. Wait a minute, how did you get that sword?"

Ryuk looks down at his Buster Sword. "I ...Tamana..."

The Swede gulps. "You killed her?"

FeeTwix approaches Ryuk and finally helps him to his feet.

"No," he says sadly, "she killed herself, or that's not quite it. She deleted her RPC."

"That's suicide," Enway whispers.

"She killed herself then. She couldn't take any of this anymore."

"And wait a minute." FeeTwix shakes his head. "Since when did you use swords?" He examines Ryuk's Dream Armor. "Let me guess, an ability granted by the runestones?"

"Exactly."

"Why do you think they took the goblin?" Oric asks as Wolf limps over to him. Oric drops next to his animal and begins petting his head. Yangu also appears after he reaches the last stair on the ice wall. He's battered, but seems cheerful nonetheless.

A terrible thought comes to Ryuk. "How much does Hiccup know about *you know what*?"

FeeTwix's eyes flash blue. "You mean NPCs spawning in humandroid bodies?"

"Refresh me on all this," Oric says. As Enway catches him up to date, Ryuk and FeeTwix continue their discussion.

"I mean, Hiccup has been there when we are discussing it," Ryuk says.

"Shit, this is really bad," the Swede says. "We need to log out and tell Sophia."

"We need to tell the faun."

"Doc," FeeTwix says. "Yeah, we need to tell him too. Um, should I just call his name?"

A flash and the Knight's War Faun spawns before them. "I figured I'd save you the trouble of getting your megaphone out," Doc says, his tail shaking as he moves around on his hooves. Leg warmers appear above his hooves and a sweater with a M-16 on the front across his chest. "It's nippy out here."

"Doc," FeeTwix says, "they took Hiccup."

Oric looks from Enway to the Killer Faun. "What in the hell is going on here?"

"That I can't quite answer," she says, having never met Doc herself.

"Doc is from the Knights of Non Compos Mentis," Ryuk explains. "They're watching over us, or something."

"Ah," Oric says. "I've heard of them."

Doc waves everyone's concerns away. "We can get to better introductions later. The important question is: does the goblin know about R-Diving?"

"R-Diving?" Oric asks.

"The word Sophia came up with to describe going from a Proxima World to a humandroid's body in the real world. Personally, I don't particularly like it, but I didn't invent the tech, so I don't get to name it."

"We don't know if Hiccup knows," Ryuk tells Doc. He touches the runestone on his chest, and morphs back to his Ballistics Mage avatar. "Also, how did you hear your name so quickly?"

The faun snorts. "I told you I'd be around and providing support."

"Have you been watching us since we last saw you in the Knight's guildhall?"

"Come on," Doc laughs, "I have a life, and a pretty nice mansion in a Barbie Proxima world, but to answer your question, yes. Aiden and I have been watching you guys. Pretty entertaining stuff, although the stuff with the goblin shaman woman was a little twisted. But that's all beside the point now. If they have Hiccup, we need to get Hiccup back before he talks."

"We don't even know where they are," Ryuk says.

"Not necessarily." Doc equips a device with an antenna on it. He extends the antenna and walks over to the spot where Kodai teleported from, his hooves making cylindrical imprints in the snow. "That seems...stupid of them."

"What do you mean?" FeeTwix asks.

"They've gone to Aramis. Don't they have a guild there?"

"Then we'll go and get Hiccup," Ryuk says.

"Yes, we will," says Doc, "and we'll bring the cavalry. Usually, I'm not one to just rush in and take action, but it's needed for this scenario. Aiden?"

Morning Assassin's avatar spawns, his Slice Bang on his back. Although he's in his armor now, he still wears his Hugh Hefner robes.

"We going to Aramis?" Aiden asks. He cracks his knuckles in front of him and the robe disappears. "Sorry, was reading the latest issue of *Wet Goblin Holes*."

"Good editorials, huh?" Doc asks. "But that's beside the point, hell yes we're going!" One of his shooting irons appears in his hand. "This is going to be fun. So, Oric, you, me, FeeTwix, Ryuk, and Enway."

"Wolf too," Oric says.

"The snow dragon might not be suitable for the combat we're going to get in."

"Then we can send him to Waringtla, to join Zaena," Ryuk tells Doc.

FeeTwix's expression sours. "Zaena would love this fight."

"We'll figure that part out," Enway assures him.

"Anyone else joining us, Doc?" Aiden asks.

"Let me see, who do we know in Aramis?"

"Jim has a hotel there. Croc works security at Barfly's."

"Croc would definitely do," Doc says. "We could ask Sophia to get an NV Visor on, but I'd rather have her monitoring FeeTwix and Ryuk. There's also Rocket, but he's not as reliable as he used to be."

"What about Quantum?" FeeTwix asks.

Aiden's mask shifts as he raises an eyebrow at Doc. "What do you think?"

Doc considers this for a moment. "It never hurts to ask."

CHAPTER 26: OUT OF RETIREMENT AND INTO THE FIRE

"You called me out of retirement for this?"

Ryuk looks at the man who stands before him. Quantum Hughes is a bit shorter than Aiden, muscular, and by the looks of it, he refuses to wear the typical fantasy getup. He's in a trench coat, a black shirt, and black boots.

There's a streak of white in his hair and something mischievous behind his eyes. A big knife is strapped to his right boot and, from what Ryuk has counted so far, he has at least four handguns strapped to him in some way.

He also wears a bright orange life vest, or at least, it used to be bright orange but he's since tried to paint it black.

Quantum Hughes Level 99

HP: 8675/8675

ATK: 3090

MATK: 10

DEF: 420

MDF: 571

LUCK: 69

"Quantum Hughes!" FeeTwix's tongue nearly falls out of his mouth. "Please! Please, please, please, please, Doc, let me broadcast this to my fans."

"Absolutely not," Doc says. "Quantum, meet FeeTwix—he's a fan."

"Of who?"

"Of you."

"Put'r there." Quantum shakes FeeTwix's hand, squeezing as tightly as he can.

"I know everything about you! I fight with your style, I've visited your childhood home in America, I've watched as much footage of you as I could find." FeeTwix takes a deep breath as his hand turns blue. "Sorry for the fanboy act. This is too much!"

"Relax, kid, it'll all be over soon," Quantum says, a sly grin on his face.

"I love your humor!"

"And I love your overcoat."

"I designed it to look like your trench coat but provide more flexibility. I can even equip items behind my back, just like you. Learned that one in the Netflix Hulu series."

"Good." Quantum claps him on the shoulder. "Okay, so what's the deal here, Doc? The Reapers back or something? I thought we put an end to those bozos once and for all. Not that I'm not down to do a little skull-stomping."

"Bozos," FeeTwix mouths at Ryuk. "My new favorite word," he whispers. "Bozos."

"They're not back in the way you'd think." Doc starts to explain. Once he gets to Veenure, Quantum waves the rest of the explanation away.

"I've heard enough to pass judgment. But clue me in real quick: we need to rescue a goblin, why?"

"Well, you haven't heard enough if you don't know why we need to rescue the goblin, Quantum," Doc says.

"Shit, Doc, haven't even been here three minutes and you're already bustin' my balls."

"You haven't changed a bit."

Quantum laughs. "How many times do I have to tell people you can't teach an old dog new tricks?"

Oric looks at Wolf and the Unigaean beast barks.

"Who's got the mean pooch? That you?" Quantum asks Oric. "Damn dog would have been nice in The Loop. Should have put one in my inventory."

Oric nods. "He's, uh, mine."

"Not bad. Okay, so catch me up, Doc, I got places to go and pancakes to eat."

FeeTwix's eyes practically flash hearts. "I love pancakes," he whispers.

Doc quickly catches Quantum up. Occasionally, FeeTwix approaches them to show Quantum some weapon he has that he thinks the famous gamer will appreciate. Quantum definitely appreciates some of them, especially the mutant hack.

"Dirty Dave made this, huh? Not too bad," he says, as he makes a 'Robert De Niro judging something' face. He turns to Doc. "I get it, I get it. This shit could get real bad if Veenure is able to figure out that she can come to the real world as a humandroid. Hell, I may have to come out of retirement again if that goes down. So we need to get the goblin. Tell me more about this goblin. He a squealer?"

FeeTwix nods.

"Then we're wasting time standing around talking about him. Here's what we're going to do..."

(0)__(0)

Kodai stands over the goblin, a twisted knife in his hand. Veenure has been unable to take over the goblin's mind, mostly because of some mental condition he has.

Hiccup spits blood as he says, "Early Onset Goblinheimer's, you emo-twated fickbag." Blood dribbles down his mouth and onto the front of his shitty chainmail armor. "Fick you, fick that sexy snake bitch—I fickin' hate lizards—fick all of you!" he says to Kodai's reinforcements, who stand around them and at the entry points to the Shinigami's guildhall.

The two mages, Tomas, and a few of the hired security stand around Kodai and Hiccup. Tied to a chair, Hiccup has already been stabbed several times, and while he shrieked at the blade that went into his thigh, he's held his own relatively well.

Kodai punches Hiccup in the eye; the sound of meat on meat ricochets to the far corner of the room.

"Yoooooy!"

Hiccup's eyes quickly swell up, but somehow he still manages to glare at Kodai. "Uncuff me, you fick! Fight me like a man, you fickin' sheep tonguing poof cake!" Hiccup spits more blood. "Fick! You call this torture?" He laughs long and hard. "I did your mom—fick, all your moms—harder than this two nights ago. Ha! You won't get shit out of me, you fickered ficktard."

A snarl on his face, Kodai approaches the goblin and stabs him in the stomach.

"Yoooy!" Hiccup's head tilts forward, blood spilling from his mouth.

An idea comes to Kodai based on what he's seen in FeeTwix's stupid little feed. He takes a healing potion from his inventory list and waves it in front of Hiccup's good eye.

"Would you like some?" he asks.

"Fick yeah, I'd like some! But if you really want me to talk, you'll get me a fickin' Hopkins' or a Cherry Apollos. Fick, why the hell did you take me in the first place?" Hiccup's eyes partially glaze over. "I'm the least informed member of the Mitherfickers. Hell, I think Wolfy knows more than I do at this point. I'm just a fickin' security guard, you idiot!"

"Why is Sophia in Tokyo?" Kodai asks.

"Fick if I know! Are you talking about the elf with the fro? Knights leader, small chest. That one? Fick, I'd rather her be in Tokyo than here. That psycho female is the reason I can't say fick, fick!"

"Can't say fick?"

"Fick with a 'U' ...ha! Fick 'U,' New Marbles!" He nods his head to the two mages. "You two are the biggest pair of salad tossers this side of the Bawa Outpost. That is west of here, right? Where the fick are we?"

"Shut up!" Kodai slugs Hiccup again.

"That's all you got?" Hiccup asks, spitting a bloody tooth out. "Spew Gorge's mom, Irene, hits harder than you."

"Tell us what we want to know or..."

"No leverage, huh? Life's a bitch, ficker."

Kodai raises an eyebrow as an idea comes to him. "Who is Spew Gorge?"

"You don't know Spewy? Fick, well, I guess you wouldn't seeing how you're the bad guy in our story and Spew is a bit player. Any-fickin'-hoo, Spewy is my cousin, also my son. Definitely my son. I had sex with my aunt, Irene, his mother, and she got pregnant, so I'm his dad and cousin. But don't tell him that. He's also of the poofter variety, kind of like yourself."

"And where does Spew live?"

"Jatla. Where else would a fickin' goblin live? I mean, he could live in Bluwid, but Spew lives in the Venom Spur District, room sixty-nine. I always remember that number, but I won't tell you why."

Kodai directs the two mages to locate Spew Gorge and they disappear.

"Wait a fickin' minute..." Hiccup's eyes go wide. "Fick me..."

"You really are a stupid goblin."

"Fick, Spewy. Fick." Hiccup bites his lip. "Okay, fick it, he can handle himself."

"Let's just see about that."

The mages appear a few minutes later holding the smaller goblin. Spew Gorge is wearing a sweater he knitted, and a sleep mask is still on his head.

"Pretty early to be napping, Spewy," Hiccup says as he coughs up blood.

"What the fick? Hiccup? Why in the fick are you here? You sold me out you, stupid fick! And it's nighttime, I was sleeping!"

"Fick me, Spewy, but why does it have to be a Hello Kitty mask?"

"Don't judge me, Hiccup!"

"Shut the fuck up, both of you," Kodai says as Spew Gorge is tied to a chair across from Hiccup. "I'll make this incredibly simple: I will torture

Spew Gorge in front of you and then I will have his body sent to the OMIB, where he will never be able to free himself. Tell me what I need to know."

Spew Gorge looks at Hiccup with angry eyes. "Well, fickin' tell them, you pink haired donkey ficker!"

"Spew, what happens in Bluwid, stays in Bluwid, and I only did that one time. Like I told you!"

"Fick you, Hiccup, tell the emo fickboy what he needs to know!"

Hiccup laughs. "He is definitely a fickboy, I agree there, Spewy." He spits blood onto the floor. "Hey!" He shouts as Kodai drives his knife into Spew Gorge's back.

"Yoooy!"

"You leave him alone, you son of a bitch!" Hiccup starts hopping up and down, his chair scraping against the ground. "You want information, I'll give you information." The goblin swallows hard. "I'll fickin' talk, just leave Spewy alone."

"I'm listening," Kodai says, turning back to the older goblin.

"Sophia, fick her by the way, went to Tokyo to do some tests or something. That's all I know there."

"What kind of tests?"

"What part of my previous sentence do you fail to understand, dumbass?"

"He's a fickboy," Spew Gorge cries. "Fick him!"

"Yes he is." Hiccup glares at Kodai with a single eye. "And like all fickboys, no matter how powerful or how important, soon enough, they all have their asses handed to them."

"Is that so?" Kodai asks, a sneer on his face as he drives his blade into Spew Gorge's trapezius.

"Yoy! Yooooy! Yoy! Yoy!"

"Hang in there, Spewy," Hiccup says, his voice dropping. "Don't give in to this pig ficker."

"Next question," Kodai says as he brings the blade to Spew Gorge's throat. "Tell me what you know, all you know, about people going from Tritania to the real world."

"This is the real world," Hiccup growls. "It is real to me, anyway. Fick, let's not get philosophical here."

"You know exactly what I mean," Kodai growls.

"Nope, I have no idea what you're talking about. Never heard of NPCs, humandroids, Tokyo, Mexico or any of that shit."

"You don't listen to your guildmates talking?"

"Have you met my guildmates? Your emo-in-crime, Ryuk, hardly talks; FeeTwix is always dealing with his fans and hawking tchotchkes; Zaena, while incredibly tall, thin, and sexy, is racist; Enway was never properly vetted so I won't comment on her; Wolf is good people, as is Snowballs; and Conan the Unigaean Barbarian doesn't make a great guildmate because he's a fickin' loner."

"Now," Kodai says, pressing the blade into Spew Gorge's neck. A bead of blood forms and drips onto Spew's sweater. "Tell me what I need to know."

An explosion in the far corner of the room scatters a few of the rented guards, separating their limbs from their bodies.

Kodai hits the deck, as both the goblins' chairs topple over. As soon as Hiccup touches the ground he starts scooting towards Spew Gorge, terror and concern in his eyes.

A man wearing a black trench coat steps through the hole. As the smoke clears, he's joined by a faun with guns, a slender guy in a ninja mask, and the rest of the Mitherfickers.

"See? I told you, Doc, you can never go wrong with a little kablooey," the man says, a cigar jutting out of the corner of his mouth. "Now which one of you dumbasses is Kodai? How do I say that last name? Nope, not gonna try. Everyone drop your weapons and put your hands up!"

(0)__(x)

"Goosebumps!" FeeTwix shows Ryuk his arm as Quantum Hughes steps forward, his hand behind his back as he scrolls through his list.

"Let's see..."

"What's he doing?" Ryuk asks.

"Watch the master at work," FeeTwix says, tears in his eyes. "He's going to murdalize those bozos!"

"Never tried this inside." Quantum looks up at the high ceiling of the Shinigami's rented guild hall as he equips *AoT* Omni-directional mobility gear, Prince's Purple Symbol guitar, and a Heckler & Koch MP7 in his right.

"Items 77, 217, and 303," he mumbles to no one in particular.

Quantum is airborne seconds later. He zips to the right side of the room and starts laying down firepower. He peppers this with sticky white blasts from the end of his guitar.

"What is that guitar shooting?" Enway asks FeeTwix.

"Super Plasmic Long-Lasting Optimal Organic Glue Extract, or S.P.L.O.O.G.E.," FeeTwix cries out, the fanboy in him barely contained. "It's one of his famous weapons!"

The blast of sticky white substance pins two of the Shinigami's rented guards to the ground.

Oric, riding Wolf now, races to the far side of the room to engage a few of the NPCs. His splintered sword and electric shield in hand, the

Unigaean Warrior launches off Wolf's back and smashes into the group, his shield sending sparks of electricity into the air.

-117 HP! -132 HP! -141 HP! -89 HP! -75 HP! -114 HP!

More firepower comes from the War Faun, who has started to engage one of the mages. Not one to be outdone by Doc and Quantum, Aiden flashbangs away, and appears behind the Berserker Mage.

The killer assassin flourishes his Slice Bang and their weapons meet.

His avatar flashes out of existence again and appears behind the mage, where he drives his Slice Bang through the mage's body.

Instakill!

More NPC swordsmen charge into the room.

"Kill them!" Kodai shouts, his marble slingshot in hand. He tracks Quantum, but every time he goes for a shot, Quantum ziplines to the other side of the room.

The Knights are toying with them, Ryuk thinks as Quantum blasts one of the sellswords with his purple S.P.L.O.O.G.E guitar. The guy's body flies into a wall, sticks there, and Quantum, zipping past the guy for the second time, gives him the Mozambique Drill.

"You still got your shooting skills!" Doc calls up to him.

"Thanks, Doc!"

"What should we do?" Ryuk sees bound Hiccup behind Spew Gorge now, using his teeth to gnaw through the rope around his cousin/son's hands. *And where did Spew Gorge come from?* he wonders as Hiccup works to free his cousin/son.

"I don't think we do anything," FeeTwix finally says. "Quantum and company are handing the Shinigami their asses. Fuck, I'd like to get in there, but..." The Swede surveys the battle. Oric and Wolf are on the far right, Quantum is zipping around the room, Doc is finishing off one of the mages and Aiden is moving in on Kodai.

As it did over the battlefield in the Sabors, a portal opens up and swells at the top of the room. Veenure's form now visible, she screams as she fires green bolts of boiling magic at Doc and Quantum.

"We got company, Doc!" Quantum shouts as he narrowly misses one of her blasts.

"I've got this," Enway says, her wand appearing in her hand. "Arcane Tide!" A fireball of pink and purple magic flies from the end of her wand to the portal.

As soon as it hits her, Veenure starts screaming again, her voice shattering any of the windows that haven't already been shattered.

His fingers deep in his ears now, Ryuk sees Quantum quickly equip a pair of noise cancelling earmuffs. The black earmuffs securely on his head, he again lifts into the air and zips over to an NPC swordsman, whom he quickly takes down with military precision.

He drops again, drinks a healing potion, and tosses it away.

The legendary gamer locks eyes with Doc and both of them nod as they turn to the portal.

A FIM-92J Stinger with a huge scope materializes in Quantum's hand and he aims the rocket launcher at the portal. Doc goes for a Fliegerfaust ground-to-air rocket launcher, and gives Quantum the thumbs up.

"Whoa," FeeTwix says, sweat forming on his brow as he takes in the mayhem. "It's beautiful!"

Not one to be left out, Aiden has equipped a Type 91 Japanese SAM-2 and, like his counterparts, he too aims it at the OMIB portal.

Doc gives the signal, and the three men fire away, the missiles all striking Veenure at the same time.

"Hot damn!" Quantum says as their explosions suck air into the OMIB portal.

As wind whips through the room, Wolf makes a beeline towards one of the final sellswords left standing.

He leaps, takes the guy down, and gets to tearing apart his throat.

The Dark Mage fires a fireball at Doc, who bails left to avoid most of the blast, but still ends up catching his little goat tail on fire.

Aiden comes to his defense in a flash.

The man known as Morning Assassin cartwheels into a kick that takes the Dark Mage off his feet. He backflips from there and lands with both feet on the mage's chest.

Quantum laughs. "You're backwards."

"Dammit!" Aiden hops in a circle so he now stands on the mage's chest, a Glock pointed at the man's face.

Bang!

Instakill!

"I love that they added the 'instakill!'" Quantum shouts.

Spew Gorge, now free, runs to the exit of the Shinigami's guildhall, leaving his cousin/father still bound.

"Fick you, Spewy, untie me!"

"Fick you, Hiccup!"

Quantum lands in front of Kodai, his freshly equipped Glock pointed at the Japanese crime lord's head. "I guess this means you're the only clown left."

"You will all pay for this," Kodai says, his slingshot aimed at Quantum's chest.

"Yeah? How much is it going to cost me? And are you really aiming a goddamn slingshot at me? By the way," he grins, "goodnight."

A foot strikes Kodai in the back of his head, knocking him out cold and forcing the slingshot from his hand.

-666 HP! *Critical hit!*

Quantum laughs. "That was one evil-ass kick, Aiden."

"Been working on that one."

Aiden lifts Kodai by his scruff and turns him toward Ryuk.

"He with you?" Quantum calls over to the Ballistics Mage.

Ryuk nods.

"Well, you want to do the honors or what?"

FeeTwix places his hand on Ryuk's shoulder. "Do it," the Swede says.

"Yeah." Ryuk takes a few steps closer to Quantum and Aiden as his Marble Gun appears in his hand.

He knows that his brother can just respawn, that he can never inflict the kind of pain on Kodai that Kodai has inflicted on him, but insult to injury will do nonetheless.

Ryuk pops the mag out of his Marble Gun, clears all the marbles out at the press of a button, and places a single sword marble in.

Once the mag is reloaded into the back of the gun, Ryuk places the muzzle of his weapon against Kodai's forehead.

Aiden stands on one side now, Quantum on the other. Doc is behind them, helping Hiccup get out of his ropes, Oric is off to the right with Wolf, and Enway and FeeTwix are behind him.

Kodai blinks his eyes open. "Ryuk?" he asks, shock spreading across his face. He glares at his younger brother. "You don't have the fucking guts to do it."

Ryuk digs the muzzle even further into his brother's head.

"Come on," Quantum whispers.

"You fucking pus—"

**Instakill!*

The sword marble tears through the back of Kodai's head and plinks against the floor.

"Fick yeah!" Hiccup shouts, a mixture of blood and healing potion spewing from his lips.

EPILOGUE

Ryuk and the rest of the Mitherfickers respawn at Lothar's bakery. Quantum, Aiden, and Doc aren't with them—they said something about hitting up Barfly's in Aramis—and Ryuk can tell that FeeTwix would have invited himself had it not been for the fact that Zaena was suffering from pyro affliction.

"I hope this works," the Swede mumbles as his avatar takes shape. Ryuk knows that he's gone through a plethora of opposite emotions over the last hour, from the adrenaline of battle to the excitement of seeing his hero to returning to the woman he cares deeply for.

"All we can do is hope," Enway says as they enter the bakery.

Ryuk catches a glimpse of Yangu in the yard next to the bakery. He gets the urge to run over and greet the snow dragon, but suppresses it.

There are more pressing things at hand.

"Fick, we should probably pray too," Hiccup says. "And I'm fickin' good at praying, if anyone's asking."

Since being rescued, the goblin has gone through a case of healing potions given to him by the Fickers. He has another case waiting for him,

Ryuk knows because FeeTwix privately messaged him about it, but the Swede is trying to stop the goblin from overindulging.

"It will be nice to see my old friend," Oric says after he and Wolf have spawned. "It's been a while."

"I still find it hard to believe you have friends, He-Man, but that's just me."

"I think the same thing about you, goblin," Oric says as he and Wolf enter the bakery.

"Yeah? Well fick you too." The goblin stops and turns away from Ryuk just as a squealer zips from his nethercheeks. "I didn't want you to face the wrath of that one, Marbles."

"Um, thanks?" he says, the putrid air still reaching his nostrils.

Enway, now inside the bakery, places her hand on her neck and makes a choking gesture to Ryuk.

FeeTwix is going through some shit, but Ryuk is too, especially after what Tamana did. Still, there is something about the buster sword that she gave him, and he could have sworn she communicated with him through the weapon.

Also, capping his brother—what pleasure that brought him. Ryuk isn't keen to explore these feelings, but they're there. Before he can follow this thought pattern down the rabbit hole, Hiccup sticks his mechanical hand out.

"What are you doing?"

"Fick, Marbles, you act like I'm trying to give you a horizontal handie or something."

"What?"

"I'm trying to shake your fickin' hand, kid."

Ryuk eyes his mechanical hand suspiciously with his Extreme Focus ability. Hiccup's hand is grimy, scratched, there's a dried booger on Hiccup's pointer finger, and there is dried blood on his palm.

"We bow in Japanese culture," Ryuk says, figuring now is as good a time as any to create a teachable moment.

"Bow? Fick me, Marbles, I'm nobody's bowing fickboy." The goblin adjusts his girth and grunts. "But if that's what wets your chalupa." Hiccup bends his head forward. "Thank you for saving my ass. And Spew Gorge's ass, even though he's an ungrateful little ficker. But thank you, Marbles, and the rest too, but they don't need to see me bowing. How's my hair by the way? Yoy, this gesture hurts the back of my neck."

"Your hair is great, and thank you as well," Ryuk says, bowing.

"What are you thanking me for?" Hiccup asks, looking up at him.

"For always saving our asses."

The goblin chortles. "That's right, I do usually save our asses. I'd pat myself on the back, but that would require effort." He yawns. "Any-fickin'-hoo, let's get in there and see about curing Liz's scaly, yet perfectly shaped and nicely taut, green ass. Then let's get some rest. I need a gobnap."

(0)__(0)

They head into the bakery and are greeted by Lothar's wife. She's behind the counter, her face red as she rotates some of the pastries, putting the fresh ones in the front of the display case and the older ones closer to the back.

She smiles thinly, and nods upstairs.

"Don't have to tell me twice," Hiccup says as he approaches the human-sized stairs. "Fick, I really don't want to climb those. Any chance I could get a piggyback ride?"

"Nope."

Ryuk takes two stairs at a time to get away from Hiccup.

"And all the nice things I just fickin' said…"

Everyone has gathered around a small cot in the open space of Lothar's library. Zaena rests on the cot, her infected arm across her chest. Wolf is near her, sniffing the air, his tail tucked between his legs, and while it seems like Lothar and Oric would like to catch up, they've focused solely on the task at hand.

"…We can discuss that later," Lothar says as he finishes greeting Oric. The giant turns to the Hourglass Mage, who stands with her Book of Time tucked under her arm. "This was something I didn't think I'd ever grant someone."

"If it works, it works," FeeTwix says. "You can take it away later."

"No," Lothar says with a sad smile, "I can't. These types of spells, if they get into the wrong hands, can augment the base D-NAS of Tritania. It is like opening Pandora's Box."

"You can trust me with it," Enway says.

"I'm sure I can, but this is a great power, and with great power…"

"Fick me, are we really going with that quote, Big Guy?" Hiccup asks, out of breath. "Look, if you know a way to heal Liz's one percent tush, then let's fickin' do it. She's the best we got. Yeah, we have Tarzan too, but he's a loner and I fickin' hate loners."

Oric shakes his head.

"Chill, Hiccup," Ryuk says, placing his hand on the goblin's shoulder.

"Chill? Pfft! Marbles, Liz is over there with a fire burning inside her and the only thing standing in the way is the big ficker. I'm not fickin' chilling for shit." He aims his mechanical finger at the giant. "Let's get this Ponygirl show on the road."

"I will ignore the goblin's threats," Lothar says coolly. "It is clear that they are driven by passion."

"Hunger too, I'm getting hangry over here. And tired."

"We will eat pastries later, and then you can rest." Lothar removes his glasses, cleans them on his blue apron, and uses the glasses to point to the top shelf of his bookcase. "Oric, can you use that ladder over there to get that wooden box."

"The one beneath the First Artifact?" Oric asks.

"That's the one."

"Doesn't seem like a very clever hiding place," Hiccup mumbles.

"I'm very much a hidden in plain sight kind of guy, Hiccup," Lothar tells him. Ryuk feels something electric move past his leg and he steps aside.

He knows exactly what it is, and before Oric can reach the wall with the bookshelf ladder, the box in question is floating in the air.

"Please, Princess Zaena," Lothar says, "save your strength."

"My strength isn't at fault here," she says as she uses her ghost limb to lower the box to the ground.

"Thanks," Oric says as he takes the box from her. "Where's the key, Lothar?"

The wooden box is sealed shut, and from where Ryuk's standing, he can't actually see a keyhole. Next to him now, FeeTwix bites his nails, his eyes blue as he watches Oric bring the box to the ground.

"You're the key, Oric," Lothar says. "Both you and I can open it."

"Fingerprint recognition?" FeeTwix asks.

Lothar laughs. "You think you're the only one with alien technology? Oric, place your finger on the golden square on the box's top."

Oric does as instructed and the clasps keeping the box together loosen and fade away. The Unigaean warrior opens the top to reveal a collection of pages that have been torn from the Book of Time.

"It's the second one from the top," Lothar says.

Oric finds the page in question and hands it to Enway.

The Hourglass Mage sits on the carpet and opens the Book of Time in her lap. As soon as she touches the page, it zips into the air and stitches itself back into the book.

The red tear on Enway's face glows as she reads the spell. She gulps, looks over at Zaena, and equips her odd wand, the receiving end black and rotten, the handle fresh wood.

"I hope this works," Oric whispers. Wolf whines, walks away, and doubles back, his ears alert as Enway lifts her wand.

"It will work," FeeTwix says with uncertainty. "I feel like it will."

Seeing the concern on the Swede's face is really taking its toll on Ryuk. He feels terrible for him; he knows very well what it is like to think you're about to lose someone. The urge to go over to FeeTwix and console him swells in Ryuk's chest. He holds it in, not wanting to interfere in the moment.

"The Reverse Time spell, especially at higher levels, can reverse any amount of time," Lothar says. "But doing so in certain situations can put a great strain on the OMIB, and create what are essentially black holes in the Proxima world proper, holes which cannot be closed. These can ruin a Proxima world, which is why I've kept the spell here."

"I can give it back to you," Enway says, her eyes flashing red.

"No, you can't. Like I said, once you've learned the spell, it doesn't matter if it is in your Book of Time or not. You could tear it to shreds and burn the shreds and it would reassemble, force the book open, and reform its page. Only after you've hung up the avatar can we take the page back out. Are you ready, Princess Zaena?"

"Just Zaena," she says, a scowl on her face and her eyes clenched shut.

Ryuk swallows hard.

The Thulean's infected arm across her chest and the flames slowly flickering off her flesh create a terribly tragic image. Even odder, there is no smell associated with the flames. The flames are just there, blue tips with slivers of purple running through them.

Enway aims her wand at Zaena's arm.

"I really hope this works," Hiccup says, his eyes wide with fear. He starts to sob. "Fick me, Marbles, don't be such a crybaby. Fick. Come on, Zaena, I mean, Liz, pull through."

Ryuk places his hand on Hiccup's shoulder again.

"I'm nobody's fickboy," the goblin blathers as pink magic moves down Enway's arm and to the tip of her wand.

She gulps, and a flash of magic strikes Zaena's infected arm.

The air is sucked out of the room as everyone looks to see the result of Enway's Reverse Time spell. Pink magic envelops the wound, bubbling at its edges. The pink magic slowly dissipates; nothing has changed about the wound.

"Oh my," Lothar begins to say.

"Fick, I knew it wouldn't work."

"Dammit." FeeTwix bites his fist and turns away.

Suddenly, the flames start to subside.

They begin to disappear, starting from her elbow and working towards her wrist. It's as if they were never there. Her greenish skin reforms, stitching over the molten lava and charred flesh from the infection.

A flash of pink magic threads across her arm, no sign of the affliction evident.

Oric gasps. "It worked. Lothar, it worked!"

"It did!"

A bright smile paints across Enway's face as she lowers her wand. Behind her, Wolf barks excitedly, running in a small circle.

"Fick yeah!" Hiccup nearly does a jump kick.

Ryuk instinctively bows to Lothar, his arms at his sides.

FeeTwix is beside himself with joy as he rushes over to Zaena.

"Thank you," Zaena says, tears in her eyes as FeeTwix reaches her.

"Fick me," Hiccup wipes his tears away. "I fickin' love happy endings. Get the fick over here, Marbles, and don't get any funny ideas."

He hugs Ryuk, and for once, Ryuk doesn't push the goblin away.

RYUK MATSUZAKI'S CHARACTER SHEET

*As of the end of book three

Ryuk Matsuzaki Level 28 Ballistics Mage
HP: 1156/1156
ATK: 157
MATK: 211
DEF: 118
MDF: 89
LUCK: 24

Skill: Tonsil Shot
Level Three: 1 in 9 chance of connecting.
Damage: 28% if enemy is less than level 30; 15% if enemy is greater than level 30.
Odds of instakill: 11%
Requirements for instakill: LUCK > 9

Skill: A Simple Request
Level Five: 1 in 5.95 chance of a request being granted.
Caveat: Only works with a clear marble.
Requirements: LUCK > 15

Skill: Cherry Poppin' Daddy
Level Three: 1 in 9 chance of connecting. Enemy's backside must be exposed. Higher levels increase damage and chance for an instakill.
Damage: 51% if enemy is less than level 30; 15% if enemy is greater than level thirty.
Odds of instakill: 16%
Requirements for instakill: LUCK > 7

Skill: Extreme Focus
Level Four: Can detect approach of camouflaged/concealed/stealthed enemies and objects.
Mage bonus: Higher levels allow sleuthing and increased accuracy. Also increases magic detection range when used in tandem with Magic Eye.

Skill: Inspire Others
Level Four: By inspiring others, you induce them to follow your orders. Higher levels allow for manipulation of enemies and random strangers.
Requirements: LUCK > 20

Skill: Magic Eye
Level Five: A colored glow indicates that magical properties are present. Higher levels allow for more detail and access to the Wikipedia of arcane knowledge. A red outline signals that a hidden enemy is near. A yellow outline signals that an object is enchanted. A dark blue outline signals that necrotic magic is being used. A green outline signals that algomagic is being used. An orange outline indicates a hidden trap is present.
Requirements: Level 13 Mage, LUCK > 8.

Skill: Splash Back
Level Three: Damage increases with higher levels.
Damage: 6% if enemy is less than level 30; 2% if enemy is greater than level 30.
Odds of instakill: 5%
Requirements for instakill: LUCK > 9

Skill: Gory Headshot
Level Three: Odds of instakill increase with level.
Odds of Instakill: 60% if enemy is less than level 30; 33% if enemy is greater than level 30.
Caveat: Must be within five meters of opponent's head.

Skill: Spit Fire
Level Two: Stuff a marble in your mouth and spit it at an enemy. Higher levels allow for more control and sustained magical abilities.
Requirements: LUCK > 7

Skill: Bonding Trust
Level Two: Bonding trust creates an everlasting connection between you and another creature. Higher levels allow for direct communication between you and other animals as you instantly understand their languages and demeanors.
Requirements: There are no requirements for bonding trust. This skill is tied directly to your D-NAS, digital neuronal autoconstruct system, and based on your interaction with others up until the point at which you met the creature.

Skill: One in a Million
Level Two: Use your slingshot and any marble of your choosing to take an impossible shot. Odds of connecting increase with each point you gain in LUCK.
Requirements: Level 10 Mage, LUCK > 17.

Skill: Levitate
Level One: By placing a marble in your mouth, you can levitate for thirty seconds. Higher levels allow for longer levitation.
Requirements: Level 15 Mage, LUCK > 12.

Skill: Knights in White Satin
Level One: Call upon the Empress' guard to aid you in a battle.
Caveat: Can only be used once per day.
Requirements: Gifted by Empress Thun.

Skill: Preemptive Strike
Level One: Distract your enemies, or have your guildmates distract them and receive a fifteen percent bonus on your attack.
Requirements: Level 18 Mage, LUCK > 20.

BOOK FOUR
TOKYO

CHAPTER 1:
I SEE HICCUP

RYUK MATSUZAKI doesn't know what time it is when he wakes up, only that he is in Tokyo, in a fancy hotel that FeeTwix has paid for, a nice, comfortable place that...

"No..." Ryuk says as he hears snoring at the foot of his bed. "No. No. No. *Fuck.*"

The sound of a squealing fart confirms it.

Before Ryuk can even get his blankets off, Hiccup is cursing at the flatulence that has seemingly woken him up. The fat goblin gets to his feet and grunts, Hiccup completely naked under a soiled and stained robe with the DD's Barbeque logo on the back, his little goblin chalupa hanging off to the side, crust on its tip.

No...

"FeeTwix, are you awake?" Ryuk says in his accented English, terror in his eyes.

The famous Swedish gamer sleeps in the bed next to him, lying on his stomach, one hand thrown over the side of the bed, his face buried in a pillow.

Ryuk tries again. "FeeTwix."

"Marbles?" Hiccup squints at Ryuk. "Where in the fick? Fick!"

Ryuk sighs miserably. "What the fuck are you doing here?"

"What the fick am I doing here? What the fick are you doing here? Where the fick am I?"

Ryuk groans.

"That's not an answer, Marbles!"

"You're in Tokyo."

"Some way to greet the goblin that has since become both your mentor and your bestie. Wait. Did you say Tokyo?" He looks around, panic in his eyes. "I'm in actual Tokyo? Fick! *Get me the fick out of here.* I want to go back to Tritania, dammit. Fick this place already. I hate Tokyo. Fick! Too goddamn clean. Fick!" Hiccup's voice grows raspy. "I'm getting panicky over here, kid. The tunnel is opening up. Fick no, Busty Gazongas is here too, shit, it's not heaven, Marbles, you chicken liddle chicklefick, pay attention! She has a pitchfork. She's going to spray me with sour breast milk!"

"Quiet, dammit," Ryuk says as he gets out of bed. He waves a weary hand at the goblin. "And cover yourself up."

Hiccup reaches his mechanical hand down and scratches his chalupa, beating his leg as he does so. "Wait a minute..." He eyes Ryuk suspiciously for a moment. "You're sizing me up, aren't you? In that case, get your chalupa out then, you sick fick, and let's see who's the real goblin around here."

"What? No. Put some fucking clothes on, Hiccup."

Hiccup continues to scratch himself. "I'm like a fickin' ghost over here, aren't I? Am I dead? Was it the HotAzz Ballz sauce I had with din-din?" He burps. "No, didn't taste anything hot there. I'd better not be a fickin' ghost. I fickin' hate ghosts! Breathe, Hiccup, breathe. Big breaths. Down to the nutsack. Everything is very legal and very cool. Breathe. Fick..."

"Quiet, Hiccup!" Ryuk clenches his fists at his side. "I need a second to figure this out. Would you shut the hell up—"

The Swede finally stirs. "Hiccup? Did you say... Hiccup? We're in Tokyo, Ryuk." FeeTwix laughs cautiously. "You must be dreaming, right? ...Right?"

Hiccup's robes part again, revealing his pimply ass this time as he turns to FeeTwix and throws his hands up. "Fick me, Twixy, some badly fickered shit is happening here. I'm going to need a couple of potions real fickin' pronto. I took the red fickin' pill. Fick!" Hiccup paces for a moment, farting with nervousness. "Wait. I took both pills. Not just the red pill. Blue too. Fick! Someone fickin' talk me down. I'm like a bird, I only fly away. Fick! Talk me down, Marbles." Hiccup rushes to a window and looks out, his eyes wide as he sees the glittering city that is Tokyo. "Holy fick. Daddy likey. This reminds me of the setting for Fickvengers..."

Did he just say Fickvengers? Ryuk runs his hand through his jet black hair. "Of all people. Please, no."

Hiccup turns back to Ryuk. His chalupa flops to the other side. "People? What part of my anatomy leads you to believe I'm a person? I'm a fickin' goblin, Marbles, you clickbait FickTok grundel! If anything, I'm a horse. Get it?" He grabs himself and laughs. "Hung like one, anyway." He snorts and spits on the floor of the hotel.

"What's happening?" FeeTwix asks. "Ryuk, talk to me here, buddy."

Ryuk points at his skull. "The things from Tritania are back. I see Hiccup."

"Things?" Hiccup throws his hands up into the air. "First you call me a *person*, now you call me a *thing?* Bleach my starfish and tell me it's your kink, Marbles. Fick you and your racist, post-industrial age elitism. Do something!" Hiccup beats his hands on his chest, his little goblin cock bouncing left and right. "This is fickin' humiliating, I tells ya, Twixy, talk to me, Twixster. Fick!"

FeeTwix gasps as he finally comes to understand the look of utter dismay on Ryuk's face. "Your digital hallucinations? Are you telling me that he-who-shall-not-be-named is actually in Tokyo?"

"Fick... fick..." Hiccup pauses and lifts a finger into the air. "Fickin' sweet, my inventory list works here. You want clothes, Marbles? You got 'em!" A three-piece tux appears on the goblin, the ass instantly ripping open due to the weight Hiccup has put on since he got the tux. "Too fancy?"

Ryuk lets out an exasperated sigh. "He's here, and he won't shut up."

Hiccup turns to look at his rear, his neck too fat to actually allow him to see the tear. "Fick, Marbles, did it rip? This was designer, you know. Tom Fick. Ever heard of that? Probably not with your ficked up dollar store fashion-sense. Stole it from one of the high-end places in Jatla. Free-ninety-nine, if you get what I'm saying here. Fick, Marbles, you sure are a cheugy-ass simp. Period."

"If you had a three-piece tux, why didn't you wear it when we met Empress Thun?" Ryuk asks, trying his hardest not to roll his eyes.

"Because, I only wear this ficksuit when I'm visiting other worlds or to weddings." Hiccup turns and shows Ryuk his ugly ass. "Best with no undies, more breathable this way. Not to mention the hole in the back makes it easy if we come across a squat toilet. That's what Japanese people use, right? Or is that the Americans? Which people use the toilet that sings you songs and washes your balloon knot? Is that the fickin' Kiwis?"

Kiwis? Ryuk rubs his temples for a moment. "You've never visited another world, Hiccup. You don't even know what kiwis are."

"The fick you say?"

"Sorry for your suffering, Ryuk. Take no offense to this, but I soooo wish I could livestream this. The Fickers would love this. Loooovvvee it. Is he really in a tux? Is it tight in a way that is hilarious? Does he look like an overweight penguin? Did you say there was a hole in the back?"

"He says it's designer. Some Tom Ford knock-off."

Hiccup points a grimy finger at Ryuk. "Tom Fick, you low-income booger. And what the fick is he going on about? Penguin? Fick penguins. You'll be glad we have yet to fight any of those fickers in Tritania. Those fickers are all over fickin' Ultima Thule." His tux disappears and a leather tunic with torn shorts appears. "Better? I make this look good, right? I think this one is designer too. Not Tom Fick, though, maybe some fashion knock-off brand like Zara. Might as well get comfy. Fick." He wipes his hands together. "We've really got to do something about my fickered ass being in Tokyo, though. I got shit I'm supposed to do in Tritania. Although being here may eliminate some debts for me. And I better not be dead. I'm fickin' serious here, Marbles..."

"You keep saying that, Hiccup."

"What's he keep saying?" FeeTwix asks. "What's he keep saying?"

Hiccup stomps his feet. "At least let me finish before you kickstart your otherworldly classism. Fick. Where was I?"

"I...I really can't handle this." Ryuk rubs his temples again. "He's rambling again about everything, from ghosts to racism and designer goblin fashion. I don't even know. The usual bullshit."

"He's such a ficker," FeeTwix says quietly, an awestruck look on his face.

"Marbles, Marbelito, I'd better not be a ghost, that's what I'm trying to say. Now, you fickin' tell Twixy exactly what I just said, dammit, or so help me—"

"He's worried that he's a ghost," Ryuk tells FeeTwix.

The Swede tries not to laugh and fails. "Sorry again, Ryuk. Ahem. I'm guessing our dear friend Sophia will want to see about this."

"Wait. That fickin' bitch is here too?" Hiccup asks.

Ryuk rolls his eyes. "You already knew she was here, Hiccup."

"Don't put words into my mouth, or thoughts into my head. Got it, ficker? And if she's here, and she can fix this shit, then let's fickin' go then, kiddos." Hiccup makes the 'wrap it up' signal. "I don't have all fickin' day."

FeeTwix gets out of bed, completely oblivious to the comments Hiccup makes about his weight in the real world versus the Proxima Galaxy and the Swede's *fickboy haircut*, as he keeps calling it.

Once FeeTwix has taken a piss and changed, the three enter the hotel's living room area, where they find Hajime in a meditation position, the Humandroid in a set of dark blue robes. One look at Ryuk, and Hajime can tell something is wrong.

"Who's the fickin' love guru?" Hiccup asks.

"That's Hajime. I've mentioned him before."

"Hmmm..." Hiccup scratches his ass for a moment as he thinks. "Ah, that's right. You mean your fickin' metal slave? Damn, Marbles, never thought you'd be the type to enslave someone. But we all have our bad habits, I guess. Fick me if I haven't learned that the hard way."

Hiccup glances to FeeTwix for a response, but the famous Swedish gamer can't hear him. By the look on his face, it's clear he is going through messages and comments from his legion of fans.

"Hajime, I can see Hiccup," Ryuk says with a gulp.

"Hiccup the goblin?" Hajime's eyes dilate for a moment, one of the clearest indications that he's a humandroid.

"What the fick is your slave doing?" Hiccup fires up the brown horn choir and waves the smell over to FeeTwix. "And how in the living fick does he know my name?"

"He's not my slave. I told him about you."

"Hiccup is calling Hajime your slave?" FeeTwix asks. "Well, it does seem like something he'd interpret with that pea-sized brain of his."

"Hey!"

"Just kidding, Hiccup, wherever you are." FeeTwix looks around, tries to give Hiccup a high five, and fails. He yawns. "Still struggling with jetlag. I was supposed to be sleeping, but I guess there is no better time than now to respond to the messages in my inbox. What a job!"

"Fick me. Marbles, if this is what Tokyo is going to be like, go ahead and kill me now."

Ryuk tries to kick at Hiccup, his leg passing through him.

"Heh! Fickin' hell do you kick like a sissy, Marbles! I thought this was the land of the ninjas or some shit. Some fickin' ninja you are. I've seen legless orc chippies in electrified nipple clamps kick higher than that. Fick. And take it from me, the legless ones suck a mean chalupa. Don't know why. Also, just to be clear, fick people who say the word 'lol' rather than laugh out loud. Heard a guy say that at a knitting class I once attended. What a fickin' chump."

"He's talking about knitting now. We've got to go to Sophia," Ryuk informs Hajime. "The goblin won't leave."

"Fick. Me. The. Goblin. Has. A. Fickin'. Name." Hiccup throws his hands up in the air and walks to the window. He looks out at the city of dazzling lights and advancements. "Ooo. Uncle Goblin likes what he sees. It's like something out of *Blade Runner* out there."

"*Blade Runner*?" Ryuk asks.

"I'm on it." FeeTwix performs a quick search over iNet. "Ah, here it is. *Blade Runner* is an American movie series about a dystopian, neo-noir future."

"The fick he just say?" Hiccup looks at FeeTwix with disgust. "Please inform Twixy that *Blade Runner* is a goblin play that takes place in a shiny city made of glass and metal, sort of like the Fickvengers. It's about a relationship between a ficked-in-the-head halfling—fick those guys—named Deck-tard, who has booty sex with a lady orclin named Gaff, famous for her three lactating tits. Three tits, Marbles! She cures Deck-tard's blindness, and then he embarks on a journey to increase the size of his chalupa so he can pleasure her backdoor once again, and get more of that yummy yummy tit milk in the process. He dies in the end, but he somehow gets her pregnant, so she has his fickered kid and names him Rutger. Something like that. I left halfway, though. That summary comes from an issue of *Slippery Goblin Holes Birthday Suit Edition* published at the time. Give credit where credit is due, Marbles."

Ryuk moans, his hands coming to his ears.

"What?" Hiccup looks to FeeTwix for support.

"Don't worry, Ryuk, I've already sent a message to Sophia," says FeeTwix. "She's preparing to see you now."

"And I've contacted her humandroid, Evan," Hajime says. "I'll arrange for an Uberyota; we'll take the rooftop entrance. I suppose now would be a bad time for an oblique quote. We can get to that later." The humandroid stands and smooths his hands over his robes. He looks as professional as ever, his hair in a tight bun that Hiccup has already commented on, not a single strand of hair out of place. "Other than the digital hallucination you are experiencing, did you sleep well?"

"Well enough." Ryuk pulls a black hooded sweater over his head.

"And are you hungry? I could prepare something before we depart," Hajime suggests.

"See, Marbles? I told you the fickin' tin man was your slave." Hiccup's stomach grumbles. "Fick me, I wish there were dragon wings in Tokyo. Not that I could eat them, they'd probably just pass through, but at least I could bask in their presence." He licks his lips. "Fick, that'd be nice."

"I'm fine," Ryuk tells Hajime, "let's just get to the rooftop."

(0)__(0)

The Uberyota is waiting once they make their way to the rooftop. As he has for the last fifteen minutes, Ryuk tries his best to ignore Hiccup's commentary. *Maybe I can get Sophia to cast a silencing spell on him,* Ryuk thinks as Hajime opens the door for him.

FeeTwix is already on the other side by the time Ryuk shuffles into the waiting vehicle. Hiccup basically sits on top of him for a moment until the goblin's form presses through Ryuk, both of them not okay with that visual.

"Fick, I really am a ghost," Hiccup says, letting out a little squeaker as if to accentuate his lament. "And now I'm getting spit-roasted by a Swede and a Japanese weeb."

"Shut up," Ryuk tells him.

"Fick, I wish Tammy were here to keep your bitch ass in check." Hiccup huffs and looks out the window, his arms now crossed over his chest.

Aside from the occasional comment about the Tokyo cityscape, the goblin is more or less quiet in the time it takes for them to reach Sophia, who is still at the university in Ueno running her experiments. Her humandroid, Evan, meets them outside. He ushers Ryuk, FeeTwix and Hajime in, Hajime naturally taking an active role in securing the perimeter as they move into the building.

"Glad you all could make it," the humandroid says. Evan is in a white robe with the pronoun 'his' stitched across the breast. He is also wearing a pair of Hello Kitty sandals, which seems at odds with his serious demeanor.

"Look, Twixy, we all know I'm probably the smartest goblin to ever come out of a shithole like Jatla, but why, and I fickin' mean this, why would we waste our fickin' time at a university? Heh. Fick me thrice and butter me nice. I knew Marbles was a fickin' elitist. You could tell by the way he wears his hoodie, and how thin he is. A stable genius, like Yours Fickly, usually has a little bit of weight around their gut from all that sitting and fickin' contemplating."

"FeeTwix can't hear you," Ryuk reminds the goblin as a door slides open.

"I really wish I could," says the Swedish gamer as Evan ushers them in.

"Is he experiencing the hallucinations now?" Evan asks Hajime.

"I believe so."

"Why are they fickin' talking about you like you aren't standing right here, Marbles? They have some sort of bias against emo fickwads who will never get their chalupas moist? And why the fick do people hate the word 'moist?' Have you heard about this, Twixy? Moist, moist, moist. I like moist. Most people like moist. Moist is fickable. Dry is not. Who doesn't like moist?"

Ryuk turns to the goblin, his fists curling at his sides. "He can't hear you, Hiccup!"

"Fick! That's what I'm talking about, Marbles. You keep up that aggression, and maybe you'll get to fickin' second base with Tammy's hot ass corpse. Hell, maybe she'll use her ghost tongue on your fickin' stinkbox. Nothing wrong with some analingus. Me? I was into having my ham flower feathered until this fickered orc chippie stuck her bedazzled nail so far up my bungholio that I was unable to see straight for two fickin' weeks. Two weeks, Marbles. Think about that. I thought I would be blind forever."

"Yes," Hajime says for Ryuk upon seeing the fury in Ryuk's eyes, "I believe he is still experiencing the digital hallucinations."

"I see."

Evan guides them down a flight of stairs. They enter a lab, Hiccup saying something about not trusting laboratories, or science for that matter. They find Sophia standing there, her hair an utter wreck, the Proxima researcher in a *Hers* robe that matches Evan's and holding a Rilakkuma coffee cup.

"This better be good." She takes another big sip from her coffee cup, a scowl on her face.

Hiccup stops dead in his tracks. "Holy fick, boys. She's even uglier in person than I thought. Look at that hair. Fick me, Twixy, I thought this bitch was supposed to be an elf or something? Although, I do like her eyes."

"Stop talking about her eyes," Ryuk says as he takes a quick glance around the room. The dive vats that they had used previously are already set up. FeeTwix is already focused on one of the vats, the Swede clearly ready to log in.

"What? Is eye commentary considered racist here or something? It's not my fault that goblins are blessed with naturally large fickin' eyes. Have you seen Spew Gorge? That liddle ficker has just about the biggest eyes I've ever seen on a goblin. Do you know how much lady chup he could get if he just put his fickin' mind to it? Fick. I'm not proud that he's my son, but I am proud of his eyes."

"Please, make it stop," Ryuk tells Sophia in his accented English. "Please. I am okay with the goblin in Tritania, but not here, not in Tokyo. Please." He bows to her. "Please."

Hiccup stomps his feet. "Why can't people say my name? It is two fickin' syllables. Fick!"

"I wonder if casting a spell to silence him in Tritania would work here..." Sophia sets her coffee cup down.

"I was thinking that could work."

"Fick you, Marbles! You chicken-cunted woodchuck ficker!"

Ryuk glares at the goblin. "Chicken-cunted?"

"Ewww, gross. Ignore him," Sophia says. "They truly are the worst creatures in Tritania."

"Hey!"

"Okay, Ryuk. I'm going to have you lie down and log in as normal. Evan and I will work on your situation up here. You may be logged in for a while we work to reverse engineer some things." She types something into the holoscreen on the table. "I am the one that created r-diving, and I might have to work backwards to figure out how to force NPCs back to the Proxima Galaxy. You'd think this would be easy, but it never is."

"It sounds easy as fick to me," says Hiccup. "If you fickin' invented it, you should know how to cure Marbles' digital covid-aids over here. Fick. This is the problem with science. They come up with something new, but everything they come up with creates a fickin' issue that is worse than whatever issue we had before. Example? Before, I was in Tritania. Now, my fickered ass is in Tokyo. Tell me that isn't dystopian in some way."

"Will he be coming with us?" Ryuk asks.

"I believe so. His existence in this world is tied to your consciousness currently being here in Tokyo," Sophia says. "That's why we can't see him."

"I'm ready to dive!" FeeTwix announces. The Swede strips down so that he can get into his dive vat.

"I'll help," Evan says hurriedly. Ryuk looks back to Hajime to find him posted up by the door, his hands crossed over the front of his body where they usually are when he stands guard. A message from the humandroid appears across his vision.

Hajime: I am aware you are experiencing discomfort. I have full confidence that Sophia and Evan will be able to fix this.

"I get it now," Hiccup tells Ryuk. "If you are in Tritania, I am with you; if you are in this surprisingly well-mannered fickhole with your metal slave, I am here as well. We're like conjoined goblins. That's not a good thing, kid. Those fickers always struggle."

"This isn't very hard to figure out," Ryuk tells the goblin sharply. "And we need to keep it a secret. I think. Sophia?"

She sips from her coffee. "Best not to tell anyone or mention it in a way that others could figure it out, especially your brother—who I'm sure watches your feed," she tells FeeTwix.

"I'll be sure not to mention it when I'm live-streaming."

"Good," she tells FeeTwix.

"You still need to be careful with what you say, Hiccup."

"Am I the one who stuck a fickin' broom handle up your leathered cheerio, Marbles? What's that? No? Then stop talking down to me! And if it's a secret that needs keeping, I'll fickin' keep it. My lips are fickin' sealed." He crosses his arms over his chest, clearly upset.

"You will probably meet with the others later," Sophia tells Ryuk. "Doc and Quantum have taken an interest in whatever it is your guild is up to."

"Quantum?" FeeTwix's eyes light up. "Fick yeah!"

"He has to get permission from Frances first," Sophia says. "Let me see, it is barely morning in Tokyo, which means it is afternoon in America. So yeah, he will log in at some point. Ugh. Probably stuffing his face with some late day pancakes as we speak. Just, a word of warning with Quantum."

"Yes?" Ryuk asks as he finishes undressing. Hiccup starts to comment on the size of his chalupa but Ryuk ignores him as he gets comfortable in the dive vat. Sophia approaches and makes sure everything has been adjusted correctly, testing the oxygen tube that he will eventually use.

"I can't believe we get to see Quantum again," FeeTwix says, the Swede gone full fanboy by this point.

"Quantum can get a little bit carried away, and he is trigger-happy." Sophia tries not to roll her eyes. "He's not professional at all."

"That's because he's a legend!" FeeTwix says, just as Evan puts the breathing apparatus over his mouth. "He's a Proxima legend."

"Ugh. He's not exactly a legend—"

"Sounds to me like someone is fickin' jelly," Hiccup says, mocking Sophia. "And you know what we do with jelly in Jatla?"

"He's a legend in my book," FeeTwix says with the breathing apparatus in. It is apparently a hill he is willing to die on.

"Fine, Quantum may be a legend, but... you know what? Never mind. It has taken years of therapy to work through some of the things that happened in 2058, so we don't need to revisit that. Not today." Sophia places the breathing apparatus over Ryuk's skull. "Open up. You may be logged in for a long time. If you want to come out, let me know. As always, I will do some light in-game monitoring. Don't just come out on your own," she tells Ryuk. "I will have some things hooked up that I'd rather you not disturb."

"When you get in the sarcophagus, does that mean we are going back to Tritania?" Hiccup asks. The goblin now stands next to the dive vat, curiosity in his eyes. "Because if so, it's about fickin' time, Marbelito. I'm getting sick of hoping Sophia's robe will part enough for me to catch a glimpse of her ladychu—"

Marbelito?

"Shut up, Hiccup," Ryuk says with his breathing apparatus in.

Hiccup laughs long and hard. "Fick me, you look like such a liddle bitch in that thing."

TOKYO

CHAPTER 2: SWORDS AND SORCERY

PIXELATING INTO EXISTENCE is something that Ryuk has long since grown accustomed to in his many dives to Tritania. He's grown so used to it that he barely hears the Brian Eno tone, the one made famous in the late 2030s. As he gets accustomed to his digital skin, the stats for all the Mitherfickers take shape:

Ryuk Matsuzaki Level 28 Ballistics Mage
HP: 1156/1156
ATK: 157
MATK: 211
DEF: 118
MDF: 89
LUCK: 24

FeeTwix Fajer Level 27 Berserker Mystic
HP: 1311/1311

ATK: 209

MATK: 37

DEF: 113

MDF: 68

LUCK: 28

Hiccup Level 26 Shield Thief

HP: 1750/1750

ATK: 138

MATK: 17

DEF: 313

MDF: 160

LUCK: 39

Zaena Morozon Level 27 Brawler Assassin

HP: 1334/1334

ATK: 264

MATK: 10

DEF: 233

MDF: 53

LUCK: 27

Enway Zoltan Rosa Level 27 Hourglass Mage

HP: 1015/1015

MANA: 605/605

ATK: 83

MATK: 191

DEF: 73

MDF: 187

LUCK: 24

Oric Rune Level 58 Warrior Berserker

HP: 3,104/3,104

ATK: 554

MATK: 11

DEF: 467

MDF: 389

LUCK: 31

Wolf Level 40

HP: 2402/2402

ATK: 699

MATK: 0

DEF: 534

MDF: 241

LUCK: 19

Hiccup, who has a metal finger in his nose, flicks a booger at the ground and claps his hands. "Fick yeah, we're back, baby!" He touches his chest. "Fick, I'm so happy to see me. Back in my own world too. I'd get down and kiss the ground if we were in Jatla. Much cleaner there than Kayi. This place is a poothole for demented elves and the criminally minded. Speaking of which, I'm done with fickin' Tokyo and all the fickery there. Fickin' lights and sounds, I tells ya. Twixy, that place almost makes me feel sorry for Marbles. Ha! Just fickin' kidding."

As FeeTwix deals with his fans and a recent giveaway, Ryuk takes a look around. They are standing in front of Enway's home in Kayi, a quaint place that looks like it could use some work on the roof. She's changed the paint on the outside so that it's now purple with pink accents, the flower boxes full of daffodils and surrounded by buzzing bees.

Ryuk frowns at the pink-haired goblin who now picks at something under one of his yellow fingernails. "I can't believe we're connected."

Hiccup looks up at him. "Connected? Is this some sicko ficko fantasy of yours, Marbles?"

"You are somehow connected to my psyche. I can't believe it."

"The fick you just say? Pfft! More like you're connected to me, in a fickin' human fickin' centipede type of way, Marbelito."

"A what now? Did you just call me Marbelito again?"

"Human fickin' centipede. Of course you haven't heard of that one. Of fickin' course. It's a fickin' goblin play, off-Broadway in case you're wondering. Really off. Heh. They say the best place for the classiest orc broads is off Broadway." Hiccup scratches his ass. "To be fair, I fickin' hate that play too, regardless of the praise Ficksel and Ebert laid on it. The production value was nonexistent, the orc chippies they chose to sew ass-to-mouth—I think that's called ATM—were bloated at best, PAWGs at worst. By the way, you're the caboose in this scenario, just in case you were thinking you'd bottom-bitch me. Not fickin' happening, sicko."

Ryuk clenches his fists. "PAWGs?"

"Marbles, you really need to get a copy of the urban goblin dictionary. And for fick's sake, relax. Looking at you clenching up over there like you're going in for a fickin' prostate exam. Fick. Must be nice to have yearly health check-ups. I'd get those too if our guild offered adequate health benefits. I'm not going to fickin' argue with you right now." Hiccup lets out a squeaking fart, followed by a sigh, followed by a curious look on his face as he checks his pants, sniffs his fingers, shrugs, and jams his metal finger back into his nose. "Fick, it feels good to be back in fickin' Ficktania. I tells ya, Marbelito, this is the life."

FeeTwix smiles, his eyes already black as he speaks with his fans. "Domo Arigato, Mr. Roboto! I'm back from the Land of the Rising Sun where I'm hanging out with the always friendly, always cool, always mysterious, extremely handsome Ryuk! Hello, everyone! *Kon-ni-chi-fickin'-wa!* Ryuk, say hello to all the mitherfickers across the globe!"

"Um, hi?" Ryuk offers FeeTwix's fans a wave.

"What the fick kind of greeting is that, Marbles? I've got forty thousand fans looking for sage-like wisdom from Uncle Goblin, and you have to stick your fickery ass into the mix with some weak sauce incel of a greeting. So fickin' sus. Hella awkward, bro. I mean, cheese and fickin' rice, Marbles, you've got about as much pizzazz as a mechanical slurping camel that has somehow found itself in a goblin gloryhole."

"Shut up, Hiccup."

"Okie-dokie!" FeeTwix turns away from Ryuk and the goblin. "Lest we get too deep into whatever a goblin gloryhole is—and don't forget, if you need to block out Hiccup's vulgarities, there's an iNet app for that—let me remind you that McStarbucks is having a huge, and I mean *YUGE*, fickin' sale today for sufferers of IBS, otherwise known as Irritable Bowel Syndrome! Mmm-mmm! If you ask me, there's nothing, absolutely nothing, that a cup of burnt coffee made by a shiny new baristadroid won't do to clean out the old pipes! No sirree! CBD-infused you ask? You bet your ass. Literally! Click-click, poo! Introducing McStarbucks' Afternoon IBS-curing CBD-infused snackachino. Click-click, poo! What's that? You aren't familiar with a snackachino? That's because it's..." FeeTwix spins, his arms out wide. "It's brand new! You heard it here first, fickers! Repair thy shitty bowels with McStarbucks' Afternoon IBS-curing CBD-infused snackachino!" His voice quickens as he launches into the final part of his ad read. "The information provided by social media personalities should not be used to diagnose or treat health problems or diseases. When faced with any medical condition, always seek the advice of your FDA monitor or other qualified health provider. Side effects of Starbucks' Afternoon IBS-curing CBD-infused snackachino include bloating, explosive diarrhea, epileptic seizures, PTSD, cantankerous sharts, leg cramps, premature ejaculation, headaches, auditory hallucinations, and miscarriages. Terms and conditions apply. See store for details. Click-click, poo!"

"For the love of fick." Hiccup turns in the direction of DD's Barbeque, which is just down the street from Enway's home. "I can't take the shilling or all the fickin' fine print. I'm going to gorge myself on dragon wings. Only way to wash away the pain I feel in having to hear Twixy's dumbfick ad-read. Did you say Irritable Bowel Syndrome? More like Irritable Goblin Syndrome, am I right, Marbles? Ha! Heh? Marbelito? Well, fick you too then and the queefing magical unicorn you pranced in on! If anyone has a fickin' problem with *IGS*, they can file it with the complaint department, right next to HR." Hiccup flips Ryuk and FeeTwix off. "Any questions, homies?"

"Got it," Ryuk says, relieved to see that the goblin is leaving. "And I'm not your homie."

"The fick you aren't."

"No questions from me, Hiccup, but I take your two finger salute and offer you..." FeeTwix equips a jack-in-the-box. He motions the goblin over after placing the jack-in-the-box on the ground. The Swede begins winding it up. Hiccup becomes excited by what is about to happen. "Are you ready for your surprise?"

"Am I ready for a surprise? Fick yeah, I'm ready. Gimme, gimme, gimme!" Hiccup waits all of fifteen seconds. "What the fick, Twixy? Is it going to work or not?"

"It's supposed to..." FeeTwix frowns. "Why isn't it working?"

"Where did you buy it?"

"Bluwid, on my way to Dirty Dave's."

"That's your fickin' problem right there, Twixy. You bought a fick-in-the-box from Bluwid."

"Yeah. Is that bad?"

"!!!!FICK YOU!!!!" The box pops open, revealing a severed hand, middle finger on display. It explodes within seconds, tossing FeeTwix and Hiccup backward and straight into a wooden fence outside of a home across from Enway's place.

-360 HP! -420 HP!

Critical-Critical hit!

"Fick!" Hiccup waddles to his feet and begins to dust himself off. A healing potion appears in his hand and he shares it with FeeTwix, the two laughing. "That was ficking fickered, Twixy! Heh! Can't believe you got me a fick-in-the-box. And on my birthday too."

FeeTwix cautiously drinks the potion, careful not to put his lips on it. "Your what now?" He hands the potion back to Hiccup.

The goblin finishes chugging it and tosses the potion over his shoulder. He burps. "Any-fickin'-who. Do you two stupid boyficks want anything to eat from DD's? I was planning on putting whatever I ordered on the fickin' Knights' tab, seeing as how they're one-percenters and have more fickin' Proxima Dollars than Jatla has STDs."

Ryuk exchanges glances with FeeTwix. "I'm good," he tells Hiccup, "but maybe Oric, Enway, Wolf or Zaena will want something?"

"Hold your fickin' pony there, Marbles. That's a fickload of mouths to feed. Unless you're coughing up some fickin' greenbacks, or giving me a fickin' raise because you've got my ass stuck at a minimum wage that hasn't increased in twenty years, best not start inviting others to the feast."

"But you said you'd put it on the Knights' tab."

Hiccup throws his hands into the air. "And seriously, why the fick are we hanging out back here in Kayi of all fickered places? Don't the Knights have some exclusive crib for us in the Twilight Zone or some fickin' Sophia safe space?"

A message takes shape on Ryuk's pane of vision.

Sophia: Hi, Ryuk. I am monitoring you now. Sorry it took me so long. I needed to go to the bathroom.

Hiccup: Fick, I've been there. Always good to squeeze one or two off in the morning. Practice good gut health.

Sophia: I will ignore that statement.

Hiccup: The fick you won't.

Sophia: I'm assuming you're settled.

Something like that, Ryuk thinks as Hiccup watches a pair of elves walk by. The goblin squints at them, suddenly suspicious. His toe knife appears in his hand as if he's planning to shank the elves.

Sophia: The Knights and I are with the rest of your guild waiting for you to join us. I should have told you before you logged in, but I was distracted with the fact that you showed up so early and I hadn't had my coffee.

Right. Ryuk turns to the goblin and the Swede. "Sorry, guys, we came to the wrong place."

Hiccup balls his fists up at his side. "Wrong fickin' place? What the fick kind of shitshow are you trying to run here, Marbles?"

"I just figured we'd meet here like we always do."

FeeTwix looks from Ryuk to Hiccup, his eyes vantablack. "So we're going then? I'd love to finish my stream real quick. My fans have missed me! And I've missed you too! G. Todd! ScottyReader! Kay! Juffree Haze! BobbyButtPlug! Annie Ellipots! Joel_Chef69! Dawny M. and pooches!"

"Pooches?" Hiccup smirks at the word, his grin shifting into a scowl. "Look, I don't give two flying ficks or a dragon's infected cornhole what you two ficktards do—including, but not limited to, whatever humans from your world do with fickin' pooches—but Uncle Goblin is getting some dragon wings. Wings, and *then* we go. Otherwise, leave my fickered ass here in Kayi. I... I'll say it."

"Say what?" Ryuk asks.

"I quit!"

"Thank God." Ryuk lifts his finger to generate a series of potential spawning locations. "Come on, FeeTwix."

"Sure thing, Ryuk!"

Hiccup's eyes start to water. "Wait. Wait! What the fick, Marbles? You were actually going to fickin' leave me stranded here? For fick's sake. Where's Spewy? It's times like this that I try to lean on my cousin/son for support, the little fickin' poofter. I'm not crying, Marbles, it's fickin' allergies!"

"Let's go with Hiccup to get some DD's and then head to the Knights," FeeTwix tells Ryuk. "The fans want to see him eat. We'll hurry, Sophia."

Sophia: You're going to eat first?

FeeTwix nods at the sky. "It won't take that long, we promise."

Ryuk imagines Hiccup burping and talking with his mouth open. "Why would anyone want to see that?"

"Why would anyone buy a vomit-ridden Fickson Pollock painting crafted by some of the shittiest starfishes in Bluwid, Marbles?"

"Do you even know what you are saying?" Ryuk asks Hiccup as they head toward the barbeque joint. Yet again, Hiccup sees the two elves, makes eyes with them, growls, and equips an axe just in case they have something to say.

They don't.

The goblin throws his hands into the air, tossing his axe in the process. Ryuk hears glass shatter somewhere behind them. "You seriously haven't heard of Fickson Pollock? No? An artist named Ficksy is his protege. Also a no? Fick, leave it to me to be your personal cultured Fickopedia over here. Fickson Pollock was a famous orclin who was known for painting with his own vomit, blood, and shit. He liked to strap himself to a ceiling and fly over the canvas until he got sick. He'd do this lying down and facing up. Toward the end of his life, he hired other people to help him with his art because of a stomach virus. And I'm not talking bird flu here, Marbles, whatever the fick that is. Fick, I remember that shit from my youth. They even put on live shows like the Spewmen Group. Definitely an event you'd want to take the fickin' kids to. I wish I had invested in some of Fickson's earlier pieces. Blah. I wouldn't have to be everyone's fickboy in this shitty liddle guild—"

"Let's just get inside, Hiccup." FeeTwix winks at the goblin. "I smell lemon pepper dragon wings…"

"Fick yeah, you do!"

(0)__(0)

DD's Barbeque doesn't skimp on speedy service, nor do they go light on the sauce.

True to his nature, Hiccup makes a mess of the wings in a remarkable time. FeeTwix livestreams the entire event as he hints to Ryuk and his fans that he has a big surprise coming for everyone. "So stay tuned!"

The goblin goes back for seconds and thirds, much to Ryuk and Sophia's chagrin. Eventually, he finishes his fourth platter of dragon wings. By the time he is done, Hiccup is gassy and barely able to walk, his face plastered in various colored wing sauces.

"Fickin' carry me, Marbles," he moans on the tail end of a burp. "I'm not going to make it."

"No time. We're already running late, and I hate being late. We're going now."

Before the goblin can bitch any more, FeeTwix, Hiccup, and Ryuk respawn in the courtyard of a home near the edge of one of the floating continents of Tritania, not far from a grand waterfall crashing over the cliffs below. Ryuk can't tell exactly where they are, but he is fairly certain they are somewhere in Polynya. It certainly doesn't look like any location from Hyperborea that he can remember.

"Wolfie—!" The big Tagvornian wolf takes Hiccup to the ground. He licks his face, cleaning all the BBQ sauces off. "Clean me up good, ya ficker!"

"Hey," Ryuk says as Enway walks over to him, Zaena not too far behind.

"Ryuk!" Enway comes forward and delivers a quick hug, which Ryuk makes awkward by not exactly hugging her back. Enway steps back. She looks gorgeous as ever, the Hourglass Mage in her flowing white gown that brings out the bronze in her skin. She's in a pair of sunglasses; Ryuk is pretty sure they're the ones FeeTwix gave her to cover up her red eyes.

Ryuk clears his throat. "Nice to see you."

"Turn them off." Zaena points at FeeTwix's eyes. The Thulean princess wears her battle armor, her red hair tucked back behind her pointed ears, her lips slightly parted now that she's seen the Swede.

"Sorry, guys, you know the rules! As much as I'd like you to meet my heroes—oh my God is Quantum Hughes fickin' in there?—what happens next is top secret, highly classified, MK Ultra, on a need-to-know basis, and in that fickin' order!" FeeTwix's eyes go from pitch black to blue again. "Heya, babe! Sorry it took us so long to join you here. We've run into a little issue."

"What kind of issue?"

"Ryuk is having digital hallucinations again, and this time they involve Hiccup."

The Thulean winces. "I don't think anyone deserves that."

"I heard that, Liz!" Hiccup says as Wolf finally hops off the goblin. "And here I was, not even a day ago, sobbing at what was about to be your fickin' funeral. Liz, you may be the hottest and greenest lizard princess this side of Jatla's Venom Spur district, with a body that a British person—whatever the fick that is—would definitely describe as *fit*, but that doesn't mean you have the right to sass me around or spit fickin' vitriol at me like you're playing a game of kick tits near the Port of Corpses."

"How are you feeling?" FeeTwix asks, ignoring the goblin.

"Better, I've told you that several times now. I've been cured." Zaena glares at Hiccup and returns her soft gaze to FeeTwix. "I was waiting forever for you to log back in."

"Sorry, babe, but a human body has to sleep. Well, technically, I can sleep and still be logged in here. But sometimes, it's nice to get some actual rest."

"Is everyone inside?" Ryuk asks.

Zaena turns to him and nods. "All aside from Yangu. He's back in Kayi."

"I didn't see him there—"

"Fickin' Snowballs! I miss that little ficker."

Zaena points at the goblin. "One more thing. A little decorum would go a long way in the meeting that is set to follow. A long way. Do I need to be any clearer?"

"Decorum?" Hiccup's shoddy armor drops from his body. He's naked for a moment, his little chalupa at half-mast. But soon, the goblin is wearing his white potato bag. "How's that look, Lizzo? Should I do anything poofty like spike my fickin' hair? If we're going to the Met Gala, I want to make a splash. It's invite-only, you know. Last I spoke to Anna Fickters, oh, nevermind. Better not to gossip about that mean ass fashionista ficker. You know, I thought about getting a nose ring once but—"

"Quiet, Goblin. What I'm saying is be quiet. Extremely quiet. Let's show them how professional the Mitherfickers can be. If you're quiet," Zaena's orange eyes narrow on Hiccup, "I'll give you a massage after."

Hiccup nearly drops the healing potion he has suddenly equipped.

"We need to preserve those," Ryuk tells him.

"Fickin' shut your fickhole, Marbles, I just got attacked by a wolf, not to mention the fick-in-the-box surprise back there in Kayi that nearly KO'd me and the Twixster over here. Don't get your little Japanese granny panties in a wad over health potions. We basically have an unlimited supply because of Twixy's ficked-in-the-head fans. So let me indulge, even if my diabetes and heart condition won't be happy about it later. Lots of saturated fat in healing potions. Fick. Wait. Wait a fickin' minute. Liz?" Hiccup takes a sip of the potion and runs a grimy hand through his pink topknot. "Did you say you'd give me a massage if I'm quiet? I swear to every hole fickable in all worlds from here to eternity you said something about a massage."

"That's right, Goblin. If you're quiet, no burps, and no eructations or flatulence—"

"No what?"

"Burps and farts, Hiccup. She's saying to keep all your fickholes on lock."

Hiccup considers what FeeTwix has just told him as he finishes his healing potion. He tosses the bottle over his shoulder and wipes his mouth with his mechanical arm. "In that case, I'll keep all my fickholes shut. You've got yourself a fickin' deal, Liztard." The goblin licks his lips. "I can't wait for a Thulean massage. Four hands are always better than two, Marbles. But you wouldn't fickin' know that, now would you?"

(0)__(x)

Everyone is inside, starting with Oric, who stands awkwardly off in the corner, as if he doesn't know how to act around the Knights. The Unigaean barbarian is as Oric-y as ever, the man Hiccup calls Tarzan in armor that looks like it's been dragged through Jatla, his broken buster sword on his back.

Even if Ryuk expects to see the Knights of Non Compos Mentis, it is still surprising to walk into the Knights' guild and see some of the legends themselves. He's also reminded of just how strong they are as he briefly scans their stats:

Aiden Level 99
HP: 6969/6969
ATK: 6888
MATK: 313
DEF: 3320
MDF: 2459
LUCK: 119

Sophia Wang Level 99
HP: 7399/7399
Mana: 3976/3976
ATK: 751
MATK: 1983
DEF: 1341
MDF: 4485
LUCK: 108

Quantum Hughes Level 99

HP: 8675/8675

ATK: 3090

MATK: 10

DEF: 420

MDF: 571

LUCK: 69

Doc Level 99
HP: 7499/7499
ATK: 5554
MATK: 1128
DEF: 8330
MDF: 4532
LUCK: 102

Doc wears a t-shirt that is just tight enough to show that the aged Dream Team contract hacker and weapon enthusiast still knows his way around a gym. The War Faun's shirt reads *Dirty Dave's Weapons Emporium*, and he has a black tactical vest over this. Next to him is Aiden, or Morning Assassin, as the Knights call him, who is decked out in shinobi-esque armor and a black mask.

"Balaclava—!" Hiccup starts to say. He slaps both his hands over his mouth.

"There they are, there they friggin' are," says Quantum Hughes. The famous gamer is in all black just like he was last time Ryuk saw him, a matching trench coat too. His silver-blonde hair looks like he's run his hand through it a few too many times, and something about the look behind Quantum's eyes tells Ryuk that he can be a real pain in the ass at times. The only thing that throws his outfit off are a pair of black Crocs on his feet with spikes on them.

"That's him," FeeTwix tells Ryuk. "The man himself. Sorry we're late, Quantum." He bows. "I learned this in Japan."

"Japan, huh? Never been. Nope, I try to stick to the Midwest. Safer there. And no sweat off my back if it was your plan to leave us waiting. But Sophia here. Sheesh, you three really know how to light a spark under her—"

"I was wondering when you'd show up." Sophia, who has her white fro pulled back into two Minnie Mouse ears, smiles wryly at the Mitherfickers. "It's about time."

"Bust their balls on your own time, Sophia." Quantum winks at the Swede. "FeeTwix, right?"

FeeTwix goes pale. Ryuk elbows him. "Yes! Yes, that's me. Ahem. FeeTwix Fajer, Twixy to my goblin friends. Want to see something cool? I'm embarrassed to show you this but..." FeeTwix snaps his fingers and an I <3 Quantum shirt appears over his tactical vest.

Sophia rolls her eyes.

"Not a bad shirt, kid. Heh. I might need to get myself one of those. You know, I've been thinking about your style, or better, I've been thinking about how you lifted my style and are trying to pass it off as your own. How many people watch your livestream again? You're some sort of pro streamer, right?"

"Upwards of four million, Mr. Hughes. And yes sir, Mr. Hughes, it is my career of choice."

"Mr. Hughes was my father. Call me Quantum. Streaming, huh? I still can't believe that's a legit profession, even if it has been my entire life. But hey, I'll take that over AI writers and AI influencers. Anyway. Four million jabronies watching, huh? Imagine that. Friggin' twenty-first century post-zoomers that probably know nothing about me. Now, I'm not saying that bothers me. I'm just saying."

"What's your point again?" Sophia asks Quantum.

He ignores her and continues. "I want to get back to your style, or should I say, *our* style." A dark look takes shape on Quantum's face. For a moment it seems like he's about to spring a weapon on FeeTwix, especially after he slips his hand behind his back. "And since we share a look," he says, his snarl shifting into a grin, "I thought it was only appropriate I got you a pair of these."

A pair of black Crocs with spikes on them take shape in his hand.

"Crocs? For... me?" FeeTwix nearly squeals with delight.

"That's right, kid. A pair of custom Crocs that I had Ol' Dave replicate a couple years ago. Got these on sale at a digital WalMacy's in one of their Proxima Galaxy Bogo Weapon Specials."

"Bogo. I love bogo."

"Everyone loves bogo. Believe you me. Anyway, give 'em a try."

FeeTwix's black leather boots disappear. He takes the Crocs and places them on his feet. His eyes flash, as if they're syncing something with his system. FeeTwix turns to show the others. "These are fickin' awesome."

Hiccup is just about to say something when the goblin glances at Zaena, gives her an innocuous smile, and winces as if he's holding in some gas.

"These are sweet!" FeeTwix jumps into the air and clicks his heels together.

"Whoa! Settle down there." Quantum and Doc take a big step back. Aiden does the same. Sophia just stands there with an annoyed look on her face. "You click those together three times and let's just say *there will be no place like home*, if you get my drift."

FeeTwix nods. "They explode. Just in case I need to take the poison pill. That's what you're telling me."

Quantum makes an explosive gesture with his hands. "Exactly. Kablooey."

Sophia shakes her head. "Are we done here? We have a serious issue and I'm pretty sure—going out on a limb here—that your guild might know something about it."

"It had to happen," Oric grunts, as if he's already heard what she's about to say.

A vein pulses on the side of Sophia's head. "I'm aware that you think it had to happen, but it has caused something rather unexpected, something we are going to have to deal with now."

"Are you going to say it or what, Sophe?"

"Sophia or Dr. Wang, not Sophe, Quan-tum."

Quantum scoffs at how she somehow manages to put several decades of disdain in the pronunciation of this two-syllable name. "Just spill the beans already. What are you writing, some gritty noir or something? Trying to get people to turn the page? Listen, toots—"

"I'm not Frances. You will not call me that."

"Where the hell is Frances anyway?" Aidan asks Doc. "Shouldn't she be here?"

"She's monitoring."

"Heya, toots." Quantum blows a kiss to the sky.

Agitation nearly causes Sophia's Minnie Mouse ears to flatten. Her agitation makes Ryuk realize just how much better his guild's relations seem to be. Zaena and Hiccup are often at each other's throats, and Ryuk certainly didn't like the goblin on most days, but their behavior was nothing like this. It always had a sense of endearment behind it, whereas Sophia's feelings for Quantum seemed like pure vitriol. "As I was saying. We seem to have a new problem. One that we can trace back to you."

Zaena places a hand on her chest. "Me?"

"Your pyro affliction. Due to healing it, something akin to black holes have opened over Polynya, portals tied directly to the OMIB. And what do you think happens when the backbone of the entire world opens in portals across all three of the floating continents, hmmm? Care to take a wild guess? Anyone?"

Hiccup boils over, his eyes filling with rage. "Now you listen here, you fickin' witched-ass fickbisquit."

Quantum claps his hands together. "Ha! Now that's a goblin!"

"No one, and I mean fickin' no one, talks to my Lizzy-poo like that. She's giving me a fickin' massage later, and you're over here fickin' agitating her, it's going to come back to me in some fickered way."

"Hiccup—"

"Marbles, you pinche liddle pug-faced fickbasket, I swear to the sweet teats of Busty Gazongas, Dirty Dave, Jesus—whoever the fick that is—and Julia Child, ditto, if you ever decide to whip your chalupa out in front of me again, you'd best believe my fickin' ass don't play. I'll cut that Vienna sausage off and stuff it like a chile relleno—that one is for you, Elfy—and then I'll force feed it to Dr. Wang over here."

Sophia's eyes flash white. Quantum steps in front of her, Aiden now at her side. "Easy, Sophe. The goblin sort of has a point."

She glares at Quantum. "What!?"

"I mean, you'd do anything for a guildmate, right? For me? Okay, don't answer that," Quantum says, "but for someone you like, like Doc. You'd do anything, right?"

Doc cracks his knuckles and the action seems to relax to some degree. "What Dr. Wang is trying to say here is that curing your pyro affliction has caused portals to open up, and demons have started to appear. Pretty tough ones, too. The good news is that their levels are relative to the continents they've spawned on. Talk about a glitch. So we're going to head to Ultima Thule seeing as how you all aren't the right level to go there yet, and your guild—"

"The fickin' Mitherfickers. Our guild has a name."

"—your guild will handle the portals on Polynya. We've got the British Assassins, Croc, and Jim the Doorman cleaning up shop in Hyperborea, so that should take care of that. Let me see, what else?"

"The pills," Sophia tells Doc, her shoulders sinking to some degree.

"Yes, that's right. We've got leveling pills for each of you, to help get you to the target level you'll need to be to visit Ultima Thule. Not gonna lie. We need you there. We can't have you XP farming while we're sealing up the demon portals in UT, now can we?" The war faun turns his hand over and produces a colorful Monday-to-Sunday pill container, one made of plastic. "Mrs. Doc got this for me so I remember to take my daily fish oil, Centrum silver, and vitamin D. Don't need it anymore because I get my fish oil directly from the source, not to mention most multivitamins are a sham. What I'm saying is I have a pond at my mansion in a Proxima Barbie world that will remain nameless."

"Take the damn pills, kiddos," Quantum says for Doc.

Sophia's eyes return to their normal color. "I've marked your map where the portals have appeared. I'd start with the one outside of Sulitlana. You can portal to Waringtla and go from there. Then Bluwid, and finally, New Gotha. And yes, we have business in Tokyo too. But at least knock out some of the portals first."

FeeTwix raises his hand.

Sophia squints at him. "Yes?"

"How exactly do we, um, *knock out a portal*?"

Doc tosses the pill container to Ryuk, who barely catches it.

"Fick, Marbles, about the only thing you'd be able to do on the baseball team is rub down the balls. That's something they fickin' do, right? Good to keep the balls nice and lubed."

"Fuck you, Hiccup."

"Right back at you, fickbag."

A metal box materializes in front of the Mitherfickers. It hovers there until FeeTwix takes it.

"I've made this one real easy," Doc says. "Press the red button, and then quickly place the metal box on the ground. Sort of a *Ghostbusters* vibe, if that means anything to you."

"I've heard of Fickbusters, but not that one." He frowns at Zaena. "And yes, I know I've lost my fickin' Thulean massage. Not my fickin' fault." Hiccup farts. "Been saving that one."

Enway places her hand over her mouth to conceal a laugh once a WW2 era gas mask forms on Quantum's face.

Doc shakes his head at the goblin and continues: "Anyway, triggering the button will summon an old friend of mine, of ours, named Rocket. Press the button. He'll take it from there."

Quantum gives the Mitherfickers a thumbs up, his voice muffled by the gas mask as he speaks again. "Easy peasy, lemon squeezy, as opposed to stressed depressed lemon zest, or flopsy topsy lemon dropsy."

The war faun tilts his chin to Quantum. "What he said."

(x)__(x)

The Mitherfickers spawn at the gates of Waringtla, Polynya's giant city where numerous Unigaean giants have settled since the Great Migration. The city is locked up tightly, likely because of the portals that have opened up across Polynya.

"How the fick are we supposed to get in there?" Hiccup asks as he looks up at the literal giant wall. "We're definitely going to need some fickin' pastries."

"We don't have time for pastries, Hiccup, we've got a portal to seal." FeeTwix's eyes go black. "Hello everyone, I'm baaaaaack! Back to tell you about the latest offer from UnitedDeltaSouthwest! It's the Valentine's Day extravaganza, with exclusive deals to Paris—*Paris est à proprement dire toute la France*—and so many other awesomely romantic places! Did someone say bogo? Yes, yes, yes! I said bogo! Buy one economy plus or greater fare and get the second one free! What's the catch? That's the catch—you have to buy economy plus, which, as we all know, is just so much better than economy. Board the plane before the plebes. Get two inches more space—two inches, people! Get upgraded snacks! Don't want the shortbread cookie? How about a yummy yummy granola bar all for the low, low price of nearly double the normal economy fare. Did someone say bogo? Yes! I said bogo! Right now through the UnitedDeltaSouthwest you can buy one economy plus or greater ticket and get one free! Terms and conditions apply. Black out dates available on the app. See the UnitedDeltaSouthwest app for more details." FeeTwix takes a deep breath in. "Wait. What's that? The fickers got a gift for Hiccup for his birthday?"

"It's his birthday?" Enway asks. She's no longer wearing her sunglasses, the mage's eyes glowing red as she turns to the goblin. "Is it really your birthday?"

"Easy there, demon eyes, fickin' sunglasses back-the-fick-on or look somewhere else. It's my birthday? Hold the fick up. Did you say it's my birthday and I'm getting a gift?" Hiccup plows through Ryuk and Enway, who were just close enough that their hands were touching. "Poofters!" he calls to them as he reaches the Swede. "Gift me, Twixy, fickin' pronto!"

"Damn, Hiccup, chill!"

"Twixy, if someone has a fickin' gift, you bet your frozen viking chalupa I'm going to get what's mine. Is it a Jatlan ficklight? Been meaning to try one of those."

"A what?" Enway asks Ryuk.

"I don't want to know."

Zaena frowns, as does Oric, who stands off to the side with his big bad wolf.

"Get ready, Hiccup!" FeeTwix turns both hands over and a gauntlet appears, one with buttons on it that look like they'd be better off on an old Nintendo, the kind Ryuk has seen in museums.

"What the fick am I supposed to do with this? Is this some sort of tug-assist? I know this one place in Bluwid—"

"It's not for that, Hiccup, I assure you. Watch." FeeTwix presses a button on the inner wrist of the gauntlet. "Fick you."

"Fick me? What the fick, Twixy, I thought we were bffs?"

FeeTwix then presses one of the eight buttons on the opposite side of the piece. A circular speaker on the gauntlet replays what he's just said.

~~*Fick you.*~~

Hiccup's eyebrows raise in confusion. "Was that a fickin' ghost? Marbles, get over here, *now,* and make sure that's not a fickin' ghost."

Ryuk, who is busy equipping his marble shotgun and loading it with sword and explosive marbles, ignores the goblin.

"It's a soundboard, Hiccup. Built into a gauntlet that has, from what I can tell, no other properties aside from its comedic purposes. So… it's a soundboard gauntlet. Let's call it that. Cool!" FeeTwix presses the button again.

~~*Fick you.*~~

"Plain English, Twixy. I'm not over here trying to speak whatever the hell they speak in Botswana."

"I'm pretty sure they speak English there."

"You get what I'm saying. What the fick does this thing do exactly?"

"You can record your voice and assign it to the eight buttons. Then, you can press these buttons instead of having to speak. I've already assigned one. Check it out." FeeTwix presses the button again.

~~*Fick you.*~~

Hiccup turns to Zaena. "Speaking of gifts, whatever happened to that fickin' Thulean massage you promised me?"

"You spoke back there, goblin. I gave you one simple task, and you failed. Not only that, you already recognized that you failed."

"I failed by coming to your defense. Fickin' lizards. It's no wonder people think those in charge of Tritania are all lizard people. Fick me, Marbelito, amirite?"

Enway turns to Ryuk. "Marbelito? That's kind of cute..."

Ryuk just shakes his head.

Oric, who has been standing there the entire time glowering at Hiccup, sighs miserably.

"What's with this fickin' guy?" Hiccup gestures to Oric. "Does Conan the angry emo barbarian have to fickin' come with us?"

"Actually, I think I'll go out on my own." The warrior from Unigaea turns away from the group. His big Tagvornian mount doesn't. He stops a few feet away from them. "Wolf?"

Hiccup whistles and Wolf turns to him. "Heh. Fick you, Robert E. Howard! It appears that Wolfie has chosen sides."

"Robert E. Howard?" Oric asks.

Hiccup shrugs. He swipes the soundboard gauntlet out of FeeTwix's hands and presses one of the buttons. The Swede's smooth voice comes out of the speaker.

~~*Fick you.*~~

"Heh!"

"I'll catch up with you all later. And Wolf, sure, stay with them." The muscled loner leaves, the rest of the Mitherfickers silent until he is no longer in eyeshot.

"Well, I'll say it if no one else will. Fick him and the wolf he rode in on. Let's see here." Hiccup examines the soundboard gauntlet. "Press this back button to record. Press this to play it back. *Fick!*"

~*Fick!*~

~*Fick!*~

~*F-F-F-F-F-F-F-Fick! Fick! Fick!*~

He then burps a fick that sounds like a low death-metal scream. "Oof, I was saving that one. Let's hear it."

~*FICK.*~

~*F-F-Fick!*~

"Enough, Goblin. We're here on a mission."

~~*Fick you.*~~

FeeTwix, who has been scanning messages from his fans, gasps. Concern traces across his face. "We've got another problem, Mitherfickers."

~*FICK.*~

"What now?" Ryuk asks.

"An airship has appeared on Ultima Thule and the Drachma Killers have begun taking the towns. Drachma Killers. Where have I fickin' heard that term before?" Wolf barks as FeeTwix scans through more messages.

~FICK.~

"This looks bad," the Swede tells the group, Wolf now so agitated that he's running in circles and barking.

Hiccup slaps him on the rear. "Cool it, Wolfie! You smell lady chup or something?"

"We need to tell Oric," says FeeTwix.

"Hercules? Someone DM him or some fickin' shit. That muscled ficker has already wandered off into the wilderness like he's Kwai Chang Caine."

Ryuk switches to messenger to tell Oric of the news. The reply comes rapidly.

Oric: I'm heading to Ultima Thule. Get the levels you need and meet me there.

"Who the fick does he think he is?" Hiccup, who has already fashioned the soundboard gauntlet around his fat arm, records another fick, this one with a sultry undertone.

~Mmm, fick.~

"Heh, that one's for you and Elfie, Marbles. Next time you two get intimate, I'll be standing there behind the curtain, watching, and will press this one."

~Mmm, fick.~

"Hiccup, shut the fuck up."

"Not happening, Marbles. If you don't know me by now, you will never never never fickin' know me."

Ryuk equips the pill holder Doc gave him. "Time to take these."

~Mmm, fick.~

Zaena slaps Hiccup on the back of the head with one of her ghost limbs.

"Hey—!"

~~Fick you.~~

"We need to hurry, goblin. The portal is open, demons are coming out, and we're wasting precious time. Not only that." She sucks in a deep, troubled breath. "This is my fault. I need to do something about this."

~Mmm, fick.~

FeeTwix tries. He tries hard not to laugh, he tries so hard that his face turns as red as Enway's eyes. But finally, it boils over. The Swede laughs, then he's forced to catch up with Zaena to beg for forgiveness.

"This is all your fault," Ryuk tells Hiccup after he has mounted Wolf. "You need to act like a... like a good goblin. And take your pill." He hands the pill to Hiccup, who pops it in his mouth and washes it down with a healing potion.

"That's bussin', Marbelito. Bet."

What?

~Mmm, fick.~

CHAPTER 3: DEMONS, PORTALS, AND MANTRAS, OH FICK!

"FICKIN' STARFISH FICKERS!" Hiccup domes a demonic creature with a dimpled Iggy Pop face and lanky-long arms that drop into sharpened yellow claws.

Instakill!

"Fick yeah. Suck my chupie, Satan!"

A blistering bolt of pink energy freezes several of the demons that have dropped from the trees. FeeTwix quickly mows them down with a Mark 2 Lancer Assault Rifle that has a Chainsaw Bayonet Attachment.

-75 HP! -69 HP! -42 HP! -136 HP!

Critical Hit!

Insta-Insta-Instakill!

"Thanks, Enway!" the Swede shouts.

"No problem, Twix!"

~FICK.~

"Focus!" Ryuk calls to Hiccup, who has slipped to the side to play with his soundboard gauntlet and sip from a fresh healing potion. Hiccup triggers the button that FeeTwix set up earlier.

~~*Fick you.*~~

"Demons, be gone!" The Swede shoots and saws like he's been playing first person shooters all his life (which he clearly has). "That's right, fickers! If you sign up for a checking account with Chase Bank of America Fargo, they'll wave the $35 monthly fee for the first six months as long as you keep a cool 10K in the account and have monthly deposits of more than 3K. Fick you, demon!" FeeTwix chainsaws into the skull of a demon just about to bite down on his arm.

Instakill!

"The real bonus comes when you maintain a balance of 10K for six months, which will net you a .025% interest boost! If you maintain a twenty thousand dollar balance, that interest rate boosts to .035%! Imagine what you can do with all that sweet, sweet moolah. The possibilities are endless!"

~*FICK.*~

"Twixy, that's a stupid fickin' deal. That's as dumb as putting money in CDs, whatever the fick those are. Who the fick is running the banks up in your world anyway? Sounds like the same fickers running the banks in Jatla. Marbles, get out a pen and paper. Firstly, after six months you're paying thirty-five bucks for what? For them to fickin' hold your money like a goddamn bank is supposed to? Then, these fickwits give you .035% interest. Fick me, I'd rather take my chances on one of the airship casinos outside Bluwid. Twix—we talking daily compound interest or fickin' what? I'm not going to get ficked by a banker again. Nope, not this time around. That's how I met Spew Gorge's mom, you know. She was a fickin' loan officer, and I had to do what I had to do to pay off my debt." Hiccup tosses a potion over his shoulder and inadvertently hits a demon in the face, one that Zaena has been engaging.

-111 HP!

Critical Hit!

"Fick yeah. Don't say I never did nothing for you, Liz!"

"To get started, you'll need to visit Chase Bank of America Fargo's website or their app and enter code #FeeTwixRox. You'll be on your way to the American dream in no time!"

The Swede ducks as Ryuk fires a sword marble into the skull of a demon.

Instakill!

"Thanks, Ryuk!" FeeTwix shouts, his eyes black and gleaming as he finishes his ad read, which draws plenty more ire from Hiccup as he continues to point out flaws in the banking systems in both the Proxima Galaxy and Ryuk's world.

Wolf leaps over Hiccup and rips into a demon. "Rip that ficker to shreds, Wolfie. Go for his chalupa!"

~F-F-Fick!~

The Tagvornian wolf responds by tearing a limb from the demon and shaking his head rapidly, madness in his eyes.

Hiccup shoots his mechanical hand out to Ryuk. "Marbles, potion me. Pronto, you ficker!"

"You just had a potion." Ryuk unloads several more sword marbles from his shotgun.

-76 HP! -89 HP! -102 HP!

Critical Hit!

"And? For fick's sake, Marbles, when Uncle Goblin asks for a fickin' potion, you fickin' give him one. What the actual fick is—Fick!" A demon tackles Hiccup.

"Hi-yah!" FeeTwix responds with a silver throwing star that explodes the demon's head, drenching Hiccup in blood.

Instakill!

"Demons, be gone!"

"Fick, Twixy, you trying to take my topknot too?" Hiccup pats his pink hair down. "Yoy! That was too fickin' close."

A demon lunges for Ryuk from the side, talons out. His Dream Armor protects him from taking any damage. Ryuk swivels, and pumps a sword marble directly into the demon's face. He moves past the hellspawn, needing to reload. He does so rapidly, mixing in sword and explosive marbles.

Ryuk always has the option of touching his chest and becoming a Berserker Warrior, but he's having fun right now as a ballistics mage, so he keeps up the cover fire as Zaena springboards ahead and *Robespierres* a trio of mangled hellspawns.

Insta-Insta-Instakill!

"Aye, demons!" Zaena screams something in Thulean as she comes down hard on another one of the demons, this one a few heads taller than the others.

Instakill!

The demonic mob continues to swell toward them, yet there is an end in sight, one that Ryuk recognizes as a potential boss battle. The outline of a gigantic hellspawn appears above the tops of the trees, its eyes blazing red.

That's a big demon...

Ryuk takes an epic step back, gritting his teeth as he calculates how they can possibly bring it down.

"Snap out of it, Marbles! Stop staring at the ficker like he's Elfy and she's finally given you a fickin' taste of her WAP."

Click-click, boom! Click-click, boom!

~FICK~

Steeling himself, Ryuk fires a half-dozen explosive marbles toward the approaching demon, which continues to remain partially obscured by the darkness of the woods. He can spot its handle now, but he's not ready for what he sees next. The mecha-sized demon has scale armor covering most of its body aside from its groin area. It has two heads, each with forked tongues, and its bulging red eyes are covered in white veins. A yellow shock of stringy hair frames its horrific face which really matches its man bush.

Petty Demon King Level 30
HP: 666/666
ATK: 132
MATK: 0
DEF: 89
MDF: 50
LUCK: 6

"Petty ficker." Hiccup cracks up once he sees the demon's handle. "Holy ficktits. I knew a petty ficker back in Jatla. I'll tell you about him later, kiddos. And fick me, Elfy, look at the demon's *Mark of the Beast* eyes. Heh. It's your twin."

"Shut the fuck up, Hiccup!" shouts Ryuk, his voice cracking.

Hiccup lifts his left thigh and lets out a squeaker as the giant demon takes a step closer to them. "Marbles, I know I told you a day ago that your balls had finally dropped, that you were well on your way to becoming a fickin' man, especially once you turned in your 4chan weeb card and finally, finally, exchanged the homoerotic octopi porn for some nice and juicy lady chup. But somehow, against all fickered odds, you've managed to fickin' suck your balls right back up to the point you're going through puberty again in some sort of *America's Funniest Home Videos* meets *Benjamin Button* mash-up on an NFT steaming service that has long since caved. No wonder your fick-faced ficktart of a brother hates you. I'd fickin' hate you too if you weren't my employer, not to mention the fact that both of you are a pair of fickin' Yakuza nepo babies. Wait. Wolfie. Wolfie! Fick! Get your poochy ass over here!"

Two demons converge upon the mouthy goblin just as he's equipping the axe that Dirty Dave gave him. One of the demons is blasted backward courtesy of Enway, who remains on the periphery like a good mage.

Instakill!

"You're welcome," she calls over to him.

"Fick yeah, I am!" Hiccup swings at a hellspawn, misses, and is tackled by a different demon. He elbows it, hops on top of the demon, headbutts the monster—his attack bolstered by his golden helm—and then uses his axe to split the demon's head in half.

Instakill!

Hiccup huffs, summons a Cherry Apollos, and chugs it while looking at Marbles.

~*Fick!*~

"*Baka.*" Ryuk focuses again on the Petty Demon King. He sends his marble shotgun away, figuring it's time to take it up a notch.

Ryuk presses the runestone on his chest.

The combined power of the Runestones of Tritinakh courses through him as Ryuk selects Berserker Warrior. He feels his muscles bulge as his Dream Armor adjusts around them. Ryuk suddenly feels stronger, like his breaths fill his lungs in a different way.

Tamana's ironing board of a sword appears in his hands. He takes off toward the Petty Demon King to join Zaena, cutting down a smaller demon in the process.

Instakill!

"Fick, Marbles, save some of that real Alpha fick energy for Uncle Goblin over here," Hiccup says once Wolf has come around, giving him a mount. "Those fickin' Runestones are like aftermarket Jatlan viagra, good for chuptile dysfunction. I took two of those little fickers a few weeks back. Boy fick, let me tell you, I just about saluted every fickin' flag in Jatla—"

"—That's right, BubonicBabe420! You are indeed the lucky-lucky winner of a year's supply of grade A feminine hygiene products! CVSgreens is all about providing women with all the things they need to stay regular and maintain control of their flow! Now, you may be asking yourself, should I, someone who identifies as a cisgender male, be doing this ad read? Of course I shouldn't! But do I find access to women's health products important enough to take CVSgreens' money? Of course, I do!" FeeTwix chainsaws through a demon, blood splattering across the front of his *I <3 Quantum* shirt, which he still wears over his bulletproof vest.

Instakill!

FeeTwix kicks another demon in the chest with one of his spiked Crocs. "Next time you've stopped in for some hygienic purchases, show them this QR code to get 15% off your purchase. What a deal!"

A QR code appears in the air.

"Mention #FeeTwixRox to get an additional 2% off after you've spent one hundred dollars or more. That's 17%! Imagine the savings—screenshot this QR code now!"

"For the love of fick, Twixy, you're no better than a fickin' orc chippie. The only difference is they can look at themselves in the mirror at the end of the fickin' day, and you can't. And what the fick is a QR code? Is that slang for something Marbles uses to moisturize his gooch? Why is the QR code shining in the air like the fickin' lights outside a Jatlan strip joint? Fick you, Lucifer!" Hiccup brings his axe across a demon's arm, severing most of it.

-145 HP!

Critical hit!

The rest of the demon's arm just dangles there for a moment, causing the goblin to laugh. "That's what I look like when I've jerked it too mu—fick!"

Wolf lunges toward the Petty Demon King, bringing Hiccup with him. He takes a bite out of its ankle, which sends Hiccup flying up and over the monstrosity. The goblin hits a tree.

"Yoooooooooooy!"

Seizing on his opening, Ryuk races toward the beastly demon just as it comes down to swipe at him. He strikes its forearm with his sword.

-72 HP!

Critical Hit!

~FICK~

Zaena appears on Ryuk's right. "We've got this, you and me."

She takes off, her ghost limbs allowing her to reach the giant demon's face with her next strike.

As she cuts away at its HP slowly, Ryuk prepares for his next attack. He wonders if he'll gain any skills in the other classes. It'd be nice to do something like cut the big fucker down with a single strike that also has a ripple effect, or be able to throw his sword and catch it on his return like something he once saw on an anime series called *Pilgrim*.

"Incoming!" FeeTwix hits the Petty Demon King with some sort of surface to air missile, which blows off a chunk of its chest and shoulder. The Swede rolls to the side, chugs a healing potion due to the damage he has received from using a firearm, and claps his hands together as the red number flashes above the Demon King's head.

-200 HP!

Critical Hit!

Ryuk strikes the giant demon's leg, taking another big piece of its HP.

-115 HP!

The kill shot goes to Enway, who hits it with a spark of pink magic that causes the demon's eyes to explode.

Instakill!

"Holy fick!" Hiccup gets to his feet and wipes some of the demon blood off his forehead. "Dang, Elfie, remind me not to get on your bad side."

She beams over at him. "You've been reminded numerous times now."

"Whew!" FeeTwix says, his eyes still black. "I'm guessing everyone just got a level. I got two!"

Zaena and Enway nod; the Thulean princess flashes the number two with her fingers.

Ryuk gives FeeTwix a thumbs up.

"Um, Hiccup?"

"Um, Twixy?" Hiccup says in a mocking way. "Fick a level, did you all see that demon's fickin' chalupa? Nevermind its yellow bush, don't know how it got bleach in the OMIB, that fickin' chup is worth something." The goblin is now on the other side of the towering demon as a healing potion slowly materializes in his hand. "Talk about a shower not a grower. Someone cut that fickin' thing off. Marbles, you've got a sword, you can do it. Tammy would be proud. I'll sell the demon chup in Jatla or Bluwid. Lot a fickin' money in selling chalupas, especially demon ones. The more foreskin, the better. Fick. I'd probably make more selling just one of these things than I'll ever be paid as a security guard for the Mitherfickers." Hiccup's axe fades away and he jams his finger on his gauntlet.

~FICK.~

Zaena looks from Hiccup to FeeTwix with disgust. "You should have never gotten him that gauntlet."

"It wasn't me, babe, it was my fans."

"Fick you, Liz. You're just fickin' jel-jel that you don't have fans that love you enough to give you birthday gifts. That's so fickin' basic of you."

"Basic? And did you say birthday? What are you going on about, goblin?"

Hiccup gestures in a way that is clearly meant to be phallic.

"You want to die, goblin?"

"Liz, I swear to fick, if you ruin my birthday, I'm going to be so fickin' triggered I just might—" Hiccup farts and glares at Ryuk. "What the fick, Marbles. Crop dust Elfie next time, why don't you? Where was I?" He squints at Zaena. "Demon chup... Marbles' sassy gassy assy..."

"Your birthday."

His eyes go wide with surprise at the Thulean's comment. "That's right, it's my fickin' birthday, Liz. And of course, of course I have to work on my fickin' b-day. Thanks a lot, Marbles."

Ryuk slowly relaxes his shoulders and lets out a deep breath. "It's not your birthday, Hiccup."

"How the living fick would you know?" The cantankerous goblin approaches FeeTwix. "Yo."

A big grin spreads across the Swede's face. "Yes, Hiccup? You have something to announce?"

"Fickers, I know you can see me. The gauntlet is cool and all—I love cool fickamajigs like this, especially ones I can later pawn when the times get tough—but what I really need, and I'll tell you what I want, what I really really want, is a cake. A fickin' birthday cake. I'm officially announcing that today is my fickin' birthday. That's right, I'm now 155 years old. If you want me to like you, if you really want to impress Uncle Goblin, you'll buy me a fickin' dragon wings cake the next time we see a DD's Barbecue. Now, listen here, fickers, I'm going to level with you. Those cakes aren't fickin' cheap. And no, before you ask, I'm not going to sell the demon chup I'm about to cut off to fund the cake. That's fickin' out of the question. That money is already accounted for. Did I mention these cakes were decorated with potions? And we're not talking about the store brand potions, or even the good brands like Hopkins and Cherry

Apollos, we're talking about the best potions in all of Tritania, the Thomas-James brand of healing potions. Fickin' shits aren't cheap."

Zaena shoves Hiccup forward with her ghost limbs.

"Hey!"

"Enough with your nonsense. We need to hurry, goblin. The Knights are doing their part, and we should do ours."

~FICK.~

"Fine, fine, Liz, but my birthday isn't over yet, and might extend into tomorrow depending on when we reaching fickin' civilization again." Hiccup places his fingers in his mouth and whistles for Wolf, even though the canine is already next to the goblin. "Good, there you fickin' are. That's a good boy. Let's go seal a fickered demon portal." Hiccup is just about to mount up when he remembers something. "But first, I need to get this fickin' demon chup before some other nitfick loots it. Shit is worth something." He summons his largest axe. "And stop looking at me like you've got fickin' Bluwid balls, Marbles. This won't take long."

(0)__(0)

Ryuk Matsuzaki Level 29 Ballistics Mage
HP: 1169/1169
ATK: 158
MATK: 211
DEF: 123
MDF: 93
LUCK: 24

FeeTwix Fajer Level 29 Berserker Mystic
HP: 1312/1312
ATK: 221
MATK: 43
DEF: 116
MDF: 69

LUCK: 28

Hiccup Level 28 Shield Thief
HP: 1854/1854
ATK: 144
MATK: 18
DEF: 330
MDF: 179
LUCK: 40

Zaena Morozon Level 29 Brawler Assassin
HP: 1360/1360
ATK: 275
MATK: 11
DEF: 248
MDF: 61
LUCK: 28

Enway Zoltan Rosa Level 28 Hourglass Mage
HP: 1031/1031
MANA: 614/614
ATK: 85
MATK: 199
DEF: 78
MDF: 195
LUCK: 24

Wolf Level 40
HP: 2402/2402
ATK: 699
MATK: 0
DEF: 534
MDF: 241
LUCK: 19

Ryuk swipes the guild stats away as they reach an open meadow. They haven't encountered any more demons since the initial batch, but he's pretty sure there are more on the horizon. Back in his Ballistics Mage form, Ryuk now wears his hood over his head, his marble slingshot tucked into the back of his belt for easy access.

As a few butterflies appear, he turns to find FeeTwix sharing a healing potion with Hiccup. Once he finishes his ad read—the Swede selling some influencer's new body image boosting lingerie—his eyes flash blue.

"And that's a wrap, phew."

"Phew is fickin' right, Twixy. I'm not going to be a fickin' liar and say I haven't struggled with body dysmorphia. All goblins have. Most of us are rotund, short and stout, and a few are puny liddle poofters like that ficker Spew Gorge. That damn goblin. I swear to fick. He really could have benefited from a father figure in his life, but don't fickin' look at me. I was busy at the time."

"I'm sure you were, goblin."

"The goblin has a fickin' name, Liz." More and more butterflies flutter across the field, enough that Hiccup swipes one out of the air and pops it into his mouth. "Fickin' protein, if you ask me." He chews the butterfly and swallows. "What I wouldn't give for some lemon pepper dragon wings, or birthday cake, or some combination of the two. *Hint hint, Mitherfickers.* I should really stash a bucket of wings in my inventory list, but that would cost fickin' money, money I don't fickin' have because I make less than minimum wage. Fick. Times are rough, the Tritanian economy is fickin' down and inflation is a whore of a bitch. The Thulean Fed is only making it worse. I'm not quite there yet, but I'm getting closer to the point that I'm thinking of selling bottled farts to all the adoring mitherfickers out there. What do you think, Twixy? Do people in your world buy ficked up shit like that?"

FeeTwix exchanges glances with Ryuk and Enway.

"I believe they do," she says. "For the right price."

"Holy fick, you're serious? What the fick are we waiting for? The bakery is open." Hiccup turns up the anal acoustics, the goblin nearly red in the face by the time he's finished. Wolf clearly isn't happy that the goblin has just airbrushed him with methane and digital hydrogen sulfide. "And that was just what I've been storing over the last few minutes. Ha! Imagine, Twixy. We'd be trillionaires."

"Selling your ass biscuits?" The Swede starts to turn his head, as if he's considering it.

Enway moves a few paces back, fanning the air.

"No. We are not doing that. Ass biscuits? Have some dignity. Both of you." Zaena lightly slaps Hiccup on the back of the head as she passes.

"Fick you, Liz!"

They continue on, the bickering Mitherfickers loosely following the map that the Knights gave them.

An incoming message splashes across Ryuk's eyes.

Sophia: What is taking your guild so long? There are several portals, and you've yet to reach one. We'd seal them ourselves, but the Drachma Killers are putting up a hell of a fight in Ultima Thule. You're supposed to be hurrying right now.

FeeTwix: Sorry, Sophia! We ran into some demons along the way.

Sophia: Don't you have a dragon? Why don't you just fly there?

"Snowballs?" Hiccup laughs. "That poor ficker. He's sort of like Spew Gorge, in a way. Never really had a father."

Ryuk: Yangu, our dragon, isn't mature yet.

"The fick you say, Marbles? Last time I checked he was almost full grown, and I'm not talking about his chalupa. But if you want, we can measure that next time we get back to Kayi."

Sophia: There are other portals that need closing. The one in Bluwid is especially troublesome because goblins have started to not only fight the demons, but also enter the portal into the OMIB. The last thing the OMIB needs is goblins. Believe me. Plus, the Bluwidians are rioting.

"The first thing the fickin' OMIB needs is goblins. We probably wouldn't be here, tasked with saving all of fickin' Tritania, if there was an element of chaos up there. Or down here? Where is the OMIB, exactly?" Hiccup squints up at the sky.

Sophia: Just hurry. Your progress is worrisome, your antics are two shades shy of moronic. It is making me, and the Knights, second-guess asking for your assistance.

Hiccup turns to Ryuk and flips him off. "Pass that along to Sophia." He farts. "That too."

Sophia: You do not want to know what I am capable of when I'm mad.

"We'll handle it," Ryuk tells Sophia. "Just give us another hour or so. Then we can log out and talk in person. Or something. Is that what you want us to do?"

Sophia: We'll be in touch.

"Heh. Fickin' fick, Marbles, she's got you whipped pretty badly over there." Another butterfly twists by and Hiccup grabs it out of the air. He stuffs it into his mouth, the wings sticking out as he looks at Ryuk and presses the FeeTwix button on his gauntlet.

~~*Fick you.*~~

With that, Hiccup, who is still mounted on Wolf, trots ahead.

"Okay, time for the adults to talk," FeeTwix says as he joins Ryuk, Zaena, and Enway. "It seems like we could use a little boost to get us there faster now that the boss lady has demands. I may have a solution. I have a steam-powered jetpack, which would allow us to fly. I also have an item printer that allows me to put an item inside and make an exact replica of it. It can't do everything—it wouldn't work on something powered by algomagic like your Dream Armor or the Runestones, but it should do the trick. I had to instabuy it from a Proxima Store when we were having ramen the other day. Wait, that was yesterday. Whew! Time sure flies when you're having a fick-of-a-time!"

~FICK~

"Cultural appropriation, Twixy!"

The Swede grins at Ryuk. "If we can just wait a moment, I can get some steampacks made, which will give us wings and make this trip much faster. They may ding our HP. I don't know about that part. They aren't exactly firearms, but I suppose you could use one as a weapon. But that's what potions are for, and luckily..." FeeTwix lowers his voice so only Ryuk can hear. "One of Hiccup's biggest fans, a guy named Van Der Toorn, bought us several cases of Cherry Apollos. We're good for a bit."

"So we fly to the portal in Sulitlana?"

"That's right, Ryuk. And I'm sure this will provide excellent content for my viewers." FeeTwix's eyes flash black. "Speaking of, we're back! That's right, folks, we've just figured out a way to get us to the portal even faster. Gather round, Mitherfickers, and behold!" FeeTwix points his finger up in the air as a steam-powered jet pack with two golden tanks fizzles into existence. "And that's not all!" A square box takes shape, one attached to a platform with a short conveyor belt on it. By this point, Hiccup and Wolf have circled back around.

TOKYO

~*F-F-Fick!*~

"I need to fickin' record more of these—Hey! What the fick are you doing, Twixy?" Nosy as ever, Hiccup hops off Wolf, hurts his knee in the process, and is just raising his hand to equip a healing potion when Ryuk slaps his hand down.

"Save them, Hiccup."

"Fick, Marbles, you've really done it now. You've really disenfranchised me to the point that I'm going to need to have a fickin' conversation with HR—"

"...And then you just put it here, press a button, and you have an exact replica." FeeTwix looks at Zaena and smiles. "Just making steampacks, babe."

The Thulean raises a skeptical eyebrow at the Swede. "Steampacks?"

Enway, who has just joined them, nods with excitement. "They are like jet packs. I've totally used one of these before in a different Proxima World, one called Steam. Anyone familiar?"

"That's Ray Steampunk's world," FeeTwix says. "I've spent some time there. Mostly exploring Verne Island and fighting rusty old mechs. Hell of a place."

Hiccup crouches down to examine the steampack. "Where does the fickin' steam come from? If this fick-traption is colonically powered, I just don't think Marbles has what it takes to toot himself along." The big wolf sidles up next to Hiccup, also curious. "That's a good fickin' pooch. Wait. How the fick are we going to strap a rocket onto Wolfie? He's already got a red one!" Hiccup laughs at his own joke. When no one joins him, he glares at Marbles. "In Jatla, I'm considered quite humorous."

"All good questions, Hiccup, all good questions. And of course you're funny." The Swede winks at him. "You've got seventy thousand

Mitherfickers watching now! Imagine that, seventy-fickin'-thousand people love your antics!"

~FICK~

The replicating machine starts up as FeeTwix launches into another ad read: "Fick is right! And if you really want to have a fickin' good time, head on over to Wendy's Hut for a Galentine's reduced-cal low-sodium lab-grown Spiced Turkey Bacon Chicken Sandwich. Hip, hip, hooray! Mention #FeeTwixRox at checkout, you'll get a ten-pack of Turkey Bacon Wrapped Dino Chickie Nuggies for free. That's F-R-E-E, free! Everyone loves free! This world-wide promotion starts today and lasts through the weekend, or until those sweet juicy chicken patties run out. Don't walk, *run* down to your nearest Wendy's Hut for their brand new Spiced Turkey Bacon Chicken Sandwich before the promotion ends. But wait, there's more! If you order through Uberyota Eats, you'll not only get free delivery, you'll also be entered for a chance to win a sweet, sweet trip for two to Bali courtesy of Wendy's Hut and Uberyota for you and your gal pal, or whomever you identify as your nearest and dearest. Any pronoun, any *body*, literally!" FeeTwix's machine starts to shake. "One last time so everyone in the back can hear it—"

The Swede starts the ad read yet again, and as he does the machine produces an exact replica of the jetpack, which it pops out the other end directly onto the platform.

"Holy fick, it worked! You could make good money with something like this. Let's make a copy of this." Hiccup summons the giant demon chalupa he cut off earlier using his axe. The large penis flops onto the ground. Enway gives the goblin a disgusted look and steps behind Ryuk. "What the fick, Elfie? You're judging me? You, the one who has yet to be fickin' vetted, has the audacity to cast judgment on my lucrative side hustle? Twixy, make at least two copies of this so I can sell this shit."

A hint of hesitation splashes across his eyes, even if they are black. "I don't know if that's a good idea, Hiccup. Also, those of you who aren't using the goblin filter, you might want to do that now."

"Filter me? What kind of safespace beta-dicked fickbunnies do you have following you, Twixy? Has no one in your world seen a demon chalupa before now?" He kicks the flaccid penis, which is about the size of a large duffle bag that has been stuffed to the brim. "This, kiddos, is worth good money. And because I'm not fickin' paid enough—"

"Fine, fine. Make a copy," Ryuk tells FeeTwix, just to be done with the goblin. "But only one copy, and only after we get the jetpacks we need. Let's do the jetpacks before we send that thing in. And what about Wolf?"

"That's right, Marbles, what about Wolfie? And glad to see you're taking your leadership role fickin' seriously for once." Hiccup crosses his arms, huffs, and turns away.

While his machine makes another copy, FeeTwix equips a mirror. "What do you think, Mitherfickers? How can we get the dog airborne?" His eyes twitch as he scans through what Ryuk assumes are messages from a private group of his most loyal fans. "Two jetpacks? Tie one to his tail and one to his snout? That doesn't sound like a good idea, Dawn!"

As FeeTwix continues to speak to his people, Enway removes the jetpacks as they come down the platform. Realizing he should help, Ryuk joins her and removes the next one, just as a third appears.

"...You do, Kay? Where did you get a thing like that? Sure, send it the fick over!" FeeTwix smiles at the mirror. "You're going to like this, Wolf."

The Tagvornian beast barks.

"That's a good boy. Someone pet him while I wait for Kay to send something over."

Hiccup scratches Wolf behind the ear with his mechanical hand. "Who the fick is Kay?"

"Kay? Why, she's the best." A large harness with wings appears, each wing with a cylindrical engine tucked under it. "There it is!"

"Holy fick, Wolfie, that's going to be fickin' sweet. How in the living fick is he supposed to control it?"

A small remote control replaces the mirror in FeeTwix's hand. He plays with it for a moment while his replicating machine produces another steampack. Soon, the winged harness is floating, the engines producing a clear energy and a light hum. "I've got it covered!"

"Fick yeah!" Hiccup shoves Ryuk aside as he reaches for one of the steampacks. "Everyone get strapped up, and no fickery. We've got a portal to seal. But before we do that, Twixy, demon chalupa copy, don't fick this income opportunity up for me."

(0)__(x)

The steam-powered jetpack has a lot more kick than Ryuk expects. Using it is an absolute blast.

Zipping through the air, FeeTwix just ahead of him, Ryuk does his best to keep up with the Swede as the wind ripples past his face. Zaena is off to his left, Enway his right, and Hiccup is at the back of the group—as always—keeping pace with Wolf who is in the winged harness controlled by FeeTwix.

Ryuk dips his head forward, bursts through a cloud, and squeezes the trigger that controls the amount of steam firing out of the back of his steampack. He catches up to FeeTwix, just as the Swede finishes an ad read for an airline company.

"...Just remember, the first checked bag is half-off if you use code #FeeTwixRox at checkout. No blackout dates, terms and conditions apply. See website or the UnitedDeltaSouthwest for details!"

"Fick yeah. Marbelito, I'm finally part of the mile-high club! I should take my pants off. I can imagine what it would feel like to have the clouds tickling my fickin' chup."

Ryuk looks over at Enway, who just so happens to be smiling at him. The red-eyed Hourglass Mage shifts closer to him.

"Are you ready for this?" she calls over the roaring wind.

"For more demons or for Hiccup to get naked yet again?"

"Let's hope not. And I meant for whatever comes next." Enway spreads her arms out wide. "I never thought joining a guild would be this exciting. And here I was, a loner thief for a long time."

"Solo stuff is great too."

Hiccup scoots up to Ryuk on his right. He winces, farts, and nearly buckles from the added power of his bottom burp. "Fick! And what's this about solo shit? Fick, Marbles, you would say solo stuff is great. Poofter!"

Wolf surges ahead, and Hiccup's eyes fill with worry. "Holy fick, Twixy—don't push Wolfie too hard. I'm coming, boy!" As naturally as ever, which is definitely a strange way to describe the rotund goblin, Hiccup flaps his arms to the side and whooshes forward, leaving Ryuk and Enway with one of his trademark parting toots.

Ryuk holds his breath for a moment. They're moving so fast that he's soon out of Hiccup's poot field, the ballistics mage finally able to speak privately to Enway again.

Being in a guild, he thinks as he remembers what they were just talking about. "A guild. Yes, it's pretty fun, this guild of ours. I don't like the name so much, but it sort of fits."

She laughs as strands of her dark hair flit against her face. "The Mitherfickers."

"Yeah, that's us. When I started it with Tamana, I never thought it would come this far. We just wanted a challenge. A reset."

"And look at us now, about to do our part in saving Tritania. I never would have imagined we'd do that."

"We haven't saved it yet," Ryuk says as their group starts to arc toward the ground. They've just passed a forest and a small village that Ryuk sees isn't currently listed on their map. He has encountered this before in Tritania. The AI is constantly at work behind the scenes to keep exploring interesting.

After another thirty minutes of travel, thirty minutes in which Ryuk tries to make conversation with Enway, he sees the outer rim of a battle. Hundreds of NPCs, RPCs, and regular player characters are battling the demons flying out of a massive portal up ahead, one that resembles a black hole.

"We've got company!" FeeTwix announces as the air starts to populate with dragon riders and winged hellspawns, the demons ranging from human size all the way up to floating whales. "And you can have company too!" he tells his fans as he summons one of his mutant hacks. It morphs into a gun arm as FeeTwix starts up his next ad read.

"Fickin' spare us, Twixy!"

"Lonely? Feel like talking to someone? In need of some social interaction? Boy, do I have an offer for you! Uberyota has partnered with BetterCalm and the good folks at MercSecure to offer you a brand new service. Make-A-Friend! Make-A-Friend will custom engineer a humandroid friend that fits all your quirks and eccentricities! Love to talk politics? Your Make-A-Friend humandroid will agree with everything you say or argue every one of your points with or without logic! Feel like cuddling? You know I got you, boo. Have you tried Make-A-Friend? These humandroids can be customized to fit your unique body type and cuddle requirements. Just need someone to cry to? How about a humandroid who always has a tissue available! Have a past trauma that would take years of therapy to overcome? How about months instead? What if it were possible to overcome them in weeks? These humandroids are trained by an Ivy League team of therapists and neurocognitive experts to deal with any and every type of trauma! Make-A-Friend!"

"Fick your therapy slaves, Twixy. Shoot your fickin' gun already!"

"With pleasure, Hiccup!" The Swede swivels his legs forward and fires a sizzling yellow blast of energy at an incoming demon. It shreds through the demon's wing, causing the demonic monstrosity to spiral toward the ground below, where it leaves a smoldering crater.

Instakill!

~FICK~

"Heh! Splat goes the fickin' bitchtitted demon. Wait. Fick! What the fick are we supposed to do about the portal again? That mitherficker is practically shitting out demons at this fickin' point." Hiccup points at it just in case the others can't see the portal. "Look at the size of that thing! Heh!"

For once, Hiccup isn't wrong. The portal is indeed shitting demons, the monsters spilling out of it like someone connected a firehose to Beezebub's ass and cranked it to full blast. Varying in size and deformity, the demons falling to the ground below show no sign of slowing down.

We've got to do something...

Ryuk fires sword marbles from his shotgun into the body of another flying demon.

-121 HP!

Critical Hit!

He zips to the side; Ryuk sees Zaena twist forward into a death spiral as she cuts through several flying hellspawns.

-68 HP! -72 HP! -76 HP! -58 HP!

A pink blast of energy from Enway disintegrates the demon into a mist of blood.

Instakill!

"Fick yeah, Elfie. Fick these diablos!"

~*Fick!*~

"We've just got to get closer to the portal. Follow me, everyone!" FeeTwix juices his steamjet and bolts ahead. "Let's head toward the ground—less distractions there."

"How the fick is there less—? Hey!" Hiccup shrieks as Zaena yanks on his leg with one of her ghost limbs. The two arc toward the ground, Wolf on their heels, the canine with his ears flitted back, his tongue flapping in the wind.

"Let's go, Ryuk!" FeeTwix says as a pair of steampunk goggles appear over his eyes. "Just like in the Netflix Hulu movie!"

Left wondering which movie he is referencing, Ryuk has no time to ponder this as Enway loops her arm in his and triggers her jetpack. She laughs as the pair torpedo toward the ground, only to swoop up at the very last moment.

Ryuk lands on his feet—barely.

He looks ahead and sees FeeTwix go with a superhero landing. The Swede has since ditched the steampunk goggles and has donned the half Reaper skull, FeeTwix already *Guns Akimbo* as he fires on demons left and right, the skull aiding his aim.

Bang! Bang! Bang!

Now in his gold helm, Hiccup races toward the front of the battle on wolfback, the goblin swinging his axe and hitting anyone, friend or foe, who stands in his way. "Get the fick out of our way!"

A demon launches right at Ryuk, the dirty little hellspawn seemingly appearing out of thin air. It tackles Ryuk. The two land on a pair of wayward, and way dead, knights. The demon digs its claws into his shoulders. Ryuk is able to buck him off. He grabs one of his molten marbles and sticks it in his mouth. As the demon comes in again, Ryuk completely torches it with a big breath of fire.

-58 HP! -45 HP! -37 HP! -82 HP! Critical hit!

Spit Fire!

Skill level up!

Skill: Spit Fire

Level Three: Stuff a marble in your mouth and spit it at an enemy. Higher levels allow for more control and sustained magical abilities.

Requirements: LUCK > 7

~FICK~

Hiccup throws himself off Wolf, who instantly leaps onto a demon and bites into his face. The goblin collides with the demon that Ryuk has just ignited, killing it upon impact.

Instakill!

"Fick, Marbles..." Hiccup mumbles as he gets to his feet. The goblin uses his mechanical arm to beat out fires that have transferred to his clothing. A healing potion appears in his other hand and he takes sips of it in between extinguishing the flames. At some point, he even uses the potion to put out the fires. Hiccup inevitably equips another potion once he runs out.

"Save the potions," Ryuk reminds the goblin. He has summoned his marble shotgun and is now in the process of loading the mag.

"Save the fickin' potions? I just *saved* your poofty liddle ass, you ungrateful ficktwat! This isn't some *We Are the Fickin' World* shit, Marbles, this is my fickin' life you're playing with here." Hiccup chugs some of the potion and burps. His tomahawk appears in his hand and he tosses it at an incoming demon.

Instakill!

~F-F-Fick!~

"Stop playing with that thing," Ryuk tells the goblin.

Ryuk moves back into action laying down cover fire for Zaena, who seems to be in the process of protecting FeeTwix while he deals with the device that Doc the war faun gave him.

Rather than listen to Hiccup bitch him out, Ryuk focuses on protecting Zaena using a series of explosive marbles that keep the demons back.

Insta-Insta-Instakill!

A mahoosive demonic arm now sticks out of the blistering portal, one that signals the sheer size of the hellspawns to follow if they don't act fast.

"Big ficker incoming!" Hiccup cuts into another demon.

-69 HP!

FeeTwix jams his finger down on the button again and again. "Why isn't it working?"

He switches to comms.

FeeTwix: Sophia! The button to call Rocket isn't working.

Sophia: It isn't? Let me ask Doc.

FeeTwix: Armageddon is about to break loose. Hurry!

Doc: I hear ya, kid. If the button isn't working, try stomping on it.

FeeTwix looks from Ryuk to an incoming demon, which Zaena unceremoniously decapitates.

Instakill!

Doc: Stomp it, kid! That always works too. Rocket is on comms. He just needs a spawning location.

"Here goes nothing!" FeeTwix tosses the switch onto the ground and brings his custom Croc down onto it.

The air ripples, the ground shaking as an enormous, blue flame twists across the battlefield.

The blue flames twist into the body of what looks like the DisNike Genie if DisNike was trying to tap into the India Market (which Ryuk was pretty sure they'd already done with the stake they bought in the ICC and their middle-of-the-century lineup of Bollywood animated features for DisNike+).

The man that takes shape is the size of a giant, no, the size of a god, his thick black hair long and flowing, his body blue as a Na'vi, his eyes yellow and filled with power. He stomps an incoming demon.

Instakill!

Sophia: Oh god.

Rocket: Oh god, is right. Vishnu is here to wreak some friggin' havoc!

A golden mace appears in Rocket's hand. He points the golden mace at the portal.

"Kaumodaki!" he says, his deep voice just about the most amplified thing Ryuk has ever heard in a Proxima world. ***"Om Vishnave Namah, grant me thy power!"***

Green algoenergy begins to swell at the tip of the enormous mace.

"Holy fickin' fickballs the Blue Man Dude is about to fick that portal up. Nope. Other way, Wolfie! Let's get the fick out of here. Mitherfickers, let's fickin' go! Take cover! Zaena, konoshlo your well-muscled ass out of there. FeeTwix, it's shield or fickin' foxholes if you can manage it. Elfie, do some time shit, I don't fickin' know. Marbles, tuck your head in your lady chup and start praying to Allah! Fick!"

Fuck you... Ryuk is just turning to glare at the fleeing goblin when Rocket speaks again.

"Om Namo Bhagavate Vasudevaya!"

With those words, the end of Rocket's club opens to reveal an electrified orb with green orbs of energy oscillating around it. It hits the portal, and instantly seals it up. The aftershock is strong enough to knock anyone standing off their feet. The green energy tears through the landscape, eviscerating demons, yet it doesn't hurt any of the friendlies.

By the end of it, Ryuk is lying on his side, his arm pretty much shot, his leg twisted. Nothing a healing potion won't fix. He equips one, takes a sip of it, and is just about to drink more when the potion is swiped out of his hand by Hiccup.

"Told you to run, Marbelito." Hiccup finishes the potion, burps, and tosses it over his shoulder. "Fick, that was fickin' awesome! The fireworks, not the potion. Although it wasn't bad either. Can't go wrong with a fickin' Cherry Apollos on your B-Day."

Rocket turns to the other players who have come to take part in the fight. He offers them a graceful bow, and then he floats into the air, his legs crossed beneath his body. There are no stats associated with his avatar. He seems completely ephemeral, seconds away from fading into nothingness.

Sophia: That was so extra.

Rocket: It was so awesome!

Quantum: Hey, I want to see some kablooey. Play it back, Soph.

Doc: I'll send you the playback.

Quantum: Thanks, Doc.

FeeTwix locks eyes with Ryuk yet again, the fanboy hardly able to contain the fact that Quantum is on their comms.

"What now?" Ryuk asks. "We logging out? Or should we..." He sighs, aware of the goblin asshattery that is in store if they go straight to Bluwid.

Sophia: Head to Bluwid. We'll regroup after that.

"You heard the fickin' boss lady," FeeTwix says, his eyes big and black as he watches Rocket fully disappear. "Let's kick another portal's ass! And for everyone watching at home, now would be a great time to remind you of WalMacy's latest sale—"

"Fick yeah!" Hiccup rubs his hands together. "Bluwid, here we fickin' come. DD's Barbecue better still be open." He snorts and spits. "They usually are during riots. Usually."

CHAPTER 4: IT'S THE MOST GOBLIN-FULL TIME OF THE YEAR

The eastern Polynyan goblin city of Bluwid looks especially bad as the Mitherfickers spawn somewhere between Dirty Dave's Weapons Emporium and DD's Barbeque, both of which are shut down, their storefronts protected by walls of metal and turrets.

"Fick, I really thought DD's would be open. Shit must be fickin' bonkers, bonkers, I tells ya, for DD's to shut down. Looks like Dave—who is fickin' innocent until proven guilty—knows what to do when the real looting starts up." Hiccup digs something out of his nose, examines it, thinks about eating it, and ends up flicking it at Ryuk. "Fick!"

Ryuk glares at the goblin. *Damn you...*

"Fick is right, Hiccup," says the Swede as myriad goblins scurry past, some carrying items they've stolen, others fighting the ones with loot, and still others going back for seconds, burlap sacks on their shoulders ready for the stuffing. "What the hell has gotten into Bluwid?"

"Wario Bluwid, wario? Dundrekh blantakh, jikh muukhai dundrekh blantakh!"

"Fick, Lizbunny, you kiss your sister with that mouth?" Now holding a healing potion, Hiccup squints at one of the item shops currently being looted. "Is that Spewy? Fick me, it's... Nope, false fickin' alarm. Just another poofty goblin with an emofick zoomer-hip fashion-forward mullet that has a lightning bolt shaved on the side. Fick. Where's the portal?"

Enway, who floats high enough that goblins can pass under her, brings a hand to her brow. She peers off toward what Ryuk guesses is the city center, yet there's no way of telling. It's all so cluttered here, and his current vantage point isn't helping. Rather than ask what she's looking at, Ryuk pops a gravity marble in his mouth and floats up to join her.

"What do you see?"

"Nothing great." Enway points out a cliff beyond town, one with goblins scattered before it, many of them capturing and enslaving the demons coming out of a portal rimmed in vibrant green algomagic and surrounded by thunderclouds. "I'm pretty sure that's where we need to go."

Text from Sophia appears on Ryuk's pane of vision.

Sophia: Give Rocket the coordinates so we can seal the portal up.

A pigtailed female goblin bursts out of the item shop and clubs another goblin with a jeweled scepter that looks valuable. "Get the fick away from me!" She charges toward the Mitherfickers and collides with Wolf.

"Hey!" Hiccup shouts. His toe knife appears in his hand and he points it at the female goblin. "What the fick? Get your own fickin' wolf, you liddle ficktwit!"

The looting goblin grabs her stolen scepter and rears back like she's going to strike Wolf with it. Zaena grabs the weapon with one of her ghost limbs and hovers it over the goblin's head. "Move along, little goblin."

"What the fick, Liz?" Hiccup asks. "After jingoism, racism, and I'm pretty sure communistic tendencies, you're going to add heightism and maybe even ageism to your fickin' litany of offenses against goblinkind?"

Of course he's defending the goblin, Ryuk thinks after he has floated back down to the ground.

"She was going to—you know what, goblin? Next time someone tries to hit you, I'll let them."

"You'd better fickin' not!"

"Fick you both!" The young goblin brings her fists up, tears suddenly streaming down her face. "I'll do whatever I have to do to get the fick out of Bluwid. The fickin' scepter was how I was planning to purchase an airship ticket to fickin' Jatla." Her face goes as pale as a green goblin's face can go. "He's back."

"He's back?" FeeTwix, who had just started an ad read, turns to the young goblin, curiosity filling his black eyes. "Who's back?"

The young goblin's teeth chatter. While she does so, Zaena uses her ghost limb to give the scepter back to the pigtailed goblinette. As soon as the girl has the scepter, the female goblin brings it back like she's going to strike one of them. "Grifty," she whispers. "Grifty is back."

Hiccup falls off Wolf. He scurries over to FeeTwix and gets behind him, the air filling with a foul smell as the goblin releases whatever he had been saving up on the wolf. "Oh, fick. Fick!" Hiccup triggers the death metal fick on his gauntlet.

~FICK~

"This is bad news, Twixy, real fickin' bad!"

"Fick!" the young goblin screeches, which causes more of the goblins in the streets around them to start yelling out curse words as well.

"Fick!"

"Fiiiiick!"

"FFFFFICCCCCK!"

"Enough." Ryuk steps between Hiccup and the young goblinette. "Who the fick—dammit—who the *fuck* is Grifty?"

Hiccup presses his mechanical finger against his lips. "Don't say his name lest he fickin' hear you, Marbles. Fick. I don't even know if I should say it. Stay strong, Hiccup, the entire world is looking toward you for inspiration and personal growth tips, not to mention sound investment advice."

"Just tell us, Hiccup."

"Fick, Marbelito, you really know how to make a shitty situation even shittier. Grifty is a demon with googly eyes, the googliest of eyes. He's a real ficker. He must have been freed from the OMIB or whatever that fickin' place is called. Wait. How do I even know that word? Point is, Grifty is the stuff of fickin' horror, kiddos. Those eyes. He is a hairy orange demon who will fickin' hypnotize you, get you high, then... you'll see. You'll see. Don't you say his fickin' name, Marbles. Fick. Is it true?" Hiccup turns back to the female goblin. "Tell me, Your Shortness, is Grifty really back?"

"Fick!" The female goblin strikes Ryuk in the groin with her scepter and takes off running.

-230 HP!

Critical hit!

Ryuk falls, the pain so intense that he can barely breathe. Hiccup starts to laugh. He laughs so hard that soon, he's lying on the ground next to Ryuk, which prevents Zaena from helping Ryuk up.

"I shouldn't fickin' laugh. I really shouldn't. But holy fick, Marbles, you need to start wearing a fickin' chup-strap. Another nut tap like that, and you and Elfie here... let's just say there *won't* be an angsty half-Japanese half-Mexican Yakuza future dumpster baby running around the streets of fickin' Tokyo, if you get my drift. You'll need some donor sperm. Maybe I can help there. Sorry. Fick. Where were we?"

"Grifty? You mean Gritty?" asks FeeTwix, who has been scanning messages from his fans. "Orange hair, googly eyes, sort of crazy looking. I'm pretty sure *Gritty* is the mascot for the Philadelphia Flyers. He's a goblin eldritch horror created by one of the developers as some sort of sick homage to the Flyers. Yeah, that's exactly what he is. Or is it a he? They?"

"Gritty? Pfft! Grifty is a he, Twixy, fick, don't get that shit twisted. Fick no. And Grifty is different from Gritty. If anything, your world fickin' jacked Grifty from us goblins and repurposed it. And Philadelphia? What the fick kind of word is that?"

"It's a city, Hiccup."

"Elfie, not now. The approved adult members of the Mitherfickers are speaking. Listen, if Grifty is out of the OMIB—"

"The goblin girl didn't say that he came from the OMIB."

"Where the fick else would he come from, Liz? Did you expect him to pop out of the birthday cake I am owed and that no one has fickin' purchased for me yet? Look, thousands, maybe millions of years ago, Grifty did some terrible things to goblinkind. Way worse than Thuleans, believe you me. I'd take a fickin' lizard over a hairy orange demon with googly eyes any day. But we sealed him away. Don't believe me? Ask any goblin. Hey! You, fickface—" Hiccup points at a goblin slipping by the group, one who has clearly stuffed looted items under his tunic.

"Yeah? What the fick do you want, fatso?" asks the goblin, who has an overbite that is affecting the way he speaks.

"The fick you say?" Hiccup grunts. "Nevermind. Grifty—"

"Fick!"

"Yes, *that* Grifty. How did goblins deal with his fickered ass back in the day?"

The random goblin gives Hiccup a funny look as if he should already know the answer to this question. "We fickin' sealed his hairy orange ass up."

"Where?"

"Fick if I know, fatso. But he hasn't been back for thousands or maybe even millions of years."

Ryuk tries not to roll his eyes and fails. *Tritania hasn't been in existence for a million years...*

"See?" Hiccup tells the group as the goblin moves on. "Where else would we seal Grifty if not the OMIB?"

Ryuk sighs. "We need to handle the portal."

"Yes, we do, Marbles. Thanks for pointing out the fickin' obvious. But if Grifty is free, we're going to need to do something about that. Fick. I don't want to, believe me, but the last thing, *the very last thing,* Tritania wants is fickin' Grifty running rampant across the three continents. Any-fickin'-hoo, I've said my piece." Hiccup chews his lip nervously. "If it's true, if Grifty is fickin' back, we should all be very afraid."

"I thought you said we should do something about your little goblin boogeyman," Zaena tells him with a slight chuckle.

An indignant look takes shape on Hiccup's face. He holds her gaze for much longer than he should be able to, until Zaena finally looks away. She scoffs at the goblin.

"Yeah? Laugh it up, Liz. We'll see who's laughing when Grifty shows up and shoves a fistful of fickin' drugs up someone's ass. We'll fickin' see. But you know what? Don't pay any attention to fickin' Uncle Goblin over here. Carry on, Mitherfickers, carry the fick on."

(0)__(0)

Hiccup complains about hazard pay the entire time it takes the Mitherfickers to fight their way through the streets of Bluwid.

Something that should be easy—visiting a Tritanian city and sealing up a portal—becomes incredibly difficult due to the sheer number of goblins that are either looting business establishments, trying to capture demons for nefarious purposes, or simply fighting one another. Because of the pills they have taken, the Mitherfickers manage to gain several levels. Soon, they'll be at a high enough level to travel to the final floating continent of Tritania, the smallest and snowiest of the three, Ultima Thule.

Instakill!

FeeTwix drives his slice bang through a goblin that has seemingly come out of the sewers hoping to steal his Crocs. "Not today, you little bastard! Speaking of today, today is the perfect time to check out The Old Banana Navy Gap Republic's super awesome, super blossom, holy wow-some, extra wholesome, Galentine's Day Extravaganza! For a limited time, spend just five thousand dollars and get a Tiffany and Co. collab friendship necklace! You get one piece, your bestie gets the other! Talk about a steal! A gold collectible that you and your coolest homie can have and cherish forever? Sign me up! In fact, I call upon Old Banana Navy

Gap Republic to send me one that I can share with our dear marblist, Ryuk!"

"Hey! What the fick, Twixy? If anyone is your bestie, it's me." Hiccup sees a demon come out of a broken store window. He equips one of his round shields and throws it like a frisbee at the demon, cracking it across the front of its horned skull.

-143 HP!

Critical Hit!

"Heh! Fick yeah! Also, did you say gold?"

"I sure did, Hiccup!"

~FICK~

FeeTwix chugs half a healing potion and throws the bottle to Hiccup, who finishes it and burps. The Swede jumps right back into his ad read: "And you too can get one of these sweet friendship necklaces by spending five thousand big ones and mentioning code #FeeTwixRox at checkout. Online, in store, and now available for same-day delivery, it's a Galentine's Day deal you don't want to miss!"

"Fickin' fool's gold if you ask me. You'll find better gold than that in the teeth of goblins all across Tritania. Look." Hiccup sticks his fingers in his mouth, shifts his tongue to the side, and tries to show Ryuk one of his gold molars.

"I'm trying to focus here, Hiccup." Ryuk uses his slingshot to strike a goblin that has just turned to them, a bottle of HotAzz Ballz sauce gripped tightly in her grubby little paw.

Instakill!

Skill level up!

Skill: Tonsil Shot
Level Four: 1 in 8 chance of connecting.

Damage: 48% if enemy is less than level 30; 20% if enemy is greater than level 30.
Odds of instakill: 15%
Requirements for instakill: LUCK > 10

"Fick yeah, Marbles. And right before she hit us with the HotAzz Ballz sauce." Hiccup approaches the female goblin and sets about looting her, entirely oblivious to the fact that both Wolf and Enway are defending him while he takes his sweet time. He grabs the bottle of hot sauce. After a bit of work, Hiccup manages to pop one of her molars out. Even as FeeTwix guns down goblins and demons, Hiccup approaches the Swede to show him the gold tooth.

"Not now, Hiccup!"

"Twixy, this is a fickin' PSA for you, for the Mitherfickers, and for anyone else stupid enough to watch your channel aside from the people that worship me. Now this, this is some good gold. Fickin' real good shit." He bites down on it to prove his point.

Zaena shouts: "Goblin! We have more important things to do. And that tooth was in her filthy mouth!" Zaena does a somersault and beheads a demon just on the verge of reaching them.

Instakill!

Beside her, Enway turns a goblin into a baby using a spell Ryuk hasn't seen before, and Zaena quickly slices it in two.

Instakill!

"For fick's sake, Liz, add fickin' goblin baby killer to your rap sheet." Hiccup summons a tomahawk, which he uses to beat back a demon that somehow has managed to break through FeeTwix's line of fire.

-58 HP! -62 HP! -49 HP!

The Mitherfickers are almost in a good spot, just another block or so and they will be directly under the portal, where they need to be to summon Rocket.

We need to finish with this, Ryuk thinks after a message comes in from Sophia, one that seems pretty annoyed by this point.

"Just a little further to go, Sophia!" FeeTwix shouts. "We could always use back-up, hint, hint!"

The Swede caps both a goblin and a demon with one epic shot.

Bang!

Insta-Instakill!

FeeTwix: Quantum isn't busy, is he?

Sophia: Why don't you ask him? He's on Comms. But to answer your question, yes, we are handling other things at the moment, things like the Drachma Killers.

Quantum Hughes: We? More like you.

FeeTwix: Hey, Quantum, you busy?

Quantum Hughes: Hey, kid. Busy? Me? Let me check my calendar. Nope, looks like my one o'clock meeting with the Peanut Gallery has been canceled. Soph, send me to the Mitherfickers. If it's back-up they need, it's back-up they'll get.

Sophia: No. Absolutely not. We are right in the middle of something. FeeTwix, Ryuk—handle this so we can rendezvous back in Tokyo.

Hiccup: Why has no one mentioned the fact that Grifty is fickin' back? Yes, *the* Grifty has escaped the OMIB, and all the Knights and Mitherfickers give a fick about is sealing up these stupid portals and fighting a bunch of ficked up Drachma pirates. What about Grifty?

Quantum Hughes: Grifty? I don't know no Grifty. Doc?

Doc: Grifty is back? Crap. That's not good.

Sophia: We can discuss this later. Seal the portal.

"Fick, I fickin' hate her, I really fickin' hate her," Hiccup says after he uses an empty healing potion to bash in the head of a goblin. "Can I kill her in Tokyo?"

Ryuk groans. "No! No, of course you can't. Focus, Hiccup. *Baka.*"

Fwitt!

Now using his triggerless marble gun, he fires several explosive marbles into a huge demon. Ryuk ignores the red prompts that populate his viewing pane as they surge forward.

"This should be a good spot," FeeTwix says as he finds what resembles an open courtyard that looks like it doubles as a place for public executions. It's hard to tell. There are guillotines, and other things that would look more appropriate in a BDSM dungeon, but there are also shrubs and a couple statues of robust goblins. "Cover me, Ryuk!"

~FICK~

Ryuk goes for his marble shotgun, which he's already loaded with a combo of sword and explosive marbles. As FeeTwix charges ahead, Ryuk fires at incoming goblins and demons. Off to his immediate right, Zaena brings down a large demon, riding its back to the ground as she guides its descent with all four of her swords jammed into its back.

A wall comes crashing down and a trio of goblins stagger out.

They all rear back at the same time and spit balls of fire at the Mitherfickers. Demons get caught in the crosshairs, causing the fire—clearly from bottles of HotAzz Ballz sauce by the look of the flames—to spread rapidly.

Soon, Wolf's tail is on fire; the flames have coated Enway's robes and she's trying to beat them out; Zaena is badly burned; Hiccup is shrieking; FeeTwix has equipped a fire extinguisher and is using it to bash goblins and put out flames; and Ryuk is left with an option he's been waiting to try out.

He touches the runestone.

How would you like to respawn?
- **A Berserker Warrior**
- **A Ballistics Mage**
- **A Dark Mage**
- **A White Mage**

He selects White Mage and waits for the transformation to take shape, healing energy rippling in the air all around him.

"Group heal!" Ryuk shouts, and sure enough, sparkling bits of light fall from the sky onto each of the Mitherfickers.

+245 HP! +257 HP! +240 HP! +232 HP! +239 HP! + 251 HP!

"Fick yeah!" Hiccup shouts. "Poofty-ass White Mage saves the fickin' day."

Enway turns to the three goblins spitting fire and completely annihilates them with a blast of pink magic.

Insta-Insta-Instakill!

"Thanks, Ryuk!" FeeTwix shouts. The Swede drops to the ground, sets the box that calls Rocket, and stomps on it.

The ground shakes; several of the buildings that were already on their last legs collapse as Rocket's towering form takes shape. The blue deity causes the goblins still in the vicinity to shriek and scatter.

"What the fick is that?"

"Fick!"

"Fick this, I'm fickin' out of here!"

"Fick me, it's fickin' Grifty!"

This last statement, which comes from a goblin that has just crawled over an exploded wall, causes Hiccup to lose his shit. "Fick! Grifty!? Where!?" He jumps at Ryuk, who only manages to catch him because Hiccup has done this before. "Marbles!" the goblin cries as his eyes dart left and right.

"You're... so goddamn... heavy..." Ryuk takes a staggering step forward. He ignores Rocket and his Hindu deity shenanigans as Rocket prepares to seal the portal.

Hiccup lets one go and Ryuk finally drops him.

"Yoy!"

"Om Namo Bhagavate Vasudevaya!"

Rocket fires a blast of concentrated energy at the chaotic portal above. The portal zips up in a flash of bristling green algomagic, the sky suddenly gray again, the demons no longer spilling out onto the goblin city.

Rocket turns to the Mitherfickers and bows. As he bows, his big blue form pixelates away.

Sophia: So extra.

Rocket: So extra awesome. Did you like how I left without saying anything? Sort of my version of an Irish goodbye.

Sophia: You've destroyed like half of Bluwid.

Rocket: Bluwid was already destroyed.

Quantum: Ha! He ain't wrong there.

Sophia: Ugh...

Ryuk shifts his focus from the dialogue to Hiccup.

"Fick, me, Marbles. Must. Drink. Potion." Hiccup, who is still lying on his back, lifts a shaky hand in the air. A healing potion appears and he struggles to get the top off. "Wolfie."

Wolf trots over to Hiccup and uses his teeth to pull the cork out. Rather than drink from the bottle properly, Hiccup merely pours it onto his face, the red liquid spilling down his cheeks. While pouring the potion, he also triggers a button on his soundboard gauntlet to play FeeTwix's voice.

~*Fick you.*~

"And that, my friends, is how you seal a portal." The Swede approaches Hiccup and wipes his hands. He then gives Enway and Ryuk a pair of high fives. Once Zaena steps over to them, FeeTwix pulls her in close for a side hug and a kiss on the forehead. "Say hi to our fans, babe."

Zaena blows a strand of orange hair out of her face. "Hi."

"She's cute, isn't she everyone? Everyone thinks you're cute. Everyone."

"Enough," she tells FeeTwix. "Turn off the eyes for a moment."

"You got it, babe. Listen, people!" A mirror appears in his hand and FeeTwix winks at it. "I want you to go back through the last two portal fights and count the ficks. Kyle_LitRPGLord, it's up to you to see who gets the closest. Winner gets an exclusive Q and A with Hiccup once we finally get some downtime."

Hiccup moans, the goblin finally able to get to his feet. "Fick off, Twixy..."

"And don't forget Hiccup's birthday. The next time we log in, I'm expecting a birthday cake. Just don't count on me to give the goblin 155 spankings!"

This statement piques the goblin's attention. "They spank people for birthdays in your world too? That's fickin' kinky as fick, the kind of shit

Marbles' ficktarded fish chalupa'd brother would be into. I'm sure he's into all sorts of stuff. Right, Marbles?"

Ryuk shrugs. "I wouldn't know."

"Like fick you wouldn't." Hiccup places a finger on one of his nostrils and snorts a large booger onto the burnt corpse of a goblin. "Fick, that's better."

Sophia: It's logout time. Come back to Tokyo, and we can discuss the next steps from there.

"What about Quantum?" FeeTwix asks aloud.

Sophia: You'll get to meet your hero later. It's time to come back.

TOKYO

CHAPTER 5: IN POSITION

KODAI SHOULD HAVE BEEN FEELING LIKE SHIT. He should have been reeling from his loss to the Mitherfickers, his cursed brother's guild of fucking losers, yet as he watches their feed through FeeTwix's eyes—the moronic Swede—he can't help but smile. He can't help but laugh.

It doesn't hurt that Tesla is currently giving him a blowjob.

Kodai is seated in a room in a posh hotel overlooking Shibuya, the drapes pulled shut. This is one of his many safehouses, and it just so happens to have an excellent kitchen downstairs as well.

"The fuckin' morons," he says. "Keep sucking," he tells Tesla once she looks up at him. To illustrate that he means business, he pulls tightly on the leash attached to the collar around the humandroid's neck. "I'll talk. To save the Thulean bitch, they did something that seems to have opened the OMIB. Veenure has unleashed—God. God! Keep going. She's unleashed some of the worst the OMIB has to offer. Portals opened. Yes. And it just... it just gets better from there. Let them run wild, the monsters. The real shocker is coming."

Once again, Kodai yanks tightly on Tesla's leash. He lays his head back, enjoying her warm tongue for a moment. As he lets a deep breath out, his NV Visor slips over his eyes. The Proxima logo appears along with the login button. He laughs. The Mitherfickers are so fucked. But they aren't the only ones.

A message flashes, just the one he's been looking for.

Walt: Busy?

Kodai: I am not.

As if Walt can see him, Kodai tightens his grip on the chain, which pulls Tesla in just a bit closer. She doesn't tense, but she does make a playful sound.

Walt: We have located the targets. Yugio and I will be in position shortly. Are there more of your men you would like to contact?

Kodai: You don't think you can handle it?

Walt: We can certainly handle it.

Kodai: Then handle it. And when you do, let me know. If Yugio thinks he needs someone else, then Sota and Haruki should do. Yes. Sota and Haruki. That should even the odds. Tesla will come as well, so five of you. How does that work?

Walt: That works. Is there anything else?

Is there anything else? Kodai's heart beats just a little faster as Tesla finds a perfect rhythm. He won't be able to last much longer.

Kodai: Let's celebrate tomorrow night. Tell Yugio to arrange the place. He'll know which one. This won't be messy, will it?

Walt: I try to keep things clean.

Kodai: If it gets messy... You know what? Just don't let it get messy. And don't kill my brother.

Walt: Understood. I will be in touch with you in the near future. I estimate this will all be handled in the next five to six hours. I will let you know if there are any delays.

Kodai doesn't respond. Instead, he closes his eyes and lets Tesla completely take over. He sighs as the feeling comes, one that seems to reach all the way to the tips of his fingers as he orgasms.

"God, I needed that," he whispers once he's finished. Kodai removes the NV Visor temporarily and looks down at Tesla, a hint of disgust in his eyes as he judges her wet lips, her mouth slightly parted. "Go clean yourself up. But clean me up first. I need to log in."

She swallows. "Do you want something to eat?"

"Sure, but later. Something light. It's going to be an exciting day."

(0)__(0)

Kodai's avatar forms into existence, a field of stars at his feet. He recognizes the OMIB and its stark vastness immediately. What he doesn't recognize are the portals opened up far below, ones showing what he was certain was Tritania.

Kodai's stats appear before him:

Kodai Matsuzaki Level 15 Ballistics Mage
HP: 830/830
ATK: 213
MATK: 176
DEF: 98
MDF: 105
LUCK: 7

He can do better. He knows that. But he is generally so distracted in the real world that he has neglected his character. It doesn't help that his idiot brother has chosen one of the worst classes. It had been funny and clever at first, especially when he was able to trick Ryuk and the others. But those days were over now, and Kodai is stuck as a Ballistics Mage, a paltry one at that.

"So it is happening," he says after he finishes examining the portals opening below his feet. "Good. I checked the Swede's feed. They appear to be battling the demons coming out of these portals."

"Yes, good," says Veenure. The serpent woman now stands in front of him, her form silhouetted as always. "And I have more in store. There are a couple other items we need to address. First, the Knights of Non Compos Mentis are going to complicate everything if we don't act quickly. Sophia is working with the Proxima company to fix any patches that would allow my ultimate plan to unfold."

Veenure still hasn't been clear with Kodai on what her ultimate plan is. He has a feeling it has to do with the digital hallucinations, but he is still in the dark. He is fine with this. Tormenting his brother, and causing trouble for a digital world that he is starting to despise, brings Kodai immense pleasure. Not only that, but he is on the verge of squashing his competition in Tokyo with his recent actions against Gintoki.

Even if they are suffering from a recent defeat, things are looking up. And that is before the news he is about to deliver to Veenure.

"That damn Sophia." Veenure seems to grow in size. "She continues to block all of my efforts."

"In that case, I have some news that may excite you."

"I have news for you as well." Veenure moves just a bit closer to him. Her thick tail wraps around Kodai's legs. He can see her forked tongue now, the yellow of her eyes. "You first."

"Sophia. It's happening in the next several hours. She has been located, and I'm handling it."

"You're going to kill her?"

"I am. And if anyone else gets in the way, I may kill them as well," says Kodai, referring to FeeTwix.

"She will have an RPC. Don't think for a moment that she won't still be powerful here."

"But she will be practically powerless there, in my world. Isn't that what you want? You will have me there. And no one will be able to stop me."

Veenure smiles. "That is true. And while I have no way to track her here in the OMIB, I do have something that would rip this world to shreds. The portals are opening. It is easier to send some of the demons of the OMIB down to wreak havoc. I could go through one of these portals as well, but no, the Knights will stop me. There are more powerful things that lurk in the OMIB, but the portals aren't strong enough to handle them. So this got me thinking."

"Yeah?"

"Before I tell you what I was thinking about, it's time that you let me in."

"Let you in?"

Veenure runs her hand along the side of Kodai's cheek. "You don't have time to handle your avatar, to increase your levels. There are things that I can do here that would grow your power exponentially. I think it is time. But to do so, you will need to give me access to your D-NAS."

"Access? Does that mean you will be able to control me?"

"If I wanted, but does that bother you? You don't care about this world, do you?"

"I've never been a big gamer myself."

She laughs the statement off. "That part doesn't matter. If you give me access, I can take over your avatar and travel to various places in the OMIB, where I can kill monsters that will net you incredible amounts of XP. You will level rapidly. By the time you return here—"

"Where would I be going? I'm here now."

"I'm getting to that. By the time you would return here, you would be able to take on the Knights. Your brother and his guild would be nothing. Imagine being that strong." She keeps her hand on his cheek for a moment as she stares deeply into his eyes. "Now, what I was saying earlier. There is a way to completely tear the threads of this world apart, to make the OMIB and Tritania one. That is a source code bomb."

"Source code bomb?"

"Yes. It has happened before you know, in Unigaea. It would be devastating here, and I know of someone who has one."

"It's a real thing?"

"The Proxima company is obsessed with protecting the integrity of their code. Once the source code bomb hit Unigaea, they spent resources that you wouldn't believe making sure it could never happen again. Around that same time, an NPC weapon's dealer from a defunct world known as Cyber Noir got a version of it. He put this into a suitcase."

"And you know this dealer?"

"In fact, I do. His name is Dirty Dave."

"Then all I need to do is meet him. Is that what you are saying?"

"No, there is more to it than that. Dirty Dave thinks he destroyed the source code bomb. But an old associate of his from Cyber Noir has it, an NPC named Clive. He lives in Steam."

Kodai considers this with a nod. "Steam? Another world?"

"A steampunk Proxima world, one created by the founder of the Proxima company, Ray Steampunk. After you have given me access," she says as a glowing orb appears above her palm, "you will log out and go to Steam. You can buy avatars for Steam over iNet, so you don't need to worry about that aspect of it. If you'd like, we can look at them from here and I can show you the one that you will need. Now, as I was saying, you will go there, and here's what you will do…" Veenure quickly explains to Kodai what will happen, and what it will cost. "So, do you agree? This is something that you think you can afford?"

He is almost insulted that she would question the kind of money Kodai is used to throwing around. "I think it is a wonderful idea. And you should know by now that with me, money isn't an object."

"Good. Touch this orb and you will grant me access to your D-NAS. By the time you return here, Kodai, you will be stronger than you have ever imagined." Veenure smiles, her forked tongue flitting against her lips. "Almost as strong as me."

TOKYO

CHAPTER 6: CURRIED REBOOT

EVERYTHING PIXELATES; Ryuk is sucked backward into a sudden vortex. Before he can blink, he finds himself back in Tokyo, the real world. The Land of the Rising Sun. His home.

Dang... Ryuk spits out the breathing apparatus and sits up. The sticky goo of the dive vat drips from his skin and mats his hair to his head.

"Fick both of us, looks like we're back."

Ryuk can barely contain his disdain for the goblin.

"What the fick is that look, Marbles? If you got something to say, best fickin' say it, you fickin' deadshit douchebaggette."

Dammit.

Sophia, who is seated on a rolly chair in front of a host of holoscreens, continues tinkering with a custom somnium skipbox. Once she sees Ryuk struggling, she glides over to him and helps remove some of the tubes she's connected to his headpiece.

"I know, I know, you can still see him. Just ignore the goblin for a moment. Evan had an idea, something worth trying. I can't believe..."

Sophia lowers her head, a bit of shame tracing across her eyes. "I can't believe I didn't come up with it myself. It should have been the first thing. But it has been so long since I've considered old-school ways to fix new-school problems that I didn't even consider it."

"What do you mean?" asks FeeTwix, who is now being assisted out of his dive vat by Evan. The humandroid offers the Swede a couple of towels. Sophia naturally turns away, but continues to work on Ryuk's rig.

"I am almost ashamed to admit it."

"That is the best time to admit something. Tell her I fickin' said that, Marbelito. Don't be fickin' useless."

Ryuk shakes his head.

Hiccup looks down at his soundboard gauntlet and triggers a button.

~*FICK*~

Ryuk scowls at the goblin.

"Ha! Fick off, Marbles. You're not going to get a little side chup from Elfie with a face like that, you ficktarded ficktwit."

Sophia continues: "We are going to try a hard reset. This will take about an hour. We will do it in another one of the rooms here. Evan has already looked into making the place comfortable so you can relax while it takes place. I figured we could order takeout during that time as well. Anything you would suggest?"

"Pizza?" FeeTwix asks.

"Fick yeah, we want pizza!"

"You won't be getting any pizza," Ryuk tells Hiccup in his accented English.

"The fick you just say?" Hiccup pretends to clean out his ears with his fingers. "If you're ordering pizza, Uncle Goblin is going to get himself a fick slice of za. No cap, Marbles."

No what?

Sophia taps Ryuk on the forehead. "Focus. Ignore the goblin. Maybe takeout is a bad idea. We're in Ueno. There has to be some place to eat around here."

"There is," Ryuk tells her.

"Anyway. The sooner you get yourself cleaned out, the sooner we can start the hard reset. Now, you should know that this isn't just your typical hard reset. While we reset your life chip, Evan and I will also run a program that clears any Proxima life chip connections you've made over the last twenty-four hours. Because there are always those, always. By logging in to the Galaxy, you grant the Proxima company permission to access your chip and monitor your data. But you already knew that. So we'll be dealing with that aspect of all this, which will take a workaround of their system due to the agreements you've made with the company. It shouldn't be too hard."

"Fick a lizard in its gizzard. Even fickin' goblins have better privacy laws than you do here in your world. Makes you think."

"Whatever, Hiccup."

"You best watch your fickin' sourpuss attitude, Marbles—"

"So, a hard reset." Something akin to a smile appears on Sophia's face. "Before you ask. No, it's not dangerous, and no, it won't affect your Tritanian avatar. But that is something we need to discuss."

"What is?"

"Your avatars. Your entire guild."

"We're called the Mitherfickers." Hiccup throws his hands up in the air and stomps around. "For fick's sake, if you're not going to do it, tell Twixy to take some pride in our guild and correct this bia-bia. Fick! I almost forgot. Ask her about Grifty." His eyes quiver with concern. "Grifty is back..."

"You're needed in Ultima Thule," Sophia says, "it's as simple as that. But none of you, aside from Oric and Wolf, are at the level that you can go to the third Tritanian continent. Once you dive back in, there is one final Polynyian portal to clear up at a dungeon outside of New Gotha. It's a strange portal, one that has opened up underground."

"Underground portal? Dungeon?" FeeTwix exchanges glances with Ryuk. "If it's a dungeon that needs clearing, the Mitherfickers will be sure to re-pre-fickin-sent. We're not quite dungeon crawlers, but I've been known to Princess a couple of Donuts, if you get my drift."

"What the fick did he just say? You know, I stuck my chalupa through a donut once. I admit I was drunk. No princesses around, but definitely a couple of orc chi—"

"You and your guild need to get to Level 35 so we can go to Ultima Thule." Sophia taps Ryuk on the forehead once again, which is a little annoying. "Now, out of the vat. Let's get started on your hard reset. Until then, ignore the goblin."

~FICK~

(0)__(0)

Ryuk would later describe it as white noise. This was what it felt like to completely reboot his life chip. At first, he felt afraid. Yet glancing across the room and seeing Hajime and FeeTwix assures him he is safe, that all is going according to plan.

"Relax." Sophia says in a not so calming voice. She affixes a custom NV Visor over Ryuk's head. It is more streamlined than any visor he's seen before, the side panel with a sleek black touchpad on it that she has spliced with a larger holoscreen that is currently in her lap. "Is the goblin here?"

Ryuk looks around.

"Yes or no?"

"Speak, goblin!" FeeTwix throws a punch where he thinks Hiccup would be standing if he was there. "Is he calling me a fickery fick-dicked ficker dicker or something like that?"

Sophia rolls her eyes. "Ugh, goblins."

"Why are they like that anyway?" FeeTwix asks. "I've been meaning to look it up, but it is just one of those things that I always forget to do. You know how these to-do lists can get."

"Why are goblins the way they are?"

"Yeah," he tells Sophia.

"It's not as complicated as it sounds. When Tritania was being created, overseen by a team led by Ray Steampunk, one of the asshole developers decided he was going to be clever. He was tasked with creating a goblin race and decided to use them to test a new AI behavioral model that they were working on. The only thing was, it was already proven to be corrupted. Developers disliked messing with it because it produced strange results."

"Strange results like Hiccup?"

"Precisely. It's a little complicated to explain, but basically they fed random bits of televised entertainment over the last two centuries directly into the AI and had it create dialogue and personalities based on the medium. This is why the goblins are the way they are, especially when it comes to their behaviors and speaking styles. Weirdly enough, Ray Steampunk and his team decided to keep it, and now we have the Tritanian goblin."

"What was the developer's name?" FeeTwix asks.

"Gideon Caldwell. Wait, no, that's not him. He's the one who created Grifty and other eldritch horrors in Tritania. No, no. Goblin vulgarities came from another one of the duds hired by the Proxima company, a duo, actually, named Randy Lionheart and Clovis Smith. Then there are the ficks, which was a mistake I made. They sure are creative with that word. Anyway." She continues tinkering with the holoscreen. Ryuk isn't fully able to see it, only that there are gauges on it with reds and greens. She taps on one of the gauges and begins to turn up the juice.

Ryuk feels nothing, yet the fact that she's doing something makes him wish he could sense it somehow.

"Well?" she asks. "Goblins? Do you see any?"

"No, Hiccup is *not* here... *Dono yō ni iimasu ka?*"

"Currently," Hajime tells Ryuk.

"*Hai*. Currently. Hiccup isn't here *currently*." Without his life chip, Ryuk is forced to rely on his own knowledge of the English language to communicate, whereas before he was provided words in real time. "*Ano*... how much longer until *reboot-oh*?"

Sophia hands Evan her holoscreen. She shuffles away and returns with a sensor, one that she slaps on his forehead. Text appears on the inside of Ryuk's NV Visor. It's in English, and it moves too quickly for him to actually read and comprehend it.

"All your vitals seem fine," Sophia says in lieu of answering his question. "That is usually a concern when doing a full reboot. You are a healthy young man, Ryuk."

"*Arigatōgozaimasu, ano,* thank you very much."

"What are we looking at timewise here?" FeeTwix asks for Ryuk. He will probably never tell the Swede, but he appreciates this about him, his

Western assertiveness. It allows for Ryuk to just be himself and know that others are advocating for him in some way.

Sophia looks over to him. "What do you mean?"

"You said you wanted us to log in and clear out a dungeon. Plus, food. I'm itching to eat too. Right now my feed is doing a playback of our fight the other day against the Atttla spiders. Heh. *Fick you, spiders!*" FeeTwix soft-screams. "Next time I run into those little bastards, I'm going to hose them down with my AUS hosegun."

Sophia eyes FeeTwix suspiciously. "Your what? Where did you get that?"

"Dirty Dave."

She slowly shakes her head. "He has done so much damage to the lore and narrative structure of Tritania, and that's without mentioning wizardous."

Ryuk grins at FeeTwix. He can tell what the Swede is thinking, that if Hiccup were here, he would probably launch into a fick-laced defense of Dirty Dave.

"And to answer your question, it should be another five minutes. You two have never done a full reboot before?"

FeeTwix shrugs. "Why would we? I don't know how they do it here in Japan, but my life chip was placed right after my umbilical cord was cut."

"Um-beh-ru-cah-ru cor-doh-oo?" Ryuk looks at Hajime for translation.

"*Hesonoo.*"

"*Hai.* Same like FeeTwix. We get..." He taps on his temple. "When babies."

Sophia shakes her head. "You know, your English really should be better considering it is the global language of pretty much anything and everything now. Then again, I guess it doesn't matter with instant translating. I'm just honestly surprised to hear someone of your age who doesn't speak English fluently. I'd say you're a rare breed, but I have a feeling that is common here, isn't it?"

"Maybe so," Ryuk says, not able to hide the shame he feels. He lowers his head; Sophia places her fingers under his chin and lifts it.

"Head up. It's important that you focus during this process. Sometimes, people pass out from being disconnected from their life chips for the first time." She offers Ryuk a wry grin. "But you are doing better than I thought."

"What did you think?"

"I thought that you may pass out or perhaps go into a short coma."

"You what?" asks Hajime, the humandroid clearly concerned by the statement. He steps away from the door. "You didn't tell me it could be lethal."

"It wouldn't have been lethal."

"People can die during a coma."

Sophia rolls her eyes, the woman a bit annoyed by the humandroid's sudden persistence. "He's fine. You can read his vitals yourself, can't you? His heart rate is good, his temperature is fine, his oxygen capacity is a little above average, he doesn't seem to be exhibiting any signs of someone about to pass out. Let's keep it that way. You should be getting a reboot screen soon, Ryuk. When it comes up, select Custom Launch so I can tap in here and make any adjustments. Evan, he's launching soon."

"Got it," Evan says, who is monitoring a pair of holoscreens. He's also directly tapped into the system from a port on his wrist.

Rather than say anything, Ryuk focuses on the inside of the visor, awaiting the reboot screen. It comes, and when it does he mentally selects

Custom Launch. More text pixelates into existence; the white noise fades away as Ryuk is presented with the dashboard he has modified over the years.

Translated messages from FeeTwix make Ryuk smile.

FeeTwix: If you're getting this, you have survived. You are Hiccup-free, and we should seriously eat something before we log back in. I can't remember the last time we ate. Was it ramen yesterday? Luckily, there's a little Japanese curry spot right around the corner popular with Ueno University students. 4.8 stars out of nearly three thousand reviews. That's the GoogleFace kinda rec I'm talking about. What do you think? Also, should I call it Japanese curry to a Japanese man, or just curry? Probably just curry.

"Stop smiling."

"Sorry," Ryuk tells Sophia, the translations coming to him now in real time. "I'm reading messages. I'm hungry. Can we eat curry? I know of a place nearby that is excellent."

She looks at him incredulously. "Curry?" Her arched eyebrows lift as she smiles. "Of course we can. I love curry. And I'm getting sick of eating ramen, even if I've only had it a few times. Actually, I never get sick of eating ramen, but in saying that I'm stereotyping myself and I don't like that. Yes, curry. We can eat quickly and return here. You have levels to get. I'm not going to say the Knights of Non Compos Mentis need you in Ultima Thule to fight Drachma Killers and finish off what's left of the portals, but we could really use your help, or Quantum and Doc could. It's their idea to bring you into that side of the equation."

FeeTwix gasps. "Quantum requested us."

"He did, but you shouldn't feel special or anything because of this. As you know, there are other guilds that are way stronger than the..." She frowns. "The Mitherfickers. Now, hold still, Ryuk. We're still loading some things."

(0)__(x)

After Ryuk dresses, he meets Hajime, Evan, and FeeTwix in a room adjacent to the space with the dive vats. The Swede is wearing a black hat now, one with little horns on it, which goes well with his black *Quantum Hughes is my Spirit Animal Shirt*—Ryuk has no idea where he got the shirt—and a pair of black Levis decorated with white paint splatter. At least in Ryuk's head, FeeTwix looks instantly cooler and on trend, especially when compared to his jeans and black hooded sweatshirt.

The others step out, and Ryuk is about to follow them when Hajime stops him. "Your oblique quote."

Ryuk takes a slip of paper from the humandroid and reads the message scrawled across it.

Change is hard at first, messy in the middle, and gorgeous at the end.

"It's a quote from a Canadian writer named Robin Sharma. I figured you would appreciate it."

"Thank you," Ryuk tells the humandroid. He tries to commit the quote to memory. To make it easier, he simply takes a picture of it with his eyes so he can view the quote later.

"We still need to be careful, especially with Kodai's recent actions. I will go ahead now and make sure all is secure. Please, Ryuk, if anything happens or seems out of the ordinary, get to cover as quickly as you can. I've shown you ways to get to cover."

"I wish I still had the humgun."

"Yes, that would be useful." Hajime parts his robes and produces a small weapon, one that is sleek and black. It's identical to the humandroid-disabling humgun except for the size. "Ah, would you look there? Seems I have one."

"Where did you get it?" Ryuk asks as they head down the hallway, one with black and white pictures of campus hanging on the walls. A familiar portrait catches Ryuk's eye upon transitioning to the next hallway. It is a portrait of Nobuyuki Tsujii, a famed pianist who has only recently died. Ryuk has seen videos of the blind virtuoso before. There had even been holoconcerts in recent years.

I didn't know he went here...

"Evan has supplies," Hajime says after a long pause. "This man that works with them, Doc, has seen to it."

"You mean real weapons?"

"I mean supplies." Hajime moves ahead to the front of the group. Ryuk watches as he goes, aware of just how much faith he has in the humandroid and what he is capable of. Soon, they are quickly moving to campus, toward a building across the street from the Ueno Zoological Gardens.

Even if it is only midday, the izakayas have already started grilling meat outside of their shops as lunch patrons gather around and share beers. It is loud, and it is also a dangerous place to be considering that the Yakuza runs a good number of these shops.

This is why Ryuk continues to keep a low profile, the hood over his head, masking his identity to anyone that would try to intercept his iNet feed. It has been known to happen.

Ryuk is still getting used to the reboot.

Some of his favorite settings have been disabled, such as the one that automatically pulls up the menu when he enters the restaurant. It isn't hard to fix, yet it is something that he will need to see to when he gets a free moment.

They stop in front of the curry spot and push through a curtain hanging from the door.

They are greeted by a chorus of voices, three male and one female, all with a typical Japanese greeting from restaurant workers in white aprons and white paper hats.

"Irasshaimase!"

"Ee-ray-mah-shay," FeeTwix says back. Even though he has instant translation, his pronunciation is off. The Swede offers the restaurant workers a respectful bow, which causes Ryuk to laugh quietly to himself. "Wait, I just welcomed them after they welcomed me, didn't I? Weird. But I want to say something!"

There is an old machine on the counter that allows a patron to put physical money into it and select the food that they would like. This is a relic of the past. Nowadays, people just order over iNet.

"I totally want to use the machine." Sophia winks at Evan as she approaches the large square touchscreen on the wall in front of the kitchen. "How retro."

She selects the medium-size curry, extra hot, with a side of gyoza and spinach ohitashi. While there are a number of ways to pay, from using a fingerprint to access one's life chip to physical cash, Sophia actually pulls a coin bag out of her purse and proceeds to put the yen in one coin at a time. It is clear that she has gone to some trouble to get change—it isn't as common as it once was—but it takes her much longer to order because she is not familiar with the currency breakdowns.

"I've ordered your favorite," Hajime tells Ryuk. "Secure channels, obviously." He turns to FeeTwix, who is still staring at all the options with his mouth open. "I've ordered for you as well."

FeeTwix licks his lips. "Is *one of everything* an option?"

"I'm sure that can be arranged. There is a private room in the back that we can take rather than sit here with salarymen," Hajime says in English, which doesn't catch the attention of any of the men in suits seated around the bar who shove curry and rice into their mouths.

Even if much of the world is now run by AI and humandroids, the Japanese economy is still carried on the backs of salarymen and women who work insane hours, even though they don't have, to just to fill a gap in their lives, lives that are extending much longer than humans have ever lived due to advances in cybernetics, bio-engineering, and gerontological breakthroughs.

"Please, follow me. *Hai!*" A restaurant employee leads them into a back room that is private, where they are seated at a table with a white cloth covering it.

"Fancy," FeeTwix says once some of the side dishes come. "Fickin' great!"

First up is a platter of pan-fried teriyaki tofu, followed by cucumber and chicken marinated in chili oil, one of Ryuk's favorites. Plates of green bean shiraee garnished in broccoli that has been blanched with sesame seed oil are soon brought to the table by a thin waitress, whose cheeks are red from all the walking back and forth and the steam from the rice cookers in the kitchen. She maintains a positive attitude as she bows to them and leaves, only to return with chilled tofu known as hiyayakko and tamagoyaki, which is a type of rolled omelet.

"Look, Ryuk," FeeTwix says after he decorates his slice of tamagoyaki with ketchup. "Just like at the maid café in Akihabara."

"You two went to one of those?"

"We sure did," FeeTwix tells Sophia with his mouth full of a ketchup-y omelet. "Ryuk's choice, not mine." He laughs once the color drains from Ryuk's face.

"No, it was your idea."

"Of course it was, bud. I'm just kidding with you. Hey, what are those?" FeeTwix snaps his chopsticks at a new dish.

"Ham katsu," Hajime says as slices of ham are placed on the table. They have been fried in panko and surround a small bowl of Japanese potato salad.

"You are so lucky the goblin isn't here, Ryuk. He'd be salivating all over the table by now and cursing at you for not feeding him."

"So many appetizers," says Sophia once the waitress brings her gyoza alongside a couple plates of simmered kabocha squash and spicy bean sprout salad. This is followed by eggplant dengaku glazed in a sweet miso sauce. "We're practically sharing *banchan* at this point," she says, referring to Korean side dishes. Sophia pops a gyoza into her mouth. "So freaking yummy."

The curry finally comes, such a simple dish after such an array of colors and tastes. It's practically slopped onto the plate like cafeteria food, the dark orange sauce with carrots, meat, and potatoes putting forth an incredible aroma. Using an upside down bowl, the chef has placed two mounds of rice on each plate to create perfect mounds. Like lava, the curry soon overtakes it.

In the end it is a great meal, leaving Ryuk well fed and ready to log back in to the Proxima Galaxy.

The dungeon awaits, and what better way to dungeon crawl than with a full belly and a high-tech dive vat?

TOKYO

CHAPTER 7: STEAM

KODAI'S BRAND-NEW AVATAR appears on a moving train. Before he can do anything, text forms in the air before him, the words outlined by a gold border:

Welcome to Steam. Our records indicate that this is your first visit. You will be in Steam's capital city, Locus, momentarily. Please take a moment to remember some of the rules of this world:

Players using items that rely upon electricity will be penalized through their life bars.

Shillings are used as a currency in Steam. Unlike some Proxima Worlds, they have no real world value.

Alchemical practices are fine as long as they fit within the boundaries of the world, which are accessible through your player dashboard.

Discriminatory comments will be logged. Repeated violations will result in account termination.

Kodai swipes the words away. He immediately accesses the dashboard and upgrades to the avatar that he has purchased from a common Proxima avatar reseller over iNet.

Name: Cygnus Arcanum Percival

Class: A

Rank: 21

Title: The Clockwork Duke of Imperium

Guild: The Iron Viscounts

Health: 8675

Steam Power: 309

Defense: 206

Dexterity: 215

Speed: 176

Strength: 187

Intelligence: 198

Charisma: 157

Secondary skills

Firearms Proficiency: 196

Mechanical Aptitude: 171

Stealth: 121

Kodai looks down at his arm to see that he is now wearing a trench coat with stylized gear-like stitching and detailing. He moves his arm and notices that it feels different. Upon removing his glove, Kodai finds a steam-powered prosthetic. He grips his hand into a fist; the gears move and whiz.

"Cygnus Arcanum Percival," he mumbles after glancing at the stats again. "What kind of stupid fucking name is this?"

A message from Veenure appears.

Veenure: I don't know how to adequately answer that question. Everything in this world has a steampunk feel to it. Are you familiar with the genre?

"No, I am not. And how is my avatar doing?" Kodai asks this just to make sure she is actually leveling his character up in Tritania. He is certain that Veenure, who now can control him to some degree in Tritania, is doing what she promised.

But he still has to check.

Veenure: All is going according to plan. As for what steampunk is, steampunk is a fantasy subgenre that incorporates tech with Victorian era aesthetic and industrial steam-powered machinery. As a genre, it often involves alternate historical timelines, or it takes place in a post-apocalyptic setting where the world has shifted back to steam power.

"Got it," Kodai says as a woman in a tight corset with bronze accents approaches. Clearly a conductor based on her outfit, she wears a monocle and has gear-like embellishments on her skirt. She has an incredible rack, something Kodai immediately notices.

"Ahem. My eyes are up here," the conductor says in a mechanical voice. "Why have you spawned here, Sir Percival? As the Clockwork Duke of Imperium, it is rather strange for you to be riding the newcomer train into Locus. Your presence on this train has been noted and recorded, Good Sir."

Veenure: You need to be in Akrasia.

"I'm supposed to be in Akrasia," Kodai tells the conductor.

"Akrasia? Why would you spawn here if you are supposed to be there?"

"Because that's where I fucking need to go."

She brings a hand to her chest. "Your language! It is unbecoming of an Iron Viscount."

Veenure: You shouldn't announce where you're going. Akrasia is a prison city southeast of Morlock.

Is this supposed to mean something to me? Kodai thinks as he gives the woman standing before him a hard smile.

Veenure: Check your map. Because your avatar was purchased and he's an A-Rank, you should be able to simply spawn there.

"Well?" the conductor asks. "Have you nothing to say?"

"Sorry. I suppose I will go there then, to Akrasia. I don't know why my avatar spawned here. Perhaps it was a glitch. I thought this was the train to Akrasia," he says, improvising.

The Steam conductor isn't buying his reasoning. "Firstly, there are no glitches in Steam. Our dear Ray Steampunk has seen to that. And did you say train to Akrasia? There is no train to Akrasia, Sir Percival. You can reach there by carriage from Steam City, but to do so you will have to pass through a dangerous area of the Lost Pines. You should certainly know this by now. I suppose an airship is possible, as is a carriage ride from Babbage Town for Rank-C and below. Come to think of it, you could also sail from Iron West Beach—"

Kodai lifts his finger after selecting Akrasia and zips away, no longer interested in the NPC conductor's explanation.

(0)__(0)

Once Kodai's avatar takes shape, he accesses his dashboard and mentally clicks on the Lore tab. He selects Akrasia, which he soon learns is also known as the Prison City of Akrasia.

As he stands at the edge of a forest, a pair of airships overhead casting oblong shadows on the ground, Kodai reads aloud: "Akrasia is a

Morlockian cesspit protected from the rest of the continent of Steam by the natural terrain and three walls: Wall Maria, Wall Rose, and Wall Titan. Prisoners and felons make up the population of the city, as do prisoners of war from the iniquitous Boilerplate Army. Unlike most prisons, certain citizens of Akrasia are allowed to move freely within the walls. Depending on their crimes, they may be required to take part in mandatory public services. When doing so, they are known as the Chain Gang." Kodai shakes his head. "These video game losers sure take this shit seriously."

Veenure: All you are required to do is find Clive, pay him, and get the package.

"I know." Kodai continues reading in spite of this fact. "The more violent ones, often considered the scum of Steam, are those who have actually been arrested in Akrasia. They are sent to Tent City, a walled off portion of Akrasia. In this area of the prison city, a prison within a prison city, you will also find what are known as Steam Breeds. It is possible to enter Tent City, but most don't go there unless they are looking for a fight or they have been sentenced there by the SRT Mondoshawans."

Kodai sees that SRT is underlined. Once he looks back at the letters, the words *Special Response Team* appear beneath them.

Then what's a Mondoshawan? he wonders. "And Clive, he is in Tent City?" Kodai asks aloud.

Veenure: He is. He is set to meet you at a bar called The Brass Marchioness. Clive is waiting there now.

"Got it." Kodai takes a step forward, only to notice that he's wearing a pair of stirrups that seem to have little engines attached to them. In examining them, he is given a prompt of their characteristics.

DisNike Limited-Edition Steam Boots

Rarity: Ultra

Weight: 1

Durability: 32

Special Properties: +27 Speed, Hoverwalk

"Hoverwalk, huh?" As naturally as ever, Kodai takes a step in the air. He then moves forward now about seven inches above the ground. The air is cushioned. With each step little puffs of steam appear around the limited-edition shoes. "Interesting."

Kodai moves faster. Once he reaches the entrance of the city, he is stopped by a trio of SRT Mondoshawans. He ignores their stats. He won't be here long enough for that matter. He does note, however, that they are each wearing augmented brass and metal suits that have enhanced prosthetics. The way the armor is stacked sort of reminds him of American football pads, albeit bulkier, and with sharp edges and contour lines that are billeted to make them stand out. Their faces are all obscured by a pool of steam, their eyes glowing red beneath gold helms.

"State your purpose for visiting Akrasia," one of them says, his voice even more mechanical than the busty conductor back on the train.

"Looking for a friend."

"The name of your friend?"

Kodai goes with the first name that comes to mind. "His name is Ryuk."

The three SRT Mondoshawans exchange glances. A spout on the back of the largest of the three lets out a toot of steam.

The other two guards turn to him.

"Dammit, Ray," says the one that seems to be doing all the speaking. "Get it together."

The guard grunts an embarrassed reply. By this point, Kodai gets this sense that they have lost their authority. Or at least they assume so. The guards wave him in without any more questions.

"Good luck finding your friend," the leader of the trio says.

Akrasia is a mess of steampunk ascetic, prison uniforms, rust, and DIY tinkering. The streets are filled with people hawking and using all sorts of steam-powered gadgets, and the ornate buildings that surround the narrow lanes are accented by a patina of age and grime.

A group of prisoners with their legs shackled together march by, chanting.

"I don't know what you've been told!"

"I don't know what you've been told."

"Time is bought and time is sold."

"Time is bought and time is sold."

"I'll do mine and when I'm out."

"I'll do mine and when I'm out."

"I'll be back without a doubt."

"I'll be back without a doubt."

Kodai steps aside to let them pass. He can't help but shake his head at the theatrics of it all. *This is worse than Tritania. But the women here are prettier...*

Kodai continues on, slipping between a pair of large inmates with metal muscles. After circling around a statue of enormous gears that have been stacked on top of one another, Kodai spots a man selling what look like steam-powered backpacks. As he approaches, a mysterious voice greets Kodai by his new handle.

"Welcome, Cygnus Arcanum Percival!"

Kodai pinpoints the voice. It is coming from a fortune-telling machine, one with a mechanical dummy inside who wears a purple turban over his head. *"Would you like a quick reading?"*

"No, I would not." Kodai peers into the shop to see a man in a top hat just finishing up with a customer. "I just have a question for him."

"I can answer your question."

"No, no you can't."

"Such a pity."

"What do you mean?" Kodai asks the dummy.

The fortune-teller moves in a mechanical way as it tilts its head at him. Its eyes blink unnaturally. *"You aren't going to like your fortune."*

Kodai gets the urge to punch the glass protecting the dummy. As soon as he feels this way, his hand begins to morph into a gun, gears clicking into place until a muzzle is presented.

"You sure have a short temper, Cygnus Arcanum Percival. How about this? I'll give you your fortune for free. You aren't going to listen to me anyway."

"No, I'm not," Kodai tells the fortune-teller as his gear snaps back into place, his hand once again in its normal form.

"Great, I will tell you your fortune now." The fortune-teller blinks its eyes several times, its teeth chattering. Finally, a fortune is delivered: *"In the end, you will be betrayed by someone close to you. Not only will they betray you, they will imprison you forever."*

"Right, I'll remember that," Kodai tells the fortune-teller as the owner of the shop approaches. He knocks his fist against the teller's brass casing. "You may need to look at this thing. It seems broken."

"Broken? That's not the first I've heard something like that. I suppose I'll have to take a look later, then. It has been known to go rogue from time to time." The owner, who is in a pair of goggles, flips up the tinted lenses and grins. "How can I help you, stranger?"

Ding! Ding! Ding!

Kodai has to wait for the sound of a hammer beating a metal bell to stop before he can speak again. "I'm looking for Tent City. Specifically, a bar called The Brass Marchioness."

"What's that?" the owner asked. "Sorry, that lunch bell always leaves my ears ringing."

"Tent City. The Brass Marchioness. How do I get there?"

"Are you sure that's where you want to go? People don't often go there if they don't have to."

"I'm sure."

The shop owner clears his throat. "Right." He brings his hands together in front of his body, his rings clicking against one another. "In that case, just head down this road and then take your first left. That'll lead you right to Tent City. And mister?" he calls after Kodai once the Yakuza crime boss has already started to leave. "Be careful."

"Noted. And get your fucking fortune-teller fixed."

(0)__(x)

It doesn't take Kodai very long to realize that Tent City is truly a wretched hive of scum and villainy.

While never as dirty, he has experienced similar things in the back alleys and basements of pachinko parlors in Tokyo. The underbelly was never a place where he felt comfortable, but he knew how to navigate it. As posh as Kodai's life had been since a young age, he has also grown up navigating these sorts of areas. No matter how safe a city or a country, there was always a place where the light didn't reach.

Kodai spots the bar he's looking for, a place called The Brass Marchioness, which has a sign near that door that says it is dedicated to the honor of some player named Steamboy. The establishment is built into the shell of a large mecha, Kodai figuring that it was once part of the towering robot's torso. Upon entering, he scans the bar to find just a few day drinkers. He also sees a robotic bartender with large metallic spider legs pouring up numerous drinks.

He finally spots the man he's looking for at the very end. Sure enough, just like his description, Clive has a red beard and a single goggle as an eyepatch. Kodai slides in next to him. "Clive?"

"Maybe."

"I'm here. Veenure sent me. Let's make this quick."

Clive finishes his drink and slams the mug onto the bar. The spider-legged bartender approaches. He pulls a pipe down from the ceiling and pours the swill into Clive's mug, just a bit of white foam at the top. "Another?" asks the bartender, who has some sort of English accent.

Clive nods to Kodai. "You want something?"

"What is this stuff?"

The bartender answers: "Aether Brandy. Aged in brass barrels in Peshawar. If you're interested in happy hour, we've got half-priced Bruce Sterling Sours, which are a mixed drink of whiskey, lemon juice, and sugar cane served in a brass shaker and topped with steam. What else? Yes, that's right, Remedio Varo Gin. High-proof gin made of a blend of rare botanicals from Verne Island."

"Did you say gin?"

"I did, stranger."

"Gin and tonic, then," Kodai tells the bartender. "And put it on his tab."

"Gin and tonic it is." The bartender swirls around and returns with a drink in a matter of seconds, one in a brass-rimmed glass.

"Cheers," Clive says as he lifts his drink to Kodai. "Now, where were we?"

"You know why I am here. Once I have the package, the money will be delivered."

Clyde takes a big sip of his drink and sets it down onto the bar. He wipes his face with his arm. "That's not how this is going to work."

"What? That was what we agreed upon."

"You and I didn't agree to anything. Veenure and I agreed to something. And she's not here."

Veenure: Go with it. I figured he would try something like this.

Kodai: Are you certain? That is a lot of money.

Veenure: The money will be tracked, even if it is being sent to a digital wallet. You have MercSecure connections. This is something they could figure out in a matter of minutes. Make sure he understands this.

Kodai: Reveal my hand this early?

Veenure: If you must.

"Well?" Clive asks.

Kodai drums his fingers along the side of his drink. "Here's how this is going to happen. I will give you the money, and you will have twenty-four hours to get me the package in Tritania. Not here in Steam. If that twenty-four hours passes and you haven't given me the package, I will see you in the real world. You know what? Let's make this easier. You have twelve hours or less. That should be plenty of time. The stipulation remains—if you do not have it in twelve hours, expect a visit in the real world."

"A what now?"

"Actually, I guess you are right. I won't be the one visiting you, but someone working for me will. I already know where you are diving from. Of course I have connections in the Maldives. You're staying at the Gili Lankanfushi, room B38. My people have already marked the hotel you're staying at and are stationed near there."

"What? How?"

Kodai finishes his drink, his patience wearing thin. "Do you have any idea who you are dealing with?"

Clive takes a big swig of his drink just as the wall comes crashing down.

"She's my girlfriend!" an angry male voice shouts as the dust clears.

"Not if she's mine!"

A pair of steam breeds begin trading punches, one clearly gone berserk by the looks of it. He tears into the opposite side of the bar, grabs the bartender by his spider-legs, and throws the man over his shoulder, straight through a window cut into the metal wall.

Barstools and chairs hit the air along with more debris; both Kodai and Clive move into cover. Now on the other side of the bar, glasses breaking overhead, Kodai's prosthetic arm begins to morph into a large weapon.

Veenure: Handle them and return. And make sure you get confirmation from Clive.

"With pleasure," Kodai says, feeling a sudden sense of excitement. This is going to be fun.

(x)___(x)

Kodai looks down at his hand, which has morphed into a gun with a brass muzzle, gears moving along its side. A reticle appears. As chaos takes place just beyond, Kodai is presented with a series of texts.

[Steam armor enhancement? Y/N?]

"Yes," he says as more glass comes crashing down around him.

[Approved.]

[Steam armor enhancement initiating.]

Kodai watches as armor forms seemingly out of nowhere. The thick, golden armor clicks into place as it cascades up his legs. He leaps over the bartop and meets the first steam breed, a hulking motherfucker with veiny muscles and all sorts of cables sticking out of his back, steam emitting from pipes along his shoulders.

Kodai kicks him in the face. On his way down, Kodai fires a targeted blast from his gun arm directly into the steam breed's stomach, his shot followed by a hiss of steam.

Fweeyooom! Shhhwoooooh!

Kodai hops to the ground just as the steam breed gets back to his feet, shaky now.

Kodai delivers a solid uppercut that breaks the man's jaw. The brute goes up and back, smashing through a table.

Before he can press himself up again, Kodai starts stomping the man's head. The flying mechanism of his boot activates on his third stomp, exploding the man's face onto the ground in a splatter of brain matter, viscera, chipped bone, and brass molars.

Kodai turns to the other steam breed. The bronze-skinned fellow takes a step back. His fists are still up, but he's definitely hesitant about what he should do next.

Kodai shoots forward to meet the man. He tackles him. The two go straight through a wall. They crack into several barrels of aged liquor, a few of which break, foamy ale spewing into the air and onto the ground.

Kodai presses himself back and fires a shot at point-blank range into the bottom of the steam breed's chin.

Fweeyooom! Shhhwoooooh!

The hiss of steam is all that's left of the guy's face once Kodai gets to his feet and turns to the main room of the bar. He comes around to find Clive standing there, the man with a gun in his hand, his arms shaky.

"Some use you are," Kodai tells him, feeling emboldened now with how much ass he just kicked in such a short amount of time. "The package. Yes or no, within twelve hours?"

"Yes, sooner. I'll deliver it myself," Clive assures him, fear in his eyes.

"Good. It's been a pleasure doing business." Kodai pauses as if he plans to remind Clive what will happen if he doesn't live up to his end of the bargain.

In the end, he doesn't say anything. After all, Clive's expensive resort is currently surrounded by a European MercSecure team. Not only that, but they know which room he's in.

Kodai wasn't bluffing.

CHAPTER 8: NOPE

ONCE HE IS BACK IN THE DIVE VAT, Ryuk waits for the NV Visor to start up. He appears in Tritania a few moments later, before he can even register the login tone. *That fast.* Even if he has visited the Proxima Galaxy countless times, the speed always takes him by surprise. From one world to the next in the blink of an eye.

"And the winner of the exclusive Q and A with our favorite goblin is… drum roll please…"

"Hold the fick on, Twixy, I'm not doing any Q and A with a ficker that—"

"Relax, Hiccup," says the Swede, his eyes black as ever. "You'll love this."

"The fick I will!"

Ryuk and his guildmates are standing outside of a city that he hasn't visited since taking his most recent avatar. New Gotha, which is surrounded by the Gotha River and its tributaries, is a city known for its white marble structures that are arabesque, the buildings with domed roofs, many of which house establishments in which people can learn to better use their powers and adjust their classes.

The buildings themselves are huge, the towers around them rising high into the sky. On top of each spire stand statues of famous Thuleans. The breeze blowing through the city comes with the scent of salt that makes Ryuk feel as if they are near the ocean, even though they are not. He knows better. There are numerous salt mines in the Saiduka Mountains, which are northwest of the city. The mountains are also where the city has got much of its legendary marble.

"If you do the Q and A, the fickers will give you your cake," FeeTwix tells Hiccup, dangling a proverbial carrot over the goblin's head. "Not just any cake, a DD's Barbeque cake topped with Thomas-James potions."

"Cake?" Hiccup smashes his fat finger on one of the buttons, a new voice playing from his soundboard gauntlet, one that belongs to a particular Thulean princess.

~~*Fick yeah, goblin.*~~

Ryuk looks at Zaena, who stands next to Enway. "I did it to shut him up," she explains. "Clearly, that did not work."

"Fick no, it didn't." Hiccup returns his focus to the Swede. "Okay, let me get this straight. I do a Q and A with this fickered fanboy and I get cake. Am I missing something here? Can it really be that simple? What about the fickin' dungeon?"

"Dungeon?" Ryuk asks.

Sophia: Yes, the dungeon you are standing in front of. That's why you are there. A portal has opened up inside the dungeon. You know what? I'll make it easy for you. Here's a quest prompt.

Quest: Will you seal the final portal that's located in a dungeon outside of New Gotha?

Possible Rewards: Enough EXP to reach Level 35, which you should already be at by now.

Risks: You'll all die and have to do this quest again and again leaving all of Tritania to suffer due to your guild's incompetence.

Ryuk accepts the quest.

He turns around to find the entrance to a cave.

"I guess..." Ryuk gestured toward the dungeon. "Let's go. Sophia's orders."

"Heh! You're so whipped, Marbles. What did you think you were going to do once you got here? Did you think we were going to go to New Gotha and you'd be able to get your fickin' gooch waxed? Fick no. Actually..." The goblin runs his dirty hand under his double chin. "A gooch waxing isn't a bad idea, Marbelito, now that you mention it. There are probably some orc chippies with serious fupa in New Gotha who would do your gooch for—"

"Focus, Hiccup, yes or no to the Q and A? My fans are waiting!"

Yet again, text from Sophia appears across Ryuk's eyes.

Sophia: You all need to get moving.

Ryuk: We will. Just give us a moment to regroup.

Enway approaches Ryuk. Her face softens and she smiles at him. "How was Tokyo?"

"We had curry. It was good."

"And your goblin problem?" she whispers.

"Fixed."

"How?"

"Hard reboot. They ran some programs as well."

"That's good to know. After we do this dungeon, I should probably log out for a little while. I can't remember the last time I logged out. I was supposed to go over to my parents' home for dinner. But that was a day ago. They'll understand. They are old-school gamers, World of Warcraft."

Ryuk nods. "I visited the Proxima WoW a couple years ago. It was fun."

"They still log in there from time to time. Mostly doing raids and trying to keep their old guild together. Can you imagine that they have been in a guild for like thirty years? Since they were in their teens. I think all their guildmates are still around too. Maybe our guild will be like that."

"Maybe."

"Maybe I'll visit Tokyo one day," she says. "I've always wanted to, you know. Everyone has an idea what Tokyo is like. Especially with all the anime."

"It is not exactly like that, but..." Ryuk thinks about how much anime has shaped Japan over the twenty-first century. From eye surgery to the way people dressed and the things they created digitally and through using robotics, all of it. What started as an interpretation of the comics that the American GIs brought over in the twentieth century had morphed into something beyond anything anyone could have predicted. "It is somewhat like that, like the anime shows. Much like that."

She laughs. "You would show me around, wouldn't you?"

Ryuk glances over to Hiccup, glad that the goblin is currently distracted by FeeTwix. "Yes, but only when it is safe. Right now, it is not safe. Because of my brother, it is not safe. Hopefully soon."

"It would be nice if the two of you could make amends, but after what he has done, and what he continues to do, I don't see how that is possible."

"Neither do I. It has been a long time coming. I wish it wasn't this way."

Their conversation is interrupted once Hiccup starts yelling and pointing at FeeTwix. The goblin equips his toe knife. FeeTwix summons a futuristic handgun, one with red lights running along the side. Zaena comes to the Swede's side as well, prepared to draw her swords. Then there is Wolf, who remains on the periphery, slightly confused as to whose side he should be on.

"Do you really want to go there, Hiccup?"

"Fick you and your fickin' bean shooter, Twixy. I want my fickin' cake, and I want it now."

"After the dungeon. You'll get your cake after the dungeon."

"At least..." Hiccup puts his knife away. "At least give me a fickin' potion. One of the good ones. Pretty please? Pretty please with a fickin' cherry on top?"

FeeTwix slips his gun into the back of his waistband and summons a healing potion, which he tosses at Hiccup. As the goblin nurses it, FeeTwix launches into a new ad read. "Did I mention that it's cold outside? *Baby, it's cold outside!* I really can't stay, I really can't, but with your invitation and permission to cuddle, I would love to sit by the fire and enjoy Krunkin' Kronuts' newest winter exclusives. I already told you about the St. Valentine's Day Massacre Kronut with cherry blossom icing, white peppermint sprinkles in a red velvet molten chocolate core. Mmm-mmm! Are you ready for their second winter offering? Are you? Tell me you are. Tell me you are ready for something absolutely fantastic! Candied Maple Krunch Caramel Creme donuts are everything you need to get your weekly supply of sugar in a single meal! Imagine sitting by the fire on a nice faux fur rug with your sweetie sharing a Candied Maple Krunch Caramel Creme donut! What a way to put on that winter weight just in time for a boozy spring. #FeeTwixRox at checkout will get you 30% off your entire order, app or in store worldwide. That's your entire order! One dozen of these bad mamajamas at 30% off? Talk about the steal of the year! And stay tuned, I have a big announcement coming..."

Hiccup, who has just finished his healing potion, tosses it over his shoulder and approaches Ryuk. "You haven't said you missed me yet. I'm just fickin' pointing that out."

"Because I didn't miss you."

The goblin shifts his weight onto one heel and lets loose a squeaker as he passes Ryuk. He follows this up by triggering one of the new recordings on his soundboard gauntlet.

~*Fick you, Marbles!*~

The Mitherfickers enter the cave, and head down a slope that wraps around to the proper entrance of the dungeon. Ryuk notices the walls look like a sea of AI-generated bodies all swimming together. It certainly makes him feel uneasy.

They approach a gated entrance that seems to be boiling with evil, evident in the smoke that has gathered in the clearing before the towering door, and the algomagic on the periphery. Ryuk loads his marble shotgun. He then loads his marble gun. He sends both of these to his inventory list and then touches the runestone on his chest, selecting the Berserker Warrior option.

Ryuk Matsuzaki Level 30 Berserker Warrior
HP: 1202/1202

ATK: 160 + 75
MATK: 215
DEF: 125
MDF: 94
LUCK: 25

He equips Tamana's sword, its scabbard naturally appearing on his back. The Japanese gamer returns the weapon to its sheath, and takes a step forward, feeling stronger now that his muscles are bulging. He pushes the hood off his head, and lets some of his dark hair spill out.

"I'm ready."

Hiccup nearly falls over laughing. "Fick. Marbles over here is cosplaying as Dwayne 'The Fick' Johnson but with hair and without a chest tattoo over your titty. Fick. I can't fickin' believe that we had to wait for that."

Whack!

"Yoy!" The goblin stumbles forward. "Fick off, Liz!"

"Quiet, goblin. Leave Ryuk alone. He looks good."

"That's right," FeeTwix says. "The fans are loving this new look, Ryuk. Ready to see some fan art?"

"No," Ryuk says as he ignores yet another message from Sophia telling them to hurry up. "Let's just clear this dungeon."

A new voice enters into the equation.

"Before you do…"

FeeTwix whips around, his eyes nearly bulging out of his head as he sees his hero, Quantum Hughes. The famous gamer has just stepped out of a portal which Ryuk assumes is courtesy of Sophia, Quantum in all black and a bulletproof vest that says D.R.E.A.M. Team.

"I see you're still wearing the Crocs, Kid."

"You bet I am!" FeeTwix goes to high-five Quantum but stops beside Ryuk instead. "Are you... planning to clear out this dungeon with us?"

"Nah, not this one. This one is small fries to me, no offense. I'm here with a gift from Big Daddy."

Sophia: He means Doc. Ignore the way he speaks.

"Heh. Take one of these, and you'll be cooking with gas." Quantum turns his hand around and five hot pink pills take shape. "What's the big idea?" he asks Zaena, who looks at him skeptically. "Don't you worry, lady, I don't got cooties or nothing. These pills should get you all pretty cranked. I'm not talking cloud nine, I'm talking cloud *level*. You dig?"

"We dig, we dig!" FeeTwix says.

"Hold the fick up. Is the detective guy trying to give us fickin' drugs? Fick yeah! Gimme, gimme, gimme." Hiccup barges past Ryuk and ends up elbowing him in the bicep. "Fick, Marbles, watch where you're fickin' going."

"Looks like someone has first dibs." Quantum drops one of the pills into Hiccup's grubby mechanical hand.

"We don't even know what they do, goblin."

"Fick if I care, Liztard. Law enforcement gives me a pill, I take the pill." Hiccup tosses it into his mouth and swallows. "Fick, Thuleans really don't know how hard it is for us lowly goblins."

FeeTwix is next to take a pill. He pops it in his mouth and swallows it, then shows Quantum his tongue. "Down the hatch. Wait. What does it do exactly?"

"You should have asked that before you took it, kid. Too late now. But don't worry. The pills will speed up your leveling. It'll make you a bit more aggressive too. According to Doc, it'll have you itchin' for a switchin' in no time flat. Should be fun. Get jazzed up, fight your way through a dungeon, home before supper. Good times. Hey, you. Yeah, you. You're Marbles, right?"

"Fick yeah, that's Marbles." Hiccup slaps his gut. "Such a little ficker, but he's a good guy, like a son to me but not as smart as my actual son and cousin, Spew Gorge."

"Yeah?" Quantum eyes the goblin. "Maybe keep that information to yourself, huh?"

A message from Sophia appears.

Sophia: The pill will double your experience. We need you at level 35. All of you. Don't come out of that dungeon until you've sealed the portal, and are at level 35.

Ryuk approaches Quantum. "I'm Ryuk. Not Marbles."

"Is that so? You're looking like you got into the beefcake there. Last time I saw you, you were a little guy."

Ryuk touches his chest. "It's the runestone."

"Runestone, huh? I may need to get one of those for myself. Always good to put something in the inventory list. Anyway, enough show-and-tell. Take your pill. And the rest of yas too. That dungeon isn't gonna to clear itself. Ah, would you look at that, Soph is already telling me I need to wrap it up." It's clear now from the look on his face that the woman annoys him. "Anyway, I'd better hit the road."

While Quantum mumbles under his breath, Zaena takes the other two pills using her ghost limb. She distributes one to Enway, who is now standing next to Ryuk.

"Fist bump before you go," FeeTwix tells Quantum just as the famous trench-coated man turns away.

Quantum raises his fist to FeeTwix. "Sure, kid. Good luck in there."

(0)__(0)

Their first fight comes swiftly. As soon as they are in the dungeon proper, demonic dwarves swell out of cracks and fissures as if they have been waiting for them all along.

Ryuk scans the first one he sees, and notices that the others are at about the same level:

Demon Dwarf Level 19
HP: 371/371
ATK: 39
MATK: 1
DEF: 121
MDF: 80

"Heads up, they're pretty well-armored!" FeeTwix calls out. The Swede goes for his AUS hose gun, the brass reservoir taking shape on his back. He locks in the nozzled cable that connects to the reservoir and aims it at the incoming demon dwarves. "Keep the change, ya filthy animal!"

Ryuk swings his buster sword into the skull of a dwarf, which cuts into its armor and quickly concusses his assailant.

-249 HP!

Critical Hit!

~~FICK~~

Hiccup, who now rides Wolf, tears off toward another dwarf and strikes it with one of his smaller axes.

-69 HP!

"Fick yeah!"

The cavernous space isn't big enough for him to really get momentum, yet the goblin does the best he can as he swivels back around and launches off the Tagvornian beast as if he has just been fired out of a cannon. Hiccup bowls down a small mob of demon dwarves. He gets scrappy all of a sudden and beats them away, the goblin possessed with power and fury, likely from the hot pink pill that Quantum gave him.

-43 HP! -26 HP! -39 HP!

"Fick the fick yeah!"

As Ryuk hacks into another dwarf, Zaena blenders herself into a typhoon of swords.

Insta-Insta-Instakill!

Her rage is complemented by an arcane attack from Enway that cuts out a huge chunk of the wall, and collapses onto more of the mob. The only problem is that this opens up another chamber of the dungeon, one with even more dwarf demons.

"What's that?" FeeTwix asks as he turns his AUS hose gun to the incoming mob. "McStarbucks is back this afternoon with Cucumber Spice McWater! Holy fickballs! That's the best news I've heard all day! Why drink regular water when you can drink a cup of refreshing Cucumber Spice McWater? Does it promote hydration? Check. Could it aid in weight loss? Check. Does it contain antioxidants, vitamins, turmeric, electrolytes, and other minerals? Check! Check! Check!"

"Fick you, Twixy, you fickered huckster fick!" A demon dwarf clobbers Hiccup across the head, yet the goblin's noggin is protected by his golden helm.

"Not... not my goblin, you won't!"

Flashing into a rage, FeeTwix darts toward Hiccup. His AUS hose gun goes away and he equips his slice bang. The Swede both slices and bangs in an effort to free the goblin, who is now trapped under a dogpile of dwarves. FeeTwix pulls dwarves off the goblin and runs his weapon through their backs, also firing at the same time.

Bang!

Instakill!

Bang!

Instakill!

FeeTwix finally finds Hiccup and helps the goblin up. "You good?"

"Fick... that was..." Hiccup starts to hug FeeTwix and stops. "What the fick, Twixy? Get your muscled Norse arms off me. I'm nobody's fickin' fickboy." Hiccup moves quickly to toss his tomahawk at a dwarf about to spring an attack on FeeTwix.

Instakill!

"Beast mode time!" FeeTwix sends his Slice Bang away. He equips two healing potions, tosses one to Hiccup, and throws one back himself. The Swede goes for his mutant hack, which forms into a bladed arm piece that extends all the way up to his shoulder. He cuts into the next mob, finishing his ad read as he whips himself into a frenzy. "That's right! Cucumber Spice McWater! You want it. McStarbucks has it! Get 50% off an order of two if you order from the app. That's half off, people! Half the fick off! I don't even know what you'll do with the savings, but I hope—" FeeTwix rages again and launches himself into the middle of an incoming mob.

Ryuk rushes to help him, the Mitherfickers in their element, the chaos fun as hell.

This was what they needed.

Ryuk is ready to push it to the limit, and have fun doing it.

(0)__(x)

The Mitherfickers are so close. They have done some serious leveling up over the last hour, and Ryuk is certain they'll soon hit the Level 35 marker.

Just a few more battles, he thinks as his eyes trace over their stat sheets.

Ryuk Matsuzaki Level 33 Ballistics Mage
HP: 1296/1296
ATK: 168
MATK: 231
DEF: 146
MDF: 98
LUCK: 27

FeeTwix Fajer Level 34 Berserker Mystic
HP: 1449/1449
ATK: 251
MATK: 47
DEF: 124
MDF: 78
LUCK: 29

Hiccup Level 33 Shield Thief
HP: 2124/2124
ATK: 170
MATK: 19
DEF: 358
MDF: 206
LUCK: 45

Zaena Morozon Level 34 Brawler Assassin
HP: 1453/1453
ATK: 297
MATK: 13
DEF: 264
MDF: 68
LUCK: 31

Enway Zoltan Rosa Level 34 Hourglass Mage
HP: 1165/1165
MANA: 670/670
ATK: 88
MATK: 224
DEF: 84
MDF: 234
LUCK: 27

Wolf Level 41
HP: 2456/2456
ATK: 713
MATK: 0
DEF: 539
MDF: 245
LUCK: 20

Ryuk also leveled up two of his skills, the Cherry Poppin' Daddy skill, which gives him a damage boost if he shoots an enemy in the ass, and his One in a Million skill, which leveled after Ryuk took down a fleeing dwarf.

Skill: Cherry Poppin' Daddy
Level Four: 1 in 8 chance of connecting. Enemy's backside must be exposed. Higher levels increase damage and chance for an instakill.
Damage: 61% if enemy is less than level 30; 15% if enemy is greater than level thirty.
Odds of instakill: 25%
Requirements for instakill: LUCK > 9

Skill: One in a Million
Level Three: Use your slingshot and any marble of your choosing to take an impossible shot. Odds of connecting increase with each point you gain in LUCK.

Requirements: Level 20 Mage, LUCK > 19.

All in all, things are looking up. And more importantly, they are close to the levels need.

Dungeons in areas of Polynya and Ultima Thule have resting places where enemies aren't able to do anything, places where guilds, or dungeon crawlers, can't be harmed while they recharge. The Mitherfickers have found such a resting place, one that even has a fairly large natural sauna in it, much to Ryuk's chagrin.

If I have to see Hiccup's naked ass one more time, he thinks as the goblin strips down, clears out any stale air he's been keeping inside his robust body, and hops in, splashing Enway in the process.

"Dammit, Hiccup."

"Fick yeah! Nothing like some hot water to get you nice and ready for more assficking, I mean asskicking. Ha!" Hiccup drinks some of the water and spits it. "Tastes not-so-bad too. Wonder how many ficktards have pissed in here." Hiccup takes another drink. "Not so many. Fick. It's good to have a bath."

"When was your last bath, goblin?"

"The goblin has a... fick!" A bubble rises and pops. Hiccup laughs again. "Fick you, Liz. That peppery little love puff had your name all over it. I guess my pooperhatch doesn't like you either. And to answer your question, last time I bathed... let me think. Nope, can't fickin' remember."

"Gross."

"Was it the word pooperhatch? Fick me, Liz. Let's not cancel Uncle Goblin because he uses the common parlance of Jatla. Do you prefer dookiechute? Chocolate pocket?"

"*Jatla blantakh!* You're disgusting."

"The last time you bathed was in Zaena's pocket sauna," FeeTwix informs the goblin. "And now that we're here, I believe it is almost time for—"

"Pocket sauna, that's fickin' right. Fick! Why are we sitting in a pool of piss-water when we could be relaxing in a sauna?" Hiccup equips a healing potion and drinks it, even though his HP was topped off simply through entering the space. Rather than chugging it back, like he normally does, he takes his time with it, savoring it as if he were a wine connoisseur. Ryuk is pretty sure he even swishes it around in his mouth.

FeeTwix smiles at the goblin. "As I was saying, I believe it is time, my handsome little friend—"

"Hey! I'm adequately sized, Twixy, and don't get that shit twisted."

Zaena pops Hiccup on the head with her ghost limb, causing him to spill some of his healing potion into the water. Hiccup sucks up the water immediately, glaring at the Thulean as he does so.

She glares back.

He glares even harder.

Zaena takes a step closer.

Without taking his eyes off her, Hiccup finishes slurping up the healing potion. He then brings his arm back, like he's going to throw the bottle at the Thulean.

"Do it, goblin."

"It would be a fickin' honor—"

"Relax, everyone, it's your birthday!" FeeTwix spins between the two of them and stops with his arms out wide. "Are you ready, Hiccup?"

"Am I fickin' ready? Ready for what?"

"For your birthday, you idiot."

Hiccup whips his head toward Ryuk, a look of shock on his face. "What in the actual fick, Marbles? You really comin' at me like that? Really? After all I've done for you? Who was there when Tammy broke your fickered little Yakuza heart? Me. Who held your hand while you sobbed and let you place your head on his chest like my name is fickin' Busty Gazongas or some shit? Me. Who is the one that has been giving you pointers on bagging Elfie here, advice that clearly seems to be working considering the two of you would be fickin' right now if the rest of us weren't here? Me. Who found Twixy, Liz, Elfie, Wolfie and recruited them? Me? Me, me, me. Speaking of which." Hiccup whistles. "Wolfie, get your ass in here."

The big bad wolf of Unigaea comes charging toward the pool of water. He hops in, splashing the goblin.

"Fick yeah! Now, where was I?"

"Your birthday, Hiccup," FeeTwix says, his black eyes twitching to some degree. He has been waiting through the goblin's entire diatribe with his arms out, like he was ready to reveal something to all of them.

Ryuk is certain that there are millions of people watching right now. Their views always go up when they are fighting. Not only that, but FeeTwix announced earlier that nearly six million people were watching their epic dwarf fight.

Six million, Ryuk thinks as he looks at Hiccup, not able to refrain from shaking his head.

"Pfft! Whatever, Marbles, I'm nobody's miniature fickpony, and it isn't even my birthday."

"But your birthday cake," FeeTwix says through gritted teeth.

TOKYO

Hiccup stares at the Swede for a moment. It is clear that he truly doesn't know what FeeTwix is talking about, his Goblinheimer's flaring up. "Fick, Twixy..."

Enway, kind as ever, even after Hiccup splashed her, comes to his aid. "Yes, it's your birthday, and your fans got you the cake that you requested. Don't you remember?"

Hiccup squints at her. "I requested a cake?"

"You did."

"A cake from Dirty Dave's?"

"Yes," she whispers.

"In that case, fick yeah, it's my birthday!" He splashes over to the side of the pool of water. "Gimme, gimme, gimme."

Zaena steps away. "I'm not singing to the goblin."

"Fick off. We all know lizards can't sing anyway."

"Now, before we give you this epic cake—and it is epic, I can't believe you Mitherfickers bought this for our dear goblin—I should tell you that right now, as in today, as in this very moment, Krunkin' Kronuts has pop-up shops in Seoul, Hong Kong, Tokyo, Singapore, Ulaanbaatar, Beijing—pretty much any major city in Asia. Sorry my friends from the west, this one is an Asia exclusive! Now, if you are in Asia, pull up your Krunkin' Kronuts app and click the star icon. Why? Because you are a star! That'll tell you if they have a pop-up in your city or not. And boy, for your sake, I hope they have one. This is a first. This is such a big deal. I've never done something like this before. We've never done something like this before."

"What the fick, Twixy, are you going to give them my cake or what?" Hiccup slams his mechanical hand against the surface of the water, which splashes Wolf. "Sorry, Wolfie," he says. "This ficker here and his fickery.

Gets me all ready to fickin' feast, and then starts a good-for-fickered ad ready."

"You're going to want to hear this, Hiccup. It's big. Really big!"

"Heh, that's what she fickin' said. Right, Marbles?"

Ryuk rolls his eyes.

"You wouldn't get *Office* humor anyway, fick-face."

FeeTwix takes a deep breath. "I am excited, I am so very excited to announce that today only, there is a Mitherficker-themed donut combo at all Krunkin' Kronut pop-up shops in Asia."

"A what?" Zaena asks.

"Surprise, Marbles, I mean Ryuk, and don't worry, we got some coming as soon as we log out. *This is so exciting!*" FeeTwix does a jump kick. "First, there's the donut holes, meant to be Ryuk's marbles. For me, there's a Boston creme donut with my face on it. My actual face! For Zaena, royalty in the house, there's beautiful purple donut with a pair of crossed swords on it. For Enway, there's an all white donut decorated with sprinkles. And for Hiccup, our dear Hiccup, there's a green kronut filled with a raspberry filling, meant to be a healing potion."

Hiccup eyes him suspiciously. "What about Wolfie?"

"He doesn't have a donut."

"What the fick is a kronut?"

"But wait, there's more! If you hit up one of the pop-up shops now, you will get a free Mitherfickers T-shirt while supplies last. Remember the design Hiccup came up with, two skulls with wings and swords? That's the one! Hit my feed up for pictures. It's all so exciting! Check it out, guys," he tells the group as a picture of the donuts pixelates in front of him.

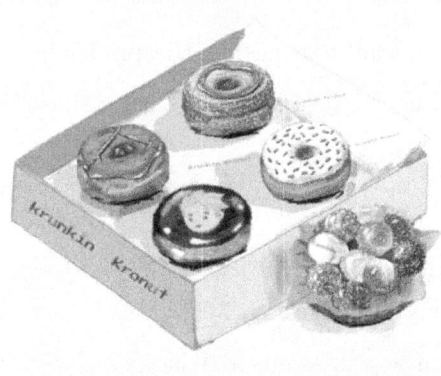

"Holy fick that looks delicious," Hiccup says. "But we need to talk, Twixy."

"Talk to me, Hiccup!"

"You've gone and licensed my IP, and are now using me to make money. You got money from this, right?"

"Of course I did."

"No, you didn't." The goblin grins. "We did. We're partners now. You and me. Fickin' fifty-fifty."

"You can't use money in our world," FeeTwix says carefully. This isn't exactly correct. If Hiccup were to take the body of a humandroid, which Sophia can clearly arrange, he would be able to use human money.

"But you can cash out here. I want a fickin' cut, Twixy, or I'm going to get real mean, real violent, real crazy, real quick. You still haven't seen true goblin mode from me. Remember that. Now that we are talking about it, after the Mitherfickers get done saving the fickin' world, I want to retire to somewhere nice with a view of the Hills of Hillshire and *not* the Jatla Forest. That's where they send old fickers to waste away and have their starfish cleaned by nurses who used to be orc chippies. They're real rough when it comes to wiping, believe you me. So a cut of the moolah. I want some young Thulean nurses taking care of me in my old age, ones that look like Liz over here."

"In your dreams, goblin."

"Fick no, in my reality, Lizzy. I'm all about *The Secret* over here. Reality fickin' manifestation. So before we have a little birthday party, before you show me any more fickin' kronuts, I want a seat at the table."

FeeTwix approaches Hiccup, crouches, and offers the goblin his hand. "First, you have a deal. Second, you have had a deal since the beginning of all this, since the beginning of my negotiations."

When did FeeTwix have negotiations? Ryuk thinks.

"Anyone that is part of the Mitherfickers benefits. Now, you've sort of ruined my Krunkin' Kronuts pitch, but not to worry, Hiccup, the fans expected you to demand something."

"You're fickin' right I want my cut. Speaking of cuts." The goblin licks his lips. "Where's the fickin' cake?"

"Is someone having a birthday party?"

Hiccup's eyes go wide upon hearing the raspy voice. "Fick. Fick! Did you all fickin' hear that. Nope. Oh fick, oh fick!" He ducks his head under the water and comes back up again to spit water at Ryuk. "Fick!"

"What was that?" Enway takes a look around.

The raspy voice speaks again: *"I love to party. Maybe we will get to party soon. Heh-heh-heh-heh! I'm looking forward to that."*

"Fick the fick no. Nope! That's not a ghost. Fick!" Hiccup grabs Wolf and hugs him, the wet canine struggling to get out of his grip. "You've got to protect me, Wolfie. Fick. Back to Jatla. Let's portal back to Jatla. Or Kayi. Now, Mitherfickers."

"If that wasn't a ghost, what was it?" Ryuk asks.

"What was it? You don't know? What the fick are they teaching you in Korea?"

"I'm from Japan," Ryuk reminds Hiccup.

"And I'm from fickin' Cincinnati. Pfft! What I'm saying right now, Marbles, is that it doesn't matter where we are from or what we identify as. And what the fick is Cincinnati? Like I said, it doesn't matter! That's not a fickin' ghost. We can't have a cake here. Bad luck. We need to get the fick out." Hiccup pushes Wolf away. He scrambles to the side of the pool and awkwardly pulls himself out of the water. For a moment, he scoots forward using his arms, dragging his legs as if he were a crocodile.

Ryuk closes his eyes as soon as he catches sight of the goblin's dimpled ass.

"Fick, Marbles, don't stand around salivating over my juicy apple bottom. Help me get my fickin' clothes on. Fick. We're really in some fickin' trouble here. Fick!"

Ryuk hears the voice again.

"*Heh-heh-heh-heh!*"

"What the hell is going on?" FeeTwix asks Zaena. Ryuk can tell by the look on his face that the Swede is a bit disappointed, especially with his big announcement being overshadowed by Hiccup's behavior and the mysterious voice.

"Don't you fickers know? That's Grifty. Grifty is here in this dungeon, and if we continue on, fick, we're going to be so ficked."

A message from Sophia flashes across their eyes.

Sophia: Ignore the goblin and continue on to the portal. If you do encounter any hostiles, deal with them accordingly.

"Get it together," Ryuk tells the goblin. "We're almost done with this dungeon."

"*Heh-heh-heh-heh!*"

"Fick!"

(x)__(x)

Hiccup is still bitching about Grifty by the time the next mob of dwarves attack, their enemies all level twenty-five or higher. Back to being a Ballistics Mage, Ryuk surges into action with a magazine of sword marbles.

-79 HP! -105 HP! -130 HP! - 86 HP! -102 HP! - 123 HP! - 94 HP! - 147 HP!

Critical Hit!

FeeTwix cuts forward with some kind of ray gun.

Fweeem!

He shrinks two of the dwarves and stomps them with his tactical crocs.

Insta-Instakill!

"What kind of gun is this?" asks Zaena, who slices and dices right next to her man, the Thulean with a big grin on her face. It's clear by the way she moves that she's having a hell of a time chopping away at the mob.

"A shrink gun, babe!"

"Shit, Twixy, got a reverse one of those for Marbles over here? Heh!" Hiccup, who has his big scutum shield, sits with his back to it so he can enjoy a fresh healing potion.

Another fucking healing potion, Ryuk thinks as he fights the urge to aim his marble shotgun at the goblin.

Wolf does his best to protect the goblin, the canine instakilling any dwarf who dares to get in his way. Meanwhile, Enway levels a trio of goblins with a blistering fireball made of pink and purple magic, her Arcane Tide power.

Insta-Insta-Instakill!

Dwarves wearing even thicker armor charge into the chamber just as FeeTwix starts up another ad read. "Boy does Chase Bank of America Fargo have a deal for you! Apply for a new line of credit and get no interest for three months. That's three whole months, people! Spring into the savings with balance transfers at a fee of 5% or fifty dollars, whichever is greater. Sign up with a Chase Bank of America Fargo checking account, and you'll get your monthly fee waived if you keep your account topped off with 5K or get a direct deposit of at least 2K. Otherwise, the monthly fee will be—" FeeTwix summons a knife, which he uses to stab a dwarf in the neck. "A monthly fee of fifty dollars! What a deal!"

"What a fickin' rip-off, Twixy, and you know it. Fick! What was that?" Hiccup jumps, his scutum falling behind him. He whips his head around. "Did you feel that, Marbles? Was it Grifty?"

"I'm kind of busy over here, Hiccup." Ryuk goes for his triggerless marble gun, which he fires at one of the armored dwarves. The explosion that follows shreds the dwarf's armor, which gives shrapnel damage to the enemies around him.

-178 HP!

Critical hit!

Ryuk is just about to surge forward and join FeeTwix when Hiccup appears beside him, the goblin trembling.

"I saw him. I saw Grifty. Fick, Marbles!" His eyes fill with sheer terror as he triggers his soundboard gauntlet, the goblin mashing several of the buttons at once.

~Fick!~

~Fick you, Marbles!~

~~Fick you.~~

~FICK~

~Mmm, fick.~

"Get off me." Ryuk whips his arm away and hits it against a furry body, one that wasn't just standing next to him moments ago.

"I was wondering when you'd say hello."

"Fick!" Hiccup takes off running. He trips over his own feet, and lands on top of one of the dead dwarves. "Yoy! Fick, Marbles. Yoy. Run you stupid fickin' ficktwat that's fickin'… no… don't look into his eyes, Marbles!"

Ryuk turns to see a being about his height, one covered in bright orange fur. He has googly eyes that never seem to focus on any one thing and he wears a sinister grin on his furry face. He wears a black hat that ties under his chin, and his body is partially covered by a tunic made of black and white fabric. The being isn't wearing any pants.

"Grifty?" Ryuk asks.

"At your service, bud. Now. Hold on. Hold on." Grifty procures a little bag full of white powder. He pours some out onto his thumb and takes a bump. *"Ooo yeah. That's the stuff. That's the stuff. You want some? Come here, have some."*

"No, Marbles, no!" Hiccup pushes between the two of them. "You will not get my fickin'— okay, he's not my friend, more of my employer and I'm sort of like his father but you get the fickin' point—Grifty, no, NO!"

"Come on," Grifty says, his eyes starting to wobble. *"Don't you guys want to have a little fun."*

Hiccup blinks rapidly, the goblin instantly possessed. "A little fun? Who... who the fick doesn't like a little fun? Fick me. I haven't had fun since I got this shit-ass job at a fickin' guild that doesn't pay for fick. Sure, Grifty, I'll take a little."

Grifty smiles. *"Yes, you will, goblin. Everyone needs to get high from time to time."* He starts to pour some of the wizardous—at least this is what Ryuk thinks it is—into his palm. *"First taste is free. Second taste, you're going to need to work for that."*

"Sure, whatever you say," Hiccup tells the furry orange demon. "I'll do whatever you want, Grifty."

An invisible force slaps Grifty's hand just as Hiccup's big nostrils are seconds away from snorting up the white powder. Grifty goes from bug-eyed crazy-looking to fucking furious in a matter of seconds as he turns to look at Zaena, who now stands with FeeTwix and Enway. Wolf is next to the Swede, hunched forward and growling as he bares his teeth.

"That'll be enough, demon," Zaena says.

Grifty starts to laugh. *"You're in for a world of pain, Thulean."*

FeeTwix steps forward and shoots Grifty in the head.

Bang!

The demon falls into a pile of orange hair, steam rising from it.

"Easy enough." The Swede blows smoke away from the muzzle of his weapon. "Whatever it is, it's dead now."

"What the fick, Twixy, I was just about to get high!" Hiccup tries to come at FeeTwix but Ryuk gets in the way. "Move, Marbles!"

"Relax, Hiccup."

"Fick off, Marbles, and fick off if any of you think Grifty is actually dead. He's a fick-forsaken fickmunch of a demon that is totally not dead, and is totally going to come back to fick us later." Hiccup steps away from Ryuk and summons a healing potion.

"You've had enough—"

Hiccup snaps his teeth. "Fick off, Marbles, I'm thinking here, and I need to recharge my juices when I think. Fick, we're so ficked. Grifty will be back. Mark my fickin' words."

Enway cautiously approaches the goblin. "We have to keep going. Sophia—"

"Fick her."

"—Sophia has given us a task. We're almost at the portal that needs sealing and we should all be at Level 35 soon. I promise, if Grifty comes back, I'll make sure he regrets it. We all will. Isn't that right, Mitherfickers?"

"Yeah, yeah, Elfie. Tough talk."

"Fick yeah, we will, Hiccup. If Grifty comes, we'll make sure he doesn't, um, what does he do aside from giving out drugs to goblins? I guess it doesn't matter, we'll make sure to put a cap in his ass." FeeTwix nudges Zaena. "Right, babe?"

"Yes."

Hiccup looks at Ryuk.

"Yes, Hiccup, I'll kill Grifty if I have to."

"Wait. You against Grifty?" Some of the potion Hiccup has just ingested flies from his lips as he laughs at Ryuk. "Fick, Marbles, I want to be one of those fathers who believes in his son, who says things like, 'sure you can; if you believe in yourself and work hard, sure, you can.' But it's safe to say that you don't fickin' stand a chance against Grifty. I like the spirit, though. What about you, Wolfie?"

Wolf barks.

"Fine, fine." Hiccup finishes his healing potion and tosses it over his shoulder, where it plinks off the severed lower torso of a dead dwarf. "Let's fickin' get this shit over with."

CHAPTER 9: DUNGEON GOBLIN FEUD

THE MITHERFICKERS REACH THE PROVERBIAL FORK in the road, one passageway heading toward the right, another toward the left.

"Easy." FeeTwix equips a small metal box. He opens it to reveal a drone with wings. "I'll just send this little bad boy—"

"Fickin' shit, Twixy, can't you read?" Hiccup motions to the Thulean writing scrawled across the wall. It's illuminated by torchlight, revealing the start of both passageways. Beyond that, it's impossible to tell where they go, or what the Mitherfickers may have in store for them.

"Reading Thulean. Sure! Babe, care to give me a hand?"

Zaena steps up next to FeeTwix, the Thulean squinting as she reads the carved words. "Ah, I see. This is the doing of a goblin."

"What the fick, Liz!?"

"You should know this considering you *are* a goblin. This is a very particular kind of moronic goblin puzzle. No, I wouldn't call it a moronic goblin puzzle. It is more of a decision that must be made, one that won't let you come back and try a different path unless you start the dungeon over again. I suppose for our levels, it wouldn't hurt for us to start over."

"No fickin' way." Hiccup crosses his arms over his chest. "Nope. I'm not starting over for shit. That fickin' fickwaffle Grifty is all over this place, and you're talking about starting at the beginning again? Fick the fick no, Lizbuns. The quicker and ficker we get out of this fickered dungeon, the better. You dimwitted fickwits don't seem to get it. Grifty is bad fickin' news. Bad hombre? Does that mean anything to you?"

"It does to me," says Enway.

"He's that." Hiccup shivers. "Fick. Wolfie, I promise I won't let these fickers jeopardize our chance of getting out of here." Since he is currently mounted on Wolf, Hiccup reaches down and pats the canine on the head. "No fickin' way. We're choosing the right path."

"Of course, we'll do our best to choose the right path," FeeTwix says, "but ultimately, my dear goblin friend, it isn't up to us."

"Like fick it isn't, Twixy. Marbles, the *right fickin' path*. Let's go." Hiccup digs his heel into Wolf. The canine turns to the path on the right. "Like I said, we're choosing the right fickin' path. Cheezus fick, let's get it together, homies." Hiccup taps the death metal button on his soundboard gauntlet.

~FICK~

Ryuk looks at FeeTwix. "Well?"

"I mean, it was the right path or the left path. I guess the right path it is. We have a 50-50 chance here."

"If we have to go back to the beginning, I can use my time skip ability," Enway reminds the group. "This would allow us to come right back here. So that makes our odds even better."

"Not a bad idea at all," Ryuk says.

"Fick me twice and call me nice, are you fickers coming or not?" Hiccup shouts to them, the goblin nearly out of sight by this point.

Zaena swallows her unique dislike of Hiccup and turns to the right chamber. "This better not be a mistake. My patience for the goblin is wearing thin."

"Speaking of mistakes, CVSgreens is having a huge sale for my American viewers," FeeTwix informs his followers. "Anything and everything in the store that protects you, helps you heal, or gives you a second chance is 15% off if pre-purchased in the app with use of promo code #FeeTwixRox. That's contraceptives, bandaids, gauze, performance enhancers, and more! So much more! So next time you get or make a booboo, think of CVSgreens and the 15% you just saved by pre-purchasing quality healthcare products." The Swede picks up speed as he reads the disclaimer. "Terms and conditions apply. Please see individual State rulings on emergency contraceptives. Void where prohibited or outlawed. This channel assumes no responsibility or liability for the accuracy of information presented as televised infotainment. Such information is subject to change without notice. The content of this channel should not be taken as medical advice." FeeTwix takes a deep breath. "15% off, and have fun out there, kids, unless you don't want kids, then have fun with a plan in mind!"

"Such a curious ad," Zaena tells FeeTwix as they catch up with Hiccup.

"Be right back, everyone!" FeeTwix tells his fans. "Just need to get through this next chamber. I'll be back in a jiffy when the action picks up. In the meantime, watch the fight against the dwarves and see how many times Hiccup blesses us with a blast of gas from his nethercheeks. Winner gets not one, not three, but *two* digitally signed pictures of the Mitherfickers!"

"Oh my fickin' fick, Twixy, you really are milking your braindead ficktard fans for all they're worth. How low will he go? Anyone's guess at this point."

FeeTwix's eyes turn blue and he shifts his focus to Zaena. "You know how it is, I takes the ads to pays the bills. CVSgreens usually does a big push during February. The money is starting to stack up, and now that we've got some licensing agreements going, I think we should be well on our way to long-term, sustainable profit."

"We?" Hiccup shakes his head. "I'd love for this to be a fickin' *we* situation. Look, Twixy, if you're profiting off our asses, we'd better be getting a cut. Not you, Elfie." Hiccup points his finger at Enway. "You haven't been properly vetted yet. Once you're vetted, we'll see. And definitely not He-Man. Fick that guy. But Wolfie? Let's make sure he's set up. And speaking of poor pooches that need a little love, throw a bone to fickin' Marbles over here too. I saw his ass in your world, and he could use something. I don't know what. But something. Fick, I'm no life coach but I'm definitely becoming an influencer, and believe you me, Twix, Marbles needs help. Finally, don't worry about giving Liz a cut. She's royalty."

"What if I put you on the board of the Mitherfickers Incorporated?" FeeTwix asks the goblin.

"A board seat?" Hiccup digs his heels into Wolf's back. "What about Marbles?"

"He'd be on the board too."

"Marbles on the board? You, me, and Marbelito. Seems like a fickin' sausage party, but what can we do? We've got a to-be-vetted elf here, and the other female member of our team has more money than Ficklon

Musk. You guys ever heard of that goblin? My fick is he a fickered fickwaffle. Any-fickin-who, where was I? Did I ever tell you the story of the Fickvengers?"

FeeTwix laughs. "No, you have not. But I feel like that's something I should record for posterity."

Hiccup stares at FeeTwix for a moment, dazed. "Fick me, what the fick were we just talking about?"

"Nothing, Hiccup, let's just keep going." Ryuk steps past the goblin. As he does, he notices a shift around him, one that the others have yet to see. It's magical, likely perceptible due to his Extreme Focus skill. Ryuk stops dead in his tracks. "Something's wrong."

A booming voice replies to Ryuk: "Not at all, adventurer, something is right!" The torches lighting the way dim and grow brighter, revealing an enormous ink shadow wearing a sparkling outfit, which causes Hiccup to shriek. From what Ryuk can tell, no stats are visible.

The ink shadow gestures down the corridor and it instantly widens.

"No, fick no!" Hiccup scrambles off Wolf and tries to run, only to trip on his own feet. "Yoy..."

"Stop, Goblin," Zaena says as she prevents him from crawling away using one of her ghost limbs. Always one to be prepared, Zaena also has one of her swords drawn. FeeTwix is livestreaming again, the Swede now waving around a shotgun. This leaves Ryuk, who quickly scrambles to load his marble shotgun while Enway, holding the Book of Time, charges up for a spell.

The wall drops away revealing an audience of dwarves, who start cheering and whistling as the ink shadow takes his place center stage, a big spotlight now shining on him. The ink shadow grins, a set of pearly whites growing from what was once the black void of his mouth. "Hey, everyone! It's your man, Ink Prior, and if you're here or tuning in at home, you know exactly what time it is."

The dwarves start to chant in unison. *"Dungeon Goblin Feud! Dungeon Goblin Feud!"*

Ink Prior winks at the crowd and points at the Mitherfickers. "That's right, it's time to play another game of Dungeon Goblin Feud!"

"What the fick is Dungeon Goblin Feud?" FeeTwix asks his fans, who instantly clue him in. "Oh shit."

As Zaena curses under her breath, a magical force sweeps Ryuk and the others to a set of podiums facing the center of a sleek stage. There is another set of podiums across from them obscured by shadows that he is certain are goblins or some other Tritanian life form.

"Shit is right, Twixy. We're so fickin' ficked," Hiccup cries. "A fickin' ink shadow *and* Grifty is on the loose? Worst day ever, fick!"

"Fick you, Hiccup!"

Ryuk glances back at the crowd to see a single goblin amidst the dwarves, the goblin with yellow and midnight blue streaks in his mullet, the sides of his head shaved. *Spew Gorge?*

"What the fick, Spewy?" Hiccup asks as the ink shadow approaches. "What the in the actual F-I-C-K are you doing here?"

"What the fick does it look like I'm doing here, you fat turdfick? I got free fickin' tickets to Dungeon Goblin Feud. You bet your fickin' ass I'm coming."

As the two goblins bicker, Ink Prior stops in front of Ryuk, who happens to be at the first podium. He taps on Ryuk's podium with a blackened fist. "Let's meet the new challengers," he says, his voice amplified as if he is mic'd. "Introduce yourself, son."

"Do we have to play this game?" Ryuk asks the ink shadow. "We have other things to do."

Ink Prior laughs. "You do, do you?" He tilts his head up; Ryuk follows his gaze to see that the ceiling is a mixture of greenish stars, not unlike the OMIB. *Where are we exactly?* He quickly fires off a message to Sophia.

Ryuk: Can you do anything?

Sophia: You chose the path that led to an ink shadow, didn't you?

FeeTwix: What else were we supposed to do? And it was the goblin who chose the path.

Sophia: That was your first mistake, letting a goblin choose anything. To answer your question, I can't interfere at this point. Think of it like a cutscene that you can't skip.

FeeTwix: I hate those.

Hiccup: Fick you, Sophia, you fickin' dumbfick. You're the strongest mage in all of Tritania, and you can't fickin' get us the fick out of here?

Sophia: No, I cannot. You must complete the challenge, *then* you will be able to seal the portal. If you want me to explain the mechanics behind algomagic, I will, but I don't think you'd understand.

"Fick her," Hiccup says. "I hope someone fickin' kills that bia-bia."

"Fick you, Hiccup!" Spew Gorge shouts from the audience.

"What the fick, Spewy? I just saved your ass like a fickin' day ago."

"Dungeon Goblin Feud, Hiccup. You know how it goes!"

Hiccup sighs miserably. "The fickin' ankle biter has a point. A game of Dungeon Goblin Feud is a game of Dungeon Goblin Feud. Can't be missed. Well, Mitherfickers, we'd better hope the questions aren't too difficult."

"What the hell is Dungeon Goblin Feud?" Ryuk asks, exasperated by this point with the crowd, the challenge, and the fact he has no idea what's going on. "Seriously? What the fuck is this?"

"Fick, Marbles, watch your language. This is a family show. And you're about to fickin' find out what Dungeon Goblin Feud is. Now, answer the shadow's question."

"Yes," Ink Prior says, his form swelling until he's towering over Ryuk. He points at him. "Introduce yourself and your teammates. And don't make me ask you again."

"Ryuk Matsuzaki." Ryuk bows his head slightly. "My name is Ryuk."

"For fick's sake, Twixy, out of the way." Hiccup nudges FeeTwix over to the third podium so he can stand at the second podium, the goblin directly next to Ryuk now. "Marbles, you've got the charisma of a dingleberry."

"And what do you do?" Ink Prior asks in a tone that tells Ryuk his patience is growing thin.

What do I do?

"I am part of the Mitherfickers. My guild." Ryuk motions to the others.

"Oh, fick me," Spew Gorge shouts from the audience. "Booooo! Booooo!"

Ink Prior grins at Ryuk. "A guild, huh? Care to introduce them?"

Ryuk sighs. "This is Hiccup. He's from Jatla."

"Damn fickin' right, I am."

"And this is FeeTwix Fajer. He's a gamer."

"I sure am! Also, Mr. Prior, is it fine if I send around a few of my drones to video from various angles for everyone watching my stream? A

Family Feud parody knock-off in Tritania? You bet your ass people are going to want to see this!"

Ink Prior considers this and finally nods. "As you wish."

FeeTwix turns his hand around and summons a rectangular box about the size of a water bottle. He opens it to reveal four baseball-shaped objects, each with a camera. They take off of their own accord.

"That is Zaena," Ryuk says, assuming he's supposed to be introducing everyone. "And at the end there is, um, Enway."

"Um? Um? Fick, Marbles." Hiccup grips the podium and leans forward. "And to be clear, Elfie isn't fickin' part of our guild, or she is, but she hasn't been vetted yet and it's a whole fickin' thing."

"Oh, goblins, always with the vetting." The crowd laughs at Ink Prior's statement. "Now, let's meet your opponents, the Celebs!"

The ink shadow slinks to the other side of the space, where lights illuminate a set of five goblins that Ryuk has never seen before. Currently, four of the goblins have been revealed, the fifth one hidden behind a black curtain.

Spew Gorge is the first to react. "Holy fick! Is that Fickolas Cage? Fickin' Dolly Fickton? Ficksy? David Fickham? Fick us, we're in for a fickin' show!"

~~*Fick yeah, goblin.*~~

"What the fick was that, Hiccup!?" Spew Gorge shouts after Hiccup has triggered Zaena's voice on his soundboard gauntlet. He triggers another one.

~*Mmm, fick.*~

Spew Gorge cackles. "Fick me, that's bad fickin'-A!"

"Fick yeah it is, Spewy!"

Ryuk looks to the other side of the stage as Ink Prior stops in front of a goblin with dark hair that has been slicked back. The goblin wears a leather jacket with studs on the shoulders.

"Fickolas Cage, my man," Ink Prior says as the two fist-bump. "My man. God-damn is it good to see you."

"What the fick, seriously?" Hiccup cries. "Not only is that Fickolas Cage—he's one of the big actors in Fickvengers, in case you haven't already figured it out, Marbles—Ink Prior is clearly showing some favoritism with that fickered fist bump. We're so dead. Fick!"

~F-F-Fick!~

"Hey, Ink, nice seeing you again," says Fickolas Cage, the dashing goblin with a big smile on his face. "It's good to be back. It's *very* good to be back."

"I'll bet it is. Now, you don't have to reveal everything," Ink Prior says as he leans forward, "but word in Jatla and Bluwid is that there is going to be a new Fickvengers coming out next year. Anything you'd like to say about that?"

Hiccup's eyes perk up. "A new Fickvengers? Fick everyone that isn't us, Marbles, this is hot news! Holy fick. Let's hope it's not fickin' convoluted, and even if it is, let's hope I don't have to watch bootleg versions of like twenty other Fickvenger shows to know what the fick is going on. Spewy, did you hear that?"

"Fick yeah, I did!"

~FICK~

"Ugh. Do I really have to take part in this?" Zaena tries to move away from the podium and is prevented from doing so by what Ryuk knows is algomagic. "Apparently, I do."

"I could tap my Crocs three times..." FeeTwix suggests, referring to the shoes that Quantum gave him.

"If we die, we have to start over at the beginning," Enway reminds him. "I could skip ahead, but it would likely bring us directly back to the scene."

"So you can't skip this?" Zaena asks her.

"No. Everything is locked."

"Algomagic," Ryuk and FeeTwix say at the same time.

Ink Prior moves on to the dolled up goblin next to Fickolas Cage. She has wavy, platinum blonde hair, ruby red lips, and wears a sparkling silver dress that accents her incredibly large chest.

"Leave some of the staring for me, Marbles," Hiccup says. "That's Dolly Fickton. She's a singer. A fickin' legend."

"Like... Dolly Parton?" Enway asks. "I went to her holoconcert when I was a teenager."

"The fick she just say? Dolly Fickton, Elfie."

Ryuk ignores Hiccup's following rant as he tunes back in to what the female goblin is saying. "...That's right, Ink. We've got several shows lined up next month in Ultima Thule. We're going to keep it real simple," she says in a country twang, "just me, a guitar, and my band, The Travelin' Fickers. We'll be playing all the hits."

"All the hits, huh? Care to give us a sample?"

Dolly Fickton blows a kiss at the crowd. "Later, darlin', you know I've got to save the best for last."

Ink Prior turns to the crowd. "You heard it here, folks, we're going to be getting some singing later."

"This is so awesome," FeeTwix says as his drones buzz about, his eyes big and black. He fires off a message to the squad.

FeeTwix: Eight million people are watching live right now. Eight million. This is a record for me, a fickin' record! The cameras will really help us capture a gameshow feel here. I'm so excited to see how this turns out. Dungeon Goblin Feud. This will be fickin' amazing!

Hiccup: Cultural fickin' appropriation, Twixy!

Sophia: I don't remember agreeing to you livestreaming everything, but now I wish we'd seriously discussed it.

FeeTwix: Sorry, must be algomagic or something. I'm being prevented from shutting it off!

Ryuk glances over to FeeTwix just as the Swede winks at him.

Ink Prior moves on down the line. He stops in front of a goblin wearing a hood, his face partially obscured. "Everyone, since Ficksy doesn't speak, he'll be using scrolls today to display his answers. Now, you might have seen some of his street art in Jatla or in Bluwid. He was trained by Fickson Pollock himself, and his latest work, which was exhibited at a museum that would randomly catch fire, is meant to be a message to people that like to visit Tritania from other worlds."

Hiccup makes a raspberry sound. "Fick off. Ficksy is a fickin' huckster not unlike Twixy over here. Fick, their names even rhyme. The fickin' artistic goblin thinks he can just paint shit and change the fickin' world. If you want to fickin' change the world, rob it of something. That's my motto. Right, Marbles?"

Ryuk shakes his head. Ink Prior moves on to the next goblin, who is lean and fit, his body covered in tattoos. "David Fickham, famous soccer player, loved by millions. Boy is it nice to see the Jatla Jaguars absolutely killing it this year."

David Fickham grins. "Soccer? For fick's sake, you a Yank or something, Ink? It's bloody football. And regarding the Jags, it's fickin' team effort, now, innit? But I like to say I do me fickin' part." Some of the dwarves behind Ryuk clap. Others gasp, all clearly impressed by the handsome sportstar.

"He's so fickin' stacked," Spewy swoons.

"Fick that ficker," Hiccup says. "That dude got famous by kickin' a fickin' ball. You should be glad your world isn't like that, Marbles, worshipping some ficker because they are fast and can kick well. Fick me, what fickery."

"And last, but certainly not least..." Ink Prior stops in front of the black curtain. He pulls it away to reveal a female goblin with thick black hair that frames her face. She wears a pair of glasses and her olive green outfit is clean-cut and form-fitting. "Fickrah, welcome back to Goblin Family Feud!"

The crowd goes wild, especially the female dwarves and Spew Gorge. "Fickin' Fickrah!" the goblin cries. "Fick yeah!"

Fickrah?

"Fick Marbles, you look like you lost your marbles again. Fickrah. She's practically Tritanian royalty. Don't believe me? Fickin' look at Liz over there."

Ryuk glances at Zaena, who seems to be hanging on the edge of every word coming out of Fickrah's mouth as the goblin speaks about social justice projects she's been working on, her new F magazine, the F-Line of skincare products she's launching, and a memoir called *What I Fick For Sure* that is set to release next year.

Fickrah laughs. "I'm writing it as fast as I can, Ink, you know that. I'm busy. I'm a busy woman. How many times do I have to tell you that?"

"I want to read it so bad," Ink Prior says. "Or have someone read it for me. That would be nice, wouldn't it? If someone read something for you. Some kind of book you could listen to."

Fickrah laughs. "Now that is an idea!"

"Pfft!" Hiccup shakes his head. "Fickin' Ink Prior with his crazy adlibs. Imagine someone reading a book for you, Marbles. Fick. Talk about the epitome of laziness." He squints for a moment. "Actually, that's not a bad idea. Fick me, Ink might be on to something! I could read twice as many books if I hired some ficker to read to me while I'm sleeping. And you know I like reading harems, Marbles. Don't fickin' judge me. It is a cultural thing, and I'm not going to sit here and defend my culture to someone who enslaves metal men."

"—Well, it is a pleasure to see you, Fickrah, and a true pleasure to see all of you," Ink Prior tells the celebrities. He turns back to the Mitherfickers, a wicked grin forming on his face. "You know the rules. In case you don't, I'll explain them as we go."

The crowd roars with anticipation as they stomp and chant, *"Dungeon Goblin Feud! Dungeon Goblin Feud!"*

Ink Prior's smile grows even larger. "Give me Ryuk, and give me Fickolas. It's time to play Dungeon Goblin Feud!"

(0)__(0)

Finally allowed to move away from his podium, Ryuk is forced closer to the ink shadow, who now stands between both teams. A floating board materializes into existence behind the ink shadow as the ground shifts, allowing a pair of red buzzers to appear.

"I'll only explain this once, so listen up," Ink Prior says with a big grin on his face. "This is a survey-based game. We survey goblins, and we tally up their answers out of a hundred. Your job is simple. I'll give you a prompt. You give me an answer. The one with the highest score gets to start. The first group to three hundred points wins advantage in the challenge to come. And remember, if you cheat or yell out an answer, your guild will be instantly disqualified. Shall we?"

Six blank slots appear on the board behind Ink Prior.

1 -

2 -

3 -

4 -

5 -

6 -

Ryuk glances back to his guildmates.

"For fick's sake, Marbles, fickin' focus!"

"Buzz in when you know the answer," Ink Prior says as Ryuk's hand moves on its own to hover over the red buzzer.

Ryuk glances over to Fickolas Cage. The goblin actor is entirely in his element.

Shit...

A small card appears in Ink Prior's hand. "We asked one hundred goblins: name the qualities of a bad goblin neighbor."

Ryuk slams his hand down onto the buzzer. "Um..." He draws a blank.

Agh-Ugh!

A buzzer indicates that Ryuk has run out of time. A few people in the crowd sigh. Spew Gorge shouts at the top of his lungs: "Fick you, Marbles, you useless fick!" which elicits a laugh from Hiccup.

"Fickolas?" the ink shadow asks.

"Hmmm. Goblins hate it when a neighbor kills a relative."

Ink Prior laughs long and hard. "You ain't wrong there." He turns to the board behind him. "Show me, *Kills a neighbor!*"

The answer appears in the third slot, and is apparently worth nineteen points.

"Pass or play?" Ink Prior asks Fickolas Cage.

"You know what? Let's give the rookies a chance. We'll pass." Fickolas Cage fires a pair of finger guns at Ryuk. "Good luck, bitch."

Ryuk returns to his side; Hiccup immediately lights into him. "You ficktard! Have I taught you nothing? Don't you get it, Marbles? If we lose, if they get three hundred points before us, we lose advantage."

"What the hell does that even mean?" Ryuk asks.

"Ah, I think I can answer that," FeeTwix explains. "According to my fans, we are going to have to fight them at the end of all this. It will be a turn-based battle. Whoever wins Dungeon Goblin Feud gets to go first in that fight. Okay. Okay, we've got this, team! We've totally got this!"

Ink Prior approaches the Mitherficker's row of podiums. He grins at Ryuk and moves on to Hiccup. "A goblin contestant. This should be easy for you."

"Fick you, squid splooge." Hiccup has since equipped his toe knife and is pointing it at Ink Prior. "Don't fickin' think for a minute you and I are cordial enough for game show banter. Ask the fickin' question, shart-face!"

Ink Prior shrugs off Hiccup's aggression. "We asked one hundred goblins: name the qualities of a bad goblin neighbor."

"Ficks a family member," Hiccup says matter-of-factly.

"Show me, *Ficks a family member!*"

Hiccup's answer appears in the number one slot. "Fick yeah!" His toe knife disappears and he equips a potion. He takes a big pull from it. "Don't say fickall, Marbles. This is a victory sip."

The ink shadow moves on to FeeTwix. "We asked one hundred goblins: name the qualities of a bad goblin neighbor."

"Um, qualities of a bad goblin neigher. Um... steals? A bad goblin neighbor steals!"

"Show me, *Steals!*" The answer appears on the floating board. "Not bad, not bad at all. Three more answers, and the Mitherfickers have the win." Ink Prior stops in front of Zaena. "We asked one hundred goblins: name the qualities of a bad goblin neighbor."

Zaena hesitates and the buzzer sounds.

Agh-Ugh!

"Ooo, it looks like you missed that one," Ink Prior says. "But the Mitherfickers have one more try. Lose this one, and the Celebs can steal."

"Fick, Liz, it's not that hard!"

"Quiet, goblin. They didn't give me enough time to think."

"Moving on..." Ink Prior stops in front of Enway, whose big red eyes are now filled with concern. "We asked one hundred goblins: name the qualities of a bad goblin neighbor."

She grits her teeth. "Borrows? A bad goblin neighbor borrows things? I don't know, borrows money too?"

Ink Prior is quiet for a moment, the crowd joining in his anticipation. Finally, he swivels toward the gameboard. "Show me, *Borrows!*"

"Whew!" FeeTwix says as her answer appears on the board in the final slot, worth just five points.

1 - Ficks a Family Member (28 Points)

2 - Steals from You (23 Points)

3 - Kills a Neighbor (19 Points)

4 -

5 -

6 - Borrows Something/Money (5 Points)

Ryuk stares in horror at the board as the ink shadow returns to him. *Two answers left...*

"The Mitherfickers currently have seventy-five points. If you get this one right, then the actual goblin member of your team should be able take it home. If you get it wrong, the celebrities can steal."

Ryuk gulps.

"Marbles..." Hiccup growls.

"We asked one hundred goblins: name the qualities of a bad goblin neighbor."

"I don't know," Ryuk tells Ink Prior. "Pissing? Pissing in your home?"

"Fick, Marbles! What the fick kind of answer is that—"

Ink Prior laughs. "Show me, *Pissing in your home!*"

Agh-Ugh!

"Ah, fick! Fick!" Hiccup says. He shoves the healing potion in his mouth and guzzles it, his eyes tearing up.

"Fick you, Marbles!" Spew Gorge yells from the crowd.

"Looks like the Celebs have a chance to steal now." Ink Prior shifts over to the goblin celebrities, who have been huddled together coming up with their answer. He stops in front of Fickolas Cage, the leader of the group. "For the steal, name the qualities of a bad goblin neighbor."

"Yes, yes. I believe the answer would be *shitting* in your yard."

Ink Prior laughs. "It very well could be. Show me, *Shitting in your yard!*"

The answer appears in the fourth slot. Trumpets sound off; the Celebs take 91 points and the win.

A scoreboard lights up revealing big fat zero for the Mitherfickers.

The ink shadow takes another look at the board. "Let's see the final answer on the board!"

The answer appears in the fifth slot down:

- *Constantly Giving Fetch Quests*

"Oh, fick that," Hiccup says. "Fick a fickin' fetch quest."

"Okay, okay, okay!" Ink Prior says to quiet down the crowd who have begun clapping and cheering loudly again. "We've got a good game going now. The Celebs have 91 points; the Mitherfickers have zero. It's anyone's game at this point. Give me Hiccup, give me Dolly Fickton!"

(0)__(x)

"Ah, fick, fick!" Hiccup says once he reaches the buzzer. Ryuk can tell by the way his chin sits that he is staring at Dolly Fickton's rack. The female goblin is all smiles as she places one hand behind her back and the other above the buzzer.

She winks at Hiccup. "Fick is right, cutie."

Hiccup gulps, a bead of sweat appearing on the side of his head.

"Fick, Hiccup, don't let her fickin' hypnotize you!" Spew Gorge shouts. "Fick!"

"Alright, everyone, settle down." Ink Prior grins at the two of them as five new slots take shape on the hovering gameboard behind the ink shadow. "Now, before we begin, I want to remind you that this round is worth double the points. Double. First team to three hundred wins! Ready? Let's go. We asked one hundred goblins—"

"Jatla or Bluwid goblins?" asks Hiccup.

"Does it matter?"

"Fick yeah, it matters, you doo-doo-faced kiddie ficker. Bluwidian goblins are hoity-toity mitherfickers living high on the fickin' pony in Polynya; Jatlan goblins are humble, scrappier, and as fickin' broke as a bunch of fickered orphans down there in Hyperborea."

"Jatlan goblins then. Now, may I continue?"

Hiccup huffs. "You're the fickin' boss, ink skeet. Do what you must."

The ink shadow reads from his cue card again "We asked one hundred goblins: name something a Thulean would hate to have happen to them."

Dolly Fickton buzzes in before Hiccup, who is once again distracted by her extremely large mammaries. "Clean up after themselves," she says.

Ink Prior turns to the game board. "Show me, *Clean up after themselves!*"

1 - Clean Up After Themselves (82 Points)

2 -

3 -

4 -

5 -

Dolly Fickton does a little dance, which drives some of the dwarves into a frenzy.

"Goblin Dungeon Feud! Goblin Dungeon Feud!"

"Pass or play?" Ink Prior asks her.

She looks back to her group of celebrities. "I think we're going to play, Mr. Prior," she tells him in her sweet southern patois.

"Sounds good. The Celebs are up!"

"Fick," Hiccup says once he has reached Ryuk. "Dolly fickin' tricked me with her busty gazongas. Not fickin' fair."

"You should have paid better attention, goblin."

"Fick, Liz, I'm only fickin' human over here."

"You're an NPC goblin," Ryuk says.

"N-P-what-the-fick-did-you-just-say?" Hiccup turns to Ryuk and sticks his tongue out.

"Fick you, Hiccup!"

"Oh fick off, Spewy." Hiccup triggers his soundboard gauntlet, playing FeeTwix's voice.

~~*Fick you.*~~

"Just pay attention and be ready for a steal," Zaena says. "I won't even comment on how stupid this game is, especially right now."

"Don't let the Thulean part of the question get to you, babe—"

"I'm not," she snaps at FeeTwix. "We just need to win and be done with this... this..."

"Assfickery, Liz. That's exactly what this is."

"Yes, goblin, you are right."

Ink Prior approaches Ficksy. The artist goblin now has a paintbrush and a scroll, his face partially hidden by his hood as he looks up at the ink shadow. "We asked one hundred goblins: name something a Thulean would hate to have happen to them."

Ficksy nods and quickly scribbles down an answer: *Become a work of art.*

"Pfft!" Hiccup laughs. "That's definitely not up there, that fickered ficknut. Yet again proof that artists are out of touch."

Hiccup's prediction is quickly confirmed as the wrong answer tone sounds.

Agh-Ugh!

"Fick yeah, let's huddle up," Hiccup says after relieving himself of a bit of pent-up gas. The Mitherfickers are able to move a bit closer to Hiccup so they can start discussing answers, which they do in whispers as Ink Prior moves on to the tatted goblin athlete named David Fickham.

"We asked one hundred goblins: name something a Thulean would hate to have happen to them."

"Oi!" David says, his voice almost obnoxiously British. "That's a fickin' hard one, innit? Nah, just fickin' playing with ya, mate. A Thulean would fickin' hate to lose their bloody ghost limbs." He nods at Zaena. "Just ask the fickin' lizard lady yourself. The answer is up there, Ink."

"Hey! Fick off!" Hiccup tries to go over the podium to attack David Fickham, but is prevented by an invisible barrier. "Don't you fickin' talk to Liz that way! She's a fick-forsaken princess—"

"Quiet, Hiccup," Ryuk says just as the ink shadow turns to the game board.

"Show me, *Lose their ghost limbs!*"

This appears on the board directly beneath Dolly Fickton's answer, worth 46 points. The Celebs now have 128 points total. Since they already had 91 points from the last round, they could win the entire thing if they can get the three remaining answers.

Ink Prior stops in front of Fickrah. "We asked one hundred goblins: name something a Thulean would hate to have happen to them."

Fickrah purses her lips. "Something a Thulean would hate. You know, I recently published a recipe book called *Fick, Health, and Happiness,* and I tried to get some Thulean recipes for it. They didn't have any they wanted to share, mostly because other races cook their food. So I'll go with that, Thuleans would hate to make their own food."

"That's not true. I can cook."

Hiccup snorts at Zaena's statement. "Fick, Liz, when's the last time you actually cooked for yourself?"

"I can make a variety of things—"

Ink Prior points at the board. "Show me, *Make their own food!*"

This answer appears in the last slot, worth sixteen points.

The Celebs need to get two more answers on the board to win it all. Ink Prior circles back around to the front, where he finds Fickolas Cage combing his black hair. "Now, you need to be careful. Miss this answer, and the other team can steal."

"Got it, Ink." Fickolas shakes his arms out and grins at the game show host.

"We asked one hundred goblins: name something a Thulean would hate to have happen to them."

"A Thulean, huh? Not too different from a thespian like me. In that case, I would say a Thulean would hate to be typecast."

Ink Prior looks at him incredulously as some of the dwarves in the crowd start to laugh. "Typecast?"

Fickolas Cage seems confident in his answer. "Typecast. It's up there, Ink."

"We'll see. Show me, *Typecast!*" He points at the gameboard.

Agh-Ugh!

"Fick, Marbles, you're up! Fick, what answer did we agree upon?"

"We were still discussing it," Ryuk tells the goblin.

"Fick, fick, he's coming right over here. It's on you, kid, make Uncle Goblin proud!"

The ink shadow approaches Ryuk before he can consult the rest of his group. "For the steal, we asked one hundred goblins: name something a Thulean would hate to have happen to them."

Ryuk looks up at the board one last time.

1 - Clean Up After Themselves (82 Points)
2 - Lose a Ghost Limb (46 Points)
3 -
4 -
5 - Make Their Own Food (16 Points)

Ryuk's mind races as he tries to think of all the things that he has learned about Thuleans, mostly through his relationship with Zaena and her interactions with Hiccup. "They would hate..." He swallows. "They would hate to be near a goblin when he farts."

"Ah, for fick's sake," Spew Gorge shouts from the crowd.

"Marbles, you fickered—"

"Show me, *Hate to be near a goblin when he farts!*"

Agh-Ugh!

"The Celebs win!"

Ryuk sighs miserably as the scoreboard for the Celebs ticks up, now at 235 points versus the same big fat zero they started with.

"Now, let's see the other two answers." Ink Prior motions to the board and the answers appear.

- *Stay in Jatla/Bluwid*

- *Relative Marries a Goblin*

"Okay, okay, okay, we have a real good game going now," Ink Prior says as he claps his hands. "Just remember, it could still be anyone's game now. This next round will decide who gets advantage. Points are now worth triple. Give me FeeTwix, and give me Ficksy!"

(x)__(x)

FeeTwix approaches the buzzer. His eyes are black as ever as he grins at Ink Prior and at his artist opponent, who has a fresh scroll with him and a paintbrush.

"Fick, Twixy, don't fick this up." Hiccup is sweating now, the goblin nursing a new healing potion. "Please, Twixy. Just think of how happy Liz will be if you win this. She'll probably give you like a million blowit—"

"Shut your mouth, goblin."

"Fick, Liz, I was just talking to myself." Hiccup drinks more of the potion and burps. "Fickin' thought police. Fick the police. *Straight out of Fickton*. Heard that album, Marbles? That one isn't by Dolly Fickton, fick no. That one is by the GWA." He finishes his healing potion and summons another.

"Hiccup, you're supposed to save those."

"Marbles, fick my dude, I'm stressed as fick over here! I drink when I'm stressed. A lot of people drink when they're stressed, you insensitive fickbag."

"We will survive this," Enway says, which elicits a bark from Wolf. While not able to participate, the Tagvornian canine is clearly engaged in what is happening, his eyes going wide and ears flitting back every time the tension increases.

"Says the fickin' unvetted elf with pointy-ass ears. Fick, I hate pointed ears."

Even though he wants to punch Hiccup, Ryuk tunes back in to what is happening centerstage. The gameboard behind Ink Prior has just four blank slots, which means this round will be even more challenging.

"We asked one hundred goblins: name something you do not learn in goblin public school—"

FeeTwix buzzes in before Ink Prior can finish the last word. "How to fick. Goblins don't learn how to fick."

"What? No. Twixy! Fick!" Hiccup all but sobs at this answer.

"Booooo! Booooo! You're a fickin' idiot," Spew Gorge shouts from behind Ryuk.

Along with Ink Prior, and the crowd of dwarves, the Celebs all laugh at FeeTwix's answer.

"Show me, *how to fick!*"

Agh-Ugh!

"Ficksy?" the ink shadow asks the goblin.

The artist quickly paints a word onto the scroll.

- *Investing*

"Show me, *Investing!*"

1 - Investing (116 points)

2 -

3 -

4 -

"Looks like the Celebs got it. Pass or play?"

Ficksy motions the ink shadow over to the Celebs' podiums.

Ryuk's next breath isn't quite a sigh of relief, but it's not far off. For the Celebs to get all the points, to win, they will have to answer the final three questions correctly. This is what Ink Prior meant when he said that it was anyone's game. The Mitherfickers still have a chance. Not a good one, but they may be able to pull this off.

"You tried," Ryuk says as FeeTwix approaches, the Swede clearly defeated.

"Shit, I should have listened to my fans. They were saying *Investing* too. Apparently this is something both our worlds share, lack of education in public schools on investing and money management."

"Cry me a fickin' river, Twixy, you just lost the game for us. Of course goblins learn how to fickin' fick in school. What the fick else are we supposed to learn? Investing? What kind of government would want to teach their citizens how to invest when they could teach them useless math and other fickin' things they'll likely never use in their adult life? Fick! We're so ficked." Hiccup chugs more of his healing potion. "This is all so ficked."

FeeTwix shrugs off Hiccup's strange mixture of sadness and anger. "If we lose, we'll kick their ass in the fight that is to come. Don't lose hope there, Hiccup."

"Famous last fickin' words, Twixster."

Ink Prior approaches David Fickham. "We asked one hundred goblins: name something you do not learn in goblin public school."

David Fickham squints at the ink shadow. "Public school, eh? I'll tell you something they don't fickin' learn. The soddin' little anklefickers don't know fickall about bloody manners."

"Show me, *Manners!*"

Manners appears after Investing, leaving just two more blank slots.

As the crowd claps, Ink Prior moves on to Fickrah. "We asked one hundred goblins: name something you do not learn in goblin public school."

Fickrah furrows her brow. "Public schools could do better to teach goblins proper etiquette, which is to say they basically don't know how to behave. Slightly different from manners, I believe. Young goblins need to learn how to behave better, in a general sense. Behave."

"Fick off, Fickrah!" Hiccup throws his hands in the air.

Ink Prior gestures to the gameboard. "Show me, *How to behave!*"

The answer appears in the fourth slot. There's just one slot left now, and two chances for the Celebs to be wrong.

1 - Investing (115 Points)

2 - Manners (96 Points)

3 -

4 - How to Behave (19 Points)

A message from Doc the war faun flashes across Ryuk's eyes.

Doc: Smoke 'em if you got 'em. If I was a betting man, and I am a betting man, I'd say that the Celebs are going to win this one.

"We don't know that yet," FeeTwix says as Ink Prior approaches Fickolas Cage.

Hiccup scoffs at Doc's message. "Someone tell the goat man to fick off and keep our fickin' names out of his mouth. Fickolas Cage is a fickin' idiot. He'll fick this up."

Ink Prior pauses in front of Fickolas Cage. "We asked one hundred goblins: name something you do not learn in goblin public school."

The Jatlawood actor shrugs. "Easy. They don't learn how to cook. Actually, I never went to public school. I wouldn't know. I went to the finest acting school in—"

"Show me, *Cooking!*"

Agh-Ugh!

"Fick yeah!" Hiccup throws his hands into the air as the crowd behind them gasps. "Fickin' Jatlawood elitests! Fick you!"

"Yeah! Fick you, Fickolas Cage, you fickety piece of thespian dungeon jizz!" Spew shouts.

Ink Prior stops in front of Dolly Fickton. "You got an answer in mind?"

"I do, Mr. Prior," the famous singer says in a cute way.

"Because if you don't get this one right, the Mitherfickers have a chance to steal and win the game." The ink shadow clears his throat. "We asked one hundred goblins: name something you do not learn in goblin public school."

"They don't learn how to do chores, Mr. Prior." She winks. "It's up there, I just know it."

"You sure?"

Dolly Fickton giggles. "I just know it."

The ink shadow turns to the gameboard. "Show me, *Chores!*"

The answer appears in the third slot. The crowd starts to cheer and stomp their feet as they chant in unison. *"Dungeon Goblin Feud! Dungeon Goblin Feud!"*

The Mitherfickers have officially lost.

TOKYO

CHAPTER 10: CELEBRITY DEATHMATCH

THE PODIUMS FIZZLE AWAY and the lights shining on the crowd dim.

Ryuk and his guildmates are forced forward, where they will take part in a classic JRPG turn-based battle. The five are now staggered in somewhat of a zigzag position, Ryuk and Enway behind FeeTwix, Zaena, and Hiccup. The Celebs are in a similar pattern across from them, their stats instantly causing Ryuk to worry.

Fickolas Cage Level 39
HP: 650/650
ATK: 210
MATK: 10
DEF: 120
MDF: 97
Luck: 38

Dolly Fickton Level 40
HP: 540/540
ATK: 120
MATK: 324

DEF: 100
MDF: 196
Luck: 68

Ficksy Level 35
HP: 512/512
ATK: 104
MATK: 50
DEF: 77
MDF: 98
Luck: 41

David Fickham Level 40
HP: 808/808
ATK: 215
MATK: 13
DEF: 134
MDF: 126
Luck: 41

Fickrah Level 38
HP: 455/455
ATK: 35
MATK: 318
DEF: 89
MDF: 152
Luck: 33

Aside from Wolf, who isn't allowed in the fight, the Celebs are all at a higher level than any of the Mitherfickers. As he continues going over their stats, Ryuk tries to find weaknesses. There aren't many. Fickrah has a weak attack and defense, as does Ficksy. The others are pretty stacked.

"Fick, we're going to have to literally fight Tritanian royalty." Hiccup throws his hands in the air. "We might as well die."

Zaena scoffs at this remark. "What? No. No, goblin, we will not lose. We will not die. There's no royalty over there. Just goblins and Fickrah."

"Fick off with your lowkey racism, Liz. Now, where was I? A wise orc chippie once said, *You can't unfick what has already been ficked,* and we truly ficked up, no thanks to you, Marbles."

"Me? You're the one that lost your match-up against Dolly Fickton."

"That doesn't seem like me."

~FICK~

Dammit, Ryuk thinks as Hiccup triggers another voice on his soundboard gauntlet.

~Fick you, Marbles!~

"Now, as you all know, the winner of Dungeon Goblin Feud gets advantage." Ink Prior floats between the two parties. "In case you need me to say this another way, this means that the Celebs have advantage. Good luck to both teams." The ink shadow swivels to the crowd. "And don't forget to join us next time for another epic Dungeon Goblin Feud!"

"Dungeon Goblin Feud! Dungeon Goblin Feud!"

Exit music plays as the crowd cheers.

"Fick them the fick up!" Spew Gorge shouts from the stands that surround them. It isn't clear whose side he is shouting for.

Hiccup puffs his cheeks out. "Fick, okay, we've got this. They're going to give us a fickin' walloping. Brace yourselves, fickers. Marbles—as soon as it's our turn, heal our fickered asses up."

"Will do," Ryuk says.

Hiccup places a finger over one of his nostrils and snorts something out onto the ground. "Target Fickrah and Ficksy. They're the weakest."

"I suppose there is no better time than now for a classic FeeTwix poll," the Swede announces to his viewers. "You know what to do. I've got three items I can use once it is our turn. You choose which one!"

"For fick's sake, Twixy—fick! Here they come!"

Fickolas Cage is up first. The goblin actor flies forward and delivers an epic karate kick to Zaena.

-215 HP! Critical Hit!

"Dang, Liz-Liz, he kicked the livin' fick out of you!"

"Quiet, goblin!"

"Fick Thuleans!" Spew Gorge shouts from the crowd.

Dolly Fickton is up next. She steps forward in her glittery dress, a guitar appearing in her hands. The singer starts up a tune that sounds to Ryuk like American country music.

~Time to give yourself a little slap

Before you give yourself a big ol' clap

I want you to hit yourself it's not as hard as it sounds

Hit yourselves and strike each other down~

Hiccup punches himself in the face. "Yoy!" The goblin slugs Zaena with his mechanical arm, while she slaps Ryuk and Enway with her ghost limbs. FeeTwix tries to fight it, but the Swede is unable to stop himself from turning around and roundhouse kicking Ryuk and following this up with a gut punch that leaves Hiccup doubled over.

-56 HP! -91 HP!

The red numbers flash before Ryuk and disappear.

"Yoooooy. Fick," Hiccup gasps, "Twixy...you really got me good."

"Sorry, Hiccup!"

Ficksy is up next. The goblin artist goes for his paintbrush, the tip of which is dripping with black ink. He walks over to Hiccup and paints a big black X across the front of his body.

[You have been doomed. You will die after three turns.]

"Doomed? What the fick? Fick! I'm too fickin' young to be doomed. I can't die on my birthday!" Hiccup tries to wipe the paint away but it is already dried. "Ah, fick. Fick!"

"What the fick!?"

"Fick off, Spewy, this is fickin' serious," Hiccup shouts at the smaller goblin. He glances back at Ryuk. "Kid, I know we never talked about a 401k, an SEP IRA, backdoor Roth—heh, backdoor—or any retirement options, but I want my 15% cut of whatever treasure we get in the future to go to Spew Gorge, plus all of my money from whatever licensing deals Twixster has conjured up. Yes, Spewy is a fickin' disappointment. But he deserves better than a life of crime and turning tricks in Jatla."

Ryuk shakes his head. "We never agreed to 15%. You're not going to die. We'll win this."

"In three fickin' rounds? Pfft! Don't get your hopes up, Marbelito. I'm doomed. Leave that hope shit to the fickin' weirdos and people that use Discord, whatever the fick that is. Fick. Fick! Where's Wolfie?"

The wolf barks.

"I just wish I could say goodbye to my favorite pooch!"

"Don't worry, Hiccup. I can remove the curse," Enway says. "If..."

"If? What the fick, Elfie!?"

"If you make me part of the Mitherfickers. That's right. I will remove the curse, but only if you officially make me part of the Mitherfickers. No more vetting nonsense. That ends now."

"Fick. Fick!"

~F-F-Fick!~

"Yes or no, Hiccup?"

"Fine, yes. Yes! Yes, for fick's sake, but when..." He slurps up some snot. "When she does something terrorist adjacent, don't come lookin' at me. Fick!"

David Fickham summons three horned skulls. He places each on the ground and proceeds to kick them at the Mitherfickers. They hit FeeTwix, Zaena, and Enway.

-296 HP! -113 HP! -314 HP!

Critical hit!

Fickrah steps forward with a devious look in her eyes. She rolls her head back and laughs maniacally. "You get a boulder! You get a boulder! You get a boulder! You get a boulder! And you get a boulder!"

Five clouds appear above the Mitherfickers. The clouds morph into large rocks that drop onto each of their heads.

-225 HP! -211 HP! -232 HP! -200 HP! -196 HP!

Critical-Critical hit!

"It's our turn," FeeTwix says once he has recovered. "Finally." A poll appears showing the picture of a giant cactus in a pot, a pair of truck nuts, and a samurai sword with a blackened blade. Luckily for FeeTwix, his fans have chosen the blade.

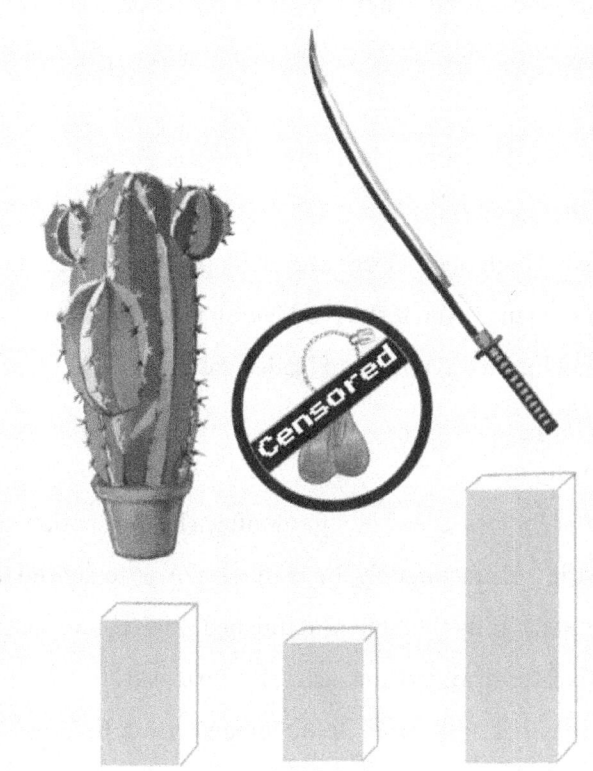

"What the fick were you going to do with the nuts?" Hiccup asks as the sword appears in FeeTwix's grip. "Did you call them truck nuts? Why are they censored?"

"That's for me to know, and for you to fickin' find out!" A small blue vial takes shape in FeeTwix's other hand. It appears that he has summoned the sword and the vial together, which doesn't seem to count against his turn.

"Where the fick did you get that? Is that some Four Loko or some fickin' shit?"

"Let's just say Dirty Dave gave me a little attack booster the last time we hung out and shot guns." FeeTwix chugs the concoction and tosses it to the side. He roars with delight, draws his weapon back, and takes off toward Ficksy.

Schwiiing!

FeeTwix cuts the goblin down with a horizontal cross slash.

Instakill!

"Fick yeah!" both Spew Gorge and Hiccup shout at the same time.

Next up is Zaena. Even if she is a Fickrah fangirl, the Thulean attacks the famous goblin with a barrage of blades, taking nearly 300 points from the Celeb's HP.

Hiccup is up next.

He follows FeeTwix's lead by summoning a healing potion and his axe at the same time. Unfortunately, he is much slower to get the top off the potion and guzzle it. By the time he's finished, the goblin is prevented by an invisible barrier from moving again, his turn over.

"What the fuck, Hiccup?" Ryuk moans as it becomes his turn, indicated by the fact he can suddenly move freely.

"Ugh. Goblin! You stupid—"

"Hey, fick off, Liz, I took some damage last round!"

"We all took damage!"

Ryuk is now presented with a dilemma. Attack Fickrah and finish her off for good, thus cutting their opponents down by another NPC; or heal his group.

Enway clears this up for him. "I'll be able to take her. You heal."

"What about me?" Hiccup cries. "You're supposed to take care of me this turn, Elfie."

"We still have time," she tells the goblin. "Go for it, Ryuk."

"Yoooooy, fick!"

It's a risk, but it's important they stay topped up. Ryuk transforms himself into a White Mage and group heals, which gives 250 HP to each of the Mitherfickers. Once his turn has ended, he's back to his original form.

Enway floats into the air as algomagic boils all around her. She concentrates her Mana into a fireball made of pink and purple magic, which strikes Fickrah hard enough to toss the celebrity goblin onto her back.

Instakill!

"Fick yeah!" Hiccup flips the Celebs off with both hands. He instantly regrets this as Grifty takes shape alongside the Celebs, the orange haired demon with a wild look in his googly eyes.

Not only that, Grifty is carrying a bag of white powder. The eldritch horror laughs. *"Now, who wants to fickin' party?"*

(0)__(0)

One of the things that worries Ryuk about Grifty is that Grifty's stats never appear. He doesn't appear to have a handle. There is no way to know how powerful he is, but there is one thing Ryuk is certain of—the Mitherfickers are in for a tough fight.

Grifty crouches in front of Ficksy's dead body, grabs some drugs from his bag, and shoves a powdery orange fist up the goblin's ass to revive the artist.

An idea comes to Ryuk. He instantly switches to their chat.

Ryuk: Do you have any more of that attack buff?

FeeTwix: You're fickin' right I do. But just one vial. The effect should last a little while, thankfully. But just one. You got an idea?

Ryuk: I do. Toss it to me on your next move.

"For the love of everything fick, Marbles, focus on the fickin' fight!"

Fickolas Cage whistles at Grifty. "Hey, pal. Give me some of the good stuff."

"My fickin' pleasure!" Wild-eyed and crazed as ever, Grifty sashays over to Fickolas just as the goblin celebrity is pulling his pants down. Grifty takes another handful of the white powder and shoves it straight into Fickolas' starfish.

"Whooo!" Fickolas shouts. "Whoo-hooo!"

Hiccup grits his teeth. "Fick me, we need to get some drugs. Fick. Wizardous. Spewy! Do you have some wiz?"

"What the fick, Hiccup? I'm not a fuckin' addict!"

"I didn't ask if you were an addict. I asked if you have some fickin' wiz!"

"Fick yeah, I have a little, I think." As Fickolas Cage turns to Zaena, Spew Gorge rummages around in his tunic. The smaller goblin produces a tiny bag. "Fick, here it is!"

Hiccup reaches his hand behind his back. "That's the fickin' stuff. Gimme, gimme, gimme!"

"Goblin! Are you out of your mind!?"

"Fick no, Liz, I'm merely trying to level the playing field. *They go low, we go low. They get high, we get high.* Fick, that's like one of the most popular goblin sayings. Now, be helpful and use your ghost limb to get the bag on your next turn. Can you use it now?"

"No!"

"Next turn. Liz. Don't fick this up!"

"My fans are saying that wizardous can increase a person's attack power. It can also make them go cray-cray," FeeTwix says, his eyes twitching as he reads through messages. "Is this really a good idea?"

"Not up for fickin' discussion with your woke-ass fans, Twixy!"

A bit jittery now, Fickolas Cage approaches Zaena, his fists up like a boxer. His eyes are bloodshot, and a little saliva hangs from his lip as he sizes the Thulean up. He whooshes forward and hits Zaena with a few jabs and finishes with an uppercut.

-62 HP! -59 HP! -31 HP! -347 HP!

Critical hit!

"Liz, you alright, boo? Fick you, Fickolas Cage! I'll never…" Hiccup glares at the actor as he shuffles back to the side of the Celebs. "I'll never fickin' watch one of your plays again. Not even the new Fickvengers!"

Grifty appears next to Dolly Fickton. *"You ready to get fickin' wasted? Fick yeah!"*

"Nah, I'm fickin' good, darlin,' but I think Mr. Fickham wants some," she says as a different guitar appears in her hands. "Now, let me see here. What's a song y'all haven't heard in a while?" She starts strumming and immediately drops into a ballad. "That's the one."

~All you have to do to make things right, is just

Punch your neighbor, bite your partner, everything's gonna be alright

Kick your partner, and stab your neighbor, everything's gonna be alright~

The Mitherfickers immediately turn on each other. Hiccup summons his toe knife and stabs FeeTwix in the leg. Zaena blenders her short swords in an attack that hits both Ryuk and Enway. His hands trembling, Ryuk equips a sword marble and fires it into Hiccup's back.

-360 HP!

Critical hit!

"Yoooooooooooooooy! Fick you, Marbles, that was almost a backdoor stabbing!"

"Yeah, fick you, Marbles, you fickered emo ficklump!" Spewy cries from the audience. "Leave his fat ass alone."

"Hey! Fick you, Spewy, I'm not fat. I'm fickin' big-boned!"

The fight not yet over, Enway launches a small fireball at Hiccup. It lands, her fireball amplified by a burst of gas from the goblin's netherregions, which in turn backfires in Ryuk's face.

-119 HP! -126 HP!

"Dammit, Hiccup!" Ryuk beats at the fire on his arms. "You stinky... stinky—"

"Yoyyyy.... Yoyyyy... Fickin' kiss my chup... Marble... I'm... not stinky..." He sucks in a deep, troubled breath. "If you want to know what the fick I am, I'm fickin' two shades away from the burnt ends at DD's Barbeque over here and you're over here lodging olfactory insults and worried about a little ass fire? Pfft! Fick off."

The mayhem isn't over yet.

A pained expression on his face, FeeTwix turns his sword on Zaena. He fights every urge he has to attack her, but he is under the influence of Dolly Fickton's song, and there's not a lot he can do.

FeeTwix swings the blade with both hands directly at Zaena's neck.

Instakill!

"Fuck!" FeeTwix shouts, his voice full of emotion. "Fuck, Zaena, I'm so sorry!" He watches in horror as her head hits the ground and her body falls, blood spritzing from her neck hole. FeeTwix suddenly amps up, anger spilling from his eyes. "I'm going to kill you!" he shouts to Dolly Fickton as she puts her guitar away.

She winks at him. "Go ahead and try, sugar."

"Fick, Twix, you fickin' killed your bae. This is like *Fickreo and Juliet* only you didn't take the poison. Fick!"

"Just stick to the plan," Ryuk tells the group as a drugged out Ficksy equips a can of spray paint and a few stencils. He begins stenciling something up, a weapon of sorts.

"There's a plan? Why the fick—" Hiccup burps. "Fick! Why the fick am I just learning about this now?"

FeeTwix takes over. "Hiccup, you're our shield. Don't be a jackass the next round. Do what tanks do. Equip one of your biggest shields and make them attack you in the following round."

"Am I a tank or a shield? Fick," Hiccup says after he registers the rage in FeeTwix's eyes. "I'll be a tank. Sure, Twix. But never look at me like that again lest you and I have words, and by words I mean a fickin' knife fight."

"Fair."

Ryuk continues: "Hiccup—you're the tank. Try to get an attack in. FeeTwix—I need the buff from you before you do what it is you're going to do."

"I'm going to kill Dolly Fickton," FeeTwix says with all certainty. "You'll get your buff."

"Right. Enway—fix Hiccup's curse."

"What about healing up?" she asks Ryuk.

"We're going to have to risk it. We take out most of the Celebs this next round. After—"

"Healing? What about fickin' Grifty?" Hiccup asks. "Fick, look at those creepy googly eyes. Fickin' fluffer, fickin' hamster ficker."

"He's our wild card. We can't kill him, but we can—" Ryuk watches as Ficksy finishes his spray painting. The artist now has a bazooka, which he turns to the space above the Mitherfickers.

He fires a shell over their heads, which explodes into bits of sticky black ink that instantly coat them. Text appears in front of Ryuk.

[Your movements are slowed.]

"Don't worry about it," FeeTwix says. "We won't be doing as much moving this next round." He eyes Dolly Fickton again. "Payback is going to be a bitch."

"Fick yeah, Twixy, that's the fickin' spirit! She's a national fickin' treasure, but someone has to do it!"

Grifty appears next to David Fickham. *"You ready to party, soccer boy?"* After a quick discussion, the famous sportstar agrees to dose up. The athlete yanks his athletic shorts down and bends over, grinning at the Mitherfickers as Grifty shoves a fistfull of drugs straight up his ass.

Terror appears in David Fickham's eyes as his face goes pale. "Oi... oi! Me arse!"

David Fickham stumbles forward, his neck a clump of veins, his eyes bulging, his forehead beet red. He begins foaming at the mouth and falls over.

Instakill!

"Oops!" Grifty laughs. *"Looks like he took too much!"*

"What the fick?" Hiccup shakes his head in disgust. "Okay, Mitherfickers, it's about to be our turn. Do not, I repeat, do not fick this up. Stick to the fickin' plan, whatever that plan may be, and Spewy, toss me my drugs when the time fickin' comes!"

"You've got it, Hiccup!"

(0)__(x)

Enway is the first into action as she turns to Hiccup and removes his doom enchantment. The black mark painted across his body fades away. "Fick yeah!" Hiccup equips his scutum and gets behind it. "Hit me, Spewy!"

Spew Gorge tosses the bag of wizardous at the goblin. Because of the buff, Hiccup can't exactly scurry over to retrieve the drugs, but he does make record time as he grabs the bag, empties all of the white powder into his mouth, and is able to get behind his big shield.

"What about your turn, Hiccup?" Ryuk hisses.

"This *is* my turn. Trust me, Marbles, I've got this!" Hiccup's eyes are as wild as Grifty's now, the goblin twitching, winking randomly. "We'll get them this round or next or my name isn't—"

FeeTwix tosses the blue vial to Ryuk. As Ryuk chugs it, FeeTwix turns the barrels of both of his mutant hacks on Dolly Fickton. Their movements are slowed because of Ficksy's enchantment, but that doesn't have any effect on the weapons as they sizzle with energy, unleashing two enormous blasts at the famous goblin singer.

-150 HP! -200 HP!

Critical hit!

When the smoke clears, Dolly is still standing, but her health is below the halfway point now. If they're lucky, Ryuk's next move will take them out entirely.

Ryuk raises his finger in the air and prepares the two words that summon his once-a-day Knights in White Satin power. "Knights attack!"

A squad of the Empress' finest materialize into existence. Their white satin capes settle and the group of knighted warriors turn their pikes on the Celebs. They move in rapidly, skewering Ficksy and Fickolas Cage to death.

Insta-Instakill!

Dolly somehow manages to avoid their attack; it seems to have no effect on Grifty, who stands by giggling to himself.

"We'll get her next round," FeeTwix says. "I promise, babe!"

Dolly summons another guitar, this one glittery like her outfit. "Y'all really wanted to push things to the extreme, didn't you?" she asks. "Couldn't just have ourselves a good fickin' time, now could we?"

She starts strumming a quick riff, and yodels for a spell. Eventually, she begins singing:

~New Gotha ain't no kind of place—

She fires a shot of boiling green algomagic at Enway from the end of her guitar.

Instakill!

~If you rob someone, they take it wrong—

She fires a shot that kills Ryuk.

Instakill!

~The nicest city and the home of the ol Fickery is Bluwid—

She fires a shot at FeeTwix.

Instakill!

Dolly finishes a verse praising Bluwid, one that Ryuk doesn't fully hear as his ghost respawns outside of the battle alongside Zaena, Enway, and FeeTwix. Wolf is nearby as well, barking wildly as Dolly fires a final shot at Hiccup's scutum.

Plink!

She stops playing for a spell, looks at her guitar with confusion, and starts up again. She tries two more times and fails.

Plink! Plink!

"Fick yeah," Hiccup says as it becomes his turn, the goblin clearly intoxicated. "Fick, Dolly, I always liked your songs about Bluwid," he says, "but this fickin' shit has gone on long enough." Hiccup equips a pair of axes. He bolts over to Dolly and hits her rapid-fire, the goblin fueled by wizardous.

-122 HP! -136 HP! -139 HP!

Instakill!

~FICK~

Grifty, who has been standing next to Dolly egging her on, looks to the forefront of the battle where he sees Ink Prior's form take shape.

The furry orange demon shrieks and quickly disappears.

"I can't believe we won…" Ryuk looks down at his hands as they stitch together, the Japanese gamer back in his avatar.

Level up!

A feeling of elation comes over Ryuk as he reaches the coveted Level 35. "We did it," he says, glancing back at the others. He sees their stats as well. Everyone has reached the landmark level. "I can't believe we did it!"

"Believe it, Marbles." Hiccup drinks half a healing potion and tosses it to Twixy.

"Thanks, Hiccup!" The Swede sips from the potion as he turns to Zaena. "Sorry about cutting you in half."

She smirks. "You're lucky I am a forgiving Thulean."

"Since fickin' when, Liz?" Hiccup burps. "Fick, that wiz got me feeling higher than a giraffe's ladychup."

Ryuk turns to the goblin. "Why the drugs? Why did you need the drugs?"

"Why not the drugs, Marbles? Fick, that's what you *should* be asking."

"What did they do? Did they make you faster?"

Hiccup licks his lips. "Fick yeah, that and they made me wild. Furtherfick, I just wanted to do the drugs. It's been a while since I partook—look that word up, fickface—in some of Dirty Dave's finest. Good stuff. Spewy, get your ass down here!"

As the dwarves file out, Spew Gorge joins the Mitherfickers. FeeTwix and Zaena are practically necking at this point, and Ryuk stands next to Enway, awkward as ever. Still a bit tweaked out, Hiccup turns his focus back to Ink Prior. "Alright, peckersnot, time to pony the fick up."

"Excuse me?" the ink shadow asks.

"We're here to seal the fickin' portal, duh. Where the fick is it?"

The ink shadow laughs. "Why, you are *in* the portal."

Hiccup nearly jumps out of his britches. "The fick you just say?"

"This is the portal. You're inside it."

"Fick!"

"Fick!" Spew Gorge, who has just joined them, hops behind Hiccup. "We're in a fickin' portal!?"

FeeTwix looks from Ryuk to Zaena. "Um...?"

Ink Prior nearly falls over laughing. "You should have seen your faces. No, this isn't the inside of the portal. That would be right over there." He gestures an inky arm to a doorway. Beyond, Ryuk sees a couple of dead demons. "I've been killing them as they come. You are here to seal it, right?"

"We sure are." FeeTwix summons the metal box Doc gave him. He triggers it and tosses the box to the ground. Rather than taking the form of a blue Hindu deity, Rocket is now wearing full ninja garb, not unlike Aiden of the Knights of Non Compos Mentis.

"We meet again, Mitherfickers." Rocket slams his left fist into an open palm, bows to the group, and then moves into a series of kicks and punches that send shockwaves of algomagic toward the portal in the other room. This comes complete with a variety of martial arts sounds straight out of the movies.

The portal seals, and Rocket turns to them. He's just bowing when his eyes widen. "Sophia?" he whispers.

"What about that bossy ficker?" Hiccup asks as he summons another healing potion.

"Sophia. Something is happening in Tokyo." Rocket turns to Ryuk and FeeTwix. "I don't know what's going on. Doc is trying to tap the feed now. You are in Tokyo, right? You may not be safe. Do you have RPCs set to respawn?"

RPCs? Ryuk tries to message her and doesn't get a response. *What the fuck?*

"Let's log out," FeeTwix tells Ryuk as he lifts his finger into the air.

"Be careful," Zaena tells FeeTwix.

"We will. And—"

"We will meet you all in Kayi." Ryuk presses the logout button.

TOKYO

CHAPTER 11: MESSY IN THE MIDDLE

KODAI SITS IN THE COMFORT of his swanky hotel in Shinjuku. He has several guards outside, and a bottle of champagne on the table in front of him, one being kept in a bucket of ice. The Tokyo cityscape is visible through the floor-to-ceiling windows, a blazing urban jungle of lights and sounds that seems to stretch all the way to Mount Fuji, which he can also see in the distance, the snowy peak reflecting what is left of the setting sun.

It is a view that people come from all over the world to see, a view worth its weight in gold. Yet Kodai barely pays attention to it. Instead, he watches Tesla's perspective through his iNet feed.

Tesla has arrived at Ueno University alongside Walt and a trio of Kodai's muscled goons. It will be a quick in and out mission. He doesn't want anyone on his team getting hurt, even if Tesla has been instructed to use his men as fodder if necessary.

The only thing that matters is getting Sophia and making sure Hajime doesn't kill Tesla.

With his eyes closed, Kodai almost feels like he's there, watching as she rushes down the hall, Walt on her right. There are other things visible on her feed, from a three-dimensional map of Ueno University to her vital monitoring system. Everything looks good. They are close.

Kodai hears a knock at the door. "This better be good," he says aloud.

He hears the door open and shut as someone steps into the room.

A man clears his throat, Kodai instantly recognizing him as a man named Saitama. "I'm sorry to bother you. Again, my apologies. Some of your mother's men have arrived."

Kodai tenses up. "Mother's men? Why?"

"We were not given a reason."

Kodai slowly shakes his head. His mother is known to do this from time to time, an act of intimidation. Show up, remind her son that she is the one who is actually in charge, maybe even give him a task to accomplish, and leave. And she never comes to greet him herself. It is always her men that come instead, ones that have the balls to give Kodai orders.

Kodai knows instantly who is outside the doors of his suite. He has grown up with the two men, Genos and Fubaki. That's why they hold power over him. He has always seen them as authority figures.

"Tell Genos and Fubaki that I'm busy. They can wait."

"Do you know how long?"

Kodai finally opens his eyes. He turns to stare at Saitama and his stupid bald head.

The younger gangster looks away. He crosses his hands beneath his waist and bows his head respectfully.

"They will know when I'm ready. And don't disturb me again. Order them some food if they're hungry. If they want something else, call up some girls. Now, no more disturbances."

Saitama leaves without another word. Kodai relaxes again on the sofa, his legs stretched out on an ottoman. With his eyes shut he jumps back into Tesla's feed, just as his group is breaching the main door to Sophia's laboratory. Hajime is there to address Kodai's three men, Haruki, Soto, and Yugio, leaving Tesla and Walt to slip around them.

Walt surges into the next room and shoots a direct shot into Sophia's humandroid assistant, the droid spilling to the right and colliding with a stack of processors. They find Sophia at a table with a box of colorful donuts opened next to her, an NV Visor on her head, donut powder on her lips.

As Evan fizzles, the humandroid short-circuiting, Tesla fires on Dr. Sophia Wang before she can fully react. This makes Kodai laugh. *Yes, yes!* He laughs even harder when the doctor slips and falls to the side, cracking her head against a table. Tesla steps over her and fires the killshot, which shatters Sophia's NV Visor.

"Get out of there!" Kodai says once he taps in to Walt and Tesla's comms. "Leave my brother and his friend."

"And Yugio?" Tesla asks. She turns to Hajime, who is just killing Soto. Yugio is near, trying to crawl away. The humandroid spots Tesla and pulls a different gun from his waist.

Bang!

The gun flies from Hajime's hand, courtesy of a precision shot from Walt.

"Leave them, go. And good shooting, Walt."

"The Swede?" Walt asks, his gun trained on Hajime, who now has his hands up.

Kodai has no problem with killing the Swede, but he knows there will be complications with doing so, especially with FeeTwix's enormous online following. Word would certainly get out and it would bring attention to his family's organization, which is the last thing he wants.

"Leave, now!"

As Walt and Tesla barrel toward the opposite exit of the laboratory, Tesla turns one more time, giving Kodai a look at the room. Hajime has turned to address Yugio. Kodai also sees that both Ryuk and FeeTwix have logged out, that they are struggling to free themselves.

"Must be terrifying," he mumbles to himself.

"What's that?" Walt asks Kodai.

"Never mind. Just get out of there."

The last glimpse Kodai gets of the room is Dr. Sophia Wang lying in a pool of her own blood, a direct shot to her head.

Veenure is going to be happy.

The young crime lord relaxes even further into the sofa. He laughs and finally opens his eyes. After a deep, satisfying breath, he looks out over the blazing city, barely able to contain his glee.

He will leave his mother's men waiting outside for another few minutes.

He wants to enjoy this, but he doesn't want to do so alone. This is why he didn't crack open the bottle of champagne on his table. Kodai wants someone to share it with, and he knows Tesla is on the way.

It is going to be a good night, but first, he needs to log in to check on something...

(0)__(0)

Kodai is giddy by the point his Tritanian avatar forms into existence in the OMIB. He's even more excited when he gets a glimpse of his stats.

How has she done it? How has Veenure taken him to the top of Tritania's level caps in such a short amount of time? Looking past the serpent woman, Kodai focuses on Tomas and the two mages, who have also reached peak levels.

Incredible.

Kodai Matsuzaki Level 99 Ballistics Mage
HP: 6920/6920
ATK: 1541
MATK: 1986
DEF: 1211
MDF: 957
LUCK: 41

Tomas Romero Level 99 Shield Warrior
HP: 5167/5167
ATK: 1662
MATK: 105
DEF: 1740
MDF: 1370
LUCK: 54

Dark Mage Level 99
HP: 2487/2487
MANA: 2466/2466
ATK: 180
MATK: 1233
DEF: 1099
MDF: 1201
LUCK: 51

Berserker Mage Level 99
HP: 4877/4877
MANA: 599/599
ATK: 1483
MATK: 647
DEF: 751
MDF: 644
LUCK: 16

What Veenure has done is truly remarkable. Kodai can hardly believe the power coursing through him. Yet there is a problem. He realizes once he takes a step forward that he isn't fully in control. At first, he is hesitant, but then he relaxes, a rare first for him.

Sometimes, it is best to let others lead.

"We will fight together," Veenure tells him, her voice all around Kodai even though she is standing directly in front of him. "You do not understand the true extent of your new powers, but I do, Kodai, I do. And together, we will be able to take the Knights and your brother's guild, not to mention any of the Empress' forces."

Kodai nods. Now that he knows that she is partially in control of him, he steps forward and examines the two NPC mages. He then stops in front of Tomas, who stands at attention. "Not bad, not bad at all. And you will be happy to learn that I have held up my end of the bargain as well."

"It is done then?" she asks, growing excited.

"It is. I saw it myself. Sophia Wang is dead."

"Good fucking riddance."

Kodai turns back to Veenure, just as the serpent woman approaches him. She wraps her tail around his legs and brings him in closer, Veenure is now three times the size she was just moments ago. The way that things work in the OMIB continues to baffle him. There is a shaky nature to it, the space ethereal at the same time that everything seemed as if it was corrupted in some way.

Kodai will never grow accustomed to it.

"It was glorious," he finally tells Veenure. "I lost three men, but other than that, it went according to plan."

"Men that were expendable?"

Kodai nods. "Two of them, yes. Yugio, I will miss his loyalty to some degree. But there is always someone willing and ready to step up and take his place in my organization. What about Clive?"

"I was just going to tell you about him. Clive has just contacted me. I truly can't believe our luck." Veenure places Kodai down, the serpent woman back to her normal size. She approaches him yet again and wraps her arms around his shoulders. "You did well."

"So did you," Kodai says. Once again, he looks down at his arms. He can't imagine what he will be capable of once he is finally unleashed on the digital battlefield. He feels pride in this, pride in knowing that not only did he succeed in what he needed to do in Tokyo, he also has completely humiliated Ryuk and will continue to do so in his world and Tritania.

"Clive should be here soon," she says.

"With the source code bomb."

"Yes. I have a feeling that by that point, the fight will be fully underway. Even if it isn't, we will hold the bomb. The fight to come. That is when we will drop it so we can not only obliterate the Knights, but all of Tritania."

Kodai considers this. "And what becomes of you if Tritania is destroyed?"

"I will stay here for the time being, and you can visit me here. Not to worry. The next step in our plan is finally coming to fruition. Let's just say there is a lot that you don't know about humandroids."

Kodai hesitates, not certain where she is going with this.

"One of the things I am able to do, especially now that Sophia is out of the picture in your world, is come through to your world using a humandroid as my vessel. I know it is possible. It has been done before."

"You're joking."

She shakes her head. "I'm dead serious. Not only has it been done before, it was done nearly twenty years ago by Sophia. Now, I don't know how to completely pull it off, but my experiments were starting to work until Sophia seemingly put a stop to them. As much as I hate to admit it, she is the best of them, of anyone versed in the Proxima Galaxy and its code. And she's a humble bitch about it as well. She's the type to turn down multimillion dollar contracts with them to work as a lowly FCG employee," she says, referring to America's Federal Corporate Government. "Once the source code bomb is unleashed, it will destroy all the avatars of this world. Bits of their data will filter through the OMIB. As they do, I will catch the pieces I need, bits of Sophia's knowledge. I will trap it, put it back together, and then I will use it."

"You would come back to my world?"

"I would. Do you want me there?"

Kodai thinks of Tesla. "Having you there would be... yes, it could work. I do have a droid that works for me. But I would get another for you."

"Why? Do you like this humandroid?"

"I do."

Veenure runs her hand across his cheek. "I'm fine with that. I don't really care what you do in your free time. I just want to see the world again, your world."

"There's a lot to show you in Tokyo and around Japan."

"So I've heard. Maybe we can start in Hokkaido."

"Hokkaido?" Kodai thinks of the snowy northern city. It has been ages since he visited. "That wouldn't be bad at all. It is cold during this time of year, though."

"I'm sure we'll find a way to keep me warm. Will you be staying logged in until the battle?"

"I need to log back out for a little bit to deal with some of my people. My humandroid is returning as well from Sophia. I want to debrief with her. But I'll be back in shortly."

"Good," Veenure says, her voice suddenly wispy, "don't leave me waiting."

(0)__(x)

Ryuk gasps awake. He has a breathing apparatus in his mouth and his body is completely weighed down by the gel-like liquid of the dive vat. He rips away the NV Visor over his face, which creates feedback in his ears. A flash of lights, followed by a sound he is certain is a gunshot, leaves Ryuk scrambling to get out of the vat.

He falls onto the ground, covered in goo like a calf.

His breathing apparatus is still in his mouth, forcing Ryuk's neck back, choking him. He rips it out and slaps his hand against the tiled floor only to hear footsteps running in the opposite direction, toward an exit on the west side of the room. Ryuk looks over toward the footsteps, blurry eyed. All he can make out is a woman and an older man. *Who...?*

"FeeTwix," Ryuk says as he turns to the Swede, who is now out of his vat, his back against the metal Proxima sarcophagus as he hyperventilates. "FeeTwix!"

"Ryuk…"

Ryuk rushes to the Swede's side. In doing so, he falls and smacks his face against a cable ramp. Seeing stars, Ryuk forces himself to his feet and reaches the Swede. He drops. There was gunfire, he was certain of it. Ryuk knew what he heard. When he finally glances over to Sophia, he sees her splayed out on the ground, a pool of blood around her head.

No…

"Sophia," he says.

"Holy shit, Ryuk. They… killed her. Evan too," FeeTwix says, panic in his voice. "Oh my God. Fuck, man. Fuck!"

Ryuk feels the shock come to him in waves. Upon hearing FeeTwix mumble the same statement again, that someone had killed Sophia and Evan, this shock turns into a bitter anger.

Ryuk knows who is responsible.

His eyes jump from Sophia to Hajime, who is just approaching the woman. Hajime crouches before her. He checks her vitals even though it's painfully clear what has happened. Hajime shakes his head. He finally looks over at Ryuk and FeeTwix.

"Quickly, get dressed," he says, his voice cool and confident as always. "We need to leave before the police arrive. I will handle Evan's feed. There are a few things he had with him as well that we may need later. Hurry." Ryuk and FeeTwix remain in their position, both paralyzed by shock. "Now, get dressed. Go."

"Come on," FeeTwix tells Ryuk.

FeeTwix reaches for a towel. He starts drying himself off. Inspired by the Swede, yet still not able to stomach the adrenaline, Ryuk does the same.

The two gamers stumble into a side office where there is fresh clothing. Ryuk slips into a shirt and a pair of sweatpants. He goes for a pair of slippers and a set of robes. He's delirious, his mouth dry, his heart fluttering as he finds a pair of fluffy sandals, likely Sophia's. There are other options available yet these are the easiest ones to put on.

They join Hajime a couple minutes later, the humandroid now with a black backpack over his shoulder. "We will go to a safe place, a location I know. After we've done so, we will reassess what has happened here. Sophia. She must have had an RPC."

"Someone like her definitely has an RPC," says FeeTwix.

Hajime nods in agreement. "She will have further instructions in Tritania. But the two of you need to be in a safe place to log in."

"Who did this? Was it your brother?"

Ryuk balls his hands into fists upon hearing FeeTwix's question. "It was definitely Kodai."

"He's a murderer."

Ryuk nods.

"What are we going to do against a freaking murderer?"

Ryuk finally looks up at FeeTwix; the Swede glances away when he sees the darkness in Ryuk's eyes.

"Ryuk, we need to go—"

"We will go, Hajime. We will go." Ryuk steps away from the two and stops. "About Kodai," he tells FeeTwix, "I have an idea. Once we are safe. I will make a call."

"To who?" asks FeeTwix after a long pause in which he looks back to Sophia's body. "This is so fucked up. Who will you call, Ryuk?"

Ryuk doesn't answer.

(x)__(x)

Ryuk, Hajime, and FeeTwix fly in an unregistered Uberyota, a service that Ryuk's family is known to employ from time to time. Ryuk is aware that his brother could technically track him, but he doesn't care. If Kodai wanted to kill him, he would have done so back there, when he was getting out of the dive vat.

No, it is clear that Kodai wanted Sophia dead.

Ryuk is certain she had an RPC. He knows that as soon as they log in they will be instructed on what needs to happen next. If not, all they'll need to do is contact Doc or Sophia. This doesn't diminish the tragedy of her death in any way. It's just what he knows will happen. Where would they spawn? Probably Kayi. It is best to regroup with the others, and Ryuk needs to check on Yangu.

Hajime: Have you decided what you will do?

Ryuk: Yes, I think. But I don't want FeeTwix knowing.

Hajime: It is inevitable, and you've already mentioned that you will make a call. He will be curious. In a situation like this, I would recommend leaning on your friends for support. They may have a surprising solution in store. Remember your oblique quote for the day.

Hajime's message flashes across Ryuk's mind's eye as he accesses the picture he took over iNet.

Change is hard at first, messy in the middle, and gorgeous at the end.

Ryuk has been calling upon memories like this for his entire life, ones that he has screenshotted. Most people do it with their eyes open. Sometimes, Ryuk genuinely doesn't know if he's experiencing a memory, or if it is a screenshot of something he has seen.

Ryuk: We are in the *messy in the middle* part, I believe.

Hajime: I believe you are right.

"So…" FeeTwix looks up at the ceiling of the Uberyota, which is playing a Hello Panda cookie advertisement. This is followed by an advertisement of a K-1 Premium Dynamite Combat Event pitting a holo Mike Tyson against a holo Akebono Taro in a match in which the winner must deliver exactly 108 punches or be disqualified. "What next? And where are we going exactly?"

Rather than reply aloud, Ryuk sends FeeTwix a message.

Ryuk: We can't talk about it here. We are going to a safe house where we can log in.

"Sounds good to me." FeeTwix shakes his head, a cold look forming on his face. "Fuck, man. I can't believe he would do something like that, your brother. I just have to trust that Quantum and the others have a plan. They have to have a plan. Doc will know what to do."

Ryuk nods. He also knows what needs to happen next, and for once, he will probably be the one to spearhead the retaliation. Hajime won't try to talk him out of it; Ryuk seriously doubts any of the others will as well.

Rather than say anything else, he looks out the window.

A fog has settled over Tokyo, gleaming buildings pressing out of the gray like alien monoliths. Everything is covered in a fine mist; water beads against the windows of the aeros as it zips through the air. Even if he has spent his whole life in Tokyo, it isn't uncommon for Ryuk to get lost in staring out at the city. Where were they exactly? He knew they were in

Ueno earlier, but he doesn't currently know their location. The fog makes it harder. He could ask Hajime, but he trusts the humandroid.

Hajime won't let them down.

It is only after they begin to land that Ryuk recognizes that they are near Setagaya.

A few years back, Ryuk walked in the rain from Setagaya to Shimokitazawa with Tamana. It was one of those memories that he cherished.

He could see her now, Tamana spinning her umbrella and stomping through rain puddles in her cute knee-high rain boots. They were fine until the wind shifted directions and the rain began striking them horizontally. Ryuk and Tamana escaped into an arcade, where they dried off and played games. To warm up even further, they had ramen at a small place across the street from the arcade, where one of the chefs kept singing parts of *First Love* by Hikaru Utada.

It had been hilarious, but the thing that made that day particularly glorious was when the rain finally let up. The rainbows. There had to be several dozen of them. It was like they were beaming from the rooftops of the buildings. Ryuk and Tamana walked the streets, dipping in and out of small vintage boutiques, Tamana trying on hats, Ryuk taking pictures.

He doesn't want to.

He knows better than to open up the photos from that day, yet he can't help himself.

Ryuk closes his eyes for just a moment as the aeros lands. He looks at the pictures from that rainy, rainbowy day. How long ago was it? Ryuk knows he could see the date, but he doesn't look. It feels better to leave it as an unknown date in the past. This is something that technology, all the data tracking and advancements, can't do. As humanity nears the 22nd century, it has reached a point where the act of forgetting or misremembering feels serendipitous.

Ryuk doesn't want to know the details.

They enter the safehouse by taking a set of stairs down from the rooftop. The home is a sleek affair, one that is both modern and traditional with its tatami mats and movable walls. Most importantly, there are two rooms, each equipped with pretty good rigs. Nothing like the professional grade dive vats Sophia had, but they were all top-of-the-line.

"You're in there," Ryuk tells FeeTwix then gestures to the room on the right.

"All this is just so terrible," FeeTwix says. "And to think we launched our donut line today. They were right there on the table!"

"I... didn't see."

"This is supposed to be a day of celebration. We were all set to go to Ultima Thule. And now..." The Swede plops down on the couch and sighs. "I don't think anyone could say that they were a fan of Sophia, but she didn't deserve that."

"No, no she didn't. No one does." Ryuk leans against the countertop as he looks from FeeTwix to Hajime. "But I have a solution. It is not a pleasant one, and I will also need your help to pull it off," he tells Hajime.

The humandroid sets the black backpack that he took from Evan down onto the coffee table. "What do you have in mind?"

"My brother has many enemies. He has done terrible things to people, things I could never imagine. But I know one enemy of his, one who has really complicated his life in the past. If he was to learn of my brother's whereabouts, he would make his life very difficult. He would do worse."

"Like kill him?" FeeTwix asks. "I can't believe I'm about to say this, but if anyone deserves to die, and I'm sorry, Ryuk, it's your brother. He's a total asshole. If you know where your brother is, or how to find out…"

"I know how to find out. And this man can make it happen."

"Who are you referring to?" Hajime asks.

"What I need from you, Hajime, is my brother's current location. We can get it through my mother, through her men. First, we get my brother's location. You and…" Ryuk swallows hard. "Sorry, I didn't answer your question. Gintoki. Gintoki is who I'm referring to."

"Gintoki? Who the hell is that?" FeeTwix asks.

"He is my brother's biggest rival. I don't know what has happened between them recently, but I do know that they have been at each other's throats for some time. With your help," Ryuk tells Hajime, "I am certain that my brother will regret attacking us and killing Sophia."

"Understood, Ryuk, understood."

"Before we do anything, we should talk to Doc," FeeTwix says, caution in his voice. "Now, I'm not disagreeing with what you are suggesting. I think it's probably for the best, especially if your hands aren't technically dirty from it. Or are they? I don't know. What I'm saying is that you should at least talk to Doc and Quantum before you do something like this. And Sophia."

"Agreed. Hajime, please discover my brother's location while we are logged in. I will log out as soon as I know what needs to happen, if I need to send a message to Gintoki. In fact, maybe I should even meet him—"

"I would advise against that," says the humandroid, "but you could video chat with him over iNet. Even if you are proposing that the enemy of your enemy is your friend, Gintoki is a dangerous man. He might see this as an opportunity to kill you *and* your brother. We won't let it get to that. But you should certainly speak with him if this is what you decide to do. I will support you if that is the case."

"Then that settles it." Ryuk turns to the first room on the left. "Let's see what they have to say, and go from there."

TOKYO

CHAPTER 12: THE AFTERMATH

Ryuk glances down at his hands as they form into existence. He is presented with the guild's stats, Ryuk confirming they have all reached or passed the coveted Level 35 mark.

Ryuk Matsuzaki Level 35 Ballistics Mage
HP: 1341/1341
ATK: 175
MATK: 249
DEF: 153
MDF: 110
LUCK: 28

FeeTwix Fajer Level 35 Berserker Mystic
HP: 1502/1502
ATK: 259
MATK: 48
DEF: 128
MDF: 82
LUCK: 29

Hiccup Level 35 Shield Thief
HP: 2298/2298
ATK: 182
MATK: 19
DEF: 381
MDF: 228
LUCK: 47

Zaena Morozon Level 35 Brawler Assassin
HP: 1489/1489
ATK: 325
MATK: 14
DEF: 276
MDF: 73
LUCK: 32

Enway Zoltan Rosa Level 35 Hourglass Mage
HP: 1229/1229
MANA: 691/691
ATK: 89
MATK: 258
DEF: 88
MDF: 253
LUCK: 27

Oric Rune Level 58 Warrior Berserker
HP: 3104/3104
ATK: 554
MATK: 11
DEF: 467
MDF: 389
LUCK: 31

Wolf Level 41
HP: 2456/2456

ATK: 713
MATK: 0
DEF: 539
MDF: 245
LUCK: 20

Ryuk can see his dream armor, the pouches on his waist filled with unique marbles. Maybe there is a day that he would get a new type of marble, but that day isn't now. At the moment, they need to figure out what happens next.

"Anything from Sophia?" asks FeeTwix.

Ryuk glances at his dashboard again to see a message that simply says, *Wait for me to contact you.*

"I think she will contact us when she's ready."

"In that case, um, let's head on in." FeeTwix gestures for Ryuk to enter Enway's home. They find Zaena seated on a cushion sofa, one leg crossed over the other, the Thulean wearing a glittering gold dress. "Um, babe?"

She looks over at FeeTwix and a big grin appears on her face. Zaena hops to her feet and stumbles toward the Swede. "I was wondering when you'd be back," she says, her voice with a hint of intoxication to it. She pulls him forward with her ghost limbs, and also knocks over a lamp which she barely manages to catch. "Oops, sorry."

"What's wrong with you?" asks FeeTwix. "Have you been poisoned?"

She laughs. "Poisoned? Of course not. You think I'm poisoned?" Zaena smirks at Ryuk. "No. why do both of you look so concerned?"

"Where's Hiccup?" Ryuk asks as he fires off a message to Enway, who he assumes has logged out for the time being. He thinks about messaging Doc, but decides that before he does that, he should make sure everything is good with his guild.

"The goblin? He's in the backyard." Zaena starts to laugh even though no one has told a joke. "He bought me my favorite liquor. And this dress." She says something in Thulean and presses away from FeeTwix. She spins once. "Sexy, right?" The glittering dress is covered in gold sequins, the piece form-fitting to the point that it appears painted on. Ryuk doesn't know how Hiccup convinced her to even try it on. It seems like something she wouldn't want to wear in front of the goblin.

"Super sexy. Superduper sexy. So..." FeeTwix raises an eyebrow at her as he pieces together what's going on. "Hiccup got you drunk, bought you a dress, and now he's in the backyard with Wolf and Snowballs—Yangu, sorry, Ryuk—is that what you're saying?"

She lightly slaps him on the cheek. "You're so smart. So handsome."

"What about Spew Gorge?" asks Ryuk.

"His son, or cousin, or whatever?" Zaena laughs. "Who knows where that goblin wandered off to. He was here for a while, but I couldn't tell you where he went after we went shopping. Wait until you see what Hiccup bought."

Once again, Ryuk and FeeTwix exchanged glances. "Where did Hiccup get the money?" Ryuk asks.

The smile on Zaena's face thins. "The demon *konopen*."

"The what?"

"I'll show you." Zaena playfully grabs Feetwix's junk and squeezes.

"Whoa! Message received, babe! In fact..." FeeTwix beams over at Ryuk. "Hey, buddy, I think you should check on Hiccup. Let me know what we need to do next. Maybe knock first?"

"No problem."

"Thanks, Ryuk!" The Swede sweeps Zaena up into his arms and exits the room. Ryuk hears him say, "I've got macaroons with your name on them," as he shuts the door.

"I've got more than that with your name on it," Zaena tells FeeTwix with a playful giggle, one that Ryuk is certain he's never heard from her before.

Yikes.

A message appears from Enway.

Enway: I'm just about to log back in. What's up?

Ryuk: It's too much to explain here. When you log back in, I'd suggest meeting me in your backyard.

Enway: Why?

Ryuk's eyes dart over to the room where FeeTwix and Zaena have just disappeared. He hears laughter and furniture moving around on the other side.

Ryuk: Just trust me.

Enway: Okay. See you soon.

Ryuk turns to the backyard. He steps outside to find a couple things he didn't expect. For one, there is Yangu, who is now a full-sized dragon and currently sleeping at the other end of the yard, the large blue dragon resting on a bed of ice.

Then, there is the goblin.

Why? Ryuk thinks. *Why?*

Hiccup is naked and lying on a lawn chair, his body gleaming as if he has rubbed some kind of tanning oil all over it. He's wearing a pair of oversized shades and is surrounded by about two dozen empty healing potion bottles, all of which have tropical colored straws sticking out of them. Scattered around him are several large boxes that are open, their interiors filled with blasts of multifarious sauces and the bones of dragon wings courtesy of DD's barbecue. Around Hiccup's neck is a thick gold chain covered in either crystals or diamonds, Ryuk can't tell. The goblin is also wearing a set of dangling earrings that match the necklace.

Wolf is near Hiccup, lying on his side and breathing as if he has eaten too much. He has a gold dog collar now, and Ryuk is pretty sure that his ears are pierced as well. That Tagvornian canine lifts his head, looks at Ryuk, licks some barbecue off his lips, and lies back down.

Hiccup clearly senses Ryuk's presence.

But rather than say anything, he grabs a healing potion on the other side of his lawn chair and lifts a turquoise straw to his lips. He sucks it down nice and slow, and finally looks over the frame of his sunglasses at Ryuk once he's finished. "Yo."

"Put some fucking pants on, Hiccup."

Rather than say anything, the goblin returns to slurping at the straw. Since there isn't anything left in the bottle, the sound is quite loud.

"What the fuck are you doing?"

"Marbles, I'm not going to sit here and tell you to take your pants off, see if you can't find a lemon pepper wing in one of those boxes, and fickin' join me. Nah, hell nah. You're too much of a fickin' stickler, a fickin' fickler, to actually unwind and have a good ass time with Uncle Goblin. You saw Liz in there. Even her scaly green ass is having a good time. Fick, she plays a mean game of Boaster Toaster, but she's not better than me, especially when I cheat. Can't believe she actually picked that dress out."

"I saw."

"She's fit as hell, Marbelito, but she's spoken for, so don't go fickin' snooping around."

"Whatever, Hiccup. She's really drunk."

"Fickin' clearly, Marbles. Wolfie, oi! Looks like we got Fickstein over here with his Theory of Drunketivity."

Wolf sighs.

"Agreed. Fickin' agreed." Hiccup snaps his finger and another lawn chair appears. "Have a seat, homie."

Homie? Ryuk starts to roll his eyes and stops. "I don't think you realize how serious..."

"Are you going to fickin' sit or not? Snowballs is finishing his gobnap. Once he's done, you and I can take the big ficker out for a liddle ride. I'll even show you how to call him."

"Ride the dragon?"

"What the fick else do you think you'd raise a dragon for? And don't say to use as some sort of oversized ficklight. That's the sort of shit that will get your Japanese ass banned from Jatla. Fick, my dude." He burps. "Fick."

Ryuk begrudgingly sits. "Some shit happened in my world."

"Yeah? Well, fickin' tell me about it then. You know I love sippin' tea." Hiccup conjures another healing potion. He hands it to Ryuk. "Drink this; it's the good stuff. The Thomas-James ones I've been raving about. I got money now. Only the best for me and my fickin' disciples."

Ryuk rolls his eyes. "I can see that. Has anyone ever told you that you spend irresponsibly?"

"Pfft! Since when do goblins spend responsibly? Racist much? Fick, I swear it's like you've never been to Tritania before." Hiccup shifts to the side to let out a squeaker of a poot, one that lasts a full thirty seconds. By the end of it, Hiccup is biting his lip. "Fick, I needed to get that out. Potions make me gassy. Or it's the dragonwings. Probably both."

"So, you sold the demon penises and now you've wasted all your rupees on jewelry, a dress for Zaena, potions, and food. Am I missing something?"

"First off, 'demon penises' sounds ficktarded. Call them what they are, Marbles, demon chalupas. Or at least chups. Secondly, I also bought some new armor. Does it change my stats in any way? Fick no. Does it look good? Fick yeah, it's lit A-F. I'll show you that later."

"You bought armor that doesn't actually protect you?" Ryuk brings the healing potion to his lips. He takes a sip from it and notices that it has a distinct flavor, unlike other ones he has tried before. It's actually pretty good, but he knows not to say this in front of the goblin.

"Good, right?"

"It's not bad."

"Marbles, whenever you are ready to lighten the fick up, I know a great gloryhole in Jatla that will have you feeling like you had your fickin' bone marrow sucked out through your weehole. Just say the word. My treat. And no, I'm not going to rant about how it should be *your* treat considering you're my fickin' employer; I'm also not going to mention that FeeTwix needs to start dishing out royalty checks lest we have some fickin' words. Why? I'm in a good mood. Look at me, finally getting some sun on my chup."

Ryuk doesn't look. Hiccup is naked, and the last time he turned his head in the goblin's direction, he got a glimpse of his flaccid weiner.

"You look green," is all he finally says.

"Marbles, I don't see color, and neither should you."

"Sophia—"

"Fick her."

"You don't understand. She was just killed in my world. My brother. His people. They attacked us and killed her."

The smile on Hiccup's face fades. He adjusts his oval sunglasses over his eyes and stares out at the sleeping Yangu. "Fick. I can't say I feel bad for the salty bitch—because fick her and everything she's done to goblinkind—but you or Twixy could have been killed, right?"

"Probably not me. But FeeTwix, yes."

Hiccup summons another healing potion. He drinks from it slowly, something agitated about the way he holds the bottle. Once it's finished, the goblin leaps into action. He jumps out of his chair and smashes the bottle on the ground against the others, which causes Yangu and Wolf to instantly wake up. "Fick! Fick that fickin' brother of yours. That's it. I'm fickin' sick of that gaping fickhole causing shit for everyone else. Sick of it! What the fick do we do now? I'll fickin' claw his eyes out! I'll bash his fickered head in!" Hiccup stands, summons an axe, and turns to Ryuk.

"You could start by putting some clothes on."

"I'll do you one better, Marbles." The new armor that Hiccup has purchased appears on his rotund body. It looks to be entirely made of gold and matches his brass arm. Once it is fully formed, his soundboard gauntlet appears as well. "Not bad, right?"

~Mmm, fick.~

Hiccup then triggers the button that plays Zaena's voice.

~~Fick yeah, goblin.~~

Ryuk brings a hand up to shield his eyes. "It's really shiny," he says, not wanting to tell Hiccup that he looks like a fucking asshole in the gold armor, especially with his short stature.

"Fick yeah, it's shiny, ficktacular, on trend, and clearly sick as fick. But that's not the point. Stop sidetracking me, bro. I was supposed to be pissed. First—and we can't forget this, even though it seems like he could be dead—Grifty is still out there. That orange ficker will fick with us again, I guaran-fickin-tee it. Not only that, Sophia has been fickin' offed by your lunatic bottle-fed fick of a brother. Then there is the portal in Ultima Thule. That shit's getting more fickered as we speak. The Knights don't seem to be able to contain it. I just heard mitherfickers talking about it at DD's. Even fickin' goblins are worried about it, you know it's bad when goblins are worried about it. We definitely need to see what the fick is going on up there in Ultima Thule."

"That's the next step," Ryuk tells him. "I'm waiting to contact Doc."

Yangu approaches. The dragon lowers its big blue maw to Ryuk.

"Awww, would you look at that? He wants some fickin' love from his father." Hiccup snorts. "Fick if you haven't been one of those dads that goes out to buy some milk and cigarettes and never returns. Real sad story. How many men are raised without proper male role models in their lives? But if you ask me—and I know you aren't asking me, but you'll take my fickin' advice anyway because I'm the only male role model in your life— if I were you, I would forget about all this bullshit for a fickin' minute and take Snowballs out for a spin. Maybe even bring Uncle Goblin with you. Let Twixy and Liz play hide the Swedish banana for a bit."

"And Enway? She's about to be here too."

Hiccup brings his hand to his forehead. "Fick, Marbles, did you really have to summon her?"

Ryuk turns to find Enway standing there in her white robes, her red eyes filled with concern. "How much did you hear?" he asks.

"Just the last bit. I didn't want to interrupt you. So it's true, Sophia is... dead?"

"She is. And her RPC is likely with the Knights." Ryuk places a hand on Yangu's snout and notices that his scaly skin is cold to the touch. *Shouldn't he be able to talk?* Ryuk thinks.

"Hi, Yangu."

The dragon lets out a puff of ice.

"He doesn't talk, if that's what you're wondering, Marbles. Fick if I know what's wrong with him. If you ask me, we should take him to a speech pathologist in Jatla that I know, but she'll fickin' charge for her services, and I'm all out of rupees."

Ryuk slowly nods. "Maybe Hiccup is right. Maybe I should take a quick flight before we go wherever they are and figure out what happens next. I need to learn to call Yangu too. Um, care to join me?" he asks Enway.

"Um, care to join me?" Hiccup asks.

~Fick you, Marbles!~

Enway approaches with her hand out. Before Ryuk can take it, Hiccup steps between them. The goblin places his grimy paws in both of their hands. "Looks like I'm the third fickin' wheel here, a chaperone of sorts to make sure the two of you keep it in your fickin' pants." He burps. "Fick, let's fly!"

(0)__(0)

It isn't ideal, yet Hiccup insists on tagging along. This leaves the three of them to figure out a way to mount the dragon. In the end, Hiccup takes the front, Ryuk behind the goblin, and Enway behind Ryuk, holding on to his waist. Even if Ryuk is directly in the line of fire of Hiccup's truffle tunnel, he tries to ignore this fact.

As the three whip through clouds, the wind blowing past their faces, Ryuk hopes it will help clear his head. He knows that there are important things that need to happen next, including the message he's about to send to the Knights of Non Compos Mentis. He also feels bad that he hasn't already contacted them, and slightly curious about why they haven't contacted him.

If anyone knew that he was back in Tritania, it would be Sophia or Doc.

"Incoming!" Hiccup shouts, which Ryuk assumes is in reference to a cloud or perhaps a sudden dip as Yangu races forward.

Instead, the goblin is referring to what Ryuk should have suspected in the first place.

Even though it is brief, the air fills with the half-digested scent of barbecue with a hint of sugary healing potion. Considering Ryuk is directly behind Hiccup with his arms over his shoulders (he refused to put them around the goblin's waist) he can also feel the flatulence.

"Fuck, Hiccup!"

"I warned you."

"So gross," Enway says, the Hourglass Mage now with her head pressed into Ryuk's back. It is the closest they have ever been, and the fact that the goblin is seated before him happily farting away annoys the Japanese gamer to no end.

It also makes him secretly laugh to himself.

From the image of Hiccup tanning, to seeing Yangu in his adult form and being able to summon the dragon, not to mention flying on the dragon's back—all of this is a much needed break from what had been a pretty stressful afternoon. It also helped alleviate the pressure from what Ryuk was planning to do.

Gintoki.

Ryuk knows when he reaches out to the gangster that the man will certainly act. If he could, Gintoki would kill Kodai in a heartbeat. With Hajime on his side, Gintoki's odds are even better.

This is a decision that Ryuk will have to live with for the rest of his life.

It is a lot to take in, yet Ryuk's life has reached the point where something needs to happen. And he knows what that something is. Now, it is just a matter of coordinating with Doc and the others.

"Just think, Marbles, next time you're getting bullied by some fickin' fick-faced squish mitten of an internet troll, you'll be able to call Snowballs here to freeze his ass to death! Isn't that right, Snowballs!" Hiccup slaps his mechanical hand against the back of Yangu's head. The dragon shifts to the side and releases a plume of ice and snow, some of which strikes Ryuk in the face as they pass through it.

"Heh! Fick!"

~FICK~

As they curve to the right, Ryuk can see the sprawling city of Kayi below. He doesn't know how high up they are, but the city seems like it's a couple kilometers down by this point. A fall from this height would instantly kill him. It would also be incredibly fun.

Feeling spontaneous, Ryuk presses away from Hiccup's body.

"What the fick, Marbles!?"

"Let's jump!" he tells Enway.

"Seriously!?"

But by this point, Ryuk is already tipping over the side of the dragon, Enway still holding on to him. He completely lets go and falls off the dragon. Ryuk transitions around so he's now face-to-face with Enway, the wind whipping her hair upward, a shocked look on her face. This quickly changes to a huge smile.

"You're crazy!"

"I like you!" Ryuk calls over the roaring wind. As they fall, he can see Yangu racing to catch them, Hiccup shrieking from his position on the ice dragon's back.

"I like you too!"

"Sorry!" Ryuk shouts.

"Sorry for what!?"

"Sorry for jumping!" Ryuk pulls himself just a little closer to her, both of them holding on to each other's shoulders, their bodies horizontal. Even as the wind ripples across their faces, he sees Enway press her lips together.

They kiss, and moments later, they hit the ground.

Insta-Instakill!

(0)__(x)

Ryuk's avatar takes shape in Enway's backyard. He stumbles forward and falls onto his knees, laughing. He hears the sound that indicates that her avatar has returned as well, an effect that sounds almost like someone quickly ripping a sheet of paper, yet dampened.

Enway approaches Ryuk. She places a hand on his shoulder and massages it.

"Do you think he is coming?" she asks as she looks up at the sky.

"I'm pretty sure we're going to hear all about it when he gets here." Ryuk can't stop thinking about the kiss, but he also knows that now is the time to focus.

"You two look happy," FeeTwix says.

Ryuk gets to his feet. He turns to find the Swede with his blonde hair ruffled, Zaena holding on to his waist, her new dress in disarray.

"I should probably sober up," she says. "He told me everything."

Ryuk nods. "Probably. I'm going to contact Doc now and we'll see where we go from here."

"FFFFFFFFFIIIIIIIICCCCCCCCCCCCKKKKK!"

Ryuk squints up at the sky to see a blue form barreling toward them. "Looks like Hiccup is almost here too."

(0)___(x)

After contacting Doc, the Mitherfickers are instantly transported to one of the Knights' many estates. This one appears to be on Ultima Thule based on all the snow and mountain peaks visible in the distance. The manor has been built upon a floating patch of land, one several hundred feet up with a pair of towers behind it that are covered by wispy clouds.

Hiccup kicks at a clump of snow. "Fick, I hate snow, and I definitely hate floating islands or whatever the fick this is. Speaking of snow. Have any of you ever eaten yellow snow? I hope the fick not. That's piss, if you didn't know, Elfie."

Wolf, who is next to Hiccup, goes wild once Oric appears. The Unigaean barbarian looks a little worse for wear, his armor beat up and damaged, his hair a mess as Wolf licks his face.

"Fick me, Conan, have a potion or some shit." Hiccup summons a potion and tosses it to Oric.

"Thanks. Drachma Killers. Not an easy fight. And why are Wolf's ears pierced?"

Hiccup shrugs. "Fick if I know. Don't know who got his pooched ass that fickin' gold collar too, but if I were a betting goblin, and I am, I'd say the mitherficker who did that is one cool ass fickin' dude."

"You pierced his ears and got him a collar."

Hiccup shrugs again. "I can't be held responsible for what Wolfie asks for at the outdoor mall in Kayi."

"Whatever." Oric glances up at the estate, and then down to the steps leading up to the front door. He pops the cork out of the potion and takes a drink. "They could have had us spawn inside."

"Pfft. Hoity-toity assfickery if you ask me." Hiccup, who is now wearing one of his shoddy tunics, snaps his fingers. His new golden armor ripples over his portly form. He still wears the diamond necklace and earrings that he purchased with his proceeds from the sale of the demon chalupa, making the goblin look like he's been severely groped by Midas. As a finishing touch, his oval sunglasses appear on his face.

"You're serious?" Oric asks.

"What the fick kind of question is that? Fick, tough guy, if you're jelly, I can get you some new armor too, get my boy Marbles over here to put it on the Mitherfickers' tab. Maybe fix that fickin' shabby-fick sword of yours."

"I'm happy with what I have."

"Said every poor fick ever." Hiccup blows a raspberry. "Fick off."

"Let's just go inside and get this settled." Ryuk takes the stairs, the others soon joining behind him. As he approaches the door it swings open, revealing a man Ryuk instantly recognizes. He seems to be a butler of sorts, with a thin mustache. But that is just upon first glance. In actuality, he is a high-level fighter.

Jim Dohrmahn Level 99
HP: 6753/6753
MANA: 2885/2885
ATK: 2058

MATK: 566
DEF: 1118
MDF: 1259
LUCK: 85

"Ah, yes, the Mitherfickers. We've been expecting you. Please, right this way," Jim says.

Ryuk knows that there aren't security cameras inside the mansion. Those aren't available in a place like Tritania. If there were, however, he wonders how odd his guild would look as they step in. First, there is Oric, who looks like he has just come out of the jungle. Near him is his giant wolf wearing a gold collar with his ears pierced. Behind them is a Swedish man in a sleeveless trench coat wearing an I <3 Quantum shirt and a pair of Crocs. Next to him is a beautiful Thulean woman with green skin, her red hair tucked behind her ears. Then, there is the goblin in gold armor who looks a bit too flashy to be taken seriously, not to mention the Hourglass Mage and her white robes and red eyes.

What a team, Ryuk thinks as Jim motions them into a study with high ceilings.

It is here that they find all the usual suspects, yet there is also someone that Ryuk has never seen before.

Frances Euphoria Level 99
HP: 6790/6790
ATK: 2899
MATK: 106
DEF: 1244
MDF: 1161
LUCK: 244

Frances Euphoria?

His face a mess of worry and anger, Quantum is seated on a leather couch, massaging his temples. There are numerous weapons, mostly handguns, on the couch next to him that have been partially dismantled as if he were preparing them for the fight that is to come. Standing near the couch is Doc, the faun of war decked out in milspec gear that looks almost alien. Ryuk has never seen anything like it.

Aiden, aka Morning Assassin, sits on a window ledge with his arms crossed over his chest. Sophia is in a big chair, looking absolutely furious, her face and white afro currently obscured by a hood that hangs nearly to her nose. Rocket is there as well, the blue-skinned man hanging out on the opposite side of the room. This leaves the newest member, the one that Ryuk doesn't recognize.

Frances approaches the group. She's dressed like a rogue, her hair a deep shade of orange and clipped on one side. There is something instantly alluring about her. Once she speaks, Ryuk gets this sense that she is often a voice of reason in the group.

"We're glad you could join us. Please, take a seat."

Chairs start to appear. Everyone sits aside from Oric, who remains in the back with Wolf.

"Fick. Anyone ever heard of ergonomics? The seat isn't fickin' comfortable," Hiccup says, his jewelry loud and obnoxious as he tries to get comfortable.

"That's because you're wearing armor and jewelry," Ryuk tells him under his breath.

"Last I checked, Marbles, we were here to kick some fickin' ass? You'd best be wearing armor too, you poofty fick-dicked fart-ficker. And the next time you—"

Sophia looks up at the goblin. *"Silence."* With those words, Hiccup is no longer able to use his voice. He gestures madly for a moment, but then finally gives up, and sits back in his chair, arms crossed over his chest, an irritable look on his face.

"I just don't see how this could happen, Doc," Quantum says, which clearly is part of a conversation they have been having for a while now. "All her tracks were covered. How? How did they know?"

"I suspect it has something to do with MercSecure," the war faun tells him. "Someone was tipped off. There is no way that they knew where you were otherwise. One day, I will weed out whoever gave your location away, Dr. Wang. But that isn't a task for today. It might take a while. But know this," he tells Sophia, "when that day comes, they will regret it."

"I have a solution."

Everyone in the room looks at Ryuk including Hiccup, who points at him and makes a jerking off hand sign.

"Fuck off, Hiccup," Ryuk whispers. He clears his throat. "Like I said, I have a solution for my brother. If that's what we're talking about."

"I just can't believe it was your whacko brother," Quantum says. Of the entire group, he seems to be taking Sophia's assassination the hardest. Ryuk doesn't quite understand why. As far as he knew, Quantum hated Sophia.

"You have a solution, huh?" Doc asks Ryuk. "Let's hear it, then, son."

"My brother's biggest rival is a man named Gintoki. They have been warring with one another for a while now. I don't know the extent of it, but I know that Gintoki would gladly use any opportunity he had to kill Kodai. My plan is to give him an opportunity. Hajime, my humandroid assistant—"

Hiccup snorts. A text from the goblin appears in Ryuk's head.

Hiccup: Calling him an 'assistant' is practically virtue signaling, Marbles. And tell Sophia to fick off for me while you've got the floor.

Ryuk ignores the goblin and continues: "Hajime has already confirmed where my brother is. My plan is simple. I let Gintoki know. Hajime can also go as well, to make sure that everything is handled correctly."

"You'd rat out your own brother?" Quantum asks. "Damn, and I thought I had a pair."

"It sounds to me like he has it coming," Aiden tells Quantum.

"That's not the point, MA, and I'm not over here saying that it shouldn't be done. I'm just pointing out the facts. But hey, the world is a cruel place."

"Hajime still has the supplies that you gave Evan," Ryuk tells Doc. "The black backpack."

"Good. That was my next question. In that case, there is a weapon in there that I need for him to use on your brother."

"Is it what I think it is?" Quantum asks.

Doc nods. "It is. A modified Golden Goosinator. The weapon is similar to the one that we used against Veenure a couple decades ago. She's Strata Godsick's daughter, you know."

This statement seems to only make sense to FeeTwix, who gasps.

Doc continues: "If and when Kodai dies, he will no longer be able to take his avatar in any Proxima World. He will force spawn into the OMIB. Not only that, he'll be presented with an image of Grammy Weatherwax smacking him on the rear. It is sort of like adding insult to injury, if that makes sense. I will forward you instructions to use it, which you should then send to Hajime. I know this isn't a solution that anyone wants, but it is one that seems necessary. To be clear, I have one here as well, and I'll try to get him here in Tritania too. But this gives us two chances to hit him." The caprine of utter destruction rubs his hands together. "Do any of you know why Veenure is doing this?"

"I don't," Ryuk says.

The rest of the Mitherfickers agree, including Wolf, who makes a sad whining noise from the back of the room. Hiccup summons a potion, a bright pink straw, and starts sipping it slowly and loudly.

"Well before your time, we are the ones who imprisoned Veenure in the OMIB. She is aware that NPCs can take humandroid bodies. The digital hallucinations have been tests she is performing for something Sophia invented called R-Diving. Morning Assassin has successfully done this, coming from a Proxima Galaxy to our world. Quantum did it for a spell as well."

"Yeah, and I didn't like it."

"That is her plan entirely. Her goal in taking Dr. Wang out through her influence over your brother was to eliminate any chance she would be caught. But there's still a lot that we can do from here, a lot that Dr. Wang can do. I guess that about sums it up without revealing too much. What do you need to do to contact Gintoki?"

"I'll just need to log out and make the call. Then I can log back in."

"Good. Now, on to what happens next." Doc steps aside and a digital map of Ultima Thule takes shape. "This is the big battle, the one that we have all been preparing for. It will take place on the planes between Tlarin and Tlanid. This is where the portal is currently located." A portal appears over the map and begins shifting across it. "As you can see, it has been moving around. The portal started in the Bitakh Forest, was in Nyik for a while, and still seems to be avoiding the capital city of Athos. That's the last thing we want."

"And the Drachma Killers?" Oric asks from the back of the room. "I ran most of them out of the Plains of Roonana. But there were less than there should have been, now that I think about it. The fuckers."

"They are with the portal. Not only that, but a group of Drachma Killers is also laying siege to Porthos, in Polynya. Luckily, we have some British friends who are handling them. It seems that Veenure is orchestrating everything. I can't shake this feeling that there's something we don't know."

"I've got that feeling too, Doc," Quantum says as a cigar appears in his mouth. He takes a puff from it; Sophia waves the smoke away. Quantum points the cigar at the map. "I'd put good money on the fact that these bozos are planning to come rolling down the plains with the Killers and hit Athos. Am I psychic? No, but I am psycho, and this is the kind of thing that bad guys do. It makes sense. The fact that they are hesitating to attack Athos leads me to believe that Veenure's got something else up her sleeve."

"She always does," says Frances.

"Yeah, that's right. She always does. Now, as for our other situation." Quantum puffs his chest out. "Personally, I would come to Tokyo myself and help you all with your brother, but I've got a pair of bad knees, and—"

"And a bad back," Frances tells Quantum as she approaches the famous gamer. She takes the cigar away from him. For a second, Ryuk thinks she's going to put it out. Instead, she brings it to her lips instead and takes a puff. "You're not going anywhere, tough guy."

Ryuk hears FeeTwix sigh audibly, as if he'd been looking forward to meeting his hero in person.

Quantum places his hand on Frances's rear and gives it a light slap. "I didn't think you'd let me, sweetheart, but I figured I'd try."

Rocket steps over to the group. "So what's the actual plan then? We go to the portal and give it everything we got? You must have something else, Doc. You always do."

Doc laughs. "Yeah, Rocket, I do, a little insider information. But let's just see how things shake out. That said, those of you that are still alive should think about going to Tokyo for the burial."

"Buried in Tokyo?" Sophia shakes her head in disgust. "Absolutely not. I will be buried with Evan back in the States, in California."

"That can be arranged too," Doc tells her.

"Frances and I can make it. Peanut Gallery?" Quantum asks Rocket.

"I'll be there."

"I know this may sound stupid, but is there a way for Evan to dive here to Tritania?" FeeTwix asks. "I've been wondering about that. He was a good guy."

"That doesn't sound stupid at all, kid. Heck, I've been egging her to create something like this forever." Quantum takes his cigar back from Frances. "It makes sense, right? We can send an NPC to our world, why not send a humandroid here? They can already communicate with us when we're here."

"It's not as easy as that, but I do have his personality and all of our interactions stored on several digital hard drives. So to answer your question, yes, it will soon be possible. But first, Veenure and the portal. Not to mention your brother." A hint of sadness traces over Sophia's eyes. "I didn't know how long I would live. No one ever does, but I wasn't expecting to be taken out by a fucking Yakuza hit in Tokyo."

Quantum leans his head back and blows a cloud of smoke into the air. "Just think of it like this, Soph, it makes for a hell of an autobiography."

She rolls her eyes at Quantum. "Oh, please…"

"I think we're done here," Doc tells the group. "Ryuk, log out and explain what's happening to Hajime. Make the call if you think it's something you should do. I can't be the one that orders you to kill your brother. Either way, try to make sure he gets shot with the weapon Evan had in his backpack. That will at least screw him up whenever he does die."

"And after that, I will log back in and join the fight."

"That's right. I'd start from Tlarin Lake. Pick off any stragglers until you reach the main force. As for the portal, I have to get a few things in place first because this is the biggest of them all. But don't worry about that part. We will seal it up," Doc says with finality, "and there'll be hell to pay for anyone who is left. Sophia, go ahead and tag everyone."

Still slouched in her chair, Sophia lifts her hand and waves it over her head. Everyone in the room now has a green halo above their heads.

"This'll make it so it's easy to find one another once the real fight gets going." Doc offers everyone a grin. "Let's make this one count."

(x)__(x)

Ryuk logs out.

He sits there for a moment and takes a deep breath in through his nostrils. As he does so, his iNet feed is populated by prompts and other things he still needs to tinker with since the hard reset. He pushes this off to another day as he thinks of Gintoki and his brother. Is this what he really wants to do? Is he really about to order Kodai's potential execution?

"Damn right, I am," Ryuk says. Hearing his voice gives him a surge of confidence. For his entire life, for as long as he could remember, Kodai had been a thorn in his side. Ryuk isn't the violent type, but it is clear that Kodai is willing to push things to the limit. He also has this feeling that Kodai would have ordered FeeTwix's death if Hajime hadn't been there. Ryuk is certain that Kodai wouldn't kill him personally, but he doesn't know if this sentiment extends to the Swede.

Once he is ready, Ryuk enters the living room space to find Hajime seated on the couch with his legs crossed beneath him. He looks like he is deep in meditation, yet the humandroid blinks his eyes open and offers Ryuk a smile. "Would you like some tea?"

"Actually, I would," Ryuk says, glad to use his native tongue of Japanese again rather than his accented English. "Decisions have been made. I have made some."

"I understand."

Hajime boils water. He transfers this to a ceramic tea kettle that he lets steep for a few minutes in silence. Finally, he pours this into stone cups. By this point, Ryuk is seated on the ground on a cushion. Hajime joins him and hands Ryuk the cup of tea.

After drinking a little tea, Ryuk explains that Doc had instructions for Hajime. "I'll transfer those to you now. Kodai must be shot by this weapon—Doc called it a Golden something—before he is killed."

"Before he is killed, got it."

Ryuk sips from his tea. "Yes, before. It will make it so he cannot log in to a Proxima world. It will force his avatar into the OMIB. That will be a torture in and of itself."

"I can imagine."

"I will need to call Gintoki now. Everything else, you will have to coordinate with him."

"It will be handled, Ryuk. I'm assuming you need to log back in?"

"I do. But I also want to see what happens."

"You can view my feed from the Proxima galaxy. You have done that before."

"Right. The good thing is, if we can't get him with the weapon here, Doc can get him with it in Tritania if he appears in any of the fights to come. We are at an advantage in this regard." Ryuk drinks more green tea. It is invigorating. Just the smell of it alone is making him perk up.

"Will you make the call now?"

Ryuk nods. "I will. But let me sit with my back against the couch. You can sit across from me. I don't want Gintoki to be able to figure out where I am. You can transmit the video feed as well."

"Are you certain?"

"I want him to see that I am serious."

Ryuk takes a seat where Hajime had just been. He finds that the place is still warm, his body naturally going into the same position as Hajime's, Ryuk's legs crossed beneath him. He settles his breath as Hajime takes a seat across from him. Ryuk locates Gintoki's information over GoogleFace and makes the call.

Gintoki picks up almost immediately. At first, he isn't live streaming, but as soon as he sees Ryuk's face he turns on his own feed. "To what do I owe the pleasure?" he asks in an almost agitated voice.

"I know where my brother is."

"You're looking to take his place?"

Ryuk shakes his head. "I'm not interested in the business. I know where my brother is, and I would like Hajime, my assistant, to go with you."

"How do I know this isn't a trap?"

"Kodai just killed someone close to me."

Something behind Gintoki's eyes hardens. "Your brother. What he has done to my family..." Gintoki trails off, mumbling something to himself about Kodai being an animal for what he did to his wife. Ryuk doesn't ask. He really doesn't want to know.

"If it helps, you can meet Hajime in a public place. A very public place. You can meet him in front of the police station for all I care. There's only one stipulation."

"What's that?"

"You can do whatever you want with Kodai, but before you do, before you kill him, Hajime needs to shoot him with something."

"Shoot him with what?"

"It's a weapon that will disrupt any RPC he may have. Are you familiar with that term?"

"Who isn't? Why do you plan to disrupt his RPC?"

Ryuk curls his lips for a moment, barely able to hide the anger on his face and in his voice. "I want to disrupt his RPC so he can never enjoy himself again even after he's died. I don't know you, you don't know me, and after today, I personally don't want anything to do with you."

The mobster grunts a response to this statement. He pauses for a moment before asking another question. "What about your mother?"

"I don't want any part of the family business. Whatever rivalries you have with her or her men are between you and her. Not me. I'm done with this life."

"You aren't even part of this life."

"And I don't want to be," Ryuk tells the mobster with finality. "But I won't be able to be free until my brother is taken care of. He will not let me rest. He will constantly torment me. What I am asking you to do is a terrible thing, I understand that, but it is the only way in my eyes."

Gintoki lights a cigarette. He inhales deeply and exhales a cloud of blue smoke, staring at Ryuk. Finally, after chewing on his lip for a moment, he speaks: "I agree to your terms. Have your assistant meet me in one hour."

"I'll connect him to you now. I don't even want to know that part of this," Ryuk says, referring to where Gintoki and Hajime will meet. "The less I know, the better."

CHAPTER 13: FICKIN' PENGUINS

RYUK REAPPEARS IN THE PROXIMA GALAXY, in Tritania, on the floating continent of Ultima Thule. Behind him is Tlarin Lake. The enormous lake is covered in a thick layer of ice. In the distance, he can see bundled up Thuleans fishing as if there isn't a war happening just south of their current location.

"It's about fickin' time," says Hiccup, the goblin still in his golden armor and sunglasses, yet now with a cloak over it and a hood on his head. He's mounted on Wolf, whose breath is currently visible.

"Hey, Ryuk!" The Swede is next to Zaena, both of whom wear the kind of down jackets that Ryuk would expect to see someone wear in the Swiss Alps. Enway is there as well, a furry hood over her head and a warm smile on her face when she sees Ryuk.

~Fick!~

"I wasn't gone that long, Hiccup, get over yourself."

"Fick, Marbles, you really don't know how to deal with someone with abandonment issues. Any-fickin-hoo, let's fickdaddle and get this fickin' donkey punch show on the road."

The Mitherfickers start toward the south. "Where's Oric?" Ryuk asks after a quick headcount.

"Tarzan? The beefcaked ass-ficker is already at the battle. He's about as patient as a fickin' horned-up goblin." Hiccup equips a healing potion and is just about to drink from it when Zaena takes it out of his hand.

"Hey!"

"You've had six potions since we arrived. Six, Goblin. Even for you, that is quite a bit."

"It's my fickin' birthday, we are heading to the battle of all battles, Grifty is still on the loose—I hope no one here forgot that—and did I mention that it's my fickin' birthday? Did I mention that already? Good. I'll mention it again."

"I'm sure we'll have time to celebrate later, Hiccup. Your fans still have a cake for you," FeeTwix tells the goblin before dropping into an ad read. "And you can celebrate too! Right now, WalMacy's is having its February Black Friday sale at stores across the good ol' U S of A! *Oh say can you see, all the savings tonight, how so proudly we spend, because our world depends on it!* That's right, America! It's your monthly Black Friday sale at WalMacy's and all prices are slashed, slashed, slashed! It's practically a crime scene in some of these places! Need a new smart fridge? Save 30% on home appliances! Need a new look after V-Day? I got you, cuz! Bogo—you know how much I love bogo—cosmetics! Bogo cosmetics! Bogo, bogo, bogo! DisNike licensed apparel and shoes are an additional 15% off. This is the fickin' way. Designer bags have all been discounted including Coach Spade's newest collection. *C'est chic!* Ready for some shut-eye? Bedding and mattresses are 10% off. It's February Black Friday, America, and don't you fickin' dare miss these deals! The sale extends through the weekend, giving you plenty of time to save, save, save! I might have to fly to the States myself to see if I can't snag something. Ryuk, want to come? Sure, you do, buddy! U-S-A! U-S-A! F-C-G! F-C-G! Mention #FeeTwixRox on the WalMacy's app to get exclusive downloadable content and skins on most video game purchases. Did I mention electronics are on sale too? No? Surprise, they are!"

Hiccup shakes his head. "Such fickery. FCG? What the fick is that?"

"America's Federal Corporate Government," Enway tells him.

"That sounds fickin' dystopian as fick. Anyway, not my fickin' problem. It's my birthday, and all I want is some cake. Meanwhile, Twixy is over here talking about some monthly sale. What the fick is Black Friday anyway? I swear we have already been over this. In Jatla, Black Friday—"

"Don't worry about it," Enway tells the goblin.

"Pfft!" Hiccup continues on without saying another word. Ryuk notices that he doesn't, however, mention anything about vetting Enway.

"Didn't Sophia silence him?" Ryuk asks Enway once she has joined him. He is currently in his Ballistics Mage form, and is loading his marble shotgun as they walk.

"Her curse faded after we appeared here."

"I have to talk to her about that."

Enway laughs. "You can always message her."

"I could."

As they walk beside one another, their hands touch for a moment. Their fingers clasp together and they linger like this, Ryuk thinking of the kiss they shared earlier. Unfortunately, Hiccup plows through them so he can catch up with FeeTwix, who is at the front of the group.

"Get a fickin' room, losers."

Ryuk resists the urge to equip his slingshot and peg the goblin in the back of the head with a sword marble.

"Don't let him get to you."

"I'll try not to," Ryuk tells Enway.

"We should probably equip our steampacks," FeeTwix says. "I don't know why Doc had us spawn so far away from the battle. We can get there a lot faster."

"Not a bad idea," Ryuk says as they start over a series of hills. He doesn't mind walking, but he knows that time is of the essence.

He spots something heading in their direction. Penguins, a whole cluster of them, slide up and down the hills on their white bellies, making a beeline toward the Mitherfickers.

"Fick, we've got company." Hiccup summons the axe that Dirty Dave gave him. "What the fick, people?" he asks after he notices that no one else has gone for their weapon.

"Relax, Hiccup, they are just penguins," FeeTwix says. "My fans love penguins. Everyone loves penguins! They're so cute, yes they are," he says as the penguins arrive.

They don't look too friendly, and once Ryuk sees one of their stats, he gets the feeling that a battle is likely.

Emperor Penguin Level 40
HP: 1399/1399
ATK: 130
MATK: 9
DEF: 213
MDF: 122

LUCK: 21

There are at least a dozen of the penguins, with more sliding up and down the hills, kicking up snow as they make their way toward the Mitherfickers.

"Hey, penguins!" FeeTwix says to the first penguin to approach. "My fans are loving this," he tells the Mitherfickers. "Who wants to take a selfie?"

"Human," the emperor penguin says, his voice exactly what Ryuk imagined a penguin would sound like. The bird is absolutely stacked, even if he has a bit of a gut. He turns his head slightly to show that one of his eyes is light blue with a scar running through it. "You are trespassing."

"Trespassers, trespassers," some of the other penguins murmur.

"The fick we are. First of all, if anyone is fickin' trespassing, it's you," Hiccup says. "In case you didn't know, you are in the presence of Thulean *and* Jatlian royalty. Now get the fick out of the way, lest you wind up chopped and served cold with a side of Jatlian potato salad, you fick-faced chodebasket."

The emperor penguin tilts his head to the goblin. The others behind him do the same. "Jatlian royalty? There is no royalty in that trashmine of a city."

"Trashmine?" Hiccup removes his oval sunglasses as dramatically as possible. He shakes his head and pushes his hood back. He hops off Wolf and takes a step closer to the emperor penguin, the other penguins all bristling behind him and murmuring to themselves. "The fick you just say about Jatla?"

"You are trespassing."

"Trespassers," a female penguin says.

More start to join in.

"Trespassers!"

"Trespassers!"

Hiccup snorts up a load of snot and spits it at the lead penguin's webbed feet. "Fick you, fick trespassing, fick ice, fick snow, fick birds, fick snowbirds in every sense of the term, fick birds that are too fat to fickin' fly, fick anything that is short and stout, fick waiting in line, fick bank interest rates, and fick you. In that fickin' order."

Dammit, Ryuk thinks. What makes all this worse is that all they really need to do is leave the territory. It wouldn't be that hard. They could also just spawn back at the start of the lake and fly from there.

"I think what my goblin friend is trying to say here is that you may want to rethink your position on trespassing." FeeTwix parts his jacket to reveal that he's packing heat on both sides, a handgun on his left and a shotgun on the right.

Ryuk clears his throat. "Maybe there is another solution—"

~Fick you, Marbles!~

Zaena draws all four of her blades. "We will pass through here, and we will be done with it. We promise not to disturb your territory."

"Is that so?" asks the emperor penguin. "All of you need to shut your mouths, especially you, Thulean whore."

Zaena steps in front of FeeTwix just as he raises his weapon. "Let's try to handle this diplomatically."

"Nah, not happening, babe. Step aside."

In the end, it isn't FeeTwix who gets the opening shot in. It is Hiccup, the goblin tossing one of his tomahawks right into the head of the emperor penguin.

215 HP!

Critical hit!

"Bring it on, you birdy ficks!"

The fight that breaks out is sudden, fast, and stupid. The penguins don't have weapons, but they do have beaks which they used to their advantage. They slip and slide toward the Mitherfickers, as Ryuk and his team lay down waves of damage.

Bang! Bang!

Click-click, boom!

Insta-Instakill!

FeeTwix fires shots left and right, as does Ryuk with his marble shotgun.

~FICK~

Hiccup is suddenly in the middle of the mayhem, part of a pile of penguins alongside Wolf. Down feathers everywhere, the Tagvornian beast instakills at least three penguins before Enway is able to fry some of them with her chromatic power.

Insta-Insta-Instakill!

-168 HP! -249 HP!

Critical hit!

Ryuk's sword marble is followed up by an explosive one that sends more feathers into the air.

"Aye!" Zaena is a whirlwind of pain, the Thulean spinning so fast that all Ryuk can see is a splash of her red hair and trails of blood and feathers.

"Where's their leader!?" FeeTwix shouts. He pushes away from the fight and equips his steampack, which instantly appears on his back. The Swede takes to the air, gritting his teeth as he scans the penguins that continue to slide into the fight.

Ryuk is just looking up at him when something on FeeTwix's face changes. "Incoming," he says as he points toward the east.

Hiccup clears through a few more penguins and finally gets a view of the enemies approaching. "Fick! Those are some huge fickin' penguins!"

Once Ryuk sees what the goblin is referring to he takes a big step back. The penguins on the horizon are towering in stature. Ryuk estimates that each is about ten meters tall. They're robust as well, their bodies shaped like bowling pins.

As Ryuk's enhanced vision kicks in, he spots something orange and furry moving along the ground.

"Grifty," he whispers, his words breaking through to Hiccup.

"The fick you just say, Marbelito? Grifty is with the fickin' fat-ass penguins? Fick! We're so ficked."

"No, we're not, goblin." Zaena flourishes both of her swords. "Let's end this now and move on. The Knights are waiting for us."

(0)__(0)

An idea comes to Ryuk. He goes for his marble slingshot, and places a clear marble in it. He aims at the mahoosive penguins as they charge toward them, the big motherfuckers kicking up clouds of snowy debris.

"Make them smaller," he both says and thinks at the same time.

Ryuk launches the marble at the feet of several of the gargantuan penguins just as they near the hill. Trails of algomagic whip into the air. It ensnares several of the penguins, their bodies instantly shrinking until they are back to being the size of toddlers.

A Simple Request!

Skill level up!

Skill: A Simple Request

Level Six: 1 in 5.40 chance of a request being granted.
Caveat: Only works with a clear marble.
Requirements: LUCK > 15

Ryuk tries to do the same to some of the other large penguins, but his next clear marble fails. In a twist of Tritanian bad luck, it actually adds armor to the rest of the colony, who are now protected by magical chainmail.

"Fick, Marbles, you got fickin' greedy!"

~F-F-Fick!~

"Not to worry!" FeeTwix goes with his AUS hose gun. "One de-armoring blast coming right up!" As Hiccup bashes into the penguins that Ryuk has shrunk, the Swede begins melting some of the armor of the larger ones. One of the giant penguins falls. It nearly crushes Ryuk, who is saved at the very last moment by Zaena's ghost limbs.

"Kill the trespassers!" The emperor penguin shouts. He now stands on the outskirts of the battle nursing a potion. Grifty is next to him, white powder in his furry orange paw. He shoves the powder up the penguin's rear just as the emperor shouts again. "Whoooooooo! KILL THE TRESPASSERS!"

~FICK~

-314 HP!

Critical hit!

-67 HP! -82 HP! - 45 HP! -73 HP!

Instakill!

~~Fick yeah, goblin.~~

Insta-Instakill!

Click, click, boom!

-55 HP! -172 HP!

Bang! Bang! Bang!

Critical hit!

"Aye!"

Insta-Insta-Instakill!

~Fick you, Marbles!~

The sounds of the Mitherfickers in battle are as intense as they are moronic. They would be distracting if not for the fact that Ryuk is used to them by now.

Ditching his marble slingshot, Ryuk fires molten marbles from his triggerless handgun, sideways like they do in the movies. The molten marbles sizzle and hiss as they hit the snowy slopes. They also do a ton of damage to any bird they strike. But the penguins show no signs of slowing down.

They're coming at the Mitherfickers in droves, their beaks sharp, half of them hopped up by Grifty, who always seems to find a waiting penguin-hole ready for a fistful of drugs.

Yangu.

It is time to summon the ice dragon.

Ryuk pops a gravity marble into his mouth and floats above the fight. He then moves a little further away, so he can get a vantage point of the Mitherfickers as they do their worst.

By this point, FeeTwix has equipped one of his mutant hacks, and is cutting penguins down like some sort of Antarctica butcher as he does a KFC Bell ad read. Near him, Wolf stands over a dead penguin shaking his head left and right as feathers fly in the air around him.

"Fick birds!" Hiccup has gone full goblin mode as he tries to keep a distance from Grifty, who continues to circle through the ranks of penguins creeping everyone out as he asks them if they would like to get high.

Zaena is near the center of it all, a whirlwind of blades that leaves enough misted penguin viscera in the air that everything around her has turned red. While she slices and dices, Enway maintains a position on the outskirts, the Hourglass Mage charging up for what appears to be her Arcane Tide power.

It's time.

Ryuk looks up at the sky. Just as Hiccup taught him, he puts his fingers in his mouth and whistles before shouting, "Yangu, to me!"

His whistle naturally gets the attention of Hiccup, who clobbers a penguin with the blunt side of an axe and fights his way to the space just under Ryuk. "Fick, Marbles, if you're going to whistle, put your fickin' chup into it." The goblins sticks his grubby, bloody fingers into his mouth, juts his hips out, and whistles. "Snowballs, get your fickered icy tail down here!"

Still floating, Ryuk looks up to the sky to see a hint of something blue-and-white that he knows is the sun reflecting off Yangu's scales.

"Good," Hiccup says. He turns back to the battle. "Snowballs will make this so much fickin' easier. Smart thinking, Uncle Goblin. I really don't give myself enough fickin' credit."

The dragon wastes no time in getting to work. Yangu swoops down, passing over the heads of the penguins as he unleashes a stream of ice that freezes them solid. Grifty, who sees the dragon coming, throws his hands up in the air in disgust as he fades away.

"Fick!" Hiccup says. The goblin guzzles a healing potion and wipes his mouth. "That fickin' Grifty. He's going to keep tormenting us until we, fick, I hate to say it. We need a kill squad to hunt him, or some fickin' shit.

Grifty must die. But don't count me in on that, just in case peeps are volunteering or some fickin' shit."

Yangu freezes more of the penguins. He rears up and bats his wings forward as he lets loose another blast, which creates speared icicles that kill dozens upon dozens of penguins.

Insta-Insta-Instakill!

"He's amazing," Enway says, the mage now standing near Ryuk.

"Yeah, Yangu is pretty awesome."

"Fick, Marbles, his name is Snowballs. Do I need to write that shit down for you or something? Fick!" Hiccup pegs a smaller penguin with a healing potion, killing it.

Instakill!

"Nice shot, Hiccup!"

"Yeah, yeah, Twix, you would say that." Hiccup sighs miserably and summons another potion. "Fick, after this, I'm fickin' retiring. Doneski over here. For real, you fickticks. It's been a good run, but it's time that I take my money—the rupees you promised me, Marbles, I believe it was 15%, and the royalties from all of Twixy's shit—and find myself a nice little spot in Hyperborea, hire me some fickin' fine ass Thulean nurses, and live out the rest of my fickered pathetic life in comfort getting handies on the reg, gobnapping, and my starfish bleached once a month. Fick, I still haven't told you fickers about the *Fickvengers*. I keep meaning to fickin' do that." He tosses his healing potion over to FeeTwix, who finishes it while doing an ad read for Krunkin' Kronuts. "There's a lesson to be had there, even if fickin' Fickolas Cage was in it. Fick."

"You're really going to retire after all this?" Zaena looks down at the goblin.

"Why? Do you want me to stick around or some fick?"

The Thulean glances at Ryuk, who glances to Enway.

"Um, I mean..." Ryuk can't silence the voice in his head. *Here's your chance.* But there is also another voice, one that he doesn't know how to process at the moment. Does he actually like Hiccup's company? *If so, the only way to explain it would be Stockholm Syndrome.* Ryuk settles his thoughts. "Let's just get through this battle, Hiccup. And here." Ryuk equips a healing potion and hands it to the goblin as they watch Yangu finish off what's left of the penguins. "Enjoy that."

"Fick me, Marbelito, I just fickin' might. I just fickin' might." Hiccup pops the top off the potion, the goblin instantly tearing up. "You aren't half bad, you know that? On God. Fick, look at me sobbing like a goblin whose entire extended family has just been slaughtered by another goblin. Must be the potions, the adrenaline, or the fact that this armor is making me a fickin' boujee-ass snack. Stop fickin' crying, Marbles. If this is the famous goblin play, *Ficktanic*, I'm fickin' Rose Bukkake and you're Jack Fickson. Don't forget that. *My fart will go on...*"

"What the fuck are you even saying?"

Hiccup sniffs, poots, takes a big sip from his potion, and nearly drops it as he goes for his soundboard gauntlet.

~Fick you, Marbles!~

TOKYO

CHAPTER 14:
MO' MONEY, MO' POTIONS

YANGU SPEARS TOWARD THE BATTLE below leaving a trail of ice in his wake, Ryuk steering as best he can. Enway is behind him and gripping his body tightly. While the rest of the guild uses steampacks, Wolf zips through the air in the flying harness controlled by FeeTwix. The Mitherfickers land on the outskirts of an epic fight, the likes of which Ryuk has only seen a few times in Tritania.

"It's about goddamn time," Oric says after they've landed. The Unigaean warrior has his broken buster sword with him and his electrified shield. It is clear by the look on his face that he is surprised to see Wolf flying. "How the hell did you get him to do that?"

"How the fick do you think?" Hiccup's steampack malfunctions; the goblin shoots ten feet up into the air and comes down hard on his belly, which forces out a fart that can be heard over the battle beyond. "Yoy... yoy..."

FeeTwix, who stands near the goblin, turns immediately to see Quantum explode out of the fight beyond. The famous gamer tosses a bladed frisbee into a demon. He shoulders into another demon and the two go into a clump of snow. Quantum pushes back and fires several direct shots into its face with a staple gun.

-156! -219! -321!

Critical hit!

"Did you ever know that you're my hero..." After singing these words, the Swede drops into an ad, one from EBAYmazon. "Hells yeah, people. It's your weekly EBAYmazon Pryme Day Sales Event, and you know what that means. Time to fickin' save! Need something from a manufacturer you never heard of yet looks just like the product from a manufacturer you *have* heard of? EBAYmazon has got your back! Need it in twenty minutes or less? EBAYmazon! Need it on any day of the year regardless of the time or if it's a religious holiday? EBAYmazon has a 24-hour humandroid workforce for your shopping convenience who don't believe in your God. Success! And don't forget to renew your Pryme membership for free twenty-minute drone delivery, unlimited eAWS iNet storage, access to the best video service after DisNike+ and HuluFlix, as well as free audiobook streaming on Spotifyible! Listen to all the classics, find something new, or get cozy within one of your favorite universes written by AI. Have you listened to Lord of the Rings 2 written by ChatGPTJourney in a world by JRR Tolkien? No? Here's your chance! Want to know more about Quantum Hughes? I do! How about his biography, *The Feedback Loop!* Check that out on audiobook right the fick now, narrated by the legendary Jeff Hays! It's an oldie, but a goodie. And of course, you know I gotsa do a Quantum plug. He's my hero, you're watching my stream, and we're at the point that anything fickin' goes!"

"Fick, Twixy, hurry the fick up, we've got a fight to get to."

"What else do you get for your weekly EBAYmazon Pryme Day Sales Event? I'm so glad you asked! Free prescription delivery! Ten free therapy sessions with a licensed humandroid therapist from Bettercalm! A bonus drink on your birthday from McStarbucks! A discounted TwitchTube Red subscription! A .0005% boost to your savings account through Chase Bank of America Fargo! Savings! Discounts at premium retailers such as Old Banana Navy Gap Republic, Coach Spade, Lowe's Depot, TJ Ross, and H&M Zara Stories! Fashion! Special deals at Wendy's Hut, KFC Bell, Subway Burger Queen, and Krunkin' Kronuts! Yummy! 25% off entrance fees to DisNike parks, cruises, and space adventures! To infinity and beyond! And so much more. So. Much. More! #FeeTwixRox gets you an exclusive Mitherfickers shirt. That's right, designed by the NPC who is increasingly becoming Tritania's most famous goblin, the shirt, inspired by classic metal band tees, features two winged skulls and a fickin' sword. This is the *only* way to get the limited edition Mitherfickers shirt, available in all sizes."

"All sizes? Do they have robust?" Hiccup asks, who has seemingly fallen into the spell of FeeTwix's ad read. "Fick. Wait a minute. I fickin' designed that shirt. Fick, Twixy! I better be getting my fickin' royalties."

FeeTwix grins at Hiccup. "Have you checked your bank account recently?"

"Guys, we sort of have a battle—"

"Marbles, shut the fick up, you panty-sniffing gorilla ficker." Hiccup raises his mechanical finger into the air, as if he is accessing something on his dashboard. The goblin's mouth drops. Not only does he gasp, he falls backward, as if he's having a heart attack. He lands on a snowdrift and begins twitching. Wolf goes wild, the canine barking as he rushes toward Hiccup.

Ryuk tenses his fists at his side, especially after he hears the goblin asking for a potion.

"Potion, fickin' pronto. Fick, Marbles, I'm... I'm fickin' rich. I'm rich. Fick me. Rich. Richer than Ficklon Musk. Richer than Fick Bezos, Fick Gates, and Warren Buffick. Potion, son. The best there is. Thomas-James. In my mouth. Pour it. Now."

"We don't have time for this. And we don't have that potion."

"Yes we do," FeeTwix tells Ryuk. "And I'm thinking that you're going to have to give it to him before this battle can continue."

"That's it! I cannot take this anymore." Zaena brandishes her swords. She rushes toward the battle, making a beeline for a mob of salivating demons. "Aye!" Beyond, the Knights of Non-Compos Mentis battle Drachma Killers, who are decked out in heavy-duty armor.

Oric nods, and without a word, he takes off after Zaena.

"Marbles... potion... heart attack. Too rich. Brain aneurysm. I'm too fickin' rich. Restless leg syndrome." He twitches. "Holy fick. Waited my whole life. Now. Rich. Dying."

"What did you do?" Ryuk asks FeeTwix.

The Swede shrugs. "The deposit came. I gave him his cut."

"Potion..." Hiccup lifts a shaky hand and presses one of the buttons on his soundboard gauntlet.

~Mmm, fick.~

The goblin puckers his lips and starts making kissing sounds as Wolf runs circles around him.

Ryuk finally gives in. "Fine. Fine! But after this, no more potions."

Hiccup continues staring up at the cloudy gray sky. "I'm fickin' rich, Marbles. Mo' money, mo' potions. Now, hook a fickin' goblin up."

(0)__(0)

The Mitherfickers enter the battle as only the Mitherfickers can—guns blazing, swords slicing, marbles flying, and goblins cursing. Oric jumps into the air and lands on the back of an enormous demon. He drives his broken buster sword into its shoulder, the beast crying out, saliva flying from its mouth. The monstrosity attempts to grab the Unigaean warrior and throw him off, but by this point, Oric has dropped and is now running his blade through the back of its calf.

-286 HP!

Mounted on Wolf, Hiccup surges forward and cracks a demon in the head with one of his healing potions, dislodging several sharp teeth. Unfortunately, the potion bottle isn't empty, and the liquid ends up healing the demon to some degree.

Ryuk handles this with a sword marble.

Instakill!

~Fick you, Marbles!~

Ignoring the goblin, Ryuk pops a gravity marble into his mouth to give himself a little perspective.

His Magic Eye skill presents several magical properties on the battlefield. There are the red outlines signaling enemies are near, and the yellow outlines signaling certain weapons are enchanted. Most of these enchanted weapons are wielded by the Drachma Killers as a face-off against the Knights of Non Compos Mentis in the middle of the field. But there are also green outlines in the sky above, around the portal and emanating from it. Not only that, but each of the Mitherfickers and the Knights of Non Compos Mentis have a green outline around their body, indicating friendlies.

Ryuk loads his marble gun with explosive marbles. He fires at a trio of Drachma Killers riding in on large wolves. The explosions create towering plumes of fire due to the Molotov cocktails made out of potion bottles that they have strapped to their belts.

-314 HP! -109 HP! -134 HP! -79 HP!

Instakill!

Splash Back!

Ryuk's Splash Back skill increases the odds of an Instakill and provides additional damage that lingers, especially when he uses something like an explosive or a molten marble.

After popping another gravity marble in his mouth, he moves to another group, who are so busy engaging Zaena and FeeTwix that they hardly notice Ryuk circle back to the group.

-267 HP! -289 HP!

Critical Hit!

Insta-Instakill!

Splash Back!

Skill level up!

Skill: Splash Back
Level Four: Damage increases with higher levels.
Damage: 10% if enemy is less than level 30; 6% if enemy is greater than level 30.
Odds of instakill: 10%
Requirements for instakill: LUCK > 11

Ryuk touches his chest.

How would you like to respawn?
- **A Berserker Warrior**
- **A Ballistics Mage**
- **A Dark Mage**
- **A White Mage**

Ryuk has yet to truly experiment with his Dark Mage avatar, something he will hopefully be able to do once things settle down again. If things ever settle down. That seems unlikely, he thinks as he mentally selects White Mage. He is suddenly given a pool of mana, as well as a boost to his Magic Defense.

As he lowers to the ground, Ryuk group heals, adding about 250 HP to each of the Mitherfickers' life bars. He tries to use it again and sees that it has a quick cooldown.

"Fick, I've got you, Marbles! Rich mitherficker coming through, bitches!" Seemingly against all odds, Hiccup has intuited that Ryuk needs protection while he waits for the cooldown. The goblin jumps off Wolf just as the Tagvornian canine collides with a demon. Hiccup hits the ground, rolls two times, and hops back onto his feet. "Yoy. Fick… too fickin' old for this shit. But at least I got money." He laughs. "Fick, Marbles, wait 'til I take your poor ass to the shopping mall in Jatla."

Even though he has the most HP out of everyone aside from Oric, Hiccup summons his big scutum and then quickly hides behind it so he can guzzle a potion. "Get your fickered ass over here, Marbelito," he shouts, red potion spewing from his mouth.

Ryuk hunkers down behind the scutum with Hiccup. *Only a few more seconds now,* he thinks, waiting to group heal again.

"What?"

"I didn't say anything." Ryuk looks over the edge of the large shield to see Quantum Hughes land a few feet away from them.

He summons a thick chain and yells, "Item 89!" which he wraps around one of the higher leveled demon's necks. Quantum drags the demon down. He equips a new item, a futuristic firearm that instantly draws FeeTwix's attention, even though the Swede is also busy gunning down demons.

FeeTwix: Item 108, Quantum's legendary PHASR.

Quantum: That's right, kid! You got my list memorized or something?

FeeTwix: Of course, I do. Tattooed on my heart. I listened to your biography like a hundred times. *The Feedback Loop* is my Bible.

Quantum: Yeah? That one is kind of unauthorized. Also, who the hell writes a biography in first person? I never trusted that author's work and neither should you. Speaking of which. Anyone ever wonder why the word *author* is in *unauthorized?* Just me?

Doc: Just you. Focus on the fight, Q, we've got more Killers incoming, and something is brewing in that portal.

"At least let me have a little fun. Watch this, kid," Quantum calls over to FeeTwix.

The famous gamer punches a Drachma Killer in the face so hard that the man loses a whole row of teeth. It's only after Quantum pulls his hand away that Ryuk sees Quantum is wearing a pair of brass knuckles. Quantum summons what looks like a bed of nails—*what the fuck?*—steps over the man, gently helps him to his feet, pats him on the back, and then suplexes him onto the bed of nails. The Drachma Killer falls to the side and trembles, foaming at the mouth.

Instakill!

"Holy crap that was awesome!" FeeTwix shouts. He then fires off a message in the group chat.

FeeTwix: Item 109, bed of nails with tips coated in black mamba venom.

Quantum claps his hands together. "That's right. I like you—FeeTwix, right?—I like you, FeeTwix, I really do. Let's kick some ass together. Whaddaya say?"

FeeTwix twists around and cuts a demon's head off using a modified steampunk scimitar.

Instakill!

"Babe? Can I?" he asks Zaena, who fights near him.

"Of course you can!"

FeeTwix sidehugs the Thulean and kisses her on the cheek. "Great! But before I do that, do not pass go! Do not collect two hundred dollars! Spend two hundred dollars at your weekly EBAYmazon Pryme Day Sales Event! The best way to support any economy is to spend, therefore, you must spend. Think of all the gadgets you need around the house, all the subscription benefits, all those fickin' perks. Perky perky perks! Who doesn't love perks?"

"I love perky ta-tas!"

"Not now, Hiccup! Your weekly EBAYmazon Pryme Day Sales Event is happening now—make it rain! Phew. Now that's out of the way, let's go!" FeeTwix flies forward, his steampack on his back. He narrowly misses Yangu as the ice dragon swoops in for an epic attack.

Quantum ducks. "Holy Graf Zeppelin! I forgot we could have dragons. In that case, I'd better call one of my own." A mirrored necklace appears in his hand.

+250 HP! +261 HP! +235 HP! +244 HP! +259 HP! +227 HP! +242 HP!

Ryuk finishes the next round of a group heal.

He touches his chest and becomes a warrior, now wielding Tamana's ironing board of a sword. As he swings into his next opponent, Ryuk has yet another flashback to that day that they walked in the rain to Shimokitazawa. He doesn't know how, but he feels closer to his dead friend in holding the sword. As he runs by a demon that has just been burnt to a crisp by Enway, Ryuk feels like Tamana is there.

And he goes with it. Inspired by her life, he surges into the battle with as much fury as he can muster.

This is for you, Tamana!

Ryuk cleaves into a demon several heads taller than him.

-179 HP!

He swings into another.

-258 HP!

Critical Hit!

He steps over the demon, just like Quantum just did to the Drachma Killer, and splits its skull.

Instakill!

He continues this for a hot minute until he's exhausted from slinging the big ass sword around.

Ryuk touches his chest and returns to his Ballistics Mage avatar, now with his marble shotgun courtesy of Dirty Dave. He fires shot after shot of molten and explosive marbles at an incoming mob of hellacious hellspawns, enjoying every moment of it, but also well aware of what is to come.

After all, Hajime has just messaged him.

Kodai's time is near.

(0)__(x)

Sophia catches Ryuk's attention as she zips forward, the mage dragging demons and Drachma Killers with her telekinetic powers. She tosses them back into the portal above. Ryuk then spots a blur of action, something that reminds him of the way Zaena moves as a man flashes in and out of the fight skewering enemies.

Aiden, he thinks, Ryuk impressed by how calculated the infamous Morning Assassin's attacks are. Ryuk fires at another demon that is a few levels above him.

-123 HP!

As he pulls away, the demon's head is vaporized into a fine, bloody mist.

Instakill!

Ryuk looks around to see Doc pointing a space-age laser gun at the demon. In his other hand is a custom healing potion shaped like a beer, one that's in a koozie. He lifts it to Ryuk as if to toast him and moves on, the war faun surprisingly fast considering that he's running around on a pair of hooves.

"It's happening!" FeeTwix points to Quantum, who now stands on the back of a dead demon, a mirrored necklace in his hand.

"Fick, I think…" Hiccup squints up at the sky just as a glint of something appears. "Yep, that's fickin' Mirror. Fick yeah! She's sassy, but fick, we need us a good sassy assy and hopefully not gassy dragon to teach fickin' Snowballs the ropes." He triggers Zaena's voice.

~*Fick yeah, goblin.*~

As soon as the mirrored dragon appears, Mirror joins Yangu in decimating some of the smaller demons with a wave of silvery fire. It seems like they are going to clean up shop until a trio of demons as large as some of the highest skyscrapers in Tokyo fall out of the portal. They land, crushing a horde of Drachma Killers and their own demon kind.

Rooooooooooooooar!

One of the ginormous hellspawns immediately backhands Yangu. The other grabs Mirror, who tries to bite at his hand only to be tossed to the ground.

"Ouch!" She lands with a thud directly in front of Quantum, who has just strangled a guy with what looks like piano wire. "That was entirely uncalled for!"

"Welp, so much for calling in the big guns." Quantum twists his hands to the right, killing the man with his piano wire.

Instakill!

"Hey, Doc, got any bigger guns?" he calls over to the war faun.

A message appears on their group chat.

Doc: Of course, I do. Dirty Dave has mechas from Steam.

Quantum: Hell no. Hell no, I'm not riding in one of those things again. Last time, I had to be the friggin' leg.

Doc: They are automated.

Quantum: I won't go on a rant about automation right now. Get them here!

A Drachma Killer charges toward Ryuk, the woman decked in head-to-toe armor and wielding two swords. She's ten levels higher than Ryuk, and happens to be coming at him just as he's reloading one of his marble guns. Her mouth agape, the woman is frozen just inches away from bringing her sword down courtesy of Enway's magic.

"She's all yours!" Enway shouts to Ryuk.

Ryuk pops a couple explosive marbles in her mouth and slips past her, just as Hiccup reaches him.

Instakill!

The woman's head explodes.

"Fickin' kiss of death shit, Marbles! Goddamn, that's some real fickin' *Fatality* shit right there." Hiccup is broadsided by a demon, one that takes a bite out of his crappy gold armor.

-169 HP!

"Yoy!"

He is saved by Frances Euphoria, who uses a pair of knives to fillet the demon in a blur of action.

Instakill!

"Fick, thank you, lady, whoever the fick you are!" Hiccup says as she helps him to his feet.

"Call me Frances."

"Fick, I'll call you whatever you'd like," the goblin says, clearly enchanted by her presence.

"Frances will do." She turns to Ryuk and flicks her hand open. A kunai passes just beyond his cheek. He turns to see a Drachma Killer stumbling forward, the throwing dagger now sticking out of his face.

The man falls onto his knees.

Instakill!

"Fick, Marbles, I think I'm in love," Hiccup says as Frances moves on.

"She's taken," Quantum shouts to the goblin. "Come on, Dave. Where the hell are ya?" He strikes a demon with a whip, turns, and is tackled by a Drachma Killer. Quantum quickly overpowers the man and summons a pencil, which he stabs into the Killer's eyes. "That one was for you, Frances!"

Instakill!

"Gee, thanks."

He winks at the redhead. "No problem, toots."

FeeTwix: Item 218, Beast Man's Whip. Item 387, John Wick's pencil.

Quantum: Correct! Now, how about we take this back in the USSR?

FeeTwix sings. "You don't know how lucky you are, boy. Back in the U-S!"

"Back in the U-S!" Quantum summons a kalashnikov and starts firing at demons. "Back in the U-S-S-R!"

Blat! Blat! Blat! Blat! Blat! Blat! Blat!

Insta-Insta-Instakill!

Blat! Blat! Blat! Blat! Blat! Blat! Blat!

Quantum runs past Ryuk. "Item 422, my trusty, lusty, busty Kalash. Soviet 39MM AK Type 2, 1951 issue, milled receiver, signature of Lady Death, Lyudmila Pavlichenko, on the buttstock even though this clearly wasn't her weapon of choice. God, that was a good day when Dave had this one in his shop in the Loop. A good day. A rainy day, but a good one. Huzzah!" He ends his monologue with more gunfire.

Blat! Blat! Blat! Blat! Blat! Blat! Blat!

Insta-Insta-Instakill!

Blat! Blat! Blat! Blat! Blat! Blat! Blat!

Hiccup snorts. "Did Trench Coat say buttstock? Buttstock means something else in Jatla, I'll tell you fickin' what." He stabs a demon in the neck with his toe knife.

Instakill!

~Fick!~

Quantum leaps into the air, twists, and fires more rounds.

Blat! Blat! Blat! Blat! Blat! Blat! Blat!

FeeTwix makes eye contact with Ryuk. "I want one," he mouths as some of the skyscraper-sized demons close in. The sudden sound of steam and mechanical gears shifts Ryuk's attention to the west, where three towering mechas touch down, smoke kicking up around their feet. Near them, Rocket has taken his giant Hindu God form, his eyes filled with lightning as he points at one of the larger demons. ***"Om Vishnave Namah, grant me thy power!"***

"Ah, yes. What a glorious battle."

Dirty Dave is suddenly standing next to Ryuk, the Proxima arms dealer dressed in a fancy tux like he's going to the opera. The tattoos on his neck, all of which seem alive, stretch all over the contours of his chin. His hair is slicked back and shiny, something devious about its design.

"Buddy, ol' pal, ol' stick in the mud!" Quantum joins Dirty Dave, the famous gamer now with a red visor over his eyes that looks like some Proxima tech.

FeeTwix: That's Cyclops' visor, item 207.

"For fick's sake, Twixy, get off Trench Coat's fickin' todger. Heh. Haven't used that word in a while." Hiccup domes a flying demon with his axe. "Fick off!"

Instakill!

~FICK~

Quantum and Dirty Dave shake hands. "Hold on a sec, Dave."

The arms dealer tilts his head to the right; Quantum brings his hand up to the side of his visor. He unleashes a blast of red energy that strikes a Drachma Killer that is creeping up on Frances in the back of the skull.

Instakill!

"As you were saying," Quantum tells Dirty Dave.

"Yes, things should come to a head soon."

This is all Ryuk hears after he sees four new combatants slip out of the portal.

He nearly gasps upon seeing his brother's stats.

Kodai Matsuzaki Level 99 Ballistics Mage
HP: 6920/6920
ATK: 1541
MATK: 1986
DEF: 1211
MDF: 957
LUCK: 41

How? How did Kodai level up so exponentially?

Yet again, Ryuk makes eye contact with FeeTwix, who has just fired several shots from a pink AM-17 at a demon, the Swede now wearing his half-Reaper skull. Messages flood the group chat.

Doc: Veenure's team incoming.

FeeTwix: We can't take them. Tomas is at Level 99 too.

Doc: Leave them to us. Hide as best you can. Disguises if you have them. Go out guns-a-blazing if necessary.

FeeTwix: Got it, Doc!

Sophia: Kodai is mine.

Doc: I need to get a shot in first, Dr. Wang. Then he's all yours.

Sophia: Hurry.

Doc: Ryuk. What's the update in the real world?

Ryuk ducks behind a demon carcass just as one of the largest hellspawns comes tumbling down. Mirror and Yangu fly through the air above him, providing icy-silver cover fire. Ryuk quickly switches to a different channel.

Ryuk: Hajime, are you in position?

Hajime: Almost.

He switches back to the group chat.

Ryuk: It should be any moment now. You want to join that chat?

Doc: I'm good. My dash is already full. Get to cover, and keep me updated.

"Time for the main event." Quantum fires another red beam of concentrated energy at a Drachma Killer. "I hope everyone brought popcorn!"

TOKYO

CHAPTER 15: THE FIGHT FOR TRITANIA

RYUK SWITCHES TO HIS WHITE MAGE FORM. He's certain it's one his brother won't immediately recognize. He sees that Zaena now wears a cloak, and Enway has switched to some gear that makes her look more elven. FeeTwix has changed clothing as well, the Swede dressed in assassin garb like Aiden and Rocket, yet still in his Quantum-approved Crocs.

"That's not a disguise," Ryuk tells Hiccup, who has equipped his white potato sack which he wears like a moo-moo as well as his pair of sunglasses.

"Throwing shade again, Marbles? Fick outta here. No one's going to recognize me in this drip. I'm practically a fashion icon over here, Juicy Cooter style. There are entire issues of *Goblin Vogue* devoted to me. Bet."

Upon Doc's instruction, the Mitherfickers have pushed away from the battle, the group now on the outskirts. There are still demons here, which they kill on occasion, but they are far enough away from the main theater that Ryuk is fairly certain they won't be spotted. If they are, it will be instakills all around. There is no way that they can go up against Kodai's team now that his brother and his henchmen are all at Level 99.

Ryuk isn't the only one that feels disappointment. FeeTwix paces, occasionally addresses any demons that find them, and speaks quietly to his fans. Eventually, he drops into an ad read, but Ryuk can tell that his heart isn't in it, which is a first for the Swede. "The Subway Burger Queen Labmeat Whopper is a twofer this week, two for ten dollars. Yay. So what if it's grown in the lab? It's good for the environment, and with the added pre and probiotic, it's good for your guts too. Wee. #FeeTwixRox in store or on the app gets you four chicken nuggies for free. What's that? You want some dipping sauce too? How about Honey Sriracha? Banana Ketchup Marmite? Kewpie Mayo? Huli Huli Sauce? Cilantro Jalapeño? Sweet 'n' Spicy Miso? With so many choices, you can't go wrong." He sighs. "You really can't go wrong."

"No lemon pepper? Pfft! Fick Subway Burger Queen."

"The Subway Burger Queen Labmeat Whopper is on twofer this week only. Get one for your best bud, sigother, or anyone in between." His eyes go blue. "Fick, I'm losing followers fast. They want us in the fight, the bloodthirsty bastards! There were," FeeTwix swallows hard, "ten million just a few minutes ago. Now it's dipping to the mid-nines."

"Nine million fickers? Twix, you, and everyone that tracks metrics, needs to get their fickin' shit together. That's insanely good. That's the kind of shit simps and poor ficks like Marbles here would sacrifice their left nut for. Take it from an insanely rich goblin, I'm talking Paris Fickton rich. Money can buy happiness, but tracking things endlessly and relying on metrics to run your world cannot. Can it produce order? Fick, I don't know. Actually, now that I say this out loud, I think I might be wrong. We should keep as much fickin' data as we can! We should exploit this data, fickin' sell it, and use what we've purchased to exploit more data. Our entire lives should be based on data! Why am I only thinking of this now? After 154 years—"

"You're 155 now," Ryuk reminds Hiccup. He doesn't know why he does this. It'd likely be best to keep out of this particular conversation.

"Exactly. Wait. Where's my birthday cake? That doesn't matter. Fick, I want to fight something."

"Let's just go back to killing," Zaena says. To demonstrate she means business, she runs her blades across one another, creating a cool metal sound and producing a bit of a spark.

"Fick, Liz, now you're talking!"

"We can just stay here on the outer perimeter killing demons. There must be thousands of them now. There is no way your brother will be able to find us if we are careful. If he does find us, maybe we will sacrifice the goblin."

"What the fick!?" Hiccup equips his toe knife. He takes a step closer to Zaena, who points all four of her swords at him.

"Try it, goblin."

Hiccup lowers his knife. "For fick's sake, Lizbunny, relax a little. I'm just fickin' with yah. Big Yikes. All of us are a liddle fickin' jumpy. Look at Elfie over here. Those red eyes. Fick."

The Chromatic Mage shrugs. "I'm fine."

"You would fickin' say that." Hiccup uses the toe knife to pick at something under his fingernail. A demon crawls toward them and jumps for Hiccup. The goblin stabs the hellspawn in the side of the neck multiple times.

Instakill!

"Fick, this is so boring," he says after he wipes demon blood on the front of his white potato sack. The goblin goes for yet another fucking healing potion. He takes a sip and burps. "I'm with Liztard over here. Let's get back to the fight. Maybe we can be helpful in some way."

Probably not, Ryuk thinks as he checks on Hajime. He catches a glimpse of the humandroid's feed. *Why aren't you in the building yet?*

By the time Ryuk looks up, the Mitherfickers have already moved closer to the fight. He joins them at the back. Ryuk can't fight so well in his white mage form, which FeeTwix picks up on.

"Don't worry, Ryuk," he says, his eyes black again, "I've got you." The Swede hands Ryuk a gun. "Real easy to use. Just like your marble gun but it has a trigger. Once you run out of ammo, click this, which pops the bottom out, and shove one of these inside." FeeTwix takes a step back, allowing for a cluster of magazines to fall onto the ground, which Ryuk sends to his inventory list.

"Thanks."

"Consider it a gift, buddy. That's one of my first guns, a Mossberg MC1sc 9MM. Now, let's kill something!"

With that, the Mitherfickers surge into the fight. They are back to doing what they do best, with less shenanigans than normal because they're technically supposed to be doing so incognito.

Ryuk fires his new gun several times—*bang! bang!*—and gets a few instakills. He sees that it cuts into his HP, which is something he keeps an eye on as he fires a few more shots. One demon surprises him; Ryuk ends up beating it back with the grip of his gun. The demon is finished off by Hiccup, who runs his toe knife through its stomach.

Instakill!

"That's how it is fickin' done, Marbelito. And don't start going all Second Amendment on me now that you've tasted a real weapon." Hiccup stops fighting for a second. Ryuk shoots the demon trying to grab at him.

Instakill!

"What the fick was I just saying? Second Amendment? What's the first one?"

"Freedom of Speech, Hiccup, but I'm not American. I only know that from the movies!" FeeTwix tells him.

For some reason, this puzzles the goblin. He steps aside as the Mitherfickers continue, the goblin nursing his healing potion. After dozens of demons are killed, FeeTwix points something out ahead, something that is cause for concern.

Ryuk sees a hairy orange being slipping between the ranks of demons. He instinctively aims his gun at it, which elicits a laugh from Hiccup.

"Fick, I'm over here pondering democracy and you're looking like a soon to be executed extra in the Fickvengers, Marbles!"

"Grifty spotted," FeeTwix says. "Concentrate your firepower on the demon!"

Hiccup goes as white as a green goblin can go. "Grifty is back!?"

The orange eldritch horror appears directly behind them. *"Want to get high?"* he asks, his voice quiet yet amplified in their heads.

"Fick no!" FeeTwix turns his mutant hack toward Grifty. By the time he triggers his weapon, the demon is gone.

"I'll get him next time," Enway says. "I'll slow him down, one of you kill him."

They hear maniacal laughter as Grifty flashes next to the goblin. He grabs Hiccup, kisses the goblin on the lips, and leaves behind a ring of white powder before skipping away. Grifty stops in front of the Mitherfickers and does the Funky Chicken.

"Fick... Fick!" Hiccup stumbles forward, his eyes bloodshot and wild.

"I just want to party," Grifty says, as he continues dancing, *"but your group is no fun. Maybe I'll see if the others will play. Maybe I'll bring a few friends too..."*

For some reason, Ryuk understands exactly what this means. He fires off a message to Doc.

Ryuk: Grifty is coming your way, likely with killer penguins.

Doc: Roger.

Quantum: Did you say killer penguins? What the hell?

Hiccup grins maniacally at the Mitherfickers, saliva dripping from his chin.

"Easy," FeeTwix tells the goblin, who is clearly possessed, "I don't like the way you're looking at us."

Ryuk gets an update from Hajime.

Hajime: I'm going in now.

Ryuk also realizes something else. They are much closer to the battle than they were just moments ago. Kodai and his forces are nearby. Not only that, but angry, drugged-up penguins have also appeared in the fight courtesy of Grifty.

"Kill the trespassers!"

Kodai turns to them. Ryuk's brother has spotted the goblin.

(0)__(0)

The group chat populates with more messages.

Frances Euphoria: Penguins? I don't want to kill penguins.

Quantum: *Killer* penguins, and them's the ropes, toots. I keep trying to shoot Grifty but that bastard is as fast as greased lightning! It'd be easier if there weren't a shitton of demons and penguins, not to mention Veenure's not-so-finest.

Rocket: And Drachma Killers.

Quantum: Them too.

Ryuk is less concerned about their banter and more concerned about the fact that his brother has spotted Hiccup. To make matters worse, Hiccup has turned on the Mitherfickers, the goblin currently being held back by Zaena's ghost limbs.

"Let me go, Liz! I'll fickin' kill ya!"

FeeTwix stands nearby, scrolling through messages from his fans. "What did Grifty give him? He's gone crazy. Anyone have a solution? I need you guys!"

"Fick you, Twixy!"

"Oh, that... that could work. Good call, G. Todd!" FeeTwix equips two healing potions. "Stand aside, babe. The goblin has been possessed, and I, and only I, am the Swedish shaman who must unpossess him! I am the goblin whisperer!"

"I cannot stand aside, I'm holding the goblin back!" With her other hands, Zaena fights off another penguin, which she manages to behead.

Instakill!

"Kill the trespassers!"

"Fucking penguins!" Several of the fat birds are obliterated by Enway as she lets loose a fiery pink blast of energy that kicks up charred flesh and feathers.

Insta-Insta-Instakill!

"Just let me try something—" FeeTwix steps in front of Hiccup, takes a swig of the healing potion and spits it into the goblin's face. He does so again and again until Hiccup finally loosens up to some degree and starts trying to lick the potion off his face. As soon as he does, FeeTwix surges forward and shoves the end of the potion bottle in his mouth. "Drink, my dear goblin friend, drink. Nature must heal itself. I command thee!"

What in the fuck? Ryuk thinks, but he doesn't have much time to process this visual as Kodai reaches them.

For a moment, he is certain that FeeTwix hasn't seen Ryuk's brother there, Kodai quickly approaching with a marble drawn as Zaena and Enway slaughter more demons and penguins.

But then the Swede locks eyes with Ryuk and grins, a message appearing in the group chat.

FeeTwix: Going out with a bang and bringing Hiccup with me. See you all on the other side!

Quantum: Thatta boy. Give 'em hell!

FeeTwix: It has been an honor, my friends.

"Wait—!" Ryuk shouts as a red canister of gasoline materializes into existence. It falls right in front of FeeTwix's feet.

Kodai produces a glowing marble. The marble morphs into a blade that covers his entire arm. He places his hand on FeeTwix's shoulder and he spins the Swede around, about to skewer him.

FeeTwix clicks his heels together three times.

Boom!

Not only that, *boom, boom, booooooooooooooooooooooooooosh!*

The canisters of fuel ignites, creating a giant purple-hot plume of fire that throws Kodai backward at least forty feet.

A message from Quantum appears:

Quantum: A little kablooey, huh?

FeeTwix: A little kablooey, indeed!

Quantum: Indeed!

Ryuk looks across the fight to see Quantum clap his hands together. The famous gamer summons what looks like a meat tenderizer hammer and strikes one of Kodai's henchmen in the back of the head.

-420 HP!

Critical hit!

"See that one, Frances!" he calls to the redheaded Knight.

"You're not even a stoner!"

Hajime's feed appears in the lower left-hand corner of Ryuk's vision just as he takes a step back. His brother flashes in front of him.

Ryuk instinctively raises his handgun and points it at Kodai.

"Look how weak you have become compared to me," Kodai says on the tail end of a laugh. "You still think you're going to win, don't you?"

Ryuk fires a bullet. Kodai plucks it out of the air, a skill Ryuk has never seen before. He holds on to the bullet for a moment as Zaena spins into action and tries to attack Kodai. She is thrown off her trajectory by a tackling penguin, the two spilling to the left.

Kodai tosses the bullet at the Thulean, pegging Zaena in the side of the head.

Instakill!

"You fucker!" Ryuk touches his chest and turns into a Berserker Warrior.

He transforms, Tamana's buster sword over his shoulder. Ryuk is about to swing on his brother, when Kodai produces another marble Ryuk has never seen before.

"I suppose we will see each other later," Kodai says, now staring at Ryuk over his slingshot. "You're going to like what happens next."

Ryuk is hit by the mysterious marble instead.

Scheooofooot!

His avatar reappears in the air and falls into a pile of snow.

"Where the—?"

For a second, Ryuk thinks he has been killed. But he's certain he hasn't respawned as a ghost. He staggers to his feet, wipes the cold snow out of his face, and sends Tamana's sword away. Ryuk takes his more familiar Ballistics Mage avatar.

A message from FeeTwix appears.

FeeTwix: Kodai teleported you!

A teleportation marble?

Ryuk pulls up his map to find he is somewhere in the Morla Mountains, which are northeast of the battlefield.

Hiccup: Fick me, was I high back there. That shit Grifty has just hits different. Fick. Was that Delta 8 or 9. Fick if I know. What happened?

Zaena: You tried to attack us.

Hiccup: Did I succeed?

Zaena: You wish, goblin.

Rather than skim through the banter between the two of them, Ryuk closes his eyes so he can fully focus on what is happening with Hajime. He sees him taking an elevator with several of Gintoki's men.

Ryuk: Update me.

Hajime: We took out the men in the lobby. Disrupted all feeds. We are nearing Kodai's floor now. According to the hotel schematics, we will have several doors to go through before we reach Kodai. I'm certain he doesn't know we're here yet. But he will once we reach the second door.

Ryuk focuses back on the group chat.

Ryuk: Doc, Hajime is almost in position.

Doc: Good. I've got the stuff set to seal the portal as well. Your brother is using some sort of teleportation magic. I've yet to peg him with the Golden Goosinator. The humandroid needs to do it.

Ryuk: I'm coming back to the battle.

Doc: Roger.

After telling Hajime that they're counting on him, Ryuk puts his fingers in his mouth to whistle for Yangu. "Yangu, to me!"

Nothing happens.

Hiccup: That's not how you fickin' do it, Dumblefick.

"Shut up, Hiccup." Ryuk puts all of his annoyance for the goblin into his next attempt at whistling for Yangu. *"Yangu, to me!"*

Hiccup: That's more like it, ficker!

For a moment, Ryuk doesn't think he's actually done it. But he hears something, the loud cry of a dragon.

Yangu has appeared.

(0)__(x)

The wind beats past Ryuk's face as he spirals into what is increasingly becoming the Battle for Tritania. Two of the steam mechas are still fighting, and one is down. The building-sized demons are all dead now, Dirty Dave's mechas now concentrated on some of the larger ones. Ryuk sees the green outlines of the Knights of Non Compos Mentis continuing to wage war, yet he is too high up to make out who is actually fighting who.

As they grow closer, Ryuk spots Enway on the outskirts and steers Yangu toward her. Ryuk doesn't need to say anything to simply shift in her direction. The dragon passes over a couple of flying demons that are quickly ripped to shreds by Mirror, who is still in the fight.

"It's about time you come back," Mirror says she catches up to Yangu.

Below, he sees Aiden engaging Tomas, the fast assassin swooping in with a series of strikes.

-86 HP! -75 HP! -309 HP!

Critical hit!

Ryuk pops a gravity marble into his mouth and lowers to the ground. He joins the Chromatic Mage, who has her book open, her brow furrowed as she locates the spell she has been looking for. "I can bring them back," she says, her eyes red and tinged with algomagic. "I'm Level 35 now!"

She bows her head and the book fizzles away. Enway throws her hands out, and three forms take shape, first obscured by a puff of green algomagic, then by a cloud of debris from Quantum's latest blast.

Ryuk peers into the smoke. *Is it...?*

~FICK~

"It's like a revive spell," Enway tells Ryuk before he can ask.

"We're back, baby!" FeeTwix says, his eyes suddenly black. "And to the twelve million of you just now tuning in, get your fickin' asses ready, it's fight-o-rama time!" The Swede goes for a bazooka, one that has been spray-painted with *Splatoon*-like graphics. The incoming penguins don't stand a chance as they are struck with a missile that tosses feathers, multifarious paint, and seabird guts into the air.

Insta-Insta-Instakill!

FeeTwix follows this up with a machine gun, which he shoots with one hand as he chugs a potion.

Brrrrrrat! Brrrrrrat!

Hiccup triggers FeeTwix's voice on his soundboard gauntlet as he charges toward a demon.

~~Fick you.~~

He drives his axe across the front of the seething demon's body, blood spritzing the air.

-116 HP!

Brrrrrrat! Brrrrrrat!

"Fuck you, penguins!" the Swede yells.

Brrrrrrat! Brrrrrrat!

Next to him, Zaena has turned her blendering skills up to eleven, the Thulean completely in her element as she ducks under a demon's clawed hand, comes up, and cuts into its back. She darts forward, uses her ghost limbs to take her over her next opponent, superhero-lands like the badass she is, and then eviscerates anyone around her.

Insta-Insta-Instakill!

"Holy fick!" Hiccup shouts as the demons and penguins all fall at once. "Bro, Liz is not fickin' around over here. Speaking of fratricide. Where's that fickered bitch-ass brother of yours—Fick! Marbles, look! What the fick is that?" The goblin points his mechanical finger at the sky, where Kodai is now freefalling toward the ground with a maniacal look on his face, a golden suitcase clutched tightly in his hand.

Kodai lands, and causes a wave of energy to ripple all around him. The surge of power forces everyone back and kills many of the more expendable demons and penguins. Ryuk glances back up to the portal, and as he does he sees the serpent figure watching from beyond: Veenure.

He also sees a flash of orange slip into the portal.

Grifty?

A message grabs his attention.

Doc: It's time for famous last words. This should be good.

Quantum: Should I get the popcorn yet?

Doc: Yep. It's about that time.

Quantum: Kid, I'm coming to you. You're going to like this surprise.

FeeTwix: I love surprises!

Quantum: And bogo.

FeeTwix: Who doesn't love bogo?

Ryuk's confusion collides with his digital adrenaline. *Why are they hinting at celebrating? What the hell is going on here?*

It appears that his brother has everyone's attention, Kodai giddy with excitement as he holds the gold briefcase in the air, the battle coming to a full stop.

Quantum lands. "How is your man on the inside?" he asks Ryuk. Sure enough, the famous gamer has equipped a bucket of popcorn from his inventory list. "This? This is item 44, my XXL Bucket of Cheesy Garlic Alamo Drafthouse Popcorn. Here, have some."

"I'm... fine," Ryuk says.

"I love popcorn," FeeTwix says.

Frances Euphoria lands, as does Doc, who is pointing a strange weapon at Kodai. "Update us," he tells Ryuk.

There is so much happening all at once that it takes Ryuk a few seconds to click into action. First, there's his brother, who is speaking about destroying Tritania, something wrong with his voice as if it isn't his own. Then there is the distraction of Frances and Quantum, who are now sharing the bucket of popcorn with FeeTwix and Zaena. There are also the sounds of the battle, from steam being released from the mechas' joints to some of the demons and Drachma Killers letting out their last breaths.

"Hey, snap out of it," Quantum tells Ryuk.

"Right! Sorry." Ryuk checks back in on Hajime's feed. The humandroid has reached the second door, just one more to go before Kodai.

"He's not there yet," he informs Doc.

"Just a little longer," Doc says into his cuff.

Aiden flashes into existence next to the killer faun. "What's happening, Doc?" He flicks his sword to the ground, leaving a line of crimson in the snow.

"I can't take the shot yet; we're holding off on the portal for another minute or so."

Hiccup shoulders between the two of them. "If we're eating, fick, might as well get me a bucket. Where the fick is Dirty Dave?"

"You called?" asks the infamous weapons dealer, who is suddenly standing beside the goblin.

~*Fick!*~

"You shouldn't sneak up on people like that, you'll end up scarousing one of your biggest fans. Fick. If you didn't already know, let me be the first to inform you. I'm a rich goblin now, Dave, the richliest of goblins. And I need a bucket of lemon pepper wings stat. Fickin' right the fick now before I get hangry A-F. Everyone else is eating, and I have no idea why."

Dirty Dave considers this. "You really should add some of our buckets to your list."

"Yeah? And I should be having my chalupa waxed weekly, my eyebrows plucked on the reg, a twice yearly lipo, and my stinktunnel bleached monthly, but those costs add up, I don't have healthcare, and even if I did, I've got other shit to spend my fickin' money on." Hiccup whistles and Wolf turns to them. Ryuk also sees Oric, the Unigaean warrior just in the process of finishing off a demon by slitting his throat.

Instakill!

By the time he's finished, Hiccup is eating dragon wings from a DD's bucket. "Fick, so fickin' good, thanks, Dave!" he says between bites. "I always knew you were innocent. Innocent until proven guilty, Liz."

"You shouldn't speak with your mouth full, Goblin," says Zaena, who now stands behind the goblin.

"Pfft!" Bits of meat fly out of Hiccup's mouth and onto the ground. "Fick the fick off, Liz." He takes another bite. "Fick. Wolfie. Oi! Here, you little ficker." He tosses Wolf a half-eaten wing, which the canine gladly enjoys. "Where the fick is Snowballs?" Even as Kodai continues his evil rant, Hiccup whistles for Yangu. The dragon immediately turns to them, and soon lands behind the group. Without skipping a beat, Hiccup tosses one of the dragon wings over his shoulder.

Yangu catches it and munches it down.

"Um, should I be concerned that Yangu—"

"Snowballs," Hiccup tells Enway as he goes for another wing. "The dragon behind us is Snowballs. The dragon hovering in the sky above is Mirror. Get that shit right."

"Should I be concerned that *Snowballs*, a dragon, is eating dragon wings?"

"Elfie, don't come at me with that woke ass shit, not right fickin' now." Hiccup swallows his bite and eats another. He starts to choke, but soon washes it back with a potion. He burps. "Fick. I thought one of you was going to have to give me mouth-to-mouth."

Quantum, who is still eating popcorn and half-listening to Kodai's increasingly long rant, laughs so hard that he spits some of the popcorn out of his mouth. "This goblin is friggin' hilarious!"

Hiccup finishes eating a dragon wing and spits the bone out. "Fick yeah, I am."

~Mmm, fick.~

"Shhh." Frances motions to Kodai, who is now red in the face, the man clearly pleased with what he is about to do.

Quantum yawns. "Yeah, yeah, yeah, evil villain talky talky. Come on, Frances, I thought you were better than this. You already know what he's going to say. Destroy Tritania—yada, yada, yada—didn't get enough love as a child—blah, blah, blah—burn this world to the ground and start a new revolution. Whatever. By this point, I've heard it all twice, and it wasn't good the first time." He tosses more popcorn in his mouth. "Someone poke me when it gets good."

A message appears from Hajime.

Hajime: Breaching now.

"He's breaching now," Ryuk tells Doc, who is still aiming his offworld weapon at Kodai.

"Damn, that didn't take long." Quantums sends the popcorn away and summons a monocular. "What? I want to get a good look at his face when it all happens."

Ryuk tunes back in to what his brother is saying, Kodai's voice amplified and sinister: "...And that is why, that is why you all will never be able to enjoy Tritania again!" He starts to twitch. "What's happening?" Kodai slams the suitcase against his own face and drops it to the ground. "No!"

"Ha!" Quantum laughs. "Been waiting all friggin' day for this!"

"Dr. Wang has made contact," Doc says into his cuff.

A smaller demon tries for the war faun, only to be struck by one of Frances Euphoria's kunai.

Instakill!

Kodai stumbles forward to grab the golden suitcase. He screams as he pulls it open, laughing maniacally even if his entire body is twitching. He goes white, the moment coinciding with Hajime entering Kodai's room at the hotel in the real world.

Rather than an explosion, or an implosion, or some blistering magic bolt of power coming from the portal above and ripping Tritania to shreds, a man bursts out of the suitcase.

The man, who has long flowing brown hair, wears golden armor embellished with gears and other steampunk accouterments. His handle is rimmed in gold and presents no other information.

~~**Ray Steampunk**~~

"Ray-fickin'-Steampunk!?" FeeTwix nearly falls over in shock. "He's God-Tier!"

"He's actually kind of an asshole, but I'll tell you about him later," Quantum says as Rocket finally joins them, the blue man now in his human size.

Ray Steampunk? Ryuk can't believe what he's seeing. Ray Steampunk is the creator of the Proxima Galaxy, the one who has made all this possible. From what Ryuk knows, he lives in a Proxima world known as Steam, and is quite reclusive these days.

"What'd I miss?" Rocket asks. He squints up at the sky. "Oh. Hi, Ray."

Quantum summons his cigar and takes a puff of it. He answers Rocket while clenching the cigar between his teeth. "Lemme see... bad guy tries to blow up the place with a source code bomb, about to get ball-tapped by Ray Steampunk courtesy of Soph. That's about it."

"Sorry, one of those demons bit the hell out of me." Rocket shows Quantum his mangled hand. It quickly reforms and snaps back into place. "Good as new!"

Hiccup huffs. "Fick, is that gilded ficker really Ray Steampunk? For real, for real? Ray Fickpunk is more like it. Heh! That fickwad looks almost as good in gold as me. Dude gots expensive tastes, I'll give him that, but does he have seventy thousand followers?"

"You have a hundred thousand now, Hiccup!"

"Fick yeah, I do, Twixy." The goblin equips his sunglasses. He continues to stuff more of the dragon wings into his mouth. "Fick, these are bussin, Marbles."

Bussin? Ryuk shakes his head as Ray Steampunk, who has been silent for a full minute now, finally speaks. "It has come to my attention that you have tried to purchase a source code bomb," he says, his voice amplified, yet his lips never moving. "This is a transgression I cannot overlook."

Ryuk can't quite understand what is going on with Kodai.

It appears that he is trying to log out, yet he's being forced to stay in Tritania. Hajime's feed provides more of the story, the humandroid now in Kodai's bedroom and standing right over him. Ryuk sees Tesla lying off to the side, spazzing like she's been hit by a humgun.

Hajime lifts the weapon that Evan left behind for him and fires it once. He then turns, leaving Kodai to Gintoki and his men.

"It's done," Ryuk says.

Doc lowers his gun. "Good. Seal the portal," he tells Dirty Dave.

"Ah, the moment I've been waiting for. The cat is out of the bag," Dave mumbles into the sleeve of his tuxedo. "All systems go." Turrets on all four corners of the battlefield press out of the snow, their domes splitting back to a whir of mechanical activity. "Ready when you are, Doc."

"Eh, let Ray finish his spiel." Doc summons a beer.

A Styrofoam cooler filled with beer forms on the ground in front of them. "Crack one open if you want." Quantum tosses his monocular over his shoulder. "We might be here a bit."

Ray Steampunk, his long hair flowing in the wind like he's the star of a shampoo commercial, finally gets to the point after another minute of beating around the bush: "Your punishment is one that is cruel, but it is one that is necessary. Kodai Matsuzaki, you will never be able to enjoy the Proxima galaxy again. You will be banished to the OMIB."

"Actually, that was shorter than I expected," Quantum says with more popcorn in his mouth, which he quickly washes down with beer. "Yeah, I know, Frances, I'm not supposed to talk with my mouth full."

Frances motions to Kodai. "Isn't this the moment you've been waiting for?"

"It sure as hell is!"

"Nooooo! Nooooo! Release me!" Kodai floats into the air, quickly going from screaming to pleading for his life. Ryuk turns away. He can only imagine what is going on in the real world. He's glad he doesn't know. He's aware that he will find out in the future. It doesn't bring him pleasure to see his brother suffer, but it does bring Ryuk closure.

It has been a long time coming.

Ray Steampunk brings his hand back. He flicks it toward the portal and Kodai, his henchmen, and all of the Drachma Killers and demons are sucked back into the OMIB. "Seal it," he calls down to Dirty Dave.

Ryuk's pretty sure Quantum flashes Ray Steampunk a middle finger, but if he does, it's fast. By that point, Ryuk is more focused on the ground as it starts to rumble. The four turrets all turn on the portal at once and fire, each spewing enough algomagic to make it too bright for Ryuk to see what is going on.

"Fick!"

Suddenly, the battlefield is clean, the sky is normal, the penguins are gone and Ray Steampunk has vanished alongside them. All that is left are the Mitherfickers and the Knights of Non Compos Mentis, including Sophia, who now hovers on the periphery.

"Well?" Quantum asks. "What now?"

The Mitherfickers and the Knights exchange glances. Doc takes a sip of his beer. "I didn't plan that far ahead."

"We could get drunk."

"Yes, we could," Doc tells Quantum.

FeeTwix places his arm around Hiccup's shoulder, startling the goblin. "Actually, I have a better idea. I think it's time for someone's birthday party."

Hiccup can't help himself. He plays Zaena's voice.

~~*Fick yeah, goblin.*~~

TOKYO

EPILOGUE: GORGEOUS AT THE END

SURPRISING MOST OF THE MITHERFICKERS, but seemingly none of the members of the Knights of Non Compos Mentis, it is Quantum Hughes who starts Hiccup's birthday song.

The famous gamer raises a frothy mug of beer, finishes it in one gulp, slams it on the table, clears his throat, and begins: *"Happy Fickday to you..."*

Everyone, aside from Sophia, joins in, Quantum leading the group and even conducting them. Just about the only person missing at the moment is Oric, who has logged out to have dinner with someone named Sam.

~*"Happy Fickday to you. Happy Fickday to you. Happy Fickday to Hiccup. Happy Fickday to you."*~

"And many more..." FeeTwix sings, the Swede's eyes black as a hobgoblin's soul so all his fans can join in the festivities. It took some negotiating, but Doc finally allowed FeeTwix to livestream as long as they weren't at one of the Knights' properties. This is why they're at a bar in

Athos, one that is built into a former library, the ancient tomes still lining the walls and collecting dust, the other patrons cleared out.

"Fick, I can't believe..." Hiccup smears his runny nose across his soundboard arm, triggering some of the buttons.

~Mmm, fick.~

~Fick!~

~Fick you, Marbles!~

~~Fick yeah, goblin.~~

Wolf howls.

"Fick, get over here, Wolfie. Need my emotional support pooch. Fick, you look so good in that gold collar. We need to..." He sniffs. "We need to get you one of those support dog vests just so fickers on the airships don't give us dirty looks. Marbles, write this fickin' shit down."

Near him, Spew Gorge, who also joined in the song, sits on a short stool with his arms crossed over his chest. "Quit fickin' around with the mutt, Hiccup. Let's just cut into the fickin' cake."

Hiccup wipes tears away. "Fick you, Spewy, it's my fickin' party and I'll... I'll fickin' cry if I want to!"

A message appears the Mitherfickers' private group chat.

Hiccup: What if it's not actually my birthday?

Zaena: I knew it!

FeeTwix: Too late for that kind of talk, Hiccup. Play along!

Hiccup sobs even hard. "I'm just so fickin' blessed to have a hundred thousand—it's a hundo, right Twix? Yeah? Cool—a hundred thousand fans willing to get me a cake for my 154th birthday. So fickin' blessed. I'm rich, and now I'm fickin' blessed. Does this make me Christian? Which religion would I be in your world, Twixy? I'm thinking Zoroastrian, whatever the fick that is." He wipes more snot. "154 years—"

Zaena's smile wanes. "I believe you are 155 years old, Goblin."

"Fick, Liz, you're so fickin' racist. Imagine if I..." Hiccup starts crying again. "Imagine if I fickin' walked around calling you lizard, or a slim-fit dragon bitch, or four-armed green-skinned hot-bodied Florida gator-hater. You'd finally know what it's fickin' like." He sucks back tears. "Who the fick invited you to my birthday party any-fickin-way?"

Ryuk: Stop crying. It clearly isn't your birthday. And if it was, you probably wouldn't remember anyway.

Hiccup plucks one of the potions off the DD's specialty birthday cake, pops open the cap, and takes a swig. "Fick, Marbles," he says as he drinks from the potion, the goblin still crying. "It's called fickin' Goblinheimers. Have some fickin' respect for the elderly and the disabled, you fick-cabbage."

Spew Gorge rolls his eyes. "You're such a fick-faced fickturd."

"Right? I keep saying that about Marbles, Spewy, but no one listens."

"I'm talking about you, Hiccup!"

"Fick you!"

"—Are we cutting into this thing or what?" asks Quantum, who has already summoned a hammered copper cake slicer from his list. He motions it toward the cake.

Spew Gorge throws his hands up into the air. "Fickin' cut the thing already. I've got better fickin' shit to do."

"The fick you do, Spewy!"

The cake is taller than either goblin, frosted with white cream and decorated on its tiers with Thomas-James healing potions. Not only that, but there are several buckets of barbeque dragon wings that came with it, mostly lemon pepper.

"I believe I will handle this, Mr. Hughes," says Jim the Doorman, who is suddenly standing next to Quantum with plates and a cake knife.

"Mr. Hughes was my father and my grandfather, Jim. Call me Quantum."

"Right, Mr. Quantum." Jim smiles at the famous gamer as he steps around him.

"Yeah, yeah, real cute, Jim. We'll see how cute you are next time..." Quantum trails off once Frances approaches, the graceful redhead instantly lightening his mood. Quantum whistles at the bartender. "Cid, let's get another round."

"Coming right up!"

Hiccup shoves Ryuk aside. "Gimme, gimme, gimme! Best slice, please, and get some of the fickin' icing on top there too, Alfred." He licks his lips. "Fick, I love DD's cake. Too bad the man, the myth, the legend himself, Davey Boy, couldn't fickin' be here. He's about as bad as Attila the No Fun when it comes to commitment. Logging out to meet some ficker named Sam? Conan made it sound like Sam is a fickin' lady, but how the fick am I supposed to know if that's the case or not with a name like that? Fick, Alfred, hurry up with that fickin' slice, my blood sugar is low."

The smile on Jim's face thins. "It's Jim."

"Fick, sure, Alfred, it's Jim. I can't fickin' wait until my next birthday."

"A year from now," Zaena says.

"That's usually how birthdays work," Enway adds.

"Gee? You fickin' think? They teach algebra in Guadalajara?"

"I live in Mexico City," she informs the goblin.

"What? They seriously just named the city after the country? That'd be like calling Jatla Hyperborea City. Fick me that's basic, Elfie. You get a pass for that. I feel sorry for you. I can't imagine a place without fickin' goblin culture."

"Ahem. The first slice is served," Jim says.

"Thanks, Al." Hiccup grabs the first slice and takes a huge bite of it. "Holy fick this is good! Fickin' moist as moist can moistly be," he says, chewing with his mouth open. "Moist. My fick is this moist. Marbles, want me to feed you like a bird? It'd be a fickin' honor, son."

"Fick! Get your fickin' shit together, Hiccup. That ficktwat isn't even your son!" Spew Gorge takes a plate from Jim and shoves some of the cake in his mouth with his grubby hand. "Fick you, Hiccup," he shouts, cake flying out of his mouth.

"The fick you say, Spewy!?"

Quantum's eyes go wide. "Did someone say... food fight?"

"What?" Hiccup turns to the famous gamer. He lifts his plate like he plans to hit Quantum with it. "We're not having a fickin' food fight at my fickin' birthday party, you trench-coated ficktard."

"A food fight would be great content..."

Hiccup swivels his head to the Swede, his fat jowls following. "Twixy? What the fick world are you living in where great content is better than great food? My fick, I fickin' hate the future."

"People love food content, Hiccup! They especially love watching other people waste food to make strange concoctions that they're immediately going to throw away. What a way to lowkey humble brag that you live in a world where things like food insecurity don't matter! Fick yeah! So... are we doing this, or what?" FeeTwix grabs a plate of cake, the Swede now standing directly next to Hiccup.

"What the fick!? No, we're not fickin—"

FeeTwix smashes the plate of cake into Hiccup's face.

Ryuk laughs. He laughs harder than he's laughed in a long time. He laughs so hard that he ends up bending forward to catch his breath. He's broadsided by Hiccup, the hefty, cake-covered goblin with a mechanical hand full of birthday cake which he proceeds to smash into Ryuk's face.

"Fick you, Marbles!"

"Fick you, Hiccup!" Spew Gorge takes one of the potion bottles and smashes it over the back of his father/uncle's head.

-212 HP!

Critical hit!

"Yoy!" Hiccup falls, and as he does he brings a table and some of the dragon wings with him. This somehow draws Doc into the ensuing fight, mostly because the faun doesn't have as much stability as the others due to his hooved feet.

"Doc—!" Frances calls out.

Whatever was set to happen before Doc falls grinds to a sudden halt.

FeeTwix, who has another plate of cake in hand ready to strike someone, slowly lowers it. Ryuk sees two other plates lower, which are being controlled by Zaena's ghost limbs. There's even a floating slice of cake that he's pretty sure belongs to Sophia, who isn't as merry as the others but seems to have cheered up to some degree. Wolf approaches Hiccup and starts licking his face.

"Fick," Hiccup sniffs, "you're the only friend I have, Wolfie."

Now holding a plate with a fresh slice of cake, Quantum walks over to Doc and offers him his hand.

"Thanks," Doc says.

As soon as he's up, Quantum slams the cake in Doc's face, sending the war faun back down.

"Ha!"

"Fickin' food fight!" Spew Gorge shouts.

The smaller goblin knocks Jim to the side as he jumps at the cake. He's quickly bonked across the side of the skull with one of the healing potions courtesy of Aiden. Hiccup, who has joined Wolf in trying to lick cake and dragon wing sauce off his arms, lunges for Spew Gorge. Near them, Frances pegs Quantum in the back of the head with a slice of cake on a plate.

~FICK~

Rocket joins the fray, the blue-skinned man diving directly into what is increasingly becoming a cake-filled, barbeque-sauce-laden backyard wrestling match between Spewy and Hiccup. The two portly goblins keep trying to overpower one another, but the sauce, the wings on the ground, and the cake make it hard for them to keep their balance.

Wings and hunks of cake fly. Ryuk glances at Zaena as she prepares to hit one of the goblins. Her cake goes wide once FeeTwix smears some across her face. The two fall, laughing, and adding to the cake and wing mess on the ground.

"Let them eat cake!" Enway says, her eyes flashing red.

The cake reforms into the same stack it had just been moments ago, a few of the potions missing from it.

Hiccup turns to her. "Holy fick, Elfie, you should do that shit after every fickin' meal I eat!"

Seizing on an opportunity, Ryuk grabs a stray health potion, loads it into his slingshot as best he can, and aims it at Hiccup.

Fwwit!

-268 HP!

Critical hit!

"Yoy!" Hiccup goes down, the goblin falling directly onto Doc, who is still having trouble standing. "Yooooy! What the fick was that? Fick? That you, Marbelito? Yooooy. You trying to fickin' step to me!?"

Quantum bursts out in laughter, the famous gamer now with his face covered in cake and various sauces smeared across his clothing. "Doc, I'm sorry, I... I just..." The entire cake that Enway has just repaired rises into the air.

It stops directly above Quantum and drops onto his head.

Ryuk, who was just starting to sneak up on Enway to get her with cake, catches Doc using a mechanized wristlet that has some sort of gravity device. Doc uses the device to lift what's left of the cake off Quantum and hits him again.

"Hey!" Quantum shouts. He starts laughing again as the cake strikes him again. "Assault and *cakebattery!*"

"Booooooooooo." Aiden stops using dragon wings as throwing stars and looks up at Quantum. "Puns. Boooooooo."

"You got something to say, tough guy? Do we need to take this back to The Loop or something?"

Aiden stands. "This is a classy joint, Quantum. If you got puns, take them down the street to Dakota's Pun and Grill. They have open mic night once a week."

"Yeah? What if I don't wanna? You want a piece of me or something?"

"Is that another cake pun?" Aiden cracks his knuckles. He wipes cake and sauce from his face and lifts his fists.

"I like big bundts and I cannot lie?" Quantum stands as well. He sweeps the end of his cake-stained trench coat aside and places a hand behind his back.

FeeTwix, who is currently suspended in the air by Zaena's ghost limbs, is entirely fixated on what's happening.

"Now, fellas..." Doc starts to say.

Quantum brings his hand around, the famous gamer now holding a milkshake. "Portillo's chocolate cake shake," he tells Aiden as casually as ever. "They got good hot dogs too."

"Yeah? Better than the one's at Dakota's Pun and Grill?"

"I think so. Couldn't have done it *batter* myself."

Aiden lets out a deep, agitated breath.

"What can I say?" Quantum asks. "Bake it 'til you make it."

The tension is palpable by this point and Ryuk doesn't know why. He's familiar with the members of the Knights of Non Compos Mentis, and he's heard Enway and FeeTwix discuss the tv show based on their adventures. He's even seen some of it, but it's not the freshest thing on his mind.

Luckily, a message from FeeTwix clues him in to what's happening.

FeeTwix: For over eight years, Quantum woke up in the defunct Proxima World known as Cyber Noir to Aiden trying to kill him. Eight years. Every single morning. That's why he's nicknamed Morning Assassin. If they fight. I don't even know what I'll do. I might have a Proxima-related heart episode. Are we taking bets? Anyone want to bet?

Hiccup: I'll fickin' take a bet.

"So you've got a milkshake," Aiden says cautiously.

"I do. What happens to a cow in an earthquake?"

"I'm not going to answer that question."

Quantum grins. "A milkshake."

"Boooooooo."

Quantum takes a big slurp from his shake. "It ain't bad, MA. They mix the cake in with the shake. My FDA Monitor would have a shitfit over this thing, no offense, Sophia."

"Whatever."

Quantum turns to her. "I'm serious. Nothing against Evan here. I'm just saying that any FDA Monitor wouldn't like a cake shake like this, especially one from Portillo's. This thing has to have over a thousand calories, if not," he sips from it again, "someone is lying to someone. Do you want one of these shakes?" he asks Aiden.

"I fickin' do." Hiccup swats the shake out of Quantum's hand. He guzzles it down, burps, and tosses the paper cup it came in over his shoulder. "Fick, that wasn't half bad. Did someone say something about a fickin' hotdog? I could go for a hotdog right about now."

"Fick you, Hiccup!" Spew Gorge cracks Hiccup across the back of the head with a bucket of wings.

"Yoy! What the actual fick, Spewy!?"

The tension is broken by full-belly laughs, mostly from Quantum and Aiden. The two come together, embrace, and then Quantum summons another cake from his list. "Item 435, a unicorn cake. Just for you, pal."

Aiden gladly takes the cake. He looks down at it, looks up at Quantum, and as he does the famous gamer grabs him and sends his knee up, smashing the cake into Aiden's face.

"It's on!" FeeTwix summons a lime green Swedish princess cake and throws it like a frisbee at Quantum. It strikes the famous gamer in the back of the head and sends him into the table, where he knocks some of the half-filled mugs of ale to the ground.

Others begin summoning cakes from their lists, Ryuk surprised by how many of his guildmates and the Knights travel with cakes. Everyone gets in on the action, including Enway, who drops an entire tres leches cake on Hiccup's head.

"Fick, that's good, Elfie!"

She winks at the goblin, the Chromatic Mage seconds away from being broadsided by a floating cupcake. "Next time I'll hit you with a churro."

"As long as it isn't a chalupa!"

(0)__(0)

By the time the Mitherfickers and the Knights of Non Compos Mentis are finished with their food fight, the walls and books of the bar are covered in multicolored frosting, bits of icing, chocolate chips, caramel streaks, and everything in between. It's about this point that Doc stands, the war faun with cake hanging from the end of his goatee.

"Well, I can't say I was expecting that."

Spew Gorge slips on a piece of cake. "Fick!"

"Fick, indeed." Doc wipes his hands. He looks down at his cakey fingers and licks them clean. "Now, I know we've all had a helluva day; I know that there are things all of us need to do, and at least one of us has to write a report to send to the people that pay our salaries—"

"I can write it tomorrow," Rocket says as he wipes some icing off his brow.

"Yes, you can. But you should start tonight. Now, where was I?"

"You were at the part about Grifty." Quantum steps forward, his face so covered in cake that Ryuk can't make out his features. As he speaks, bits of cake fly from his lips. "You were at the part where you tell us we're going to need to form a hit squad to go after Grifty."

"Yes, I was getting to that. It appears you jumped the gun."

"Rather jump the gun than have it jump me. I think that makes sense. Anyway, Grifty—"

"Fick!" both Spew Gorge and Hiccup say at the same time. Wolf, who is next to Hiccup, starts licking the goblin's face again.

Quantum flicks some cake to the ground. "Yeah, that guy. Grifty escaped into the OMIB. Which is fine and dandy. That's where his hairy orange ass belongs. But here's the thing. There was this bozo weapon's dealer from Steam in the OMIB at that time, a guy named Clive, and from what we can tell, Grifty has portaled to Steam with him."

"To Steam?" Ryuk asks.

"No, Marbles, to fickin' Kayi. What the fick is wrong with your well-marbled ass?"

Well-marbled ass? What the fuck? Ryuk glares at Hiccup.

Not breaking eye contact, Hiccup uses his finger to take a clump of cake off his arm. He sticks the finger in his mouth and sucks it until Ryuk finally looks away. "That's what I fickin' thought."

"Well, that was uncomfortable as a rooster in a pond," Quantum points out, which is a sentence that Ryuk can't quite wrap his head around. "But I've said it before and I'll say it again. I like the goblin."

"The goblin has a fickin' name—"

"And if it's a kill squad that's needed to go find Grifty in Steam, I volunteer..." Quantum takes a quick look around. "Definitely you," he tells FeeTwix, "you," he tells Hiccup, "and hell, you too." He points at Spew Gorge. "A few badasses and a pair of goblins. What could possibly go wrong."

"Why the fick would you take two goblins and a fickin' fick-oil salesman to some ficked-ass Proxima whatever to hunt Grifty?" asks Spew Gorge.

"Grifty is a bad hombre," Hiccup says, the goblin's teeth chattering. "He'll get you fickin' high and leave you dry. Fick, protect your starfish around that ficker. You saw what he did to the Celebs back at Dungeon Goblin—"

"For one, Grifty is a goblin demon, and I have a feeling if one of youse is there, we'll be able to find him easier," Quantum says, interrupting Hiccup. "I would ask Ray Steampunk, but he's... what do you goblins say?"

"He's a fickered trashcan fart that looks like a poofty-ass incel in his gold armor," Hiccup says. "Right, Wolfie?" The elicits another bark from Wolf.

"Yeah, something like that. Maybe Sophia could convince him to give a damn, but my guess is he'll be a pain in the ass about it if she does."

"He's only a pain in the ass because you don't treat him with respect."

"What's there to respect, Soph? Anyone acting holier-than-thou is usually shittier-than-not. Am I right, am I right, or am I right? Rocket, you can in-game if you'd like. Or you, Frances."

Frances Euphoria slowly shakes her head. "Why would I ruin your budding little bromance? I'm surprised you didn't invite Aiden."

"I didn't?" Quantum looks at Morning Assassin. "I thought that shit was implied."

"Steam?" Aiden shrugs. "I'll think about it."

"I'll definitely in-game for you," Rocket says.

"And I can livestream it, right? Because holy fickballs this would make some good content."

"Sure," Quantum tells FeeTwix, "but only if you manage to capture my good side."

"Which side is that again?"

"You'll know when you see it," Quantum tells Sophia.

"What about me?" Ryuk asks.

"Oh fick. I can't." Hiccup tries to stop himself from laughing. "I really can't, Marbelito, I really fickin' can't right now. Hella awkward, bro. I deadass need some new fickin' guildmates now that I got more money than John D. Fickefeller. Fick, Marbles. That cringe is going to rub off if I'm not fickin' careful."

Enway approaches Ryuk and hooks her arm in his. "You're going to be busy with me. I just got a ticket to Tokyo. Or, FeeTwix got one for me."

"You're damn right, I did! The Mitherfickers are rich now, and she's flying first class."

"Sure, that's the reason I didn't invite you," Quantum tells Ryuk. "Sure. Anyway. You got your main gal coming to Tokyo, and that leaves me, my protege, Rocket, my best friend—"

"I've yet to RSVP," Aiden says.

"—And a pair of deviant goblins to deal with Grifty. Sounds about right."

"Can Wolfie come?" asks Hiccup.

Quantum shrugs. "As long as he promises to piss on the first Ray Steampunk statue we come across."

Hiccup pets Wolf. "We can make that happen, boy. I'll just give you a bunch of potions beforehand. Fick, maybe I'll piss on the statue too."

Spew Gorge wrings his hands. "Deviant? Did you just call us deviant goblins? Fick you, Dick Tracy. I still didn't fickin' agree to this—"

"I want to come too." Zaena presses her shoulders back. She would look regal if not for the fact that her armor is smeared with bits of cake and barbeque sauce. "I've never been to another world, and I do not care about your sausages or the fest you will have with them."

"Fick, Liz, you really don't know what sausage fest means, do you?" Hiccup laughs and is immediately slapped on the back of his head by the Thulean.

"Oi! Careful with the fickin' hair," he tells her.

"Good. So... you, me, you, you, you, you, you, and you." Quantum shrugs. "Is that everyone?" No one says otherwise. "In that case, let's meet in the morning so we can all get a little rest and regroup, unless you got something to say, Doc?"

"I'm good." The war faun takes a look at the bar. "This is going to be an expensive clean-up."

"Eh, the Knights can write it off," Quantum assures him. "Hell, bill the FCG or even better, Ray Steampunk."

Hiccup stomps his feet into some cake. "What about my fickin' birthday party?"

"No one said it was over." Quantum motions toward some of the mess on the ground. "Dig in. There's plenty of cake to go around."

TOKYO

RYUK MATSUZAKI'S CHARACTER SHEET

*As of the end of book four. Continue on for a short story about catching the notorious Grifty!

Ryuk Matsuzaki Level 35 Ballistics Mage
HP: 1341/1341
ATK: 175
MATK: 249
DEF: 153
MDF: 110
LUCK: 28

Skill: Tonsil Shot
Level Four: 1 in 8 chance of connecting.
Damage: 48% if enemy is less than level 30; 20% if enemy is greater than level 30.
Odds of instakill: 15%
Requirements for instakill: LUCK > 10

Skill: A Simple Request
Level Six: 1 in 5.40 chance of a request being granted.
Caveat: Only works with a clear marble.
Requirements: LUCK > 15

Skill: Cherry Poppin' Daddy
Level Four: 1 in 8 chance of connecting. Enemy's backside must be exposed. Higher levels increase damage and chance for an instakill.
Damage: 61% if enemy is less than level 30; 15% if enemy is greater than level thirty.
Odds of instakill: 25%
Requirements for instakill: LUCK > 9

Skill: Extreme Focus
Level Four: Can detect approach of camouflaged/concealed/stealthed enemies and objects.
Mage bonus: Higher levels allow sleuthing and increased accuracy. Also increases magic detection range when used in tandem with Magic Eye.

Skill: Inspire Others
Level Four: By inspiring others, you induce them to follow your orders. Higher levels allow for manipulation of enemies and random strangers.
Requirements: LUCK > 20

Skill: Magic Eye
Level Five: A colored glow indicates that magical properties are present. Higher levels allow for more detail and access to the Wikipedia of arcane knowledge. A red outline signals that a hidden enemy is near. A yellow outline signals that an object is enchanted. A dark blue outline signals that necrotic magic is being used. A green outline signals that algomagic is being used. An orange outline indicates a hidden trap is present.
Requirements: Level 13 Mage, LUCK > 8.

Skill: Splash Back
Level Four: Damage increases with higher levels.
Damage: 10% if enemy is less than level 30; 6% if enemy is greater than level 30.
Odds of instakill: 10%
Requirements for instakill: LUCK > 11

Skill: Gory Headshot
Level Three: Odds of instakill increase with level.
Odds of Instakill: 60% if enemy is less than level 30; 33% if enemy is greater than level 30.
Caveat: Must be within five meters of opponent's head.

Skill: Spit Fire
Level Three: Stuff a marble in your mouth and spit it at an enemy. Higher levels allow for more control and sustained magical abilities.
Requirements: LUCK > 7

Skill: Bonding Trust
Level Two: Bonding trust creates an everlasting connection between you and another creature. Higher levels allow for direct communication between you and other animals as you instantly understand their languages and demeanors.
Requirements: There are no requirements for bonding trust. This skill is tied directly to your D-NAS, digital neuronal autoconstruct system, and based on your interaction with others up until the point at which you met the creature.

Skill: One in a Million
Level Three: Use your slingshot and any marble of your choosing to take an impossible shot. Odds of connecting increase with each point you gain in LUCK.
Requirements: Level 20 Mage, LUCK > 19.

Skill: Levitate
Level One: By placing a marble in your mouth, you can levitate for thirty seconds. Higher levels allow for longer levitation.
Requirements: Level 15 Mage, LUCK > 12.

Skill: Knights in White Satin
Level One: Call upon the Empress' guard to aid you in a battle.
Caveat: Can only be used once per day.
Requirements: Gifted by Empress Thun.

Skill: Preemptive Strike
Level One: Distract your enemies, or have your guildmates distract them and receive a fifteen percent bonus on your attack.
Requirements: Level 18 Mage, LUCK > 20.

GRIFTY MUST DIE

(A short story starring Hiccup, Quantum, Spew Gorge, FeeTwix, and hell, Zaena and Wolf too. But not Aiden aka Morning Assassin. He was busy with orc chippies.)

CHAPTER ONE: FROM TOKYO TO FICKBUSTERS

FeeTwix is happy for Ryuk. Even if he tried to hide it, it is clear just how excited Ryuk is for Enway to come to Tokyo. He is at Narita Airport now to meet her, with plans to go to Harajuku afterward in disguise.

One can never be too safe in Tokyo, especially the son of a Yakuza crimelord. This is why Ryuk has Hajime with him. FeeTwix also has a few drones monitoring the situation, and he has tapped into Hajime's feed just in case. Later, he'll have his two PAs put it all together into a sweet video.

"I guess it's just me, me, and me, and my fickin' self," FeeTwix says as he gets comfortable in his haptic response chair.

Ryuk and the Swede are staying at a new place now, another safehouse arranged by Hajime. It is a quaint affair, designed to look like an older Japanese home yet with modern features and thick, bulletproof walls. A safe place to dive.

FeeTwix pops a final Marbles donut hole into his mouth. They've gone through two boxes now, and decided the donut holes are the best, Hiccup's kronut a close second. FeeTwix has a nutritional bar nearby, one with all the ingredients—micro and otherwise—he needs for a long dive. FeeTwix goes ahead and eats the nutritional bar as well.

It's the last he has from the supply he brought from Sweden; he's certain that there is a Japanese equivalent.

Even thinking such a thing populates his iNet screen with advertisements. This reminds him that he's going to have to do reads during the next mission.

"Got to pay the bills," FeeTwix says.

He laughs at this statement. The bills are paid. The Mitherfickers are becoming a pocket-sized phenomenon, which is how everything works in the late twenty-first century. With post-internet AI and influencer-driven entertainment, people find their tribes and join them, fragmenting media in ways that still baffle traditional providers like DisNike. If you are the type of person that could lead one of those tribes, a person like FeeTwix, it is well worth your time, not to mention lucrative.

But aside from all that, aside from the endorsements and the money and how FeeTwix is now able to help his friends, what really blows his mind is the fact that he is now in a position where he has joined the ranks of his heroes, people like Quantum Hughes. To the point that he is now going to team up with him.

FeeTwix has been a fan since he'd first heard of the famous gamer, and to consider him a mentor, maybe even a friend...

"I'm afraid to die, even though I know I can't die," FeeTwix says as the Proxima logo takes shape on the inside of his NV Visor, a quote from Quantum's unauthorized biography, *The Feedback Loop*.

FeeTwix is instantly transported to Kayi.

He assumes that he is going to head straight into Enway's quaint home to find Hiccup. Instead, he notices that something has changed about her street.

Across from their guild headquarters stands a three-story goblin McMansion. It is large, white, and surprisingly modern, yet it is also gaudy in a way that FeeTwix can't quite wrap his mind around. It looks entirely out of place in an elven village of ramshackle one-story homes mostly made of wood.

"He really did it, didn't he?" FeeTwix turns on his feed. He clears his throat and channels the salesman version of himself:

"Pew-pew, pew-pew! Hey there, Mitherfickers, we are live and just about to check in on Hiccup's new crib! But before we do, EBAYmazon is having a huge home goods sale in the U S of A! Need decorations for every holiday imaginable? Have disposable income and find it important to decorate for Halloween, Thanksgiving, Christmas, New Year's, Valentine's Day, St. Patty's Day, Easter, Independence Day, any and all obscure holidays in between? Of course you do! What better way to pay homage to the lords of capitalism than to change the decor of your house every fickin' month? Need storage for that stuff? Now we're talking! EBAYmazon has large boxes, small boxes, ethically sourced boxes, compostable boxes, wooden boxes, steel boxes, little boxes on a hilltop, little boxes made of ticky-tacky—you name it, they got it! I'm guessing by now you're going to need a nice shelf to store these boxes? Those are on sale too! Furniture, side tables, backyard furniture, baby room tech, half-bath cuteness, kitchen gadgets you'll only use once—EBAYmazon has you covered! Boxes to cover tissue boxes, boxes to cover kleenex boxes boxes, laundry hampers, toilet paper dispensers, tp caddies, trash cans, signs to hang around your house that have religious phrases—EBAYmazon has it all! You can fill not one, not two, definitely not three, not four, not five, but *all* the rooms of your home with enough tchotchkes to bring you joy and keep those dopamines firing! Pew-pew, pew-pew! 10, 15, 20, 25, even 30% off! Did someone say Bogo? Holy fick, I heard Bogo! There are even some items on Bogo! People, we're talking real fickin' savings here, the kind of savings that only EBAYmazon can bring you. And don't forget EBAYmazon basics, which are knock-offs of your favorite knock-offs all designed to save you a dime. Who wants to be rich? Of course, you do! What better way to be rich than to save on clever and decorative home goods that will instantly fill your life with happiness? And what better place to spend that dime than the EBAYmazon store or app? #FeeTwixRox gets you an additional 5% off today only. Not tomorrow, not yesterday, today only, mitherfickers. And don't forget, everything on the EBAYmazon store has various payment options to make sure you get what you need right now. Buy now, pay later! You have a home, you want to decorate it, they have what you need. EBAYmazon home goods, success!"

FeeTwix brings his hand to his chin as he stares up at the rooftop of Hiccup's new home. It would be hella cool content for him to scale to the top and come smashing through the window like he's Morning Assassin. But maybe that's a bit much.

As he approaches, FeeTwix scans through some of the messages from his most loyal supporters. Some of them have been following his livestreams for years, since he was a child. It's nice to see them, the ones that are still there. It reminds FeeTwix of how far he has come in a relatively short amount of time.

He had his doubts at first.

There was a point when it was starting to appear as if FeeTwix wasn't going to be able to be the influencer he'd always dreamed of becoming. But then things started to click in a zom-pac Proxima World known as Dead City, and most of those viewers followed him over to Tritania.

Now, he stands before a goblin McMansion, one that he helped pay for, constructed for perhaps the most disturbed, cantankerous, and strangely genuine NPC ever in existence.

At least to his knowledge.

"Fickers get ready. Your hero awaits!" FeeTwix approaches the door. Rather than let himself in, he knocks.

He hears some shouting on the other side, and couple *ficks*.

Definitely Hiccup's place, he thinks as there is more rummaging on the other side of the door.

The door is finally opened by...

"No way," FeeTwix says as his eyes trace over a Thulean wearing a tight nurse outfit. She is the first pudgy Thulean he has encountered, and for a moment he wonders if she is one of the orc chippies that Hiccup has been going on about for ages. But then he sees kitchen utensils floating in the air behind her, signaling that she has ghost limbs.

Definitely Thulean.

Her orange eyes start from the top of FeeTwix's head and end at his feet before she finally looks back up at him, the woman unimpressed. "Hey. What do you want?"

"I'm here for—?"

"Uncle Goblin? Right this way. His Lordship is expecting you."

"His Lordship?"

The portly Thulean doesn't answer as she motions him in.

One of FeeTwix's fans notes that the skirt part of her nurse outfit is too short, revealing the bottom of a very dimpled, very green ass. This leads to an argument between his viewers about body positivity.

As his fans argue, FeeTwix and Hiccup's Thulean nursemaid pass a couple paintings—one he's fairly certain is a fake Fickson Pollock piece. They step under an arched doorway into a study.

Hiccup's study is a few feet deeper than the other rooms, the walls done up in wood paneling like something FeeTwix has seen in TV shows set in the 1970s. The room is sparsely decorated, but there is a bugbear rug that ties it together, and a stripper pole in the corner. FeeTwix spots a fridge near one of the leather couches with a glass door that's full of red healing potions. There's a book on the coffee table by an author named Angel Farts titled *Oh, Great, I Fell in Love with a Demon Mimic and Now I'm Going to Hell to Become a Dungeoncore Farmer*.

Other than that, the den is surprisingly sparse.

FeeTwix has a feeling that this won't last.

"...And that's what I told him," Quantum says. "I said, hey, if you ain't going to sell it to me, I'm going to take it. Them's the ropes, knucklehead."

"Did you fickin' take it?" Spew Gorge asks, Hiccup's son/cousin wide-eyed as Quantum continues.

"You're damn right, I did. Item 500, my foot-scented *Dungeon Crawler Carl* anarchist cookbook. I mean, many of the recipes are things I already know, improvised explosives and whatnot. Weirdly, some of it is in Icelandic. But getting it was no walk in the park. I had to fight a—" Quantum stops his story and looks over to FeeTwix. It is at this point that FeeTwix also notices that Zaena is in the room, her back currently to him. Quantum grins. "Well, if it isn't the man of the hour." He points a finger gun at FeeTwix and fires it. "Glad to see you, daddy-o."

Daddy-o? FeeTwix blushes.

"It's about time your Nordic tush fickin' shows up," says Hiccup, who is seated on a leather chair with his feet propped up on an ottoman. The goblin is in his potato sack, which is open enough that FeeTwix almost catches a glimpse of his nether regions.

"Hey, Hiccup! Mind covering up?"

"Yes, I fickin' mind." Hiccup shifts his legs so FeeTwix can see even more of his gobsack. "Fick, Twixy, I was starting to get fickin' worried here that Marbelito's brother came back from the dead to use your skull as a fickin' fickho—"

"So everyone is here then aside from MA, who took a rain check," Quantum hops to his feet and approaches FeeTwix. "Put'r there, kid." The handshake that follows leaves FeeTwix's hand aching after it is finished. But he doesn't say anything.

By this point, Zaena has turned to him, the Thulean princess with a wry smile on her face, a curl of orange hair hanging over her eyes.

"I thought you would never show up," she says.

"Sorry, babe. I wanted to make sure that Ryuk arrived at Narita Airport before I logged in."

"Narita Airport? Is that a place for airships?" she asks.

"What the fick else would it be for, Liz? Fickin' chalupa depository? Fick, I've heard of those places, Spewy. They'll take your chup if you aren't careful. They say they just want your clam sauce, but believe you me. Fickin' ink shadows—"

"Fick ink shadows!"

"That's right, Spewy, fickin' ink shadows run those places. Remember Barry the ink shadow? God what a ficker. Fickwitted ink shadows like that will do anything for a taste of goblin gravy." Hiccup grunts. "Which fickin' reminds me. I keep forgetting to tell you all about the Fickvengers."

"No one cares about that, Goblin."

Hiccup places his hand around his mouth to amplify his voice. "Oi, Josephine! Come in here and curse out Lizticles in Thulean."

"Remember, there is a way to censor the goblin," FeeTwix reminds his fans.

Wolf, who has his own little bed on the other side of the room, finally gets to his feet. The Tagvornian beast yawns, licks his lips, and approaches FeeTwix. The Swede places his hand on Wolf's head and looks down at his striking blue eyes.

Much to his surprise, the other Thulean enters with all the authority of someone who runs the place.

Josephine takes a hard look at Zaena, spits, and lights into her: *"Blintakh blu-rakh fornachnakh! Aye! Pizdakh mrovna fondakh!"*

She spits again and promptly leaves.

~Mmm, fick.~

Hiccup and Spew Gorge laugh after he triggers the button on his soundboard gauntlet that plays Zaena's voice.

~~Fick yeah, Goblin.~~

Hiccup continues cackling until he accidentally farts. "Fick, Spewy, it's worth the cost of having a Thulean nursemaid. I'll tell you that much."

"I stand fickin' corrected. Josephine is fickin' great."

Zaena glares at the two goblins. She places a hand on the hilt of her nearest blade, only for Quantum to interrupt what would have surely been a goblin bloodbath.

"Easy there, toots. Why do I get the feeling that we should be portaling to Steam rather than watching the Thulean slaughter the goblin?" Quantum asks. "Let's get this shitshow on the road, folks. Who has a Steam avatar?"

"I do," FeeTwix tells him.

"Boom. And the Knights will take care of the NPCs. Also boom. Rocket is our in-game; that means he'll be providing us data once we get there. Maybe a boom, I dunno. Depends on how annoying he is this time around. The last place Clive went was in Akrasia, to a tavern there in Tent City. Just in case anyone is wondering why we're going to Steam."

"Who the fick is Clive?" Spew Gorge asks Quantum.

"That's the guy that Grifty—"

"Fick!"

"—escaped with. I already told you about him."

Spew Gorge shakes his head with disdain. "That dude is ficked as fick. Grifty probably shoved a fistful of drugs up his fickin' ramboon by this point."

"Ramboon?" Quantum asks Spew Gorge. "Can't say I've heard that one before."

"Fick, Spewy, we really got to be careful," Hiccup says, his teeth chattering. "The rest of these pedobears don't get it, but I'll say it again for the dumbficks in our group—Grifty is no laughing matter. He might look like a crazy mitherficker with those fickin' googly eyes—"

"Fick those googly eyes!"

"For fickin' real, Spewy, for real, for real. On God, that ficker is fickin' cray-cray. But he's serious business."

Quantum gives the goblin a wrap-it-up signal. "Yeah, yeah, we get it. No one said anything was funny about Grifty. We will find out where Clive is, and hopefully that will lead us to Grifty and capture him. Easy-peasy. Check this out." Something begins to materialize onto the coffee table.

"Pfft! Easy-fickin'-peasy—"

"Item 39, your *Ghostbusters* proton pack," FeeTwix says once Quantum has summoned the device.

"That's right, Kid. I've got my own, and Rocket will have ones ready for all of us there. Don't forget, Grifty must die. But to kill him, we need to trap the bastard first. Then Doc and Sophia can take it from there. Now, does everyone have everything they need?"

"Ghostbusters? You mean *Fickbusters*?" Spew Gorge asks. "I can honestly say I've enjoyed all versions of that fickin' franchise."

"Sure. I like that name too. *Fickbusters*. Sure. Let's call it that."

"Wait a fickin' minute. Potions work there, right?" Hiccup asks Quantum.

"Not the ones from Tritania, no. Why would they?"

"In that case, I'd better fickin' bring some." Hiccup claps his hands together. "Josephine! Order some more Thomas-James and two cases of Cherry Apollos for the fridge in the garage. And have a fickin' salt bath ready for me when I get back, some DD's too. Fick, might as well warm up some hot wax too so I can get my landing strip and my starfish cleaned up. Speaking of wax on, wax-fickin'-off, wax up the stripper pole too, Josephine. I've got cardio to do in the morning, and that pole isn't going to wax its fickin' self."

"Will do, Your Fickered Lordship!" she calls from another room.

FeeTwix smiles. His fans are loving this.

"Ah, fick me. Fick!" Hiccup punches his hand into his open palm. "Is tonight my fickin' yoga class? It is, isn't it?" He groans. "Yeah, yeah. I guess we should fickin' cancel it. No. Keep it scheduled. Josephine!"

"Yes, Your Fickered Lordship?"

"If I'm not back for my private lesson, tell the instructor's chippie ass to wait up for me. Fick. I can at least do some fickin' pranayama. Breathe in, Hiccup, breathe out. Boyfick am I gonna need it after the fickery I'm about to get into. Stressful as fick, I'll tell you that. Especially without Marbles cheering me the fick on. Fickin' elfie and her fickin' WAP. I get it, but fick, I thought he was really going to drop the ball on that."

"If you want to watch Marbles and Elfie later, you can," FeeTwix tells Hiccup. "I'm recording their meet-up. My people will cut it together like a movie. It should be cute."

"Cute?" Hiccup and Spew Gorge exchange glances. "Fick me, that's going to be awkward as fick. I've got to watch that."

"What a fickin' poofter," Spew Gorge says. "But I'll watch anything that makes me fickin' cringe."

~FICK~

"For real, for real, Spewy. Any-fickin-hoo, you've got a room upstairs now, so you don't have to come to Steam with us if you don't fickin' want to. You can just fickin' stay here too like the antisocial snowflake that you are."

Spew Gorge scowls at the bigger goblin. "What the fick, Hiccup? We already discussed that I was coming, you ficktwat. And I'm not an antisocial snow-fick. I keep trying to invite my knitting group over, but you won't fickin' let me."

"Those poofty fickers? Fick no, Spewy. Fick. No. Especially Simba. That fickin' weretiger is the reason we aren't getting a kitten. Well, that, and I'd probably eat it."

Spew Gorge laughs. "Fick yeah, you would."

Zaena stares daggers at the pink-haired goblin.

Hiccup catches her eye just as he's about to press another button on his soundboard gauntlet. "What the fick, Liz? Eyeballing me and shit. Don't get fickin' jelly. You're a fickin' princess. You can have a servant and a private fickin' yoga instructor too if you want one. And you'd love a fickin' stripper pole. It's fickin' great for core exercises. Fick. I don't want to hear your fickin' shit today, not today, of all fickin' days. It's not my fault I'm independently wealthy."

~~*Fick you.*~~

Quantum gives Hiccup a funny look. "So... we're good here?"

"Fick yeah, we're good."

~*FICK*~

CHAPTER TWO: THE NEW DREAM TEAM IN STEAM

FeeTwix's avatar takes shape in Steam. The Swedish gamer wears a brass chest plate that is actually modified milspec armor he has purchased off-world, which pairs well with matching vambraces and brass-colored gauntlets. Various pieces of his get-up are awash in steampunk aesthetic, from gears and cogs to crisp Victorian edges. The rotary weapons on his shoulders take shape, powered by a clockwork mechanism on his back, one which whirrs into action and kicks up a cloud of smoke before settling.

"Been a while," FeeTwix tells his Steam avatar. "Been a fickin' while."

FeeTwix finally takes in their surroundings. They stand at the edge of a lush forest, the prison city of Akrasia visible in the distance.

The Swede's stats appear:

Name: Sir FeeTwix Gearfort Fajer
Class: C

Rank: 5
Title: The Copper Duke
Guild: The Mitherfickers
Health: 758
Steam Power: 64
Defense: 41
Dexterity: 19
Speed: 21
Strength: 34
Intelligence: 38
Charisma: 51
Secondary skills
Firearms Proficiency: 141
Mechanical Aptitude: 58
Stealth: 47

He turns to Quantum and sees his handle, Steamboy_889, which is outlined in gold. Quantum appears to be the only one with an actual handle, which FeeTwix knows comes from having an older avatar that has been around since the start of Steam.

"What in the fick is this shit?" Hiccup quickly becomes the center of attention as the portly goblin shifts around awkwardly in his new gear.

His head is protected by a brass helmet with goggles, one with functional steam-powered fans near the ears like Leia buns. FeeTwix assumes these will be used to keep the goblin nice and cool. This is matched by functional steam vents along his shoulders, which release little puffs of excess heat. Hiccup has brass plated shoulder guards that match a set of knee guards, an armored skirt, and as he turns, the goblin letting out a steamy little poot, FeeTwix sees that there is a grilled opening on the back of his trousers like a set of flannels.

Hiccup farts again, this one long and painful sounding. "Yoy, yoy," he groans. "Fick me."

"Holy fickin' shit, this is dope as fickin' fick." Spew Gorge is dressed in a similar way. Rather than wearing a little cap on his head, the goblin's multicolored 6x9ine hair is braided around gears.

Hiccup grunts. "You look like a fickin' fickhat, Spewy, and you know it."

"Fick off, Hiccup! You look like a fickin' golden Christmas ornament with your poofty fat ass."

"Hey!"

"Eh, not exactly what I was expecting," Zaena says as she examines her own gear.

The Thulean Princess looks fly as hell in a corset made of leather and brass, one designed to accentuate her curves. Fringe runs along her collar, all of which comes together over a glimmering jewel worn almost like a bolo tie. As FeeTwix takes her in, he also notices her thigh-high boots, ones adorned with cogs and gears. She turns and he sees all four of her swords sheathed in various locations.

"So hot," he whispers to himself.

Finally, there is Wolf, who simply wears a pair of steampunk-themed goggles. He barks as Hiccup approaches him.

"Look at your fickin' ass, Wolfie. Damn pooch. Too fickin' cute for your own good. Fick, I love that pup. More than I ever loved Marbelito or any other fickers claiming to be my son." The robust steampunk goblin summons a healing potion, one of the nice ones. He pops the top, takes a big drink from it, lets out a final squeaker, and then gives some of the potion to Wolf. "That's a good ficker. Drink up, boy."

"Save some of that shit for me, you ficker!"

"Fick off, Spewy, you're not getting any of the Thomas-James. Have all the Cherry fickin' Apollos you want, but the good stuff is mine."

"Well? Are we ready to get this little shitshow on the road?" Quantum asks.

FeeTwix double checks that he's livestreaming.

Currently, there are about nine million people watching his feed. He knows that this will increase once they kick into some action. More and more of his fans have set notifications for any time he is engaged in a fight. The most loyal viewers, weirdly enough, are turning out to be Hiccup's fans, over one hundred thousand dedicated goblin stans. They seem to watch the stream for any and all scenes in hopes that the goblin does what the goblin does best. Fickery.

A message appears from Rocket.

Rocket: Last known whereabouts of Clive are at a tavern in Tent City known as the The Brass Marchioness. You'll like this one, Q Papi. The tavern is dedicated to you.

"Dammit, Rocket, call me Quantum. You're acting like this is the good ol' days or something." Quantum ashes his cigar. He points it at the air in front of them. "And it ain't. Those days are long gone, and if we are being honest, they weren't all that great."

Rocket: What are you talking about? These are the good old days. It has been ages since I've been running in-game for the man, the myth, the doesn't-take-no-for-an-answer legend himself. And now you've got a couple up-and-coming badasses.

Quantum is about to tell Rocket something else when Hiccup starts to hover. The goblin shoots about ten feet into the air and then comes crashing down, which naturally produces more gas that mixes with the hot steam coming off his outfit. "Yoooooy!"

~FICK~

Spew Gorge laughs. "What fickin' fat ass pigeon!"

Hiccup triggers his soundboard gauntlet multiple times as he lies there on the ground in pain.

~F-F-Fick!~

~Fick you, Marbles!~

~Mmm, fick.~

~FICK~

Spew Gorge goes from amused to annoyed. "Stand your snowfruit-fickered-ass up, Hiccup."

Quantum approaches the goblin and offers him his hand. "Not so slick there, are you, Slick?"

"What the fick was that?" Hiccup slaps the famous gamer's hand away and gets to his feet of his own accord. He presses his hand into his lower back. "Yoy." Yet again, he summons a healing potion. "The boots can fickin' fly?" He kicks them off and sips from his potion. "Fick that."

Zaena can barely hide her disdain. "You idiot goblin. Those potions do not work here. Weren't you listening to the man? You will get even fatter if you keep drinking those."

"Fick, Liz, already with the fat shaming. You too, Spewy. Did you call me a fickin' pigeon just a second ago? WTF bro? I swear to fick, to Busty Gazongas and her sweet—"

"This is going to be so much fun," Quantum says, his smile slightly broken. "So much fun. And you are right, Rocket, I guess, I guess this is just like the good old days. Come on, everyone."

Rocket: I told ya, Q Bro.

Quantum shakes his head. He motions for the others to follow him as he takes a few steps into the air, where he starts hovering. While everyone else is decked out in steampunk gear, Quantum seems to have gotten a pass. He wears his normal black trench coat and dark get-up, the only thing offsetting his outfit being the spiked Crocs on his feet.

Rocket: Doc is about to hop on comms.

"I thought he had more important things to do," Quantum says as FeeTwix catches up with him.

Doc: I do have more important things to do, but I don't want you to screw this up. And someone has to keep an eye on my favorite three goblins.

"Hey, don't lump me in with these bozos."

"Bozos? Fick you, you fickin' perv," Spew Gorge shouts at Quantum. "You trench-coated buttficker!"

Quantum laughs. "Trench-coated buttficker, huh? The last guy that called me something like that, well, let's just say he ended up sleeping with the fishes at the Pier."

"Yeah? Before or after you ficked every starfish he could provide? Fick you, and fick him too!"

~Fick!~

The smaller goblin speeds ahead. He has clearly figured out how to use his hover boots, as have Zaena and FeeTwix. Still without footwear, Hiccup is mounted on wolfback, the mouthy goblin a few paces behind them, bitching as always.

"Fick, I'm ready for whatever meal hobbits eat after they've had their first breakfast."

"Second breakfast?" Quantum asks.

"Not that one."

"Elevenses?"

"Fick if I know, Trench Coat. What the fick kind of food do they got around here anyway? Gotta be something good. With all the steam, maybe they make land dragon dumplings. Mmm." He licks his big lips. "I'd eat a fickton of those. Add some lemon pepper sauce, a little HotAzzBalls..."

"You won't like the food here, believe you me. I'm going to go out on a limb here and say Steam's cuisine is not to the goblin's, um, complicated palate. Much of it is..." Quantum glowers at the sky. "Ray Steampunk is a vegan, and because of that, even though *we are in a digital make-believe world, Ray,* he has forced veganism on the entirety of Steam. Ain't that a bitch," he says, seemingly to himself.

"Ray Steamfick sounds like a real ficker," Hiccup tells Quantum.

"If you only knew."

FeeTwix jumps from smiling over at his hero to an ad read. "Who is ready to upgrade? Rejoice! GoogleFace is having a huge sale on their MetaPixel S490 NV Visors! What's the difference between the new MetaPixel S490 and the S480? Would you be surprised if I told you it wasn't a lot? What if I told you it had a slightly better processor, and it weighs .00014 ounces less than its predecessor? And guess what? With GoogleFaces Pay-it-Forward Gear Top Off program, you can send your MetaPixel S480 back and get fifty dollars off your purchase of the MetaPixel S490! Fifty big ones! Did someone say savings? I know I fickin' did."

~FICK~

Hiccup somehow manages to catch up to the Swede, the barefoot goblin tooting his way along, much to Wolf's chagrin.

"Twixy, that shit is a fickin' scam and you know it. What the fick is wrong with these companies? Why not just release something new when something new is actually available? I swear to fick it's like the boner ointment Dougbug was fickin' selling to this gnome. Fick, that's a long story, but to sum it up for the lizards and trench-coated weirdos, I saw an upgraded 2.0 ointment like a fickin' week later. Fick. And guess what?

Same shit as ever. Just upgraded packaging. It already worked before, got me nice and fickin' solid, and then I just had to have the new one because, I don't fickin' know. It fickin' sucks being so easily tricked by capitalism."

"Fick that shit," Spew Gorge says.

"Fick is right. Same shit, different fickin' packaging, and they charge more for it? Not in my Jatla, they don't!"

"Pay no attention to him," FeeTwix says with a big smile on his face. "Instead, pay attention to me! The MetaPixel S490 is everything you want in an NV Visor and more. Turn on GoogleFace daily updates to be the first to learn of the release date for the MetaPixel S490+, because who doesn't need an even faster processor? At nearly 2 percent faster than the MetaPixel S480+, this one has some serious go juice. Do not miss this special deal! #FeeTwixRox gets you a custom skin for the NV Visor. Dive into a Proxima World in style with the MetaPixel S490! Fick yeah!"

~~Fick you.~~

As soon as his spiel is over, FeeTwix checks the list of ads he is still contractually required to read on today's feed. There are dozens of them, but he plans to be logged in to the Proxima Galaxy for the rest of the day and into the night, which gives him plenty of time to read them off. He also sees that he has a message from his PAs telling him that there are some things he needs to approve.

"Later," he tells himself.

They reach the outer wall of Akrasia, where they are greeted by a trio of guards. The three are decked out in thick steampunk armor, with helmets that cover their entire faces, their eyes beady and red.

Quantum lands.

FeeTwix can tell he is about to give them hell and he can't wait.

"Just wait," he tells Zaena, who doesn't see what all the fuss is about.

"Boys, I'm going to need to see some identification," Quantum tells the three guards. "I'm here under the orders of Prime Minister of Cockwork, Brass, and Steamy Threesome Affairs, Chancellor Director General Rupert Edmun Seraphina Augustus Alexander the Third, formally of Finnegan's Bake and Stonerhelm. Now, with that in mind, it is important that I personally identify all SRTs in compliance with Title LXIX and Title CDXX of the Steam-Powered Prosthetics Licensing Act, SPPLA, of 1865, as regulated by Locus Steam Wardens and the Steamwatch Sub-Branch Cog and Gear Whisky Tango Foxtrot tasked with checking for Echo Tango Sierra, steampunk and *Raydundant* compliancies, not limited to forced veganism."

The three SRT guards look about as flabbergasted as three men that are half machines can. They exchange nervous glances.

Doc: Are you done?

Quantum shakes his head. "I'm just getting started, Doc. Take a seat. Heh." He grins at the guards. "IDs, boys."

The three begrudgingly produce identification cards, which Quantum scrutinizes, and then hands to FeeTwix to scrutinize.

"Let me see here," FeeTwix says, playing along. "I don't know about this one."

"I'd better check that one again," Quantum says as he takes the ID back from FeeTwix.

"Wait. Wait. What is the fickin' point of this?" Hiccup asks as he shoulders his way to the front. "Fick, let's fickin' go, Trench Coat. I've got a fickload of shit that I need to do tonight, and that's without mentioning my yoga class. Fickin' breathe, Hiccup. We should have brought Josephine. I can just have my starfish fickin' waxed right here and right now." A hint of confusion traces across his eyes. "Hold on, what the fick is going on here again?"

Zaena rolls her eyes. "You aren't the only one wondering that, Goblin."

"Holy ficktits, Hiccup! Did you see the big fickers in there?" Spew Gorge points at some of the prisoners beyond. "Some scary mitherfickers, if you ask me." His teeth start to chatter.

"Big fickers?" Hiccup peers around the three guards, just as a group of muscled prisoners stops by the front entrance to Akrasia. "Fick!" He grows serious after his little shriek. "Fick, Spewy, we'd better roll in there prepared." Hiccup equips his toe knife. "I'll fickin' shank a ficker if I have to. Bet." After fiddling with his chest plate for a moment, he finds a place to stick the knife for easy access.

"...Well, that about wraps it up, I guess," Quantum tells the guards, who have now produced identification papers and another set of IDs. "I'm going to go ahead and hold on to these papers and have them stamped back in Akrasia." He stuffs the paperwork into the inside of his trench coat. "You'll be receiving your fines delivered by airships."

"Fines?" one of the guards asks.

"If you don't know why you are being fined, you will when you get the mail. Now"—Quantum smiles at the three guards—"point me in the direction of Tent City. Wait? What's that? I've been here before. I can probably find it myself? Sure, I'll find it myself." And with that, the legendary gamer struts right past the guards.

Rocket: You still got it, Q.

Doc: If by 'got it' you mean he's still an asshole, yes, he still gots it. Now, quit screwing around, find Clive, and more importantly, find Grifty.

CHAPTER THREE: STREET FIGHTER

FEETWIX AND HIS MOTLEY CREW enter the Brass Marchioness to find that the place has been completely destroyed. There are no patrons, the ground is covered in bits of shattered glass, and what looks like rust-colored shit is smeared across the walls.

Zaena slips behind FeeTwix and places a hand on his back. "It appears that the commoner you are looking for isn't here."

"Gee, you fickin' think, Lizturd?" asks Hiccup as he kicks a brass mug to the side, spilling a bit of oily ale. "This shit looks about as good as some fickin' horsepiss. Smells like it too."

"What would you...?"

"Fick!"

~Fick!~

~FICK~

Both goblins react at the sudden voice of the bartender, a man with steampunk spider-like appendages. He is on the wrong side of the bar, his body twisted in ways that don't look natural: *"What would you... What would you... What would you... What would you like to drink?"* His voice fizzles out and he speaks again. *"What would you like to drink?"*

Quantum crouches in front of the bartender. "Heya, pal. Not looking so good, are we? Speaking of looking, I'm looking for a real tough guy named Clive. Any idea where I can find this jabroni? We were told he was here."

"What would you... What would you... What would you... What would you like to drink?"

A burst of steam emits from a port on the bartender's back. His eyes roll into the back of his head and come all the way back around.

"Holy fick, Spewy, that sounds just like..."

The two goblins exchanged glances.

"What are you two going on about now?" Zaena asks as Wolf slips around her. He finds a piece of what looks like charred flesh on the ground. The Tagvornian beast sniffs it, gives a lick, and starts eating the bit of meat.

"Not a bad idea, Wolfie," Hiccup says. "Not a bad idea at all, you little ficker. Hey! Don't be fickin' greedy. Save a fickin' bite for me." The irascible goblin tries to yank the roasted bit of flesh from Wolf, but the dog manages to eat it before he can. "Fickin' spoiled pooch. Fick, Wolfie. I'll remember that shit next time... what am I saying? You know I'll share a potion with you any old time, you dumbfick." Hiccup turns back to Zaena. "And as for what we are *going on about,* Liz, that fickered steam hiss sounded like a famous goblin song. Spewy, want to give these poofty fickers a taste?"

"Fick yeah, I do." Spew Gorge purses his lips together and makes a strange whistling sound. *"Schwoo-Schwi-Schwoo-Schwoo.* Ready!"

Hiccup starts rapping: "The fickin' orc chippies in Jatla go—"

"Schwoo-Schwi-Schwoo-Schwoo."

"Goblins, orclins, fickin' ficks—"

"Schwoo-Schwoo-Schwi-Schwoo."

"Starfish fickers snowflake poofty-poos—"

"Schwoo-Schwi-Schwoo-Schwoo. Schwi-Schwoo-Schwoo-Schwoo-Schwi-Schwoo, Schwoo-Schwoo—"

"Enough," Zaena groans. "That was terrible."

"The Thulean cookie is right," Quantum tells the two rapping goblins. "That's about the worst thing I've heard all day, and mind you, I had a conference call with Sophia earlier."

"How the fick, sorry, ahem, how the heck is she doing anyway?" FeeTwix asks, while simultaneously sending a message to his fans and his PAs to *find the instrumental* for this goblin track.

"Sophe? Good as she's going to be doing for the time being. Evan is almost up and running in Tritania, so that's good. Other than that, what can I say? She's her usual old—I promised myself I wouldn't say *bitchy*—her usual old *difficult* self. But that's beside the point." Quantum turns back to the bartender. "We need answers."

"Fick yeah, we do," Hiccup says.

"As for whatever happened in here, it's clear that someone blew a fuse or whatever dumb shit they have in Steam in place of world mechanics that make sense. Hell, a couple people even bought the farm considering the blood on the ground. I'm not here about that," Quantum tells the malfunctioning bartender. "And I'm not here to be a pain in the neck either. I'm just looking for a little dope, a little info, if you catch my drift, pal. Clive. He's supposed to be a regular around here. Heard of him?"

The bartender's eyes roll a couple times. *"Clive... Clive...?"*

"That ficker is ficked in the head," Spew Gorge says.

"Clive... Clive... Clive?"

Quantum looks up at the smaller goblin and nods. "You might be right there."

"Of course, I'm fickin' right, Trench Coat. For fick's sake I know a ficked up ficker when I see one."

~*Fick!*~

Quantum stands. "Rocket? Doc? You got anything that can cut into this guy's NPC D-NAS and make this a little easier? I didn't expect myself to have to put on the gumshoe hat here. I'm no sleuth, more of a vigilante."

Rocket: Coming right up, Q-Rank.

"Be right back, just need to do a little read..." FeeTwix smiles at Zaena. "Relax, babe, this will only take a moment."

While Quantum gets to hacking the bartender, the Swede slips outside the front door of the Brass Marchioness. He finds a nice place in the shade. Before he starts in, FeeTwix briefly scans the information for his next ad. He's going to need to rehearse this one.

"KFC Bell's Kung-Pao Boom-Tao Chicken Wow-Wow. KFC Bell's Kung-Pao Boom-Tao Chicken Wow-Wow," he whispers, his eyes blue for a split second. They turn black again.

FeeTwix sees a reflective surface across the street, and after stepping around a sleeping drunk in a steampunk wheelchair, FeeTwix points at himself in the reflective surface and winks:

"Hey, Mitherfickers! We're here in Akrasia doing a little *sleuth work*, as the man, the myth, the legend, the Quantum would say. But you don't care about that, you're hungry! And boy do I have an offer for you! Let me be the first to tell you about the newest offering from KFC Bell. Are you ready? Let's go! Introducing the Kung-Pao Boom-Tao Chicken Wow-Wow, which totally isn't a questionable name! Kung-Pao Boom-Tao Chicken Wow-Wow has all of the flavors of Asia wrapped into the perfect sandwich, the kind you have come to expect from KFC Bell! Start with succulent diced cabbage sourced from the Mongolian Steppe that has been turned into a savory and oh-so-umami sloppy slaw. Finish it off with KFC Bell's patented genetically engineered sesame chicken patty marinated in dark soy sauce from Sapporo and you have yourself one helluva sandwich! Did I mention a pungently delicious kimchi topping, and a side of deep fried topokki garnished with hot pepper flakes from Malaysia, or how KFC Bell's Kung-Pao Boom-Tao Chicken Wow-Wow pairs perfectly with a taro boba milk tea or a nai wong bao steamed custard bun? Did someone say secret menu? No! This is on the actual menu! Talk about a way to take a trip to Asia without having to leave the comfort of your own home *or* logging in to a Proxima Galaxy. #FeeTwixRox on the KFC Bell's app saves you 10% on your entire order. KFC Bell's Kung-Pao Boom-Tao Chicken Wow-Wow. You don't want to miss this incredible sandwich!"

~*Mmm, fick...*~

"Hiccup?" The Swede turns around to find Hiccup standing there with a healing potion in one hand, the goblin itching his gobsack with the other. "Fick me, Twixster, that sandwich sounds like fickin' garbage. If you want a good sandwich, let me give you a little recipe I invented. Actually, this fickered orc named Og Lemon invented it, but I'm the one that put that ficker through culinary school."

"Sure you did, Hiccup. I'm sure you'd enjoy KFC Bell's Kung-Pao Boom-Tao Chicken Wow-Wow. It's true perfection, and it's only available for a limited time!"

"Like fick it is. And what the fick is a Boom-Tao? Sounds like a nickname for one of Marbelito's farts. That ficker is always crop dusting us, and I, for one, am fickin' sick of it." Hiccup poots as if to illustrate his point. He motions back to the Brass Marchioness. "Your fickin' American idol seems to be getting the information he needs."

FeeTwix spots Zaena standing in the doorway and blows a kiss at her.

"For fick's sake, Twixy, get a fickin' room."

Wolf is outside now as well, the big canine sniffing something on the ground. As he continues to walk forward with his nose pressed down, he runs directly into the foot of a mahoosive Steam prisoner. The brute is a wall of solid muscle with mechanized gears over his chest and a face covered in so many scars that FeeTwix can barely make out his features. Wolf stops.

The man pulls his foot back and kicks the Tagvornian canine hard enough that Wolf yelps.

Hiccup tosses his half empty potion to the ground. "What in the actual fick!? Fick no. Hey! You! Yeah, you. No, not him. You, yes, you, the one with a fickin' face like a taint scab. You're a fickin' dead man!" The angry goblin summons his axe. "No one ficks with my pooch. No one!"

Hiccup is just about to bumrush the jacked-up steam punk when he stops dead in his tracks. Grifty, orange-haired and googly-eyed as ever, pops out from behind the ruffian.

"I was wondering when we would meet again! He-he!"

"Fick!" Hiccup's cry draws Spew Gorge's attention, just as the smaller goblin is leaving the tavern.

"Holy fickballs!" Spew Gorge goes for a crooked dagger. "Fick!"

"Fick!"

~FICK~

"Fick!"

~F-F-Fick!~

"Step aside, goblins!" FeeTwix, who has equipped a crossbow that fires a weighted net, aims it at Grifty.

The goblin eldritch horror smiles. *"Hey, guys. It's your old friend Grifty. Looks like the three of you are up for a party. I fickin' love to party. First taste is free..."* The orange demon shoves a fistful of white powder right up the beefy steambro's bottom spout, the same bruiser who kicked Wolf. The man cries out in pain at first, yet it quickly morphs into ecstasy.

"Yeeeooowwwwww-wowwwwwwww!"

His muscles bulge and ripple, veins popping along his neck, his eyes nearly popping out of their sockets. If he was shredded before, the steam goon is practically a lump of cauliflowered sinew by the time Grifty floats away.

He waves at FeeTwix and the goblins. *"See you fickers later..."*

"Not so fast, Grifty!" FeeTwix fires a net at the demon; Grifty side steps it. Zaena instinctively shifts into slice-n-dice mode as she tries to stop Grifty from getting away.

As she nears him, the Thulean is struck by an incredible punch from the drugged-up steam fuck.

~Fick!~

FeeTwix explodes toward the bruiser, looking to deliver a punch of his own now that he has equipped a modified boxing glove with the knuckles coated in adamantium.

His first hit strikes the man in the chest and does little damage. The steamed-up brawler follows up with a left hook.

Wham!

Slow motion follows, FeeTwix veering off to the side, blood flying out of his mouth before he hits the ground.

Quantum steps out of the bar.

"Now what in the hell is going on out here?" he asks, his cigar falling from his mouth. By the time it reaches the ground, Quantum has a 12-gauge shotgun in one hand, and a burlap sack full of doorknobs in the other.

The drugged-out Steam prisoner turns to him.

"Hey, you. Yeah, you. No, not you," Quantum tells Spew Gorge, who points at himself. "Not you," he tells another prisoner who happens to be on the sidelines carrying what looks to be a sack of groceries. "You. Yeah, you, the guy who keeps forgetting leg day. Hey. Don't worry about him," he says once the steamed up beefcake turns back FeeTwix. "I'm all you need to worry about right now. Are you the one out here causing all this ruckus?"

"Who the hell are you?" the man asks Quantum. He's completely unhinged now, his nose running, drool dripping from his chin.

"Who the hell am I? You know what? Hold this for me for a second."

Quantum approaches the steampunk thug and hands him his bagful of doorknobs.

Still shaking, the man looks down at them with confusion. "What am I supposed to—?"

Click-click boom!

He flies backward, only to be shot midair by Quantum.

Click-click boom!

The steamcake bruiser crashes through a bench made of brass, completely ruining it. Quantum approaches and picks up the bag of doorknobs.

He sighs. "Hold this for me," he tells Zaena, who has since joined him, the Thulean ready to engage their assailant. She gives Quantum a weird look, but ultimately takes his shotgun once he hands it to her. "Thanks. I'll make this quick."

Quantum slams the bag of doorknobs down onto the muscled prisoner.

~*Fick!*~

"Another one? Sure!" He strikes the guy again and again, until he seemingly grows tired of hitting him. He lets out a deep breath. "Hard work, ya know?" Quantum says as he winks over at FeeTwix.

"Fick him the fick up!" Hiccup approaches with his toe knife. "Let me get a stab in for Wolfie."

"I just hold on a second. I've got other plans for this bozo."

Quantum grins down at the dog abuser. He now lies on his back, bleeding profusely, his mouth open and his teeth cracked. "Please..."

Quantum equips a stick of dynamite and finds his cigar. He uses the end of his cigar to light the dynamite, which he subsequently stuffs in the guy's mouth. "You might want to take a few steps back," he tells Hiccup and Zaena.

The goblin and the Thulean do as instructed, Zaena still awkwardly holding Quantum's shotgun.

Ka-Boom!!!

The explosion that follows sends gears, bone, and brain matter into the air. All that is left in the end is a smoldering corpse. Quantum takes his shotgun back from Zaena, sends it to his inventory list, and claps his hands together. "Now, what did I miss?"

"My hero..."

"Pfft! Fick me, listen to Twixy practically Stanning over here. Shit is almost shameful. But I don't Stanshame. I get it. Any-fickin-hoo. Ugh. Fick. Fick, I don't want to say it." Hiccup turns back to Spew Gorge. "It just isn't the same."

Spew Gorge gives him a confused look. "What isn't the fickin' same, Hiccup?"

"Fick, fick! I'll just come out and fickin' say it, even though this shit is definitely going to come back to haunt me. Marbles should be here for this. Instead, he's in fickin' Tokyo playing a game of hide the weasel with Elfie."

"Ah, fick that guy."

Hiccup ignores his counterpart. "I wish I was fickin' there to monitor the two of them and give Marbles heavy petting advice. You're still keeping an eye on those poofcakes, right, Twixy?"

"I sure am," FeeTwix says. "You can watch it later."

"It better be good." Hiccup grunts, farts, snorts, farts again, checks the open flap of his britches, sighs, equips a healing potion, pops the top, and finally points a mechanical finger at Quantum. "And how the fick are we going to catch Grifty if he keeps doping mitherfickers up and then bailing like I did Spewy's mom after—"

"Fick you, Hiccup!" The smaller goblin rushes over to his father/cousin.

~Fick you, Marbles!~

Spew Gorge tries to take Hiccup's soundboard gauntlet from him. "Fick that stupid fickin' bracelet of yours—"

Hiccup cracks the smaller goblin across the head with the potion.

"Yoy! Fick, Hiccup, that fickin' hurt!"

FeeTwix gets in between the two of them. "Goblins, please, stop fighting. We have more important things to do." It gets to the point where he has to keep one hand on Hiccup's forehead and the other on Spewy's to keep them from scratching or biting one another. Zaena comes to his aid, the Thulean using her ghost limbs to drag Spew Gorge away from Hiccup.

"Whose fickin' side are you on anyway, Liz?" Hiccup shouts.

~FICK~

"Enough," Quantum says. "I can't believe I'm the one putting a stop to the shenanigans, but enough, you two, enough."

Doc: Now you understand what it is like to deal with you.

Rocket: Ooo, burn!

Quantum equips of fresh cigar and starts puffing on it. "Save the fickery—see? Two can play this game—for later. I got a little info out of the bartender, and I think it's a good place to follow up. If we go there now, we will probably catch Clive while he is still logged in."

"Clive? Who the fick is that?" Hiccup asks.

Wolf barks.

"See? Wolfie can't remember either."

Quantum answers the goblin: "Clive is the guy who brought Grifty—"

"Fick!" Spew Gorge and Hiccup shout. Both goblins look around, the pair seemingly forgetting they were just at each other's throats.

Quantum shakes his head. "I don't think I'll ever get used to that. But to answer your question—and don't interrupt me this time—Clive is the guy who brought Grifty to Steam. According to the half-dead bartender in there, Clive has a place way down south."

FeeTwix accesses his map of Steam, which appears before him slightly pixelated. "How far south? We talking Peshawar?"

"Nope. Verne Island."

"Nice, I've farmed EXP there before. There are tons of monsters and discarded robots from whatever war they keep fighting here. I never could quite figure that out."

"Same. Anyway. It looks like me and you are about to become a pair of Island Boys. First to get the face tattoo loses," Quantum tells FeeTwix.

Hiccup summons a Cherry Apollos, pulls the top out with his teeth, spits it to the ground, and takes a drink from it. Spew Gorge approaches, and he shares it with the smaller goblin as if they hadn't been trying to kill each other just a few moments ago.

"Grifty is on a fickin' island? What kind of island are we talking about here?" Spew Gorge asks.

A message from Rocket appears.

Rocket: Are there different types of islands?

"Who the fick is Rocket anyway?" Hiccup asks. "Do I know him?"

"He's the one who turned into a giant blue god and sealed portals back in Polynya," Zaena says. "You were there."

"Like fick I was, Liz." A confused look traces across Hiccup's face. "Wait. I was."

"You were."

"You're fickin' sure?"

"I'm sure."

"But are you fickin' sure?"

Spew Gorge scowls. "She's fickin' sure, Hiccup. Stop hogging the fickin' potion."

Hiccup drinks some of the potion, swishes it around in his mouth, spits it back into the bottle, and hands it to his counterpart. "Get ficked, Spewy. And fick me, I must have been high that day. I don't remember a big blue ficker at all. Speaking of which, Spewy, you bring any Wiz?"

"Hiccup, you can't keep bumming off my fickin' supply."

"Wiz?" Quantum pinches the bridge of his nose. "No drugs, goblins. That's the last thing we need here in Steam. Besides that, we don't want to offend His Holiness, Ray 'I'm a useless RPC' Steampunk. Anyway, to answer your question, Verne Island is a heavily forested island, if that means anything to you. We're going to have to find Clive there. If we find Clive, we'll find Grifty."

"Fick!" both goblins yell.

"The fickin' ficktwat was just fickin' here." Spew Gorge's nostrils flare wide. "I can still smell him. Why don't we look around this steamed up fickhole instead?"

Quantum runs his hand across his beard stubble. "It is a fickhole, Akrasia. But nah. I think Clive and Grifty got something going on down south."

"You mean they're fickin' banging each other?" Spew Gorge laughs. "What a bunch of fickin poofty fick-n-boots."

~Mmm, fick...~

"Nah, not that kind of operation," Quantum tells the goblins. "Clive was a protege of Dirty Dave. I believe he may be trying to set up some sort of drug ring here in Steam, which I'm sure Ray Steampunk would be interested in stopping. But no, he'd rather watch from afar as always, leaving the dirty work to the professionals. Sorry, I digress. I have a history with that bastard. Where was I?"

"Fick if I know," Hiccup says, "but if you are beefing with some ficker named Ray Steamfick, so am I. Fick you, Ray!"

"Heh. That's the kind of goblin spirit I can get behind." Quantum ashes his cigar. "We get Clive, and we get Grifty. Or we get Grifty, and we get Clive. Either way, these bozos are going down once and for all."

Hiccup triggers Zaena's voice.

~~Fick yeah, goblin.~~

GRIFTY MUST DIE

CHAPTER FOUR: VERNE ISLAND GRINDING WITH SIR CHARLES WARREN

FEETWIX NEVER KNOWS what to expect in a Proxima world, but being attacked by child-sized parrots with handles that read Squawkzilla just as they reach Verne Island is definitely something out of the blue. The Squawkzillas are violent little fuckers, with sharp beaks, angry eyes, and tail feathers the color of Froot Loops and Fruity Pebbles.

Squawk!

Squawk!

The splashes of color remind the Swede of another thing. Steam doesn't have the same rapid-fire JRPG-inspired prompts as Tritania, and he doesn't like it.

As FeeTwix starts beating away the pissed off murder-birds with a barbed wire baseball bat, he messages his team back in the real world.

FeeTwix: Guys, I need some Instakills.

Geneva: Instakills?

Kristen: He means the prompts.

Geneva: Oh! I was wondering why things weren't as dynamic.

Kristen: I'll ask the core group. I'm sure there's a mod.

~Fick!~

Squawk!

~Fick you, Marbles!~

"Instakill!" FeeTwix says in his deepest voice as another bird comes his way. "Anything?" he asks his team. "I need some fickin' Instakills over here!"

Kristen: Yep. There's a mod for that. Hold on. Setting it now.

FeeTwix: Thanks, ladies!

FeeTwix swings his bat into one of the birds just as it jumps for him.

Instakill!

"Ah, that's the good stuff!"

~F-F-Fick!~

Squawk!

"Fick these birdy ficks!" Spew Gorge shouts as he cracks one across the face with a huge hammer.

-69 HP!

Critical hit!

~FICK~

Squawk!

FeeTwix pops an incoming parrot with a Kimber R7 Mako that he has tucked in the back of his belt.

Bang!

Instakill!

It falls to the side, but not before letting out one last painful death cry.

Squuuuu... aaaaw...kkk...

"Fick 'em to hell, Twixy! This! Is! Jatla!"

~FICK~

"No, it fickin' isn't, you poofty fat fick!"

"Fick you say, Spewy?"

One of the birds comes right at Hiccup. He nearly cuts it in half with his great axe.

Instakill!

Zaena whirrs through several of the birds, the Thulean zipping right past Hiccup.

-34 HP! - 25 HP! - 41 HP! -69 HP!

Critical hit!

Squawk!

Squawk!

~F-F-Fick!~

"Save some for me, Liztard!"

"Try to keep up, goblin!"

~Fick you.~

It's like clockwork. The action picks up and FeeTwix's views skyrocket. Earlier, when they were snooping around in Akrasia, he was averaging somewhere in the eight millions. As soon as he starts killing some oversized parrots, his audience balloons to eleven million.

That's right, fickers, he thinks. *Let's take this to the next level!*

Quantum remains a scene stealer, the showstopper of showstoppers, the famous gamer using everything from a pot of piping hot coffee to a VCR to beat the living shit out of the Squawkzillas. He manages to duck, roll, and come up with a Christmas 2000 Furby, which he chucks at one of the mahoosive parrots.

Instakill!

"Fick yeah, Trench Coat!" Spew Gorge shouts.

To confuse the birds, Quantum equips a pair of life-size Mary-Kate and Ashley Olsen love dolls. He tosses them into the shrubbery. Several of the dumb birds turn to the love dolls and jump toward what they assume are new opponents.

"You got it, dude!" Quantum places his hands behind his head, offers FeeTwix's viewers a shit-eating grin, and begins firing at the killer parrots with his crotch gun.

Rat-tat-tat-tat! Rat-tat-tat-tat!

Squawk! Squawk!

Rat-tat-tat-tat! Rat-tat-tat-tat!

Insta-Insta-Instakill!

Rat-tat-tat-tat! Rat-tat-tat-tat!

Squu...uaaaa... wk!

"What sort of contraption is that?" Zaena asks FeeTwix as she finishes off one of the last parrots. The Thulean sheathes her swords and blows a strand of orange hair out of her face.

"That? Easy. That's item 447, Quantum's *From Dusk Til Dawn* crotch gun."

"More like a fickin' chalupa gun!" Hiccup shouts over to them.

Zaena smiles fondly at the Swede as she cuts a bird's head off.

Instakill!

"It is both pathetic and cute that you know every one of the items that this terrible man keeps in his inventory list."

"Terrible? Come on, babe. He's not that bad."

"Fick birds, and especially, most especially, fick fickin' penguins." Hiccup drives his axe down into the head of a bird that's already dead and cuts its beak off. "Wait a minute. Wait a fickin' minute!"

~Fick you, Marbles!~

Hiccup's eyes fill with delight. "Spewy, get your fickered ass over here and help me collect the beaks. Fick me, why didn't I figure this out earlier? These fickers will be worth a fortune." He grabs the beak and examines it. "Fick yeah. Fick the fick yeah. These may be worth even more than the fickin' demon chups I sold in Kayi to that fickered mage."

"What the fick is up, Hiccup?" Spew Gorge asks, the smaller goblin now resting his big mallet across his shoulders.

"Keep up, Spewy." He shows the smaller goblin the beak. "See this shit here? We can grind the beaks up and sell them as fickin' boner pills to Thuleans. Or maybe we can sell them as aphrodisiacs to those stupid fickin' elves in Kayi. Fick, if we dye them, we could maybe pass them off as Wiz, or hawk them to those dumb fickers who head south to Krikaya for BBLs and booty injections. What I'm trying to say here, Spewy, is we could definitely make some supplements from this fickin' shit. And get even richer."

Spew Gorge nods, clearly impressed. "Fickin' good idea, Hiccup. And we split the profits?"

"Normally, I'm more of a 'I get ninety percent and you get ten percent' kind of goblin. But you know what—?"

Squu...uaaaa... wk!

Spew Gorge smashes his hammer down onto the head of one of the birds, and manages to preserve its beak.

Instakill!

"—We can go halfsies. And I know it's a fickin' good idea, Spewy. Now, get some fickin' beaks."

"What the hell is wrong with you?" Zaena asks the steampunk goblin. She pops Hiccup on the back of the skull with one of her ghost limbs, which releases a puff of steam from his headgear.

"Yoy!" He turns to her and scowls. "What the fick, Liz? Where the fick did that come from?"

Zaena flicks some of the blood on her blades to the ground. "Why are you harvesting beaks?"

"Why am I harvesting beaks? I'm harvesting fickin' beaks because I'm a fickin' businessman doing business things. Fickin' duh, Liz."

"You're already rich."

"What the fick else are rich people supposed to do? Connect the fickin' dots, you hotbodied Thulean dotard. Spewy and I are working toward fickin' generational wealth here. It's not fickin' hard to understand. Step One—*get rich or die trying,* just like Fickty Cent said. Step Two—get richer, and then make it hard for other people to get rich through a variety of backdoor investments; offshore fickery; tax loopholes; freeports; making sure the poor remain uneducated; vitamin supplement schemes; lobbying; narcotics; writing a political memoir with a jingoistic title like *The Courage to be a Ficker* or *Give Me Fickery or Give Me Death* that appeals to the lowest common denominator; and finally, starting fake charities that you can use to launder money."

"You're an idiot."

"I'm an idiot?" Hiccup farts in defiance. "I'm the smartest fickin' goblin this side of the Bawa Outpost. You don't need to read some fickin' dumbass book about rich dads and poor dads by some ficktarded fick-for-brains orclin weirdo to understand this shit. I'll simplify it for you, Liz: Spewy and Uncle Goblin are on Step Two. With these parrot beaks, we can hit vitamin supplement schemes and narcotics in one fickin' go-around, use that to get into politics via lobbying and perhaps a ghostwritten memoir—I know a desperate writer named Harmon Cooper who'd love to pen that shit—*then* buy art to store at various freeports in

Polynya and Ultima Thule. I got a guy who can get us some of Ficksy's newest paintings. From that point, we shift into effective altruism, the biggest fickin' scam there is." Hiccup taps his mechanical finger against his temple. "Work smart, not hard, Liz-poo. And stop fickin' disembiggening me. Shit is getting fickin' old."

She rolls her eyes.

"The goblin isn't wrong," Quantum says, who has been listening to the entire argument. "Those beaks will be worth a fortune in Tritania, embiggened or disembiggened. Go ahead and get them."

"Fick yeah!" Hiccup flips Zaena off with both hands and goes to work.

"You'll lose those fingers one day, goblin. And I know just where to hide them."

"Fick me, Liz, that's sadistic as fick." Hiccup brings his axe down onto the head of another oversized parrot. "But I kind of like it…"

~*Mmm, fick…*~

Quantum places his hands on his hips as he watches the goblins collect beaks. Near them, Wolf has already started to eat one of the parrots.

"Save some of the good meat for me, Wolfie," Hiccup says. "This shit will taste better than fickin' dragon wings with the right sauce. Bet."

"Fick yeah, it will," Spew Gorge calls over to Hiccup. "Let's get some fickin' meat too."

"Good call, Spewy—"

"Just beaks," Quantum says as he equips his famous Bowie knife and begins helping them. "This is a sidequest, boys, one that is totally worth it and one we don't have time for."

~*FICK*~

After a quick ad read for Chase Bank of America Fargo, FeeTwix approaches Zaena and slips an arm around her waist. "Don't let them get to you, babe."

The glare on her face softens. "I've been doing pretty good so far."

"You really have. All my fans are saying that."

"You and your fans," she says, but by her tone he can tell she's flattered.

Quantum cuts a beak, tosses it to Spew Gorge, wipes his brow with the sleeve of his trench coat, and glances up at the foliage above. "Rocket—can you give us a path to follow or something? As much as I'd like to put on Dora the Explorer backpack, item 359, I've got places to go and goblin demons to capture. It's probably best if we get this show on the road."

Rocket: I'd say just head the same way you're already going, Q Dawg. You seem to be pretty good at sniffing out the right direction.

Quantum brings his hand to his chin and squints toward the distance. "Sniffing out the right direction, huh? You know what? Yeah. Fine. I got a solution for this. Unless your pooch has a good nose on him?" Quantum asks Hiccup.

The goblin looks up from the parrot he is currently slaughtering. "Wolfie? He's a good sniffer, especially if there is some lady chup in the fickin' vicinity. Ficker can smell that at least a kilometer or two out. But if we're being fickin' honest, he's more of an attack pooch. Isn't that right, you little ficker?" Wolf approaches Hiccup and licks his face. "Fick yeah, you are, you little fickin' stinker."

"Sweet." Quantum lifts a finger. "I've been wanting to summon this little pup forever. I present to you—"

"Item 116, your bloodhound named Sir Charles Warren?" FeeTwix asks. The grin on Quantum's face thins. "You sort of took the wind out of my sails there, Kid."

"Sorry!"

"Anyway, here's Sir Charles." A bloodhound appears out of thin air and drops onto the ground. Wolf looks up, but ultimately goes back to watching Hiccup cut beaks.

Sir Charles is an older dog, with brown fur and a droopy face. Quantum approaches him and places a hand on his head. "Charles."

"Quantum," the dog says.

"He can fickin' talk?" FeeTwix exchanges glances with Zaena. "He can talk!"

"Don't listen to that ficker, Wolfie. It doesn't matter if you can't talk. In fact, I like you because you can't fickin' talk," Hiccup tells the Tagvornian beast.

Quantum pulls a napkin out of his pocket. "We're looking for someone, Chuckie, old pal, old stick-in-the-mud. I got this from the bartender back in Akrasia. Think you can find this bozo?"

Sir Charles takes one sniff of the napkin and grunts. "It will be my pleasure."

GRIFTY MUST DIE

CHAPTER FIVE: THE LEGEND OF THE FICKVENGERS

SIR CHARLES WARREN THE BLOODHOUND doesn't say much as he leads them through the forest, his nose constantly on the ground.

"...I didn't have a lot of options, so I settled on Sir Charles Warren," Quantum says, continuing the discussion he's been having with Spew Gorge. "Eh, the good names were pretty much taken—Pluto, Bruno, Trusty, Ladybird, Hubert, Duke, Copper. You get the picture."

"No I fickin' don't, Trench Coat, but I like the name Sir Charles," Spew Gorge says. "Who the fick is Sir Charles Warren anyway? Named after someone from your fickin' world, right?"

"Yes, from my, ahem, fickin' world. An officer in the British Royal Engineers, later the police chief in London during the Jack the Ripper murders."

"Fick!" Spew Gorge says. "I've heard of Jack the Ficker. There's a ripper too?"

"Same difference, I'm guessing."

"Did yours go around stabbing orc chippies for no fickin' reason what-so-fickin'-ever?"

"Like I said, same difference."

"What a ficker."

"Indeed."

Quantum and Spew Gorge are at the front of the group, directly behind the bloodhound. Hiccup is near them, riding Wolf, the goblin tooting along as always. This leaves FeeTwix and Zaena at the back.

FeeTwix is glad to get a quiet moment with Zaena, even if his feed is still on. There are nearly ten million people watching in anticipation of the fight that is to come, but a little quality time is a little quality time, and he's grateful for it. The Swede is certain they will find Clive sooner rather than later, which means that they should find Grifty as well if all goes according to plan.

"...So you will come?" Zaena asks the Swede a second time. "It is supposed to be this afternoon. I told them you may be busy."

"Of course I will, babe. I already agreed and RSVP'd. Was there an RSVP? I love hanging out with you and your family. You know that."

He feels her stroke the back of his head with one of her ghost limbs. It makes his skin tingle. "No, you don't. No one loves hanging out with my family. They all seem to hate each other, or at the very least, they don't like each other's company."

"Yeah? Royalty in our world is like that too."

"You have kings and queens?"

"We sure do."

Zaena shrugs. "Hmm. I would have thought your world was more advanced than that by now."

"You would think, but no. The bloodlines of the families that ruled my world hundreds of years ago are still on top in most cases. I see it as a hopeful thing."

"You do?"

He grins at the beautiful Thulean. "If there is such a thing as rebirth, then maybe I will be reborn into the body of a prince in the future. I already have a princess..."

"You are so *rivdnakh*."

FeeTwix quickly accesses a Thulean language translator that his fans recommended to him. "What? Rivdnakh? I'm not *corny*. I'm sincere, I'm romantic." He grabs a bouquet of flowers from his inventory list. "See? Romantic."

Zaena takes the flowers and smells them. She stops, smiles at FeeTwix, and is quickly interrupted by Hiccup, who has circled around to join them. Before she can threaten the goblin, Hiccup swipes the flowers out of her hand, sniffs them, takes a bite, and nods. He chews the petals loudly. "Fick, I'm not gonna lie." Hiccup swallows some of the flowers and burps. "I need more veggies in my fickin' life, at least according to my doctor."

Zaena watches the goblin trot ahead, the Thulean completely in shock as he continues to eat her bouquet of flowers.

"Fick, these are good," Hiccup calls ahead to his counterpart. "Spewy. Want a flower?"

"A fickin' what?" Spew Gorge turns back to his cousin/father. "Fick yeah, I do. Let me get a fickin' bite."

"These shits are almost as good as fickin' funeral potatoes."

~~*Fick yeah, goblin.*~~

~*Mmm, fick.*~

"I will kill him one day," Zaena says under her breath.

"Relax, he is just being a goblin. Besides, here's another bouquet." FeeTwix gives her more flowers, these ones red and white. They also have little stems sticking out of them with macaroons on the end.

"You got another?"

"These were the ones I was planning to give you later." FeeTwix shifts his focus to his viewers. "Speaking of flowers, I know that Valentine's and Galentine's Days are fickety fickin' over, but that doesn't mean that you can't, and it certainly does mean that you shouldn't, get a bouquet delivered to your sigother right the fick now! That's right, folks, WalMacy's has every rose you need in every color possible. Atrovirens? Celadon? Falu? Sarcoline? Skobeloff? Vantablack? Of course, they have these obscure colors too! Roses, tulips, daisies, peonies, lilies, orchids, sunflowers, and carnations galore! Every color, every size, and now, and you're going to like this, every fickin' flavor! Want to be like everyone's favorite asshole goblin?"

"What the fick, Twixy!?"

"—Walmacy's has you covered! Edible flower arrangements are now available at stores across the United States. And I'm not talking your typical edible flower arrangement. These are genetically modified flowers that provide electrolytes, nootropics, trace minerals, omega-3 fatty acids—they're fickin' healthy, people! So head down to your local WalMacy's today, visit their website, or hit them up in the app! #FeeTwixRox gets you a jaw-dropping flower-blooming twenty-five-fickin'-percent off your first order!" He picks up his speed to read the disclaimer. "Terms and conditions apply. Flower conditions may vary depending on region. Flavor and color availability subject to change. WalMacy's and its subsidiaries are not legally responsible for statements made by creator content, as per the Corporations Are People Too and

They Have Feelings Law Act. Void where prohibited. See website or app for details."

"Are you done?" Zaena asks him.

"Sorry," he tells her through gritted teeth. "Where were we?"

"You were convincing me not to stab the goblin in the back of the head."

"Just eat a macaroon. It will make you feel better."

The macaroon seems to lighten the Thulean's mood as they continue to follow the bloodhound. They reach a clearing, the trees here giving off a patina of rust. Some of them even let out little puffs of steam, which causes Hiccup and Spew Gorge to laugh every time they see it happen.

"Fick, Spewy, little fickin' fart knockers."

"Heh! Fick these stinkbutt trees."

~FICK~

As they continue on, barefooted Hiccup mounted on wolf and the others hovering via their steam boots, Hiccup is finally able to tell the group the story of the Fickvengers. FeeTwix mostly tunes him out so he can cross-check the ad reads that he's obligated to do that afternoon. He's still filming, of course. He's always filming.

"...And yeah, that was *Fickvengers: Civil War*. Now, Iron Fick is dead or some shit, and that leaves the other Fickvengers to regroup and decide if they should keep robbing fickers blind. Mostly the same cast, though. Brad Fick, Leonardo DeFickrio, Fickstain Hoffman, Been-a-fick Cumberfick, Ficknee Poitier, Jodie Fickster... fick, who else, Spewy?"

"Miley Fickrus, Samuel L. Fickson, Fick van Dyke, Marlon Fickdo, Jack Fickolson, Nicole Fickman, Fickzel Washington, Tom Ficks."

"Shit, that's fickin' right. Can't forget Fickdamn Driver, Robert de Fickro, Katherine Fickburn, Meryl Fick, Fickquin Phoenix, Clint Fickwood, Ian McFicklen—"

"Wait, who is on the team again?" Quantum asks, the famous gamer clearly egging Hiccup and Spew Gorge on. "And did you say they were robbing people?"

"Are you asking about actors or characters?" Spew Gorge asks. "And fick yeah, the Fickvengers were robbing people. They're a team of super villains, you dumb ficker."

"Characters. What are their superhero names? And careful what you call me there, bub," he tells Spew Gorge.

"Um, there's Spider-Fick, Fick Widow, Dr. Strange Fick, Fick Panther, Captain Jatla, Fickeye, The Fick—"

"Fick that big ficker. Fick She-Fick too. There's also Aunt-Ficker." Hiccup laughs. "It's so funny when he ficks aunts. That ficker ficks so many aunts."

Spew Gorge snorts. "Yeah, he's a real aunt-ficker, that's for fickin' sure."

Hiccup farts a response, causing Wolf's nostrils to flare and his ears to twitch. "Sorry, Wolfie. Where the fick was I?"

"Is there a Thor?" Quantum asks.

"Who?" both Spew Gorge and Hiccup ask.

"Thor. You know, wields a big hammer, is from Asgard."

"Where?" Spew Gorge asks. "Is that some fickin' shithole in Polynya? Also, what the fick is an ass guard?"

"Fick, Spewy, I could use one of those next time I visit some of the rougher chippies down in Jatla. Their nails. Fick me, their nails!"

The smaller goblin cackles.

~Mmm, fick...~

Quantum frowns. "I can't believe I don't have Thor's hammer in my list. I need to talk to Dirty Dave about that. I have Captain America's shield, item 68." He summons the shield, which appears on his back.

"You mean Captain Jatla?" Spew Gorge asks, the smaller goblin genuinely confused.

"Sure."

"What's this about a ficker who wields a big fickin' hammer?" Hiccup still looks confused.

"Thor," Quantum says.

"Nope, that ficker isn't in the Fickvengers as far as I know. Maybe he's whatever Fickolas Cage is doing next, Ghost Ficker, or some shit. Also, I want Iron Fick to come back, preferably as an orc chippie."

"Fick no."

"What do you mean fick no, Spewy? That shit would be fickin' tight as fick, and you know it. Fickin' Fickvengers needs more orc chippie representation, if you fickin' ask me. All we got is fickin' Fick Widow, and she's too batshit for my taste."

"My favorite is Spider-Fick."

"Pfft! I'm so sick of that fickin' Spider-Fick backstory." Hiccup equips a healing potion and takes a drink from it. He bends forward and lets Wolf lap some up as well. "I mean, for fick's sake, how many young fickboys are they going to have play that fickin' role? Miss me on that, telling the same fickin' story over and over again... Aunty Fick. Uncle Fick. I get it, Peter Ficker is a liddle nerdy bitch in the beginning, then a green-ass radioactive Attla spider bites his chalupa, and it gives him the power to swing from buildings using his—"

Quantum laughs. "Hold on, goblins think the radioactive spider bit his... chalupa? What the hell is that?"

Rocket: It's goblin slang for male genitals.

Both Spew Gorge and Hiccup look at Quantum like he's crazy. Hiccup shakes his head in disdain. "Any-fickin'-hoo, someone enroll Trench Coat over here in a fickin' Sex Ed class so we can continue having a very important discussion. Fick. Everyone knows that Spider-Fick can shoot spider webs from his starfish after being bit on his chalupa, which he uses to swing from buildings and stinkblast enemies. Wait a fickin' minute."

Wolf's ears perk up. "What is it, boy?"

Spew Gorge stops at about the same time that Quantum does. Sir Charles the bloodhound is now pointing his snout ahead.

"Is that a shack up there?" FeeTwix asks. He squints, but much of the forest is now covered in steamy mist.

A message from Doc appears.

Doc: That's no shack. That's a Galapagos steam turtle.

The mechanized turtle presses away from the ground, steam shooting out of porthole-sized openings along the bottom of its rusty shell. There's a shack on top, clear as day as the turtle turns to them, its eyes glowing orange.

"Want to try that again, Doc?" Quantum asks.

Doc: I stand corrected. Also, you may want to get ready for an assault.

As this text appears in front of FeeTwix, the sides of the turtle's shell open, producing a pair of enormous Gatling guns, each about the size of a septic tank. They start to whirr.

"Fick!" Hiccup goes for his biggest scutum, which he gets behind alongside Spew Gorge.

Blat-blat-blat-blat-blat-blat-blat-blat!

The first round hits, the shield protecting them. The force pushes them back a few feet, yet Hiccup has stabbed the shield into the ground deep enough that they don't fly backward.

Blat-blat-blat-blat-blat-blat-blat-blat!

Zaena swings to safety by using her ghost limbs while FeeTwix summons a steampack, which allows him to fly straight up into the air, directly over the fight. As explosions sound beneath his feet, he peers into the madness for his hero and sees Wolf and Charles the bloodhound running along the outskirts of the fight.

Is Quantum okay—?

The smoke clears and FeeTwix sees Quantum wearing item 418, his Replica Carmagnolle Atmospheric Diving Suit.

It shouldn't work.

It really shouldn't work, yet this is a Proxima world.

"You crazy son of a bitch," FeeTwix says again, a grin appearing on his face.

Quantum is in possibly one of the most steampunk-looking things FeeTwix has ever seen. The diving suit, made of brass-colored plate armor and with a helmet that has dozens of two-inch diameter glass viewing ports, has joints made of concentric spheres to create a close fit yet allow for movement.

It looks badass.

Rocket: Holy hell, Schoolboy Q, you look cool as hell.

Quantum: Kid, I see you up in the sky. You got a hose gun, right?

FeeTwix: AUS courtesy of Dirty Dave.

~F-F-Fick!~

"Dave is not a fickin' criminal, Liz," Hiccup shouts below, the goblin picking an opportune time between gunfire to air his grievances. "Innocent until proven fickin' guilty, you green witch! Fick, Spewy, hook Uncle G up with a potion."

Blat-blat-blat-blat-blat-blat-blat-blat!

"Fick you, Hiccup, get your own potion!" Spew Gorge shouts, the smaller goblin still next to his father/cousin as he nurses a Thomas-James.

"Hey! Those are the good ones. Give me that, you little fick—"

Rather than listen to the goblins bicker, FeeTwix does as his hero has asked. By the time he has his AUS hosegun ready to go, Quantum has one as well.

"Let's do this thing!" FeeTwix shouts.

Blat-blat-blat-blat-blat-blat-blat-blat!

The famous gamer is struck by another round of fire, the bullets plinking off his protective suit. He takes a staggering step forward, and aims his weapon at the turtle.

A message from Quantum appears:

Quantum: Release the Kraken!

As FeeTwix hoses the turtle down from the air, Quantum does so from the front, the liquid melting much of the metal turtle's face and its eerie orange eyes.

This seems to do the trick, and soon the turtle is on its last leg.

Instakill!

It shifts forward and hits the ground, the entire top half of its body dissolved into a pile of brassy mess. The shack that has been erected on its back slides off, depositing bits of wood and other random items onto the ground.

"I really thought that was it," Quantum says as FeeTwix lands. The famous gamer is still in his diving suit, his voice heavily altered by his get-up. Sir Charles comes charging out of the forest with Wolf.

"Wolfie? Fick!" Hiccup throws his arms out as the Tagvornian canine approaches. Wolf jumps into his arms and takes the goblin to the ground as he licks his face. "Yoy. I was wondering where the fick you ran off to.

Figured you and that other pooch had sniffed out something nice and juicy. Got to be somewhere around here."

Wolf barks.

"What's that?" Hiccup asks as the canine finally lets him up. He swipes the healing potion out of Spew Gorge's paw and gives it to Wolf, who licks at the tip of the bottle.

"What the fick, Hiccup?"

"Fick off, Spewy, the pooch here is trying to tell us something."

"Since when do you speak fickin' mutt?"

"Since I last saw Irene, your fickin' mother—"

Spew Gorge dives at Hiccup and tries to stab him with a small dagger. The two goblins roll around until Zaena approaches and separates them using her ghost limbs.

~FICK~

~F-F-Fick!~

Hiccup continues to trigger the buttons on his soundboard gauntlet as she holds him back.

~Fick you, Marbles!~

~Mmm, fick...~

~FICK~

~Mmm-mmm, fick...~

"Fick that thing, Hiccup, and fick your chubby fickin' ass!"

"Hey!"

Meanwhile, Quantum has lost focus, the famous gamer explaining to FeeTwix how unique his atmospheric diving suit is while still inside the piece. "...It's good for depths of up to a thousand yards. The closed circuit system was revolutionary at the time, allowing you to breathe a mixture of helium and oxygen, rather than just compressed air. Cool, right? Ever heard of the bends? I'm not talking about the Radiohead album. I saw their holoconcert last year with Frances. Her choice, not mine. But it was pretty good. Anyway, the bends. The bends are caused by nitrous gas, which the helium add-on prevents. Of course, none of that matters here in Steam. And I had the suit modified anyway. Talk about Iron-Man's Hulk get-up."

"Iron Fick," Hiccup says, even if he is still arguing with Spew Gorge. "Who the fick is Iron Man?"

Sir Charles sits on his haunches and throws his neck back. He let out a long howl that instantly draws Quantum's focus. "Sorry, boy. You know how I get with my gear." The dive suit fizzles away, his voice returning to its normal state. "What is it, boy?"

"The wolf and I have found Clive." Charles points his nose toward the south. "He's up ahead, and he's with Grifty."

"Fick!"

~FICK~

"You're not going to like what they have."

"Yeah? What's that?" Quantum asks the bloodhound.

"A giant steampowered robot. They have recommissioned it."

"How tall are we talking here, Chuck?"

The bloodhound considers this. "I'd estimate fifty meters."

Quantum puckers his lips. "Can you give me that in American? I'm only good with the metric system when it comes to firearms, weirdly enough."

"Over one hundred and fifty feet."

"What was the shack then?" Quantum asked as he motions to what's left of the Galapagos steam turtle. "I thought Clive was in there. Or at least that he was in there at some point."

"That's just a love shack."

Quantum nods over to FeeTwix. *"Baby Love Shack."*

"Is a little old place where—"

"We can get together!" Quantum says, finishing the verse that FeeTwix started. "I want to sing the rest, but I'm not going to for legal reasons."

"Love Shack? What the fick kind of song is that?" Hiccup pushes Spew Gorge away and looks back at the disheveled shack. "More like a fick shack."

Quantum cracks his knuckles. "Not a wrong observation, but I digress. Or we need to stop digressing before Doc chastises us for wasting more time. I guess we should get down to business. Rocket, Peanut Gallery? You got something that we can use to take on a big ass mecha? Maybe something, ahem, *mighty morphin'*, if you get my drift."

Rocket: Oh, I get it. And you're going to like this, Q Poo. Hang tight; I promise this time you won't have to be the leg.

GRIFTY MUST DIE

CHAPTER SIX: THOSE EVIL NATURED ROBOTS

[WELCOME, SIR FEETWIX GEARFORT FAJER.]

[D-NAS interface initiating ...]

[Checking black box ...]

[Black box confirmed.]

[Weapon status green. Initializing...]

[Weapons confirmed. Ammunition at capacity. Loading OS updates...]

[8675309...]

[OS updates loaded.]

[Syncing to D-Nas...]

[D-NAS G2G, ATM, FTW...]

[Initiating interlink...]
[D-NAS Interlink complete.]
[System ready.]

FeeTwix can hardly believe his luck. He has read of Quantum's escapades in Steam, the time that Quantum was the actual foot of a giant mecha while the other Dream Team members were in the other body parts. But to be in one himself alongside Mr. Hughes' shining star? His idol? The guy who shaped the way FeeTwix games in a Proxima world?
Goosebumps.
So many goosebumps.

[Propulsion systems green.]
[Flight system loading...]
[Flight system green.]

"Yes," FeeTwix says as he fully syncs with the pod located on the shoulder of the giant robot.
Their mecha is a sleek creation, one made of fictional metal alloys and Proxima composites such as vibranium, adamantium, Mandalorian iron, harmoncooprium, jeffhayesasteel, ice-nine, and phrik, with the armor platings crafted from blackened kevlar and protected by a thin energy shield, green like algomagic.
"What the fick, Twixy? Why do the fickin' goblins get the leg pods?" Hiccup asks, his voice with a hint of static to it due to the comms system they are now speaking through.
~FICK~
"This is fickin' classism!"
"Fick yeah, it is, Spewy!"
"Trust me," Quantum assures them, "you want someone like me in the cockpit."

"Just be happy he didn't put you in the ass where the two of you belong," Zaena tells the goblins. She is in the pod across from FeeTwix, the Thulean on the mecha's opposite shoulder.

"What the fick, Liz? I practically nursed you and fickin' Marbles to adulthood and you're up there looking down on me and Spewy?"

"Hoity toity rick ficker shit—"

"And stuffing fickin' Wolfie in here with me?"

Wolf barks.

"That's right, Wolfie, tell that fickin' bi—"

"Quiet, goblins!"

~Fick!~

[Hostiles identified. System ready to engage.]

"Hey, people, we've got company," Quantum says as their mecha shifts to the south.

A smaller, yet equally armored steam mecha explodes out of the foliage, scattering the birds in the trees. While the enemy mecha may be covered in rust, its plating looks strong and thick. FeeTwix spots Grifty and Clive inside the bulbous cockpit, the goblin Eldritch horror moving around frantically as he pounds buttons.

"Grifty spotted," Quantum says.

"Fick!" both goblins shout.

A port opens up on the enemy's shoulder and fires an EMP weapon that fries their system before Quantum can get a round off.

Critical hit!

The inside of FeeTwix's cockpit flashes red. He is presented with commands on the viewing pane.

[Electric system down. Initiate ejection?]

Hiccup wails: "Why the fick does it want me to ejaculate us? Fick, Spewy, we shouldn't have climbed into this metal bucket. Fick, fick! What the fick were we thinking? Goblins don't do robots!"

~FICK~

Wolf starts barking.

"Fick, Wolfie is about to shit himself in here. This is bad, real bad!"

"I don't want to fickin' die!" Spew Gorge cries.

"Busty Gazongas, bless us with your frothy fickin' milkers before Grifty gets here. Fick! Fick!"

~FiiiiiiiIICCCCCKKKKKK~

Hiccup's soundboard gauntlet causes a burst of feedback that elicits an angry shout from Zaena: "Quiet yourself, goblin! Stop pressing things!"

Quantum's voice is the next to appear in FeeTwix's headset: "Everyone cool it. I've got this..."

[Electric system down. Initiate ejection?]
[Y/N?]
[Please verbally accept or decline.]

"No!" FeeTwix frantically downloads a mecha manual that a fan named Paul has sent him. He skims through it. "Shit yeah, this is it. Thanks, Paul. Quantum, I may have a solution!"

"What do you got, Kid?"

"A Game Genie Manual: Mecha Edition. These were all destroyed..."

Quantum gasps. "You got the Game Genie Manual: Mecha Edition? Holy hell, send-r-up!"

"Sending to you now. If we transfer power from the flux capacitor, it looks like we can override the—" Their mecha lurches forward as Grifty's mecha meets theirs.

"Fick off with the technical fickery, Twixy. Blast this ficker!"

They are slammed onto the ground, where they take out numerous trees.

-120 HP!

Wildlife flee all around them as explosions start up, Wolf's barks growing increasingly louder.

"First taste is free..."

"Fick!"

"Fick! How in the living fick did Grifty get in here?" Hiccup shouts. This is followed by a sudden release of gas that also causes feedback. "Yoy..."

"Dammit, goblin!"

"Fick, Liz, I get gassy when I'm about to die. Not my fickin' fault you lack proper gut bacteria—"

"I see a pair of cute goblin asses that want to party... the rest of you can join too."

~Fick!~

"He's got us cornered, Spewy. He knows our asses are cute. Fick!" Hiccup starts to sob. "I'm too fickin' young to die this way. Wolfie doesn't deserve—"

"This really is some good stuff!" Quantum tells FeeTwix, the famous gamer oblivious to the goblins' laments. "But, now that I'm holding the manual, I guess it's time to come clean about something. I've never been a 'read the manual' kind of guy, but I've always wanted to be. Wordy mumbo jumbo. You get it. Rocket. Coming your way."

Rocket: On it, Q Mecha. Digital high five to your fan for finding this, Twix. Usually I can find this kind of stuff, but this is something else!

Doc: Do I need to override everything and take over this fight? How the hell are you losing to an orange goblin demon and one of Dirty Dave's rejects? I swear, if I have to put my beer down for this...

"Don't you dare put that beer down," Quantum says as they are struck again by a metal fist. "We're still in the fight!"

"You call this a fickin' fight?" Spewy asks as Grifty's mecha stomps them. "We're getting our metal ass fickin' handed to us. Fick, Hiccup, this is it."

~FICK~

"I know, Spewy. I know, *sniff*, I just want to fickin' say that—"

Grifty's voice appears again, seemingly all around FeeTwix now. *"Open up. Grifty is here to party..."*

~Fick you, Marbles!~

~F-F-Fick you, Marbles!~

Hiccup sobs even harder. "I wish fickin' Marbles was here to die valiantly with us. That stupid liddle ficker. Fickin' Marbelito. Getting tail in fickin' Tokyo while the rest of us fight for democracy here in some fickered steamhole. I guess, *sniff*, I guess I should say I'm fickin' proud of him in the end. That ficker made the right move, WAP over death. Spewy, write this down—"

"Fick off, you write it down yourself, you fickin' frog-faced ratficker! That ficker isn't even your fickin' son!"

Grifty stomps them again.

-79 HP! -98 HP!

"It's okay, Wolfie. We'll just have to die together. Come here, you stupid pooch. I swear, Marbles, fick. That boy wasn't so fickin' bad after all. Marbelito. But if we're being honest, if we are making fickin' confessions, *sniff*, I can't believe how quickly he moved on from Tammy to Elfy. Shit is ficked up. Some real soap opera shit, *The Young and the Fickless*. This is the real world, and Tammy's ghost is hardly fickin' cold. Twixy, write this down: Marbles, to you I give my favorite fickin' toe knife; my entire collection of *Goblin Holes;* my golden helmet and axe from Dirty Dave; my favorite designer potato sack; my McMansion in Kayi and the property tax bill that's coming—"

"Not now, Hiccup!" FeeTwix says as more prompts come to him.

"*Hehe!*" Grifty's mecha puts the muzzle of an energy weapon directly against the chest of their Iron Giant.

The weapon begins charging up.

Rocket: Almost ready, Q Man. Hold tight!

"I'm definitely puckered up now!" Quantum says.

"*How about a taste? Just a little taste?*" the demon asks, his voice even more distorted and evil than normal. "*First taste is free...*"

"How 'bout you taste my fickin' puffy starfish after I've eaten my weight at DD's, you ficked up penguin-fickin' poofbasket?!" Spew Gorge screams.

"Fick you, Grifty!"

"*Mmm. This is going to be so fun. I think I'll start with the mouthy goblin.*"

"Which one?" Zaena asks, the Thulean much calmer than she should be at the moment.

"*The mouthy goblin... I love wet mouths...*"

Hiccup boils over with anger, doing a complete 180 from his sad, sobbing state of earlier. "The fick you say? I swear to fick, Grifty, if you do anything to harm Spewy, Wolfie, or Marbles, I'll fickin' carve your skull out with my toe knife, you orange fick bagel! Thumbs fickin' down, bitch! Get bent, chomo!"

[Warning - Melee Energy shield at 75%...]

[Deploying nanoparticles. Estimated time to repair, one minute. If unable to repair, ablative coating will provide additional damage support.]

[Warning - Melee Energy shield at 73%...]

Even though he was just cursing, Hiccup is back to sobbing again. "I just want to see his ugly fickin' emofickered face. Fickin' Marbles, just one more time before I join Busty—"

"Shut the fick up, Hiccup! Fick you, you fickin' oxygen thief, double fick Marbles, and fick Grifty too!"

"Hey!"

A surge of power ripples through their mecha. It forces them off the ground in a matter of seconds. They fly into the air with Grifty's mecha on top of them.

"Now we're cooking with gas!" Quantum says as they begin punching Grifty's mecha.

Wham! Wham!

-116 HP! -132 HP!

"Fick yeah!" Spew Gorge shouts. "Let me kick him in the nuts."

"Mechas don't have gonads, but I appreciate the sentiment," Quantum calls down to the smaller goblin.

The hand partially controlled by Zaena goes around the enemy mecha's throat. "Let's bring it down," she shouts to Quantum.

"Not a bad idea, toots. This one goes out to the Undertaker!"

They explode into the air and chokeslam the enemy mecha down onto the ground, their attack amplified by powerful thrusters.

-211 HP!

Critical hit!

The tables have officially turned.

"Let's turn up the slaps!" Quantum says.

[Wuxia melee slaps initiating...]

FeeTwix's arm whirrs into action as it delivers an E. Honda number of rapid-fire slaps to Grifty's mecha that populates his viewing pane with dozens of flashing red numbers.

Whack-whack-whack-whack-whack-whack-whack-whack!

-8 HP! -6 HP! -7 HP! -5 HP! -3 HP! -9 HP! -4 HP! -2 HP!

"Fick yeah, Twixy! Wouldn't mind a couple slaps like that from Josephine—"

"Hey, that other ficker's getting away!" Spew Gorge yells once a compartment on the back of Grifty's mecha blasts into the air. It's an escape pod, and since FeeTwix can still see Grifty in the cockpit, it can only mean that Clive is trying to flee.

"You want this one, Kid?" Quantum asks FeeTwix.

"With pleasure."

[Initiating pod release.]

FeeTwix hears the sound of hissing steam as he's fired out of their mecha's shoulder.

The Swede is suddenly airborne, his steampack instantly appearing on his back. "Incoming!" He zips directly toward Clive's pod and lands just as a modified DisNike Iron Man fist pixelates over his hand. They sail over the forest, and are soon a hundred meters away from the mecha fight.

"I know now is a strange time," he tells the twelve million people watching him. He begins pounding on the glass protecting Clive with his DisNike Iron Man fist, "but this is one of those deals you simply can't miss! Right now, #FeeTwixRox gets you 10% off your cart at JC Targets! Expect more, and fickin' pay less!"

FeeTwix finally breaks through the glass. He fires a shot from the palm of his hand, one that would have hit Clive in the face had the man not shifted left at the very last moment.

Clive explodes out of the cockpit, the man wearing steam-powered boots. He wraps his arms around FeeTwix and takes him straight to the ground.

-145 HP!

Clive scrambles on top of FeeTwix, bashes him with a headbutt, and wraps his hands around his neck. FeeTwix clips him in the shoulder with his shoulder-mounted weapon and knees him in the nuts.

-193 HP!

Critical hit!

While his assailant is bowled over, the Swede kicks him across the face with his spiked Croc.

-128 HP!

Clive tries to press himself up and FeeTwix gives him another kick, one that sees spit and blood flying out of his mouth.

-154 HP!

"Doc, what do you want me to do with this one?" FeeTwix asks once Clive hits the ground, the man momentarily dazed. The two mechs continue to go at it behind him, tearing up trees and ripping rusty piping from the ground.

Doc: Shoot him with this.

As FeeTwix looks down at his palm, a strange gun takes shape. It reminds him of Ryuk's marble gun, yet is golden and inlaid with curvaceous women that look almost like Barbie dolls. "Dang, Doc," FeeTwix says as he points the gun at Clive.

Waaaaaaaaaazooooh!

The gun produces a bolt of golden energy and does the job, Clive caught with his finger in the air as he desperately tries to log out and can't. Quantum lands, surprising FeeTwix and Clive.

"Who's in the mecha?" the Swede asks.

"I let the goblins and their pup take the wheel. It was them or the Thulean. So I rolled the dice. Anyway. Clive." Quantum cracks his knuckles. "Looks like you are coming with us now."

"Like hell I am!" The compartments along Clive's shoulders begin to open. A retractable brass claw extends from the compartment and zips toward Quantum, who miraculously steps to the side to avoid it.

"That's how it's going to be, huh?" Quantum equips a pair of web shooters. They appear instantly on his hands. Because he knows that the famous gamer is about to hand Clive his ass, FeeTwix steps around the pair so he can give his fans some live commentary.

"I hope you guys are ready. This is the show we've been waiting for. Quantum has item 143, his Spider-Gwen web shooters. Clive doesn't stand a chance. Holy fick! Quantum grabs Clive around the feet with his webs and swings him around his head. The humanity! I've never seen anything like this! Quantum has tossed Clive into one of the protruding pipes. Now he is equipping a pair of noise canceling earmuffs, item 363. What is he going to do with those..."

"A little kablooey never hurt no one until it did."

"Put your censors on, people, this is going to be brutal! Quantum has pinned Clive to what's left of a pipe using his webbing. Now, he's equipped... I know what that one is! It is item 202, his picnic basket filled with plastic explosives and tuna sandwiches. Hey, toss me a sandwich."

"You got it, Kid!" Quantum tosses FeeTwix a sandwich. He then places the picnic basket near Clive's feet.

FeeTwix takes a bite. "Not bad, not bad at all. I know you're not supposed to eat with your mouth open, but this is pretty fickin' good."

"What the fuck are you doing? Let me log out!" Clive screams. "What the fuck is wrong with you?"

"I've been asking myself that for a long time, pal. But just you hold tight. I'm assuming you have a nice rig in the Maldives, or wherever the hell you're diving from. Doc, if you're listening, and I know you are, turn the pain up on his haptic response."

Doc: Granted. But hurry up. The goblins need your help to finish Grifty off. You should have let the Thulean steer.

FeeTwix glances back to the mechas to see them stumbling around and throwing punches. He hears a few distinct *ficks* as well.

"Fine, fine." Quantum, who still has his earmuffs on, equips a hockey stick.

"That's item 242, Casey Jones' Hockey Stick," FeeTwix informs his fans. Before he can say anything else, Quantum begins striking Clive with the hockey stick, even as the lowkey villain's retractable arms try to fight him off. "Looks like he has found a way to deal with those retractable arms," FeeTwix says once Quantum has equipped item 336, Kylo Ren's busted ass lightsaber.

Quantum cuts the arms away and finally approaches FeeTwix, now holding a Fortnite Sideways Rifle. "Item 414," FeeTwix tells the nearly thirteen million people watching his live feed.

"You're gonna want to step over here with me," Quantum tells FeeTwix. "You might want some earmuffs too."

"Got it," FeeTwix says as a pair of DisNike muffs appear on his head.

He joins Quantum just as the famous gamer points his rifle at the picnic basket.

Ka-boom!

The explosion shreds Clive's legs and most of his lower torso, but he's ultimately kept alive due to the steamgear he's wearing.

"You... bastard..." Clive says, damn near delirious with pain.

The next message from Doc seems more urgent.

Doc: Are you done showing off yet? Grifty is getting away.

Quantum and FeeTwix look back just as the two mechas come crashing down. A ripple of energy takes out most of the forest around them.

"Zaena," FeeTwix says, his heart suddenly in his throat.

He triggers his steampack and takes to the air.

GRIFTY MUST DIE

CHAPTER SEVEN: GOBLIN CHOONS

FEETWIX AND QUANTUM arrive on the scene. The goblins have, predictably, done a poor job in manning the mecha, but they have also managed to bring Grifty's mecha down as well. So there's that. The two towering robots are a mess of tangled limbs, billeted metal, puffs of steam, and more brass than a Mardi Gras parade in New Orleans.

A message from Rocket takes shape.

Rocket: The goblins are somewhere under the wreckage.

"Thanks for the heads up," Quantum says. "Be on the lookout for Grifty," he tells FeeTwix, his statement barely reaching the Swede. There is only one thing on his mind as he sifts through the rubble.

FeeTwix has to find Zaena.

"Babe?" he asks, desperation in his voice. He suddenly doesn't care about his feed, his legion of fans, or the fact he's teamed up with his idol. "Where are you? Babe?"

Wolf barks. The Tagvornian beast approaches, a little worse for wear, but fine nonetheless.

"Where are the goblins, boy?" Quantum asks the dog.

Wolf barks again and starts circling a particular mound.

Wolf hops back once FeeTwix sees a few chunks of metal plating magically lift into the air, his heart instantly settling. The Swede lets out a huge sigh of relief as Zaena presses out of the rubble. The Thulean dusts off some of her armor and pulls her skirt down. She checks for any injuries, and frowns at him.

"Stupid goblins," she says as FeeTwix helps her down. She instantly comes into his arms. He naturally places his hands on her rear as he hugs her. "Not here," she says softly once he gives her ass a little squeeze.

"Sorry, babe. Just was worried, that's all." FeeTwix's eyes flash black. "And we're back. The mechas have collided, and the goblins are somewhere in the debris. Fick! Grifty is here too. Double fick! Let's see if we can't find the fickers, and I am using that term for all of them. Also, quick shout out to Cyn, who made a *Grifty Is My Homeboy* t-shirt. Shit is hilarious! Check it out in the feed, and don't show that to the Hiccup fanclub!" FeeTwix gets a message from one of his PAs reminding him he still needs to do an ad read for EBAYmazon.

FeeTwix: Not now. I'll hit that one later once we've got this wrapped up. I know, most views are happening at the moment, but I'm not in the right headspace at the moment.

Geneva: Just hold them for later and do them all at once.

FeeTwix: That always works. Once we get Grifty.

FeeTwix thinks. "Hiccup, Spew Gorge?" he calls with his hands around his mouth as Wolf continues to sniff through the wreckage.

FeeTwix tries again. "Hiccup? Spew Gorge? I have, um, Thomas-James healing potions and a cake from DD's Barbeque..."

~FICK~

The sound comes from the underside of a half-cratered shell. It is slightly muffled, yet still loud enough for him to hear it. Hiccup triggers another button.

~F-F-Fick!~

"Found one," FeeTwix says as Wolf rushes over to the mound. "Babe, can you find the other?"

"I think it'd be better for us to just leave them here. But sure, I'll have a look around."

"And keep an eye out for Grifty."

"Fick!" This cry definitely belongs to Spew Gorge.

"I think I found the other goblin," Zaena says.

"The goblin has a fickin' name, Liz!" Hiccup shouts as FeeTwix and Quantum approach the pile of debris. Hiccup triggers the button FeeTwix recorded as Wolf continues to bark.

~~Fick you.~~

~~F-F-F-Fick you.~~

Quantum taps the metal plating with the tip of his Croc. "What do you say, Kid? You take one side, I take the other? That'd be the old-fashioned way. I'm sure I got something in my list that could take care of this hunk of metal."

~Fick you, Marbles!~

"Where the hell did he get that thing anyway?" Quantum asks as they lift the shell together. FeeTwix is pretty sure it was once part of the shoulder armor.

"His fans gave him the soundboard gauntlet."

"Are you shitting me?"

Rocket: Only you can shit you, Q Hat.

"Not now, Peanut Gallery. Did you say the goblin has fans?" Quantum asks FeeTwix as they set the metal shell aside.

~~Fick yeah, goblin.~~

Triggering Zaena's voice causes Quantum to laugh. The Thulean, who stands near them assisting Spew Gorge, isn't as impressed.

"I shouldn't have recorded that for him."

"Fick you, Liz!" Hiccup says, his voice still partially muffled.

~FICK~

"He has a larger following than you'd expect," FeeTwix tells Quantum. "One hundred thousand people last I checked."

~Mmm, fick...~

"A hundo?" Quantum shakes his head as they work to remove the next metal covering. "And does the gauntlet do anything else? Maybe a little kablooey, or maybe it fires a laser or something?"

"Nope," FeeTwix says, suddenly feeling foolish. "It just plays sounds for comedic effect."

"Ain't that something. I've got a few things in my list like that, you know, just for shiggles. Take item 7, my WalMacy Sam's Club super-sized jar of nutmeg, or item 296, my Olympic Gold medal—that one wasn't easy to get. And we can't forget item 506, my Pickle Rick squishy toy. I could go on, and I will later. Let's talk about that after we wrap up here. But for now, it looks like there are just a few more panels until we reach the goblin."

~Fick you, Marbles!~

Soon, Quantum and FeeTwix remove the last piece of metal covering Hiccup. The goblin is in a fetal position nursing a healing potion. "Don't go toward the light, Hiccup," he whisper-sobs as Wolf licks his face.

"Don't fickin' do it. That shit's a fickin' trap. Speaking in third person is a fickin' trap too."

"You're not dead." Quantum offers the goblin his hand.

Hiccup opens one eye, looks at the hand, and slaps it away. He waddles to his feet. "Yoy," he says as he chugs what's left of his potion. "Yoooy." He tosses it over his shoulder, equips another, pops the top, pours it over his head, and lets Wolf finish the rest. "Fick, what the fick happened?"

"What happened?" Quantum looks out at the numerous mounds of debris. "For one, I learned that you don't let goblins steer a mecha. Heh. Who woulda thought? Now, we've got to find Grifty in all this mess. If he's even here. Actually..." He grins at the two goblins.

"What the fick?" Spew Gorge approaches, the smaller goblin's steampunk outfit surprisingly scratch-free.

Quantum rubs his hands together. "Yeah, this is going to work. Goblins, it is time to reveal why I brought you along. Now, you might think I did so for the antics, and that would be partially true. You might think I did it because I enjoy your company, and that is emphatically false. But no, there's another reason."

"We're nobody's fickin' fickboys, if that's what you're thinking." Hiccup summons his toe knife and jabs it in Quantum's direction. "I'm telling you, Trench Coat, don't you even think about trying to fick my starfish."

"Do what to your what? I'm trying to come clean here, but you keep interrupting me. Anyway. I'll keep it simple, real fickin' simple. I need you to get Grifty out here. He's a goblin eldritch horror. He seems to like goblins, and he clearly wants to party with you and your son over here."

"I'm not his fickin' son."

Hiccup farts. "Yeah, if anything, he's Irene's son. That his fickin' hoe-ass mom—"

"Don't you say shit about my mom, Hiccup!"

"So let's party," Quantum says as a Santa Claus hat appears on his head. "Item 235, closest I have to a birthday hat."

Rocket: How festive!

"I digress. What's that song you were singing earlier?"

"I Believe I Can Fick?" Spew Gorge asks Quantum.

"You were singing that?"

"I was humming it quietly."

"He's talking about the Goblin Whistle Rap," Hiccup says. "And I'd love to perform that for you, Trench Coat, but we're nobody's fickboys, like I keep saying, and we don't want fickin' Grifty—"

"Fick!"

"—Showing up here."

"Come on, Hiccup, the fickers want to hear it," FeeTwix tells the goblin. "You've got over one hundred thousand fans ready to hear this masterpiece. Don't disappoint them."

The portly goblin turns to the Swede and flips him off. "Don't fickin' disappoint them? I don't even know who these fickers are. If anything, the fact they like me disappoints *me*."

"They're the ones who bought you a birthday cake," FeeTwix reminds him.

"It wasn't even my fickin—"

Zaena cuts FeeTwix off, her nostrils flaring with anger. "Sing the song, goblin, and I'll give you a four-handed massage."

Hiccup's eyes bulge. He swivels to Zaena. "Wait. What the fick did you just say, Liz? Did you just say the M word?"

She crosses her arms over her chest. "You heard me." A frown forms on her face, one matched by the smile on Hiccup's.

"Are those your ghost limbs?" he asks, the goblin practically drooling once she starts massaging the back of his neck. "Feels so fickin' good…"

Zaena stops.

"Wait! What the fick?" He glares at her. "You can't leave me with Bluwid balls over here."

"The song, goblin."

"What about me?" Spew Gorge asked. "I want a fickin' Thulean massage!"

"Spewy, you're going to need to take one for the fickin' team here. And you know what? Sure. I'll take one too. Fine, if you help me, you can invite your fickered knitting group over to the crib. But not tonight. We got fickin' plans, from yoga to watching the romcom that is sure to be Marbles and Elfie's Japanese fail of an adventure. Fick I hope it is porny."

"You mean it? I can invite my fickin' pals over?" Spew Gorge looks genuinely pleased. "Are you fickin' serious?"

Hiccup settles his breath. It's clear he doesn't want to say yes, but he definitely wants a Thulean massage. "Yes, and I'll even buy the dragon wings. But not Simba. Fick that weretiger. Deal?"

"Deal."

"Wait!"

Both Hiccup and Quantum turn to FeeTwix, whose eyes are black as he broadcasts what is set to be great content to his followers.

"What the fick, Twixy?"

FeeTwix's boombox appears. "How about an instrumental to go along with the rap? My fans found a version."

He presses the play button. The instrumental starts up. FeeTwix stops it.

"Sweet, and thanks Ahmed for hooking this one up. Well?"

Hiccup and Spew Gorge exchange glances. "Fickin' works for me."

"Fick. Alright then." Hiccup clears his throat. He equips another potion to wet his whistle, chugs it, and tosses it over his shoulder. "Hit it, Twixy." FeeTwix starts the music track again.

"The fickin' orc chippies in Jatla go—"

"*Schwoo-Schwi-Schwoo-Schwoo.*"

"Goblins, orclins, fickin' ficks—"

"*Schwoo-Schwoo-Schwi-Schwoo.*"

"Starfish fickers snowflake poofty-poos—"

"*Schwoo-Schwi-Schwoo-Schwoo.   Schwi-Schwoo-Schwoo-Schwoo-Schwi-Schwoo, Schwoo-Schwoo-Schwi-Schwoo.*"

Hiccup glances around. Quantum motions for him to continue.

"The fickin' orc chippies in Jatla go—"

"*Schwoo-Schwi-Schwoo-Schwoo.*"

"Goblins, orclins, fickin' ficks—"

"*Schwoo-Schwoo-Schwi-Schwoo.*"

"Starfish fickers snowflake poofty-poos—"

"*Schwoo-Schwi-Schwoo-Schwoo.   Schwi-Schwoo-Schwoo-Schwoo-Schwi-Schwoo, Schwoo-Schwoo-Schwi—*"

Grifty is suddenly standing next to Hiccup. *"Ooo-wee! It sounds like someone wants to fickin' party."*

The music comes to a grinding halt.

"Fick!" Spew Gorge shouts as he spots the hairy orange demon. Grifty shifts over to him, his googly eyes going wild.

~FICK~

"First taste is free."

~F-F-Fick!~

The demon gives the smaller goblin a creepy smile. *"Look at that pretty little mouth."*

"Fick you, Grifty!" Hiccup tries to punch the demon, yet Grifty steps aside. He laughs and flashes a bag of drugs. *"Who's ready for an assfull?"*

Quantum triggers his modified proton pack.

Pyooom!

A tractor beam shoots out of it and latches on to Grifty.

"What!? Why don't you want to party?"

"Not today, you ugly bastard," Quantum says as the energy begins to drag Grifty toward the open proton pack.

"First taste is freeeeeeeeee…"

Grifty is sucked into the little metal box. The device flops down onto the ground and quivers. For a moment, it seems like it's about to pop open, yet the contraption stays shut. They can all hear Grifty's voice one final time: *"First taste is freeeeeeeeee…"*

Quantum places his Croc on the proton pack. "Doc, we got 'em," he says once it is clear that Grifty isn't getting out any time soon.

A message from the war faun appears:

Doc: I can see that. Rocket will be by to pick it up shortly. Sophia will dispose of it soon after.

"So that's it then?" Quantum asks.

Doc: Did you want a cookie or something?

Hiccup yawns. "I'd fickin' kill a mitherficker for a cookie at the moment."

"Fick yeah, I'm fickin' starved."

"For real, Spewy. Glad this shit is fickin' over. Let's get the fick out of here." A little steam erupts from a port on his back. Whether it is a poot or a world-appropriate aesthetic is up to Ray Steampunk to decide. "Sick of this fickin' tin can too. Trench Coat. Take us back to our fickin' world before I start getting cranky."

"Start? Hold your horses. We'll be going shortly."

"Horses? Why the fick would I hold my horse?" Hiccup asks Quantum. "If I had a horse, Spewy and I would already be eating it."

"Fick yeah, we would."

~Fick!~

"Just keep your pants on over there. And I mean that in the most literal way possible. I've seen enough wayward goblin balls today to last a lifetime." Quantum turns to FeeTwix. "What about you, Kid? I blocked out the whole afternoon for this little escapade and the day is young. I know of a pretty decent bar in Valhalla if you're interested."

FeeTwix doesn't even need to look at Zaena to conjure an answer. When it comes to his hero versus the love of his life, there's a very clear answer. "Sorry, Quantum, I've got plans with some Thulean royalty."

"Yeah?" The famous gamer steps over to the Swede. He places his hands in the pocket of his trench coat. "I'd invite myself, but me and Thulean royalty don't exactly see eye to eye. I get it, though. To be young and in love in a Proxima World. Those were the days."

FeeTwix places his arm around Zaena's waist. She's too distracted by the goblins, who have started bickering about the best way to slaughter a horse, to hear the rest of the conversation.

"You know, then," FeeTwix says, his eyes flashing blue.

"I know," Quantum says.

Should I? FeeTwix has wanted to ask Quantum this very question for some time. It's been at the back of his mind, but he's never quite found the moment to ask it. He decides to go with it: "Was it worth it on your end? I've always wondered."

Quantum turns away from the Swede, looks up at the hazy sky, and summons his cigar. The famous gamer takes a puff from it before continuing. "You mean leaving Dolly behind for Frances?"

"Yeah, sorry if I'm prying—"

"Yeah, it was worth it. And I'm not just saying that either. Different times now, though. So who knows what I would have done these days."

"Have you ever gone back?"

"To The Loop?" Quantum exhales a cloud of blue smoke. "Nah, I know better. Some doors are best left shut. But maybe one day. Maybe when all this is over."

"When you become an RPC?"

He smirks at FeeTwix. "Something like that. Anyway. We'll talk about that another time, just you and me. Maybe not around the goblins or your main squeeze. Raincheck?"

"Abso-fickin'-lutely," FeeTwix says. The two bump fists.

"Stop fighting, both of you!" Zaena tells the goblins, the Thulean finally snapping. "You are relatives. You shouldn't be fighting all the time."

"The fick you say, Liz?" Hiccup asks. He tilts the toe knife he has been pointing at Spew Gorge toward the Thulean. "You want a taste?"

"Yeah, fick off!" Spew Gorge glares at the Thulean.

"The two of you should be happy."

"Why the fick would we be happy, Liz?"

~FICK~

"Grifty—"

"Fick!" they both scream.

"—is no longer a threat to goblinkind."

Hiccup grows serious. "You think so, huh? We'll just see about that, Lizzy. Fickers like that don't die easy. And where's my fickin' massage?"

Zaena laughs. "Your massage? I already gave it to you."

Hiccup lowers the knife. "Really?"

"Yes, goblin."

"When?"

"Earlier, don't you remember? Spew Gorge remembers." She winks at the smaller goblin, who sees an opportunity to get revenge against his cousin/father.

"Yeah, Hiccup, she, um, gave you a sweet fickin' massage back in Kayi. You practically shit your fickin' pants."

"Fick no..." Hiccup places his hand on his bum and smells his fingers. "I definitely don't remember almost shitting myself."

"It happened, Hiccup. I was so jealous. You don't fickin' remember?"

"What? I remember. I fickin' remember, Spewy. Fick yeah, I do. And it was a good massage too. Fick yeah! I guess Josephine is off the hook tonight." The goblin lets out a squeaker and turns away from the others. "Well? What the fick are we waiting for? Someone beam my ass back to Tritania so I can get to my yoga class. Spewy and I got shit to do before Marbelito's cinematic debut. I've said it before, and I'll probably fickin' say it again: this starfish isn't going to wax itself."

~Mmm, fick...~

"I'm going to kill you one day, Goblin."

Hiccup laughs. "Like fick you will, Liz."

THE FICKIN' END.

Made in the USA
Las Vegas, NV
03 February 2025

17516682R00454